Reviews of *Picking Up The Brass*

"Nugent is a swine and a rabble rouser. He should be tied to the wheel of a field gun carriage and horsewhipped for the prevalent offence of having an opinion different to mine."
Major General (Retd) Tarquin B Razzamatazz OBE, KFC, Pre-Op TS.

"You tell 'em Eddy. What a brilliant f*cking book. They're all a bunch of tw*ts."
Craftsman Herbie Doorjam, D Wing,
Military Corrective Training Centre, Colchester.

"No, no, no. Nugent has it all wrong. He has painted a picture of the army of the 1980s entirely inconsistent with what I believe to be the case. Where is the harsh-but-fair RSM, the lovably eccentric officer? Where are the grimy-faced Tommies who'd help an old lady across the road? Though I've never served, I reserve the right to believe that young men simply can't spend so much time masturbating and drinking heavily."
Reverend Simon Runtigan, Ipswich.

"I have not read this book and I have no intention of so doing. Good day to you."
Air Chief Marshal Sir Aubrey Garstang-Batter
DSO PMSL RSVP RAF, Chief of the Defence Staff (Retd).

Some *real* reviews (by people who bought the first edition of *Picking Up The Brass* on Amazon)

I laughed until a little bit of wee came out. FB

Hilarious… I just couldn't put it down. DS Jones

Is this the funniest book ever written? Had me snorting, giggling uncontrollably and rolling around. RN

Had me in stitches on various occasions, and I'm not even a squaddie. Mantis

Just finished reading it… what a book. Loved it. Diane

I was warned that my delicate female sensibilities may not appreciate the humour and language. However, I nearly pi$$ed myself laughing from start to finish and couldn't put it down until I'd read it from cover to cover (much to the chagrin of my nearest and dearest). Can't wait for the sequel. Bungling Sidekick

One of the funniest books I have ever read. I've never laughed at a book so much. Betty Boo

Unlike many a book on Army life, Picking Up The Brass *tells the real story of what life is like for the average soldier. A great book and essential reading for any potential recruit.* ArmyYed

A brilliant book. S Gourley

Brilliant. Well worth the 5 stars I and the majority have rated it at. Nicholas L. Barnard

Don't be fooled into thinking that Picking Up The Brass *is only for ex-squaddies… It is as valuable an insight to the mentality of the average military man as the reader is likely to ever get.* T Lucas

Got to be one of the funniest books I have ever read. I was crying laughing and I really did think I had wet myself. A book by squaddies, for squaddies. Dale The Snail

Absolutely brilliant read. Filbert Fox

Not since reading Irvine Welsh's Trainspotting *10 years ago have I enjoyed the experience of another language, ie 'Squaddie Speak'. Rich humour pervades Eddy's story. His wit and observation are subtle but hilarious, and I couldn't put it down. Top Notch!* Salford Boy

The most realistic book on army life I've read. Still trying to tape my sides back up. I Wells

A work of genius. Bugsy7

Fantastic book, read it from cover to cover in two days. Indiadeltaonezerotango

The funniest book I've read in a couple of years, causing me to cry laughing and struggle to catch my breath in places. Dozy Bint

Not to be read whilst eating or drinking, as there's every possibility of involuntary regurgitation through the nose. Quite simply the funniest thing I've read for a very long time. D

PICKING UP
THE BRASS

EDDY NUGENT

Monday Books

© Charlie Bell and Ian Deacon 2008
First published in Great Britain in 2008 by Monday Books

A CIP catalogue record for this title is available from the
British Library

ISBN: 978-1-906308-03-2

Printed and bound by CPD Wales, Blaina
Typeset by Andrew Searle
Cover Design by Paul Hill at Kin Creative

www.mondaybooks.com
info@mondaybooks.com

In memory of Gunner John Robert Parker Ravenscroft,
Royal Artillery 1939 to 2004.
Charlie Bell

In memory of Les Deacon (Flight Lieutenant RAF)
April 9 1922 to November 22 2007.
The nicest bloke I ever knew.
Cheers, Dad.
Ian Deacon

Contents

Preface

The British Army is famous for a lot of things – among them its ability to make a brew in any conditions, its inability to provide soldiers with edible food in any conditions and for being the best fighting force in the world, pound-for-pound.

But anyone who has spent time in and around the British military fraternity will tell you that its defining characteristic is humour. If there are no sacred cows in comedy then this is never more apparent than in the pranks, jokes and one-liners delivered by the men and women who stand ready to defend our country.

This book, we hope, reflects that humour. It's the story of Eddy Nugent, a gangling, naive youth from Manchester who decides, almost on a whim, to join the Army. Like all young lads who join up, he finds to his appalled horror that the recruitment posters suggesting he'd spend his service windsurfing in the Caribbean don't tell the full story: the reality of basic training is a life of terror and accidental hilarity at the hands of a group of right bastards.

But gradually – as most do – he finds his feet and settles in to life as a soldier.

Eddy is fictional, just about; he might as well not be. His career path reflects ours exactly – everything he does, sees and hears is something that happened to one of us or one of our close mates.

We first met in Belize, where we were stationed with the Royal Corps of Signals. While there, we drank enough rum to generate moderate back pain, enjoyed the company of the locals and occasionally did some work. The rest of the time we spent discussing our love of comedy literature, and how it was strangely absent from the military genre – with the notable exception of Spike Milligan. Bumping into each other in Northern Ireland a couple of years later, we continued that conversation and after we'd left the colours we kept in touch and started to formulate our ideas for a book.

Picking Up The Brass is the result.

We have focused on the humour of soldiering, and on life for those who don't end up in the SAS, learn to kill people with a toothpick or become an underwater knife fighting instructor.

We're deeply indebted to Carol and Alison for supporting us throughout the lengthy process from conception to the point we find ourselves at today. Love to Jack, Holly, Chester, Casey, Bryher and Caleb and thanks for not throwing too many objects at your dads as we tried to write. Much gratitude to Chris Lee, Neil Brogan, Mark Bloxham, Nick Barnard and Andy Lamont for being our military guinea pigs and reading our manuscript instead of your newspapers at lunch. Many thanks to Terry Christian, Mike Garry, Andy Johnson, Andrew Critchley, Phil Beckett, Matt Baker, David Graham, Paul Bell, Liam Walsh, Bob Dickinson and Graeme Hawley for their support.

Best wishes to all the men and women of the British Forces. You don't know it now, but the memories you are creating today will serve you well for the rest of your lives.

To anyone out on operations, read this book and have a laugh, then come back home safe.

Lastly, thanks to Monday Books for spotting our first efforts on the Army Rumour Service website, where the Good and Bad COs had allowed us flagrantly to peddle our wares.

Charlie Bell and Ian Deacon, July 2008

NO MORE SERGIO TACCHINI

I'm still at a loss as to why I actually joined the Army.

Nobody I knew was in the Army.

Nobody I knew wanted to join the Army.

Attitudes towards the forces amongst my schoolmates ranged from mild apathy to outright hostility. I attended one of the biggest Catholic, all-boys schools in Manchester. Lots of the lads were of Irish parentage and had been brought up on stories of horrors visited upon their ancestors by the evil, British Imperial Forces. Personally, I found myself in the apathetic camp. The only contact I had with people from the Armed Forces was when they'd send a recruitment wagon to the local fair in Platt Fields Park. This always panned out the same way. A four tonne lorry, covered with a camouflage net, would be parked up on the grass with kids swarming over it like smelly locusts as a disgruntled corporal tried to keep them all from destroying it.

Even to my untrained, 15-year-old eye, it was clear that to be handed this particular gig you'd have to be the soldier who'd been in the most shit that week. When he wasn't clawing small boys from under the bonnet of the wagon, he was having to answer stupid questions from their older brothers.

'So what's it like then, Mister? Have you ever killed anyone?'

'No.'

'Do you have to fire a gun?'

'Yes, it's the Army. One of the things you get given is a gun.'

'Do you get to do karate?'

'No.'

'Can you fly a helicopter?'

'No.'

His answers would be delivered with the same deadpan expression and monotone voice. A tiny throbbing vein, just above his left ear, was the only indication that this guy was close to losing his rag. Just before it happened, the parents would come along and clear the kids off the truck, and the Corporal would think he was saved. Only to have a dad or two saunter up, stand next to him, rock back and forth on their heels, and say, 'So…you're in the Army, then?'

'Yes.'

'I used to be in the Army.'

'Yeah?' The Corporal's brain would be sounding out a frantic internal warning: *Say nothing that will encourage this guy to regurgitate his entire National Service experience.*

'Yeah. Course, it were a few years ago. Summer of '56, to be precise.'

'GET OFF THAT TRUCK, YOU LITTLE FUCKERS!'

As a recruitment technique, it was fundamentally flawed, but it was preferable to hearing another story about blanco and bromide.

They came to the school once as well. It was quite an interesting talk, full of loud bangs and promises of excitement. This time it was a fat old Sergeant, who was quite enthusiastic about the whole thing. Though he came a cropper when it came to the question and answer session. After the usual chat about guns, helicopters and karate enquiries, our English teacher, Mr Brooks, tore him a new arsehole. A bit of a bearded campaigner, straight from Central Casting, Brooksy proceeded to ask this guy probing, and extensively researched, questions about the British presence in Northern Ireland. It was like shooting fish in a barrel. Other than calling him a hippie a couple of times, the Sergeant gave Mr Brooks the floor, enabling him to demonstrate to us all his ability to ask probing, and extensively researched, questions. My only clear memory of the debate is that it made us late for metalwork.

The point is, the Ministry of Defence had done no effective groundwork to get me to embrace its cause.

The first time I gave it a bit more thought, was after seeing a documentary series called *The Paras*. The episode that had a profound effect on me, featured the recruits getting beasted for what seemed like the entire programme. The instructor was bellowing at them throughout and they all looked like they were just about to die from exhaustion. But despite this, I couldn't help thinking that it did look like a bit of a laugh. There was no logical connection between these two things, but there it was.

Providentially, or not, I found myself in the city centre the weekend after.

It was a regular excursion. Three or four us would go into town, with little or no money, and hang about the Arndale Centre for most of the day. The ulterior motive was to chat up girls, but I was completely crap at it, and avoided all female contact like the Plague. Myself and Jimmy Connolly, who was at my level of romantic handicap, would shoot off and find something else to do, at the first opportunity. Usually, we'd go into Dixons. They always had the latest video games on display and you could get five minutes playing on them, until an acne-riddled shop assistant with a wedge haircut chased you off.

On this fateful day, we found ourselves wandering up Market Street, back towards Piccadilly Gardens. Just before Lewis's we turned right, down Fountain Street. About halfway down on the left, and just after The Shakespeare Pub, was the Army Careers Office. We had a look in the front window, and were greeted by cardboard cut outs of young blokes windsurfing, abseiling and generally having lots of fun. Another guy, looking suitably dirty, was firing a big bazooka, with a huge grin on his face. The last cut out was of a bunch of lads, drinking in a bar, raising their glasses to the camera. It all looked pretty interesting, though one nagging thought struck me. The lads in the bar looked very 1970s. This was 1985, and to a lad like me, having the correct amount of Sergio Tacchini or Ellesse clothing was of critical importance. It didn't occur to me that the display was a bit out of date. I assumed that squaddies wore some sort of civilian uniform as well, one that followed contemporary fashion but with a seven-year time lag. I found out later, that this is a recurrent problem within the Forces. Torn between the need to recruit, and the reluctance to spend money on anything that doesn't actually kill people, they always tended to wring every last drop out of every video/presentation/slideshow or cardboard cut out. All the brochures and guides I was subsequently given to entice me featured blokes in flares with big sideburns. By the mid 1980s, only snooker players were dressing like that – Manchester was wall-to-wall Sergio Tacchini, Goths and die-hard mod revivalists at that time.

Nevertheless, the display was alluring enough for me to want to know a bit more. 'Shall we go in Jim?' I said.

'Fuck that.'

'Come on, we'll just ask a couple of questions.'

'Go on, then. You first though.'

I laughed and made my way to the door. As I was pulling it open, a guy came out, a big, bullet-headed, shifty-looking fucker. I moved out of his way.

'Alright, lads?' he said. 'Don't do it. You'll fucking regret it.'

But I'd stepped inside and, before I knew it, I was on one side of the door and Jimmy was on the other. The door was thick glass so I couldn't hear him, but I watched his shoulders shake with silent laughter as he walked off down the road.

'Come in son, take a seat.'

It was the same fat Sergeant who'd been to the school a couple of months before. He was sat behind a large, highly-polished wooden desk, with a brass name plate announcing grandly that he was Sergeant Pete Chapman, King's Regiment. There were two flags on the wall behind him, a Union Jack and The British Army standard – a lion and a crown on a red background. I shuffled towards the desk as he stood up and stretched out his hand. It was the first time I'd ever shook anyone's hand and it made me feel older.

'What's your name?'

'Eddy Nugent,' I said.

'Nice to meet you. I'm Pete Chapman – Sergeant Chapman, but you don't have to call me Sergeant yet. Sit yourself down.'

We sat down at the same time, and remained there in silence for a second or two.

'Thinking of joining us then, eh?'

I thought nervously for a second or two. 'Nah, not really, just thought I'd have a look at a couple of brochures or something.'

He started moving into his tried-and-tested sales pitch.

'It's a great life you know, son. Twenty years I've been in, and I've enjoyed every last minute.'

I looked at him dumbly – my natural resting expression – and waited for more. 'I'm not saying it's easy, but it's a fantastic way of becoming a man and seeing the world at the same time.'

'What parts of the world?'

'Oooh, all sorts. Germany, Cyprus, Belize, Norway, Ireland and loads of others.'

At the time, I didn't notice that he'd left the word 'Northern' out when mentioning Ireland. Maybe he thought this subtle omission would dupe potential recruits into thinking that a portion of their career would be spent fishing in Galway.

'How old are you, son?'

'I was 16 in January.'

'So you'd be 17 next January?'

'Er… yeah.'

'Well, you're too young to join up as an adult, but there are other options. You could become a Junior Leader or an Army Apprentice.'

Both terms meant absolutely nothing to me, so I allowed my jaw to slacken a little more, giving him another cue to carry on.

'If you've got enough brains about you – and you look like a smart lad – you can get accepted for an apprenticeship. It will mean two years at an Army College and you'll come out qualified to take up a position in either the Royal Corps of Signals, Royal Electrical and Mechanical Engineers or the Royal Engineers.'

'What are they like, these Colleges?' To tell the truth, although I was academically reasonable, I was never a big fan of school and wasn't very studious. The idea of another two years of it didn't appeal at all.

'They perform all the functions of an ordinary College. On top of that, you get paid, get to take part in lots of adventure training, and train as a soldier concurrently.'

To my ears that sounded pretty good, but I'd remember that description later on, usually when being fucked about for a minor indiscretion. I didn't realise it at the time, but he'd made no special observations about me that led him to suggest this career course. This was because everyone my age who went in that week would have been offered the same thing, to fill whatever the latest quota requirement was. If I'd gone in the week before I'd have been a helicopter pilot; the week after, I might have become a Gurkha.

'Sounds alright,' I said, trying to sound non-committal.

'Course, to go any further you'll need your parents' permission, but I'll give you all the usual bumf. You can show it to them and come back when you're ready.'

He started to collect various pieces of paper and leaflets from drawers in the desk.

'So what'll happen next?' I was interested enough to want to know that.

'Get your Mum and Dad's signatures, and come back to take some tests, then we'll take it from there.'

This felt like a natural punctuation mark, so I stood up.

'Just a couple of questions to get out of the way before we go any further,' he said.

'Oh. OK.' I sat back down abruptly.

'Are you a homosexual?'

I looked at him blankly. I wasn't sure what answer he wanted, but I thought I'd better opt for the truth.

'No.'

The truth was, I wasn't really an anything-sexual. All I'd done was a bit of wanking, having refined my technique using the only acceptable pornography in a Catholic household, my Mum's Grattan catalogue. At a stretch, I suppose I could have claimed masturbatory promiscuity, in that I occasionally preferred the see through lingerie on page 186 over the basques on page 150 but at that age even the odd 18-hour girdle photo could do the trick. I still don't know how I never got caught. Once or sometimes twice a day, I'd emerge furtively from the toilet, with an 873 page catalogue under my arm, and stroll nonchalantly over to put it back where it belonged, near Mum's magazine rack. I never went to the trouble of preparing an alibi, so I don't know what I'd have said if I'd ever been asked, 'What were you doing in the toilet with the catalogue?' I suppose, 'Working out what I'd like for Christmas,' would have been truthful, in a way.

'Sorry to ask,' said the sergeant, 'but it's Army regulations. We wouldn't want any poofters sneaking in, would we?'

I wasn't sure how much sneaking would be required to answer a question 'No' instead of 'Yes', but I understood the point he was trying to make.

He leant forward, and his face expression became earnest. 'What about drugs? Ever taken any?'

'No.' Once again, this was the truth. Like most of the lads at my school, I drank and smoked in moderation. A packet of ten Craven A would last me a week, and the under 16s football team I played for all used to go for a pint in the Crown in Hulme after our Sunday games. Back then, pre-ecstasy and before coke was easily available, the narcotic progression, in order of severity, was weed, glue and heroin. Weed smokers used to talk a lot of bollocks and eat a lot of Kentucky, but it seemed unlikely that someone sitting there stoned off his face could suddenly get that Damascene moment and float off to the Careers Office. I had no experience of glue, but we used to have to run past the smackheads in the Hulme flats every Sunday morning on our way to the football. We'd unconsciously conserve some of our energy during the match to ensure fleet-footedness on the return trip. Again, soldiering probably wasn't the first moneymaking scheme that sprang to a junkie's mind when he needed to make a few quid, quick.

'Ever been in trouble with the Police?'

'What do you mean by "trouble"?' I asked, guardedly.

'Anything serious? Ever been arrested or charged with an offence?' He had his pen at the ready, primed to write any response down.

'I got cautioned when I was fourteen, but not charged.'

'What for?' He jotted something down.

'Swearing at a policeman,' I said, sheepishly. Every summer, they used to have an Ideal Homes exhibition in the park. There was nothing there for kids, really, except for those rubbish art stalls where you could make your own pictures. After allowing you to squeeze a few blobs of paint onto some paper, they'd stick it in a centrifuge and turn it on for a few seconds before – hey presto! – your masterpiece was revealed for the bargain sum of 40p. It was always a ghastly combination of the four primary colours, forming a passable representation of an enormous tropical insect splattered on a windscreen. Other than the art stand, the exhibition was a great opportunity for fooling around and annoying the vendors. The trouble was they used to charge a pound for entry. Bearing in mind that that sum was enough to buy chips for six hungry men, we used to sneak in through an open drainage outlet which started halfway down Brighton Grove and emerged in the park. It was 400 metres long, probably eight feet wide and up to six feet high, and a small river of polluted water ran down the centre with raised paths to either side. You would inch along the path, with matches to light your way, or in complete darkness if you were feeling particularly brave. It was quite spooky – it became known as 'Witches Tunnel' – and for the kids I knocked around with, getting through it was a real rite of passage. The first time I went through I was ten. I thought I was going to die of fright and I'll never forget the feeling of relief when we rounded the last bend and saw a stab of light from the park. Of course, by the age of 14, I was an old hand, and the tunnel was just a convenient means of access and egress. We even used to eat our chips down there. To sneak in to the exhibition, you simply emerged out of the end of the tunnel, hopped over a two foot fence, and you were in. On this occasion, and by complete chance, a copper happened to watch us all come out of the tunnel. By the time we'd spotted him he had hold of me by the back of the neck. The rest of the lads were straight back over the fence and into the tunnel, disappearing into the darkness like rats in school uniform.

'You fuckin' bastards!' I shouted behind them.

Unfortunately, the copper thought I was talking to him. Despite my remonstrations, he took me down to the station on Platt Lane and cautioned me in front of Mum and Dad. They were both mortified. On the way home, a walk of about a quarter of a mile, Mum wouldn't talk to me. I had to walk a couple of paces in front of them while they walked behind, discussing me. Every now and again, my Dad would take a casual swipe at the back of my head with his right hand, cursing under his breath. I was hardly Clyde Barrow, but it was enough to get me to behave from then on.

'I shouldn't think that'll set you back too far,' said the sergeant, with a grin. He put down his pen. 'That's enough for now, son. Get yourself home and we'll see you for the tests when your parents have signed.'

I stood up and we shook hands again. He gave me the various leaflets he'd assembled. Then I turned round and walked out.

* * * * *

Walking back towards Market Street, I was in a bit of a daze. I wasn't sure whether I'd applied to join the Army or not. And Royal Signals? Royal Engineers? What was all that about? In my naivety, I thought you just joined 'The Army' and maybe decided what you wanted to do later on, when you'd had time to think about it.

I didn't say anything for a few days to Mum and Dad. I wasn't nervous or anything, just a bit uncertain about the whole thing really. This went on for about a week. Eventually, I just thought, Fuck it, I can decide not to proceed at any time. That particular phrase was splashed all over the leaflets. Apart from 'Fuck it.' Maybe they'd had people who'd thought they were conscripted as soon as they looked in the window, and the caring, sharing Army wanted to assure everyone else that this wasn't the case.

Mum and Dad were good about the whole thing. Dad started off with his popular opening salvo of, 'What the fucking hell do you want to go and do that for?' before slamming down his paper and staring at me like I was an idiot. I had no idea of the answer, so I let him get on with it. 'A brainy lad like you shouldn't join the bleeding Army. It's for ex-cons and people who can't get on in life.'

I'm not sure what he was using as his points of reference, but it seemed a bit outdated.

'But Dad, have a look at the leaflets,' I said. 'It's not like that any more. I'd be at the college for two years getting a trade and learning loads of stuff.'

'He's right for once, Pat,' said my Mum, thumbing through the papers. 'It does look worthwhile. And he can always come home if it doesn't work out.'

Nice one, Mum. Ever the realist, she'd sussed that this was the one chance she'd have of pushing me into any sort of further education.

'Hmm.' Dad made a big display of ignoring the leaflets and going back to the paper. He conceded the argument quietly over the next few days. I saw his glasses on the leaflets one day, where he'd left them. Another time, as he was coming in from work and I was on my way out, we met at the front garden gate.

'So you fancy this Army Apprentice thing then?' he asked quietly, looking at the handlebars of his bike.

'Looks alright, Dad. I wouldn't mind a go.' I looked at the side of his head hopefully.

'I'll tell you why I've got misgivings, son. I've known a few soldiers in my time, serving and retired. I'm not saying they're all the same, but most of the ones I've met were arseholes.'

'What sort of arseholes?'

'Big mouths, mainly. They've got a fucking story for every occasion. Whatever you've done, they've done better. Give me your word that you won't turn out like that, and I'll sign the form.'

'No problem, Dad, it's a promise.' We parted.

The form got signed and sent off. The next thing I got from them was an instruction to come for a written exam, back at the Careers Office. I turned up at the date and time specified, and was led in to a room full of desks, 14 or 15 of which were occupied by fellow potential Field Marshals. They represented quite a cross section of Mancunian society: several missing links, a bubble-permed Brian May look-alike and a fat, camp chap with his glasses round his neck on a string. The rest were a selection of spotty teens like me, at various stages of an acne coup. I took my seat, and the show began.

The ever-present Sergeant Chapman came in and started handing out the question papers whilst going through his hackneyed stand up act.

'Remember lads, no cheating, you'd only be cheating yourselves. You can look down for inspiration and up in exasperation, but don't look side to side for information.'

He explained that the Army currently had 170 career choices available. The worse your score on the test, the less choice available. Very straightforward. I don't remember the questions exactly, but it wasn't difficult. I handed in my paper, then went in to another room and had a brew. After a while, all the papers had been collected and marked, and we got called in one by one. My interview was brief. I'd achieved the score required for my selected trade, and could continue to the next stage, which was the medical.

I got another letter about a week later. It contained instructions to attend the Territorial Army Centre on Lloyd Street on the first of May at 9am for my first medical examination. Attached to the back of the instruction was what was supposed to be a map with directions to the centre, but which actually looked like one of the clues off *3-2-1*. It made no sense whatsoever. I showed it to my Dad, who'd lived in Manchester all his life, but he was stumped, too.

'Maybe it's an initiative test?' he said, doubtfully, whilst turning the paper for the fifth time. That hadn't occurred to me. I examined it with renewed enthusiasm. After a while, Mum got sick of listening to us trying to work it out and got the A-Z out of the top drawer in the front room sideboard. After a minute or so, she folded the book open in front of us, at the right page, with her finger pointing to the correct spot.

'Good thinking, Barbara,' said Dad.

She went back to what she was doing, shaking her head slowly.

When the day of the medical arrived, I was outside the TA centre 15 minutes early. We'd been told to dress smart, so I had on my one-and-only suit, a blue, cheap-and-nasty affair that I'd worn to my cousin's wedding. It was too big for me, but I'd been told that I'd grow into it. When I was about 42. The TA Centre was a big Victorian building, with a huge set of wooden double doors with a smaller door cut into the right hand one. As I hung around, a few more lads showed up in ill-fitting suits until at five-past-nine a soldier emerged, carrying a red clipboard.

'Morning fellas,' he said. 'I'm Corporal Smythe. Are you all here for your medicals?'

The group nodded assent, and he went through his list of names. There were six of us, with one no-show; as soon as the corporal was happy that he had the right number of bodies he put his pen away.

'Right, follow me,' he said, disappearing back through his little door. Inside, the building resembled an old gym. This, he explained, was the drill hall. It smelt musty, and could have done with a good clean. We walked through into a corridor, and were told to sit down on a bench that ran the length of the wall.

'Listen in for your names,' he said, 'and go through there when you're called.' He pointed down to a black, wood-panelled door. Then he disappeared, leaving us alone with our thoughts. I didn't know it then, but this was to be one of the major features of my military life. Regardless of the situation, be it a medical, an inspection, a meeting or an operation, you would always be required to arrive at a pre-determined time and place before being left standing around until someone in authority would eventually find the time to wander over with more instructions. The further instructions would usually involve being told to wait some more, until somebody with further instructions arrived.

'Nugent!' I was stirred from my torpor by the return of Corporal Smythe. He was standing in the corridor, now armed with a green clipboard. I stood up and walked slowly towards him. 'Come on, son,' he barked. 'Get a fucking move on or we'll be here all day.'

I sped up, as requested. As I reached him, he flicked his head in the direction of the door. 'In you go. Just do as you're told.'

I went through and found myself in an extremely old-fashioned looking office. Behind an oak desk, in front of a big bay window, was a very old man, who I assumed to be the doctor. I had been expecting someone of military bearing, but this guy looked just like Charles Laughton might have if he'd combed his hair with a toffee apple. I walked over to the desk, stood by the knackered wooden chair in front of it and watched as he squinted at a sheet of paper on the desk. He was having some trouble, apparently, but eventually he looked up and said, 'Edward Nugent?'

'Eddy, yeah.'

'Let's get off on the right foot, Mr Nugent. I may not look like an Army Officer, and I can't begin to tell you how pleased I am about that, but you can call me Sir from now on.' His rebuke was delivered in a friendly tone, but I got the message.

'Yes, Sir.'

'Take your shirt off, there's a good man.'

I did as I was told, whilst he hobbled round the desk towards me, pulling a stethoscope out of one pocket and some half-moon specs out of another. He took so long to get round to me, that I'd started to get a bit cold. But eventually he started his examination, tapping his fingers on my back and listening intently, before moving round to the front and feeling my hands and arm joints. He then took a step backwards before muttering, 'Good, good, now drop your trousers please.'

I undid my belt, and my oversize strides flopped straight to the carpet.

'And the underpants please.'

I complied, exposing my tackle for his inspection. He cupped first the right testicle, then the left. I kept my gaze firmly on the wall opposite me. Funny that isn't it? If he'd been putting stitches in my arm or checking my reflexes, I'd have been all eyes. But a strange man caressing my nuts induced in me an air of feigned detachment. Perhaps, somewhere deep down, I thought that taking an interest might be construed as a come-on. As he fondled, I looked out of the bay window, across the road to a row of shops. I could see a painter at the top of a ladder, touching up the eaves of the building directly opposite. Thankfully, he was more concerned with staying on the ladder than watching me having my goolies groped.

The doctor finished the examination and told me to put my clothes back on. Then he motioned to the chair.

'No problems at all there, young Nugent. I'll sign you off as fully fit, and you can continue with your quest to take the shilling,' he said, signing an otherwise unidentifiable piece of paper with an elegant flourish.

'The shilling, Sir?'

'Join the Army.'

'Oh… right.'

'Off you go then.' He dismissed me with a wave of his pen, and I made for the door.

Corporal Smythe must have been listening at the keyhole, because he shouted the next name before I got back out into the corridor. The next victim strode past me as I drew level with the Corporal. 'In you go,' he told the lad, before turning his gaze to me. 'Something the matter?'

'Sorry, I just wondered what I do next?'

He rolled his eyes theatrically. 'Go home. They'll get your medical results and contact you with further instructions.'

'So there's nothing more to do today?' I said.

He fixed me with what he probably considered his hard man stare. It wasn't a bad one, actually.

'Are you still here?' he growled.

I took his point, and made my way out of the building.

FRANKIE SAY NO WAR

I felt good on the bus home, like I'd jumped some sort of hurdle. Dad was in the living room reading his paper when I got in.

'How'd it go?' he said, trying to pretend he wasn't all that interested.

'Alright. The doctor was a bit weird, but he said that I was fully fit and that I could continue with my application.' I sat down next to him on the sofa.

'Fit as fucking fiddles, our family. You won't have any problems there, son.'

He started reading again, muttering something about 'fucking space shuttles'.

A couple of weeks later, another brown envelope arrived, with the MOD stamp on it. I took it into the kitchen and opened it. They started off by congratulating me on passing the medical, and then gave me a date to attend a selection course at the Army Recruiting Centre in Sutton Coldfield, together with a rail warrant that would get me there and a badly-photocopied map. Whilst there, it said, I would generally get fucked about for a day and a half. There'd be a written test, a chest X-ray and various physical exercises – sit-ups, pull-ups, a standing jump and a one mile run. If I passed all of this, I'd be interviewed. If I passed that, I was in. The letter recommended that I train for the physical stuff. I wandered over to the calendar on the wall. Fuck me. It was only 21 days away.

Over the next two or three weeks, I did a bit of training – not to Rocky III standards, but I got a few miles done and checked to see if I could do sit-ups and pull-ups. I didn't know what a standing jump was, but it didn't sound too difficult so I omitted it from my strict regime.

As the day drew close, my nerves grew and I showed my Dad the letter they'd sent me. 'Nothing to it, son,' he opined. 'There's nothing on there you won't be able to do, take my word for it.'

I wasn't convinced. 'I just wish I knew more about what's going to happen, Dad.'

'Listen, you're a clever lad and you're fit. You're as good as in. You don't think the Army can afford to be that choosy do you?'

When the day finally arrived, I was ready to go. I caught the bus into town and walked up the short hill to Piccadilly train station. It was just after 9am. My train wasn't due to leave for another thirty minutes, so I'd have had time for a quick brew, but I was too nervous to relax. I made straight for the platform and sat on a bench near the train. I'm not sure what I was expecting it to do, maybe bugger off up the track as soon as I wasn't looking, leaving me stranded and potentially jobless, but it comforted me to keep it within visual range. Ten minutes before departure, the doors opened with a rush of escaping air and I got on, stowing my holdall underneath a seat and sitting down. I'd always been told that the way to get a double seat to yourself on any form of public transport is to give a wide smile to anyone that approached. People would generally assume that you were doolally and move on. I employed the tactic to good effect, and was able to stretch out and put my feet on the opposite seat as soon as the train pulled out.

The journey down to Brum was uneventful; I even nodded off for a while, waking up with a nice pool of drool on my shoulder as we passed through Walsall. I got into New Street just in time to make the connection for Sutton Coldfield, which was unusual for the ubiquity of people very like myself: lads and young men with short haircuts, white shirts and nervous dispositions. Lots of blokes, in fact, who looked lost in their own thoughts, dreaming up ways in which they were going to fuck this selection up for themselves. Before long, the train eased into Sutton Coldfield and everyone alighted. As I was making my way off the platform, the first military man of the day hove into view. And earshot.

'Anyone who's here for the Army Personnel Selection Centre, make your way over to me please,' he barked. He didn't mean the 'please' bit, but I suppose he didn't want to scare us off just yet. As lads made themselves known to him, he swung his pen-holding right arm back in a long arc. 'On the coach over there, fill up from the back.'

The vehicle he'd described as a coach looked like something from a very early Norman Wisdom film: a huge green charabanc that didn't look capable of forward movement. Still, people were clambering aboard, so I followed and found an empty seat. Almost immediately, another lad, with shockingly wiry, ginger hair, parked his arse next to mine.

'Alright, mate. Whatchoo here to join then?' he enquired in a comical, Cockney twang whilst moving his feet to rest on the top of the seat in front.

'Hopefully the Royal Signals if everything goes alright. You?'

'Fackin' Greenjackets, mate. Best Regiment in the Army.'

I didn't have the first clue what a fackin' Greenjacket was, so I just nodded and smiled in admiration.

As the coach filled up, the soldier climbed on, and stood next to the driver, facing down the aisle. He began to address us in a broad Yorkshire accent. 'Listen up everyone. My name's Sergeant Graham. I'll just go through the nominal roll and then we can get going.'

He rattled through his list as quickly as our inability to answer would allow.

When he got to the Cockney's name – which was Jordan – the Cockney replied, ''Ere, Sarge.'

Sergeant Graham glared at him. 'If you think you're fucking clever enough to address me by rank, call me Sergeant, you little Cockney cunt,' he shouted.

'Yes, sergeant,' whispered Jordan in response.

'And get your fucking feet off that chair, or I'll make you eat this fucking clipboard.'

The newly humbled Londoner did as he was told and dropped his head so he could stare at his knees.

Jesus, I thought, *and this is treating us with kid gloves*. I needn't have worried; Graham was simply employing a tactic, used the world over, in every industry where lots of men work together. Identify the bloke with the biggest gob, humiliate him in front of his peers, and gain control of the entire group. The sergeant was perfectly polite to everyone else after his little demonstration of verbal firepower, and the journey to the barracks was as short and pleasant a drive as can be had through Birmingham.

* * * * *

As soon as we arrived, we were all ushered off the coach quickly. There were five or six Sergeant Graham clones standing around now, all shouting and cajoling at once. Eventually, they corralled us into a fairly neat formation of three ranks, with each rank containing approximately 20 men. Then the clones moved off to one side and stood in a row. The one at the end then detached himself and moved to the front of our dishevelled bunch. He identified himself as Sergeant Major Jones and welcomed us to the APSC. He then ran through a prepared briefing, outlining all the dos and don'ts to be observed during our stay. Mainly don'ts. Immediately after this we were marched to our rooms. I say marched, but what actually happened was that the clones did a lot of shouting, and our group sort of ambled in the direction they were walking. There were one or two lads who must have done some time in the cadets, as they were trying to march properly, arms swinging back and forth etc. They were wasting their time, and just succeeded in getting filthy looks off the rest of us, for trying to be fucking clever. Yet another funny thing... as I write, I realise that some of the most important military lessons were learnt right at the start. Such as, *In the Army, do not, on any account, try to show initiative. Ever.* It's a lose-lose situation. If your attempt at individual mental enterprise turns out to be successful, you'll gain the grudging appreciation of the men in charge, and the hooting derision of your compadres. If it turns out to be a stupid idea, every bastard gets to laugh at you. Don't bother, and save yourself some heartache.

The rooms were exactly as you'd expect – long dormitories with ten sets of bunks to each, laid out on either side of a central aisle containing a table with four orange plastic chairs.

'Pick a bunk, dump your bags and get back outside please, lads,' said the latest clone, positioning himself by the door. We did as we were told and were soon loosely assembled in our squad, awaiting further direction.

This came from Sergeant Graham. 'You will now be taken to the cinema to watch a short film,' he announced, grandly.

We were shepherded over to a small cinema and filed in. Everybody took their seats quietly. The lights had been pre-dimmed and some identifiably military music was being piped through the PA system. When everyone was seated, the Sergeant Major stood at the front and opened up. 'Right, fellas. If you look under your seats, you'll find a programme of what you're going to be up to while you're here. It's all very straight forward. Do as you're told and get where you're supposed to be on time, and we'll all get along fine.' The implied threat was clear and we didn't miss it. 'You will now be shown a short film about Army life, after which you will be taken to the gymnasium for your physical tests. Has anyone not done any training?'

The question was unexpected and nobody replied. He chuckled malevolently. 'We'll see, we'll see. Enjoy the film, gents.'

He moved to the side of the screen, simultaneously giving the thumbs up gesture to the projectionist. The screen flashed to life. The film lasted for ten minutes and was, in hindsight, hilarious. It consisted of brief clips showing all the great, adventurous things we could expect to do during our tenure. There were people windsurfing, abseiling from helicopters, rock-climbing, sky-diving and scuba-diving. This was all accompanied by a cheesy soundtrack that sounded like Pearl and Dean had put it together. Short-haired young men lazing about on a Caribbean beach, or playing volleyball with local kids. Could it get any better than this? I couldn't wait to sign up. The final scenes were unforgettable. The camera cut to another bunch of blokes propping up the bar of what must have been a NAAFI pub. As it panned in closer, the central character, a fat-faced corporal, slowly turned to face us. He raised his half-full pint pot to us, winked into the lens and said, 'All this, and pay as well!'

Over the ensuing years, I'd repeat this phrase a few times, usually through gritted teeth whilst up to my neck in shit.

As soon as the film finished, the Sergeant Major moved back in front of the screen. He was smiling. I wonder why. 'Right, lads,' he said. 'There you have it. I couldn't have put it better meself. Every man an emperor, every day a holiday, every meal a feast. I wish I was the same age as you lot, 'cos I'd get to do it all again. Now, get your arses back over to your rooms, get your PT kit on, and wait to get called.'

There was a flurry of activity and the clones roared into life again, harrying us till we were back in the rooms. 'Come on, fellas,' shouted a Sergeant Rogers, demonstrating the British NCO's ability to conceal words of encouragement within a generally abusive patina. 'Get a fucking wiggle on.'

We got changed as quickly as we could. A few lads, like myself, had the usual footy shorts, footy socks, trainers and plain t-shirt on. A few wore rugby tops or hockey shirts and there was the occasional flash of DayGlo lycra. One or two had brought pop band t-shirts, and a couple of really brave bastards had political comments. Each bloke had to run past Sergeant Rogers to get out of the door, and he had an absolute field day. The first one he pulled up got the full treatment.

'Frankie Say No War? *Frankie fuckin' Say NO FUCKIN' WAR?* Where the *fuck* do you think you are, son? Greenham Common? Get back to your fucking holdall and get a top on that doesn't make me want to punch you.'

'I haven't got another sports top,' said the lad.

'I couldn't give a shit if you've got to do press-ups in a fucking sheepskin, son, get it off.'

As soon as 'Frankie' spun round, another target presented itself to Rogers. One of the blokes was trying to jog past him with a pair of Union Jack running shorts on. In no way did they float the sergeant's boat.

'What the *fuck* have you got on there?' he bellowed.

'Shorts,' came the bemused reply.

'They are not fucking *shorts*, son. They are a defacement of your country's flag.'

The short wearer was game. 'They're just shorts,' he repeated.

Rogers blew his stack. 'No they are fuckin' *not*! They are your single-handed attempt at overthrowing the government, aren't they?'

'Eh?'

'That flag has flown over some of the finest buildings in the world. It was carried by men in battles that they couldn't possibly have won, but did anyway. And you think that that same flag should now be used to cover your shitty little arse while you run round the gym. Do you? *Do you?*'

Fuck me, he'd really gone in at the deep end. I couldn't believe he'd flipped his lid quite so spectacularly over something as mundane as a pair of shorts. It was another lesson to be learned over the coming years. Some people took all of that blindly patriotic bullshit quite seriously. Rogers was obviously one of them. The wrongdoer changed his shorts.

Almost everyone got varying degrees of abuse but I got off quite lightly. 'You could have given them trainers a scrub, son.' That was it, no comparisons with war criminals or references to Genghis Khan.

Outside, we assembled into our loose squad again and jogged, en masse, over to the gym. I quite liked the jog over, it was the first thing we'd done which felt vaguely martial. Sixty men, all running, sort of in step. I was quite surprised that nobody broke out into one of those American 'Sound off, 1, 2, 3, 4' cadences. I'd learn later that the British Army didn't perform those 'let everyone know you're here' chants as it was considered vulgar. 'And besides,' as one physical training instructor put it, 'If you've got enough energy to sing, you can fucking run faster.'

We came to a halt outside the gym and were again addressed by the Sergeant Major.

'When you get inside, do exactly as you're told by the PTIs. You'll know which ones they are. They've got big muscles and they're all extremely handsome. As long as you don't get between a PTI and his mirror, you'll have no problems.'

With that we were ushered into a huge, hangar like gymnasium. Set up all over its floor were various pieces of apparatus… chin-up bars, ropes, medicine balls, benches and mats all strategically placed. Dotted around, numbering about eleven in all, were the aforementioned Adonises. As described by the Sergeant Major, they all appeared to be perfect physical specimens. Dressed in identical white plimsolls, blue stirrup pants and white vests with red piping, they all bristled with recently-exercised muscle groups. There was something faintly sinister in this look. It conjured in my mind black and white images of Aryans doing mass public displays of exercise at Nazi rallies in the '30s. I felt distinctly weedy, with my thrown-together outfit and twig-thin legs. The spell was broken when the lead hunk stepped forward and identified himself. Instead of the expected Bavarian tones, his words poured out in best Blackburn.

'Right, fellas. Welcome to my world. My name is QMSI Rixon. You're here to perform some basic physical tasks, so we can establish that you're not complete knackers. Failing any of the tests will seriously jeopardise your chances of joining the Army. You've all received advance warning of what to expect, so there is no excuse for not being prepared.' He paused and looked at us. 'Has anybody not done any training?'

Reply came there none.

'Good, good, good. All magnificently-trained and honed to perfection then? From here you will be assembled into groups of six and taken round the various apparatus where you will do your tests, and be marked accordingly. As per your instructions, you will be expected to execute seven sit-ups on an inclined bench, three underarm pull-ups on the beam, and an 18-inch standing jump. You will also be doing a one mile squadded run in 10 minutes, immediately followed by the same run done with individual best effort. The time limit for this portion of the run is 7 minutes. The run will be carried out tomorrow morning, immediately prior to your final interview. Any questions? Good. Listen in.'

With that, the other PTIs sprang to life and ran over, quickly setting about dissecting our group into the manageable chunks of six that their boss had mentioned. A big black guy came my way, made a chopping motion next to my left shoulder, and swept me and the five guys to my right to one side. 'Right, you're my lot,' he said. 'I'm Corporal Fox... follow me'.

He turned on his heel and ran off, so we ran after him. Whilst running over to the first piece of apparatus – the pull-up bar – I had just enough time to weigh up the physical condition of my cohorts. Of course, we weren't in direct competition, as it was an individual physical assessment, but it was always a good morale booster to have a Billy Bunter around to make you look a bit better. No such luck. The other five lads all looked pretty similar to me, pasty and skinny, but with no evidence of spare tyres. Fox stopped us just before the bar and pivoted round smartly. Panting slightly, we waited for his next instruction whilst looking at the bar with some trepidation.

'First three, up to the beam.'

I was in the first three, so I moved forward and stood directly underneath it.

The corporal dropped his clipboard, jumped up to the beam, and caught it, underarm, in a firm grip, with his arms shoulder-width apart. 'When I give the word, you will dangle from the beam like so, making sure your arms are fully extended. When I say "up", you will heave yourself up until your chin is above the bar.' He performed the activity as he spoke. 'You'll stay there until I say "down". If I catch anyone resting his chin on the bar, I'll chop his fucking legs off. When I say "down", you'll drop back into the start position. Complete that three times, and that's you done.'

He released his grip and landed, cat-like, in front of us. (By cat-like, I don't mean that he started to lick his own balls, but that he landed gracefully.) 'OK, jump up to the beam.'

I'd done a bit of training so I was quietly confident. My trio stepped forward as one and we jumped up to the beam and proceeded to dangle in the prescribed military fashion. It seemed like an age before he gave the command to pull up. We did so immediately. As the middle man. I used my peripheral vision to check on my colleagues' progress. The first one was no problem for any of us, but the second made the guy on my left struggle a bit, and pull a gurning face as he barely got his chin above the bar. He then made the mistake of resting his chin, just for a second, on the bar. Fox spotted him immediately and proceeded to berate him.

'Fucking stop it you, or you'll have me hanging off your legs for the last one.'

The gurner quickly complied and we were instructed to drop down again. He left us dangling for three or four seconds and called 'up'. I heaved myself into position and waited. The three-second wait had done for the gurner, who was trying to pull himself up in instalments. He'd go up a little bit on his left arm, then a bit more on the right. All of this was accompanied by loud grunts, more like you'd expect on a maternity ward. His legs were kicking frantically, as if riding an imaginary unicycle. Corporal Fox, completely unimpressed, stood in front of him, staring up into his eyes.

'Are you pulling faces at me, son? I fucking hope not. Get up there you fucking waster, you're keeping your mates waiting.'

Which of course he was. I'd been resisting the incredible urge to let my chin drop onto the bar for about ten seconds now, and my puny biceps were beginning to pack up. The bloke on my right seemed to be going through the same sort of pain, and sounded like he was trying to pass a particularly large shit.

'For fuck's sake, get up there. Put some effort in. You're starting to embarrass me.'

After another three or four seconds of primal screaming, the gurner finally got his chin above the bar, and we were allowed to drop down.

Corporal Fox stood in front of us, scribbling on his clipboard, before pointing at us. 'Pass, Pass, Fail. You'd better work hard on the rest of the exercises, son, or you'll be fucked. Next three, up to the bar.'

He redirected his gaze to the next rank, giving us our cue to shift out of the way and watch. They completed their pull-ups without incident and we followed Fox round the gym to the sit-up bay. This element of the trial posed nobody any problems, so we headed off to the standing jump. This exercise involved a single jump. Each of us would stand on tiptoes with right arm extended, fingers pointed, palm flat against a small blackboard. The PTI would chalk on the board to indicate the extent of the reach before each 'athlete' crouched down and leapt upward, re-striking the blackboard. The difference between the two marks had to be at least 18 inches. I now know that this is used to measure explosive power, and can identify numerous physical shortcomings, but at the time I was totally perplexed. It didn't seem to make any sense, other than to establish your promise as a basketball player. Maybe there was some sort of future military requirement for this skill? I had visions of a platoon of hard-bitten Tommies trying to throw grenades through a window, only to find it was just too high. From out of nowhere comes the regimental standing jump expert, who positions himself by the wall and crouches down before, in one balletic flourish, leaping skywards and dispatching the grenade through the open window, thus saving the day.

I was shaken from my daydream, as usual, by somebody shouting. 'Don't you dare bob down, you little cheat. Full extension of the arm, on tiptoes.' Corporal Fox was roaring at the gurner, of all people. He was trying to load the dice a little in his favour by trying to appear shorter. That hadn't even occurred to me. (It would be a while before I understood the concept of 'Skive to survive.' It is every soldier's tacitly-sworn oath to cut corners whenever possible during a PT lesson. This is never done because of the soldier's lack of fitness, but primarily as a bit of a 'fuck you' to the PTIs. Additionally, during a ferocious PT beasting, you never know just how much more is round the corner. It's simple common sense to conserve energy whenever you can. Of course, the downside is that, should you be caught, no mercy is to be expected. You will be given more exercise than everyone else, and your skive will prove to have been counterproductive.)

I managed my jump without too much drama, as did most, and that completed the tests apart from the run. We were herded back into the original group and addressed again by the QMSI.

As he spoke, he looked at his clipboard, shaking his head occasionally. 'Right, most of you have passed everything, but some of you are a shower of shite. Where's the bloke who couldn't do one pull-up?' An arm slid up, reluctantly. 'You, son, are a shabby excuse for a potential soldier. You should be fucking ashamed of yourself. My Granddad is 93 tomorrow. He's got Alzheimer's and diabetes and one of his arms is still on the Somme, but even he can do more pull-ups than you.' The arm crept back down ashamedly as barely-suppressed laughter escaped from the ranks around it. 'That's it for the gym today. Next bit of exercise is tomorrow's run. Those of you who did badly in here had better fucking impress me tomorrow or you'll be up the road.'

We were then taken, en masse, to a scruffy white Portakabin for our chest X-rays. By the time we'd all been through, it was about 3.30pm and I was wondering when we might knock off. Of course, we weren't quite finished yet, and Sergeant Major Jones filled us in with the details of the next thrilling instalment.

'OK, lads. Last activity of the day. After you've got cleaned up, we're going to take you over to the main hall, where you'll do your written tests. After that, you'll be taken to the cookhouse for your tea. Then, until tomorrow morning, your time's your own. Your dormitory sergeant will show you where the NAAFI is. You can use the phone or get something to eat there. Those of you who are old enough can have a beer. Don't get pissed. If anybody turns up tomorrow morning smelling like a magic marker, he will not be allowed to do the run.'

With that we were spirited off to the dormitory again. After a quick shower and change, we were paraded back outside and taken over to the main hall. It was just like our assembly hall at school. As I'd just started my O levels, it had a very familiar look: long rows of single desks, with lots of cheat-denying space between them. Once everyone was seated, we were addressed by an officer, a dapper-looking Education Corps Captain who spoke with a clipped Home Counties accent.

'Hello, fellas. I'm Captain Turncroft. Hope you've had a nice day so far?'

No response.

'Yes… well then. Read all the questions before you start and stop writing when I tell you to. You have an hour.' After a suitably grandiose pause, he added, 'You may begin.'

I'm not sure what the tests were designed to identify, but they were not difficult. I don't remember any of the questions specifically, but it was all multiple guess so the worst case scenario gave you a one-in-four chance of getting the answer right with a complete stab in the dark. I'm not particularly clever, yet I sailed through it and was left with 20 minutes of thumb-twiddling before the clock ran down. I looked round the room and spotted several stereotypical examinee types. There were those like me, who'd finished early and wanted the world to know – tapping pencils on the desk or exhaling loudly, hoping someone would notice how smart they were to get done so quick. Then there were those guys, fiercely protective of their own work. Despite the fact that there wasn't another person within eight feet of them, they were hunched over their desks, one arm furiously crossing boxes, the other shielding their precious output. Some had the look of the damned about them, like they'd been given a different paper to everyone else, one on quantum physics, maybe. They'd be staring at a wall or looking up at the ceiling, wondering what sort of a job they'd get now they'd found out they couldn't even pass an Army test.

By the time Captain Turncroft coughed lightly and said, 'Five minutes,' almost everybody had finished. One guy at the front was still intermittently chewing his pencil and writing: he was either a bit thick, or being really thoughtful about his ticking style. The rest of the time drained away, and Turncroft reappeared, to say to nobody in particular, 'Time up, stop writing.'

The clones swooped in from all directions, scooping up question papers as they darted between the desks. Then it was back outside again, and as the Sergeant Major had promised, we were taken over to the cookhouse for our first taste of Army food. It was pretty good actually, a couple of choices of main course, a couple of puddings and as much bread and cordial as you could down.

It was the first and only time that I was to encounter polite and affable cookhouse staff. The men and women of the Army Catering Corps are pilloried incessantly by the rest of the Army as being responsible for more military deaths than any amount of enemy action. The old adage is that theirs is the hardest course in the British Army, because no one has ever passed it. As a result of all the abuse they get, they are turned into the bitterest of soldiers, without a good word for anyone or anything. They seek little victories over their customers by subjecting them to strict food rationing at the hotplate. Woe betide any man who tries to take more than one sausage at breakfast, or fancies helping himself to a couple of extra slices of bread. But obviously the cooks had been briefed to be on their best behaviour at the APSC, lest they scare any of us off, and they couldn't have been more chummy. After feeding up, we were taken back to the dormitory and left to our own devices. It was only 5.30 pm, but it had been a long day. I had a bit of a kip on my bed, then went down to the NAAFI to phone home. I joined a short queue at one of a line of four phone booths, and waited for my turn.

When I got in the booth, I whacked in a bit of change and punched our home number. After three rings, Dad answered.

'Hello.'

'Alright, Dad?'

'Who's this?'

'Eddy!'

'Eddy... mmm I used to have a son called Eddy. He left home years ago.'

'Dad!!!'

'Alright, son. How's it going?'

'Not bad, passed all the tests so far.'

'Told you you'd be alright. What else is left?'

'Just a run tomorrow morning, then an interview.'

'Piece of piss, get an early night and you'll scream round.'

'Hope so.'

'Everyone treating you alright?'

'Yeah, they all shout a bit, but I haven't done anything to attract attention to myself.'

'That's the trick. There's always some other daft bastard who'll get himself noticed, and when he does, make sure you're on the other side of the room.'

'OK.'

'Good luck for tomorrow then, son. Shall I put your Mam on?'

'Yeah.'

He placed his hand over the mouthpiece but I could still hear his muffled voice. 'Barbara, Barbara, it's our Eddy. Mummy's little soldier wants tucking in.'

I heard the footsteps tapping up the hall, then the sound of the handset changing owners.

'Hiya, son. Are you alright?'

'Fine, mum.'

'You've not been firing guns or anything yet have you?'

'Ha, ha, no not yet.'

'It's not funny Eddy, they're dangerous, them things.'

'I know Mum, I won't get my hands on anything like that until I actually join, though.'

'Good.'

'Did you go and see Gran today?'

'Yeah, you should have heard her when I told her about you. *Don't let any o' them buggers bully him, Barbara, or they'll have me to answer to.* Bless her.'

'Jesus.'

'When will you be back?'

'Sometime in the afternoon.'

'Ok, son. Take care, sleep well.'

'Bye.'

I hung up and made my way out of the booth, holding the door open for the next man.

I followed Dad's instructions and, after getting cleaned up, I got an early night.

* * * * *

We'd been told to be ready by seven thirty, but by twenty past everyone was sat on their beds. One guy had a Walkman glued to his lugs and was lost in some tinny music. I couldn't tell what he was listening to at first, as his attempts to sing along were just oblivious mutterings, but it was confirmed as Prince when at one point he shut his eyes, grimaced and shouted, 'THIS IS WHAT IT SOUNDS LIKE WHEN DUST TRACK!'

While he listened to the diminutive newly crowned Prince of Pop the rest of us nervously awaited the arrival of the shouting men. They duly arrived and verbally steered us outside where the QMSI and his pantheon of muscular gods were waiting for us.

'Right, good morning to you all. I trust you slept well? Good. OK, you all know the score for the run, but for those of you with no brains I'll go over it again. From here, we'll go to the start point at the parade square. We will then run, walk, run for one mile. This will take exactly 10 minutes and will be considered a warm up. You will then have thirty seconds to sort yourselves out. You will then turn round and run back over exactly the same route. This time, you will have seven minutes to complete the distance. This is not difficult and is only two-thirds of what we refer to as the Basic Fitness Test. One of the PTIs will run round in exactly this time. If you finish behind him you've failed. But what I don't want to see is a load of blokes jogging one pace ahead of him. Best personal effort, gentlemen. If I catch any fucker cruising, I will make him eat his own trainers. I'll be stood watching at the finish line. I want to see some aggression in those spotty faces. You should be trying to catch up with the man in front of you right up until the last second.'

His speech just made me feel even more nervous. I'd done the training and knew I could make it round in the time specified, but I had no idea it was going to be like *Chariots of Fire*. As soon as he finished speaking, we were assembled in to the standard three ranks and jogged over to the start line. Without further ado, the QMSI pressed a button on a ridiculously large stopwatch and we set off. It became apparent that we were going to do two laps of the camp's huge parade square. The first third of the test wasn't in the least bit difficult. There was a lot of nervous hawking, coughing and spitting, but nobody appeared to be tired. I was about five back from the front of the left hand rank, and could see the QMSI at the front setting the pace; he ran like an Olympic dressage horse, with lots of flamboyant knee-raising, all done for show and to demonstrate his superior physical prowess. We did our two laps and came to a halt, back at the start line.

'Right,' he said. 'If anyone needs a piss, have one quickly.' A couple of blokes nipped to one side to relieve themselves. The QMSI was studying his stopwatch intently. 'Hurry up, hurry up,' he shouted to the nervous-pissers as they packed themselves away. His urgency was transmitted to the crowd, now no longer in ranks but all vying for pole position on the start line. There was lots of semi-polite elbowing and then some outright shoving. Fuck me, it began to feel like the Grand National or something.

'Remember, gents… best effort. Standby… GO!'

We were off. The BFT, or Basic Fitness Test, is not difficult, which is why it's called basic. Though we were running a shortened version, it was clear that any young person with a modicum of fitness would have no problems running a mile and a half at around a seven minute mile pace. The trouble with the BFT is the start. Peer pressure makes everyone go off like greyhounds. This is alright for the cross country runners who'll end up doing the whole thing no slower than eight minutes whatever happens, but when you get a 10-minutes-30 man running off at the same pace, he's setting himself up for some serious pain. The trick is to set yourself a decent pace and pound that out for the first mile; over the last half mile, if you're feeling fit, you can open up a bit. Of course, whenever you spot a PTI lurking you're obliged to put in a bit more effort. You don't actually run any faster, but you create that impression by swinging your arms a bit more or contorting your face into an expression that looks like you're approaching the vinegar strokes of a vicious wank. Sadly, I didn't learn all of this until some years later, so, like everyone else, I sprinted like a bastard as soon as the QMSI said *Go*.

Of the 60 runners, I found myself in the lead group of about 10. The man right at the front was putting distance between himself and the rest of the group with every step he took: he was running so aggressively that from the side he would have looked like a human swastika. By the time we'd got half way round the first lap, I'd already started to get knackered and was slowing down. A few lads edged past me, so I just started looking at the floor and plodded on. By the time the start line came in to view, I'd regained a bit of composure and was still in the top 20. There were lots of people around the area of the start line, shouting at the runners as they passed through for the second lap. The shouts alternated between encouragement and outright abuse.

'Come on, lads. One more lap to go, keep it going!'

'Get moving, you fat cunt!'

'Excellent, you in the red top. Now get after the next man!'

'Fuckin' hell, son. Douglas Bader could get round quicker than you!'

As I passed through I got my second wind. With only a third of a mile to go, I felt confident enough to start putting in some real effort and passed a handful of people on the way round. By the time I'd done another circuit and had entered into the home straight again, I was about 15th. I sprinted for the line. The QMSI was timing at the finish line and shouting the time out every ten seconds. As I crossed he yelled out, 'Five minutes, fifty'.

I stumbled to a halt and adopted the standard pose: bent over double, with my head almost between my knees and my hands resting on my thighs. I got a smack across the top of the head and looked up, startled, to find one of the PTIs growling at me.

'None of that bollocks,' he said. 'Stand up straight and take deep breaths.' I did as I was told, though the temptation to crouch down was overwhelming. Some blokes were vomming copiously. A couple were dry-retching, producing nothing but a bit of bile and bulging eyes for all their effort. The PTIs were going mad at the spewers. 'Don't you fucking *dare* be sick on a parade square,' one PTI roared at a dry-heaver. The lad was doing his best, his hand clamped over his mouth. 'If you're sick, I'll make you pick it up and carry it back to your room.' The potential spewee now had both his lips firmly clasped between his fingers, but started to relax when he realised he'd won the battle with his gag reflex.

All the while, the QMSI was running down the clock. As the time got to seven minutes, we were all ordered to encourage the rest of the runners in. I turned in the direction of the home straight, and counted about ten men, some quite a way back. 'C'mon, you fuckers,' bellowed the QMSI. 'Six minutes 40! Six minutes 45!'

Those runners within earshot flew into a blind panic, and began to sprint like demons. As he was shouting 6.55, five of them crashed over the line in unison and collapsed in a sweaty heap. They were immediately upbraided by the assembled training staff. 'NAAFI break is it? How come you lot are resting? The time you fuckers took to get round you must have already stopped for a brew?'

Only three blokes failed to make it within the allotted time. They were quietly drawn to one side and had their names taken. After another thirty seconds of people standing around getting their breath back the QMSI piped up. 'Not bad lads, not bad at all. Only three failures out of 60. Your results for all the tests will be passed to the personnel selection officers. You'll now be taken back over to the rooms to get scrubbed up. Then it's back in your best clobber for your interview. Any questions? Good. Get 'em away!'

There didn't appear to be any reason to rush back to our rooms but, as usual, Sergeant Rogers hurried us along anyway, displaying his accomplished command of swearing with aplomb. 'Come on, you lot. Stop dragging your feet, you've only been for a little fucking run. Hurry up and get fucking dressed.' As soon as people started donning their shirts and ties, or suits, he warmed up. He spotted one bloke in a musty-looking, black, single-breasted two piece that looked a touch on the small side. 'Fuck me, son. Did you get that off a dead body?'

It's only a hunch, but I don't think anyone had been to a gentleman's outfitter. I donned the same suit I'd worn to the medical; I'd filled out a bit since then, but not enough to avoid Rogers's sartorially critical eye.

'What's your name, son?'

'Nugent.'

'Right, lads. If anyone's forgotten his suit, there's enough room in Nugent's for one more.'

The bastard. I scuttled past him as quickly as I could and waited outside. I'd never get the chance to see how he dressed when off duty, but I'll bet he was no Cary fucking Grant.

With the entire complement assembled, we were walked over to a single storey block adjacent to the cinema. As we walked, I had to admit that Rogers was right about us. We did look shit, even in our best clothes. The mid 80s was not a good period for fashion, and there were some real crimes on show. Worst of all was the abundance of Dynasty-style false shoulders: guys who'd looked like Charles Hawtrey on the run had been transformed into American footballers and the squeak of patent leather shoes must have been audible on the other side of the camp. It didn't help that most people were still sweating from the run and there was lots of finger-in-the-collar head twitching going on. We stopped outside the block and waited.

Sergeant Major Jones emerged and began speaking immediately. 'This is your final interview, lads. Please address the Personnel Selection Officer as "Sir". Your future depends on it. Don't be nervous.'

With that useless bit of encouragement he ducked back inside. When they shouted for the first bloke, it was obvious that it was going to be done in alphabetical order. I don't know about other organisations but it's a real advantage in the Army to have a name beginning with an early letter. Nobody in the military has the imagination to do things differently, so the As and Bs get everything first – pay, jabs, kit, rations, they're seen to before the rest of us.

My middle of 'N' wasn't too bad, but you were fucked if you were W or later. They got round to me after about half an hour. I went in and was pointed towards a slightly ajar, badly-veneered door by one of the Sergeants. I knocked, and entered. The PSO stood up and greeted me quite warmly, introducing himself as Sergeant Major Robinson.

'How have you found it all then, Mr Nugent?'

Another first, I'd never been addressed as Mister before, unless you counted sarcastic history teachers.

'OK thanks, Sir.'

'I've had a good look through your results. You don't appear to have struggled on anything in particular. Good scores on the written tests and no problem on the physical. I watched you on the run this morning, you did seem to be cruising a bit at the end of the first lap?'

'I just wasn't sure of the distance, Sir, and I went off a bit quick at the start.'

'Not to worry, you'll have plenty of opportunity to hone your pacing techniques. Now, you're down to join the Royal Signals as an Apprentice, correct?'

'Yes, Sir.'

'I'm happy to tell you that based on your results, I'm prepared to offer you a place at the Army Apprentices' College, Harrogate.'

Fuck me, that was it. I was in. In the couple of seconds before he started talking again, I went through a range of feelings. Delight, of course, quickly followed by horror, trepidation and excitement.

'Are you prepared to accept this offer?'

'Yes, Sir.'

'Good, congratulations. The College has two more intakes this year. You can either join in June or September. Which would you prefer?'

'September, Sir.'

I may have been sixteen and on the verge of an exciting period of my life, but there was no way I was missing out on the Summer holidays. The Army could have me after I'd had a couple more months pissing about.

'The paperwork will be sent to your parents for signatures. The only thing remaining is your attestation. This is where you swear allegiance to The Queen. It will be done at your local careers office between now and your joining date, which will be September the third. Have you any questions?'

'No, Sir.'

'Well then, Nugent, that's it.' He stood up smiling, and offered his hand again. 'Well done, and good luck.'

I shook the proffered hand vigorously. 'Thank you, Sir.'

'Transport to the train station will be leaving in a few minutes.'

He picked another folder up from the desk and starting reading it, and I took my cue to leave. I was feeling slightly bewildered as I got back outside. Incredibly, I already felt a little bit different to the lads still waiting. I was in, and they weren't yet. You'd think I'd passed SAS selection, or been promoted to General. I was directed on to the same ugly green bus I'd arrived on. It was half full and the lads scattered around were engaged in happy conversations. I presumed they'd all received the same nod as me. The gurner from the pull-ups bar was sat on his own about three seats up from me, looking despondent out the window. It was pretty obvious from his demeanour that he hadn't been so lucky. My counselling skills were at quite a rudimentary level at this stage of my life, so I thought better of saying anything to him and contented myself with a smug, self-satisfied grin which I wore all the way to the station.

I just had time at Birmingham New Street to call home.

'Hello.'

'Hiya, Dad, it's me.'

'Everything OK, son?'

'No.'

'Eh? What's happened?'

'They said I didn't try hard enough on the run and to come back when I could show some more effort.'

'The dirty bastards. Who do they think they are? I'll fucking go down there I will. Where is it?'

'Only joking, Dad. I've been accepted.'

'Ha ha ha, you little bugger, wait until I see you. Well done, Eddy.'

'I'd better go, me train's due.'

'Right, I'll tell your Mam. See you when you get home.'

Mum was a bit subdued when I got in. I know she was pleased for me, but she had the obvious heartache of losing her boy to the Forces.

I had a whole three months before my joining date and had a great time. I kept myself fit, usually going for a run every couple of days. I was one of the few in my crowd at school who had something sorted out. With school now over for most of them, the prospect of no employment hung over the less fortunate ones. In the time before I left, a couple more started the process of joining up, encouraged by my bragging into thinking it was a brilliant career choice. A few of my mates were going on to College.

Despite the fact that they were the sensible ones (well, as sensible as you can be when looking like Robert Smith), who were setting themselves up for success in later life, all they actually saw at the time was a further two years of school, while I was disappearing for a swashbuckling life of adventure on the open seas, or its land-based equivalent.

About six weeks before my joining date, I received an instruction to attend the Careers Office in Fountain Street for my attestation. As usual, I was told to dress smartly for the occasion and to be there for 1.30pm on the 23rd of July. This time, as I walked through the door of the office, it was with a bit more confidence. There were a couple of lads hanging around outside, examining the shoddy, cardboard displays in the windows. I was cocky enough to tip them a wink, and say, 'Alright, lads?' as I strolled through the door.

As with my last visit, the first person I spotted was Sergeant Chapman, wedged into the seat behind the desk. He got up and was just about to launch into his welcoming speech but then he stopped and looked at me, one eye half-closed, Columbo-style. 'You been in before, son?' he said.

'Yes. I'm Eddy Nugent, I'm here for my attestation.'

'Right, right. So you did it then? Well done.'

'What do I have to do for the attestation?'

'Oh it's straight forward enough. You'll go upstairs and have a quick interview with the attesting officer and then you make a declaration, to serve The Queen and do as you're told. Let's have a look at who the attesting officer is today.' He glanced down at his desk, and ran his finger down a single sheet of white paper, stopping halfway. His brow furrowed slightly. 'Oh… right. You've got Major Hathaway.'

His tone worried me a bit. 'Is that a problem?'

'Oh no, he's just a bit odd. He can get a bit short-tempered. He's probably got a piece of shrapnel stuck in his brain or something. I'll tell you what, don't do anything to antagonise him, and you'll be out of there in five minutes'. Once more, a Senior NCO's attempt to reassure me had had the opposite effect. 'Take a seat over by the stairs, and I'll give you a shout when he's ready.'

'OK.'

I sat down, feeling uncomfortable in my low quality suit, and waited. Nervously, I thumbed through a couple of leaflets which suggested I should 'Be the best you can be,' and urged me to 'Pick a life, not just a career.' They were obviously preaching to the converted but there was nothing else to read. After a couple of minutes, Sergeant Chapman called over.

'You can go up now. Remember – be polite.'

I nodded anxiously and walked up the two flights of stairs that led to the first floor offices. I walked down a short corridor, glancing at each name plate, before coming to Major Hathaway's office at the end, on the left. I straightened my tie, wiped the front of each shoe in turn on the back of its opposite trouser leg, and knocked lightly. There was no answer, so after a wait of about ten seconds, I tapped again, this time slightly harder. Still nothing. Maybe he wasn't in? I turned the handle of the door and pushed it open far enough to poke my head through.

Shit, he was in there.

He was stood with his back to me, looking out of the window. His left hand was behind his back and his right was holding a big pipe. I was just about to sneak back out and knock again when he turned round, and I froze. He was one scary-looking man. He'd have been in his late 40s, and about five foot ten, and he had the same face as the straight man from the Laurel and Hardy films. You know the guy, the one who always turned to camera with one eye shut in apoplexy at being outwitted or injured by Stan and Ollie. I think he was called James Finlayson. Anyway, that contorted, angry face was Major Hathaway's default expression. His face was topped off by a set of eyebrows in which you could have lost Denis Healey; it looked like someone had nailed two Yorkshire Terriers to his forehead. Above the eyebrows, his head was dazzlingly bald, apart from a little Hitler moustache above each ear. I feared for my life.

'Who are you, boy?' he scowled. As he was an officer, I was expecting a posh accent, but he sounded like a cross between Brian Glover and Fred Dibnah.

'Eddy Nugent.'

'A "Sir" on the end of that is forthcoming?'

'Err... Yes, Sir.'

'Where's your manners, Nugent?'

'Pardon, Sir?'

'In the Army that I joined in nineteen-hundred-and-sixty, it was considered polite to knock on someone's door before entering their office.'

'Well, I did knock, Sir,' I said. 'A couple of times, Sir.' I stayed close to the door, ready to leg it if things turned proper nasty.

'I haven't served twenty five years in this man's Army, in order that a limp-wristed, can't-knock-on-a-door-properly little bugger like you can backchat me,' he said, in tones of unmistakeable menace.

Despite the fact that he was six feet away from me, his tobacco impregnated breath was making my eyes sting. By now, he'd moved to stand behind his desk. On the wall, behind his head was a picture of The Queen. She looked about thirty years old and, incredibly, the artist had managed to make her look attractive. Hathaway swung his arm in her general direction and said, 'So you're here to take The Oath of Allegiance to Her Majesty, are you?'

'I think so. Yes, Sir.' My voice was trembling.

'You bloody *think* so? You're not joining the cubs, lad. You'd better bloody know so.' He turned away from me and looked toward the picture. He stayed focused on it for a full 10 seconds before turning back to me. He had tears in his eyes. This was not a well man. 'It's not something to be taken lightly lad. I took mine a quarter of a bloody century ago, and I can still remember it like it was yesterday.'

He placed both hands on the desk and stared at me intently.

'What I want to know, son, is are you a quitter?'

'Pardon, Sir?'

'A quitter, are you a quitter?' His accent made the word come out 'kerrwitter'. 'I'll not let anyone take The Oath of Allegiance if

I don't think he means it. Too many of you lads joining now are only doing it for a laugh.'

'I'm not a quitter, Sir,' I ventured, timidly.

'Good, prove it to me then. Can you do star jumps?'

I had no idea what he meant and told him so.

He explained. 'A star jump is a physical exercise where you crouch down and then jump up throwing your arms and legs out. Like so.'

He walked round the front of the desk and demonstrated one for me. When he reached the arms and legs out bit, he looked like he was going to burst out with a big show tune or something. He stopped and fixed me again, with his deranged stare. 'Start pushing 'em out.'

In case you've never served, I ought to explain at this point that the average soldier's experience of taking The Oath was as follows: walk in, shake hands, read Oath of Allegiance whilst holding Bible, shake hands again, depart. This usually took three minutes. I'd obviously picked the wrong day, and the wrong man. I'd already been getting bollocked for five minutes, and now I was about to have an impromptu physical beasting whilst wearing a nylon suit. I started performing the exercise. After doing about five, I paused and looked at The Major. He returned my gaze and, with an alarmed look, shouted, 'Did somebody say stop?'

I carried on. I could feel myself starting to sweat through my suit and each time I jumped up my tie flapped around in my face. After another couple of minutes, I started to get tired. Instead of doing the exercises with the vigour demonstrated by Hathaway, I started to falter. He was quick to spot the downturn in effort.

'So you are a bloody quitter?' he said, in triumph. He'd moved to stand right in front of me, and at the end of each repetition my face was level with his.

'No, Sir,' I shouted back.

It went on for another minute or so. By the time he said stop, I was completely fucked and was really only bobbing up and down a bit and throwing my arms back like John Inman feigning surprise.

He put his hand on my shoulder and said quietly, 'Stop, lad. You've done enough.'

I was a complete mess. The top button of my shirt had fallen off, my tie was wrapped right round my neck, and my suit jacket was hanging off me. I looked like I'd been thrown out of a bad nightclub. Whilst I was stood there gasping like a newly-caught fish, he produced The Bible and the card with The Oath written on it. I was forced to recite it whilst having to take a breath after every two words. I can't remember its exact content. Suffice to say, it involved agreeing to do exactly as you were fucking well told, no matter how stupid or needless the said order was. I'd have read whatever he put in front of me if it meant I could leave once I'd finished. As soon as I'd completed it, he whipped both the items away and placed them in the top drawer of his desk. Then he picked up his pipe and wandered back over to his window. He casually turned round and nodded sagely in my direction. 'You can go now, lad.'

I straightened myself out, and made to leave. As I put my hand on the door handle, he called to me. 'Nugent?'

'Yes, Sir?'

'I hate quitters.' Oh no, I was going to get some more. I thought fast.

'Me too, Sir'.

He turned to face me again, and looked at me quizzically, exhibiting superhuman strength by raising one of his eyebrows. Then he smiled and said, 'Tell Sergeant Chapman to send in my next patient.'

I practically ran down the corridor and down the stairs. When I got to the foyer, there was another lad waiting in the seat that I'd previously occupied. I was just about to warn him, when Chapman spoke from his seat behind the desk.

'Right, Morris, you can go up. Don't antagonise Major Hathaway, he's a bit short tempered. Just be polite and you'll be out of there in five minutes.'

Morris got up and made his way upstairs, the poor bastard.

Sergeant Chapman came round to stand in front of me. 'What did he make you do?'

'Star jumps. He's fucking mad.'

'You were lucky. He had one lad running on the spot for 45

minutes last week. I didn't want you to say anything to Morris. To tell the truth, you're better off not knowing. So that's you all done then.'

'What happens now?'

'You've got your joining date?'

'September the third.'

'A few weeks beforehand, you'll get sent travel details and a train warrant to get you where you're going.'

'Right.'

'Best of luck then.' He took my hand and shook it.

'Thanks.' I made my way out of the office and back onto the street. I got the bus home and was still sweating from Hathaway's treatment when I got in 20 minutes later.

* * * * *

In my last month and a half of freedom, I continued to train, and threw in a couple of things that I thought I might find helpful. I got Mum to show me how to iron clothes and started setting my alarm clock early, to see what hauling myself out of bed at 6am would be like. It was shit, and something I could never see me getting used to. I consoled myself with the thought that maybe all that getting up early and people saying, 'You 'orrible little man,' only really happened in *It Ain't Half Hot Mum*. It would be safe to say, in hindsight, that the Sergeant Major character that Windsor Davies played was a watered-down version of some of the people I was going to meet.

About halfway through August, I received the hotly anticipated joining instructions and travel warrants. The assorted leaflets went into great detail about what to bring with me for recruit training. Ominously, it stated that I wouldn't need any of my civilian clothes for the first seven weeks, so not to bring too many. They must have had some real dimwits turning up, as they felt it necessary to list every little thing they wanted you to bring. 'Please ensure you arrive with adequate amounts of underwear' was one of the instructions. It suggested that you sew or mark your name in all of your clothing as well. I disregarded this bit of advice, and was to regret it later.

A week before I joined, I went and exchanged my travel warrants for train tickets, at Piccadilly Station. I left them on the window ledge of my bedroom, and spent the rest of the week looking at them every time I went in there, with a growing sense of foreboding. It was only really dawning on me, right at the death, that I was about to take a huge step in my life, and it was beginning to scare the shit out of me. My date to join was September the third 1985. It fell on a Tuesday, and Mum and Dad had a party for me on the weekend before I went. It was round at the house, and the place was mobbed with various aunties, uncles, cousins and mates, all there to wish me well, and get pissed, although Nan did insist on watching *3-2-1* despite the clamour. She had a bit of a love-hate relationship with Ted Rogers. On one hand his tan and rugged be-wigged good looks swept her off her feet, on the other, his explanations of the ridiculously obscure clues would leave her raging. 'The lying swine!' she would shout as someone ended up with the bin.

By midnight, I had lots of watery-eyed relatives telling me how proud they were of me. My Auntie Mary told me that I'd make a great soldier, though I don't know how thirty years working in a biscuit factory had qualified her to make such a judgement. Her husband Jim won the award for being the most sozzled bloke at the party. He'd collared me at about nine o'clock as I was coming out of the kitchen.

'Yer a fucking smasher, Eddy, 'ere you go.'

He dug into his pocket, almost losing his arm in the process, and pulled out a two pence piece. He placed it carefully into my hand and closed my fingers around it, winking conspiratorially all the time. In his advanced state of drunkenness he must have thought he was back in the 50s, when two pence would have bought something more than a Bazooka Joe. By midnight he was asleep on the back lawn.

Mum got a bit maudlin just before bed-time. I had to have a dance with her, and she started to cry a bit, with her head on my shoulder.

'Don't cry, Mum. I'll be back on leave after a couple of months.'

'I know, son. I just worry about you that's all.'

'I'll be OK.'

The next couple of days were spent packing and repacking my suitcase. It's always been a habit of mine, checking things that don't need checking. I'd packed the case myself, but I still went through the little inventory to ensure I'd remembered everything. I found myself doing this every four or five hours until Dad got sick of it on Monday morning and said, throwing down his newspaper, 'For fuck's sake, Eddy. Give it a rest. If you check that case one more time before tonight, I'll shut you up in it.'

For the rest of the day and evening I just sort of hung around, too nervous to do anything but pace around. On Dad's recommendation, I decided to get an early night and went up to bed at around nine o'clock. Mum and Dad were just getting ready to watch the news. I stood in the doorway and whispered quietly, 'Night Mum, Dad.'

They both looked round. I could see from Mum's eyes that she was holding back the tears and Dad seemed to be wavering behind his own familiarly stoical mask.

'Night, son,' they said in unison, and looked away quickly as I closed the door quietly behind me.

My sleep was incredibly fitful. I had all sorts of odd dreams that I couldn't recollect in the morning, or now. I remember lying on my back under the duvet, with both arms behind my head, willing myself to sleep. I must have got off at some stage, because the next thing I remember it was broad daylight and it was time to join the Army.

AN EXTREMELY FAIR MAN

Dad gave me a lift to the station. Neither of us spoke during the drive: the silence was only broken by the Bruno Brookes show crackling out of the one working speaker of the car radio. Somehow, *Walking On Sunshine* didn't fit my mood. I was extremely nervous about what was waiting to greet me at Harrogate, and Katrina's joyous crooning about her baby loving her wasn't hitting the spot. I didn't feel the love, and it didn't feel good. We got to Victoria Station with 15 minutes to spare. Dad helped me to the platform with my bags. He had to be at work, so he couldn't hang around to see me off. He went to shake my hand, but when he took it, realised that something more than that was required. He pulled me close in to him and hugged me. We stayed like that for a few seconds and when he pulled back, he had tears in his eyes. I'd never seen him cry before and was taken aback so I tried to reassure him.

'I'll be alright, Dad.'

He smiled, with an effort. 'I know, son. Now listen. If this isn't for you, don't be bloody scared to say so. The world's full of people doing jobs they don't like. If it gets too hard, or it doesn't turn out like you thought it would, you can come home and try something else.' I nodded, picking up my cases. 'Mind you,' he said, 'don't give up too easy. I can't imagine that it's going to be pleasant, but us Nugents have never been quitters.'

There it was, that word again. I gave an involuntary shudder and climbed aboard the train. I stashed my bags and went back to the door, pulling the window down.

'Right then, Dad. See you soon, hopefully.'

'OK, son. I need to shoot off to work now anyway. Take care of yourself and keep your head down. Don't get noticed and you'll be alright.' He ruffled my hair with his right hand. 'Go on. Get sat down or you'll lose your seat.'

I looked around and saw that the carriage was starting to fill up. We said our final goodbye and Dad spun smartly on his heel and strode quickly up the platform. I watched him get to the ticket inspection point, then I shut the window and made my way to the seat.

In the 10 minutes before we left, a few more Harrogate recruits boarded the train. They stuck out like sore thumbs among the commuters, with their new haircuts, uncomfortable shirts and over-abundance of baggage for your average 16-year-old lad. One lad had almost an entire football team of relatives seeing him off: he pulled himself away like a Beatle dodging autograph hunters and boarded the train one carriage down from me. Several others, cutting it fine and with no one to see them off, had to open doors that the guard had already shut to make it on.

When the whistle finally went and the train pulled off, I still had a double seat to myself. I tried to settle down, despite my nerves. I had my travel instructions tucked safely into the arse pocket of my trousers but still took them out every few minutes to check. An hour to Leeds, then we'd change for Harrogate. I spent the entire journey gazing out of the window, attempting to take in a bit of the scenery. Every now and again we'd go through a tunnel and my reflection would stare back at me. It seemed to be saying, 'You daft twat.' The only other thing I remember from our passage through West Yorkshire (apart from feeling sick after eating two Cabana bars back to back), was a sign outside a farm which said, 'Half a pig, fifteen quid.' It seemed to confirm that I was moving from one world to another.

According to my instructions I had 20 minutes at Leeds in which to be on platform 5C, but I ran anyway, blundering through the station with my bags like an old lady with an eye on a jumble-sale bargain. The pointless dash left me with a quarter of an hour to kill so I found an empty bench and sat down, wearily, looking at the silent, waiting train. Gradually, the platform filled with the same young faces, all nervously smoking or introducing themselves to others, hoping to glean snippets about the forthcoming experience to help allay their fears. Just before the train doors hissed open, I was joined by a lad who was struggling with six bags. I immediately started worrying about what I might have forgotten. I had a good look around the platform and took some solace in the fact that, like me, everyone else was averaging two or three cases. I nodded to the lad, a stocky guy with a ginger flat-top. 'Fuckin' hell, mate,' I said. 'You've got a lot of stuff there.'

He looked at me quizzically. 'All essential gear, mate. You only got the two bags then?'

'I've got everything they put on the list,' I said.

'Oh, I didn't go off *their* list. Me Dad's in the Green Howards, so he told me what to take.'

I was going to find out the hard way that being the first soldier in the family had its drawbacks. Knowing someone who'd been through the same training, who could provide hints and tips that would help avoid the pitfalls that I was going to stumble into with every step, would have been useful.

A metallic voice from the train announced the service as the doors opened, and everyone started gathering up his luggage and cramming it onto the two-carriage express. By the time I got on, all the seats were taken, so I dropped my bags and stood by the doors. The train moved off, almost silently. The journey only took half an hour; as we travelled through Burley, Kirkstall, Horsforth, Weeton, Pannal and Oatlands, the mood grew palpably more sombre, and conversation dwindled to a few hushed exchanges. As we slid in to Harrogate station, everyone was waiting, bags in hand, for the stop. We all spilled through the open doors and on to the platform.

As I lumbered down the concourse, I noticed an elderly man in Army uniform. He was holding a clipboard and directing some of the lads who had got off the train before me to go outside. As I drew nearer, I saw that the old codger had a name-tag that read 'Lang' on his chest. He also had a black cane with a metallic end under one arm and a black armband emblazoned in red with the letters 'RP' on the other. I looked him up and down discreetly. He had the gaunt, craggy features of Old Man Steptoe. Before I could speak, the old coot looked up and barked, 'Name?'

'Eddy. Eddy Nugent.'

He scowled at me, and shot back, 'Eddy Nugent, what?'

I panicked, thinking he wanted me to give him more details about myself. 'Eddy Nugent,' I said, 'from Manchester, er, Sir.'

'SIR! Fucking *Sir*! I'm not a fucking "Sir", Nugent. I work for a living. Do you understand?'

No. 'Yes.'

'Yes, fucking *what?*' he screeched, pointing at the single chevron on his right arm.

I wasn't stupid, and I knew that he wanted me to call him by his rank, but I didn't have a clue what it was. My stomach was in knots: I'd only been off the train for five minutes and I was in the shit already. So I just pulled a rank out of my head.

'Yes… Corporal.' Just about the only others that I knew were Squadron Leader, Admiral and Centurion.

'That's more like it you horrible, lazy bastard. Now get on that fucking green bus in the car park, and I'll be watching you, lad.'

I shuffled outside and climbed aboard. The coach was spartan, with uncomfortable, thinly-padded, green bench-seats that had metal rails for headrests. Everyone had a double seat to himself, and nobody was mixing or talking to anyone else. I found a seat and soon after a chubby kid sat down next to me. *At least there's one guy I can beat on a run*, I thought. It's amazing what gives you comfort when you think you're in dire straits.

Once the bus was full, the driver started the engine and the old corporal climbed abroad. The pneumatic doors closed behind him with a hiss and he braced himself in the aisle. When what little conversation there was had died down, he sneered,

'Right, you little fuckers! You're in the Army now! So when I speak to you, you will call me "Corporal". Do you understand?'

'YES, CORPORAL!' came the loud reply, in unison. Except for one lad, who deviated from the required response. A tall bloke, two seats in front of me, had also noticed Lance Corporal Lang's similarity to Steptoe Senior. Instead of shouting 'Yes, Corporal!' with the rest of us, he called out, 'You *dirty* old man,' in the manner of Harry H. Unfortunately for the would-be comic, by the time we had said our bit, his lone impression was still in full flow, and the 'old man' part trailed away into silence. Then he realised just how badly he had fucked up. Lang turned scarlet with rage: he was about an inch away from having steam coming out of his ears, to the accompaniment of the noise from a locomotive whistle. The bus was deathly quiet aside from the occasional suppressed snigger, but the majority of us were shocked into wide-eyed silence. I was just thinking that this would be a smokescreen for my minor altercation, when Lang took a step forward.

'What's your fucking name?' he bellowed at the joker.

'Smith, Corporal.'

'Right, Smith. Me and you are going to have fucking words.'

Then to our surprise, Lang just sat down and the bus pulled out of the car park and headed towards camp.

I stared at my troubled reflection in the window as we wound through the light stone houses of the town and out into the dark greenery of the countryside. We climbed a foreboding hill and then headed down a lane with a small housing estate and the huts from *Tenko* on the right. Shortly after that, the camp perimeter came into view on the left. It seemed to be in the middle of nowhere, making it extremely open to the elements.

The bus slowed and we turned through the gates, me gawping at everything – even the guy on gate, because he'd passed basic training and I hadn't. I was snapped out of my gawping by the bus jolting to a stop outside the guardroom. Then Lang stood up and shouted, 'Right, Smith! You funny fucker! Get off the shagging bus!'

Smith didn't move at first and just looked around the bus as if one of us would offer some advice, but we were all as scared as each other and could be of no use. Then Lang called out again, 'Come on, you cunt. Get the fuck off the fucking bus now!'

Smith slowly stood, and Lang harangued him all the way down the aisle. 'Take your fucking time, Smith! Don't hurry whatever you do, you cunt. I've got all shagging day!'

Smith sped up and jogged along the aisle and down the steps. Once outside and on the tarmac, Smith was subjected to Lang's full arsenal of insults. Then, to my horror, he was marched into the guardroom jail at a ridiculously fast pace. A minute or so later, Lang came back out of the building and got back aboard the bus. He looked very smug. 'Any other comedians?' he shouted. When there was no reply, the bus set off again, passing a large boiler house with a chimney and a strange round building with a sign saying 'NAAFI' outside it before a series of four storey accommodation blocks came into view.

We stopped at the corner of two blocks. Lang read out a list of names. 'You're in Scott Squadron,' he said. 'Now get off the bus.'

As soon as the Scott Squadron guys filtered down the steps, they were verbally set upon by a group of young junior ranks yelling, 'Hurry the fuck up!' and 'Sort your fucking shit out!'

I watched as they were then herded into one of the blocks and out of sight.

Then Lang read out another list of names; when mine was called out, my heart skipped a beat.

'Right, you lot are Rawson Squadron, so get the fuck off the bus.'

We all stood up and made our way down the aisle. As soon as we hit the Tarmac, another group of blokes, a year or so older than me, sprinted out from the block and started to shout abuse at us. There was a mad scrabble for our cases from the belly of the coach. As soon as I had my baggage, I just turned and followed the person in front of me. There were so many NCOs shouting so much abuse, and so loud, that – as we clambered up the stairs of the block – the hollering seemed to form one unintelligible downpour of swear words and threats. I didn't dare look at any of the instructors, for fear of some unspeakable reprisal.

When we reached the first floor, we were directed through some brown double fire doors. We were told to give our names and lined up along the wall in alphabetical order. We were stood perfectly still and looking above the heads of the NCOs, but they still shouted at us for some imaginary crime, all the while stalking the corridor and eyeballing us menacingly. Before long, another coach-load of recruits turned up and were integrated into our group through the same medium of loud swearing.

We were each assigned a bed – eight of us per room – and then herded back downstairs into the quadrangle formed by the accommodation blocks. After the palaver of trying to form three ranks, we were turned to our left and marched to the cookhouse for our first taste of Army cuisine. None of us were in step and the ripple effect of our pathetic attempt at marching resembled the legwork of a drunken millipede. After a short while, we reached a covered walkway, the approach to the cookhouse. One of the instructors called for the squad to halt, and numerous comedy collisions took place, with some stopping dead and others continuing to march. Our woefully disorganised state earned us more grippings.

'You useless bastards! You cunts can't do fuck all! Now line up against the glass wall on the right, and get in single shaggin' file!'

The desperate, scrabbling transition from three ranks to single file was mayhem but we sort of made it. I ended up in the middle of the line, and we started edging to the cookhouse.

Inside, I sneaked a brief look around. There was an illuminated hot plate with a line of cooks in stained whites standing behind it. Some of the tables had soldiers sitting around them. These blokes looked across at us and laughed whilst making the odd comment about us being a 'bunch of wankers.' One of the NCOs caught me looking and was immediately in my face. 'What the fuck are you looking at, you cunt?'

'Nothing, Corporal!' I replied. Luckily he had the same rank as Lang, so I knew what it was.

He pointed to the guys in uniform who were already eating. 'Don't you fucking dare look at them, you're not worthy.'

I don't know what he expected me to do. If I wasn't worthy of looking at anybody who was out of basic training, I'd be spending most of my time with my eyes shut. Surely this would raise some serious safety issues, especially when undergoing firearms training. But I just looked ahead of me and said, 'Yes, Corporal!'

Then he was away to grip someone else for an equally trivial crime.

After a while, I bore down on the hotplate. The meal itself resembled a school dinner, with the usual staples like chips, sausage, pies, beans etc. But the people serving it were very different. As opposed to the red-faced, friendly dinner ladies I'd known in school, these people, while still red-faced, were cantankerous borderline psychotics with all manner of skin disorders. I made a mental note to stay clear of the cornflakes at breakfast. As I moved along the line, I was met with scowls from the chefs to the point where I began to feel that they personally hated me. I just got my scoff as fast as I could and took it to an empty table where I began to eat at a leisurely pace.

I was halfway through my meal when the NCOs stood up and shouted, 'Right, Rawson Squadron Recruits. Get outside now!'

Not one of us had finished our food, and we looked around at each other in dismay. But the instructor who had just shouted the order, reiterated his point. 'FUCKING GET OUTSIDE NOW, RAWSON RECRUITS!'

Spurred on by the level of the NCO's rage, we all dashed for the exits, even blokes who were just coming off the hotplate with a tray full of food. Our first lesson had been learned: get your food eaten as fast as possible, because the NCOs went through first, and as soon as they had finished theirs it was time to leave.

This lesson meant that, come the next meal, there was plenty of physical jostling for a good place in the queue. If you were last to get served, table manners were suspended and you ate as you went down the hotplate.

Once back outside in the walkway, we were put into three ranks again and 'marched' out past the back of the accommodation where the bus had dropped us off. From there, we went back down the road in the direction of the guardroom, looking like Napoleon's retreat from Moscow. On passing the boiler house again, we turned right down towards a large, derelict-looking building and came to a shambling halt at its doors. I noticed the word 'CINEMA' above them – an ambitious claim, I thought. To the left of the main entrance was a wall-mounted poster, informing us all excitedly that *Trading Places* was coming soon. It was only three years after everyone else had seen it.

I still wasn't used to the constant yelling, and jumped a little when one of the instructors roared, 'Front rank, file in.' There was a picosecond's pause, before he screamed, 'Get a fucking wiggle on, you lazy fucking gobshites.'

Harried witless, the front rank did as it was told, followed by the middle and rear, under constant vocal bombardment. Glancing timidly left and right as we went through the foyer, I could see that, as cinemas went, it was a bare-arsed affair. Dour shades of purple and blue reigned, with none of the usual accoutrements like a popcorn stand or a gorgeous, thick-skulled ticket lady. We were herded down the central aisle to the front and were instructed via points, threats and grunts to file into the first empty row. Sitting down in those surprisingly comfy seats was bliss, regardless of the abuse, and I took the liberty of having a quick look round. On the wall to my left was a collection of dark wooden panels, listing, in gold lettering, the names and tenure dates of all the Commanding

Officers of the college. On the right were similar boards giving the same information for the AT RSMs. Once sat down, our numbers seemed quite impressive. With the four Squadrons' intakes combined, there were about 400 of us. The NCOs lined the back wall, glaring. One of them caught me looking over. 'Can I get you a fucking choc-ice?' he sneered.

I turned round quickly and tried to sink into my seat, just as a huge man came striding down the aisle. He was at least six-foot-three and he marched so purposefully that he made it to the front in about eight paces. He turned and regarded us grimly. A hush descended, to a new level beyond mere silence. He opened up in a Glaswegian baritone which sounded like he'd been gargling glass. 'Good afternoon, gentlemen.' Without waiting for a response, he continued. 'My name is Company Sergeant Major Hendricks of Penney Squadron.' He turned to stare at the Penney Recruits who were sitting to his left near the back. 'Those of you in my squadron will get to know me very well over the next two years. I'm not very good with names, so those of you whose names I can recall will either have done something to impress me, or acted the cunt. Either way, you'll remember me.'

Hendricks was scaring the shit out of me at a distance of 40 feet. This was getting to be a like a bad joke: every newly introduced member of the DS was worse than the previous one. It was both well-choreographed and utterly depressing.

His voice shook me out of my fugue. 'The rest of you will meet your Company Sergeant Majors soon. They are all as nice as me, so you won't be disappointed. You're here now to meet the two most important men in your life for the next two years. You will be addressed first by the RSM, and secondly by the Camp Commandant. When the RSM walks into the room, I will give you the command, 'Sit *up*'. You will then sit up so straight that all your vertebrae will fuse simultaneously. Understood? Good.'

He moved to the side of the cinema, and stood, poker straight, with his eyes looking expectantly towards the entrance. There was utter silence, punctuated only by a tiny, nervous fart from someone in front of me. Then I heard the foyer door being pushed open and glanced at Sergeant Major Hendricks just in time to hear him shout his command. The entire room stiffened,

400 sets of peripheral vision trying to clock the RSM as he boomed down the aisle. As he got to the front, he executed a perfect parade ground halt, no doubt doing additional damage to an already threadbare carpet. He then spun round, in a perfect about-turn and slammed his right foot down to complete the movement, almost putting it through the floor. It was a full three seconds before he spoke and he cast his gaze critically on a sweeping panorama of the room. He wasn't as tall as Hendricks, but he was built like an all-in wrestler. His stable belt was wrapped round a prodigious beer gut, which was straining to escape both above and below it, his pace stick was jammed tight under his left arm and his boots were shinier than it was possible for non-metallic objects to be. He obviously subscribed to the little man-big hat school of thought, and he peered at us from under an enormous peak, denying us eye contact and increasing his aura of danger. His voice, when it emerged, took us by complete surprise.

'Good afternoon to you all. My name is Warrant Officer First Class, Regimental Sergeant Major Banning, of the Coldstream Guards.'

There was a trace of a Cornish accent, but his tone was light and almost too quiet to hear clearly.

'I am responsible for your discipline and well-being whilst serving at this training establishment. I am an extremely fair man, with high standards both given and demanded. If you try your hardest and endeavour to honour the words in your oath to Her Majesty the Queen, you will find me to be no enemy.'

That sounded fair enough to me. His delivery was calm and measured and made me feel that perhaps there were small pockets of sanity existing in the place. But, of course, there was more, and it made my dread return immediately. He removed his pace stick from under his arm and pointed it in our general direction. With no change in his manner, he said, 'However, if any of you besmirch the good name of this College, or bring the smallest aspect of the Army into disrepute, I will stick this pace stick right up your arse. It will need two strong men armed with bolt croppers to retrieve it, and when they do it won't be me that cleans the shit off it.'

It was at that supremely inopportune moment that someone coughed loudly. The result was predictable. The RSM turned to face him, and asked him quietly, 'Do you think it's polite to interrupt a Regimental Sergeant Major while he's speaking?'

The guilty lad was beyond speech, and simply sat and stared, and waited for whatever was coming next. The RSM raised his voice to the Senior NCOs at the back of the room. 'Sergeant Bolton, please remove this man to the guardroom and ensure that he understands his folly.'

For the capital crime of performing a reflex bodily action, the guilty party was ordered into the aisle and marched away, probably forever.

As if nothing had happened, RSM Banning made a polite enquiry. 'Would anyone else like to cough?' He took our terrified hush as a No. 'There you have it in a nutshell, boys. Stick to the rules and you'll have no problem. Fuck me or any of my staff about, and you will receive no quarter.' He glanced at his watch. 'The Commandant will be entering the building shortly. I will give the same command to sit up that Company Sergeant Major Hendricks gave you earlier. Make sure your response is equally observed.'

He moved to stand by CSM Hendricks and adopted an identical pose. Despite all the fear that they'd managed to instil into me, It was at this point that I started laughing at my predicament – internally, of course. They looked such a pair of cunts stood there. You'd have thought God himself was about to walk through the door, if their chin-jutting expressions were anything to go by. I got the sneaking suspicion that thinking this way was going to be a useful release valve.

We were all anticipating the sound of the doors opening, and when they did, we made ready to brace ourselves up after the RSM's command.

'Sit *up*.'

From the back, it must have looked like an attempt to break the 'most people being simultaneously executed in Texas' record as the Commandant moved quietly down to the front. As he neared the RSM, Banning sprang to life and made a show of marching three feet towards the Commandant before completing another exaggerated drill movement. In tones barely higher than whispers, the RSM informed the CO that the new intake were awaiting his instruction. The RSM then retreated to his initial position by the stage after being thanked by the CO. Whilst this short pantomime was being enacted, I checked out the Commandant. He was shorter again than the RSM, probably about five foot seven, and his build was slight. He was in Number Two dress and looked pretty snappy. A pair of well-polished, brown shoes finished the look. The only person I'd ever seen dressed like this before was the Brigadier from *Doctor Who*.

The CO removed his hat and turned to face his audience, knocking us completely off-guard by producing a huge smile.

'Sit at ease please, boys,' he invited. I only relaxed a fraction, letting my shoulders slump slightly. He continued to smile without speaking, as though mentally preparing an off-the-cuff speech. After a few seconds, looking up and down the rows of shell-shocked faces, he began.

'Good afternoon, and welcome to Uniacke Barracks, home of the Royal Corps of Signals Army Apprentice College Harrogate. My name is Lieutenant Colonel De La Tour and I am the Commandant of this fine establishment.'

His accent hovered somewhere near 'wannabe aristocrat,' like he was putting it on a bit. At school, I'd once had to drop off a note at the staff room and I'd gone in, after knocking, to find Mr Lever talking to his bank manager on the phone. When he was teaching us French he had a slight West Lancashire accent, but the bloke at Barclays must have thought he was talking to a minor royal. It seemed like De La Tour was labouring under a similar verbal idiosyncrasy.

He looked at the RSM and then back to us. 'By now, you've met a couple of the personalities that make up our little family. The thing that you must always bear in mind is that we are here to help you in your undertaking to become trained soldiers. None of my staff are paid to mess you around unnecessarily and they will endeavour to help you find your way without having to resort to threats or punishment.'

Now I was confused. This didn't seem to tally up with anything we'd experienced so far.

'However, if you are failing to achieve the standards laid down by me, then I fully expect my NCOs and Senior NCOs to encourage you – along, perhaps, with some gentle chiding.'

The RSM's face was totally inscrutable, but I could see that Hendricks was cracking into an almost imperceptible grin. Just like the Queen supposedly thinks the world smells of fresh paint, the Commandant had a slightly lopsided view of 'his' College. As soon as he was around, the shouting and abuse stopped and was replaced by constructive criticism.

'There will be times when some of you feel homesick or that you are simply unable to continue, for many reasons. If you find yourself in this position, inform any permanent member of staff and you will receive a sympathetic hearing.'

The light chuckle coming from the line of NCOs at the back, was quickly strangled by a ferocious look from the RSM.

'Don't forget to try and enjoy this experience. You are embarking on an adventure that will see you emerge in just under two years as trained soldiers and tradesmen in our esteemed Corps. It's not for the faint-hearted, and no doubt a few of you will fall by the wayside, but those of you who complete your training will have gained something to be fiercely proud of. I'll now leave you in the capable hands of the RSM, and would just like to congratulate you all on choosing a career in the Royal Corps of Signals. Carry on RSM.'

'Sit *up*,' bellowed Banning, and we complied immediately as the Commandant took a leisurely stroll back up the cinema aisle, smiling.

As soon as he was through the double doors and out of earshot, the dark cloud that had temporarily been dispersed returned with vigour. Of course, it was Army policy that none of the NCOs or the RSM would publicly disagree with anything the Commandant said, particularly in front of junior ranks. Nevertheless, the sniggers and grins made it quite apparent, to anyone with the tiniest amount of perception, that they all thought he was spouting utter bollocks. He probably thought we were going straight back to the block, from the cinema, for a big sing-song with the staff.

We hadn't been sat at ease since the Commandant left, so the RSM left without requiring us to stiffen up theatrically. When he'd gone, CSM Hendricks waited for a few seconds and followed him without another word. The second the doors closed behind him, the braying returned immediately. We were 'encouraged along' and 'gently chided' by the NCOs until we got back outside the cinema. Once again, they optimistically tried to get us to march as a squad, presumably to give them some more abuse ammunition, as if they needed it.

When we made it back in front of the block, we were halted in the quadrangle facing the Squadron offices. At this point, all of the ATNCOs gathered in front of us. This was one of the things I'd never be able to reconcile myself with throughout my time at the College. I'd love to have met the bright spark at the MOD who thought it was a great idea to put 17-year-olds, who'd been in the Army a year, in charge of their younger colleagues. It was a revelation of man-management, straight from the William Golding school of social studies. They loitered around, eyeing us up for an excuse to give us an ear-bashing. But we had already learned to avoid eye contact and to say fuck all, unless something was asked of us.

Then, after a couple of minutes, what looked like a werewolf in a dress and a tramp in uniform came out of the Squadron offices.

The tramp spoke. 'Good afternoon, gents. I am Corporal Timms and I am in charge of the Squadron stores. So when you get your webbing, your lids, and all that, you will get it from me. I will also give you all of the shit that you need to keep the block clean. Is that clear?'

'Yes, Corporal!'

He pointed a shaking hand to the cross-dressing lycanthrope. 'And this lovely lady is Dawn. She is the Squadron Clerk, and will deal with all of your administrative problems. So you will treat her with respect. Is that also clear?'

'Yes, Corporal!'

Timms really was a scruffy bastard. His uniform looked like he had just pulled it off a dead body, and he himself had the appearance of having been on a dirty protest with nothing to keep him company but a year's supply of meths. His ensemble would have been complete if he'd been using a length of electrical flex to hold up his trousers. My blind respect for anyone with rank had just taken its first knock.

Dawn seemed like a nice enough girl. Although a bit timid, she was of a pleasant disposition. But, fuck me was she hairy. Not the downy ladies' fluff that's noticeable on some women if you catch it from the wrong angle; no, this woman had whiskers you could light a match off. If she'd have been a man, she'd have been charged for not shaving.

Following the introductions by the cast of *Carry On Screaming*, two other permanent staff came out of the office. They were both medium-sized men, again in uniform, but they were carrying pace sticks and wearing a blue sash each that ran diagonally across their chests. They looked like also-rans from a military beauty contest. Both also wore forage caps (more commonly known as 'Twat Hats'), with the peaks running straight down their faces, thus compressing their noses and obscuring their eyes. They had to tilt their heads back and look down their noses at us to speak. The one on the right spoke first, out of the side of his mouth. 'Gentlemen!' he boomed. 'I am Sergeant Atkins. And this,' – he gesticulated to the other sergeant with his stick – 'is Sergeant Bailey. Soon you will be split into different Troops. One of us will be your Troop Sergeant, and from that moment forth, you will fucking hate us. Do I make myself understood?'

'Yes, Sergeant!' we hollered. But amidst our call, a single, whining, unlucky voice could be heard saying, 'Yes, Corporal.'

All the instructors, both permanent staff and junior soldiers, heard it, and in a flash had congregated around a pencil-thin kid who looked a bit like a girl.

'What the fuck did you call me?' screamed Atkins.

'Corporal, Sergeant,' replied the quivering youth.

'*WHY*? Do I *look* like a Corporal?'

'No, Corp… er, Sergeant.'

Atkins stepped forward until he was almost nose to nose with the unfortunate youth.

'What's your fucking name?' he hissed through gritted teeth.

'Rose, Sergeant.' He was close to tears.

'Are you sure it's not Pansy? Do you play any musical instruments, Rose?'

'Yes, Sergeant. The guitar, Sergeant.'

'Bollocks, you play the fucking pink piccolo. Or is it the blue veined flute? You'd better sort your fucking shit out and start fucking sparking, Pansy. Or you will end up in a *world* of hurt.'

With that, Atkins, Bailey and all the other non-recruits moved off to the sides, and the final introduction of the squadron hierarchy took place.

Three men walked out. The first, who was also wielding a pace stick, had a badge on the sleeve of his right arm. The other two had their rank atop their shoulders. The first man, with the stick, screamed a word of command. 'SQUA, SQUAAAAAAAAA, CHAAA! Standstill!'

This unintelligible noise was like a sound effect from a karate film, but it made all the other people in uniform spring to attention. Then the smallest of the three men stepped forward, his rank denoted by a crown on his epaulettes. He spoke in 1950s BBC English. 'Ah, yes, gentlemen. Welcome to Rawson Squadron. You will soon learn that this is the best Squadron in this College, and that to let the standard slip would be a terrible error on your part. I am the Officer commanding the squadron, Major Tatchell.' (He pronounced it 'Tetchell'.) 'This' – he pointed to the other Officer – 'is Ceptain Bessett, my second-in-commend.'

Bassett was much older and bigger. He had a badly-broken nose and he looked like he had been in the Army since the Battle of the Bulge.

Finally, Tatchell gestured to the third man who had come out with them, and who had made the strange shouting noises. 'And this is Sergeant Major Horton. You will get to know him very well in the future, gentlemen. Just make sure that it is for all the right reasons.'

SSM Horton could have been Tatchell's brother. They were both short, slender men, with hook noses and hooded eyes, and each radiated an air of a wholly unpleasant persuasion. Like a couple of evil Smurfs, or a pair of goat-bothering trolls.

Tatchell looked up and down our group of scruffy youngsters, then he sniffed the air, spun on his heel. 'Carry on, Sergeant Major!'

'SAH!' replied Horton, as he snapped up an immaculate salute. When both officers had gone, he turned to Sergeants Atkins and Bailey and told them to get us processed. Then he, too, returned to his office.

The two sergeants had a conversation with the junior instructors and Dawn, who then went up into the accommodation block.

Then Bailey spoke. 'Right, gents. When I fall you out, get your lazy arses up into your shaggin' rooms and get the documentation that you were told to bring. Then be out in the fucking corridor before I arrive, or there will be *hell* to pay!'

He paused, sucked in a lung-full of air then made the same kind of noises that the SSM had made earlier. 'SQUA, FAAAAAAAAAAALLLLLLLL, ITE!'

As soon as he had given the word, the junior NCOs started shouting and herding us up the stairs, occasionally slipping in an assisting boot up the ring.

We sprinted up the corridor, panting and frantic. The corridor itself was split into three parts, each separated from one another by double doors, and containing three sleeping rooms, one set of toilets, one drying room and one set of showers and sinks. I was in the middle room of the corridor, so I got to my kit quite quickly. Luckily I had stashed my documents at the top of my bag, so I got back out into the corridor well within time. The NCOs had wedged the double doors back, so the corridor was open to its full extent and I could see Dawn at the far end, sitting behind a table laden with files.

When Sergeant Bailey came up the stairs, there were still some lads rummaging frantically through their kit to find their documentation.

Bailey went mad. 'WHAT DID I SAY? WHAT THE *FUCK* DID I FUCKING *SAY*? BE OUT IN THE CUNTING CORRIDOR, WITH YOUR FUCKING DOCS, BEFORE I GET UP HERE. AND YOU CAN'T EVEN FUCKING GET THAT RIGHT! YOU FUCKING *WANKERS*! THIS IS A VERY *FUCKING* BAD START, GENTLEMEN, VERY BAD IN-FUCKING-DEED!'

I felt a wave of collective trepidation sweep through us. Bailey waited until the last man was out in the corridor with his papers.

He then told us all to turn to our right, and the first man at the head of the line then dressed forward with his birth certificate, and Dawn processed him into the Army. After what seemed like an eternity, I was next in line. I gave Dawn my documents, she yawned and scratched her chin. It sounded like a path being swept with a stiff broom. I closed my eyes and shuddered, but all I could visualise was a big pig, rubbing its side up against a tree. I was pulled out of that hideous mental picture when Dawn told me my Army number. 'Don't forget it,' she said.

I returned to my room, repeating it over and over in my head; it helped drive out the last remnants of the swineful visions.

ELEPHANTS' NESTS AND
COW PAT BERETS

I was the first back, so I took the opportunity to survey our room. There were two doors leading in. On entering from the first door there was a bunk bed with two lockers on the right, opposite an identical arrangement next to the window. This layout was duplicated around the room, except for the back right hand corner where there was a single bed with a locker. That one was made up, unlike the bunks which were bare of even mattresses; I didn't know who it belonged to.

My exposure to the other guys in the room had been negligible, as we had only passed each other as we dropped our bags off, or picked up our documents. But soon they started to filter in.

They were all just nondescript kids like me. Most of them were scrawny, although one of them was a bit overweight. We were all quiet and engrossed in our own troublesome thoughts when one of them piped up in a London accent. 'Alwight, lads. We've got to get to know each uvver, so I'm Paul, Paul Jones.'

I followed next and just told them my name, then the rest of the lads took it in turns. The fat kid was called Alistair McKenzie and was from an obscure village in Hampshire. There was Steve Keets from Nottingham, Tom Galbraith from Glasgow, Colin Mortimer from Newcastle, and finally, two friends who had joined up together in Warrington, Barry Nash and Neil Moody.

The initial conversation was brief and nervous. Cockney Paul was by far the loudest and most vocal, and he seemed very confident. He and Alistair had been in the Army Cadets before joining up. None of the rest of us had that kind of experience, so they took on an air of superiority and started trying to give us an impromptu drill lesson. I just gazed miserably at them as they marked time on the spot, shouting at themselves. It just looked like one more thing I was never going to get the hang of. The display was cut short by the instructors screaming for us to get out into the corridor again.

Once out there, we were told, with another fanfare of shouting, that we were being issued with bedding and shown how to assemble our bed blocks.

What the *fuck* was a bed block?

Whatever it was, I was already betting it wouldn't be something pleasant, designed to make our lives easier. We were taken down to the store, adjacent to Corporal Timms' grotto. Twenty minutes later, we were back in the room with our newly-issued kit: two pillows, two sheets, two pillowcases, a counterpane and four grey blankets. None of which looked remotely inviting. Both my pillows had decorative slobber stains, the counterpane was a hideous orange, 70s thing and the blankets, like a really scratchy loft insulation, were almost too painful to carry.

I ditched them all on my bed, the bottom bunk near the door. The mattress was clean and white and had green stripes running the length of it, making it look like a Pacer. Steve Keets took the top bunk and started to put his gear on the mattress. Barry and Neil, being mates, buddied up across the way, and the two ex-cadets, Paul and Alistair, decided it would be a good idea to share. That left the last bunk to Tom and Colin. Tom asked the question that was on all of our minds.

'What's a bed block then, Paul?'

In his capacity as military attaché to Room 4, Recruit Troop he began to explain.

'It's just another thing to fuck us about with. It's a way of folding your blankets and sheets for inspection. It looks like a big liquorice allsort and it's a cunt to get the hang of.'

Oh good. Just as he was about to go into a bit more detail, the 'corridor' shout came again, and we dropped everything and rushed out of the room. Neither of the permanent Sergeants were around now, so we were entirely in the hands of the AT NCOs. There were six Lance Corporals, three Corporals and a Sergeant. The Sergeant's special status was defined by a red sash and pace stick, and he quickly introduced himself.

'Afternoon, tossers. I'm AT Sgt Bramhall and my sole job in life for the next fourteen weeks is to fuck you about until you hate me so much you'll want to kill me.'

I'd only known him for eight seconds, and I'd have happily done him some serious physical damage. That is, if I'd been quite a lot harder; he couldn't see my face and I could blame someone else.

'Tonight, your room NCOs will be in charge of you. Sergeant Atkins will be going round the block at eight o'clock tomorrow morning, and your rooms will be fucking *spotless*. If they're not...' He trailed off for a second and smiled. 'Well, we'll see what fucking happens. Before tea, Corporal Edgeley will come round to your rooms, one by one, and show how to get your bed blocks ready for the morning. When I say "go", get back to your rooms. Oh, and by the way, if I catch any fucker sitting on a bed or leaning against a locker between now and December I'll throw him out the nearest window. GO!'

We ran back into our room and tried our hardest to stand around in a military fashion. It seemed a bit unfair about the bed and locker thing. There were only four chairs round the table, so those of us that didn't get one had to just stand around like drunks waiting for the pub to open.

Twenty minutes later, Corporal Edgeley wandered in with a sneer on his face.

'Right, the lot of you... round the table in a semi-circle *now*.'

Of course, we weren't quick enough to respond to the command, and found ourselves pushing out the press-ups for a minute or so until he got bored and stood us up again. He pointed at Tom.

'Have you been issued your bedding?'

'Yes, Corporal.'

'Fucking hell, not another Sweaty Sock. Go and get it and bring it over here. Quickly.'

Tom ran to his bed space, even though it was only five feet away and he could have made it over there in one step. I suppose he was just showing willing. He returned with his full complement of bedding, and was reprimanded immediately by Edgeley.

'Did I say bring your fucking counterpane? Did I?'

The changes in Tom's expression took place in an instant. His first reaction was one of consternation – ie *'You told me to get my bedding, so I brought the lot, you cunt.'*

His mind quickly computed that this wouldn't have been a clever answer. It altered immediately to one of vacant capitulation, as he – like the rest of us – started to learn the game.

'Sorry, Corporal.' He managed to make it sound genuine, even though we all knew that he was punctuating the words internally with the phrase, 'You fucking wanker.'

'Right then, get it on. You can be the ghost of the counterpane.'

For the rest of the display, Tom wore the counterpane over his head like a psychedelic trick-or-treater.

Edgeley assembled the bed block with ease and a running commentary. Even as I watched him folding blankets and sheets to millimetre perfect dimensions, I knew that this would be the first of many things where I would fail. He used three blankets, separated by the two sheets, to create the bulk of the block. He then employed the fourth blanket as a sort of wrapping to the whole affair, folding it in such an ingenious way that I stopped trying to suss it out immediately. The whole process took him about three minutes and when he finished he was left with a solid chunk of best Army bedding, trussed to the point of bursting.

'This is a fairly quick job. What I want yours to look like is this.'

He left the room for a second and returned with another bed block and placed it on the table. It was a complete set-up, compressed so tightly and neatly that it was two-thirds the size of its cousin. It must have taken somebody days, equipped with elaborate measuring tools and a banding machine, to produce such perfection. I had the feeling that if anyone pulled at one of the sheets, there would be an almighty explosion and people would be picking pieces of bed linen out of their hair for days.

Edgeley continued with the lesson. 'You'll place your bed block at the head end of the bed, with the pillows on top. Any questions?'

Tom's muffled voice emerged from beneath his disguise.

'What about the counterpane, Corporal?'

'Oh yeah, forgot about that. Give it here, Spooky.' He took the counterpane off Tom's head and dragged it over to his bed. He then covered Tom's mattress with it and began to tuck it in.

'What I'm doing here are called hospital corners. This is the way you'll make your bed for the rest of your military careers. Those of you who are here for more than a week, that is.'

That bit looked fairly straightforward, and when he'd completed pulling it tight, from underneath the bed, he placed the bed block and pillows on top.

'Da daaa! There you go. Piece of piss.' He looked at Tom. 'What's your name again, Jock?'

'Galbraith, Corporal.'

'Well, yours is all made up already, Galbraith. Looks like it's your lucky day.'

'Yes, Corporal.'

'Is it *fuck*!'

He then proceeded to dismantle Tom's bed block down to component level, taking special care to shake the blankets out thoroughly. I'm sure that his reasoning was that he didn't want to lend Tom an unfair advantage and not that he was just an utter cunt who took great pleasure in making lesser mortals miserable. When he'd finished, Tom's bunk looked like a Moroccan carpet shop, with blankets hanging from the lights and lockers. Edgeley then left, heading gleefully for Room 5, the perfect bed block under his arm, to repeat the display.

As soon as we could hear him shouting next door, we knew the coast was clear, and started talking quietly. Colin helped Tom get his bedding down as we discussed the finer points of the bed block.

'What a fucking gobshite,' said Tom, folding his blankets back to their original size.

'I think they're all gonna be like that, mate,' said Paul.

I ventured my own opinion. 'I'll tell you what, I've got no fucking chance of making one of them things.'

This brought a laugh of assent from Steve. 'I'm with you there, Eddy. I reckon we'll get shat on tomorrow morning.'

'Don't worry about it, lads,' said Paul, with undeniable accuracy. 'We'll get shat on however well we do.'

And there it was, though I didn't know it at the time. The secret of basic training. There *is* no correct answer. The sooner you learned that, the better. Some got it in days. It took me a couple of weeks. Others went through the entire three months thinking they'd done something personally to upset the instructors. The fact was, all punishments and prizes were pre-ordained. How an inspection went was not down to how much cleaning or polishing you'd done – the staff had already decided, over a brew, exactly what standard you'd achieved. The inspection was academic – a smokescreen to justify whatever punishment they had in mind for that day. For the fortunate ones who learned the secret early, it took a lot of the pressure off. Only you knew if you'd tried your hardest to do something correctly – an NCO screaming in your face on some flimsy pretext wouldn't change that.

The next 'corridor' shout came about 20 minutes later. We were told to put all our spare civilian clothes, minus socks and shreddies, into our suitcases and stow them in the case room. That left me with just the clobber I was standing up in until we were issued our uniforms. Putting your civvies away seemed like a far more emphatic step towards being in the Army than signing papers or chanting attestations. All the instruction and running about took us up to tea-time, and we were quickly assembled back outside for a piss-poor march to the cookhouse for the evening meal. The food maintained the same ropey standards of lunchtime, although there was a slight difference. Instead of chips and sausages, we got chips and pies. Still shit, just different. It also transpired that to ask, 'What's in the pies, Chef?' of one of the slop-jockeys would see you larded with four-letter words by way of reply.

On our arrival back to the block that evening, we discovered who else would be sleeping in the other bed in our room. Lance Corporal Baker was one of the junior instructors. He was about seventeen-and-a-half, which – when you were a sixteen-year-old recruit – put him somewhat on a pedestal. He was about six feet tall with dark hair and a permanent shadow on his jaw that meant that he needed to shave every day. Unlike the rest of us; though we were forced to shave on a daily basis, it was by no means a task that was born of necessity. Baker would sleep in the room and be the first line of discipline. He started his introduction as he meant to go on, by telling us to 'shut-the-fuck-up' and to 'listen-the-fuck-in' and to 'start shagging sparking.'

Then he continued. 'Right, gents. I will be your room NCO during basic training and to that end I am responsible for the state of you fuckers and this room. So for the rest of the shagging night you are going to be taught how to clean the room, the corridor and the ablutions. You will also be taught how to behave when a senior rank enters the room, and how to lay out your lockers. At the end of the night you WILL write a shagging letter home telling everyone how fucking great it is here, and you WILL have your shagging heads down at twenty two hundred hours local fucking time! Do you understand?'

He had a stronger Mancunian accent than mine, but I couldn't see us being mates for a while.

'Yes, Corporal!' we shouted, as loud as we could.

'*LOUDER* YOU LAZY BASTARDS!'

'Yes, Corporal!' we shouted back at exactly the same volume as before.

'That's better. Right, firstly you've got to learn room etiquette. If you see an NCO walk into the room, the first thing you do is stand to attention and shout "UP!"' He bellowed the 'up' part. 'Right, we'll practise that for a bit.'

I could hear sporadic shouts of 'UP!' Coming from the other rooms; no doubt their etiquette lessons were already in full swing.

Baker scowled, and left the room. We all looked at each other bemusedly, but before we could say anything he had come back in through the other door, right next to Alistair McKenzie. Alistair just stared back at him and gawped, open-mouthed and frozen with fear. On seeing Baker, I went rigid and shouted, 'UP!' All the other lads did the same, but Baker was bearing down on McKenzie in a rage. Before addressing Alistair, he shouted to the rest of us, 'Keep fucking shouting it! You're going to need the shagging practice!' So we continued to shout rhythmically at the tops of our voices. I felt like a bit of knob, but if it stopped me getting a gripping, then it was worth it. Baker was really going to town on him.

'Why the fuck didn't you shout when I entered the room?'

'I don't know, Corporal.'

'Well you'd better start knowing, Goat Jugs. Or you're going to shit out!'

'Yes, Corporal!'

'Right, the rest of you shut up. McKenzie, carry on.'

All eyes were on Alistair as he started to shout. 'UP! UP! UP!' He was very self-conscious and was close to tears. Despite this, Baker showed no sign of letting up. 'Come on, McKenzie! Get some air in those pudgey pregnant dog tits and get shouting.'

Eventually, Alistair paid his penance, and for the next 30 minutes, the NCOs spent their time just wandering in and out of each other's rooms to keep us on our toes and ensure that we could grasp the concept of standing up and shouting.

Then Baker took us through the intricacies of shining the floor with sickly-smelling yellow floorwax and an ancient looking manual bumper. The bumper consisted of a solid lump of metal with a soft brush base and a long wooden handle that protruded from the top of the weight. Baker described how we could use the bumper to bring the brown lino floor up into a shine. 'Right, gents. Get a cloth each, with a good fucking scoop of wax, then get on your shagging knees in a line and smear that fucking shit in to the deck in a circular motion.'

We did as we were bid and – after a while – Baker continued with his instruction. 'USE YOUR FUCKING NOGGIN, GENTS! ONCE YOU'VE COVERED THE AREA IN FRONT OF YOU, MOVE BACKWARDS UNTIL THE WHOLE FUCKING FLOOR'S COVERED. JESUS-FUCKING-H-FUCKING-CHRIST! IT'S NOT FUCKING ROCKET SCIENCE!'

Once the floor was covered, the wax was left to dry. The method of shining it was very simple: just push and pull the heavy bumper over the wax, very fast, for a very long time, whilst under a constant verbal assault from Baker. Those of us that weren't on bumper-duty were cleaning the washrooms and the toilets. It was relatively straightforward. All you had to do was scrub and polish everything in sight. The other jobs – like cleaning the showers, the corridor and the drying room – were shared amongst the other two rooms in our section of the corridor.

Every now and then we would have to swap over, and take turns running the bumper. I was nervous about this; Barry Nash and Neil Moody had already done a stint, and when they'd staggered from the room they looked like they had just been released from the Bastille. I was no different. Each push and pull of the vile instrument drained my strength. The fact that I was as skinny as the bumper handle itself didn't help matters, and each motion felt like it was shredding my arms and hands.

'I fucking love bumpering, Nugent,' said Baker, as he sat on his bed. 'Do you?'

'Yes, Corporal!' The two words were broken up by gasps for air.

'Do you know the one thing that I like more than bumpering, Nugent?'

'No, Corporal!'

'Watching people bumper for me! Now that gives me wood! Does it give you wood, Nugent?'

'Yes, Corporal!'

'Fucking good man, Nugent! Right, repeat after me at the top of your voice. One-two-three-four, I must bump the floor!'

I repeated everything he wanted me to, and each chant got more bizarre. The final slogan, to the tune of *I Love To Love But My Baby Just Loves To Dance*, went, 'I love to bumper, 'cos it gives Corporal Baker wood.'

By the time 9.30pm rolled around, we were all knackered and smelling like school janitors. I couldn't believe how spotless the room was, but Baker told us that it was in bog-order. 'It looks like the main stage at the world shit-juggling championships,' he said, with a critical air.

Finally, he made us all sit down and write a letter home. I didn't really know what to put, so I just said I'd arrived safely and that the food was OK. My mind was in a bit of turmoil, and that was probably evident in the banality of my writing.

Once we had all finished, Baker took the letters and we all went to bed, with an enforced lights out at 10 pm. We whispered quietly for a bit. Hushed questions shot back and forth to find out where guys were from and what they thought of the Army so far. When I wasn't involved in a conversation, my mind would wander and I took stock of my current predicament. In the middle of one of my thoughts, Tom was describing life in Scotland and after finishing a swear word laden sentence, he finished it off with, 'D'ya ken what I mean?'

After 30 seconds of silence, Paul's cockney accent cut through the dark like an 18 certificate Dick Van Dyke. 'Who the fackin' 'ell's Ken?'

I dropped off as Tom explained the origins of Glaswegian gibberish, only to be woken, three seconds later, by Baker smacking the shit out of my bunk with one of his mess tins. The metal-on-metal clanging was horrendous, and it woke the entire room immediately.

'Come on, you lazy tossers. Hands off cocks and on socks. Get out of them fucking scratchers. There's work to do.'

I jumped out of bed and checked my watch. It said 5.30am, but I couldn't believe that I'd been asleep. A shocked Steve, slip-sliding down from the top bunk, obviously had the same thought in mind. Within three or four seconds, all eight of us, in a selection of unsightly undercrackers, were stood at the end of our beds, shivering slightly, while we waited for Baker to say something else.

He started laughing. 'Look at the fucking state of you lot. The Army's had it, I tell ya.'

He had a point. Standing there to attention, thrusting our chests out, dressed only in Y-fronts, we were a sorry display of manhood. Tom Galbraith was stood on the other side of the room, directly opposite me. He had his eyes fixed on a point somewhere above and behind my head and his right spud was hanging outside his gruds, in mid-air, like a turkey's wattle. I averted my gaze and watched Alistair McKenzie trying to keep his gut in. There was no sign of a tan anywhere. Col Mortimer, whose skin had been subjected to 16 years of sub-zero Geordie winters, was particularly white. He looked like he'd been Tippex-ed. After shaking his head a bit more, Baker continued. To nobody in particular, he shouted, 'Stand up straight, you fucking dregs. Right, it's half-five, you've got until seven to get this place in order. You'll then be taken down to breakfast. At eight o'clock, Sergeant Atkins will be round. If you've got any problems or you need help with anything, ask someone who gives a fuck.'

With that, he retreated to his bed space. He opened his locker door and lay down on his bed. Leaving the door ajar created an effective barrier between him and us.

Paul Jones, as usual, was the first to speak up. 'Let's get scrubbed up first, then we'll get on with it.'

I grabbed my towel and washkit and followed the rest of the lads into the ablutions. Rooms 5 and 6 shared the sinks and toilets with us, so 24 blokes were waiting on eight washbasins and three showers. I got in line and waited while a poor kid with acne had his first shave. He looked like he was going to need a transfusion when he was finished and when I got to the bowl after him I was sure I could see little lumps of flesh in the plughole. I had never shaved in my life, but, mindful of the joining instructions – *It is an offence not to be cleanly shaven in the British Army. All personnel will arrive with adequate shaving equipment for day one of basic training* – I'd arrived equipped with a couple of Bic razors and a big can of shaving foam. The trouble was, I didn't have anything to remove, not even a bit of bum-fluff. I lathered up my face until I looked like Father Christmas, then went through the motions, somehow managing not to slit my throat. By the time I'd had a quick shower, got back into the room and got dressed in my day-old civvies, it was just short of six o'clock.

Baker made an appearance from behind his door. 'I'll tell you what lads, I'm not hearing many cleany-cleany noises. You'd better get a fucking move on. Nugent, what are you doing, you fucking knob-gobbler?'

I was just making a start on my bed block, and told him so using the method familiar to all recruits – looking at the ceiling and shouting as loud as was humanly possible.

'I'M DOING ME BEDBLOCK, CORPORAL.'

'Well, it's fucking shit. Sergeant Atkins is going to love you.'

Over the next hour, we all flitted around from bed blocks to sweeping to dusting to cleaning to polishing to bumpering to cowering to worrying to bed blocks again. By breakfast time, we'd achieved the sum total of fuck-all and we were browbeaten down to the cookhouse by Baker and his mates. I was pleasantly surprised by the morning offering. In a radical departure from the previous day's lunch and dinner, the food looked OK and tasted of something. The choices were, as they always would be, cereal, toast, a big greasy fry-up or a combination of the three.

I went for the fry up. There were various hotplate trays holding bacon, sausages, fried eggs and fried bread and a steaming cauldron of baked beans at the end. You were supposed to help yourself; within two seconds, I'd made the biggest mistake in the Slop Jockey code of practice. I'd stuck two sausages on my plate and was going back in for a third, but as soon as the tongs hit the skin of the frazzled banger one of the cooks appeared from nowhere and stuck his head through the counter until we were nose-to-nose.

'Two sausages only, you fucking stroker.'

He was absolutely fuming – it was as if he was paid in sausages, and I was eating his wages. I dropped the tongs immediately and scuttled down the hotplate to get away, carefully adding one piece of bacon, one fried egg and one piece of fried bread to the plate as he glared at me. I couldn't decide whether one or two ladles of beans was the correct amount, so I opted for none, the only safe bet.

The rest of the lads from the room had got round one table, so I squeezed on to the end after helping myself to a brew from a silver Burco boiler near the entrance doors. The room NCOs had allocated us 45 seconds to eat our meal, so conversation was at a minimum. Barry had enough time to lick his plate, but I was just tucking into my second sausage when the shouting started. I managed to gobble it down as we were herded back outside. Baker was waiting for us when we got back to the room. He was shaking his head ruefully.

'Half-seven lads. You'll just have to tell Sergeant Atkins that you were too busy filling your fat fucking bellies at breakfast to get the room done properly.'

We spent the next 25 minutes trying to get the room up to the imaginary required standard. By 7.55 am, my bed block was still hopeless: it looked like a dead badger. No-one else's was much better.

'Right, stop fucking about now. You've had as much time as you're gonna get. He'll be round in a couple of minutes, so stand by your fucking beds.' We did as we were told.

'Nugent?'

'YES, CORPORAL.'

'I want you to stand outside the door. When Sergeant Atkins has finished with Room 3, I want you to stand to attention. You will then shout "ROOM, ROOM, SHUN", to bring the rest of the lads up. Do you think you can do that?'

'YES, CORPORAL.'

He turned to the rest of the room.

'When Nugent shouts ROOM, ROOM, SHUN, you will all stand up straight as your spongy little spines will allow. Understood?'

'YES, CORPORAL.'

I was quite impressed by just how loud seven blokes shouting at the same time could be.

'We'll see.' He turned back to me. 'You will then say to Sergeant Atkins, "Good morning, Sergeant. Room 4 Recruit Troop, ready and awaiting your inspection." That's when the fun starts. Got it?'

'YES, CORPORAL.'

I waited for further instructions. The only one forthcoming was, 'Well? Fuck off then.'

I positioned myself outside the room door and looked along the corridor. To my front I could see one bloke from each of rooms one, two and three adopting an identical stance to my own. I didn't dare look around, but presumed this was being duplicated down to Room 10. Before Atkins arrived, I had a couple of minutes to go through my lines. There wasn't much point really. I knew I was going to fuck it up, I was that nervous.

When he came through the double doors adjacent to Room 1, he was accompanied by Corporal Timms, who was self-importantly carrying a clipboard. It was hard to eavesdrop whilst trying to stand perfectly still, but the guy outside Room 1 seemed to say the right things and the entourage moved inside, followed by the room NCO. For about five seconds there was relative silence and I thought maybe it was going to be alright. Perhaps they'd go easy on us, it being our first full day and all that. The first sign that this wasn't going to be the case was a bed block being thrown into the corridor. Even when it landed and slid to a stop against the wall, it still looked better than mine. It was followed by Sergeant Atkins roaring at the owner.

The guy outside Room 2 looked round at me. The expression on his face said it all. He simply mimed the words, 'Oh, fuck.' I had to stifle the urge to laugh, despite my growing sense of dread. The destruction of Room 1 took about three minutes. I heard the same process being repeated eight times. First there would be a couple of questions from Atkins, the volume rising dramatically with each word. There would be a short nervous answer, interrupted by what sounded like a bear roaring. The unmistakeable noise of furniture being up-ended was next, followed by a short period of silence as Atkins moved to the next bunk. The system was employed identically in Rooms 2 and 3. As soon as they'd moved in to next door, Baker came out and stood beside me.

'You'd better get it fucking right, Nugent.'

I was shaking like a leaf. I counted eight sets of the familiar banging and clattering and readied myself for the onslaught.

Atkins emerged from Room 3, red-faced and angry. He made a bee-line for me and stopped no more than a pace away. I looked at him and started breathing in to say, 'Good morning.'

'Don't you fucking look at me, sunshine. Do you fucking fancy me or summat?'

I switched my gaze to a point above his head and shouted, 'Good morning, Sergeant.' I stopped, because he was shaking his head angrily.

'What I think you're trying to say is ROOM, ROOM, SHUN.'

Steve and the rest of the lads responded immediately to the authority in Sergeant Atkins' voice. I realised my mistake and started to shout, 'ROOM, ROO...'

'Too fucking late, don't bother. And never mind the "good morning" bollocks either, you've already fucked it all up beyond redemption.'

He turned to Lance Corporal Baker. 'Get a grip of your blokes, Cpl Baker, or I'll get a fucking grip of you.'

He moved past us both and into the room. Baker followed him, shooting me a filthy look as he went by. I hadn't really dropped him in the shit, it was all just a big blag between the DS, but I wasn't to know that. I was just starting to feel sorry for myself, when Atkins screamed. 'Whose fucking bed block is this?'

I didn't really need to look, but I did anyway. He had impaled the offending article on the end of his pace stick and was inspecting it with grim fascination.

'MINE, SERGEANT. NUGENT.'

'Jesus Christ, this is the worst one I've seen so far. It's like a fucking elephant's nest. Did you have boxing gloves and a blindfold on when you did this?'

'NO, SERGEANT.'

'Well, you should have done. You might have done a better fucking job. Bad start, Nugent. Bad fucking start.'

He lobbed it over his shoulder like a farmhand shifting straw bales. It bounced off my head and onto the floor at my feet. He continued to move through the room, voicing unsurprising opinions about our hygiene, stupidity and genetic make-up, all done at town-crier decibels. Only Col Mortimer came in for a similar amount of flak as me. He'd had the great idea of disagreeing with Sergeant Atkins.

'Whose is this one?' said Atkins, prodding Col's bed block.

'MINE, SERGEANT. MORTIMER.'

'Think you've done a good job do you?'

'ERM, YES, SERGEANT.'

'Well, I think it's shite.'

He pointed to a bulge at the back of the arrangement, that shouldn't have been there.

'What the fuck's that? It looks like you've trapped Arthur Askey in there. So you think that's up to standard do you?'

'YES, SERGEANT.'

'So, I'm a fucking liar am I?'

'What? ERM, YES... NO SERGEANT.'

The rest of us were shouting silently, *'Shut the fuck up, Col,'* but he'd already stitched himself up.

Atkins continued with the theme.

'So, what you're saying is you know better than me. A spotty, little Geordie gobshite, who's not even been in the Army for a day, knows better than me, a Sergeant in the Royal Corps of Signals with twelve years' service under his belt?'

'NO, SERGEANT.'

'I'll be fucking watching you, Mortimer. No one likes a smartarse. Especially one with a grid like a pizza. Corporal Baker, sort this fine bunch of wankers out.'

He left the room, with Timms in his wake, urgently scribbling on his clipboard. As the melee began in Room 5, Baker debriefed us. 'Fucking cheers, lads. That's me in the shit. Well fuck youse lot. When I'm in the shit, you're in the shit. I'll get you sparking, don't worry about that. Right, put your stuff back together and wait for the next corridor call.'

We started reassembling our bed blocks and putting the mattresses back on the beds. It looked like we'd been burgled by gorillas. Baker got called out by the NCO from Room 3 and left us to our own devices. We were all in our own little worlds, panicking about what might happen next, when Paul Jones shouted across to Col. 'I carn't fackin' believe you called 'im a liar, Col.'

Before Col could protest, we erupted into laughter. Fuck, did we need it.

'What about me, I've got a fucking elephant's nest,' I said.

This got them all laughing even louder. When Alistair reminded us of the insult Atkins had levelled at him about his weight, we were giggling like schoolgirls. He did quite a good impression of the Sergeant as well. *'Fuck me, McKenzie. You're a bit of a fucking blimp aren't you. When you go to the zoo, do the elephants throw peanuts at you?'*

It relieved a bit of the pressure and, by the time the next corridor shout came, I was feeling less depressed. This time we were taken down to the MRS for our medicals. The med-centre consisted of a 20 seat waiting area, a couple of examination rooms, a small dental clinic and a ward with eight beds for in-patients. You'd hope that, as a medical practice, it might be a repository of human kindness on the camp, but you'd be wrong. It was run by an old Scottish dragon, a Major in the QARANCS. She wore a pair of horn-rimmed specs, suspended on a chain around her neck, and introduced herself in unfriendly, 'Miss Jean Brodie' tones.

'Welcome to the Medical Reception Station. My name is Major Lines. You're here for your medical today and we will process you presently. For the rest of your two years, this is where you will come should you ever need to report sick. I am well aware that our services are often abused by skivers and malingerers, who always report here in large numbers whenever a cross-country run is looming. You may rest assured, boys, that if you report sick and I, or the doctor, find nothing wrong with you, you will be for the high-jump. And in this instance, the high-jump will not be a preferred alternative to long-distance running.'

She had a small self-satisfied giggle to herself. Eighty blank faces stared at her. The first 20 lads were seated whilst the rest of us filled up the space behind the chairs and the entrance corridor. Whilst Major Lines was talking, a little man had appeared behind her. I suppose he was a soldier, since he was in uniform, but he had the military bearing of Ronnie Corbett. He wore a pair of shiny black shoes and dark green, barrack-dress trousers. He also wore a starched white, short-sleeved white smock of the sort that dental nurses wear. A single, silver-metal chevron on the right sleeve indicated his rank. He can't have weighed more than seven stones, and most of that was hair. He had a classic comb-over, though in the absence of the raw materials required for such a 'do' he looked like he'd been combing it out of his ears. Major Lines nodded to him. 'Lance Corporal Nesbitt will make sure order is kept whilst you are waiting. When I call out your name make your way to the examination room.'

With the roll being called alphabetically, I was the last one from our room to go through. The medical was fairly standard and was conducted by a disinterested, septuagenarian doctor, as the Major looked on and took notes. I did all the same tests that I'd completed prior to joining, presumably to make sure I hadn't blagged my way through. With the treatment we'd been receiving, it was beyond my comprehension that anyone would consider cheating to get in. It would have been like someone pushing in in the queue for the guillotine.

As soon as I'd finished, I got dressed and made my way out into the waiting area. Baker clocked me straight away. 'Back up to the room, Nugent. Carry on tidying.'

When I walked in, all the lads were gathered round the window, looking down on to the parade square. A squad of 30 lads were being drilled by a sergeant. They were moving in perfect unison and responded to his commands with complete precision.

It looked fucking cold, that square. It was roughly the size of a couple of football pitches laid side to side, with a small inspection dais on the left. When the squad was stood still, the flapping of their trousers indicated that the wind was tear-arsing across the barren expanse of concrete at a rate of knots.

'That looks pretty difficult,' said Steve.

'Nah, mate,' said Paul. 'Just takes a bit of getting used to. We'll be that good in no time.'

I appreciated the confidence he was placing in me, but watching the skill levels required on the square I assumed (correctly) that drill would be something I could place on my list of 'things that I am shit at.'

'What's happening now then?' I said, to nobody in particular.

'Baker told me that we'll be getting our kit issued in the indoor arena.'

I liked the sound of that. It would be nice to actually stick a uniform on, if only to make me feel like I belonged a bit more. From all the running about in the same set of civvies, I was getting some major BO fumes from my shirt.

Baker turned up 20 minutes later and fell us in downstairs with the rest of the troop. The indoor arena was adjacent to the gym, and as we halted outside it a squad of about 15 apprentices were coming in off a run, in Army PT kit. In their red v-neck tops, huge blue shorts, green socks and white plimsolls, they looked like the winners of the 1926 FA Cup Final.

The inside of the arena was huge, about a third the size of the parade square, with rows of supporting pillars up to a three-storey ceiling. Lots of large blue crash mats were propped up against the far wall to our right. At the bottom end of the building, a line of tables ran its full width. Each was piled high with lots of items of clothing and kit, in varying shades of green.

We filed forward, one rank at a time. The store men had obviously been through the same kind of traumatic experience as the cooks. They were surly bastards who treated the items to be issued as their own personal belongings. The first bits of kit I received were two sets of camouflaged trousers and jackets. The man behind the table scrutinised me for about a second, then spoke some clothing sizes and handed me my outfit. It was painfully obvious that they wouldn't fit me. Even at an initial glance I could tell that they would be too wide and too short and had been designed for Bella Emberg. Next came two pairs of olive green trousers and jumpers, followed by a dark blue beret that was the size and shape of a freakishly large cow pat.

Adjacent to the berets was a stack of shirts. Although they were the same dull green as the jumpers, they gave off an occasional glint, as a sharp piece of the fabric caught the light. When the shirts were stacked on top of the clothing pile that was now perched on my outstretched arms, I placed my chin on them for support: it felt like having fibre-glass ground into my neck. It was the most uncomfortable cloth I had ever felt, as though made out of unwanted sandbag stock-piles from the Second World War.

The weight of items being supported by my spindly arms was now reaching critical mass, but I saw with relief that the next desk was piled high with kit bags. My heart sank when I realised that these 'sausage-bags' were to practical carriage what the KF shirt was to comfy clobber. After the sausage bag came the holdall, into which I deposited my stockpile of items (including the sausage bag itself), swiftly followed by a plethora of towels, eating irons and Robin Hood-style green thermals. Finally we were given our PT kit, which comprised one white and two red t-shirts, two pairs of shorts and a pair of white road-slapper plimsolls. These had soles so thin that they offered no cushioning whatsoever. You'd get bruises on your feet walking on ants.

Fully laden, I felt like a pack mule, bent double under the weight of all my kit. This didn't cut me any slack with the NCOs. As soon as I came out into the daylight, I was harangued back to the block by Baker and his mates.

Eventually, we all filtered back to the room, all in the same state, panting and wild-eyed. Five minutes later, Baker came in and took us through the process of laying out our lockers. He folded everything perfectly and placed it on its pre-designated spot on the shelves. After half an hour of demonstrating this, he set us to the task of doing it ourselves. The results didn't satisfy him and he called us idle fucking wankers as he emptied every shelf from every locker. 'Do it again,' he yelled, 'and this time, try to make your shagging lockers look a bit less like a thalidomide jumble sale!'

By the third time our kit had hit the deck it was lunch, so we marched to the cookhouse again, this time armed with our own knifes, forks, spoons and porcelain mugs.

After the meal we were halted outside the accommodation where the troop Sergeant shouted, 'Right, gents. You've got one minute to get up those shagging stairs, get your diggers washed and get out into the corridor for an inspection!' He surveyed us. 'Well don't just stand there! Get fucking moving!'

The whole squad did a bomb-burst and charged up the stairs. Some lads were trampled underfoot as we surged on like a herd of terrified wildebeest. There was a scuffle for the taps to clean our utensils, then we were out into the corridor and stood to attention. The NCOs moved up and down our line, inspecting every knife, fork, spoon and mug. The majority of the pot mugs were sent smashing to the floor. The other diggers were scattered the full length of the building.

'You minging bastards! Next time get the fucking things dried and cleaned properly!' one of them shouted. Soon the lessons would be learned, and it wasn't long before we could get all of our items cleaned and dried in a minute. There were always a few trample-victims after every basic training meal, though.

The rest of the afternoon was spent queuing, yet again, for more equipment issue. This time it was from the squadron stores. The inside of Corporal Timms' domain was dark, foreboding and had a slight aroma of Bell's whisky. The shelves were stacked with various items of stout green cloth webbing, helmets and sleeping bags, all of which was issued to us as one big pile. We were then taken outside onto the grass, where we were shown how to assemble the multitude of belts, straps and pouches.

The webbing was incredibly archaic '58 pattern,' indicating its year of design rather than its revision. It was virtually impossible to adjust in size and any exposure to moisture would cause it to triple in weight. Aside from this, it had a negligible carrying capacity. When we were given the list of items that we had to pack in the various pouches, I couldn't help but think that unless the inventor of the TARDIS had designed the stuff we would be shit out of luck. This would become more apparent on our first training exercise.

After a tussle with assembling the webbing, we were shown how to pack and unpack our sleeping bags. My bag was suspiciously light, and, when I unfolded it I found it the size of a moth pupa and as thin as a sheet of used toilet paper, with a similar scent. I looked around despairingly. It seemed that there was a direct correlation with the bag sizes and their new owner. The smaller the guy was, the bigger his sleeping bag, and vice versa. It appeared that I would spent the next two years of exercise sleeping in an involuntary foetal position.

The icing on the cake for the afternoon's issues were our helmets. They were identical to those issued in the Second World War, and they came with the novel invention of an inch-and-a-half spike protruding downwards from the inside towards the skull. I stared at the spike in disbelief. Surely this was some mistake? The trauma was softened slightly by an item known as 'The Spider', which looked just like its namesake and clipped inside the helmet and onto the spike. It consisted of a central hole for the spike, with eight evenly spaced plastic 'legs' that ran down the head, so that the helmet would be seated properly on your noggin. The spider was good for two things. Firstly, it reduced the spike penetration into your head from an inch-and-a-half to just half an inch. Secondly, you could place it on your head by itself and run around pretending to be a pre-war American footballer. When accompanying the spike protrusion with the bouncing caused by the elastic chinstrap, it made running in the helmets feel like having a furious woodpecker stuck to your head.

I didn't even bother to check my respirator. After the trauma of the helmet, I imagined there to be something equally hideous inside the gasmask. I'd had enough shocks for one day, so I just put the 'resi' into its relevant pouch and bundled everything together.

It was with a relatively heavy heart at the prospect of two years of torture that I carried the last of my issued kit up to the room.

A BAND OF SWAPO REJECTS

Kit doesn't iron itself. Baker used Alistair's uniform to demonstrate the required technique, meticulously starching perfect creases into his shirts and trousers. By the time he'd finished, they were immaculate. He looked around at us. 'Got the hang of that, gents?'

We all nodded blankly, not wanting to rock the boat by asking any questions. Baker must have known this. 'Well, we'll soon see,' he said. 'You scruffy cunts'll probably turnout like The Billy Smart's Clown Liberation Front.'

His gaze then fell on Alistair. 'I bet you're chuffed to have a set of decent working dress, eh, McKenzie?'

'Yes, Corporal!'

'Well, I'd better sort that out then!'

Grinning gleefully, Baker ironed a massive set of tramline double creases down the front of Alistair's trousers. 'I tell you what, McKenzie. I'm a right *cunt*, me. Those will be a *bastard* to get out!'

He buggered off, chortling, and left us to it.

From then until lights out, we took it in turns on the iron. When we weren't doing that, we polished our boots. Baker had offered us plenty of advice about breaking the boots in so that you didn't get blisters. He suggested that we mark time in a bath full of water for half an hour or fill them full of piss. This would ensure that the leather would be supple. It turned out that these particular hints had been handed down through generations of soldiers and were only really suitable if yours were the sort of boots worn by squaddies taking part in the relief of Ladysmith.

To familiarise us with the various types of uniform, the NCOs used the evening to take us through quick-change parades. These were exactly what they sounded like. We'd be told a certain dress code – PT kit, for example – and given a certain timescale in which to get dressed. This would be abbreviated thus: 'One minute, PT kit, GO!'

We would rush to our lockers and scramble into the required clothing and parade back into the corridor, only to be met by, 'Too slow. One minute, combats, GO!'

And so it would continue.

I suppose it served a purpose, but once the dress code became a bit more cosmopolitan then the whole thing went a bit. One of the more exotic parades was 'Robin Hood dress', which meant green thermal top and bottoms (tucked into green socks), green water proof poncho cape and green cap comforter (a rolled-up piece of cloth that looked like the old commando headdress). This one paled into insignificance next to 'Mess Tin Order'. Which was nothing but a green Army belt worn around the waist, looped through the handles of your mess tins, one to cover your arse and the other your wedding tackle. Admittedly, it was easy and quick to get into, but it let the wind in something fierce and there were hygiene issues to consider.

Next morning, Baker woke us and instructed us to put on our 'combats'. I'd heard the word during the blizzard of quick changes, but I couldn't for the life of me remember which bits of my newly-issued kit were required. I stared helplessly into my locker. Steve Keets stood a few feet away, gawping at me with a look that said, 'I hope you fucking know, 'cos I don't.' Only Paul had started to get dressed and, of course, Baker quickly spotted this. Exasperated, he started shouting. 'Fucking hell, is Jones the only of you knobbers with a memory? *Combats*, you *cunts*.'

He caught me sneaking a look over at Paul to get a couple of tips. 'Stop eyeing him up, Nugent, he's not your bird. I'll say it one more time. Combats. This includes, one pair of Army socks, one pair of boots-combat-high, combat trousers, combat jacket, shirt KF, and that farcical fucking excuse for a beret.'

As he shouted it out, I pulled it on to the floor so I couldn't forget. He chivvied us along with his brand of tough love, and five minutes later we were all dressed in the requisite outfit.

We looked various degrees of ridiculous.

As usual, Paul and Alistair looked OK, but the rest of us looked like DPM tramps. Either we'd shrunk as we slept, or the uniforms were living things, and had spent the night growing a couple of sizes. It was hard to say who looked the silliest as we all stood to attention at the end of our beds, trying to project some military bearing.

My clothes were the most ill-fitting. Barry Nash won the prize for the worst-shaped beret. The rest of us had opted for the, 'plop it on your head, then smooth it down over your right ear,' look. This gave off a sort of martial Frank Spencer vibe. Barry had spent so much time smoothing his down that it nearly touched his right shoulder. The band of the beret should have been just above his left ear, but his over-enthusiastic preening left a gap of about four inches. I'd seen photographs of WW2 Tommies wearing them like that, but it was safe to say that that style was no longer in fashion.

Baker started laughing when he saw it. 'Jesus, Nash. What the fuck is that?'

'Don't know, Corporal.'

'Neither do I. You look like you're just back from El Alamein. Get it fucking sorted out.'

Barry did as he was told, pulling the band until it was directly over his lug. This made the bit that was touching his shoulder stick out until it was parallel with the ground. You could have landed a small helicopter on it. The 'improvement' had only succeeded in making him look a bigger twat. As Baker checked the rest of us out, he continued to chuckle. Not benevolently.

After he gave us the nod, we clumped into the corridor and outside for a recruit troop parade. I don't suppose the boots were especially heavy, but I'd never worn anything like them before and had to consciously think about each step I took, lifting my legs in the exaggerated fashion of Neil Armstrong on the moon. When we were all on parade, in three ranks, the effect was no less unimpressive. It seemed like everyone had someone else's uniform on – we looked like the North Yorkshire detachment of a badly-equipped central African rebel force.

All the apprentice NCOs were there. They were dressed in boots, lightweights and navy blue sweatshirts, with a Royal Corps of Signals cap badge embroidered over the left tit. I presume they were dressed differently so that nobody could possibly mistake them for recruits, though given the state of us that was highly unlikely.

When Sergeants Atkins and Bailey appeared, they were similarly attired. 'Good morning, gents,' said Sergeant Bailey. 'We're going to take you on a run round camp. Don't worry about it, it's not a test or anything. We'll use it to get you used to running in step and to point out the various buildings and areas that you'll be using. Do as you're told and pay attention when you're given information. Listen in to my word of command.'

He was about to shout something, but obviously realised we didn't even know the basics of drill. So, in a more conversational tone, he said, 'Turn to your right, and keep fucking still.'

Three or four blokes managed to fuck this simple order up. As I turned to my right, the bloke to my left spun the wrong way, and stood there, facing me. For a second you could see him thinking, *Maybe I'm the only one that's right?* The torrent of abuse from the NCOs soon clarified matters for him. Sergeant Bailey then moved to the head of the squad, shouted, 'By the right, double-march,' and set off.

As he had promised, it wasn't physically demanding. We ran round the camp at a pace only slightly faster than a walk, and I enjoyed it. It was the first time I'd felt remotely 'soldierly'. There's something indefinably satisfying about running along in a squad, even if you look like a band of SWAPO rejects. Perhaps it's the sound of eighty heavy boots hitting the ground at the same time, or at least roughly the same time. As the ATNCOs bemoaned our lack of coordination, Bailey would occasionally bring us to a shuffling halt before pointing out a feature of the camp.

The main camp was a rectangle of about a kilometre by half a kilometre. The parade square was bang in the centre and most of the buildings clustered around it on all sides. To the west were the accommodation blocks. Behind them were the cookhouse and Baker Block, where the single, permanent staff below the rank of Sergeant lived. To the south of the square were the four three-storey education blocks where we would learn our trades. To their left was the gym, the swimming pool and indoor arena. Tucked in neatly behind there was the outdoor arena and assault course. The all important NAAFI was at the north-west corner of the square. The cinema and guardroom were at the north-east corner, adjacent to the camp entrance. The camp's most distinctive geographical feature ran flush to the square's western edge. There were three churches running along the perimeter, all triangular in shape. In the centre, forming a huge wigwam of glass and concrete, was the C of E church. To its north was a much smaller Catholic version, and a similar building to the south catered for interdenominational services. Behind these were the playing fields, bordered by the Officers' and Sergeants' Messes.

Out of the camp, and up Pennypot Lane was another area where we would receive field-based telecomms training, but Bailey didn't trust us on a public road and opted for a brief description of that location. Throughout the run, he offered unsettling glimpses of the purpose of each landmark he pointed out. Of the NAAFI, he pointedly observed, 'Don't fucking worry about remembering this place, you won't be spending much time in it.'

He simply scowled as we jogged past the Officers' Mess, but brought us to a reverent halt outside the WOs' and Sergeants' Mess. 'Think about it, fellas,' he said, in solemn tones. 'Keep your noses clean and, in 10 years or so, you may get to enjoy all the things the Mess has to offer.'

It wasn't very Churchillian in its power to inspire. Never mind a decade, all my powers of concentration were focused on lasting the day.

He took great pleasure in showing us the assault course. It consisted of all the usual obstacles – a set of monkey bars, a wall, a bigger wall and an even bigger wall, with an extra-big wall behind that one. Right near the end was the comedy sketch staple, the rope swing above a deep pool of pungent-looking water. Throughout the remainder of my years in the Army, this would be the point on every assault course where spectators would congregate. Always the penultimate obstacle, when a soldier arrived there he was generally ballbagged, unless he was a racing snake.

The previous soldier would be on the other side, still holding the rope. The idea, as demonstrated by the PTIs, was that the soldier in possession of the rope would push it back, allowing the next man to grab it and swing athletically across, landing with a comforting, two-footed thud and keeping hold of the rope to repeat the exercise for the man behind him. It sometimes worked like this but regularly didn't, hence the expectant crowd.

There were various ways it could go wrong, all resulting in observers crying with laughter and a fall into a shit-stained pool for the unlucky acrobat.

In the 'Marcel Marceau', the rope despatcher was a little too vigorous in his throwing technique. Holding the rope by the bottom, he'd bring it back over his shoulder and chuck it powerfully towards his mate. This would put a kink in the rope, which would usually flick it upwards just before it got to the other side. If he hadn't predicted this, the jumper would have already leant forward to grasp something that was no longer there. All the way down to the water, his hands would still be holding an imaginary rope.

Even if the throwing part was done correctly, there was plenty more that could go wrong. For a textbook example of 'The Reluctant Fireman' the rope was generally quite wet from use or weather. If the jumper didn't grab it tenaciously, he'd just slide right down it, usually over the centre of the pool. This would result in a couple of hefty rope burns on the hands, which would be quickly soothed by four feet of borderline sewage.

If a man caught the rope and didn't slip off, he might make it across, but only if he didn't catch it too high or too low. Too high, and he'd perform 'The Town Hall Clock.' This involved just swinging back and forth with no chance of making it to either bank. Eventually he'd come to a stop and then resign himself to the inevitable. Too low, and the jumper would demonstrate a 'Queen Mary,' ploughing through the pool, leaving a wake like one of Cunard's finest before halting at the far wall, and sinking without trace.

The sturdy bloke who avoided all these pitfalls was still left with one to beat – 'The Stretch Armstrong'. If he didn't time his jump off perfectly, he was up shit-street. If he let go too late, the return swing would have begun and he'd be left with his toes gripping the edge of the wall for all they were worth, whilst his arms held on to the now immobile rope which left him suspended right over the water. A strong lad could hold on for a good thirty seconds in this position, toes trying to burst through his soles for a bit more purchase. You'd think there was only one course of action here: surrender and let your feet fall into the pool, quickly followed

annoyed the drill instructor to this extent was deemed
it coming' and, in fairness, he would have completed
nd 3 before being awarded the top prize. The first
at he was going away was a barely intelligible shriek
illpig to, 'Staywhereyoufucking*ARE*!' The recruit
pt to halt, usually badly, compounding his error. The
ould then accuse him of deliberately sabotaging the
shaking his head and turning to one of the ATNCO
h the immortal words, 'Get him off my square.'
ruit would immediately be dragged out of the
told by the ATNCO to remove his beret and belt
em in his left hand. I'm not sure why. It might have
e was no longer fit to wear his headgear. It was
to be that it made him look a bit more of a tit.
rds, 'Listen in to my timing,' the recruit would be
jail at 40 miles an hour. The horrendously quick
ed for people on their way to clink, was known as
.'

got to the jail, he was handed over to the reviled RPs
ave a list of shitty jobs for him. He'd stay there until
he lesson, usually an hour or two. At the end of his
one of the ATNCOs would come and get him and
ack to the squad.
l to conform, I considered the injustice of it all. How
posed to know this stuff? I wondered if there was a
sman, and managed to tick off the first two levels of
id so. I'd already been shouted at from a distance a
nes and had instinctively shrunk to make myself a
t. Whilst I was formulating the words to my official
missed another shout, bracing my shoulders around
after everyone else. This made Bailey as mad as a
he stormed over to me, bellowing, nose-to-nose. I
his breath – a combination of low quality hot
nd high quality tabs which produced a heady
at smelt like shit.
our fucking name?'
T, SERGEANT.'
ed me in the chest with his pace stick.

by the rest of your body. I did see someone try an alternative once. He let go with his hands first. With his feet hooked behind a course of bricks, his body formed a lovely arc as it swung back and twatted the wall, leaving him knocked out and still dangling, with his head underwater. As a couple of his mates hauled him out, preventing his certain death, the assembled crowd shrieked and chortled.

After the tour, and just before Sergeant Bailey fell us out for lunch, he informed us that we would be getting our first drill lesson that afternoon, in working dress. Thankfully, Paul was able to remember what we had to stick on.

Stood outside in boots, lightweights, shirt, jumper and beret, we waited to commence our long and painful relationship with the square and the myriad joys of marching up and down in straight lines. The two Sergeants took the lesson, with the ATNCOs assisting. Predictably, we were utterly hopeless and smashed all previous 'wrath incurred per second' records. We weren't the only squad on the parade ground that day. All the other squadrons' recruits were undergoing a similar baptism of fire. The indiscriminate roars of Drill Sergeants came from all directions. To begin with, it was hard to tell which Sergeant was bollocking which squad, but it didn't take long for us to pick out Bailey and Atkins' individual styles, like a brood of new-born chicks identifying their mother's call.

Being our first time, all they wanted to do was basic foot drill. It didn't even involve marching. Standing easy, standing at ease and standing to attention was all we had to learn.

As usual, there was a broad spectrum of competence on display, with the ex-cadets showing strongly. The only way I could judge my individual performance was by mentally measuring the yells I received on my internal 'screamometer' in comparison to those my peers got. This simple yardstick put me in the bottom ten. With the permanent staff giving all the commands, the ATNCOs took on the responsibility of monitoring the recruits from their own rooms. Steve Keets and myself took the most shit off Baker. I don't know what it was about drill – maybe my heart was never in it. We had it repeatedly explained, that it was the most efficient way of moving a large body of men from point A to B. I couldn't argue with that, but there always seemed to be an unnecessary amount of fucking about, taking in the rest of the alphabet before finally getting to the second letter.

'Standing at ease' is a misnomer. It involves standing with legs shoulder-width apart, arms behind the back, the right hand being held by the left at the base of the spine. The chin is supposed to be slightly raised. It isn't the stress position, but there are more comfortable ways of standing – leaning against a convenient wall or lamppost, say.

From there you can go one of two ways. With the command, 'Stand Easy,' you can relax your shoulders and drop your chin a bit. This is as indolent as drill gets in the British Army. There was never any further instruction to 'Just chill out for a bit, lads.'

The other option is 'Attention.' The instructor roars the word 'SQUAD.' In a millisecond, eighty chins jut up and one hundred and sixty shoulders brace. He then repeats the word, this time in a strangled, elongated fashion. This is to let you know that an executive word of command is shortly to follow and no action is yet to be taken.

'SQQUUAAAAAAAD.'

A second or so later, the word 'SHUN,' is screamed.

In a lightning-fast response, eighty right legs lift until the thigh is parallel to the ground, before slamming the foot back down to rest adjacent to the left, with both feet forming the 'ten to two' position. Simultaneously, the arms move from their position at the back to be pinned tightly at the sides, fists clenched with the little finger to the rear, and the thumbs pressed tightly on the index fingers.

Each drill instructor has his own way of delivering the 'SHUN.' It allows them to express themselves creatively, within the strictures of the parade square. Some just shout extra loud for that bit. Others raise their voices, going from tenor to falsetto in the space of a single word.

The strangest ones – Sergeant Bailey was one of these – opt for a complete disfigurement of the word, paired with the high-pitched delivery. In his case, the instruction would come out as, 'SHHOOOWWNNNAAA,' and just needed the word 'muthafuckas' on the end to complete the 'New York pimp' effect.

Our lesson didn't go as Bai[...] they got progressively more a[...] anything correctly. We started pi[...] start.

'SQUAD,' he roared unexpect[...] within the designated time, but m[...] seconds later.

'AS YOU WERE.'

This was our cue to go back to t[...]

He abused us for a few mo[...] command, 'SQUAD,' I want shit-[...] again.'

Without further warning, he [...] YOU FUCKING WERE. Right, y[...] grip my shit.'

He then went through a blu[...] impossible to keep up with. 'SQ[...] ASYOUWERESQUADASYOUW[...] QUAD.'

At the end, none of us were sure[...] I initially opted for standing easy. [...] gave the impression that everyone [...] ease. Like I was on *Runaround*, I ch[...] the majority. We spent 20 minutes [...] with Bailey getting redder and redde[...] sluggish reactions.

The insults were always vulga[...] recipient, and represented the first le[...] square. They began from a distance. [...] a more personal approach, applied [...] wasn't enough incentive to get your[...] taken out of the squad and humilia[...] demonstrate your atrocious drill in [...] display. The ultimate punishment, [...] were beyond drill redemption, was j[...] being able to move your legs or ar[...] slightly excessive, but it was all in the[...] apparently.

Whoev[...] to have 'ha[...] levels 1, 2[...] indication [...] from the [...] would atte[...] instructor [...] lesson bef[...] pissboys v[...]

The r[...] squad an[...] and hold [...] been tha[...] more lik[...] With the [...] marched [...] pace, res[...] 'Pokey I[...]

Wher[...] who wo[...] the end [...] punishm[...] pokey hi[...]

As I [...] were we[...] Drill Or[...] abuse a[...] couple [...] smaller [...] compla[...] five mi[...] bastard[...] could [...] bevera[...] concoc[...]

'W[...]

'NU[...]

He [...]

'Start getting it right, Nugent, you cock. I've seen quicker reactions from a waxwork.'

'YES, SERGEANT.'

With that, he retreated, taking his demonic breath with him. By the time we moved on to, 'Coming to Attention,' both Sergeants were at an increased level of animation. The ATNCOs mirrored their mood, throwing in continuous barbed criticisms of every lacklustre knee raise or tardy brace. Knowing that I'd progressed through levels 1 and 2, Baker focused his attention on me, finding increasing fault with everything I did. It was a tactic borrowed from professional football. I was the defender on a yellow, Baker the striker trying to get me sent off. I thought I was doing it right, but it wasn't long before Bailey had me stood out in front of the squad, demonstrating my shoddy skills. I was compared to a variety of old-fashioned, camp stereotypes including Liberace, Danny La Rue and Larry Grayson, largely due to my inability to make much noise when my right boot slammed into the concrete on the completion of the movement. As I continued to repeat the actions, Bailey addressed the rest of the lads. 'I want to hear a noise like a fucking shotgun going off when I shout, "SHUN". Not like this cunt. I could make more fucking noise banging me bellend on the armoury door. Get back in the squad, Nugent, you're on your last chance.'

I marched back in to the anonymity of the squad as quickly as I could and made a superhuman effort to do everything correctly. My problem was that the spirit was willing, but the flesh was weak. I wasn't the only one fucking up, and it was a toss up between me and a few others as to who would be the one to push Bailey over the edge and get sent to jail. The question was answered half an hour before the lesson finished, when my beret fell off. It had been a bit windy, but not enough to remove headgear. The constant drill movements and flinching had caused the band to ride up from my left ear. I'd been too scared to adjust it and had spent a couple of minutes trying to manoeuvre it back into position by waggling my ears, but that didn't work. At the same time as I completed my millionth 'SHUN', a small gust of wind caught the underside and blew it off my head. It rested by my foot, stolidly refusing to jump back on my head despite my telepathic commands. As soon as

Bailey saw it lying there, he went ballistic. 'Nugent, not you a-fucking-gain,' he howled. 'I've had enough of you, you fucking leg-iron. The only thing you're good at is being shit. Lance Corporal Baker, get him off my square.'

Nobody in the squad actually moved, but I could feel them all pulling subtly away to eliminate any guilt by association. If it had been allowed, they'd have all been looking in 80 different directions, whistling. Baker appeared with undisguised glee. 'Right, Nugent, pick your beret up and get it in your left hand.' I obeyed as quickly as I could, hoping it might earn me a reprieve. Unfortunately for me, my fate had been decided. He continued. 'Listen in to my timing. By the left, quick march.'

With that, we were off, Baker's timing turning the words into one, barely understandable racket. 'Lefrighlefrighlefrighlefrigh-lefrighlefrighlefrighlefrighlefrighlefrighleffft.'

I was trying to match his pace and swing my right arm in time, which was impossible: I suspect I looked like Charlie Chaplin. It was 200 metres to my final destination, and we got there in less than a minute. Baker's shouts must have alerted the trolls in the guardroom, because they were waiting to greet me. Foremost, of course, was Corporal Lang, who beamed, revealing a set of teeth like a fighting patrol, all blacked out and five metres apart.

Baker and Lang had a brief conversation as I stood there, panting. Once Lang had established that he had me for 30 minutes, I was released into his custody. He wasted no time.

'Right, you little shagbag, get in that fucking guardroom. There's some bumpering to be done.'

I started to march, but Lang told me to run or he'd kick me up the arse. Needing no further persuasion, I ran into the guardroom, where a couple of fat old Lance Corporals were reading the tabloids and eating hardboiled eggs. A bumper appeared, and Lang shouted, 'Right, fucking get on with it. I want to see my face in this floor when you're done.'

I couldn't think why he'd want that: he was a grotesque little cunt. But I wasn't arguing. Having done my share the previous night, I was confident that bumpering was at least one thing I'd be able to do without criticism. Frankly, it didn't seem like a punishment. I was now off the square and away from Bailey and

Baker's beady eyes. Sharing personal airspace with Lang wasn't pleasant, but it was preferable. I was young and naive, of course: the Army is far too clever to make a punishment more desirable than regular work. I was already doing the standard bumper sweeps when Lang stopped me. His tone was scarily amiable.

'No, no, no. That's not how you do it. Let me show you.'

He then positioned my hands correctly and I realised that I wanted to go back on the square. I was standing with my left hand at the top of the bumper handle and my right at the bottom, just above the bumper itself. It was an extra long handle, and I had to be at full stretch to implement Lang's orders. 'Lovely,' he said. 'Carry on like that and you'll do a great fucking job.'

He then sat with his egg-eating mates and enjoyed the show. I spent the remaining 25 minutes of my punishment walking up and down the room in this agonising position. It was back-breaking and I was sweating through my jumper within a couple of minutes. It was hard to tell from the angle I was at, but it didn't seem to get the floor any shinier, either. Occasionally, Lang or one of his cronies would give me a bit of condescending encouragement. There was a big clock on the back wall, and every now and again I'd get a glimpse of it. It ticked interminably slowly, and by the time my ordeal was over I felt like I'd been there a week.

When Baker came to get me, Lang told me to stand up. I released the bumper handle but found myself locked in position. I straightened myself up, letting out an involuntary yelp as my back snapped back into line.

'Never mind that, you fucking girl,' Lang said. 'Come back anytime you like.'

By the time Baker had pokeyed me back to the lads, they were just about to be marched off the square. Sergeant Bailey greeted me cordially. 'Ah, Nugent. Enjoy the hospitality in the guardroom?'

'YES, SERGEANT.'

'Good. They aim to please. Think on for next time.'

I joined the back of the squad and we were taken back to the block, where I was debriefed by the rest of the lads. Like the kid who gets the strap at school, I found that my punishment had accorded me a bit of celebrity status. I went into great detail and it made my roommates shudder and laugh in equal quantity.

That evening was a simple repetition of the one before. The only change was that the standards expected were now higher, as we were now such veterans. There was method to some of this madness, though. Our joint tribulations were already sticking us together as a room. By lights out we'd achieved what we judged to be a decent job. Baker's opinion was less effusive. 'Better than last night, but still fucking shit. Call it a hunch, but I don't think Sergeant Bailey will be impressed. Get a good night's sleep anyway, fellas, you've got PT tomorrow.'

* * * * *

Baker's intuition proved to be spot on, and the room was turned upside down again. It was a good demonstration of the law of diminishing returns. The room trashing was expected this time, so it didn't bother us so much. For the second time in two days, my bed block bounced off my head before falling to pieces on the floor. As soon as they moved on to Room 5, we started straightening the place up, on auto-pilot. Baker had left us alone, so we indulged in a bit of banter. Paul shouted across to me.

''Ere, Eddy? What's the facking score wiv' you an' that bed block then?'

'Fuck knows, mate. I reckon someone's nobbling it while I'm having a shave.'

'Yeah, that'd be right,' shouted Tom. 'When I went for a shit last night my kit was spotless. I got back and some cunt had ironed it all wrong behind my back.'

This brought roars of laughter. Tom was going to be the tramp of the room, that was clear. He couldn't iron, and he always looked like he'd slept in his clothes. Fortunately for him, he didn't worry too much about it.

Baker came back in and screamed at us to get into our PT kit, so we scrambled around in our lockers with the now familiar panic-tinged haste. Once attired in our baggy shirts and shorts and plimsolls, we looked ready to take on Roger Bannister on the cinder track of his choice. We were fallen in outside the squadron offices and marched down to the gym. On arriving at the end of the 400m walk in our paper-thin daps, every man-jack of us had shin-splints.

by the rest of your body. I did see someone try an alternative once. He let go with his hands first. With his feet hooked behind a course of bricks, his body formed a lovely arc as it swung back and twatted the wall, leaving him knocked out and still dangling, with his head underwater. As a couple of his mates hauled him out, preventing his certain death, the assembled crowd shrieked and chortled.

After the tour, and just before Sergeant Bailey fell us out for lunch, he informed us that we would be getting our first drill lesson that afternoon, in working dress. Thankfully, Paul was able to remember what we had to stick on.

Stood outside in boots, lightweights, shirt, jumper and beret, we waited to commence our long and painful relationship with the square and the myriad joys of marching up and down in straight lines. The two Sergeants took the lesson, with the ATNCOs assisting. Predictably, we were utterly hopeless and smashed all previous 'wrath incurred per second' records. We weren't the only squad on the parade ground that day. All the other squadrons' recruits were undergoing a similar baptism of fire. The indiscriminate roars of Drill Sergeants came from all directions. To begin with, it was hard to tell which Sergeant was bollocking which squad, but it didn't take long for us to pick out Bailey and Atkins' individual styles, like a brood of new-born chicks identifying their mother's call.

Being our first time, all they wanted to do was basic foot drill. It didn't even involve marching. Standing easy, standing at ease and standing to attention was all we had to learn.

As usual, there was a broad spectrum of competence on display, with the ex-cadets showing strongly. The only way I could judge my individual performance was by mentally measuring the yells I received on my internal 'screamometer' in comparison to those my peers got. This simple yardstick put me in the bottom ten. With the permanent staff giving all the commands, the ATNCOs took on the responsibility of monitoring the recruits from their own rooms. Steve Keets and myself took the most shit off Baker. I don't know what it was about drill – maybe my heart was never in it. We had it repeatedly explained, that it was the most efficient way of moving a large body of men from point A to B. I couldn't argue with that, but there always seemed to be an unnecessary amount of fucking about, taking in the rest of the alphabet before finally getting to the second letter.

'Standing at ease' is a misnomer. It involves standing with legs shoulder-width apart, arms behind the back, the right hand being held by the left at the base of the spine. The chin is supposed to be slightly raised. It isn't the stress position, but there are more comfortable ways of standing – leaning against a convenient wall or lamppost, say.

From there you can go one of two ways. With the command, 'Stand Easy,' you can relax your shoulders and drop your chin a bit. This is as indolent as drill gets in the British Army. There was never any further instruction to 'Just chill out for a bit, lads.'

The other option is 'Attention.' The instructor roars the word 'SQUAD.' In a millisecond, eighty chins jut up and one hundred and sixty shoulders brace. He then repeats the word, this time in a strangled, elongated fashion. This is to let you know that an executive word of command is shortly to follow and no action is yet to be taken.

'SQQUUAAAAAAAD.'

A second or so later, the word 'SHUN,' is screamed.

In a lightning-fast response, eighty right legs lift until the thigh is parallel to the ground, before slamming the foot back down to rest adjacent to the left, with both feet forming the 'ten to two' position. Simultaneously, the arms move from their position at the back to be pinned tightly at the sides, fists clenched with the little finger to the rear, and the thumbs pressed tightly on the index fingers.

Each drill instructor has his own way of delivering the 'SHUN.' It allows them to express themselves creatively, within the strictures of the parade square. Some just shout extra loud for that bit. Others raise their voices, going from tenor to falsetto in the space of a single word.

The strangest ones – Sergeant Bailey was one of these – opt for a complete disfigurement of the word, paired with the high-pitched delivery. In his case, the instruction would come out as, 'SHHOOOWWNNNAAA,' and just needed the word 'muthafuckas' on the end to complete the 'New York pimp' effect.

Our lesson didn't go as Bailey and Atkins planned, and they got progressively more angry at our inability to do anything correctly. We started pissing Bailey off right from the start.

'SQUAD,' he roared unexpectedly. Some of the troop reacted within the designated time, but most of us braced up a full two seconds later.

'AS YOU WERE.'

This was our cue to go back to the 'Stand Easy' for another go.

He abused us for a few moments. 'When you hear the command, 'SQUAD,' I want shit-off-a-shovel reactions. Let's try again.'

Without further warning, he shouted again. 'SQUAD. AS YOU FUCKING WERE. Right, you wankers. You're starting to grip my shit.'

He then went through a blur of commands which were impossible to keep up with. 'SQUADASYOUWERESQUAD-ASYOUWERESQUADASYOUWERESQUADASYOUWERESQUAD.'

At the end, none of us were sure of what position to stand in. I initially opted for standing easy. A furtive glance left and right gave the impression that everyone else had gone for standing at ease. Like I was on *Runaround*, I changed my position to go with the majority. We spent 20 minutes on that particular movement, with Bailey getting redder and redder in the face at our continued sluggish reactions.

The insults were always vulgar and funny to all but the recipient, and represented the first level of punishment on the drill square. They began from a distance. Further transgression merited a more personal approach, applied at point-blank range. If this wasn't enough incentive to get your act together, you would be taken out of the squad and humiliated slightly, usually made to demonstrate your atrocious drill in a 'here's how *not* to do it,' display. The ultimate punishment, reserved only for those who were beyond drill redemption, was jail. Going to prison for not being able to move your legs or arms as instructed may seem slightly excessive, but it was all in the best interests of the recruit, apparently.

Whoever annoyed the drill instructor to this extent was deemed to have 'had it coming' and, in fairness, he would have completed levels 1, 2 and 3 before being awarded the top prize. The first indication that he was going away was a barely intelligible shriek from the drillpig to, 'Staywhereyoufucking*ARE*!' The recruit would attempt to halt, usually badly, compounding his error. The instructor would then accuse him of deliberately sabotaging the lesson before shaking his head and turning to one of the ATNCO pissboys with the immortal words, 'Get him off my square.'

The recruit would immediately be dragged out of the squad and told by the ATNCO to remove his beret and belt and hold them in his left hand. I'm not sure why. It might have been that he was no longer fit to wear his headgear. It was more likely to be that it made him look a bit more of a tit. With the words, 'Listen in to my timing,' the recruit would be marched to jail at 40 miles an hour. The horrendously quick pace, reserved for people on their way to clink, was known as 'Pokey Drill.'

When he got to the jail, he was handed over to the reviled RPs who would have a list of shitty jobs for him. He'd stay there until the end of the lesson, usually an hour or two. At the end of his punishment, one of the ATNCOs would come and get him and pokey him back to the squad.

As I tried to conform, I considered the injustice of it all. How were we supposed to know this stuff? I wondered if there was a Drill Ombudsman, and managed to tick off the first two levels of abuse as I did so. I'd already been shouted at from a distance a couple of times and had instinctively shrunk to make myself a smaller target. Whilst I was formulating the words to my official complaint, I missed another shout, bracing my shoulders around five minutes after everyone else. This made Bailey as mad as a bastard and he stormed over to me, bellowing, nose-to-nose. I could smell his breath – a combination of low quality hot beverages and high quality tabs which produced a heady concoction that smelt like shit.

'What's your fucking name?'

'NUGENT, SERGEANT.'

He prodded me in the chest with his pace stick.

'Start getting it right, Nugent, you cock. I've seen quicker reactions from a waxwork.'

'YES, SERGEANT.'

With that, he retreated, taking his demonic breath with him. By the time we moved on to, 'Coming to Attention,' both Sergeants were at an increased level of animation. The ATNCOs mirrored their mood, throwing in continuous barbed criticisms of every lacklustre knee raise or tardy brace. Knowing that I'd progressed through levels 1 and 2, Baker focused his attention on me, finding increasing fault with everything I did. It was a tactic borrowed from professional football. I was the defender on a yellow, Baker the striker trying to get me sent off. I thought I was doing it right, but it wasn't long before Bailey had me stood out in front of the squad, demonstrating my shoddy skills. I was compared to a variety of old-fashioned, camp stereotypes including Liberace, Danny La Rue and Larry Grayson, largely due to my inability to make much noise when my right boot slammed into the concrete on the completion of the movement. As I continued to repeat the actions, Bailey addressed the rest of the lads. 'I want to hear a noise like a fucking shotgun going off when I shout, "SHUN". Not like this cunt. I could make more fucking noise banging me bellend on the armoury door. Get back in the squad, Nugent, you're on your last chance.'

I marched back in to the anonymity of the squad as quickly as I could and made a superhuman effort to do everything correctly. My problem was that the spirit was willing, but the flesh was weak. I wasn't the only one fucking up, and it was a toss up between me and a few others as to who would be the one to push Bailey over the edge and get sent to jail. The question was answered half an hour before the lesson finished, when my beret fell off. It had been a bit windy, but not enough to remove headgear. The constant drill movements and flinching had caused the band to ride up from my left ear. I'd been too scared to adjust it and had spent a couple of minutes trying to manoeuvre it back into position by waggling my ears, but that didn't work. At the same time as I completed my millionth 'SHUN', a small gust of wind caught the underside and blew it off my head. It rested by my foot, stolidly refusing to jump back on my head despite my telepathic commands. As soon as

Bailey saw it lying there, he went ballistic. 'Nugent, not you a-fucking-gain,' he howled. 'I've had enough of you, you fucking leg-iron. The only thing you're good at is being shit. Lance Corporal Baker, get him off my square.'

Nobody in the squad actually moved, but I could feel them all pulling subtly away to eliminate any guilt by association. If it had been allowed, they'd have all been looking in 80 different directions, whistling. Baker appeared with undisguised glee. 'Right, Nugent, pick your beret up and get it in your left hand.' I obeyed as quickly as I could, hoping it might earn me a reprieve. Unfortunately for me, my fate had been decided. He continued. 'Listen in to my timing. By the left, quick march.'

With that, we were off, Baker's timing turning the words into one, barely understandable racket. 'Lefrighlefrighlefrighlefrigh-lefrighlefrighlefrighlefrighlefrighlefrighleffft.'

I was trying to match his pace and swing my right arm in time, which was impossible: I suspect I looked like Charlie Chaplin. It was 200 metres to my final destination, and we got there in less than a minute. Baker's shouts must have alerted the trolls in the guardroom, because they were waiting to greet me. Foremost, of course, was Corporal Lang, who beamed, revealing a set of teeth like a fighting patrol, all blacked out and five metres apart.

Baker and Lang had a brief conversation as I stood there, panting. Once Lang had established that he had me for 30 minutes, I was released into his custody. He wasted no time.

'Right, you little shagbag, get in that fucking guardroom. There's some bumpering to be done.'

I started to march, but Lang told me to run or he'd kick me up the arse. Needing no further persuasion, I ran into the guardroom, where a couple of fat old Lance Corporals were reading the tabloids and eating hardboiled eggs. A bumper appeared, and Lang shouted, 'Right, fucking get on with it. I want to see my face in this floor when you're done.'

I couldn't think why he'd want that: he was a grotesque little cunt. But I wasn't arguing. Having done my share the previous night, I was confident that bumpering was at least one thing I'd be able to do without criticism. Frankly, it didn't seem like a punishment. I was now off the square and away from Bailey and

Baker's beady eyes. Sharing personal airspace with Lang wasn't pleasant, but it was preferable. I was young and naive, of course: the Army is far too clever to make a punishment more desirable than regular work. I was already doing the standard bumper sweeps when Lang stopped me. His tone was scarily amiable.

'No, no, no. That's not how you do it. Let me show you.'

He then positioned my hands correctly and I realised that I wanted to go back on the square. I was standing with my left hand at the top of the bumper handle and my right at the bottom, just above the bumper itself. It was an extra long handle, and I had to be at full stretch to implement Lang's orders. 'Lovely,' he said. 'Carry on like that and you'll do a great fucking job.'

He then sat with his egg-eating mates and enjoyed the show. I spent the remaining 25 minutes of my punishment walking up and down the room in this agonising position. It was back-breaking and I was sweating through my jumper within a couple of minutes. It was hard to tell from the angle I was at, but it didn't seem to get the floor any shinier, either. Occasionally, Lang or one of his cronies would give me a bit of condescending encouragement. There was a big clock on the back wall, and every now and again I'd get a glimpse of it. It ticked interminably slowly, and by the time my ordeal was over I felt like I'd been there a week.

When Baker came to get me, Lang told me to stand up. I released the bumper handle but found myself locked in position. I straightened myself up, letting out an involuntary yelp as my back snapped back into line.

'Never mind that, you fucking girl,' Lang said. 'Come back anytime you like.'

By the time Baker had pokeyed me back to the lads, they were just about to be marched off the square. Sergeant Bailey greeted me cordially. 'Ah, Nugent. Enjoy the hospitality in the guardroom?'

'YES, SERGEANT.'

'Good. They aim to please. Think on for next time.'

I joined the back of the squad and we were taken back to the block, where I was debriefed by the rest of the lads. Like the kid who gets the strap at school, I found that my punishment had accorded me a bit of celebrity status. I went into great detail and it made my roommates shudder and laugh in equal quantity.

That evening was a simple repetition of the one before. The only change was that the standards expected were now higher, as we were now such veterans. There was method to some of this madness, though. Our joint tribulations were already sticking us together as a room. By lights out we'd achieved what we judged to be a decent job. Baker's opinion was less effusive. 'Better than last night, but still fucking shit. Call it a hunch, but I don't think Sergeant Bailey will be impressed. Get a good night's sleep anyway, fellas, you've got PT tomorrow.'

* * * * *

Baker's intuition proved to be spot on, and the room was turned upside down again. It was a good demonstration of the law of diminishing returns. The room trashing was expected this time, so it didn't bother us so much. For the second time in two days, my bed block bounced off my head before falling to pieces on the floor. As soon as they moved on to Room 5, we started straightening the place up, on auto-pilot. Baker had left us alone, so we indulged in a bit of banter. Paul shouted across to me.

''Ere, Eddy? What's the facking score wiv' you an' that bed block then?'

'Fuck knows, mate. I reckon someone's nobbling it while I'm having a shave.'

'Yeah, that'd be right,' shouted Tom. 'When I went for a shit last night my kit was spotless. I got back and some cunt had ironed it all wrong behind my back.'

This brought roars of laughter. Tom was going to be the tramp of the room, that was clear. He couldn't iron, and he always looked like he'd slept in his clothes. Fortunately for him, he didn't worry too much about it.

Baker came back in and screamed at us to get into our PT kit, so we scrambled around in our lockers with the now familiar panic-tinged haste. Once attired in our baggy shirts and shorts and plimsolls, we looked ready to take on Roger Bannister on the cinder track of his choice. We were fallen in outside the squadron offices and marched down to the gym. On arriving at the end of the 400m walk in our paper-thin daps, every man-jack of us had shin-splints.

The NCOs left us in our shit-scared silence outside the gym and in a couple of seconds, a pack of knuckle-scrapers filed out of a side door and descended on us in an ominous manner. This was it, this was the beginning of The Planet Of The Apes: a bunch of silverbacks had escaped from Twycross and were masquerading as the camp's PTIs. On closer inspection, they turned out merely to be ridiculously-muscled psychopaths, suffering from acute narcissistic rage. I found this out as one of them, in a white and red-piped gym vest, put his broken nose to mine and whispered, 'You're fucking weak, aren't you?'

'No, Corporal!' I lied.

He glanced at my arms: I looked like the poster child for a Red Cross famine appeal. The PTI snorted in disgust and moved on to the next lad to dish out an equally unnerving insult. The air was broken by a broad Scouse accent. 'Right youse' guys, I am QMSI Johns, and I run the physical training on this camp. In a minute you will be fallen out into the gym for your first PT lesson. Once that happens, you are the property of my instructors. One piece of advice, gents. Never walk during a PT lesson.'

Then, with a 'carry on' to his troop of simians, he walked back into the gym.

The largest and angriest of the instructors stepped forward. 'Listen in. When I give you the command "Fall out", you will turn to your right, march three paces and get into the gym as fast as your pathetic bodies will carry you.'

His already huge chest filled with air, and he bellowed, 'FAAAAAAAAAALLLLLLLLLLLLL OUT!'

Before we had even started our turn to the right, the shouting started, 'Come on, you lazy cunts! Get in that shagging gym! Are you walking!? Are you fucking walking!? You'd better-fucking-not be!'

This took us by surprise and everyone tried to do a runner for the gym at the same time. It was bedlam; we ran like a nest of startled woodlice scurrying for cover. The squeeze through the gym door was horrendous as we trod all over each other in the effort not to be last to fall in. The result of this was that every set of white plimsolls was covered in dirty footmarks.

We'd all assumed that, once we were in the gym, we would be beasted and that would be it. It would be horrible, but predictable. As usual, we were sadly mistaken. There was an inspection first. Unsurprisingly, the NCOs went howling mad at the state of our kit. Given that we had been half crushed to death whilst entering the gym, I thought we weren't too badly turned out. It goes without saying that I didn't air my views.

The chief ape walked out in front of us. 'You idle fucking bastards! You are the worst turned-out group of recruits I have ever seen, and you are going to pay the price, gents, you mark my words! Tonight, you will parade back here at 1800 hours, with your kit ironed properly and your fucking pumps whitened! Do I make myself clear?'

'Yes, Corporal!'

'PT lessons are a parade ladies! And as such, you lazy cunts will be well turned out. Now, I was going to give you a nice easy lesson to get you used to the gym, but seeing as you can't be bothered to turn out in good order for my class, I can't be bothered to take things easy on you. NOW GET ROUND THE FUCKING GYM AND TOUCH ALL FOUR CORNERS, GO!'

Then it began. Everything we did, be it press-ups, sit-ups or whatever torture the instructors could think of, the order would come as, 'Exercise... begin! TOO SLOW, DO IT AGAIN! YOU'RE NOT IMPRESSING ME, GENTS!'

After an individual was deemed to be 'not impressing' the PTIs for the third time, he would be sent to hang off the wall bars until he saw the error of his ways. At one point or another during the lesson, everyone had done a stint on the bars. My turn came whilst in the middle of my hundredth nodding head/arse thrusting, straight-armed press-up. The instructor told me that I wasn't trying hard enough, and that he had my number. After that, it was a matter of seconds before he lost his temper with me. 'Get on those fucking wall bars you idle cunt, Nugent!' I wanted to run to the bars, but I just staggered across the floor as if I'd just got off the waltzers.

I had actually been trying my best at the time of the gripping, and this punishment taught me the benefits of 'skive to survive,' immediately. From then on, if the instructors weren't looking, I rested. As soon as they turned around, I grimaced dramatically and put on my best vinegar stroke face.

At the end of the session, everyone looked ravaged. We were all sweating profusely, red of face, and the previously pristine v-neck of our PT shirts had now stretched to form a huge 'U' that was exposing at least one nipple.

The worst thing was we had to get back to the block, sort our kit out, and go back to the gym to suffer it all again.

Our return trip to the gym that day was not as physically demanding as before, but it was 10 times worse all the same. During the first lesson it had begun to rain, and when we returned at 1800 hours it was lashing down. They kept us standing out there for 10 minutes. By the time two of them came out, the whitener had began to run off our daps and was making a white river on its way down to the drains.

'Well, gents,' said one of them. 'Seeing as you can't get your clothes clean, we may as well get them dirty for you. Now fall out and start running around the assault course.'

We didn't actually attempt the obstacles as we were clad in only t-shirt, shorts and daps. What we did was run up and down the side of the course until the mud became ankle deep. We were then made to get into the prone position and crawl up and down until we looked like 1950s B-movie mud-monsters.

With the importance of PT kit maintenance thoroughly drilled home, we were marched back to the block where we scrambled to get our washing done in time for the next lesson.

On arriving back to the room, Baker was waiting with his arms folded and shaking his head. He summed up his feelings about our current plight in one word: 'Cunts.'

I went to sleep that night feeling heartily sorry for myself. There was absolutely no way on this planet that I was going to be able to withstand these levels of abuse for 14 weeks. Like every other recruit in history, I nodded off, safe in the knowledge that I was easily the biggest arsehole to ever have graced the uniform.

THE BUTT PARTY

The camaraderie created by mutual adversity got me through, along with various other dead legs. As the days went by, things seemed to get incrementally better. You couldn't have plotted this progress on a graph, but I began to see the light at the end of the tunnel. Baker's use of the word 'cunt' was as frequent, but seemed to lose some of its venom. I found, to my immense surprise, that my body actually had the building blocks of co-ordination, and that occasionally I could march in a straight line and halt at the same time as everyone else. I hesitate to say it, but by the time I'd been there a couple of weeks, part of me was starting to enjoy the training.

We were lucky in Room 4, as all the other rooms appeared to have a duty fuckwit whose task it was inadvertently to spoil everyone else's hard work. Room 6 had the biggest fuckwit. He was called McDaid, and he hailed from somewhere in the far north of Scotland that was closer to Russia than it was to Harrogate. His particular trick was to leave shitty undercrackers around. Never considered to be a particularly high social grace, in a recruit troop setting it is apt to get the entire room murdered. As soon as his little habit was discovered, Sergeant Atkins always paid special attention to McDaid's locker. He struck dark gold one morning, when 'Skiddy,' as he soon became known, had dunked a pair of particularly clinker-infested gruds into one of his boots in the couple of seconds immediately preceding the 'Room, room shun.'

'Where have you left 'em this morning, McDaid?'

'Pardon, Sergeant?'

'Do I have to go fishing with my pace stick, or are you going to give me a clue?'

After a couple of moments, Skiddy sighed. 'Ma right boot, Sergeant.'

Atkins shuddered. 'You dirty bastard,' he shouted. 'I don't know what it's like in fucking Latvia or wherever it is you're from, but in the British Army we do not keep our soiled underwear in our boots, or anyone else's for that matter. Right, get 'em on your 'ead, you can wear them all morning.'

Tom Galbraith was the closest we got to a fuckwit, but his brilliant sense of humour compensated for his shortcomings. He always made me laugh, even when I didn't know what the fuck he was on about. He told me one of the jokes from his Scottish cabaret whilst we were cleaning the bogs on a bull night and I didn't get it until the next morning.

'Hey, Eddie, ya cunt. You'll like this ain. What's the difference between Bing Crosby and Walt Disney?'

I was concentrating on removing a particularly adhesive bit of shit with the back side of the scrubbing brush. 'I dunno, mate. What?'

'Bing sings, and Walt disnae.' He roared with laughter slapping me on the back when I just stared at him, dumbfounded.

'Ya miserable fucker, ye. Walt *disnae*,' he said.

I carried on removing shit from the toilets, for Queen and country.

It was mildly comforting to know that the Army did not expect us to endure our hardships without any kind of reward. To that end, we were paid the princely sum of ten pounds per week. However, in typical Army fashion, obtaining and spending the money was not made easy.

Our financial reward was administered on an official pay parade at the end of every week and took place in the block. The squadron 2IC would be sat behind a table at the end of our corridor, flanked by Atkins and Bailey, like two vultures just waiting for one of us fuck up. In front of the officer would be a tin of money, a pen, and a register of our names. We would line up in front of him in single file. At his behest, the recruit at the head of the line would spring to attention, march forward, halt in front of him, salute, give his name and number, accept the ten pounds, check it, announce, 'Pay correct, Sir!', salute again, about turn and march away, all to be carried out with regimental pauses of 'one-two-three-one'. It all sounded straightforward enough, but the reality was different.

Any mistakes would be picked up by Atkins or Bailey and the offender would be sent to the back of the line where he would wait

15 minutes for his next turn. Should someone be unlucky enough, or just totally shit at drill, to be picked up three times, then they would be sent to jail. 'Grippable' offences would include: a lacklustre spring to attention; a step on the march forward or away that had an inadequate heel-dig or arm-swing; sloppy saluting (Skiddy was particularly prone to this – he saluted like a depressed New Romantic, sweeping his flick from his eyes).

Once armed with our fortune, we still had to purchase our boot polish, plimsoll whitener, boot-bulling cloths, starch and all other manner of kit maintenance stuff from it. Which left negligible change for anything else. Any trip to the NAAFI was only to be done by one person per room, and they were not allowed to buy any confectionery for themselves or the rest of the chaps. To enforce this, the room NCOs would search any NAAFI run bags when the designated shopper would return. This led to most of the guys developing the ability to drink a freshly opened 1.5 litre bottle of Irn Bru and eat ten Mars bars in one minute. You'd be burping up fizzy pop sick all night, but it was worth it for the sugar rush.

Another weekly routine was the Sunday church parade. The Army considers itself religious, and in the spirit of tolerance and acceptance, if it is religious, then so are you.

Atkins and Bailey would have us all outside at 9 o'clock for an inspection. God demanded that we be in our best clobber, so we wore barrack dress. This was pretty much the same as working dress, but instead of the dreaded KF we wore the far more civilised brown No 2 dress shirt. We also wore barrack dress trousers, in place of our lightweights. They were a horrible bit of kit, their only plus point being that they didn't take much ironing, being fashioned from some sort of weird plastic-textile-hybrid material. Once pressed with a suitably hot iron, they held their crease for three or four years. Walking in them was like having your legs rubbed with a Brillo pad, and marking time for more than a few seconds would leave you with severe carpet burns on your thighs.

All recruits had to attend, and although we didn't have to wear a military uniform to church, a rigid dress code was enforced. It was 1985, and perhaps they were petrified that we'd all show up in Cameo cod-pieces or Spandau Ballet suits. Anyway, the college hierarchy had decided that each squadron needed a civilian uniform as well. Rawson's was the worst. Smart 'get-you-into-a-club' trousers were combined with a white shirt topped with a fetching purple jumper and tie combo. The jumper had a yellow eagle motif on the left tit, and the tie had diagonal yellow stripes of smaller eagles running across it. You looked like you were off for a couple of rounds of pro-am golf with Tarby and Brucey. To add insult to injury, these items had to be purchased from the PRI with a significant portion of the apprentice's meagre wages.

Three quarters of the recruit troop fell into the C of E category. This included anyone who wasn't sure, and those atheists who didn't want an argument. The rest of us were Catholics, or as Sergeant Atkins put it, Ratcatchers. Conveniently, Sergeant Bailey was also a 'Roman Candle', so he always took our squad. The C of E service was taken in the big church, by the College Padre, whilst our mass was taken in the smaller church to its left by a priest who drove in from Harrogate. As we filed in to the chapel for the first time, I was a bit slow in removing my beret, which caused Bailey to growl, 'Take your hat off in the House of the Lord, Nugent, you cunt.'

Once you were inside and sat down, sanctuary was achieved for the duration of the proceedings. For 30 minutes, you were left alone with no-one shouting at you. As long as you didn't fall asleep or fuck about, it was a well-earned break. As the priest droned on, it was possible to drift off and relax. He would relate anecdotes about life in Harrogate while we took the opportunity to look at some of the eye candy on show. Permanent members of staff would bring their wives and children to the services. Most of the wives were on the big side, but some of the daughters provided a welcome change from having to look at squaddies all the time.

One unsettling aspect of the service, upon which a half-decent theologian could have written a dissertation, was that the priest was a grass. If he ever spotted anyone, especially a recruit, nodding off, he would bring it to the attention of one of the Sergeants hovering at the end of the pew. How a man of the cloth could do this, in the safe knowledge that the sleeper would soon be undergoing a punishment far outweighing his crime, was beyond me. After every service, as he shook hands and smiled at his departing parishioners, five or six lads would be doing star-jumps on the grass behind him whilst one of the SNCOs berated them for not displaying the Christian virtue of good listening.

Our mass always finished a quarter of an hour earlier than the C of E, so we were allowed to go and have a cup of tea in the refectory next door whilst we waited for the rest of the troop. It was a nice skive and it was quickly spotted by the other lads. As the weeks went by, a conversion took place the likes of which would have had Billy Graham strutting about with his chest out. Six weeks into training, almost half the troop were declaring themselves Catholic on a Sunday morning. Atkins and Bailey had never bothered to count numbers, but they started to get suspicious by week 10 when only Atkins and eight recruits were heading over to the big church. A glance to the left allowed them to witness the massed ranks of unbaptised Catholics squeezing in next door, all eager to enjoy a sneaky brew with only their immortal souls as payment. They put a stop to it eventually by checking names against a list of everyone's official religious beliefs.

* * * * *

A few weeks into training, we were introduced to the primary role of the Army, military training. This was a heady mix of weapons handling, including stripping, assembling, loading and unloading various rifles. All of this led to the natural conclusion of firing them on the ranges. As range day drew closer, my trepidation grew at an exponential rate. We had been filled with all sorts of stories as to how the SLR was an elephant gun just waiting to dislocate every bone in your body – all the normal shit that people who have done something feed to those that haven't. Once we were all deemed competent with the rifles, we were loaded onto four tonners and whisked off to the sunny climes of Whitburn ranges on the North Sea coast, or 'Whitburn-sur-la-Merde' as it should have been known.

We were all sat down and broken into two groups, one which would be shooting first and the others who would be operating and repairing the targets. This second group was known as the 'Butt Party', which drew several laughs.

I was in the butt party first off, which only made the build-up to shooting even more ominous. I shouldn't have been so nervous, but I'd never fired anything with a calibre larger than an elastic band in my life and I didn't know what to expect. So when the first 'crack and thump' of the rounds whipping overhead snapped me out of a tit-and-fanny daydream, it only threw fuel on the fire of my anguish.

Still, it wasn't all bad. Colin Mortimer tried to cheer me up by pointing to a six-inch diameter glue pot and saying, in his thick Newcastle accent, 'How, Eddie man. Ya see that pot o' glue? Well, that's your arse, that is.'

It soon became monotonous. The guys would shoot, we would tot up the scores and then repair the targets, and so it would continue. It soon occurred to me that shooting first would be better, as you would have all afternoon to get your weapon clean afterwards. Not that it would make much odds, because any instructor who inspected your rifle would say that it was in 'bog order,' regardless of its actual condition, and you would be sent away to re-clean it. If it was clean you wouldn't bother to touch it again. When you took it back for re-inspection, the instructor would say, 'That's fucking better! Why didn't you do that properly in the first place, you lazy cunt?', but that was neither here nor there.

The transition from butts to shooting took place at lunch. We all congregated behind the firing line, near an old hut which was staffed by an old guy, the range warden. He looked like a wookie with mange, and at first I thought he also stank to high heaven. It transpired that the God-awful smell was coming from a small kitchen inside his hut. One of the instructors asked him what the source of the whiff was. He replied, 'Don't you worry about that, son. I'm just cooking up a few starfishes for me dog.' With that, he pointed down to his side, but there was no dog there. He was obviously insane.

The moment of truth eventually came at two o'clock that afternoon. I got into the prone position behind my long black rifle and followed all of the instructor's orders to load and make ready. It was just like being in the classroom, and I soon forgot my worries. Until I fired the fucking thing. It kicked like a barge mule in my weedy grip, and the rear sight leapt back and split my eyebrow open in a flash of blood and white pain. Needless to say, I held on to it for grim death after that. When I dressed away from the firing point, one of the instructors noticed my bleeding eye and called me over. I explained myself and he offered some encouragement. 'Well you won't fucking do that again, will you, you dickhead?' he said, and he was right – I never did.

We were also taught field craft, the art of seeing without being seen, like when you're drunk and dancing naked in the street but are convinced that you are invisible. There were practical and written lessons in first aid and nuclear, biological, chemical warfare. Instruction in the latter culminated in us being gassed in a small chamber filled with CS. When it was my turn to remove my respirator, I held my breath as long as possible. The instructors were onto me and started bombarding me with questions, with the result that I took in an involuntary lung full of the stuff and spent the next five minutes choking and spluttering, with two 12 inch-long snot strings hanging from my beak.

The only other time I caught the full force of CS was during the 'canister change' drills, when I panicked. Despite my best efforts to get the filter secured back in place by cupping my right hand over its mounting hole, it still got cross-threaded on re-attachment and I got a full hit of gas inside my respirator.

The whole mil' training extravaganza was overseen by a group of moustachioed instructors who were only one step down from the PTIs on the 'angry-at-the-world-ometer'. Their rage would peak every time one of us fucked up on a test, and the most common example was magazine loading. This was a practical exam that involved kneeling with an empty magazine between your legs, and an up-turned helmet full of 20 rounds on the floor in front of you. When the instructor said go, the panic began and with it a desperate, shaking finger scramble to bomb up the mag with the loose rounds in the allotted time. The last couple of rounds were the worst as you would have to chase them around the inside of the lid and force them into the magazine, resulting in skinned fingers and knuckles.

We were split into sections for mil' training. Ours consisted of my roommates and, much to my horror, Skiddy McDaid. Our instructor, Corporal Havers, was a large, but relatively reasonable man. Unfortunately, Skiddy's inability to carry out even the most basic instructions often saw Havers flip into a rage that resulted in our section running around camp with our rifles above our heads. It wasn't until Tom and Barry threatened Skiddy with a good shoeing that his level of competence rose from 'no use to man nor beast and an affront to God and nature' to the dizzy heights of 'dreg of society'.

One of Skiddy's more memorable fuck-ups was on our first 'contents of webbing' inspection. The crux of packing your webbing was for everything to be as compact and portable as possible. To that end, for a shaving kit, everybody would pack a brush, a soap stick and a razor inside their mess tins. Skiddy, however, rocked up with a 33% extra free, 1 litre can of Erasmic moisturising shaving foam. The can was coloured in the well-known camouflage combination of lurid red and white, and it stuck out of his kidney pouch and up his back like a full-size barber's pole. Once again, it caused Havers to lose his rag and another jaunt around camp was on the cards.

All of our military training came to a head with our basic training exercise, when we packed our hopelessly inadequate webbing, clambered aboard the four tonne trucks and headed off to Catterick Training Area. As soon as we got off the four tonners, another flaw in the webbing came to light. We were told to lie down in the all-round defence formation. As soon as I went prone on the deck, my backpack rode up and pushed on the back of my head, forcing my face into the ground. I couldn't see more than two feet in front of me, and that was only by rolling my eyes up as far as they would go. Eventually, I managed to rest the front lip of my helmet on the rear sight of my rifle. This took the bone-breaking pressure off my neck and also increased my field of vision from two to three feet. Even so, I was no use to anyone. If we'd been attacked, the order to open fire would have to have been, 'Don't shoot until you see the blacks of their toe-caps.'

We were taken to an area known as Rabbit Wood where we were shown the basics of building 'bashas' out of our ponchos.

The example that Havers built was perfectly formed and looked like a proper tent. Our attempts, on the other hand, were more like a shanty-town for pissheads on the edge of Sao Paulo's worst favela.

As we were now deployed on exercise, we had to cam-up with shit-smelling brown 'cam-cream'. The instructor explained how you could use too much, too little, or just the right amount of cream. He then press-ganged three recruits, including me, and did a practical. I was fortunate enough to be the 'too little' fellow, and ended up looking like the Dallas Cowboys quarterback, with a single dark stripe under each eye. Tom dipped out and got the 'too much'; he looked like Al Jolson, with Havers taking great pleasure in grinding the cream into his ears whilst singing 'Mammy'. Barry was 'Mr Right' as Havers called it. Once the cream was applied he had about half of his face covered in short brown smears, and he looked like, for the first time in his life and to everyone's surprise, a soldier.

Once we had re-built all of our bashas to an acceptable standard, and were all cammed-up, we were taken through compo rations. These field rations came in tins, and as a general rule were bland in the extreme. The only glimmer of hope was in the sundries pack that came with the box, because there was the familiar site of a packet of Rolos. These were a massive morale boost, although I was a bit dubious of their authenticity, given that all the writing on the pack was in Arabic. The other sweets in the box were some Foxes glacier fruits. They were impossible to separate from their wrappers and were invariably consumed with at least half of the plastic still on. Other delights from the boxes included a horrible processed cheese that became known as 'cheese possessed' and bacon burgers that were simply a solid lump of fat and scrag meat. There was also a single slop-like substance which in one tin would be called 'chicken curry' and which would reappear in another tin, identical in appearance and taste but called 'chicken in brown sauce'.

The king of compo food, however, was steak and kidney pudding or 'babies heads' as it was affectionately known, due to the soft indented feeling to the pastry when cooked.

The cumbersome tins of compo stretched our already overloaded webbing to its limit and meant the only available storage space for the Rolos and other sweets was in the respirator pouch. This was dicing with death, as we were told from the start that nothing, but nothing, other than NBC equipment was to go in the pouch. It seemed a shame, as it was large enough to house a family of Vietnamese boat people. The sweets in the pouch thing worked great until the first afternoon, when Havers threw a lit CS tablet into our harbour area and roared, 'GAS, GAS, GAS!'

There was a flurry of activity from all of us, and in my attempts to avoid the effects of the gas I pulled out my respirator with all of my strength from its pouch. Sweets were scattered over a 10 foot radius like an explosion at Willy Wonka's. As soon as I had my respirator on, I started trying to pick up the sweets before Havers noticed them. As I did so, I noticed that the vision in my left eye was blurred. I assumed the outside of the eyepiece was dirty, but rubbing it had no effect. I stared quizzically at the stain for a second or two before the true horror hit me: a melted Rolo was stuck to the inside of the mask, and there was CS gas everywhere so I could do fuck all about it. Driven on by blind fear as to what Havers would do to me if he saw the offending sweet, I tried desperately to shift it, nodding and shaking my head furiously and blinking at the same time, trying to catch the offending chocolate in my eyelids. Quite how painful it would have been if I'd succeeded, I dread to think, but it wasn't working and, after a minute or so of doing this all I'd achieved was to invent a mad dance that was suited only to a northern soul all-nighter. So I gave up and spent the rest of the time avoiding the instructors or tilting my head away from them. When the gas all clear was given, I whipped off my mask and cleaned it as quickly as possible. It had been a close shave and I had certainly learned a lesson.

The rest of the day was taken up with practising section attacks. This entailed alternate members of the squad running forward to attack an imaginary enemy. It was knackering, especially as you tried to avoid sheep shit and puddles when hitting the deck.

Come last light, we had the mandatory stand-to and then we cooked our compo evening meal. It wasn't the best-tasting food ever, but the hot chow did the trick on our weak and tired bodies.

That evening, a guard roster was drawn up, and we settled into night routine.

At around 2100 hours, the heavens opened and we got drenched. I remember lying in my sleeping bag, feeling waves of water lapping against my body. Later, in the light of day, we found the area was four inches under water. Everyone, including the instructors, was soaking wet, as was all of our kit. It went without saying that morale was rock bottom. Virtually no one was talking, and any words that were passed were in the form of a massive whinge. Most of the guys must have been thinking the same as me, which was, 'Fucking hell, if all exercises are going to be like this, then it's going to be a nightmare.' To that end, it was decided by the DS that we would go back to camp. It was, after all, only supposed to be a two-night, introduction to the field, and they would have two years to beast us over the various training areas of Great Britain.

It turned out that the whole of North Yorkshire had been subject to severe flooding in one form or another. Of course, Baker gave us the now inevitable hard time and told us that in his day they would not have been brought back in. He tried to justify his statement by giving us hugely-inflated tales of hardship on exercises so cold that the flame on his lighter froze. But the whole fabrication fell on deaf ears.

The last remnant of exercise life came in the form of 'compo shits,' which were large dungs caused by the arse blocking effects of the rations. They hit most of us about 12 hours after being back in camp. The strange thing about them was that they all smelled the same. One such cack was so huge that we were paraded into the corridor, then marched into the toilet one at a time and forced to look at it. It was incredible, like two cans and one bottle of Newcastle Brown Ale end-on. It would have been three cans of brown, only the bottle is better shaped to give the natural taper of the log. It wouldn't pass down the U bend and had been left there: inevitably the blame fell on Skiddy, and he was given the dubious task of disposing of the beast. By all accounts he had to chop it up into manageable pieces before it would flush.

As Christmas drew closer, so did the end of training. In the last few weeks, we endured a constant ratcheting-up of expected standards. Our admin skills had improved beyond recognition, and the ATNCOs and Sergeants increased their nitpicking to combat our new-found abilities. Baker took the lead in these matters, excelling in the discovery of things that weren't there. Even with Tom Galbraith's ropey contribution, we were on top of our game and the room was generally gleaming. In the absence of any real problems, Baker simply invented them. During one inspection, he brushed his hand carefully across the top of my locker. When he brought it down, he inspected it before gleefully showing its contents to me.

'What the fuck is that, Nugent?'

A solitary pubic hair nestled in his palm and it was obviously a plant: the colour match with Baker's hair was nearly perfect. I had a quick mental flash of him stood in the toilets just before he came into the room, selecting which pube to pull out. It wasn't worth challenging a person who would go to these lengths to drop you in the shit.

'It's a pube, Corporal.'

'Oh, fucking *really*? And there's me thinking it was a fucking guitar string. What the *fuck* was it doing on top of your locker?'

For a fraction of a second, I entertained the notion of replying, 'You brought it in with you, you weird fucking bastard. It's one of yours, freshly-plucked from your bush five minutes ago, you scary halfwit.'

Instead, I replied, 'I must have left it up there and forgot about it, Corporal.'

He wasn't sussed enough to realise that I was taking the piss, but Steve Keets couldn't stop himself from emitting a short, loud laugh. This caused the entire room to join in for the briefest of moments, before Baker screamed for order. 'Fucking funny is it, Keets?' He was blazing mad, and from experience, was apt to do anything.

'No, Corporal.'

'Like Nugent's pubes, do you?'

'No, Corporal.'

'Well, you can have it. Here you go.' With that, he stuck it to Steve's forehead, his anxious sweat holding it in place perfectly. It looked like a comedy frown line.

By that stage of the game, impromptu pubic hair decoration seemed like a minor indignity and Steve didn't seem to suffer any ill effects.

Under threat of punishment, time was set aside for us to write home. Though not physically censored, we were always encouraged to write about the more positive aspects of the experience. This made for extremely short letters and I used to pack mine out with whining. Moaning about my circumstances was cathartic but probably made quite grim reading to Mum and Dad. They used to write their letters jointly, and they took on an almost conversational tone, as Dad would respond to comments further up the page by Mum. For some reason, the pen would run out at least once during every single letter. Instead of stopping as soon as the ink began to wane, my Dad always wrote something like, 'Bloody hell, this pen's abo...' before recommencing in a different colour. The running commentary wasn't essential, but it always made me smile.

Getting letters from friends and family was fundamental to maintaining a modicum of mental health. The training staff were well aware of this and loved to piss people about on the weekly mail calls. The whole troop would be paraded and Sergeant Atkins would stand there with a huge pile of mail in his arms. The letters were in no particular order, so he'd just shout out the name and the recruit could run up to receive the highly-prized item. The whole thing took about half an hour. Some lads would get upwards of ten letters but as the pile dwindled, those yet to get a letter would start to get twitchy. I usually got one or two a week. The regular missal from home would occasionally be supplemented by a note from one of my mates. Gran wrote from time to time, though her bad eyesight and terrible spelling meant that I couldn't read them without an Enigma machine. Barry Nash obviously had three or four girls on the go, and by the time he went up to collect his eighth letter of the week, he would be getting scowled at by the less fortunate. One lad, Dave Norrington, hardly ever got a letter and Atkins used to love winding him up. The tricks were the same every week, but due to Nozzers' undiminishing optimism, he fell for them every time.

'Norrington.' Atkins would be waving an alluring blue envelope.

Dave would run up like the excited school kid I suppose he'd recently been. As Atkins passed him the letter, he would deliver the blow, smiling and to a big roar from the troop. 'Give that to Nash, will you?'

As Atkins got to the last bits of post, he'd shout Dave's name out once more.

'Norrington?'

'Yes, Sarnt?'

'No mail.'

If you were stood behind him, you could watch him deflating. It was that unsettling combination of funny and cuntish that made you feel a bit of a twat for laughing.

In these pre-mobile phone days, the only other form of contact with home were strictly-rationed phone calls. It was a privilege that was withdrawn at the drop of a hat, but as a reward, it used to make us work our bollocks off. We didn't get anywhere near for the first six weeks, but during week seven our entire room was allowed down to the two red booths that stood outside the cinema. Chaperoned by Baker, we were allotted ten minutes each, 'and no fucking more.'

I'd spent most of my money on polish and Brasso anyway, so keeping it short wouldn't pose a problem. When it was my turn, I went in with a small pile of 10p pieces and dialled home. As soon as the connection was made, I heard my Mum's voice say 'Hello,' and it affected me more than I thought it would. Though my Dad's use of profanity was liberal and inventive, it was an unwritten rule that I didn't swear in front of my Mum. Unfortunately, having spent the last month and a half in a cursing workshop, where every second word, and sometimes every *single* word, was 'fuck,' I couldn't help myself. It was great to hear the tones of a friendly female who meant me no harm.

'Hiya, Mum. It's really nice to hear your fucking voice,' I replied.

'Pardon?'

I was horrified with myself and blushed hard enough to steam up the inside of the booth.

'Sorry, Mum. I'm not thinking straight.'

'I hope that's not all they're teaching you, son?'

'No. Sorry, Mum, everyone swears a lot round here.'

'Maybe you can teach your Dad some more new ones when you come home. That'd be nice.'

I got to speak to them both on five or six occasions before the end of training and it took Herculean efforts to keep the conversation expletive-free. The chats were always short and sweet but they never failed to put a spring in my step. Mum's concern for my wellbeing was comforting and Dad always had me laughing with stories about work and his eccentric views on current affairs. On one occasion, Gran was round having her tea when I rang. She tied up my whole ten minute allotment telling me details about the death of a cat that belonged to a woman I'd never heard of before hanging up because her food was getting cold.

* * * * *

The two main bullshit factors of basic training were the drill badging parade and the Squadron Commander's block inspection. Both would be overseen by the evil, troll-like OC, Major Tatchell, taking a couple of days off from goat-bothering to plague the recruits one last time.

The purpose of the badging parade was to ensure that every man jack of us could not only perform adequate drill but also recite Corps history parrot fashion. Presumably this was preparation for the unlikely event that one of us would make it onto *Mastermind* and choose 'Uninteresting Facts About The Royal Corps Of Signals' as our specialist subject.

Our reward for passing badging would be the Royal Signals cap badge, which would help us to stop looking like new members of the French Resistance.

At the start of the parade the OC stood at one side of the square, with our entire squad facing him at a distance of 20 paces. Two recruits would then come to attention, march forward out of the squad, salute to the left, salute to the right, halt, and salute to the front before answering a barrage of questions about the Royal Signals. With the job done, they would salute again, about turn, and march back into their original places leaving Bob as their uncle.

However, in classic Army fashion, if the bloke you were partnered with were to fuck up then you both failed.

To that end, I spent several minutes each week praying that I would not get saddled with McDaid as a partner.

The day of the parade was unseasonably hot and sunny, with a slight heat haze rising from the square. We were lined up in our pairs and I was partnered with Barry Nash. The OC started to appear in the distance, slowly getting larger. It took him ages to get there: it was all quite reminiscent of Omar Sharif coming out of the desert in *Lawrence of Arabia*.

Barry and I were in the best place to be for any kind of drill – in the middle of the group, giving us the kind of anonymity only dreamed of by right-hand markers and people whose surnames began with an A or a Z. Tucked away in the centre of the pairs, we started to arse around. When the OC was in his final approach to the examiner's position, Barry began to talk quietly out of the side of his mouth, in a high-pitched voice. 'Hello, my name is Major Tatchell, and I am an evil troll.'

I started to giggle, but Barry carried on regardless. 'I live under a bridge and eat goats, just after I've bummed them to death.'

The more I thought about how much trouble I would be in if I got caught, the worse it was.

'If your drill is not up to standard, young Nugent, that would be a very grave error on your behalf! Because you too shall receive a good bumming! Now march over my bridge, because I am a troll wanker!'

'For fuck's sake, Barry,' I whispered. 'Shut the fuck up, you cunt.'

Luckily he stopped, and I had composed myself by the time it came round for us to do the test. It went swimmingly, with no slip-ups on the drill. The OC asked us the generic questions we'd been told to memorise. He asked me to name the slow and quick marches of the Corps and got Barry to describe the cap badge in intricate detail. After our successful attempt, we had the opportunity to watch the rest of the guys go through their paces. As predicted, Skiddy fucked up monumentally, saluting to the left when it should have been to the right and producing a halt which, instead of a precise check pace, one-two, was just a random sequence of flailing legs like something from *Riverdance*.

Two days later, we had the bullnight for the OC's inspection. The brown lino floors had never been so shiny. Each armed with a tin of dark tan Kiwi Parade Gloss boot polish, we got on our hands and knees in one long line and polished the floor like a giant boot. Everyone worked their plums off and anyone going into another room without a good reason was met with anger and possible violence for the capital crime of fucking up the floors. We pretty much worked the whole night through without stopping, save for an interim inspection by AT/Sergeant Bramhall at 10 o'clock. The inspection was unnecessary as we all knew the score with bullnights by this point, but Bramhall insisted that it go ahead, and who were we to protest? At the appointed hour, he sauntered into the room leaving scuff prints on the deck, whilst we all stood to attention and watched our work go down the tubes. He checked absolutely everything and could find no fault. In a last-ditch attempt to dig up a grippable offence, he picked up the metal waste paper bin and peered inside. It was spotless, but nevertheless, he went into an insane rage. 'Who the fuck was supposed to clean this?' he called.

Alistair stepped forward. 'Me, Sergeant. McKenzie, Sergeant.'

'Come here, you lazy fucker, and look in this fucking bin.'

Alistair did as he was told and Bramhall continued. 'Well, Goat Jugs. What the fuck do you see?'

'Er, I don't know, Sergeant.'

Alistair's reply was cautiously quizzical because there was not a spot of dirt in the receptacle. The bin was surgically clean. Bramhall roared. 'Well, I'll tell you, you shitdick! FEZZ! That's what it is, it's fucking FEZZ! Look!' He forcefully up-ended the bin onto the white surface of a table and lifted it, expecting to see a pile of dust and dirt. But the table remained clean. So he repeated the action, this time following it up by smashing the base of the upside-down bin with his pace stick. Again, nothing. At this point he went scarlet with anger and began thrashing the bin in a frenzy of long, looping blows. Eventually, he stopped and stared at the now pockmarked base, which looked like an aerial photograph of Ypres. Then he took on the appearance of a vindicated man: on the table was a tiny flake of paint that his assault had knocked off the inside of the bin.

'Right, McKenzie,' he said. 'Get your lazy fat arse into the corridor and bring in the large bin from the ablutions.'

Five seconds later, Alistair returned with the family-sized round metal bin. Bramhall then made him stand to attention, with the bin over his head, as he subjected it to the same deranged attack. I swear that each time the stick hit the bin Bramhall's feet were off the floor. It was apparent that some of his punishment ideas were cartoon-based.

The next day's inspection was carried out, again, by Major Tatchell, but this time it was done when we weren't there. We were given a run down on his findings when we returned from mil' training that afternoon. Our room had come top – the only thing he could find wrong was that one of the beds was missing a spring, no doubt shaken loose by years of masturbation.

Later that day, we were awarded our cap badges. They had a strange design flaw – three lumps of metal protruded through the inside of the beret and dug into the wearer's forehead – and the NCOs were kind enough to emphasise this point by making us stand to attention in our berets and hitting the cap badges with the palms of their hands. After this we all had three small dents in our noggins to remind us of the momentous occasion.

Having the cap badge seemed to make a huge difference to our status. From the moment we were 'badged' we zipped up the food chain, all the way from amoebae to plankton. Although the bollockings and punishments still came thick and fast, the emphasis started to shift. There was a subtle perception that those who had got this far were likely to make it through basic and take up positions as apprentice tradesmen. Even strokers like Baker went a little bit easier on us. I presumed that there was an element of self-preservation to this stance. As soon as we finished training, his rank would mean pretty much fuck all, and the desire for recriminations might surface. I didn't think I was capable of taking him on physically, but Tom Galbraith was relishing the prospect. One of his favourite topics of conversation was what he was going to do to Baker if he ever saw him in a pub.

'I'll tell ya', lads, if I ever get the chance to sort him out, he'd better hope there's someone walking round Harrogate with a bollock donor card.'

He was a great laugh, Tom, but I wouldn't want to have been in his bad books.

As we moved into December and closer to the passing off day, we seemed to spend more and more time fucking about on the square. Although my drill was adequate, I took a bit of pride in the fact that I wasn't much good at it. There were a few lads in the troop who loved it, and they could be seen practising on their own in the corridors, in the hope that one of the ATNCOs might spot them and award them a few arse-licking points. The rest of us saw it for what it was, one great big ballache which we'd do our best to forget as soon as we didn't need to know it.

Getting through basic training was a process of continual assessment, there were no big exams towards the end. The instructors had us convinced from the start that we could be kicked out just for farting at the wrong time. The reality was that as long as you generally tried to do as you were told, and didn't fuck up royally all day every day, you would probably get through. As we trudged through the three months, our numbers did diminish for various reasons. Some lads decided that the Armed Forces just wasn't for them and took the opportunity to voluntarily discharge themselves. Another handful disappeared when medical problems surfaced that hadn't been picked up in the selection process. With a couple of compassionate discharges and one disciplinary sacking, our numbers were reduced to sixty-two by the end. The troop sack-of-shit, Skiddy, sailed through, to everyone's amazement. In hindsight, he was the perfect bloke for the Army, less the dubious personal hygiene habits. Despite his ability to mess up any given task, he never gave up trying and earned, from upwind, the grudging respect of the staff.

A week before pass off, we were paraded for our recruit troop photograph. As with everything else in the Army, the photograph was structured by rank. The OC and the recruit troop officer were sat plum centre, flanked by Sergeants Atkins and Bailey and the ATNCOs. To maintain symmetry, a couple of shortarsed recruits were placed in the seats on either side, to bulk up the front row, and the rest of us were arranged in order of height to give an even look. Basketball players were bang in the middle of the back row, and the size gradually diminished until it got to the Cornish contingent on the ends. The photographer took a couple of shots whilst everyone tried to give him a hard man stare. Then, in an attempt at state-controlled fun, we were told to 'mess about', so that the snapper could take a jokey photo. For most of us, turning a photo from serious to humorous would have involved exposing the right or left plum, preferably resting on the head of the man in front. Before anyone thought of it, Atkins ruled it out. This left us with the hilarious choices of putting our hats on back to front or winking at the camera.

In the last week, we were allowed to phone home every night. Mum, Dad and Gran were coming over for the pass-off. All our conversations were taken up with the massive logistical operation that would see three people travelling from Manchester to Harrogate on a train. Mum was full of questions that I didn't have an answer for. 'Should I wear a hat?' 'Are all the other Mums going?' 'Can we take pictures?'

Dad was more laconic and simply wanted to know if he was going to be able to buy me a pint after. Gran had assumed that one of the royal family would be in attendance and was disappointed when I gave her the news that the highest dignitary would be the big fat Mayor of Harrogate.

'Ooooh, that's a shame, Eddy. Are you sure?'

'Yeah, Gran. We had a look at the plan for the ceremony yesterday. There'll be a couple of Colonels and a Brigadier, plus the Mayor and his wife.'

'You'd think one of 'em would have made the effort, the lazy buggers. What about that Princess Michael of Kent, you know, the Jerry. She's never doing anything, except pretending to be nice. She could have popped up.'

'Sorry, Gran.'

'Not to worry. I can't wait to see you in your uniform Eddy.'

I had visions of her ruffling my hair in front of my new mates, or cleaning something off my cheek by gobbing on a hankie.

We were dragged on to the square every day for more drill rehearsals. Once we were sized off for our pass off positions, I managed to secure myself a nice cosy berth in the middle rank, with Col and Tom close by. We were told what would happen on the day in fine detail. The four squadrons of recruits would form up closest to the flimsy wooden inspection dais, which would be struggling under the combined weights of the Mayor and his missus. Behind us would be four squads of back up troops, comprised of older apprentices. They were there solely to fill up the square a bit and reduce its barren wasteland appearance. To their rear was the college band, a ramshackle collection of drummers, pipers and sick bay rangers. (Throughout my time in the college, the band was synonymous with skiving. 'Bandrats,' got out of all sorts of duties and sometimes exercises. They were always disappearing out of camp for some performance or another. The downside was that it was a deeply uncool thing to do. In the overwhelmingly macho world of the Army, being in the band would mark you out as lacking in moral fibre.) They only attended one of the rehearsals, and that was two days before the event. We followed a boringly familiar routine. Our four squads marched on first, closely followed by the support troops. The band wheeled round to the back and halted. The RSM was on the square to check that everything was being done properly. With him around, the Seniors were jittery and blokes were getting gripped and jailed left, right and centre. There was a constant trickle of comedy marching over to the guardroom, throughout the practice. With us all in position, the razzer explained that we would be stood there for forty-five minutes, whilst the Mayor did his inspection. He would stop to chat every now and again.

'If he stops to talk to you, speak to him clearly and look at him. I will be stood right behind him, so if anyone tries to give him a smart fucking answer, I'll be on hand to throw them into prison. Just think how much your mummies and daddies would enjoy watching me marching you away.'

It was probably correct to assume that if we were getting a specific warning not to do something, it was because someone had done exactly that in the past. I'd love to have met the bloke who was that determined to be a smartarse, despite the massed brass of the college being on hand to hear him. I hoped it had been worth the jailtime.

To keep the crowd entertained, the band would play a medley of tunes during the inspection. They went through their repertoire for us and – try as I might – I couldn't find any running theme or connection in the tunes. They started off with a bagpipe solo of *Amazing Grace*, followed, inexplicably, by *The Age of Aquarius* by Fifth Dimension. I was expecting soldierly tunes that would exhort me to puff my chest out, but we got, in quick succession, the theme tune from *Coronation Street*, *Eye of the Tiger*, the Corps quick march, *Louis Louis* by The Kingsmen, *Colonel Bogey* and *Rio* by Duran Duran. I'd not heard a military arrangement of the synth-pop classic before, and it took me quite some time to name that tune.

The inspection finished, we came to attention and did a march past of the dais. On the day, the crowd would be directly behind the platform and this would be their chance to get a few photos. The march past complete, all that was left was the clichéd inspirational speech by the Commandant. For the practice, the padre pretended to be Lt Col De la Tour, and took the opportunity to do a bit of holy rolling to his captive audience. With that, we marched off to the haunting strains of *The Lion Sleeps Tonight*. It was an imaginative rendition, with the tuba player contributing the 'wim-o-weh' sounds, but I felt a bit cheated. Where were all the military classics? They never played any of this shit before kick off at Wembley.

The last night before pass off was a bit of a non-starter. Because Mum and Dad were only a couple of hours away, they were just going to travel over on the day. The parents of lads like Skiddy from the frozen North and blokes from the West Country were filling up b&bs all over Harrogate and anyone who had folks coming that night was allowed out to have dinner with them. If the rest of us had known this, we'd have all been lying like NAAFI watches but as it was, they were all slipping out the door at seven as the rest of us were in the corridor getting on with a half-hearted bull night. Skiddy passed us in his best clobber, trailing a cloud of Blue Stratos behind him. He had a white shirt and grey suit on, and it was tight in all the wrong places. Paul Jones shouted, 'Fackin' 'ell, it's Alexei Sayle.'

Steve Keets chipped in. 'Apparently, you can't tell his Mum and Dad apart.'

'What do you mean?' I said innocently.

'Fucking hell, Eddy. Let's put it this way. If you come from the same place as Skiddy and your Mum, wife and sister add up to more than two people, you're not a local.'

Recruit McDaid did have that distinctive 'hillbilly' look to him.

Amazingly, that evening, Baker tried to ingratiate himself with us a bit. Nothing spectacular, but when he entered the room and I shouted, 'Up,' he waved his hand and said, 'Don't worry about it. That's all finished with now. Just get the room squared away and we'll leave it that.'

Cue seven bemused faces. When he went out about an hour later, we talked about him. 'You know what?' said Tom Galbraith. 'I take back all I said about Baker. That one act of generosity has changed my opinion of him completely... he fucking wishes. What a cunt. Does he think we've all got goldfish memories or something?'

That was the thing with Baker. Getting bollocked, shouted at and punished for nothing were all part of the game. We understood that implicitly, and wouldn't be holding grudges against everyone. The subtle distinction with Baker was that you knew he really got off on the power trip. I'm sure he went off for a hand shandy every time he shouted at someone.

The last thing to do for the evening was to press our kit for the parade. The best outfit you can wear in the Army is your number-ones. They're smart as fuck – high-collared jacket with gold buttons and trousers with a red stripe down the side – and they come with a guarantee that says you will look sexy to gullible women. Trouble was, you only get to wear your number-ones at weddings, or if you're going to meet the Queen.

The next outfit down is your number-two dress. This is quite snappy – a sort of muddy-greeny-brown colour, worn with a brown shirt and tie. It doesn't sound too hot but once accessorised with collar dogs, silver buttons, a lanyard and white belt it looks the bizz. We didn't get to wear that one, either.

We were left with the dreaded barrack dress. The only embellishment for the parade was a black plastic belt worn with a silver Corps buckle and to be cleaned with a special foam, available only from the NAAFI at hyper-inflated prices. They were tossbags in that shop. They had a hotline to the squadrons and anytime you needed something desperately you could catch them changing the price stickers when you got in there to buy it.

It rained on our pass-off, not enough for them to change the programme to the indoor arena, but enough to get us all wet and miserable. It was still exciting, though, and when we formed up out of sight of the crowd, we were given a pep talk by the RSM.

'Right, gentlemen, you've earned this, so enjoy it. Let's see bags of swagger out there today, and please don't make me jail you.'

All our drill was spot on, and we got in to our positions without a hitch. For the expected 45 minutes of the inspection, I tried to spot my Mum and Dad and couldn't. It can't have been any easier for them: in the reduced visibility of the drizzle, we must have been impossible to tell apart at a distance of 40 metres. The Mayor and his wife went straight past me, but spoke to the next man. The band were just launching into their third tune, but I could earwig on the conversation. It was scintillating stuff.

'So, young man, where are you from?'

'Bedford, sir,' said the recruit, Bloxham I think it was.

'Oh, we love Bedford. We have friends there.'

Bloxham left it for five seconds before realising he was supposed to reply. 'Smart, sir.'

The RSM glared at him, but the Mayor had already moved on, oblivious to the sarcasm. When the inspection was over and we were piss-wet through, we did our march past. We went past the dais twice, chucking up the obligatory eyes-right both times.

Before we were marched off, the Commandant got up and made his speech. It was jam-packed with clichés. 'Recruits of 85C,' he said. 'I say to you, well done. You've all been through the mill in the last three months and have come up trumps. Your parents and I are all very proud of you today. But the proudest people here should be yourselves. You've grasped the bull by the horns, and stuck it through to the end.'

Blah blah etc fucking blah.

He went on like that for five minutes, including every sporting and military metaphor in the popular canon. I stopped listening after a bit and finally caught sight of my parents. There they were, right on the end of the third row of the stand. I couldn't work out how I hadn't pegged them before, then realised it was because Dad was wearing a suit, not something he did often. Gran was to his right, talking to someone in the row behind. The RSM calling us to attention, snapped me out of it again, and we marched off, taking the opportunity to join the tuba during the 'wim-a-ways' this time.

As soon as we got off the square, we were dismissed, and we all ran to the NAAFI to meet up with our families. I found my three straight away. When Dad spotted me, he waved, putting his pint down. He looked more excited than me. I made my way over to them and a group hug ensued. The scene was being repeated all over the NAAFI. Soldiers were getting their hair ruffled and rubbing lipstick off their cheeks; shouts of, 'Ooh, don't you look smart,' and 'Can you get me a jumper like that?' bounced off the walls.

After the initial few seconds of adrenaline had gone, Dad reverted to type and searched for something to find fault with, whilst Mum and Gran twittered around me.

'Ahhh, look at you, Eddy,' said Gran. She planted a hairy kiss on my face. 'I'll bet there isn't a smarter looking boy in the whole Army, eh, Barbara?'

Mum smiled, nodding. As she was about to speak, Sergeant Atkins came up and introduced himself. 'I was Recruit Nugent's Troop Sergeant for his basic training,' he said, all smiles and just about stopping short of putting his arm round my shoulders. It made me feel queasy. My Dad insisted on buying him a pint, whilst Gran asked him bone questions. He replied to them all professionally, but as soon as Dad returned with his beer, he made his excuses and moved on to the next family. Whenever I spotted one of the lads from my room, I got them to come over and say Hello. They were all politeness personified; Tom Galbraith nearly charmed the bloomers off Gran.

'What a lovely lad he was. So mannerly,' she said, as he walked away. I didn't tell her he'd been flicking tagnut-encrusted pubes at me a couple of days ago.

After a couple of beers and a few more impromptu speeches from various squadron personalities, we were allowed to shoot off. Whilst Mum and Gran sat in the car, Dad gave me a hand getting my gear from the room. He took quite an interest in the room and had a good look round. The only comment he could think to make was uncannily accurate. 'Bloody hell, nine of you in this little room? It must have smelt like an open fucking drain.'

I had two whole weeks off and at the start of my leave, it felt like the camp and all its horrible inhabitants were a million miles away. I spent significant chunks of my holiday boring the tits off my mates, with alcohol embellished-anecdotes about my newly-acquired warrior status. They were all pleased to see me and interested in the stories to begin with, but as soon as I started using sentences entirely comprising of military abbreviations, their attention naturally wandered. Any time I saw this happening, I simply ramped up the fabrication percentage of each tale until they listened again. It meant that the 'Rolo in the eyepiece' incident had become a life-threatening event, with the CS gas being replaced with something far worse which I simply invented on the spot. I think they knew I was bullshitting, but at the time it was slightly more interesting than sixth form college.

I really did see myself as being far more grown up than my civilian contemporaries, but in hindsight I was probably just being a tosser.

I took full advantage of the relaxed home regime. Mum and Dad were probably expecting me to leap out of bed before them every morning before doing all the ironing, but I immediately reverted to my pre-Army, slovenly ways. I stayed in bed till lunchtime every day, waking up to an empty house. Whilst Mum and Dad were at work, I tried my hardest to clean out the fridge, whilst watching the finest soaps that Australia had to offer. I'd have tea with them when they got in, then ring round my mates, trying to persuade them to come out. A few beers later I'd roll in with a bag of chips, which I'd promptly fall asleep into, before beginning the cycle again. It was a pattern of behaviour that wouldn't change for my entire Army career, and my Dad could never understand it. Surveying my Beirut style bedroom, he'd make the same point. 'There's no way they'd let you get away with this in the Army.'

He was absolutely right, and it was precisely why my room was a tip. As soon as I got home, the last thing I wanted to do was be tidy. Mum had to regularly pull me up about my language, as I used military-level cursing to cope with any domestic crises. I couldn't find my door keys before going out one night, and had already broken the world record for using the word 'fuck' before I spotted Mum's horrified stare and stopped. Swearing was, however, not the most embarrassing habit that Mum picked me up for. On several occasions she would say something on the lines of, 'Eddie, leave yourself alone!' At which point I would look around the room and reply, 'What?' On closer inspection I would realise that I was walking around the house with both of my hands down the front of my tracksuit bottoms, cupping my plums soothingly. I would then adopt the 'How did they get in there' facial expression and slink off to my room.

One night, I went out for a game of snooker with Dad. He was a lot better than me and augmented the difference by cheating whenever he thought I wasn't looking. It was little stuff like giving himself an extra point, or pretending not to notice that he'd nudged a red with his elbow. While we played, he asked me about Harrogate. 'I have to tell you, son, I didn't think you'd stick it. When I was putting you on that train, you looked too little, and it seemed like it was going to be a bit too much for you.'

'It wasn't that bad, Dad. After the first couple of weeks, it was the same old shit, and it was just a case of hanging in there.'

'I must say, though, I'm bloody proud of you.' He was about to take a shot, but paused. 'I know I don't say much, but you should hear me go on about you at work. They're all sick of me reading out your letters.'

He took the shot and went to mark up his score. 'So what happens with you now?' he said.

I noted that he'd awarded himself five for a red and green. It must have been a hard red. 'I go into trade training for a year and a half, then graduate from the College. I can do pretty much what I want from there.'

'How do you mean?'

'The trade that I'm doing, Radio Telegraphist, is really well spread out through the Corps, so I can apply to be posted almost anywhere in the world. I've got to qualify as a tradesman first though.'

I lined up a pot as he spoke.

'Don't you worry about that, son. They won't want to let you go after they've trained you up. Looking at some of them cro-magnons in your squad, I don't think you'll find it too hard to keep your head above water.'

I hoped he was right, but we had been warned that passing through basic training was only the beginning of the Harrogate experience.

Christmas and New Year came and went really quickly, and before I knew it, I was packing my bags to go back to camp. I shouldn't have been too bothered. It wasn't as if I was going to be one of the newest blokes there any more.

A new intake would be arriving as soon as we got back, and all the DS attention would be focused on them. Even so, I'd have liked a bit more time off, and it was a solemn train ride back to Yorkshire.

SEX LIARS AND SAMUEL MORSE

The return trip to Harrogate was, as usual, fraught with worry. I was anxious as to whether I'd be any good at trade training, but my immediate concerns were more about my new roommates. After basic training, our entire troop had been disbanded and redistributed amongst the rest of the squadron, spread randomly through the rooms occupied by older soldiers. Some of us would be lucky enough to end up with a couple of friends, others might find themselves the only new boy in a room of hairy-arsed mentalists. My fears were slightly allayed once I got into camp and checked the squadron orders board: Barry Nash was in with me, though I didn't know any of the other occupants. It was a who's who of unfamiliar names, McInerney, Ellis, Barnard and Collins. The room NCO was AT/Lance Corporal Derby.

The older blokes didn't really pay us much attention, but every now and then, Barry and I would be referred to as 'stroppy rooks'. As time went on, we were gradually accepted and integrated into the room pecking order. The natural life cycle of the college continued and, after a couple of weeks, another recruit troop was in progress on the lower floor, meaning that we weren't at the bottom of the food chain anymore. As bad as it may seem, it cheered me up to see the new recruits getting beasted. From my lofty vantage point, I couldn't believe how shit they were at drill, and everything else for that matter.

As the lads gradually accepted us, we came to know them as individuals. They were all just older versions of the characters from my recruit troop.

Paul McInerney was a mad jock, very similar to Tom Galbraith. The most morally bankrupt member of the room was Graham 'Spud Gun' Ellis. Spud, a porn fiend extraordinaire, possessed an outstanding repository of filth, or 'art' as he called it. Many a time I'd be snoozing on my bed, only to be awoken by Spud holding open the Readers' Wives section of *Fiesta* an inch from my face. 'Look at that, Eddie. Look at it. Now that is hot,' he would enthuse. Staring back at me would be 'Rita, from Tamworth,' legs akimbo, airing her admirably-furred display of genital topiary. 'What do you reckon to that fadge?' Spud would continue. 'Look at the state of the bastard, it's like a hairy nappy. Hey, Eddie, it's like a wolf with its throat cut. Here, if you like that, look at page 42, there's two fat lezzas having a baked bean and custard fight.'

This behaviour was only a scratch on the surface of Spud's depravity. His most notable idiosyncrasy had been the thing that had spawned his nickname. He had a scrotum that, when stretched to its full extent, was of record-breaking proportions and he used it to perform a series of amusing tricks. The opening trick of his repertoire was to stretch his ball bag over the top of a pint pot and play it like a tom-tom drum. Anybody not suitably impressed by this could not help but be bowled over by the finale. Spud would get hold of one of his testicles, stretch it as far as it would go, then fold it back under his legs and push it up his arse. Any spectators that hadn't passed out at this point would be treated to him firing the bollock out of his ring piece with a large fart. I often wondered how he'd discovered this talent in the first place.

Spud's polar opposite was Nick Barnard, an ice-cool customer with the ladies. Even at 18 years old, his trapping skills were legendary and I'm almost certain he never had to resort to sticking his bollocks up his arse to impress some fluff. Nick would just stand at the bar, like a Greek god with a badly-drawn bulldog tattoo, and let the ladies do the work. The pinnacle of his tupping came when he was promoted to Apprentice Sergeant and given his own room. It was like giving an American postman his own gun shop. Nick's already illustrious exploits went through the roof, mostly because his latest conquests didn't have to worry about seven other blokes watching the action. The icing on the cake came when the orderly Sergeant discovered him firing one up one of the female permanent staff. In a world where shagging a woman was a major event, getting some action off a decent looking instructor was enough to promote a young lad to the hall of fame. Even the Sergeant Major only gripped him half-heartedly: he couldn't help but quiz him on the size of the woman's breasts and her technique and compliment him on his conquest.

Andy Collins was a bit of an enigma. He was quiet, a grey man within the room, who – ironically – spent half of his time in the grey bar hotel, under the watchful gaze of Lang and his cronies in the guardroom. Andy's problem was that when he got beered-up a transformation of David Banner proportions took place. Once drunk, if he wasn't pissing his own bed it would be someone else's. If he wasn't fighting with bouncers, it would be with the police. He was otherwise a good soldier, and that was the only thing that stopped him getting booted out. It was strangely admirable that he never offered any kind of viable excuse for his actions. His defence always followed a set pattern. When asked why he had committed these acts, he would just shrug and say, 'Well, sir, somebody's got to do it. These beds won't piss themselves you know.'

He even used it after being caught having an affair with one of the instructor's wives. In his normal fashion he told the OC, with a perfectly straight face, 'Well, sir, somebody's got to do it. These marriages won't wreck themselves you know.'

We never really got to know Lance Corporal Derby. He kept himself to himself, drawing his blanket curtain across his bed space as soon as he got in from trade. Spud reckoned he was a bit religious and frowned on the various excesses on display in the room. He didn't bleat about it though, and he never attempted to convert any of us.

All in all, it wasn't a bad room. This certainly did not leave me devoid of troubles, though. I had the remaining 18 months of my training to get through yet.

The college year was split into standard terms, with a nice big leave period separating each one and coinciding with normal school holidays.

The syllabus was absolutely jam-packed. Each term was crammed with an intimidating amount of telecommunications trade training, education lessons, external leadership courses, military training exercises and telecomms exercises, known as Mercuries, which would put our trade knowledge to the test under field conditions. All of this was topped with a light dusting of mandatory hobbies, weekly bull nights and enough PT to slake the thirsts of even the most self-obsessed PTIs. It made for a richly diverse stay.

Trade training filled a sizeable chunk of the curriculum. During term, when not on exercise or EL, most of our time was spent trying to absorb the skills that would turn us into competent tradesmen and more importantly, earn us the extra pay that came with qualification. The college taught various trades but the main split was technicians and operators. In its simplest terms, the techs fixed the radios and the operators broke them.

My particular trade was Radio Telegraphist. It was a mishmash of all the operating skills and well-regarded in the broader corps. Most of our training took place in the operator wing and was conducted by a variety of instructors. Half were serving SNCOs, with the remainder comprising JNCOs and civilians. The civilians were usually retired soldiers who never forgot to remind us that things were much harder in their day.

We were taught how to use all the radios in the Corps portfolio. Even in 1985, the Clansman range was beginning to look a bit dated. When we were first shown round the 353 room, I assumed we were in a museum. The VHF radios looked archaic and made peculiar noises whenever you flicked a switch or turned a dial. The HF range was no better. The internal whirring and clattering that accompanied any operation was comparable with a difference engine. Notwithstanding their aesthetic shortcomings, all the radios were robust and functioned as they were supposed to do, unlike the apprentices.

We were taught the cabalistic intricacies of British Army voice procedure. At face value it all seemed straightforward enough, but it was incredibly easy to say the wrong thing at the wrong time. The VP instructor, a retired YOS called Brimble, always took great pains to remind us of the potential consequences of our actions. Of course, it's true that a grid reference or name sent in clear language on an insecure net constitutes a security breach, but his overreaction made us want to do it more. We would sit in his class, separated into little booths, with our headsets on. After being given a callsign each, he would tell us what to do.

'Zero, I want you to direct the net and get an acknowledgement from D30. B10, I want you to then ask permission from Zero to send a long message to A20.'

With that, the 45 minute lesson would commence and voice traffic would fly back and forth, with constant interjection and advice from Mr Brimble. As soon as someone made a mistake he would be up on his feet, pointing at them. 'You, son, have just had men killed. You sent a grid reference in clear. As we speak, one of Ivan's missiles is heading right for that spot and everyone there will be dead. How do you feel about that, eh?'

He struggled with our bad habits, learned from Hollywood films, too. 'We don't say *over and out* in the British Army,' he'd scream. 'How many fucking times?'

It was his misfortune that Vietnam films were getting quite a showing in the cinemas around that time. He endured a constant battle against enthusiastic apprentices trying to call in air strikes on villages or informing him that 'Charlie was behind the wire'.

Another key discipline was the sending and receiving of Morse Code. We were told constantly that, in the event of a nuclear war, the first form of communication to be re-established would implement this century-old skill. Learning it was a major headache, and I used to dread the lessons. It wasn't particularly difficult, but I always felt that my napper was being damaged by weekly exposure to this repetitive noise. Sending was a doddle in comparison to receiving, and at least it gave you the opportunity to do something with your hands. Our Morse instructor was a grumpy bastard who'd served on Arctic convoys in the war. The lessons always ran like clockwork and we'd start as soon as we walked in the door. He was the only ex-forces member I have ever met who could not be distracted by questions about his service. We'd try every week, to no avail.

'Hey, sir. It must have been really interesting in the Second World War.'

He'd just ignore us and start piping Morse into our headsets, and we'd wearily begin jotting the translation onto message pads. One year, on our last lesson before Christmas, in a great display of magnanimity, he replaced the Morse tape with a Johnny Mathis yuletide medley. It was the only time in the two years that I missed the Morse.

Another skill that the Radio Telegraphist needed was the ability to type at 36 words per minute. Trying to square this with one's self-image as a warrior was a tough task. The instructor, Sergeant Warnell, tried to convince us unsuccessfully as we sat hunched behind medieval T100 teleprinters, waiting for the lesson to start. 'Don't knock typing, lads. The ability to produce a long message without errors, under enemy fire, is not something to be scoffed at.'

Perhaps he was right, and the age of the typist was moving away from a secretarial monopoly. The two things – soldier and typewriter – just didn't fit together, though. I'd never seen one used as a weapon in any war film. We were taught on keyboards without embossed letters so that we'd learn to touch-type. According to Warnell, this was so that we could type in a 'lights-out tactical situation.' Two or three lessons in, I made a mental note of never mentioning it to anyone who I was trying to impress.

One of the more interesting courses was Antennas and Propagation. In the classroom we learned all about the characteristics of radio waves and how best to use their idiosyncrasies to our advantage. All our practical work was done near the football pitches behind C block. The instructors were all radio hams and watched our attempts at antenna construction with undisguised horror. As they shook their heads, we'd try and assemble half-wave dipoles out of copper wire slung from 12-metre masts. The chief A and P instructor was a big Yorkshireman who'd just left the Corps after 22 years' service. My efforts at putting up a sloping wire earned the following accolade from him. 'Fookin' hell, Nugent, it's all ovvert place. Like a crazy woman's shite.'

As with every syllabus, the easiest lessons were the ones we enjoyed most. There were lots of little subjects that only took a term or so to learn and they came under the umbrella of 'basic signalling skills'. The two Lance Corporals who took these lessons were a proper double act who didn't really give a fuck. In the two years I was there, nobody failed one of their tests, primarily because all the answers were given out prior to the exams. This allowed the Lance Corporals more time to drink brews and smoke tabs at the back door of the classroom whilst we arsed about waiting for the lesson to finish. The only thing I remember was something called the 'back of the hand test.'

My memory is sketchy but it was a way of testing to see if a vehicle was electrically live or earthed appropriately. Before climbing into a box body or wagon you were supposed to brush the back of your hand against the outer skin whilst your feet were still on the ground. If you were going to get a shock, the perceived wisdom was that when your muscles spasmed your fist would clench but not grab hold of anything. Do it with your palm and you would end up gripping the door handle and holding on until you died or someone brayed you with a GS shovel.

* * * * *

Once a term, our new-found knowledge was put to test in the field. The aforementioned Mercury exercises were a combination of trade and military training. They all had the same basic format but concentrated on different skills; some focused on HF and Morse, others on VHF and RATT. They were all equally traumatic and an abject lesson in sleep deprivation. Every exercise was preceded by an equipment check. Because all Mercuries were conducted with the additional comforts of working from a vehicle, you might think the kit list wouldn't be quite so important or exhaustive as on other manoeuvres. If only. The instructors approached the kit inspection with the fundamentalist vigour of the Crusaders.

I'd be standing in line with my entire exercise kit laid out in front of me, shitting myself, as the Corporals went down the line screaming at any kind of deviation from the sacred list.

'What the fuck is this?'

'My sewing kit, Corporal.'

'I know that, you fucker! Why have you got two needles and one pin, when the list clearly states three needles! And another thing, why aren't your PT daps properly whitened?'

'Because we are going on exercise, Corporal. I didn't think …'

'Exactly, you scruffy, idle bastard! Now get your shagging gat above your head and get round that football pitch until you see the error of your ways!'

And woe betide the man whose water bottle wasn't full to the lip.

Even if you had all of your contents down to the last item, you would get gripped for a purely fictitious infringement of the rules. Paul Jones spent weeks preparing his clobber for these exercises. He went to extreme lengths, and had even vacuum-packed some of his gear to ensure water-proofing. This still wasn't good enough. He got picked up for the fingers on his gloves being too long. Added to that, his packing technique had supposedly ruined the non-existent insulating properties of his military clothing.

When it came to the list, we were *all* born with original sin.

The bread-and-butter of exercise life involved operating the radios from the backs of the vehicles, mostly staying awake for hours on end whilst listening to white noise. Every 12 hours or so we would tear down and move location, setting up again immediately on arrival at the new destination. Sometimes the next location was miles away, but at other times it was only a matter of inches. Moves of less than 10 feet were a sure sign that the instructors were pissed off with you. Moving location may sound relatively straightforward, but it was the mother of all fuck-arounds, and its pain-in-the-arse factor was increased 10-fold at night.

On tearing down the detachment, all camouflage netting, generators, 12-metre masts, tents and tools had to be packed away and all the trenches filled in. Then our instructor would drive us to our next spot. If it was a bit of a distance, you'd get your breath back and maybe catch a five-minute doze. Our hearts would sink on the short moves. We'd all jump in and he'd start the engine. We'd set off and everyone would have their fingers crossed hoping for a good long drive. Immediately after completing one rotation of the wheels he'd cut the ignition, and shout, 'Right! Out you get, you fuckers. Get set up.'

The worst application of this torture happened to us on Mercury Four. We spent almost the entire exercise, in a very hot June, baking in full NBC kit, including respirators. All the detachments spent the entire week-and-a-half of the exercise in one field moving in synchronisation. Each time the radio message was sent for the move, every detachment would up sticks and move to the spot that their neighbour had just vacated. For ten days, we literally just went round in circles, the depression increasing exponentially each time the call came.

I doubt that such an act of soul-destroying suffering and banality has been perpetrated on anyone, anywhere, before or since.

The whole spectacle took place under the watchful eyes of the instructors and the merciless sun and the heat in my respirator – filled with the stench of cam-cream, CS gas and sweat – was unbearable. The sweat had worked itself into a lather which made the mask slip around on my face, and putting up a 12-metre mast in those temperatures was hideous. But although the mask magnified the problem, it also provided the anonymity behind which to whinge and look downtrodden without the instructors noticing. At first I thought it was just me who felt like this, but I walked past Colin Mortimer once, and all I could hear coming from his respirator were angry mutterings. He was hammering a mast stake into the ground badly and was whining to nobody in particular, 'Howay, ye bastad. I divn't like this fookan respur-reat-a one bit, like!'

Col was a constant source of amusement to me. He was always mumbling to himself, and even though I only understood half of his rants, I still found them hilarious. I remember after watching *Karate Kid* in the camp cinema, he did an impromptu crap karate display whilst walking back to the block. He then turned to me and said, 'How, Eddy, man. I reckon I'll buy me sel' one o' them Bonzai trees, like. Ye knaa, like that owld Jap blerk off of that film.'

'But aren't they expensive?' I said.

Col looked at me like I was retarded. 'Nah, man,' he said. 'They're ownly small, like.'

As well as having to tear down and set up the detachments on a regular basis, the radio networks always had to be active. The permanent staff constantly monitored the nets to ensure that pointless traffic was being sent regardless of the situation.

The biggest nightmare on the location moves was the manipulation of the camnet. It was an absolute bastard to deal with, particularly when wet, and I remain convinced that it was woven from the devil's arse-hair.

Its mesh-like attributes meant it snagged on absolutely everything – particularly clothing buttons and weapon sights. If you found yourself caught up in it, the only way to free yourself was to wail pathetically until one of your oppos came to free you. Struggling only worsened the situation and it was possible to find yourself snared in eight or nine different places. I remember as a young boy watching *Spartacus* and thinking that a net was a bit of a poncey weapon to have if you were up against a bloke with a sword. As soon as I'd spent fifteen minutes trussed up by my webbing and rifle, I reviewed my opinion.

I used to have nightmares whilst on exercise that I was snared in the nets or even worse, that the flywheel to the generator had caught the net and had sucked all of our cam into its engine. Like some unhinged 'Nam vet, I'd wake up with a jerk, only to realise that I shouldn't have been sleeping in the first place because I was on radio watch. I'd then have to check my watch to see how long I'd been asleep, and scribble fraudulent entries into the radio log book to account for the relevant time period. I was once in the process of such an act of counterfeiting when a training Corporal, Brady, came charging into the back of the wagon. He accused me of being 'a lazy spotty bastard' who'd been 'gonking on stag.' He backed this up by saying he'd been calling me over the net for the last 10 minutes. As cool as a cucumber, I told him that I had been out checking the generator for petrol and that I had informed the net of my intentions. He must've been having a wank or a shit, or maybe both, during the period that I'd sent this fictitious message, because he let it lie. Luckily, he fucked off straight afterwards, because five minutes later the genny packed up, rendering my lie completely transparent.

I knew he hadn't believed me and he got his revenge later in the exercise. One night, we filled the detachment's metal washbowl with compo and had a big stew cooked over a kero heater. It tasted lovely, but the burnt on charcoal-food-hybrid on the base of the bowl was physically impossible to clean off. We used tons of Scotchbrite and parts of our weapon cleaning kits, but we couldn't shift these caked-on bacon burgers. Barry Nash even tried hitting it with a shovel, but the stuff was as hard as diamond. In a desperate attempt to minimise our gripping from Brady, we decided to lob the bowl away and say we had lost it on the last move. Losing kit in a tear down was far more forgivable than getting it into the shit state that it was in. Our location at the time was called Bishop Monkton and we were right on a riverbank. It was decided that we would chuck the bowl into the raging waters in the dark, and let mother nature dispose of the evidence. Colin Mortimer did the honours. On returning to the tent he said, 'We wivn't see that fookan' thing again, man.'

We waited with confidence for the morning inspection by Brady. As soon as he turned up, he had us parade outside the vehicle and face the river. What had looked like a fast-running torrent the night before seemed more like a millpond in the cold light of day. Floating directly in the centre of its glassy surface was our washbowl, in all of its shitted-up glory. I remember a hot blast of adrenaline lighting up my stomach as I realised the 'bang to rights' nature of the situation. After making us all swim out to the bowl and back in full combat gear, Brady had us move location every hour for the next day, totalling an exact distance of 24 feet.

* * * * *

Although the Mercury exercises were necessary to prepare us for the job we were actually going to do when we left training, I preferred mil' training. Although it was hard work, I felt like a bit more of a soldier going through the disciplines common to every member of the Army.

With our only previous foray into mil' training exercises taking the form of a one-night, shortened baptism of lukewarm water, it was with some trepidation that we went on to our next – and reputedly hardest – battlecamp. Exercise 'Warrior Dig' was a one-week trench-digging exercise with a combined 'potential accumulation of sleep' rating of about five hours. This was not good, and the nightmare stories that the older lads fed us only served to heighten the feelings of dread amongst our still fresh-faced intake.

It was the arse end of February. We were all lined up in the boiler house carpark with our kit spread out in front of us as the instructors went howling mad during the inspection. The weather was atrocious. Raging sleet and snowstorms lashed us, as we held out one item at a time for the scrutiny of instructors.

The only consolation was that most of the lads from the basic training room were still in my section. Col was standing next to me, which was good for two reasons. Firstly, he was a good laugh, his dry humour never failing to cheer me up. Secondly, because he was upwind of me, he was bearing the full force of the snow. All the flakes that had my name on them were coming to rest in his right ear. He was shaking violently and there was a large stream of snot hanging from his hooter. Every now and then he would mutter to himself through gritted teeth, 'Aaaahh howay, ya fookan bastad! This is nee laffin matta!'

I never thought that I would be glad to get on a Bedford 4 tonner, but by the time they all rocked up I was so cold that even their torn and useless canopies offered welcome sanctuary from the elements. Once all of the wagons were static, Corporal Havers shouted, 'Right, gents. Get on the shaggin' Robert Redfords.'

I managed to nod off on the drive to the training area, and woke up feeling like dog-egg. Still, it was all sleep in the bank for the forthcoming week.

Catterick training area had changed not a jot since I had last seen it, apart from the liberal sprinkling of snow hiding the bleak tufts of moorland grass that caused you to go over on your ankle.

We were rousted into our sections and set off one group at a time towards the platoon harbour areas. Every now and then someone would stumble and mutter, 'Ya fuckin bastard!' as they lurched to their feet with their ankle tendons screaming foul play.

After an hour of walking and falling we arrived in the exercise area. The plan was to spend the first day digging our trenches, bashering out that night in the woods. We would use the following day to complete the excavation. Once we were in position, we brewed up and waited for the instructors to take us to the trench locations. That time came much quicker than I would have liked. It seemed like I'd just finished my brew when Havers dropped an armful of picks and shovels in front of us and with what could only be described as a shit-eating grin said, 'Right, ladies. Pick a shovel, any shovel, and follow me.'

He took us to an area that was about half a mile from our bashers. It was completely exposed and overlooked a valley. We paired up, and I stayed with Colin. We were then allocated an area each into which we would dig our trench. It was with considerable happiness that I noticed a familiarly shaped dent in the ground, right next to our allocated position. The indentation indicated an old trench, which usually meant loose, easily-diggable earth. Colin obviously shared my thoughts, as he was smiling from ear to ear, and we were waist-deep in our new house before the majority of the other lads had got down to their ankles. It wasn't long before we had dug to the required depth, so we stood there for a while, leaning on our shovels and looking at the other lads cracking on. There was no finer job in the world than watching other people work, and we warmed to our task, making witty comments about everyone else's shortcomings. The slowest progressing hole belonged to Skiddy and Rose. They were hacking at the rock-hard ground but getting nowhere fast. Rose looked red faced with emotion, as they had already been gripped by Havers on a number of occasions. The last time he'd been past, he'd thrown a big clod of earth at Rose, shouting 'You'd better get that shaggin hole dug, Pansy, or I'll have you using shit for cam cream. Now geldi-fucking-geldi.'

The use of different languages in his motivational speeches always impressed me.

When enough trenches were dug, we were shown how to use a kip sheet. A mesh of pegs and string were bashed into the ground at one end of the trench, through which would be woven the sheet itself. The whole thing was then covered in dirt. The theory was that a well-installed sheet could cope with having a Land Rover driven over it. Rumours were rife that we would have to take it in turns, cowering under our shelters whilst the instructors tested the manufacturers' claims. Colin articulated all of our concerns with a shout of, 'Fuck that!'

The vehicle stress test didn't actually happen, but the instructors did jump up and down on top of the shelter whilst one of us sat underneath it. Although not ideal, the thought of having a size 10 pair of leather personnel carriers landing on your head was preferable to being crushed to death by a three-quarter tonne vehicle.

By the end of the day, only half the trenches were finished and we traipsed the half mile back to the basher location. Colin and I got the midnight till 1am stag. Not the best, but by no means the worst. We spent it talking in hushed tones. Strictly-speaking, it wasn't the brightest tactical move, but it was better than falling asleep on stag and getting a shoeing off Havers. Our conversation was typical of young blokes of the time. Colin told me how Sam Fox 'needed it' and that, in his professional opinion, the blonde one from The Human League would beat the dark-haired one in a fanny-licking contest. Her 'prize' would be a severe tupping from himself.

As teenage as the discussion was, it did the job of keeping us awake. One of the later stags was less vigilant, and we were awoken by a barrage of thunder flashes being thrown into the harbour area. Some twat had wobbed-out on shift, so there had been no reveille. The DS went fucking rhino, and although it was the fault of only two blokes we were all beasted to near death. For the first time in my career, the reality was actually worse than I'd been able to fear. We were made to don full NBC kits and then given a PT session the QMSI would have been proud of. The pinnacle of the punishment was what seemed like an endless run in respirators over the moors. I was really chinstrapped and sucking in as hard as possible through the canister. This only impeded the airflow and induced near panic: it was with great mental effort that I controlled the urge to remove the mask and managed to regulate my breathing enough to keep my major organs functioning. It could have been worse. Alistair McKenzie yakked up in his mask. No one realised until the rising vomit lake became visible, sloshing around in the eyepieces of his respirator. He eventually tore it off, the honk spilling out like the breaching of the Moehne Dam. Despite this, the instructors still gripped him for taking off his resi' without permission and he received additional punishment.

After this, the rest of the exercise – although filled with fatigue, cold and damp – didn't seem so bad. The beasting had been terrible enough to create a talking point for years afterwards. Next to it, standing in a trench freezing your plums off and up to your ankles in mud was comparatively pleasurable.

The only other type of exercise we went on was External Leadership, or EL as it was unsurprisingly known. It sounded like a bit of a skive, a break from military and comms training for a week in the Lake District or Cairngorms. During the course of my apprenticeship, I was scheduled to go on three different leadership exercises. They were loosely described as canoe, rock and snow. They were one of the highlights of my time at Harrogate, despite the instructor's best efforts to spoil them.

The first one I went on was 'snow'. It was meant to be a week of skiing near Aviemore. I'd never skied before and had visions of myself Franz Klammering down lethal slopes. Those lucky, rich or smart enough supplied their own equipment. The rest of us took our chances at the storeman's hatch. Huge strides had been made in the development of outdoor clothing in the early 80s. Breathable, waterproof garments were freely available. Rucksacks were becoming lighter and more comfortable, with fresher, more ergonomic designs every week. Companies like Berghaus and Karrimor were designing boots that moulded to the foot of the wearer, providing a snug, blister-free walking experience. All of these innovations had passed by the Army Apprentices College Harrogate without so much as a backwards glance. There were only four design parameters to which the military manufacturers had adhered. All the clothing had to be capable of holding comedy amounts of water. It had to be garish in colour and capable of third-degree chafing. Finally, when the whole outfit was worn, it was important that the apprentice looked like an overgrown Austrian schoolchild. We were given orange 'windproof' smocks, red, knee-length socks and grey corduroy breeches. An enormous grey woollen balaclava topped off the natty ensemble. The walking boots that accompanied the outfit were ridiculous. Each weighed the same as a car battery and had laces eighteen feet long. The only other bit of kit we were given was an ancient blue rucksack, fabricated with maximum discomfort in mind.

On the first morning of the exercise, everyone going on the adventure paraded on the familiar testing ground of the boiler-house car park at 6.30am. The EL staff then performed a kit-check that went down to the last sock and shaving stick, as though trying to outdo each other in achieving ever higher levels of pedantry. I never did understand their attitude: they had perhaps the best job in the Signals, and yet they were always miserable. For 48 weeks of the year, they didn't wear uniform and got to enjoy some of the best climbing and walking terrain in the world, yet they still wore the expressions of people who'd discovered dogshit in their pockets.

After the kit-check and the obligatory bollockings for those of us who'd forgotten those all important things like a ninth pair of underpants or a spare pair of laces, we got ready to board the coaches. Stood there, in our just-post-Victorian clothing, we could have been mistaken for members of Ernest Shackleton's ill-fated Antarctic team.

Driving up to Scotland in those bone-crunchingly uncomfortable coaches took forever. Those with a bit of initiative had brought books to read, but the rest of us were reduced to examining the contents of our deathpacks for the 12-hour journey. Every now and again, someone at the back would read out a particularly juicy excerpt, from the letters page of a bongo-mag, which would raise morale for a short while. If the sound levels ever went up too far, one of the instructors would shout lazily from the front to keep the fucking noise down. (Why do people in positions of responsibility always sit at the front of the coach? Is there a practical reason, or are they just big kids who like to pretend they're driving?) We stopped once, at a nondescript motorway services near Newcastle, to stretch our legs and get a brew. Everyone had sneaky slashes in nearby bushes. Nobody wanted to go into the main building, as we looked like such twats. For the rest of the trip, most of the lads got their heads down. By rotating my balaclava until the hole was at the back, I fashioned myself a bit of personal airspace and slept until we arrived.

The snow exercise was remarkable only in that someone had obviously forgotten to book the integral ingredient of the downhill experience – snow. Ever resourceful, the instructors simply replaced all skiing activities with huge walks through the mountains. The Cairngorms were absolutely beautiful and, although the hiking was extremely hard work, I loved it. Because it was the middle of winter, it felt like our group of eight were the only people in the hills at some times. When we did come across someone, they'd always smile politely and say hello. As we slogged past, it was easy to see the pity in their eyes as they gazed at our low-quality threads.

Throughout the walks, our instructor would ask us challenging, map-related questions, such as 'Where are we now?' After 30 or 40 wild guesses, with us jabbing his map like inquisitive primates, he'd give up and show us, but he didn't seem to mind too much.

The only activity we did that nodded in the direction of winter sports was an hour's ice-skating in Kingussie. When I handed over my boots for a pair of ice-skates, the assistant couldn't get them in the pigeonhole and had to leave them on the floor, assuring me, unnecessarily, that they wouldn't be stolen. Some of the other lads spent the hour chatting up the local girls, despite being dressed like identical tramps, but I thought I'd give it a go. I'd never skated before and after whopping my head off the ice a couple of times, I jacked it in and spent the rest of the time in the café nursing a cup of tea.

The rock climbing and canoeing ELs were a great laugh. Both were extremely draining, but being solitary disciplines each allowed for a bit of individual flair. I was a bit of a natural at the climbing, being in possession of the perfect 'skinny but strong' physique. My downfall was the dreaded 'disco leg'. I'd be perched on the rock, just about to make the crux move in the climb, when my left pin would start shaking so badly it looked like the opening bars of *Jailhouse Rock* were about to kick in. It wasn't a nervous thing and was just down to tired muscles, but to the bloke doing the belaying on the ground it looked I was shitting myself, and the directing shout of, '10 o'clock, disco leg, Eddy Nugent,' would go up, followed by roars of laughter from everyone on the deck. The twats.

You could look quite cool whilst canoeing. Anytime I walked around in shorts or trunks, I was painfully aware that my legs were hanging down from my arse like a pair of matchsticks with shoes on them. But in a canoe, everyone had the same build. I had a fairly strong upper body and got the hang of the stroke quite quickly. On the first day of the canoeing week, before they let us go anywhere, the staff organised a confidence test. Each canoeist had to capsize his canoe 50 metres from the shore. The confidence part of it was that you weren't allowed to right yourself – you had to slap your hands on the bottom of the canoe until someone came to your rescue. I was one of the first to go. It was strangely disorientating; it only took 20 seconds for someone to get out to me, but by then I was beginning to shit myself and puff my cheeks out to conserve air. Then I had the pleasure of watching everyone else. It was an ideal opportunity for the staff to take out any grudges they'd been holding about particular apprentices. Dependent on where their name appeared on the scale of cuntishness, people could be left drowning politely for anything between 10 seconds and a minute. It was always funny to watch the tapping on the bottom of the canoe becoming more and more frantic, and a couple of people naturally just lost it and emerged coughing and spluttering before the rescuer could get to them. Their lack of bottle was plain for all to see and their shame was compounded by the loud cheers coming from the shore.

* * * * *

Sadly, these exercises were few and far between. It was obvious, even to the sadists in charge of the college, that subjecting us to an academic syllabus entirely consisting of Morse Code and lessons about radios would send some or all of us mad. In an attempt to break things up slightly, the officers of the Royal Education Corps were drafted in to inject more interesting information into our reluctant brains. The lessons were, to some extent, a blessed relief from the death-by-viewfoil tedium of trade training. We were schooled up to City and Guilds standards in various subjects, including English, Maths and General Science. Most of the lads were sporting a slack handful of 'O' Levels anyway, so it wasn't too challenging and the education centre had a trump card. It had a complete monopoly on good-looking female instructors. In a camp where the only other women soldiers were the soup dragons in the cookhouse, the pretty lieutenants and captains of the Ed Corps caught everyone's attention. There wasn't a man-jack on camp who hadn't thrapped himself silly thinking about them.

They would give lessons where their entire classes learnt absolutely nothing. Instead, 15 unlikely scenarios were being concocted in 15 heads, all with the same disgusting ending. One particularly attractive Captain taught maths. I remember her explaining an equation to me once; she'd leant over my desk, exposing the briefest glimpse of bra strap. This was wankers' paydirt, and instead of listening to her spiel all I could hear was a voice in my head repeating, *Must-see-the-rest, must-see-the-rest.*

The lessons were all conducted in C block. The rooms were identical to the trade theory classrooms, save the odd dog-eared poster. The blocks were orientated in such a way that the sun came blasting through the windows at around mid-afternoon. On hot days it was very difficult to pay attention, and it was hard not to wob out mid-period.

On top of the usual subjects, we were also exposed to the new-fangled world of computer studies. I'd done a tiny bit of this at school, but our one computer had usually gone missing once a month. As soon as the insurance paid out, the replacement would be proudly unveiled. Word would hit the street within a couple of hours, and the duty junky would be going in through the window shortly after the caretaker had gone home that night.

There were no such security risks at the college. The computer room was a secretive bunker with darkened windows housing the latest BBC machinery: huge, cream-coloured machines like props from *Blake's 7*. They were shite, to put it mildly, and used almost all of their processing power just starting up. However, they did have one redeeming feature. It was very easy to make them display line after line of obscenities. You typed in a swear word of your choice on line 10 and then instructed line 20 to 'Go to 10.' A swift tap of the 'run' key, and – hey presto! – you were provided with infinite lines of your favourite adjective from the dockers' dictionary. It was the first lesson learnt by apprentices, and the only one remembered by most, and was best put to use at the end of a lengthy 'programming' lesson. When someone made the mistake of going to the toilet, his hours of painstaking work could be deleted by his next-door neighbour. When he returned from the traps he would be greeted with a pleasant, 'Fuck off, you wanker', streaming up and down the screen.

All in all, though, education was just viewed by the lads as a lovely doss and a break from the more important aspects of training. The rodneys from the Education Corps were soft touches. We were used to being shouted at and threatened with execution, and their more cerebral approach was open to abuse. They were primarily teachers and the uniform was just an occupational necessity. Enforcing discipline didn't sit well with their self-image and it was always amusing if one of them lost it and tried to bollock someone. We'd been gripped by the best, so it was impossible for a mild-mannered girl from Sussex to reach the standards set by tattooed Glaswegian sociopaths.

To my mind, the combination of theoretical instruction and field training constituted a more than ample workload, but the college authorities were keen to minimise any spare time and filled it with as many jobs and chores as possible.

Every four weeks, we took our turn being Duty Squadron. For that seven days we did all the college jiff jobs and guards. On Sunday evening, the board would go up in the office window detailing everyone's fate. Duties were meant to be divvied up equally, but you could be guaranteed one of the shittier jobs if you'd fucked up in the preceding month. There was a sliding scale of cushiness. The easiest job possible was the WRVS NCO and the most onerous the much-feared Sunday cookhouse. Sandwiched between the two extremes were fire picquets, weekday guard, weekday cookhouse and weekend guards.

Best of all was when you realised you'd only copped for one WRVS. All you had to do was report to the WRVS woman at seven o'clock in the evening and be there to give her a hand with anything until she knocked you off at 10. At the time, the Women's Royal Voluntary Service had old biddies stationed all round the world, serving hot beverages and homespun philosophy to the Armed Forces. The delights on offer, like table tennis and bar billiards, only attracted the serially skint or terminally bored, so it made for a simple duty. You just had to sup cups of tea whilst ensuring that no fights broke out over the billiards.

It was unusual to be dealt the prize hand of a single WRVS, though. I generally found myself with a couple of guards to do during the week. The 10 apprentices who constituted the guard had to parade outside the guardroom just after tea to be inspected by the duty Sergeant, the severity of the inspection depending entirely on his recent sexual successes or failures. The best turned-out soldier got knocked off and escaped the duty which sounds like a reasonable incentive. The trouble was, some blokes had the family connections or thieving abilities to ensure they had loads of spare clobber handy. They could afford to have a set of ridiculously-starched combats hanging in their locker, waiting to be whipped out when duty called, while the rest of us tried to press creases into trousers that had spent two months at the back of a top box, folded to the size of a matchbox.

As soon as the winner was thinned out, the guard roster was drawn up by the duty Corporal and the stags began at 6 pm. They always worked a two hours on, four hours off rota. Three of the guard would look after the front gate, taking a two hour turn by the barrier, whilst the other six did 'prowler' in pairs. Prowler was the better option. The book said that you were providing a 'visible security deterrent to any potential intruder, and a first line of defence in the event of a terrorist attack.' It sounded pretty impressive, but the reality was a bit different. Ours was a big camp, with lots of nooks and crannies to provide comfortable harbour to the serious skiver. On the early evening shifts, up to NAAFI closing time, you had to be on the ball, as there were lots of people milling around. When the clock struck twelve, the idleness could begin. My favourite hiding place was the kit store next to the outdoor arena. The lock on the back door was buggered but it still looked OK, which meant that nobody ever fixed it or knew about it. The store was full of crash mats and me and my prowler buddy of the evening would lie down on one of these, pull another over the top of us and snooze there until 15 minutes before shift end. We were at the end of a radio, but the duty Corporal could be relied upon to be too lazy to come out and physically check up on us. Every few minutes we'd be disturbed by a radio check, asking us for our location. I'd rub sleep out of my eyes and speak into the handset. 'This is D10, we are at the assault course and heading for Bradley Squadron.'

This would satisfy him and he could go back to reading the year-old *Razzle* or dog-eared Sven Hassel book that could be found in any guardroom drawer.

The front gate was a trickier prospect for the career layabout. The box, about the size of your average lift, was situated 20 metres from the guardroom. It had windows on all four sides, making the occupant clearly visible. There was absolutely nothing to do, except to keep awake at all costs, and a two-hour shift lasted for approximately three months.

There was a telephone, and a button for raising and lowering the barrier, and that was it. At night-time, incoming traffic dropped to zero and you were left with your own limited imagination for 120 long minutes. Masturbation, the great ennui reliever, was off limits to all but the most accomplished. There was subtle graffiti, but it only took a minute or two to read and was all cry for help stuff: *'Why the fuck am I here?' 'This place is fucking shit.' 'I agree wholeheartedly.' 'Who fucking asked you?' 'Fuck off, then.'*

In my two years I did the gate three times and fell asleep once.

I was on from 4am to 6am. It was freezing outside and as soon as I got into the warmth of the box, my eyes starting getting heavy. I held out for 15 minutes, the nodding dog cycle becoming more pronounced with each passing moment. I drifted off and was woken what felt like a second later by a tooting horn. I peeled my face off the inner window and jumped up in my seat. It was one of the cleaners on a moped. I slid back the window and said, 'Morning. Can I help you?'

She showed me her pass and I raised the barrier. I watched her go over a couple of the speed bumps and prayed to God that she was going to turn left for the Officers Mess. Unluckily for me, the old bag couldn't wait to get to the guardroom and bubble me. She had a brief conversation with the Corporal, it was Chester from the gym. Five seconds later he burst out of the door and headed straight towards me. I smartened myself up, just before he banged on the window.

'Out here, you.' I came out and offered him my best creepers grin. 'That cleaner says you were a-fucking-sleep when she came to the gate.'

There was no way on this planet that I was going to admit it. Falling asleep on guard was one of the biggest no-nos possible. There was a principle at stake. Nod off on a poxy camp college gate and get away with it, and you would be sure to get all your mates killed at an unspecified point in the future.

'No, Corporal. I wasn't.'

'You fucking liar, she said she waited there for five minutes watching you before she bibbed her horn.'

'I wasn't, Corporal. She must have been mistaken.'

I was bricking it, but couldn't go back. The tremble in my voice was obvious, but it was going to boil down to my word against a fat, 79-year-old dwarf from Knaresborough. Chester knew this. He hadn't been watching me, or he'd have said. He'd probably been pulling the head off it in the toilets, taking advantage of the quiet time. He jabbed his right index finger at the name-tag on my combat jacket and glowered. 'Right then, Nugent. I'll have to give you the benefit of the doubt. But I don't fucking believe you for one minute. Your face needs ironing and you've got slobber on your collar. The next time I get you in the fucking gym, I'm going to beast the fuck out of you.'

He was true to his oath, but it was a small price to pay.

In between shifts we had to sleep in the back room which we shared with the fire picquet. Fire picquet was a bit of a laugh. You spent the whole week living in the guardroom, turning up there after tea each evening. There was no work to do as such. You were on standby to react to any fire that occurred, as a stopgap before the emergency services arrived. There were lots of hydrant points around the camp and every evening the duty officer would call out the picquet for a drill. If you happened to be walking past at the time, it provided great entertainment. Eight blokes would come flying round the corner, frantically pushing a big red handcart. As the Duty Officer timed and supervised them, they would try and get the hose fixed to the hydrant. The exercise was over when they got water coming out of the end of the hose. It was a classic example of, 'too many cooks.' They'd all be shouting and telling each other what to do without actually accomplishing anything. Somebody would be rooting round in the boxes on the cart, trying to find the correct lump of metal that provided the link between hose and hydrant. When it was located, he'd hold it up like the FA Cup, to a big cheer. As soon as it was fitted, someone else would turn the tap on, sending water spuming forth straight from the hydrant, having blown the incorrectly-attached hose 15 feet down the road. It's a matter of divine providence that they never had to tackle a real blaze.

The guardroom sleeping area was horrible. There were 14 blokes in there at any one time, in varying states of unconsciousness, kipping on green, sweat-generating, rubberised, piss-proof mattresses. The stench in there went right off any available graph. Fourteen sleeping bags, 28 feet and 14 sets of cigarette-induced halitosis concocted a murderous smog which was almost impossible to sleep in. I'll carry the smell with me to my dying day.

The job to be avoided at all costs was the weekend cookhouse. It was an appalling experience from start to finish. Unlike the weekday version, where you just worked the mornings and evenings, you had to be there all day, from 6am until the last chip pan was sparkling, usually somewhere around 9pm. Blokes would do anything to get out of it. Claims of a family bereavement or self-amputation were common. I was only ever stung for one Sunday during my stint, but that was more than enough. I don't know what I'd done to deserve it, but when I saw my name scrawled in blue chinagraph in the appropriate box, the blood drained from my face. Worse still, I was on with Dave Preston, the biggest 'sex-liar' in the squadron. Not only was I going to be elbow-deep in gristle and gravy all day, I was going to have to put up with Dave's eccentric stories. I met lots of sex-liars down the years. They were always the same. Superficially good-looking, they gave off some sort of female-repulsing pheromone that made all women run a mile. In the same way that nobody ever saw a cat having a shit, nobody ever saw a sex-liar cop off. Terry Waite was getting more sex than Dave Preston, but if you listened to the tales of his leave adventures, it seemed like his knob was doing overtime.

The worst thing about the cookhouse was the cooks. It wasn't so much the head chef or any of the seniors, who were quite aloof and spent most of their time ignoring you. The real fuckers were the privates and lance-jacks who gave you jobs to do. They hated everyone, but reserved their deepest vitriol for the apprentices. They'd made the wrong choice at the careers office and knew that they were sentenced to military purgatory, in suffocating heat surrounded by the permanent smell of fried eggs. This was the one time we were allowed a glimpse into the hell of their normal lives, and boy did they love showing us.

Myself and Dave turned up at the hotplate promptly at 6am. Dressed in shirtsleeve-order working dress, we were ready to go. The head chef met us. 'Morning, ladies,' he said. 'Report in the back to Private Greenwood and she'll give you your jobs for the day.'

We went round the back of the hotplate and looked for our taskmaster. There were six or seven sloppies moving back and forth, carrying breakfast items to and fro, and Greenwood was moving past us with a tray of streaky bacon, when I spotted her nametag.

'Private Greenwood?'

She ignored me, and carried on to the hotplate. After depositing the tray into its requisite cavity she came back drying her hands on a manky cloth. 'Are you two the cookhouse bods for the day?'

'Yeah,' I replied.

'Yes, fucking *Private*. Right?'

'Yes, Private.'

I'd forgotten that absolutely everyone outranked us on the camp, even fat female Danny Devito look-a-likes. Clearly a graduate of the, 'one for you, one for me' school of cookery, she must have been pushing 12 stones despite being five-foot-fuckall.

First off, she had us cleaning all the empty trays as they came back in from the front. Armed with wire wool pads and Deepio cleaner, we got to work. The huge, stainless steel sinks were full to the top with almost boiling water: any cooler, and it would have no effect on the congealed grease from the substandard food products which had been superglued to the trays minutes before. It was too hot to bear for more than a few seconds, so I sprint-scrubbed, identifying parts of a given pan that I would go for and plunging both arms in for a few moments of frenzied scrubbing. Then I'd pull them back out before the skin on my forearms sloughed off like a debutante's glove.

Dave seemed to have lower temperature water or a higher pain threshold and paddled merrily whilst working. 'What do you reckon to that Greenwood, then?'

'She's a fucking Yeti, Dave. Why?'

'I did someone who looked just like her on my last leave. I did her mum as well.' Without any encouragement, Dave continued with a Baron Munchausen-approved anecdote which finished with a healthy percentage of the female population of Torquay having been thoroughly serviced by him.

Every time we got the pan pile down to zero, Greenwood showed up with more and it was a good two hours before we got finished. My hands were translucent by this time, and the Deepio had softened my nails worryingly.

Greenwood sent Dave off with a mop somewhere and had me peel my way through a four foot pile of spuds in one of the back rooms. I'd mistakenly imagined that disrobing spuds by hand had ended with National Service, and I was in bits by the time she let me back out. The paper-thin skin on my hands was now full of cuts from the peeling knife I'd been wielding so ham-fistedly, and the fat troll went bonkers when she saw the results of my carving.

'What the fuck is this?' she shouted. She was holding up one of my finished articles between her thumb and forefinger. It had started life as a volleyball-sized King Edward but I'd pared it down until it looked like an albino conker. 'Right, you fucking tossbag. If peeling spuds is too difficult for you, I've got a better job.'

Keen to dispense summary justice, Greenwood dragged me to another room. There were three black plastic bins, the household variety. Two were empty and one was full of breakfast cereal. Smiling benignly, she said, 'Some daft bastard's mixed the Frosties up with the Cornflakes. You can sort them out till teatime.'

She walked off chuckling as I worked out the best way to approach the task. I spent five minutes thinking of elaborate, scientific methods that might be employed, or contraptions, purpose-built for the undertaking. After much deliberation, I settled on the only foolproof method. I picked up a single flake, examined it for the presence or absence of sugar frosting and deposited it into the relevant bin. A clock in the back left hand corner of the room ticked loudly.

It wasn't all bad. I was sat down and I had Frosties on tap. I'd always loved them as a kid but they were reserved as a treat by Mum and Dad, placed in the same food group as Lucozade, Ribena and Aeros. Now I could scoff as many as I wanted and I duly did so, selecting only the choicest and most coated ones for consumption. When Greenwood came back to send me for my tea, I wasn't hungry and my pupils were heavily dilated.

Tea was followed by three more hours of panbash. Cracks were beginning to appear in the skin between my fingers and the Deepio was getting into the spud peeling cuts. I asked Greenwood if I could have some gloves but her reply would have made a navvy blush.

By the time we were finished I thought I was going to need arm transplants: it felt like I'd been using them to transport uranium.

As we were leaving, I commiserated with Dave. 'God, that was fucking awful, eh?'

He winked at me and pointed down to his ball-sack area. 'I don't know about you, mate, but I enjoyed it.' He leaned in closer. 'I only shagged that Greenwood.'

My clothes and my boots were covered in a thick layer of sludge – when I tried to put some polish on them that evening, it just slid off. I stank of the cookhouse for a week, despite obsessive showering.

The head-sheds were aware that any leisure time would be spent wastefully. With the main pastimes being masturbation and soap watching, sometimes simultaneously, it was their opinion that our youthful energies needed to be channelled positively. They contrived to limit potential hand-shandy time by making us attend 'hobbies night' every Tuesday and Thursday between 6pm and 9pm. Tuesday night was compulsory, with a failure to attend punishable by instant, overnight jailing. Thursdays were ostensibly voluntary, but it was Army voluntary, which meant compulsory. Any apprentice who was caught up the block on a hobbies night was right up shit creek.

At the start of each term, the troop Sergeants would assemble everyone and force us to choose our hobbies. The popular ones were instantly oversubscribed. Cycling, archery, sailing and clay pigeon shooting had an abundance of volunteers, and you had no chance of getting in unless you knew the instructor. As the options dwindled, Barry Nash and I were trying to decide which would be the least bad. It was a bastard of a decision to make as they were all as shit as each other, reading like a roll call of interests likely to get you ostracised from normal youths of your age.

Chess, guitar (non-electric), war-gaming, radio ham, bagpipes, woodwork, computers, painting and bird-watching.

The more you looked at the list, the worse it got. It was the troop Sergeant's job to ensure everyone got a slot and he would start making decisions for us, selling the subjects with the enthusiasm of a circus barker.

'Right, AT Gantry. You look like a musician to me. Just think how much you could impress the birds if you tell 'em you can play the guitar.'

'Yes, Sergeant.'

'Lovely, I'll stick your name down then. Report to Mr Kelly in Room 5, C Block. Nash and Nugent, you can fucking join him.'

That was that. You were allowed to swap round at the end of each term, which meant we were lumbered with learning the guitar for three months.

Mr Kelly took a roll call every time and if you weren't there you were reported to the Squadron. There were 24 of us in the guitar lessons and learning was a slow process, hampered by our militant lack of enthusiasm or talent. By the time it came to change round, all he'd managed to teach us was the first four lines to *Morning Has Broken*. I can still play it, but have yet to find it of any use.

The tough lessons learnt in the previous term made me determined to pick a decent or skivable option second time round. In the weeks running up to the swap, an informal intelligence network sprang up, weighing up the relative pros and cons of each hobby. Was the instructor a pushover? Could you arrive late and leave early? Could you make a baseball bat in woodwork? All the info helped you towards a decision.

I was planning to pick bird-watching next. Apparently it was quite interesting and Mr Harrop only kept you for an hour, but before I could stick my name down for the twitchers I was put in the chess group, with the comment that I 'looked like a fucking egghead.'

I knew enough about chess to know that I didn't want to know any more and the instructor was a proper bastard. Mr Henly was an ex-RSM who taught radio principles in the operator wing and he was always out to drop people in the shit. Unfortunately for him, he picked the second week of that term to have a massive heart attack and die. It's cruel to take pleasure at someone's death, but we were all doing guilty back-flips. In the haste to backfill his official position and get him buried, his hobbies group was completely forgotten and we had twelve weeks of doing shite-all. We turned up at six o'clock every Tuesday and Thursday as required, safe in the knowledge that, barring miracles, we could piss off after half an hour, our duty done.

I got caught up the block a couple of times that term, once whilst watching *Star Trek* and another time on my way back from a leisurely thrap. I dropped my wanking manual and toilet roll as the duty Sergeant appeared out of nowhere and roared, 'What the fuck are you doing?' The evidence was plain to see and before I could answer he followed up. 'I can see what your real hobby is, but why aren't you at fucking chess?'

As agreed with the rest of the class, I stated simply that we'd finished early.

'Right,' he yelled. 'I'll check with the instructor.'

Then he stormed off, looking for someone else to catch out. It could've been worse, though. Whilst being rumbled 'post milk' was embarrassing enough, Barry Nash had it even worse once. Unbeknown to him, one of the instructors had been stood, arms folded, in the corridor watching him practice his robotics dancing in front of the washroom mirrors, with Barry resplendent in mirrored shades and popping to *System Addict* by Five Star.

By the following term they'd managed to find another leader for the men of chess, but by that time I'd moved on again. I'd managed to get myself into the cycling club by schnecking unashamedly with Major Danby from the Education Corps who took us for English. He ran the hobby and every time I was in his lesson I'd drop hints that I'd been born to ride bicycles. It worked and he made the casual suggestion that I should stick my name down. I was in like a shot and stuck with the bike riding till the end of my time at the camp. We didn't actually ride them on Tuesdays and Thursdays. That was all done on the Wednesday sports afternoons. On the two evenings we did maintenance, though most of us just farted around whilst the more serious members got on with oiling chains and pumping up tyres.

PASSING OUT

Eighteen months can pass remarkably quickly when you're in a routine, and this was borne out by my remaining stay at the camp.

The weekend hangovers, united with the highs of catching people wanking in the bath and lows of someone vomming on you during a run, helped the weeks speed by, despite the regular beastings in PT and the weekly hobbies and bull nights.

Once each term, the senior term of lads would graduate and our intake would always do our bit as back-up squads. It had the effect of punctuating each incremental rise up the food chain. Seniority amongst the apprentices was mainly due to time served. There was a ranking structure that mirrored the non-commissioned table, but any rank attained was lost on graduation. Horror stories were always circulating around camp about apprentice Sergeants who had forgotten to show appropriate deference in their new working units. All the anecdotes finished with the upstart being given a shoeing by a liney. As the old lads went off one end of the conveyor belt, we moved along and a new intake of 16-year-old civvies would appear, cowering at the beginning.

Each night before graduation, the out-going troops would sweep through the rooms like a herd of buffalo that had been drinking from a watering hole contaminated with Woodpecker cider. They'd tip all the new boys out of their beds and destroy all manner of fixtures and fittings. The first time I experienced it it was quite alarming, but after a new recruit troop had moved upstairs I had nothing to fear as the sprogs would take the full force of the beatings.

It wasn't until Nick, Spud and a whole host of other characters left that it dawned on me that soon it would be my intake's turn. Spud's departure was as gross as one could imagine. At his leaving do, he did his farting bollock trick for a final time. In an obviously pre-rehearsed fashion, he took a stack of 10p coins and forced them into his foreskin. He then proceeded to rhythmically thrust his hips forward so that a coin flew out on each upstroke. He called this ritual 'tank slapping', and with each swish of his knob, he enthusiastically encouraged us to try and catch the warm coins. Naturally we gave it a miss, restricting our compliments to shouts of 'Ole'.

As with all 16- to 18-year-old lads, socialising played a large part in our lives. Mad drinking on a Friday wasn't considered wise: next morning we had compulsory sports, and anyone smelling like a magic marker was heading for the pokey. But every Saturday night there would be queues of several hundred youths waiting to book out of camp or catch a taxi. Most were dressed in grey slip-ons, white socks, chinos and shirt with the occasional Colonel Abrams/El Debarge-style padded shoulder suit. The over-dressing wasn't a lifestyle choice the lads had adopted, it was a compulsory dress code imposed by the college. It was a rule that some guys would go to extraordinary lengths to get around, including climbing the fence or wearing jeans and a t-shirt under their hideous 'wedding outfits'. The guardroom Corporals never seemed to notice when guys went out weighing 14 stone and came back wearing different clothes and three stones lighter.

This formal dress code made it incredibly difficult to blend in with the locals, and making conversation with a Harrogate girl whilst denying being in the Army was almost impossible when surrounded by a Spandau Ballet impersonator's club. I found I wasn't too bad at chatting up girls. I'd be nervous to begin with, but after a couple of beers I could hold a decent conversation without making too much of a plum of myself, even when having to shout over Hazell Dean at full volume. My attempts were usually futile though. Even if I was doing well, the final nail would be driven into the chat-up coffin by Barry Nash. Just as it looked like I was getting somewhere, he'd appear and put his arm around my shoulder. The Union Jack t-shirt with 'These Colours Don't Run!' emblazoned on the front introduced him nicely. His torpedoing would generally go as follows:

Barry: 'Wheeeyyyy, get the fuckin' beers in, you cunt!'

Me: 'Er...'

Girl: 'Who's that?'

Me: 'Er, I don't know, I've never seen him before in my life.'

Girl: 'He looks like he's in the Army.'

Me: 'Yes, he does a bit, doesn't he?'

Barry: 'What are you talking about, Eddy, you daft wanker.'

Girl: 'Eddy? But you said your name was Dave?'

Barry: 'Here, Eddy, where's your bird going?'

Me: 'I tell you what, Barry. One of these days I am going to bray you.'

Barry was a good egg, but he loved getting blokes blown out.

Any town with a camp of junior soldiers nearby will always be troubled with violence between the locals and the military. In a garrison town with soldiers that were grown men, the sides were evenly matched, but we were the only military unit in the vicinity and we were short on punching power. Unfortunately, the Army environment made lots of the lads think that they were infinitely harder than they actually were. It goes without saying that some skinny, flame-haired 16-year-old Jock built like a Sudanese Locust is no match for an 18 stone piss-tank-warrior brickie from Leeds. This didn't deter some of the more foolhardy from gobbing off. When they did, it was usually to completely the wrong bloke and they would often return to the block with black eyes and loose railings for their troubles. The injuries would be explained away, fraudulently, the victim claiming to have fought off dozens of knife and chain-wielding nutters.

Many of the past clashes with local youths had attained legendary status, details being added with each telling of the stories. One such anecdote probably originated in a bout of normal Saturday night fisticuffs, but by the time I heard it it was an epic tale of blokes being tied to a pool table and pushed out of second storey windows. All of which had apparently resulted in the entire college booking out, dressed in boots, lightweights and PT kit, then being ferried into town by four tonner and tearing the place apart. The fact that the local papers had neglected to cover this momentous event never dented the enthusiasm of people recounting it to wide-eyed listeners.

There is no denying that my nights out in Harrogate were good fun, although a little frustrating due to my inability to tap off. The cheesey-named local hot spots – Champers, the Kings Club and Christies – were a laugh, and certainly chocker with enough skirt to fire me up for a milk when I got back to camp. Some of the guys were more successful with the ladies, and those who didn't have the fieldcraft training to smuggle their partners on to camp would find a quiet bush or use the bandstand in the Valley Gardens Park to do The Lord's work with their birds.

* * * * *

Four months before graduation, we were given the opportunity to select our postings on completion of training. The selection involved completing what was known as a dreamsheet. Trying to decide where you wanted to go in the world was a thrilling choice, but it wasn't called a dreamsheet for nothing. Like hobbies, it was blindingly obvious that everyone was going to go for places like Cyprus and Brunei, and a lucky handful would strike oil. The majority of lads would spend weeks humming and hawing over which sun-kissed part of the planet they'd choose, only to find that manning and records had completely ignored their request and were packing them off to an armoured div near the East German border. As always in the Army, it was purely a matter of head count. If someone in Akrotiri was struck by lightning at the exact moment your request hit the posting officer's desk, you might get the dream draft. Otherwise you could expect to be trying to hide from a German winter behind a malfunctioning kero heater.

There were quite a few interesting units in the Corps. 30 Signal Regiment were known as 'The Globetrotters', and were always going away on UN operations. 249 Signal Squadron were ski troops and spent considerable time in Norway, refining their Arctic Warfare techniques. Both seemed interesting, but the one that really caught my attention was 5 Airborne Brigade Signal Squadron. They were a mainly parachute-trained unit, whose job was to supply the Brigade with comms, jumping out of planes with radios. It made no bones about what was required of you on the display. Any one going to the unit had to attempt the physically-demanding P-Company course. On successful completion they would be awarded the coveted maroon beret before going on to get their wings on the parachute course at Brize Norton. There were a couple of instructors who'd served time at the unit, and they walked round camp in their maroon lids and parachute smocks looking, in my opinion, the dog's bollocks. That was enough for me, and I stuck my name down. Because it was a volunteer unit, they were always short of blokes and there was no danger that I'd be turned down. It would mean I'd stay in the UK, as they were based in Aldershot. As well as the prestige of serving in such a unit, it would mean I didn't have to disappear into the vortex of a BAOR posting.

As we came to the end of training we went through the trade board. All of the skills we'd learnt over the last two years were formally tested. The stakes were high. Anyone who failed would have to stay at the college for a course of remedial training prior to a reattempt. It was hard, but if you failed you would be treated like a major duffer by all and sundry. There was loads of cheating going on. People were entering into reciprocal agreements with colleagues who had the opposite strengths and weaknesses to themselves. Crib sheets and whispers were the order of the week and most of us got through, sometimes with the tacit assistance of a benevolent instructor who couldn't be bothered with the hassle of re-testing apprentices.

By the time came to leave, we'd been issued our number two dress. I was really looking forward to moving on and speaking to Mum in the run up to graduation encouraged me further.

'We're so proud of you, Eddy. You've done really well to stick with it.'

'Thanks, Mum.'

'Even your Auntie Mary and Uncle Jim are coming across for the parade. Your Dad's hired a little minibus.'

I hadn't realised I was the focus of such proud attention; it had to be a special day to prise Mary away from the McVitie's factory in Levenshulme.

The day of the graduation was great. It was the back end of July and, unlike for the pass off, the sun put in an appearance for the whole show. I always found the camp unfamiliar on sunny days, it was almost pleasant. We were all excited but we feigned indifference to maintain street cred. We were sent down to collect weapons an hour before and queued impatiently outside the armoury. Lance Corporal Lang was on weapons duty that day and he came in for a stack of abuse, from the anonymity of the queue. He was trying to keep order in his endearing way. 'Keep the fucking noise down, or there'll be no weapons and no fucking graduation.'

He was wasting his time. It had been two years since he bollocked us at Harrogate train station and the interim had given us all time to figure out where his place was in the pecking order.

'Fuck off, Lang, you coffin dodger.' The shout had come from someone far braver than me, and nearer the back. Lang was furious, and ran up and down the line demanding to know who'd insulted him. The wall of blank faces told him he'd get no answer. There was great pleasure to be taken in having one up on the little Nazi. He realised he was wasting his time on blokes who two hours from now would be able to give him a dig in the NAAFI if he got lippy. He turned back towards the armoury door, and the same voice from the rear encouraged him to get back to work. 'Just give us our guns, you jittery old knacker.'

He stopped for a moment and then thought better of it, moving behind the counter with previously unseen speed.

As we got into our two's dress in the block, the cameras started doing the rounds and people started adopting unnatural poses for the viewfinder. Men in various states of undress were pointing rifles menacingly around the room in the hope they'd look hard in the picture. Blokes who didn't smoke were dangling lit cigarettes from their lips to increase the delinquent effect. Of course, the unit 'photograph spoiler' was on hand to lower the tone and quality of any snaps. I recently dug out my Army photo album at Mum's and had a good look through, recounting the circumstances of each exposure. What I did notice as I flicked along was that every single photo had been ruined by someone in the background. Every single one. My Mum's albums are full of smiling people, gathered at various family occasions. All the subjects behave impeccably. Mine all have someone doing rabbit ears behind my head, or exposing a hairy spud. One of the photos, taken on the morning of the graduation, shows our entire recruit troop room, all kitted out, ready to go. We looked the business, the eight of us. One of the lads from the intake below used my camera to get a couple of snaps for me. After getting the film developed, I sat on a bench in Piccadilly Gardens to examine the pictures. The one of Room 4 Recruit Troop was the best – with our laughable, hard-man stares there was a real bonhomie to our little group. I smiled fondly. And then that I noticed that someone had managed to climb on top of the lockers behind us and drop his kecks. Pulling his cheeks as wide as they would go, he was exposing his anus perfectly. I don't know who it was, but he must have had some photographic training as his ricker was plumb top-centre. It was going to rest on Paul Jones' head for eternity.

We formed up for the parade in the road near Bradley Squadron, hidden from the stand and viewing platform by Penney Squadron's accommodation. As soon as the band started playing, the support troops marched into position and awaited our grand entrance. Listening in to the orders being roared by the RSM, we moved onto the square to the tune of the Corps quick march. Once we halted, we treated the spectators to a display of static weapons drill. We had it boxed off fairly well, and each crisp movement drew 'oohs' and 'aahs' from our families. After that came the obligatory standing still for an hour.

It was a new Mayor doing the inspection and he really took his time, revelling in the opportunity to dress like Henry VIII without attracting the attention of mental health professionals. The bandmaster was keen to show that his finger was on the pulse of any recent popular music developments, so we were treated to a bizarre brass version of *The Final Countdown*. Eight blokes collapsed in the heat, two from our squad. We'd been told to rock back and forth gently within our boots to keep the circulation going, but the heat and inactivity bred prime conditions for fainting. Every five minutes or so, my ears were drawn to a banging and clattering as another apprentice bit the dust. Whenever it happened, a couple of seniors ran on to the square and grabbed hold of the bloke under the arms, before dragging him off and taking all the precious bull off his boots in the process. I think the Army would have liked to charge people for fainting, citing some obscure legal transgression like 'showing disrespect to the Queen by hallucinating and breaking all your teeth in front of the colours.'

Instead, the fallen had to endure the derision of those who'd managed to stay on their feet. I was feeling a bit wobbly myself and breathed a huge sigh of relief when the inspection party finally moved back to the dais. It was great to get moving again and we completed the march past. When we got to the corners of the square furthest from scrutiny, discipline broke down slightly and discussions took place about any eye candy in the crowd.

'Did you see that blonde one with the big knockers in the Smiths T-shirt,' shouted someone behind me.

'That's my fucking sister, you,' came the irate reply.

'Sorry, mate. She has got big knockers though, eh?'

'Fair one.'

All was quiet again as we marched past for the second time, doing a snappy eyes right as the Commandant saluted and the Mayor tried to.

When we came off the parade ground we were marched behind the stands. After a count of three, everyone threw their hats in the air with a heartfelt cheer. That sort of thing always looks great in the films, but I spent the next five minutes looking at the names in scores of lids until I found my own. Several people took advantage of the situation to swipe hats that were in better condition than their own.

The Nugent gang descended on me as soon as I was spotted. Auntie Mary reached me first and smothered me in kisses, laughing and crying at the same time. 'Eddy, you were brilliant. I told you you'd make a good soldier.' Her prediction, written in the biscuits, had been accurate after all.

Uncle Jim and Dad were stood behind her, smiling benignly. Gran had brought a 'gentleman friend' with her, an old soldier called Alfie Silver she'd met down the British Legion, and he'd clearly enjoyed himself. He stepped forward and shook my hand firmly. He had a chest full of medals above the breast pocket of his Royal Engineers blazer. 'Well done, son. That parade was splendid. Takes me back to 1940 it does.'

Before he could get started on his wartime record, Mum interrupted. 'Come on, Alfie, let me get to him.'

She hugged me and kissed me gently on the forehead. 'Well done, Eddy. I'm so proud of you.'

Dad joined her, putting an arm round both our shoulders. 'It was smashing that, son. I'm not sure about the music, but all that drill with the weapons looked the bees knees.'

I said my goodbyes to the lads, and we swapped earnest but ultimately doomed promises to keep in touch from our new units. And then I climbed into the mini-bus for the journey home.

Dad had brought a crate of beers and we drank and sang all the way back to Manchester. It only took a couple of hours, but Alfie took full advantage of the free ale on offer and was boozed up and waffling by the time we got to Leeds. The chest full of medals he displayed testified to the contribution he'd made during World War II, but he couldn't resist colouring in his stories a bit. With all the eyewitnesses out of the picture, his imagination had free reign. Pointing to one of his brightly coloured gongs, he said, 'Do you know what I got this one for, Eddy lad?'

'No, Alfie. I know they're all WWII medals but I don't know what each one means.' For the rest of the run in, he told me amazing stories about his adventures in the war. Some were heartbreaking, others hilarious. I can't recall the details now but one of his anecdotes had what is possibly the best opening line I've ever heard. 'I was on the piss in Nazareth,' it started.

It was impossible not to be captivated by the charming old codger, reliving memories of his youth. It was unimportant that he was making some of it up, and when my Dad pointed out that El Alamein and the Dieppe raid happened around the same time he was shouted down by the rest of us and Alfie continued with his story.

I had a whole month before I had to report to Aldershot. I trained almost every day, following the curriculum suggested in my joining instructions. I ran in the mornings and did some work with a Bergen in the afternoons. There were no hills in our part of town, so I was reduced to running back and forth over a railway bridge near the local B & Q. I looked a knob and got regular abuse from schoolkids. I never responded, mainly because I agreed with their comments.

I didn't let the training programme get in the way of my number one pastime, and managed to fit in plenty of beer drinking. Now that I was receiving trade pay for my qualifications my wages had gone up, and I didn't have to sponge off Mum and Dad as much. Despite having busy working lives, they tolerated my drunken behaviour with good grace. Dad only saw red with me once. I came home from a club one Saturday night at about 3am. When I realised that I didn't have my key, I tried to climb in the downstairs toilet window. I'd managed to squeeze my way through the small aperture. It was usually left open as Dad always liked to drop a depth charge just before bed and Mum thought that the draught might stop the paint from peeling.

I got my hands either side of the sink that sat just below the window and started to bring my legs through. Just when I thought I'd cracked it, I caught the bottom of my jeans on the handle of the window. I couldn't get it free or push myself back up. I struggled for five minutes before giving up with my head resting in the sink and my feet still outside. There was only one thing for it, and I meekly started shouting for help, the call muffled by the porcelain. I heard the lights upstairs being switched on followed by the noise of Dad stomping down the stairs. When he opened the toilet door, he was hopping mad and was just about to launch into a hefty bollocking until he saw my predicament and started laughing. 'Fucking hell, Eddy. What time of night is this to be washing your hair?'

He grudgingly helped me down and went back to bed, but marked my card the next morning.

I made sure there were no recurrences and concentrated on getting my fitness up for the trials ahead.

ALDERSHOT

I travelled down to Aldershot on a miserable Thursday morning. My rail warrant took me all round the houses on a tour of all the nondescript, dormitory towns dotted all over the South East.

Years later, I had a heated regionalist argument with a mate from Woking who was slagging off northerners for all he was worth. I'd been proudly listing all that Manchester was famous for: he was countering in an annoying combination of a faux Cockney accent and an inability to pronounce the letter 'r'.

'Fack off, Eddy, you're talking wabbish.'

'Go on, then, name one thing that Woking can be proud of?'

He could have said 'The Jam', but, after pondering for a few seconds, he announced, proudly, 'We've got the biggest cemetewy in Euwope.'

I have no idea if that's true, but the accuracy of the statement is unimportant. It was the fact that he considered it more significant than the invention of the computer (1947, F. C. Williams and Tom Kilburn, Manchester University) that impressed me.

When the train finally emerged at Aldershot, I hauled my bags down and struggled out through the exit doors. I had no idea how far it was to the camp so I walked over to a taxi driver who was leaning on his car, smoking.

'Scuse me, mate. I'm looking for Arnhem Barracks.'

'Do you want directions, or do you want me to take you there?'

'Is it far?'

'It will be with all them bags,' he chuckled.

'Fair enough.'

He popped the boot and I slung my two holdalls and daysack in. It was only a short journey but I got his life story on the way. Like lots of garrison towns, Aldershot was extensively populated with old soldiers, tied to the place by marriage to a local. My driver had been in 3 Para for 12 years before leaving in the mid-70s. He was quite fat now, no doubt due to the standard cabbies' diet of kebabs and Coke, but he still looked quite capable of handling himself, with his number two haircut and an impressive selection of tattoos which looked like they'd been done with a blue crayon.

Looking in the rearview mirror, he interrogated me. 'Arnhem barracks, eh? What are you then, Signals?'

'Yeah that's right, first day today.'

'Just out of training then?'

'Yeah, I've been at the Army Apprentice College in Harrogate for the last two years.'

He wrinkled his nose up at that one. 'Sounds a bit wank all that, mate. Are you here to do P-Company?'

'That's right, I'm posted in to the Signal Squadron, but as a volunteer for Airborne Forces.'

'Fit lad are you?'

'Not bad, I've been doing a lot of training.'

He smiled, and shook his head slowly. 'You'd better be ready for some pain.'

He headed out of town and up a short rise called Hospital Hill, leading on to Queen's Avenue. About 100 metres down on the right was a huge Victorian building, and he pulled up next to it. He looked over his shoulder at me and jerked his thumb at it. 'That's Maida gym. You'll get to see lots of grown men crying in there, yourself included,' he chortled. He then pointed down to his left. 'That's the NAAFI on the left, and if you look a bit further down on the right, that's the Sig Squadron offices. That's £2.60 please, mate.'

I gave him three quid and told him to keep the change. Then I got my gear out of the boot and watched him spin the car round and head back into town.

I stood there for a moment, getting my bearings. The camp looked like an enormous, badly-designed housing estate full of ugly concrete buildings. Back then there was no fence around the camp, and you could walk on to it at any point. (A year or so later there was an escalation in PIRA activity on the mainland, so a two-metre fence was erected around the entire place. For months afterwards, people were cutting through it – not terrorists, just pissed-up squaddies who didn't want to have to walk the long way round after a night out. One particular patch of the fence – by the

9 Para, Royal Engineers living quarters – was breached and repaired almost daily. They tried to stop it by posting two poor bastards in a 9 x 9 tent to watch it every night, but they weren't a great deterrent. Blokes from 9 Sqn would just turn up with a set of bolt croppers and snip a big chunk out of the fence right in front of them, offering to snip a big chunk out of the guard if they said anything. The guard commander would come to check on them during the night, and would rightfully want to know why there was a huge fucking hole in the fence when it was their job to prevent that precise event from occurring. Rather than grass on the fence-cutters, the guard would then pretend they hadn't seen anything, and that they'd only noticed the hole when the guard commander pointed it out to them. This would all be done silent movie-style, with lots of exaggerated eye-rubbing and hands-on-hips incredulity. Eventually, 9 Sqn started walking round to the back gate like everyone else, and the short-lived and completely ineffectual 'fence-picquet' were stood down.)

I gathered my bags up and walked down towards the Signal Squadron offices.

It was just after lunch, so lots of blokes were coming in and out of the NAAFI. I saw a few Signals cap badges along with medics, engineers, REME and a couple of Ordnance Corps blokes. The only thing they had in common was the maroon colour of the beret, which I found myself gazing at in admiration. I found out later that a controversial rule had just been passed within the Brigade. Previously, only those in the Brigade who were parachute-trained, and had therefore passed P-Company, were entitled to wear parachute wings and the maroon beret. Anyone else serving in the Brigade was obliged to wear their normal headgear until the courses were passed. The new rule was that anyone posted-in to the Brigade could wear maroon. It was probably done with the best of intentions – to make everyone look the same and engender a good esprit-de-corps. Of course, it had the diametrically-opposite effect. Soldiers who had actually earned the beret bitterly resented others wearing it without going through the same trial. Conversely, lads who had only volunteered for the brigade in order to work for something which was coveted and respected objected to having to wear it just as bitterly. Of course, there were quite a few who enjoyed getting to wear the gear without having to do anything for it; fat blokes walking round in badly-shaped maroon berets were absolute punch-magnets, and would regularly get assaulted without ever understanding why.

Eventually, a way was found by which the beret kept its cherished status. An unwritten rule was introduced: anyone in the Brigade could wear the bog-standard stores-issued job, but only parachute-trained soldiers could wear the higher-quality leather-banded affair, available for purchase at the Victor's shop in Aldershot. It wasn't an ideal solution, but I'm sure it kept a lot of lardarses from getting a good kicking.

I carried on past the NAAFI and walked over to the Signal Squadron. I stopped at the base of a flagpole with an Airborne Signals' flag fluttering from the top and dropped my bags. There was no-one about so I had a good look around. I was standing on a parade square about the size of half a football pitch. Behind me was a two-storey building, with an external spiral staircase leading to the first floor. Dotted all over the building were blue doors marked with blue and white squares. The writing on the squares gave details of the pleasures to be had inside: 'Clothing Store', 'Bedding Store', 'Armoury', 'QM's Department', 'Squadron Offices'.

On the opposite side of the parade ground was the side wall of the cookhouse. The third side of the square had another row of two-storey offices, with signs on the doors reading 'Line Stores', 'Alpha Troop' and 'Bravo Troop'.

There didn't appear to be too much more to the place.

As I was stood there wondering what to do next, the door marked 'Alpha Troop' opened and a very large man came out and headed towards me. By the time he'd completed the walk of about 50 metres, I'd had enough time to identify his rank (Sergeant) and demeanour (threatening). Unlike everyone in the Apprentice College, he didn't have a nametag on his jacket.

'Who are you?' he snapped.

Throughout my time in Aldershot, this was the standard opening shot in any conversation with a stranger. It was meant to put the respondent on the back foot immediately, and it was very effective. I learned later that the correct response to the question, leaving both parties with honours even, was, 'Why, who are you?'

At this early stage in my education, such a response would have resulted in some sort of physical pain, so I opted for burbling nervously. 'Sig Nugent, Sarnt.'

'Posted in?'

'Yes, Sarnt, from Harrogate.'

'Craphat then, yeah?'

'Err, yes.'

'There's no fucker about at the moment. Everybody gets back off block leave on Monday morning. I think Kenny Rogers is over in the stores, stocktaking or something. If you go over and see him, he'll sort you out with some accommodation. Do you know who you're supposed to report to?'

'Staff Sergeant Herbert.'

'Right, well that's a bit fucked up. He's on leave 'til Monday as well.' He stood there for a second, wondering what to do with me. 'Look, go see Kenny and get your bed space. Get him to show you around a bit if he's got time. Other than that you can do your own thing 'til tomorrow morning.' He crooked his thumb in the direction of the door he'd just exited from. 'Come and see me at eight o'clock, in normal working dress, and I'll find you some jobs to do.'

'Right, Sarnt.'

With our conversation complete, he moved off back towards his office, before stopping and shouting back. 'Nugent?'

'Sarnt?'

'Try not to talk to anyone, you'll only annoy them.'

'Errr, right, Sarnt.'

He moved off and left me alone. I headed towards the bedding stores door and knocked. The shout that came from inside was not Texan, but deepest, darkest Brummie.

'What the fuck do you want?'

Slightly taken aback, I shouted through the closed door, 'It's Sig Nugent from Harrogate. The Sergeant told me to come and see you to get some accommodation sorted out.'

'Which Sergeant?'

'I don't know his name. He was a big guy, a Scouser.'

'Bryson?'

'I don't know.'

'Fucking wanker, thinks I've got nothing better to do.'

There was a brief sound of footsteps before the door to the store was unlocked. It was a long process – it sounded like several padlocks and at least three rows of bolts being undone before the door swung open. I checked it was the bedding store, and not a repository for some priceless antiquity.

Kenny Rogers' head emerged from behind the door. He was a gargoyle of a man, with a skinhead which exposed various lumps, bumps and stitchmarks on his skull. An oft-broken nose and a set of bad teeth completed the look. 'What is it you want then?'

'Sergeant Bryson said to get a bed space.'

'Fuckin' *did* he?'

'Yeah.'

He softened slightly. 'Sorry, mate, not having a go at you. I've got loads of work to do and I know for a fact that that fucker is just sat up in his office looking at himself in the mirror, and it's his fault that I'm the only fucker not on leave at the minute.'

'Why's that then?'

'He brought a mattress in last week and tried to exchange it, but I wouldn't let him. He tried to say he'd spilt a brew on it, but you could tell he'd pissed it.'

'How did you know?'

'The only way that could have been a brew stain is if he'd been drinking out of The European Cup. The whole fucking mattress was piss wet through. Only the corners were still white. If it was tea or coffee the stain would have been brown, but it was as yellow as a Post-it. So I billed him the fifteen quid for a new one.'

'And he didn't like that?'

'Did he fuck. Whilst he was signing the chit, he says to me smiling, "I'll be doing the guard roster for the block leave period today, Rogers." So that was me fucked.' While he was talking, he'd opened the door fully, and was now going through the elaborate process of making it secure from the outside.

'Sorry to hear that, mate.'

'Ahh, it's not too bad, I've caught up on a lot of me work, and I get to fuck off as soon as the rest of 'em come back. It's always mad here the first week back after block leave, so it'll be good to be out of the way.' He moved the last padlock into place and snapped it shut, before turning back to me. 'Right, I'll take you over the block. Probably stick you up on the top floor. There's a few more coming from Harrogate isn't there?'

'Yeah, five I think.'

'Yeah? I'll stick you all on the top floor, you'll be a bit more out of the way, and the meatheads might leave you alone.'

'Meatheads?'

'Meatheads, cassette-heads, empty heads, Aldershot orphans... call 'em what you want. It's all the blokes who never go home. They've either got no parents or family, or no parents or family who like them. All they do is work here, and go down town and get pissed at all other times. They hate craphats, and they like to pay visits when they're leathered. Nothing too bad really, usually just a bit of drunken fist-waving, and the occasional bit of mayhem. If I stick you on the top floor, they might be too drunk to make it up that far.'

'Are you a craphat?'

'No I'm fucking not. What do you think these are?' He pointed at the set of parachute wings, sewn neatly on to his jumper at the top of the right sleeve.

'Sorry,' I replied. After what Sergeant Bryson had said, I was very scared of offending anyone, but Kenny started laughing.

'Don't worry about it. I tell you what, though, a lot of people are really touchy about who is and who isn't, especially since all the hats are wearing maroon lids. You'll find all this out. There are some blokes who will flatly refuse to speak to you if you aren't para-trained. Most blokes will tolerate you, but would rather have someone para-trained in your slot. Then there are blokes like me who don't give a monkeys who I work with. I've passed the course so I've got nothing to prove to the meatheads, but I can't be arsed being shitty with someone just because they haven't got their wings. The best thing I can suggest is you get Pre-Para and P-Company out of the way as quick as you can. Then you don't have to worry about it.'

'I think Pre-Para starts next Tuesday.'

'Yeah, that'd be right. Have you been training?'

'Quite a lot, yeah?'

'That won't matter. It'll still be fucking murder,' he smiled. 'I wouldn't want to go through that again.'

In the time it took to have the conversation, we'd arrived outside my accommodation block. It was a forbidding looking building.

'Here you go, Prisoner Cell Block E. Rumour has it that the architect who came up with this scheme is doing time for designing a load of flats that fell down in Bradford.'

'Seriously?'

'Don't know, might be a load of bollocks, but if this camp is anything to go by he'll be getting buggered in strange ways in Strangeways, ha-ha! Like I say, I'll stick you in one of the eight-man rooms on the top floor. When any of the other Pre-Para lads show up, I'll send 'em in the same direction.'

He bent down, picked up one of my bags and turned to the door. I grabbed the other two and followed. There was a rudimentary, push button combination lock on the door. He ignored it and pulled the door straight open. 'Don't know why the fuck they bother with them. The combination is always the same, 1, 2, 3, 4, but you still get blokes who are too thick or pissed to remember, so they just boot it off with a size 10 master key. It gets fixed every Monday and smashed every Friday.'

He laughed, shrugged his shoulders and headed up the stairs. The stairwell seemed quite clean and tidy, and I was beginning to get my hopes up that the interior was going to be more welcoming, after my first impressions from outside.

'Seems quite clean, Kenny?'

'This is the best you'll ever see it. Before any block leave, there's a big clean up. The head-shed threaten you with keeping you back unless it's done. The razz man comes round, the morning of knock-off day and inspects. It's the only time anyone bothers their arse. All the shit gets crammed into lockers, into the false ceilings and under beds. He usually just has a bit of a skim round, makes sure there's no blood on the walls or bodies in the drying room. I tell you what though, if he opened one of the lockers, he'd get killed by a shit avalanche.'

'So there's not too much bullshit then?' I asked, hopefully.

'Nah, mate, it's not that sort of place. They concentrate more on running and tabbing than drill and inspections.'

Well that was good news. After Harrogate it was going to be nice not having to worry about shiny boots. Unfortunately Kenny carried on talking. 'Anyway, you'll be that ballbagged from getting beasted all over the training area you wouldn't have the energy for drill if they tried to get you to do it at gunpoint.'

I got that queasy feeling in my stomach. *What have I got myself into?* I half-hoped Kenny was feeding me a bit of a line to scare me, but he didn't seem like that sort of bloke.

On the second floor, Kenny turned right and opened a fire door leading into a short corridor. He pointed. 'You want the first door on the right. Just pick an empty bed space and sort your locker out.'

'Cheers, Kenny.'

'No probs. Wash areas through on your left, and there are three other rooms up here. You'd better stay out of them. All the lads are away, but you don't want anyone catching you skulking around their kit. I can tell you for a fact that they won't be very understanding. I'll see you about.'

With that parting shot, he left me to it. I lugged all my bags into the room. There were four beds to each side of the room, each with a locker, top box and side drawers next to it. I was going to be afforded about the same amount of privacy as I'd had in Harrogate, ie none, but it all looked OK.

I chose one of the beds nearest to the big, square window and, after a brief gawp outside, I started stashing my gear in the locker, reading the weird graffiti left by previous tenants. *'Clash, Cash, Hash, Gash, Keith and Sarah'* said one scrawl. I still haven't got a clue what it meant; a list of Keith and Sarah's needs, perhaps. After I'd done my locker, I lay on the unsheeted mattress and had 40 winks.

Until the Squadron came back in its entirety, the next few days were boring and strange. I'd never been on an empty camp before and it was mind-numbing enough for me to make a mental note never to drop myself into enough shit to get me held back during block leave.

I did a bit of work for Sergeant Bryson, painting a couple of Land Rovers in an imaginative combination of black and green. I went to every meal in the cookhouse, where an industrially fat slop jockey Corporal dished out heavily-fried food to the slack handful of blokes that were knocking around.

I took walks into town on Saturday and Sunday – during the day, of course. I'd heard enough about the nightlife not to attempt a boozing spree single-handed.

Over the weekend, the other five Pre-Para lads showed up.

I was able to help out a bit, showing them the various parts of the camp that I'd discovered. By Sunday night, all six of us were in the room, apprehensively discussing what lay in store. Other than Davey Bovan, Willie Edwards and Scouse Marriott from Harrogate, there was Joey Donaldson from 30 Sigs and Shuggy Tennant from 211 Signal Squadron in Germany. During any conversation of this sort, everyone is secretly trying to establish that they are not the most unfit, haven't done the least training; and are not the most disorganised.

I was alright on the first two points, but I lagged behind the rest of them when it came to organisational skills. Davey, Willie and Scouse had all done a lot of training at Harrogate and during the big summer leave, and were raring to go. Joey was on the Corps cross country team and had wanted to serve with Airborne Forces for five years. Shuggy, on the other hand, had a beer gut. It came out during the conversation that he'd only volunteered to get out of Germany.

'How do you mean?' asked Scouse, perplexed.

'Well it's a volunteer posting, innit,' said Shuggy, 'I was fucking sick of Germany. I've been there six years, straight out of training, and I had another two to go before me next posting. They call it the Iron Triangle, 1 Div, 3 Div and 4 Div. Once you're in you never get back out. If you stick your name down for a volunteer unit and pass the course, they've got to let you go.'

'There's one little flaw in your plan there, mate,' said Davey.

'What's that?'

'Pre-Para and P-Company are a cunt to pass. We're going to be getting ran absolutely fucking ragged for the next six weeks. Are you up for all that?'

'I should be alright. I've done a bit of training, I can pass me BFT and all that.'

It sounds tight to say it, but I was heartened by the fact that I could be 100 per cent certain that somebody was going to be behind me on the runs.

At about 10pm, people starting sorting themselves out for bed for an early night. At about quarter past, the door opened and a short man squeezed himself through into the room, smiling slightly. He was about 5ft 6in tall and the same width across the shoulders. He was dressed in boots, lightweights, shirt and maroon beret, and round his waist was a Signals' stable belt, with an Airborne buckle. He also had a green and yellow lanyard on, instead of the normal Signals blue. His short sleeves allowed him to display his extensively tattooed and muscled arms; he looked friendly enough, in a no-nonsense way. He also looked capable of beating us all up with one hand tied behind his back.

He took his beret off, to reveal a number two, the choice of the discerning paratrooper, and introduced himself in a strong Northern Irish accent.

'Evening, lads. I'm Staff Sergeant Herbert. I'm the training wing Staffie and I'll be taking you for Pre-Para for the next three weeks.' We gathered round him, leaving a bit of a respectful distance. 'There are seven more on the course. Two officers and five lads who failed the last one. I hope for your sakes you've done a lot of training.'

This received some nods in agreement and a comedy gulp from Shuggy.

'Well, we're starting tomorrow, so I hope so. I want you all formed up on the square at 0730 hrs, underneath the flag. Dress is red PT tops, lightweights and boots. No watches, no jewellery, no make up.' He had a quick glance round. 'Looks like we'll have a haircutting party tomorrow as well.' He looked over at Davey and shook his head. 'You've got more hair than Bonnie fucking Tyler. Not to worry, we'll sort that out. Make sure you've all got a white material patch on the front of your shirts with your name clearly visible. Tomorrow morning it will just be a light run and a bit of battle PT to see what sort of condition you're all in. You'd best get some sleep.'

He stuck his beret back on and trundled out, leaving us to ruminate on his words. I was bricking it a bit; I'd rather have started there and then than wait 'til the next morning.

* * * * *

The alarm went at 0630 hrs. I was out of bed as soon as it went off and getting washed, shaved and into my gear. I didn't fancy breakfast; the idea of running around with a load of pigswill sloshing around my guts didn't appeal. At 7.15am we all walked over to the square. The camp was bustling with activity. All the units were back in from block leave, and there were people milling about all over.

We were immediately identifiable, in our red PT tops, as Pre-Para fodder, and we attracted quite a lot of looks, mainly of the pitying sort. By twenty-five past, all thirteen of us were stood in front of the flagpole. The two officers, sparkling white tops on, looked like standard Sandhurst, rosy-cheeked teenagers.

A couple of minutes later Ssgt Herbert came out of the first floor offices and down the stairs with two, younger, bigger blokes behind him. They wore maroon t-shirts, and no name tags.

When he got in front of us, he introduced himself again. 'For those of you who didn't get to meet me last night, my name is Ssgt Herbert. I will be looking after your mental welfare for the next three weeks.' The two other men stood slightly behind and either side of him. He swept his hand to the left indicating a tall, ginger man with more tattoos and even less hair. 'This is Corporal Griffiths.' Then he indicated to his right, 'And this is Lance Corporal Frankson.' Frankson had slightly fewer tattoos but was taller and harder-looking than the other two.

All the time that Herbert was talking, the two Corporals glared up and down our lines, daring anybody to make eye contact. Nobody did.

Herbert continued. 'You all know what you're here for, so I won't give you any long speeches. Passing Pre-Para will entitle you to attempt P Company. We're not in the business of sending people to Depot Para who we don't think will pass. It makes us look bad. Pre-Para is not an easy course, but lots of people have passed it so it's not impossible. Turn to your right and listen in.'

We did exactly as instructed, immediately. Ssgt Herbert walked to the front man and addressed him. 'Stay with me. Stay exactly half a pace behind me. If you get any closer, I'll assume that you all want to run faster.'

Without further fanfare, he started to run and we followed. For three weeks.

The whole of Pre-Para was a blur of mud, pain and launderettes.

Right from the first morning, they set out to murder us. They were working on the unscientific premise that anybody who was left standing at the end would consider P-Company as a bit of time off. The light run that Herbert had mentioned the night before consisted of an eight mile cross-country slog. The route we took became achingly familiar within a couple of days. Under the Arnhem Barracks archway, down the road past Normandy Barracks, over Pegasus Bridge, and down past the Wellington Memorial and onto the training area. This was a massive expanse of MOD-owned land covered in hills and intertwining paths, with little physical tests designed to further deplete the visitor. The first of these was called 'Spiders'. We'd already pegged it two miles and were starting to feel the pace when Herbert called us to a halt at the bottom of a small hill. Well, he said 'Halt,' but what he *actually* meant was for us to stop running forwards and start marking time at the double.

'Get your fucking knees up,' screamed Frankson. They weren't happy until we looked like a mad, Irish dancing troupe.

Spiders was so-named because of the myriad paths that ran over and around it. The usual script is that one of the instructors will run up and down the paths, crossing the peak of the small hill regularly for about five minutes. He'll then swap with another instructor who'll take the next shift. Of course, unlike the instructors, the students don't get to take a rest, and are thoroughly chinstrapped after a couple of goes around. The most horrific thing about it was the fact that it didn't count towards anything. You didn't get any points or backslaps for completing it. It was just something you did on the way out to the training area.

After our introduction to Spiders, we simply formed back up in a squad and carried on with the run. If you were particularly unlucky, you'd do it on the way back in as well; whenever I hear someone utter the expression, 'I'm scared of Spiders,' I get a flashback and have a little shudder.

Various other attractions in this theme park of pain were Hungry Hill, Miles End Hill, Flagstaff, Zigzags, Long Valley and the Mulberry Bush. Funnily enough, they all involved running up and down hills until you thought you were going to regurgitate your heart and lungs. When I wasn't looking at my own feet, I'd occasionally look around me frantically, hoping there would be a big cliff that I could just jump off, or a nice pothole in which I could break my ankle.

The first morning's run was just the start. We covered every fucking blade of grass on that area. Sometimes in PT kit, sometimes with bergans, sometimes carrying each other, but always knackered.

As well as the joys of the training area, there were the murderous 90-minute gym sessions. We'd frantically change into our 'Tupper of the Track' shorts as roars started echoing inside the cavernous gym, emanating from an increasingly impatient Frankson or Griffiths.

'Come on you lot, hiding won't do you any good.'

'The longer you take, the worse we'll make it.'

Joey Donaldson was the fittest lad on the course, he sailed round all of the runs, but the gym sessions had a weird effect on him. When the Corporals started screaming at us to get in from the changing rooms, he'd get all upset. He'd start jogging on the spot with a look of horrified panic in his eyes.

'What do you think we'll do today?' he'd ask, in the hope that someone would suggest a nice game of volleyball.

The answer was always the same. We would get crucified. The sessions always started with a warm-up that left me more fucked than any complete PT lesson we'd done in Harrogate. Then came the kneeling gun drills. If ever an exercise was designed by The Devil it was this one. Originally it was for Artillery gun crews and would assist in getting them fit for the arduous drills required to fire a fucking great lump of metal at something over the horizon. Some sadist from another unit in Aldershot must have caught sight of it, recognised its misery-inducing potential and hijacked it for 'all arms'.

You start off in the kneeling position, left foot planted flat, right foot tucked under right arse cheek. From there, keeping the head and back straight at all times, you leap gracefully into the air before dropping down into the original start position, but with the feet reversed. Then you simply continue this until you are dead, or dying. Very quickly, our thighs would turn to concrete and despite all the instructors' protestations we would find our leaps becoming less and less graceful with each repetition. After a couple of minutes, we looked like we were trying to tie our shoelaces and have a shit at the same time. I believe it got banned eventually, because it turned peoples' knees to mush.

After the gun drills, they would just run us up and down the gym doing shuttles for eternity.

Every possible permutation was employed. Press ups, sit ups, star jumps, burpees, sprinting on the spot, bunny hops, seal crawls, leopard crawl, monkey crawl. By the end of the lesson, we would have usually stopped sweating and would be staring, bug-eyed, at the instructors. We'd have all that lovely white cack round the outside of our mouths that's only normally found on marathon runners or the criminally insane.

The instructors' favourite trick was to knock us off to get changed and then call us back because somebody had committed a minor (ie non-existent) transgression, like not running properly out of the gym or failing to hallucinate correctly. We would then undergo a further 10 minutes of punishment, usually on the ropes. Anyone caught trying to cheat on any of the exercises, for a couple of seconds of respite, would be ordered to the wall bars where he would be made to hold on with both arms and raise the legs until the body formed an L shape.

Occasionally, Herbert might send us off with a word of encouragement, but all I could ever hear was a big thumping sound in my head where my brain was trying to escape.

When we finally escaped their clutches, people would fall on to the benches and wonder how the fuck they were going to summon up the energy to take their clothes off to change.

Of course, the meat and drink of the Airborne Forces is bergan humping, and Herbert and his staff made plenty of time for that, too.

We would generally run-walk-run between six and ten miles every afternoon, carrying a 35lb pack and a drill weapon of about

10lbs. With water and everything else, it usually totalled around the 50lb mark. The weapon always had to be carried in the high port, with the index finger of the right hand over the trigger guard. The 'carrying handle', despite its name, was never to be used. It didn't make any sense, but I don't remember anybody, during the whole three weeks, being argumentative about anything. The tabs took the same routes as the runs but were much harder because of the additional weight. We'd always get strung out after a few miles, and would end up resembling a line of refugees attempting a border crossing.

Other physical activities formed regular punctuation marks between the gym and the training area. We were taken round some of the P Company events, notably the steeplechase and the assault course.

The steeplechase wasn't too bad. It was two mile-long laps of a Weil's Disease-infested mud bath to the rear of the football pitches. There were knee high hurdles and huge water jumps all the way round: lads would get submerged in what looked like drinking chocolate but smelled like cow shit, before emerging like the Creature From The Black Lagoon with kids' bikes wrapped round their necks. We had 18 minutes to get round twice and by the end we'd be caked in so much mud that we looked like disinterred corpses. With about as much energy.

The story was that the assault course had been designed by a committee of psychologists and fitness experts to ensure that runners were stretched to their physical and mental limits. Perhaps they were out-of-work Nazis doing a bit of post-war freelancing. It wasn't the worst I've done but, fuck me, I knew who my mates were whilst I was on it. We had 7min 30sec to do three laps. There weren't any big gaps between obstacles, so the only way to overtake people was to barge them out of the way or climb over them. The first obstacle was a six foot wall, and when the shout went to start everyone hit this at the same time. Best mates were happily hauling each other off and stepping on heads to get a quicker start. From there, it was a case of clattering round as best as I could. Every now and again, Frankson or Griffiths would berate me for not overtaking the man in front. Fortunately, by the second and third lap, all the wood on the course was good and wet from everyones' boots. At some stage, the guy in front would go flying when his feet hit something slippy, allowing me to breeze past without having to break his nose. The same thing would happen to me on the next obstacle, and a kind of status quo would be maintained with the training hounds kept at bay.

For safety purposes, we had to wear helmets on both the steeplechase and the assault course. That sounds sensible, but wasn't. With the constant jumping up and down, the front of your lid would repeatedly drop over your eyes, leaving you with a good chance of running into a tree.

The pace throughout the three weeks was relentless, like a macabre version of *Groundhog Day*. Though not everything was the same. To their credit, the instructors were quite inventive. As soon as you thought you'd been subjected to every possible agony, they would produce another.

One afternoon, halfway through, Herbert informed us that instead of a tab we were going swimming. We turned up at the pool in the Royal Engineers barracks at Cove thinking that at last we'd been given a bit of a break. The optimism of fools knows no bounds. It was just as terrible as the gym. The shuttles were exactly the same, only water-based.

Until that session, I didn't think it was actually possible to sweat in a swimming pool. It went on for an hour. Anytime we got out of the water we were not allowed to use the bar to aid our climb. We were supposed to haul ourselves up and out using only our arms, with the right leg swinging on to the poolside at the last second. This was OK at the beginning, but by the midpoint of the beasting the only way out was with a freak wave to wash us ashore.

The last thing they had us doing was the butterfly. My method was to give it a quick spin of the arms before going under, whilst swallowing as much water as I could. Just as I was about to drown, I'd summon enough energy to kick and push my head to the surface. Another lacklustre attempt at the arm movement would follow, and I'd grab another quick breath before heading for Davey Jones' locker again. It took me three minutes to complete a length, and I came second.

Another afternoon, we were doing battle PT on Queens Parade. This consisted of fireman's lifts, 50 metres there, 50 metres back, then swap and get carried by your oppo. I was carrying Willie, and I dropped him. Frankson went berserk.

'Nugent, Edwards, fucking get here.'

We ran over as fast as we could.

'Right, you funny cunts. Think it's a fucking joke do you? See that big tree?' He pointed back over our shoulders. I turned round. I looked for a big tree but couldn't see one. Queens Avenue is a vast grassed area, usually covered in football pitches. Then I spotted a lonely old oak, off in the far distance – at least half a mile away. It had to be the one he meant. I quickly turned back round and said, 'Yes, Staff.'

'Good. Round the tree and back again, GO!'

We ran off at a sprint, but the pace dropped off as soon as it appeared that the tree wasn't getting any closer.

'Where the fuck is it, Eddy?'

'Right by the fence, you can just about see it.'

He was 200 metres away, but Frankson's superhuman hearing picked our voices up and he screamed after us like Duncan Norvelle's twisted younger brother. 'Got time to fucking *talk*, have you? Don't make me chase you.'

We picked up the pace, and eventually ran the mile it took to get back to the squad. Frankson was waiting for us, smiling. 'Too slow,' he said. 'Go round again.'

Off we went. To tell the truth, it was the first time I managed to laugh on the course. Once we were near the tree, we were well out of even Frankson's aural range. I said to Willie, between ragged attempts to breathe, 'I've never been this fucked in my life, mate.'

He took a deep breath before producing his reply. 'All this,' he gasped, like a whooping cough victim, or a 90-year-old miner. 'All this... and pay an' all.'

* * * * *

I'm making it sound like hell on earth, and in many ways it was. But you learn to laugh at hardship and privation in the Army, and this was a volunteer posting so we had no business complaining. And there *were* good points. There were no bullshit inspections, mainly. As long as your boots and kit were clean and ironed, that was enough.

Every evening after tea, we'd head down town as a bunch and chuck all our laundry at the woman in the Posh Wash on Grosvenor Road. While she attempted to remove half the steeplechase from our kit, we'd nip off to the McDonalds. Despite having just eaten our tea, we'd be hungry again and would usually find room for a couple of Big Macs and a skipful of chips. This would leave just enough time to down one or two pints of Guinness before picking up the washing. Straight back up Hospital Hill and back to the block. By the time we'd got all our ironing done, it would be about 10 o'clock and time for our lovely beds. I've never slept so deeply before or since. I'd shut my eyes, and two seconds later the alarm would go off at 6.55am. I used to feel completely cheated, until Davey came up with a great idea. We started setting the alarm for 3.30am. As soon as it went off, we'd sit up and revel in the fact that we had another three hours kip before Herbert could get his hands on us again.

'It's like the bloke talking to the old tramp,' said Davey. 'The tramp tells him his shoes are four sizes too small for him. The bloke asks him why and the tramp says the only pleasure in his sorry life is taking the fuckers off at night.'

It sounds daft now, but it worked.

We had the weekends to ourselves. This gave us a couple of days to recharge our failing batteries for the following Monday, and it was conducted in the time-honoured tradition of getting leathered. Herbert recommended that we go for a couple of light runs on Saturday and Sunday to keep the joints oiled but we had another form of lubrication in mind. I think a few of us would have cracked up if there weren't a few beers to look forward to after spending a week working harder than Esther Rantzen's toothbrush.

Great care had to be taken whilst on the pop in Aldershot. It wasn't a welcoming place for the non-para-trained. The pubs were divided between the various units in the Brigade: anybody wandering in off the street, either not from the unit or not friends with someone in the unit, was likely to be challenged, and – if lucky – chucked out. If it was a bit later on in the evening and people were pissed, or if the trespasser had a particularly punchable face, then a bit of a kicking might ensue. It was primitive in the extreme, but as long as you knew the rules you could avoid trouble.

There were only a handful of places that weren't off limits to craphats like myself, the most popular being The Queens and The South Western. The Queens was a decent place used by all units – they had a disco on every weekend and lots of loose women could be expected to attend. The South Western was a right dive – always three quarters empty and in severe need of redecoration. The important factor for us in both was safety. Paras love a fight – an absolute fact! They don't care who the fight is with, and being heavily outnumbered doesn't bother them. After a night on the ale, the slightest provocation – actual or perceived – spells trouble. Local folklore tells of the time when riot police turned up to prevent the Paras from destroying Aldershot during Airborne Forces weekend in 1986. The police formed up at one end of the road and faced off with an equal number of soldiers about 100 metres away. The cops then started their usual routine of shield-beating, before advancing menacingly towards the mob. Unfortunately, these tactics were designed to intimidate the wavering Greenpeace protester; a crowd of drunken paratroopers were a different prospect altogether. They saw the shield-beating as a bit of a challenge and performed their own advance. Instead of the rigidly-disciplined movement of the Old Bill, this was more like a Highland charge by a pack of wild gorillas. Apparently, the police line broke and retreated immediately, leaving helmets, batons and shields scattered everywhere. In the absence of an easily-identifiable enemy, blokes from the Brigade would turn inwards and fight each other, picking fights with other guys from the same unit just for a laugh. While we were on Pre-Para we managed to avoid trouble, but I witnessed at least four fights a night.

The black dog of depression would begin to descend somewhere around Sunday afternoon, when we realised that our next beasting was less than 24 hours away. The evening would be spent putting white zinc tape all over our blistered feet and the various places on our backs where the bergans had rubbed skin away. It was good stuff, zinc tape, but it was an absolute bastard to remove – taking it off took persistence and an impossibly high tolerance to pain. The only thing that hurt more was tincture of benzene. 'Tinc-benz' was absolutely brilliant for foot blisters, but the agony involved in administering it was beyond compare. The procedure is as follows: Lie the patient down on the floor. Remove the boot and sock from the given foot. Insert the toe end of the boot into the patient's mouth and tell him to clamp it between his teeth. Puncture the blister with a sterile hypodermic needle and draw out any liquid. Remove the needle and suck up a couple of mils of tinc-benz from the bottle. Instruct four large blokes to take hold of the patient's limbs, pin the fucker down and hold on for dear life. Inject the tinc-benz into the blister cavity. Retreat quickly whilst the four men try to contain the boot chewing patient who is now a human bucking bronco. It worked like a dream though. You'd never get another blister on that patch of skin again, so the pain was worth it.

As the three weeks drew to a close, it was apparent that most of us were going to pass this phase. The two Rodneys and Joey had no problems and were at the front for everything. Then there was a group of seven, including me, who struggled like fuck for the duration of the course but managed to stay with it enough to get the nod.

Three lads failed. Two blokes on their second attempt gave up halfway through and were quickly posted back to their units.

Then of course there was Shuggy. Right from the start he was lagging behind, last on everything. Every time we went on a tab, he was getting dragged along by his bergan straps after a mile or two. I think he earned the grudging admiration of the training staff by flatly refusing to jack it in, despite it being obvious that he was never going to be fit enough to attend P-Company. He must have *really* hated Germany. He did manage to introduce a new word into the local dictionary. We were doing a BFT round Queens Parade. Shuggy went off like a shot and was matching Joey Donaldson pace for pace. For about 300 metres. His speed deserted him as soon as his lungs started burning, and the rest of us, pounding out the distance at a more regular pace, soon closed up with him. As I passed him, he started to vomit. I say 'vomit', but nothing was actually coming out. He was just making horrible retching noises with every couple of steps. In a timed event like the BFT, you don't have the luxury of pulling over for a spew, so Shuggy attempted to keep running whilst his digestive tract went into spasm. Each time he made a renewed effort to bring up his entire diaphragm, his right knee would slam up to his chest, involuntarily. He would stumble on for a few paces before repeating the movement. He looked like the victim of someone with a Voodoo doll and an itchy pin finger and ran like this for a couple of hundred metres before his constitution settled down. Ever after, if someone was afflicted with a similar complaint, he was said to be 'Shuggying' (verb, 'to shuggy'). I'm sure it made him quite proud, and served as some consolation when Herbert gave him the bad news and despatched him back to the loving embrace of the 'Iron Triangle'.

On the last Friday of the course we were treated quite well and after a farewell punishment session in the gym, we were addressed by Herbert. 'OK, lads. Well done over the last three weeks.' It was the first and only time he gave us any indication that we'd pleased him. He quickly qualified his praise. 'You've not been the worst, but you've certainly not been the best. Having said that, 10 is a very good number to be sending down the road to Depot Para. You've all done enough to prove you can pass P-Company, but you'll have to graft. Remember, only three more weeks and you're finished. Don't make the mistake of failing. You'll only have to do this all over again.' The thought horrified the squad, and we visibly shuddered. 'Have a good weekend, and standby for Monday.'

P COMPANY AND BONGO BATTERY

We had a good piss up on the Friday night. Everything from 9 o'clock onwards was a blur of beer and pizza. We spent the rest of the weekend getting our gear together, and by Sunday night we were all ready to go. Sitting around on our beds at 10 pm, we discussed what our fate would be.

'Do you reckon it'll be much harder than Pre-Para?' asked Scouse Marriott.

'That isn't possible,' said Davey.

'Our kid did it about five years ago,' said Joey. 'He said it wasn't too bad.'

'Yeah, but I bet he was a fucking racing snake like you? What about the rest of us slugs?' Willie had a low but realistic opinion of his abilities.

Scouse said, 'Like Herbert said, I'll be fucked if I'm doing this again. Just keep ticking off the days, lads.'

Next morning found us outside the Parachute Regiment Depot at 7am. Two guys from 1 Para were manning the vehicle checkpoint at the front gate. They had a good snigger as we approached them. 'P-Company is it, lads?'

'Yeah.'

'Ha, ha, ha, fucking scaley craphats. You'll be back by tomorrow night.'

'Yeah, with a lovely big payslip,' said Scouse.

'Wankers,' said the 1 Para lad. One of the bugbears that other units in the Brigade had about the Signals was that we got paid loads more than them. It was a bit of a misconception. Some of the Techs were on a really good wedge compared to your average Infanteer, but the rest of the trades didn't clear too much more money than their opposite number in an Infantry Regiment. Still, it was always a good way to wind someone up quickly, and Scouse had used it to good effect. We crossed Alison's Road, past the

WW11 Dakota aeroplane that stood guard outside the barracks, and walked into 'Depot'.

P-Company was fundamentally similar to Pre-Para, in that it involved getting run into the ground and shouted at a lot. There were more people involved, though – some 90 candidates from all over the Army. RCT, Ordnance Corps, RE, Signals, Artillery, REME... there were even two guys from the Pay Corps. I could just see them parachuting into some hot spot in the middle of nowhere with a bergan full of money for the lads.

All the instructors were Senior NCOs from the Parachute Regiment. As with Sutton Coldfield, with the passage of time they've all sort of morphed into a single character in my mind's eye. Six foot tall. Build of a light heavyweight boxer. Freddie Mercury moustache. Black hair cut in the same style as an Action Man's. Their dispositions were all frighteningly similar, too: they got paid for behaving in ways that would get you sectioned in any other industry. When approached by a student, they would answer his question politely. Underneath, and visible to all watching, they would be bristling with the desire to beast them for having the audacity to engage them in conversation.

The days consisted of gym sessions, tabs and runs. You couldn't skive in the gym. There was a big balcony at the back where extra training staff would assemble. They would be assigned a few of us to watch, and as soon as the lesson began they would be screaming at anyone seen not to be trying. On the first morning, there were 23 of us hanging from the wall bars, wailing like prisoners in a medieval dungeon.

The tabs got longer and faster each day. On the Monday of the second week, we were taken to the South Downs. Not for the scenery. That day's work was a 15-mile speed march. I never got to the end – on foot, anyway. The halfway point was called Chalk Hill. The squad was mostly still together by this stage, but one of the REME lads in front of me was getting loads of jip from one of the instructors.

'Number 44, get hold of that fucking weapon properly.' We all had numbers, painted with pump whitener, on the map pockets of our lightweights. It saved the P-Company staff having to remember anyone's name. Mine was 38. The REME bloke was obviously feeling the pace and had started to exhibit an unusual characteristic that I'd seen on a few guys as they started to get more and more exhausted on a tab. His neck and head seemed to be getting further and further from his bergan. Whether it was from the weight of the bergan pulling itself off his shoulders a bit, or whether it was a subconscious attempt to distance himself from the thing which was causing him such intense misery, I don't know, but he'd started to resemble a tortoise on its hind legs, stretching for a lettuce leaf that someone was holding just out of reach. Unfortunately, he was dropping down to a tortoise's pace, too. The instructor came right up to his earhole. 'You, you annoying fucker, are making the people behind work harder. Catch up with the man in front, or I'll fucking launch you.'

The idea is you're right behind the guy in front, nose touching bergan. The instructor grabbed the back of the REME's bergan and shoved him along till he caught up. It was fruitless. Within a couple of seconds, he was lagging again. After four or five cycles of this, you could tell that he was close to jacking it in. From my point of view, this was all quite beneficial. The little tableau to my front was taking my mind off my own exhaustion.

Finally, the instructor spoke again, more quietly this time. 'Fucking quitter are you?'

I was instantly transported back to the Careers Office. I was glad I wasn't having to do this tab in a suit.

'No, staff.'

'Get in the fucking jack wagon, you're slowing everyone down.'

'NO, staff.'

'It's not a fucking request 44. Do as you're told. Fall out, bergan off, and wait for the wagon.'

The REME lad knew the consequences of jacking and didn't want any of it. It may have changed now, but back then on P-Company if you got three black marks you were RTU'd. Failing to complete an exercise, or coming in outside the time required for a particular event, got you a mark. I'd already got up to two – one for not finishing with the squad on the first tab and the second for dregging on the mulberry bush run the previous Friday.

'Fuck off, I'm alright,' he screamed back, which tipped the instructor over the edge. He grabbed the lad by the back of the bergan and spun him round, presumably hoping to extricate him from the squad and fill him in. Number 44 realised he'd given the wrong answer and started trying to escape a hiding by losing himself in the squad. This might have worked if we all had 44 written on our trousers, and shared his surname, which was emblazoned across the front of his chest. The rest of us were still tabbing along, staring open mouthed at the Buster Keaton scene to our front. Number 44 got about a yard away from the instructor before he was grabbed again. The instructor was screaming unintelligible expletives at Olympic pace now, but 44 was still struggling. All of a sudden they both went over on their arses and we all piled into them. It was like Becher's Brook, and I found myself at the bottom of about six bodies. By the time we got up and got moving again, I was way behind the squad. By the time I got to the rest point at the top, the rest of the lads were getting ready to move again and the medics looked bored. One gave me a lukewarm brew and an instructor came over with absolutely no fanfare to inform me that my number was up. There was a similar lack of ceremony back at the depot. They'd seen thousands of abject failures, and they processed me with the appropriate apathy.

And that was P-Company finished for me. Four weeks for nothing.

* * * * *

I was out of Depot Para by the end of the day. Scouse and Willie helped me carry my gear back to Montgomery Lines. They didn't say much, just dropped the gear by my bed and before they left and gave the universal shrugged shoulder movement that means 'Tough shit, mate,' before heading off down town to do their washing.

Truthfully, it was a blessing in disguise. I don't think I had the mental rigidity required to get through P-Company. It wasn't just a fitness course, otherwise the whole Brigade would have been manned by cross-country runners. The course had been designed to test our ability to keep going whilst under lots of additional pressures, and I'd found myself lacking in this department.

The next morning I had to report to Ssgt Herbert at 8.15am. He was less than sympathetic. 'Go on then, let's hear it,' he said, sarcastically.

I explained what had happened while Herbert rolled his eyes, tutted and shook his head at me with a 'heard it all be-fucking-fore' stare. Eventually, he held his hand up to silence me. 'There are two types of soldier in this unit, Nugent,' he said. 'Airborne and non-Airborne. If you're Airborne, that's great. If you're not, nobody wants to hear your excuses.'

'Right, Staff.'

'It's just tough shit. You'll get sent down again – if and when we let you. We've just had word from Manning and Records that you've been posted in, so pass or fail, you're with us for the next four years.'

This was news to me. I assumed I'd be posted out for failing. It turned out that units were short of blokes of my trade, and para-trained or not, I could operate a radio and do Morse code.

'You'll be in Bravo Troop, otherwise known as Bongo Battery. Go over there now and stick your feet in Ssgt Jeans' in-tray.'

He dismissed me with a wave of his hand and went back to inventing new forms of torture.

So Aldershot was going to be my home for the foreseeable. After what Kenny had told me, I wasn't too sure it was what I wanted but I needn't have worried. Despite the fact that I never did pass P-Company and get my wings, even after another attempt, I had a great four years. I got promoted – just – I got myself fit and I learnt that there was plenty of fun to be had, once you'd escaped training and got into a working unit.

As soon as I got over to Bongo Battery, Ssgt Jeans welcomed me with the words, 'Fucking great, another craphat. I'll stick you on one of the RATT dets. Go down and see Tin Can Ally and ask him where RATT Delta is.'

'Yes, Staff.'

I quickly excused myself and walked down the stairs to the Bravo Troop locker stores. As I opened the door, I was confronted with a handful of blokes leaping around like jumping jacks. It was quite clear that they'd been sat around skiving until they heard me on the stairs. They must have assumed I was Ssgt Jeans – one guy was feverishly sweeping a perfectly clean floor and another, who'd obviously been kipping on a rolled-up cam net, was jumping up and down on it as though trying to cram it into a smaller space. The second they caught sight of my 18-year-old sprog features, they stopped the charade and fell back into their previous positions.

I piped up. 'Is Tin Can Ally around?'

The cam-net squasher, shook his head in remonstration. 'Fuckin' 'ell, mate. Don't call him that if you want to see another NAAFI break. It's Cpl Allinson to you.'

'Sorry, Ssgt Jeans told me to ask for Tin Can Ally.'

'Yeah, well he can get away with it, you can't. He's out the back sorting out one of the Rovers. 18 GB 64 I think.'

I headed out to the Land Rover bay. I could see a row of about 15 of them, all with trailers attached. Dotted sporadically around them were soldiers in green coveralls. Some were painting, some were checking tyre pressures and others just seemed to be loafing about, like the guys in the stores, ready to burst into action if a figure of authority appeared. The Rover marked 18 GB 64 was directly to my front, and a large, coverall-clothed arse was sticking out of it. I tapped on the side panel of the vehicle and said, 'Cpl Allinson?'

The guy inside jumped, and there was a fizzing noise, before he emerged rubbing the back of his head with a filthy right hand. 'For fuck's sake, mate. Never bang on a wagon when someone's doing batteries.' He climbed down and shook my hand. 'Pete Allinson.'

'Eddy Nugent. Sorry about that. Ssgt Jeans told me to come down and see you to get put on RATT Delta.'

'This is Delta.' He grinned and crooked his thumb back over his shoulder to the vehicle he'd just been working on. 'I'm the Det Commander, so it looks like you're me new sprog.'

He looked like he'd really been in the wars – his nose was squashed flat and his whole head looked slightly out of shape. I found out later what had happened: he'd been working under a trailer which was held up by a jerry can when he'd accidentally kicked the jerry can away. The front end of the trailer had come down on him, with the big towing eye catching him smack in the face. It had been lunchtime, so he'd lain there for some time, with just his nose and mouth protruding from the centre circle of the eye, trying to call for help. With his face being so compressed in the eye, his screams had been reduced to a quiet, 'Hoooouuullp.' After 15 minutes, a Troop Staffy had stopped by the compound to warm down after a run and heard someone calling. He later said that it had sounded like a Dutch child. When they got the trailer off him Pete was fairly bashed up, and he'd had to have extensive chunks of steelwork put into his face to keep it all together. Hence, 'Tin Can Ally'. He never got called the nickname to his face, mainly because he was on the Army Boxing team and was quite capable of doing Land Rover trailer-style damage to the face of anyone brave enough to try it. But he was a spot-on bloke, and he looked after me on the Det until he got posted out a couple of years later.

Life in the troop was fairly easy going. A standard day consisted of turning up for parade in normal working dress, which consisted of boots, lightweights, shirt and jumper in the winter, and boots, lightweight and shirt in the summer. The decision to change from winter to summer dress, or vice versa, was always taken without any regard to the weather. It would just appear on orders that the following Monday, May 1st, summer dress would come into effect, regardless of the fact that a hailstorm was expected that day. Blokes would be walking round in the pouring sleet with a flimsy KF shirt on and nipples like a fighter pilot's thumbs, whilst others would be hiding under cam nets in the troop stores, trying to conserve their body heat. At the end of the summer, the reverse decision would be made, and everyone would don jumpers in a heatwave. The first parade was usually at 0815 hrs. The troop would form up, and there might be a cursory inspection, just to make sure that nobody was in a really shit state.

After the parade you'd be fallen out to do first works parade on the vehicles. This was a bit of a joke really. You were supposed to do various checks on the wagons – lights, oil, brakes, indicators etc – but it was just a job creation scheme for the serially inactive. There isn't a lot that can go wrong on a Land Rover that's been stationary for 24 hours, but – by fuck – we'd make certain. Occasionally, you'd find an indicator lens gone. These were always getting accidentally broken. Solution: unscrew the fucked one, toss casually over the shoulder, approach the next wagon in the row, look round furtively, unscrew your new lens, look round furtively, put it on your wagon.

The victim would usually find out the next morning and shout, 'Who's nicked me fuckin' rubies?' to be met with blank stares all round. As soon as there was nobody looking, the victim would begin the cycle again.

At about 0900, a rickety old burgundy Salvation Army wagon would pull up at the back and the first brew of the day would be purchased. The wagon – the 'Sally Bash' – was staffed by the oldest man in the world. He got smaller every week. When I first got there, he could only just see over the counter and after six months he had to stand on a box to serve me. His fingers were covered in warts, and if you were really lucky, one of his spoon fingers might enjoy a quick dunk when he stirred your tea. It was best not to look, really. He also sold an assortment of rolls. Well, more of a straight choice – cheese or ham. I remember someone asking him if they could have cheese *and* ham. He looked like someone had walked across his very small grave.

Consumption of the Sally Bash brew would be spun out until about 0940, leaving you only 20 minutes to push until NAAFI break. Sometimes Pete would use this time to give me some instruction in the ways of the HF det. In Harrogate the only vehicle-mounted HF radio they'd taught us was the 321. This was a combination of TURF, SURF and radio. It took up a little corner on the breadboard in the back of the wagon and was as quiet as a mouse. The 322 was a much weightier beast. It was basically a souped-up 321, with a 250w amplifier and associated equipment. It took up the entire breadboard and generated more noise than a landing Chinook. The first lesson Pete gave me was on how to assemble it all. It looked ridiculously complicated, but Pete simplified it immediately.

'Just stack 'em all up like this.' He positioned all the separate pieces of equipment in their relevant places on the breadboard. 'Bolt 'em together.' Each piece of kit had a bracket on its base, to secure it to the item beneath. 'Then join 'em all up.' He pointed down to a huge, black ball of assorted leads. I stared, goggle-eyed, from the leads to the radios and back. I couldn't begin to work out how they went together. Pete started laughing. 'Don't look so fucking stupid, it's a piece of piss. If it'll go on, it's the right lead. Try it.'

Using his method, I selected a lead and had a look at the end. I then matched it up with a similar-sized cavity on one of the radios or amps and connected it. Incredibly, it worked, and within 10 minutes I'd successfully set up my first 322 det. I don't suppose it mattered that I didn't have a clue what I'd just done. Pete whacked the power on and it all made the right noises, so we were happy. When I stepped back out of the wagon and looked at the 322 in all its glory, it resembled the controls on Flash Gordon's spaceship, only more dated, with its clunky black dials and brass, right-angled connectors. Whirring noises would sporadically emerge from the radio, barely piercing the overpowering jet engine noises of the fans on the amp. It was state-of-the-art stuff, and no mistake.

After one of Pete's impromptu radio lessons, it was time for NAAFI break. There'd be a bit of a sprint on, as the NAAFI didn't stock too many of the nice pies. The contract had been won by Ginsters. If you got to the shop early, you could enjoy a beef and onion slice or a steak and kidney pie. If you got held back, it was the dreaded ploughman's pasty. They were minging, and obviously in plentiful supply. A lot of people would then retire the stores to eat their snack. This was more convivial than the NAAFI, but you did have to be on the lookout for sneak thieves. It only happened to me once. I'd just got back in the stores with my Ginsters and a bottle of Lucozade and I left them down on a bench while I nipped to the bog. I couldn't have been gone for any more than 30 seconds, but when I got back I found both had been nicked. Whoever had done it had screwed the lid back on the empty bottle and carefully re-inserted the little silver pie tray into the wrapper. Sitting on top of it was a Post-It note. I picked it up and read it. 'Mmmm,' he'd written. 'That was nice. Cheers, loser.'

I had to take my hat off at his speed and audacity.

By the time NAAFI break was over, it was half past ten, leaving us with an hour-and-a-half to push until lunchtime. Unless there was something specific to fix, or pretend to fix, somebody would think of a stupid job for us to do. One new OC Squadron decided we should change all our cam-nets. Cam-nets always looked the same. A large expanse of green netting, covered randomly in brown and green cam squares made of nylon. They were draped over vehicles in the field to break up the outline. This officer announced that squares were not naturally-occurring shapes in the wild, and that we should change them for triangles. I think the MOD had just spent £20,000 teaching him this on a course, and he was keen to apply his new knowledge. Nobody pointed out that triangles were equally uncommon. A normal cam-net was about the size of the penalty area on a football pitch, so this was no small task. We had to cut off every cam square, snip them in half and then re-attach them in a random pattern. It took us about a week, with everyone chuntering for the entire duration. The combined under-the-breath muttering of over 100 men is something to behold.

Then the nets were inspected with great ceremony. They all passed, apart from the one prepared by Dave 'Crazy Legs' Crane. Dave was the Corps Orienteering Champion, but I've never met anyone thicker. He was legendarily stupid: on one famous occasion, he took a boot to the stores to exchange. When asked where its partner was, he replied that there was nothing wrong with that one. When it came to the nets, he'd let no-one down. He'd done exactly as he was supposed to do, but when he sewed the triangles back on he thought he'd be clever and pair them up to make squares. The RSM hollered at him for about 10 minutes.

A year after the great cam-net switch, it was decided by another new OC Squadron that triangles were not naturally-occurring shapes in the wild and that we should revert to the squares. Maybe Dave was just ahead of his time.

Lunch was from 12 till 1pm. Some of the keener lads would manage to squeeze in a run instead of eating. The rest would troop off to the cookhouse, followed by a quick watch of *Neighbours* before getting back down on parade by five-to-one. The received wisdom about British squaddies, that they are hard-headed, dangerous individuals with a penchant for casual violence, could have been completely undone by a bit of fly-on-the-wall in Bongo Battery 1310hrs. Large men would be engaged in earnest conversation as to whether Scott was really right for Charlene, or whether Madge just needed to clear her throat to stop sounding like Marlon Brando.

The afternoons were just a longer version of the mornings, where we tried to find things to do until 1630. The Sally Bash would show up around three to serve another round of wart-poisoned brews to break the monotony, but the idea was, if possible, to get yourself sent on an errand. This meant, effectively, the afternoon off. One day, I was sent to the Marconi factory in Southampton to return some equipment that the unit had been trialling. Joey Donaldson came with me. He'd passed P-Company by then and was now resplendent in his wings and leather-banded beret. We turned up at Marconi, parked the Land Rover at the front of the building and walked in. The receptionist had more than a passing resemblance to Olive from *On The Buses*.

'Can I help you?' she squeaked.

'We're here to drop some kit off.' I looked down at the delivery note. 'To Ken Sharples.'

'I'll see if he's in.' She picked up the receiver of her desk phone, punched in four numbers and waited for a response.

'Oh, hello, Ken. It's Diane on the front desk. I have two men here with some equipment for you. Pardon? Hang on, I'll ask. Are you from the Army?'

We were wearing camouflage and berets and we looked at each other quizzically before Joey responded. 'Yeah, just tell him we're from 5th Airborne.'

She nodded and returned to the call. 'One of the gentlemen is called Cliff D'Airborn.'

We laughed all the way back to Aldershot. I always thought that if I ever took up acting I'd use it as my stage name.

Finally, at 4.30pm each day – excepting the obligatory Wednesday sports afternoons – we'd form up as a troop and be knocked off for the day. Everyone would go to the cookhouse for tea, and then your evening would be your own. This riveting itinerary went on for week after week. The big exception to this routine was during the run up to an exercise. Because of the nature of the unit, people took going on exercise quite seriously, so they'd have you preparing for one week prior to deployment. Lots of inspections, making sure everybody's archaic radios were good enough for one more roll of the dice, and that all the gear required had been packed. The wagon kit list for a two-week exercise was enormous. By the time you'd crammed it all in to the Land Rover and trailer, there was just enough room for a couple of humans to shoehorn their way in. We looked like the Beverly Hillbillies when we were driving out of camp.

Most of the exercises were done on Salisbury Plain, with occasional diversions to Otterburn or Catterick (Hatterick as it was known to the para-trained lads). Prior to leaving, we were forced at gunpoint to watch a video which detailed the environmental dos and don'ts on Salisbury Plain Training Area (SPTA). Officers would be stood at the door of the lecture theatre with bayonets fixed to prevent us leaving. It was mind-numbing in the extreme, and consisted of a Robin Cook look-alike pointing at signs of various colours and shapes and then explaining their meanings in earnest tones. His intentions were good, but had the opposite effect to the one desired. Telling belligerent squaddies when and where they can't shit is asking for trouble. After 45 minutes listening to Cooky preaching, you could see the resolve materialising on peoples' faces and you knew that, first chance they got, they were going to curl one down on some rare flower.

We'd usually get to our exercise location in the middle of the night. The convoy of Land Rovers were supposed to slip quietly into position but unfortunately the locations were always in the middle of the woods somewhere so there would be lots of cursing, bumpers hitting trees and guides frantically waving torches to try and direct the vehicles. As soon as we got into our location, we would set the detachments up. Our portion of the headquarters consisted of four vehicles, backed on to a 12x12 tent. The tent had two canvas socks at either end, and these were fixed over the rear of the Land Rovers to provide a light-proof seal. Tables and seats would be set up in the floor space of the tent to provide an area where we would process and distribute the messages we received over the teleprinters.

Our HQ was pretty far back from the action. In fact, the only formation further back from the front line was the Brigade Maintenance Area or BMA. The abbreviation was more commonly translated as Bloody Miles Away in reference to its proximity to the trenches.

For the para-trained lads, it was rather different. They would jump in from a C130 Hercules, with a bergan full of radio batteries and kit strapped to their legs that weighed about the same as a Fiat Uno. Once they'd landed, if they hadn't shattered all the bones in their legs, they would chuck the bergans on and tab to a pre-designated spot, usually six or seven miles away and then set up comms when they got there. That was what all the Pre-Para and P-Company training was about.

Back in Delta Group Headquarters, as soon as we had set all our masts and radios up, we dropped into a standard shift system of four hours on, four hours off. If you weren't on shift you were supposed to eat or sleep. Both activities were carried out in your shell scrape, which had to be dug as soon as comms had been established. Once the set-up had been completed, things were quite dull. A regular flow of practice traffic would be transmitted to demonstrate the availability of the circuits to the command structure. About the only highlight during a given 24-hour cycle was waking the next guy up for shift. You were supposed to give him a shake 10 minutes before you came off, to give him time to come round and make his way back to the tent from his scratcher. Obviously, whoever you were waking up would be as grumpy as fuck and really unhappy at the prospect of leaving his beautifully-warm sleeping bag to go and sit in the back of a freezing Land Rover having loud Morse blasted into his tortured ears. When you woke him up with a bit of a prod from your boot, the response would come, from deep inside the bag, 'Right, I'll be there in a minute.'

You'd go back to the tent and wait for five minutes. Then you'd go back out to him and get a bit more vocal.

There'd be loads of this to-ing and fro-ing, and by the time you handed over to him 15 minutes of your precious sleep would have been eaten up. Of course, when he came to wake you up four hours later, the pantomime would be repeated.

In the mornings we'd have the usual stand-to at first light. If you were on shift you didn't have to bother, but if you were sleeping you had to get up. The Squadron were keen on this sort of stuff. No staying in your sleeping bags. They wanted you lying down, out of your bag, and in a good firing position. The RSM and the OC Squadron would tour the shell scrapes, and anyone caught dozing would get a rollicking. They always took the same route, so you could spot when they were getting close. I used to lie on my back, facing into the compound with my helmet on back-to-front and my rifle pointing back across my shoulder. This gave the impression, in the limited light of breaking dawn, of a perfectly good defensive position. That allowed me to stay warm in my bag until the RSM was about three scrapes away. I'd then adopt a more conventional pose, and he would pass by without a word.

You were always be waiting for Endex to be called. Speculation would always circulate that for some, unspecified reason, the exercise was going to finish early. It never did. The exercise would always finish as planned, usually on the Friday morning. There would be a quick teardown, followed by a mad rush back to camp. The role of the unit dictated that nobody would knock off until the wagons were all ready to redeploy. This meant that you only had the rest of Friday to turn the whole detachment round. The blokes would work like Trojans to try and get finished before four o'clock. Some wanted to get home to various parts of the country and had mental images of traffic jams getting longer and longer. The rest of us just wanted to get a shower and get out on the beer. If a payday had occurred whilst you were out in the field, the desire to get it spent enhanced the work frenzy. Clean all the kit, washdown and POL the wagon, get all broken kit into the techs, re-pack the trailer and sort out the cam-net. The OC would come round once all the work was complete and inspect all the dets. If they were to his liking, he'd give an eagerly-anticipated nod and we were free to go.

During one of the turnarounds, an accident occurred that helped me understand what Pete had been on about when he told me never to bang on a wagon when someone was doing their batteries.

One of the jobs was to get the radio batteries disconnected and check their electrolyte levels. The four 12v radio batteries, each about the size of a portable telly, were connected in series and parallel and sat underneath the breadboard with a gap of about three inches between them. The proper way to remove them was to take all the radio equipment off the breadboard and undo the four bolts that held the breadboard in place. You could then move it out of the way and gain free access to the batteries from above. Of course, this was far too sensible for most of us. To save ourselves having to mess about with the radios, we would prefer to take our chances with the tiny gap between the bottom of the breadboard and the lugs of the batteries. It could be done, but it was akin to safecracking. To remove the connecting leads from the lugs took watchmaker-like precision. You would have to lie on the floor of the wagon and crawl forward until you could get your arms in over the top of the batteries. Your head was crooked sideways to get a good look at what you were doing. Using an adjustable spanner, you would then start loosening the lug bolts. The restricted space available meant that you could only turn the adjustable a couple of centimetres before removing it and putting it back on the bolt. To add to the excitement, parts of the breadboard were made of metal. If the adjustable touched them, an excellent electrical connection was made, resulting in lots of blue sparks and burnt facial hair. It was customary when walking past a wagon, where this nerve-wracking operation was taking place, to give one of the side panels a good whack with the flat of the palm. It was what is known in the trade as a cunt's trick. The person inside, already on tenterhooks, and with a single bead of stress-induced sweat about to drip off the end of his nose, would jump, causing him to twat his head on the underside of the breadboard and arc the batteries.

This is what happened to Jimmy Curry.

Unfortunately for him, when the battery arced, it blew up. I was in the next wagon along. The contained percussion was similar to the sound of a depth charge exploding. There was a gap of about half a second before Jimmy came piling out of the back of his wagon, clawing at his face, screaming, 'My eyes, my eyes.'

Some of the acid from one of the batteries must have got in there. He went off, blindly running round the wagon compound. He was a bastard to catch: by the time he ran into the wing mirror of one of the other Land Rovers, there were six of us chasing after him. We pinned him down, writhing and gnashing like Linda Blair in *The Exorcist*, and Brummy Jenkinson ran to the med-centre to get one of the butchers as Pete Ellinson shouted, 'Get some water to rinse the acid away.'

We all ran to our wagons, got the water bottles out of our webbing and started emptying the contents into his eyes. It started to have some effect and he began to calm down, until I drained a pint of super-strength Screech into his red-raw peepers. He started yelling like a Japanese soldier on a suicide charge. The Screech must have had a higher PH value than the battery acid, and they were combining to melt his face like a Nazi who'd just opened the Ark of the Covenant.

Fortunately for Jimmy, and me, a medic quickly turned up with loads of eyewash and distilled water, and sorted him out. They said later that the acid hadn't been too bad, but the Screech could have permanently blinded him.

Unfortunately for Jimmy, as far as the Squadron was concerned the accident was his fault, so they charged him £85 to replace the busted battery. When he went in on Orders to sign the charge sheet, he still had patches over both eyes and had to have his hand directed to the document by the RSM. He could have been signing anything.

Everybody learnt a valuable lesson from the experience and always accessed their batteries in a safe way from that moment onwards. Did they fuck. At the end of the next exercise, there were more blue sparks and acrid smoke issuing from the back of the wagons than ever before. It was like the welders' section of a School of Construction.

* * * * *

As soon as the OC had given the Caesarean thumbs up, everybody would bomb-burst from the square as quickly as possible. There was a good reason for this. You were guaranteed that one of the Senior NCOs or Officers would remember a job that needed doing and the slowest Tom would get gripped and find himself working for another hour or two while the rest of us got scrubbed up and headed down town to blow our wages.

Despite the fact that I was in Aldershot for four years, my non para-trained status meant that some of the pubs were permanently out of bounds, and going drinking could still be a risky venture from time to time. On the whole, though, it was a great place to go out, get drunk and meet ladies of dubious moral fibre.

A normal night out would start in McDonalds, a bit of pre-session carbohydrate being considered the height of good planning. People complain that McDonalds has homogenised the High Street, making everything look and taste the same no matter where you are in the world. There is obviously some truth in that, but you only had to look out the windows of the Aldershot branch to know exactly where you were. There was always some sort of drama unfolding on the street. Usually it was a domestic dispute, but occasionally it would be something more juicy. I remember sitting in the window once with a couple of lads. We were having a laugh at a guy from 3 Para who was having a kip in Rumbelows' doorway. It was 7 o'clock on a Saturday evening, so he'd obviously had a bit of a day of it. As we were watching, a Military Police Land Rover rolled up quietly beside him. The two occupants smiled to each other as they climbed out of the vehicle and donned their red forage caps. We all looked at each other and Willie Edwards said, 'Fucking wankers, he'll be in jail tonight.'

'Brave bastards aren't they?' said Scouse Marriott. 'They'll only pick up the ones who are sleeping. There's probably a brawl going on in the Rat Pit, but you won't catch 'em anywhere near that, the tossers.'

MPs aren't well thought of generally, but they were particularly despised in Aldershot. They seemed to spend most of their time catching people urinating in bushes or staggering home from the pub. It was dead easy for them to get a bloke bounced for the catch-all charge of 'bringing the Army into disrepute.' It was nothing to them, but for whoever had been charged it meant jail time or a fine, or both. If there was anything happening that required bravery to deal with, they could be relied upon to be on the other side of the county.

Sniggering, one of the monkeys approached the dozing Para while the other called it in on the radio. It was an easy pinch for them, an additional drunk to add to the quota. Or so they thought. God knows what he'd been dreaming about, but as soon as the MP touched him, the Para was on his feet and swinging. The first punch landed dead centre in the MP's face and sent his cap spinning across the pavement. The second shot was an awesome right-hand haymaker which caused the monkey to bounce his head off the Rumbelows window and collapse to the floor.

McDonalds was double-glazed, so we were watching without the benefit of sound. It added a surreal touch to the proceedings and made it all the more riveting. The whole of the clientele and staff were glued. As soon as it was apparent that monkey number one would play no further part, everyone's attention switched to the other one, who was now jabbering into his handset like a Vietnam-era US Marine calling in a contact. If he'd played it a bit cooler and kept quiet, the drunken Para might not have noticed him. Now, he headed for the vehicle. The MP dropped the handset and plotted his escape. A lethal game of 'tig' began. It was like watching a couple of kids chasing each other around a kitchen table. The MP had obviously called for reinforcements and was trying to keep as much of the Land Rover as he could between himself and his attacker. The Para was equally determined to put lumps on the monkey before his mates arrived for having the cheek to wake him up. Various spectators in the restaurant with us were adding touches of commentary.

'Ten quid says he fills him in.'

'Nah the rest of 'em will be here in a minute.'

But then the monkey fell for the oldest trick in the book. As he went round the back of the wagon and out of sight for just a second, the Para switched back and ducked low. They met by the passenger side door, right in front of the burger-eating crowd. Before he had time to turn round, the MP received two jabs to the chin and dropped like a stone, to the accompaniment of an impromptu 'Hurrah!' from the McDonalds seating area. The Para was eager to finish him off and moved towards him, fists clenched. He was just drawing back to deliver the next punch when he suddenly stopped and looked up and down the road like a meerkat. We couldn't hear the sirens but he obviously could. He pinpointed the direction the sound was coming from and went off like a roadrunner in the other direction. Ten seconds later, an identical MP Land Rover crammed with the red-hatted scoundrels flew past. I don't think they ever caught him, and of course nobody in McDonalds had seen a thing.

Another time, we saw two blokes from 1 Para having a bunny hop race the length of the high street. Not especially interesting, you'd think, but it was one o'clock on a Sunday afternoon, and the only clothes they had on were their socks. The good, church-going people of Aldershot were rightfully horrified by the shrivelled cocks and bad squaddie tans on display. The next time I saw the pair was the following Tuesday. They were getting marched to the cookhouse by an RP Sergeant at an incredible rate of knots with saucepan helmets on their heads and no laces in their shoes. Somebody had obviously been waiting to wave them over the finish line.

After the McDonalds, we'd usually conduct a general tour of the pubs, drinking as much beer and avoiding as many fights as we could. The Queens and The South Western, obviously, and maybe The Trafalgar, and onto The George for last orders. The George was really strange, in that one side was for craphats and the other was for para-trained personnel: you transgressed at your peril.

On the way back, I'd always stop for a pizza. No matter how drunk I was, or however close I was to death from alcohol poisoning, I could always say, 'Large ham and mushroom, wi' extra mushroom.' It must have been some weird culinary auto-pilot. I remember being back in the room one night, scoffing my last slice, when Joey Donaldson came back in, sporting a bust lip and a crazy hairdo.

'You'll never guess what's fuckin' happened, Eddy?' Without waiting for me to reply, he carried on. 'I've just been mugged by three blokes from 1 Para.'

This was surprising. Despite there being lots of crime in Aldershot, it was all of the drunken brawl variety. Theft of property or money from the person was far more rare.

'How much did they get?' I said.

'Fuck all, they just nicked my Kentucky.'

In the true spirit of the man who has had too much to drink, Joey had bought himself a bargain bucket, with enough chips and chicken for four starving dockers. He'd been tucking into it, on his way up Gun Hill which ran to the left of the hospital. It was a particularly dark stretch of road, but a good short cut. When he was halfway up, the three muggers had jumped out from a bush and confronted him.

'They said, "Give us your food",' Joey continued, whilst applying a fat wad of toilet roll to his lower lip. 'I told them to fuck off and they jumped me, the bastards. They gave me a bit of a shoeing, but once they were sure I was going to stop fighting, they just grabbed the scoff and bimbled back towards town.'

'What did you do?'

'What could I do? They were all twice my size. I did what anyone else would do in the situation. I waited 'til they were about 50 metres away and shouted "wankers" after them.'

I started laughing. 'That's it, mate. You fucking tell 'em.'

He'd started to see the funny side and smiled. 'As soon as I said it, one of 'em came running back up the hill. I thought I was going to get another panelling, but he only wanted the wet wipes. They must have fell out of the bucket while they were doing me over.'

When the rest of the Squadron heard about the mugging, Joey was ribbed mercilessly for two weeks by blokes walking past him doing chicken impressions. Everybody that used Gun Hill for the next month or so was careful to have eaten their takeaway before they started the ascent, and any member of 1 Para encountered on guard for a long time after was viewed with suspicion.

If you were lucky, you got the chance to take something more than a pizza back to the block. Lots of the women who frequented the bars in Aldershot were renowned badge collectors, and were attempting to achieve the proud personal goal of shagging someone from every Corps or Regiment in the town. This could work to your advantage. No matter how grotesque your haircut or dated your fashion sense, if your cap badge was on her 'to do' list, you could still see some action.

I spent entire evenings wandering up to women, ready to work my limited charms on them, only to be rebuffed at the first attempt. 'Alright there? Haven't seen you in here before. Can I get you a drink?'

'What unit are you in?'

'Erm, 5 Airborne Sig Squadron.'

'Sorry, love, I just need a Gunner to complete the set, then I can move on to the Navy.'

When you did strike lucky, you counted your blessings. Let's face it, a squaddie isn't much of a catch in the copping-off stakes. She wasn't going to get whisked away to a bachelor pad and serenaded for the evening before being made love to in ways she'd only seen in her dreams. No, she'd be taken to a squalid room full of empty pizza boxes and shagged badly on a single bed whilst the guy in the next bed shouted at her to keep the fucking noise down. To make matters worse, you could be guaranteed that someone else would be watching silently over the partition, with his eyes set to 'record', doing a bit of research for his next wank.

Incredibly, some girls actually wanted to stay the night. Sharing a single bed was no fun. After making a few unsuccessful attempts to get comfortable in the spoons formation, you'd generally give up and go for something more practical. Top to toeing wasn't the most romantic way to spend a whole night in bed with a woman, but it meant you got a decent night's sleep, even if your companion would have nightmares about your P-Company-ravaged feet for months.

In the morning they'd leave. To get out of camp from the Signals block meant a stroll through the entire grounds before you reached the camp exit. You'd see them leaving on a Saturday morning if you were on back gate, and they always looked a bit forlorn. The outfit they'd been wearing the night before, in which they'd looked like a million lira, had spent the evening on the floor of the singlies block, after being unceremoniously removed by her lover. There would be stains all over it, some identifiable, others more mysterious. This was OK if they were only walking round the corner, but travelling home on the bus looking like one of the dancers from the *Thriller* video can't have been much fun.

For a little while, some crackpot from one of the other blocks used to get busy with an air rifle. It only happened a couple of weekends running, but he managed to gain the name 'The Saturday Morning Sniper'. He always got women as they headed up the path towards the cookhouse and he exclusively went for 'bum shots'. The average Aldershot lady made it almost impossible for him to miss. I remember leaving the cookhouse one morning and heading back to the block with a brew. I chanced upon two women adopting excellent Section battle drills to escape his attentions. Their movements drew a small crowd, who couldn't help but admire their speedy dashes and effective use of available cover. The fact that it was all done in high heels and mini skirts was all the more impressive.

OFF TO BELIZE

The routine of weeks of tediously pretending to work on wagons, followed by rapid bursts of activity, prior to, during, and after an exercise continued, and before I knew it a year had flown by.

I'd managed to pass another Pre-Para and fail another P-Company in that period. There was no injury to hide behind this time. I hadn't prepared properly and only got through by the skin of my teeth. I spent an hour convincing Ssgt Herbert that I wouldn't let him down in Depot Para and didn't even last a week. I nearly went AWOL: the idea of explaining myself to Herbert made me shake like a shitting dog. When I went up to his office, he saw me through the glass panel in the closed door. He was on the phone, but stopped talking the moment he spotted me. He said a couple more words and hung up. He got up from his desk, visibly angry, and lumbered towards the door. I nearly ran for it, but he'd have caught me so I didn't bother.

He opened the door, and spoke slowly and quietly, through gritted teeth. 'What... the... fuck... are… you… doing... back... here?'

The only thing to do was be brave and take my bollocking.

'I've been sent back, Staff.'

'Why?' His voice was still quiet, but the threat was palpable.

'Everybody was running faster than me, Staff.' I didn't mean to sound flippant but it just came out that way.

'Nugent, you are a fucking disgrace. If I had my way, I'd post you out today, with the word SHITBAG tattooed across your forehead in red ink.'

I was no barrack room lawyer, but I knew enough about Queens Regs to know that this wasn't a permissible punishment.

'Staff.'

He shook his head in disgust. 'Get your excuse for a body out of my sight. Report back to Ssgt Jeans in your troop.'

He shut the door in my face and went back to his desk. The reception I got back at the troop was a bit kinder. I'd worked hard enough over the year to be quite well thought of, and despite still being a craphat had made quite a few friends. I got loads of earache for coming off the course and was called various exotic names, the most splendid being a 'lazy, shit-munching wankbag.' It abated after a month or so. I'd obviously performed better than I thought, because – just over a year after I arrived – I was tipped the wink that I was going to be promoted to Lance Corporal. Out of a pool of 12 Siggies, there were three of us: myself, Joey and Mark Gorse, an older soldier who'd been sweating on promotion for a couple of years.

Ssgt Jeans gave us the news early, and warned us to keep quiet about it. It was a Wednesday, so we had Squadron PT the next morning, but Joey wanted to celebrate the news. The plan was to have four or five pints and toast each other's success. Of course, it never worked out like that. We had ten pints and bought a pizza before starting the walk up Hospital Hill to the back gate. There was a building site halfway up the hill, and for reasons known only to himself, Joey wanted to eat his pizza in one of the house shells that were springing up in the compound. In my drunken state, it seemed like a splendid idea. I climbed the fence first. Joey threw the pizzas over and followed. We sat in the footings of a soon-to-be living room and ate our scoff.

'Turn the fucking telly over, Eddy,' Joey shouted from his breezeblock armchair.

'Do it yourself, I'm checking out the drinks cabinet.' I'd found a standpipe and took a long swig from the tap, hanging there like a calf on a teat.

We finished our food and got up. As we stepped over the footings and headed back to the fence, Joey stopped and, with a look of pissed concern, said, 'Did you set the burglar alarm?'

'You're always asking me that, course I did,' I replied. We neared the fence, laughing at our own hilarious double act.

'Hey, Eddy, fucking check that out.' I looked over. Joey was stood by the edge of a great big hole, about eight feet in diameter and of a similar depth. A foot or so of oil-stained water sloshed about in the bottom. As I peered over the edge, watching my footing, Joey nudged me. 'Give us a hand with this.'

He'd spotted a cement mixer that was teetering on the edge of the hole, and his intention was plain. My sense of social responsibility had disappeared with the ninth pint, so I gave him a hand and we shoved it into the hole, taking great satisfaction in watching it almost disappear beneath the water. As we turned round, my balls dropped. They'd dropped already, obviously, immediately prior to the onset of puberty, but the shock was great enough to make them retract as far as my ribs before they tumbled back into their appropriate scrotal sacs. A military police car was parked right by the fence. The lights were off and they'd obviously seen everything. They got out of the car with undisguised glee on their faces.

'Good night out, lads?' asked the one nearest to me.

'Nice bit of criminal damage to round it off?' his mate chipped in.

Joey looked at me with the sort of expression he'd worn before the PT sessions on Pre-Para, but I was no use to him. We were absolutely bang to rights. Even as I contemplated a runner, another monkey wagon pulled up on the other side of the building site and all the fight went out of me.

We were put in front of the Squadron OC the next morning and warned for orders. Everyone I met for the next two days bollocked me and we actually got charged on the day we were supposed to be promoted. Mark Gorse went in before us and came out beaming after winning the first tape of his career. As soon as he went past us, the RSM rounded on me and Joey. Stood there in our two dress, we wilted under his verbal onslaught. 'Right, you pair of fucking halfwits, listen to me. I'm fucking glad you got caught. The idea of two little fucking vandals like you getting a promotion makes me want to commit murder. You've dragged this Squadron's reputation through the dirt, and you will fucking pay, of that you can be certain. Listen in to my word of command.'

We were sprint-marched into the OC's office and made to mark time for a whole minute before we were given the halt. We stood there panting and received another rifting from the OC, only this time with less swearing and longer words. The sentiment was the same. Our punishment was a £150 fine each and seven days' ROPs, which were to start that night. We were bounced out of his office at the same speed and sent back to the troop.

ROPs are a bastard. ROPs that start on a Friday night are a bigger bastard, and ROPs that start on a Friday night on Montgomery Lines are the biggest bastard of all.

It was only seven days, but we were worked like dogs, doing the shittiest jobs possible. We had to weed the parade square. We painted bollards black, then green, then black again. We cleaned toilets with wire wool. We had to scrape of all the wax floor polish that had accumulated on the skirting boards of the guardroom, armed with only a cookhouse spoon.

Mixed in with all of this was a number two dress inspection at 0630, a working dress inspection at 1200 and another two dress inspection at 2200. All the inspections were done by the duty SNCO of the day. If he was a tosser, we would get called back for repeat inspections until he was satisfied.

It was a nightmare.

As a deterrent though, it was marvellous. I didn't drop another disciplinary bollock for the rest of my time in Aldershot. This wasn't down to any age-related increasing maturity, but an overwhelming fear of crawling on my hands and knees across an area of concrete the size of an airport runway pulling up dandelions.

After my punishment, I knuckled down in the troop and kept my nose extremely clean. When another nine months had passed, I got the delayed promotion and became Lance Corporal Nugent, Royal Corps of Signals.

I was now only 16 ranks away from becoming a Field Marshal.

Within the Squadron, my life didn't change perceptibly as a result of my new rank. I remained on RATT Delta, working under Pete. The only real advantage of being a LCpl was that I was less likely to be dealt shitty jobs. Added to that, I suppose, was the slight increase in pay, which meant, in real terms, that I could afford an extra couple of pints of beer a day, and an additional, non-meat topping on my pizzas.

As soon as I'd been promoted, I was obliged to attend the Royal Signals Detachment Commander's Course (RSDCC) at 8 Signal Regiment in Catterick. It was a four-week ball-ache. Signals units from within UKLF would send all their newly-promoted men to be taught in the ways of the Corps. There was a huge cross-section of ability and intelligence on show. A lot of the lads who showed up had been in Harrogate at the same time as me. The emphasis throughout the four weeks was on leadership and military skills. Due to the role and amount of training conducted in Aldershot, lads from our unit always breezed the course. You were expected to get, at the very least, a top five finish, and we regularly provided the top student. I came fifth on mine, which I was quite happy with.

After getting back from Detties, I fell back in to the troop routine. I'd now been in the Squadron a couple of years and was considered 'not a new bloke any more'. This was nowhere near the coveted title of 'old sweat', but enough to gain a bit of respect and know everyone in the Squadron. Not being para-trained was always going to hold me back, and there was always pressure from the Training Wing to get on the next Pre-Para. They used to run about three courses a year, in January, June and September. I was keeping myself fit, but I wanted to be sure I was going to pass on my next attempt. I started training a lot harder, running distance most evenings and at weekends. This was augmented by Squadron PT. There were generally three sessions a week, Tuesday and Thursday mornings and Friday afternoons. The Friday afternoon didn't always happen if there was a lot of work on, but when we did do it, it was always a tab of anything from six to ten miles. We'd get finished at about half past three and knock off for the weekend. The Tuesdays and Thursdays were a bit more unpredictable and relied entirely on the whim of the Training Wing. It could be anything from a game of volleyball in the Gym to a six-mile Cross Country run at breakneck speed, or sometimes a go on one of the P-Company events, usually the Steeplechase or Assault Course.

There was always a huge dilemma about going on the beer the night before Squadron PT. Everyone would be scrabbling around to find out what we'd be doing, but it was very difficult to obtain information. The Training Wing enjoyed wielding this bit of power and were keen to keep the morning's activity under wraps until the last possible moment.

Generally, people thought 'fuck it' and went on the beer anyway. Most of the lads were fit enough to cope with it and were happy to suffer from some Olympic standard shuggying as a consequence of a good night out. There was a small group who actually made a point of it. As soon as they were told that we were on a BFT on this or that day, they would make plans to get absolutely blootered on the night proceeding the run. This was solely so they could say, and it was the archetypal Aldershot mentality, 'Ha, ha, seven minutes forty five, and I was on the fucking lash all night.'

Occasionally, very occasionally, we'd get an easy session. We'd turn up at Maida Gym at 0730. If the parade was at the Gym, it could be anything. A run starting in the car park, indoor assault course, circuits or battle PT, all of which were potentially knackering activities. It was too much to hope for that we'd do something dossy, but it did happen from time to time. Medicine Ball Tennis was the best laugh, though it resulted in similar injury figures to that of a company attack up a well-defended hill. A line of vaulting horses would be placed side to side across the middle of the Gym, forming a halfway line. Scores of medicine balls would be placed on the horses. The Squadron would then split into two teams who formed up on either side of the line. The game was simple. When the PTI blew the whistle, the clock would start. The aim was for the other team to have more medicine balls on their side of the line when the whistle was blown again, usually one minute later. The approved method of despatch was, with your back to the horses, to squat down with the med ball on the floor between your legs. Using your arms and legs as pistons, you would then explode upwards, launching the bugger as far and high as physically possible. There would be 30 people on each side of the line duplicating this manoeuvre, and it was always bedlam. As well as trying to get your own balls over, you had to dodge all the incoming from the other side – a bit like a recreational version of a sustained mortar attack. A medicine ball is made of old brown leather and weighs about the same as a newly-born hippo. If one landed on you from a reasonable height, it would flatten you. By the end of the game, there would always be a slack handful of people lying around on the floor groaning, and the worst injury sustainable was a direct hit to the head from immediately above. If you didn't see it coming, the medicine ball would force your head down through the gap between your shoulder blades leaving you looking like Sandy Toksvig or Gladstone Small.

I had a really good Christmas that year. It was my Dad's 50th birthday party, and I did lots of catching up with mates and family that I hadn't seen for a while. As soon as we got back though, we were straight back into it. There were enough exercises going on to take us all the way through to summer. Having continued to increase my strength and fitness, I'd asked to stick my name down for Pre-Para in September 1990. About a month before, I was upstairs in the troop offices, putting all the mail into the relevant pigeon holes. I overheard Ssgt Jeans talking to one of the other Lance Corporals, Johnny Bergsen.

'You've got no chance, I'm never going to get a replacement now.'

'Honestly Staff, I wouldn't ask if it wasn't really important.'

Johnny was due to be going out to Belize the following week. The squadron manned three rear link detachments on a six-month rotational basis. It was considered a real swan, and this was the first time I'd ever heard anyone trying to get out of it. This was Johnny Bergsen, though. He was the most henpecked soldier I'd ever encountered. His wife used to turn up at the troop sometimes and berate him for committing unspecified crimes. As well as having to listen to his wife, he'd also be able to hear the rest of the troop, behind her back, making the universally-understood 'Hock Tssshhh' sound whilst brandishing imaginary whips to indicate his put-upon status. As time drew close to their enforced half-year separation, which Johnny must have been looking forward to immensely, she'd started trying to scupper his escape. This had resulted in him having to beg his Troop Staffie not to send him to Belize because his wife couldn't cope without him. What he actually meant was that she wouldn't have anyone to shout at without him.

'Right, well, if you can find someone who fancies it, fair enough, but I can't see it,' said Ssgt Jeans dismissively.

'Cheers, Staff.'

As he left Jeans' office, I blocked his path with my grin. 'I'll fucking do it.'

'What?'

'Your Belize, I'll do it.' There was no chance I was going to let him past me to ask someone else. There was no need to worry, he was as chuffed as I was.

We knocked back on Staff Jeans' door and got asked in.

'What's it now, Lcpl Bergsen?' he said impatiently.

'Lcpl Nugent says he'll take my spot, Staff.'

Jeans looked over at me and then back to Bergsen. 'That was a bit fucking quick. Did you have this set up before you came to see me?'

'No, Staff. Eddy was outside doing the mail.'

I nodded in assent.

Jeans sat there for a few seconds. 'OK, Bergsen you're off the hook. Nugent, go and see Corporal Smith. Let him know what's going on. There are six of you including him. You'll need to get your skates on. All the rest of the lads have had their jabs and been issued their troppies.'

'No probs, Staff.'

'Get going then, if you get sorted quickly, you can get off on a few days leave before you have to emplane.'

Fucking hell, it just got better and better. A few days' leave, followed by a six month holiday in Central America at the taxpayer's expense. I immediately went and found Mark Smith and put him in the picture. He was unfazed by the change to the plans, and gave me a list the length of my arm of things to do before I went on leave... injections, malaria tablets, clothing. The tropical combats were actually quite smart and comfortable – the first piece of kit I ever got out of the stores that I didn't hate the sight of. The jungle boots were quite nifty too. Well, one was. Kenny Rogers tried to fob me off with an 8 and a 9 but I was getting a bit long in the tooth to fall for any of those tricks.

The next day was hectic, but once I'd got all my gear MFO-ed and cleared from the Squadron, I was allowed to go home. We were flying out from RAF Brize Norton the following Friday, so I had a whole week off. I spent every minute I could on the beer with various family and friends and managed to steer every conversation onto Belize. It was one of those countries that you'd heard of, but whose location you couldn't point to in an atlas. I became an expert in the construction of Central American maps with ashtrays and beer mats. By my last night, my Dad knew more about the place than me. Over a final couple of pints on the Wednesday night, he said, 'I don't mind telling you, Eddy. I'm bloody envious.'

'Why's that, Dad?'

'Why do you think? You're going to be having a whale of a time in the sunshine, drinking out of coconuts and what have you. We'll all be freezing our bloody bollocks off over here.'

'It won't all be fun, there's plenty of work to do you know.'

He burst out laughing. 'My arse, you'll be on the pop from sunup to sundown. The only work you'll be doing will be on your tan.'

We both laughed, then went quiet for a couple of seconds, before he said, more seriously, 'It'll be weird, not having you around at Christmas, son. Make sure you keep in touch as much as you can. Your mum'll appreciate it.'

'I will, Dad.'

Amidst the euphoria of getting such a plum detachment, I hadn't really thought of the impact it would have on my folks. I was 21 now, and they'd got used to me being away, but not for such a long time and it would be our first Christmas apart. I made a mental note to write at least once a week and phone whenever availability and coin permitted.

The next morning, they both came with me to the train station. We had an emotional group hug on the platform, and I got on the train. As it pulled away, I could see that they were both mouthing something to me. Mum's was easy to decipher. It could only be 'elephant juice' or 'I love you'. I presumed the latter and mimed it back to her, smiling.

Dad's was a little bit more obscure. It looked like he was saying 'We are jolly'. As the train picked up a bit of speed, he could see that I hadn't yet understood, so he started to enunciate flamboyantly, like a kid trying to impress a music teacher.

The penny finally dropped.

'Wear a johnny.'

GLOSSARY

58 Pattern
Collection of belt-mounted, modular and thoroughly spongelike pouches which were first issued in the same year that Elvis did his basic training.

Army Apprentice College
Junior Army training and education facility, where soldiers learn vital skills such as weapon handling, drill and wanking undetected in an eight-man room.

Army Careers Office
First point of contact for anyone wanting to join the Army. Staffed by people who could sell a year's subscription for *Razzle* to Mary Whitehouse.

Army Catering Corps
Slop Jockey central. Attractive military employment opportunity for people who like being covered in blue plasters and having hands like *The Singing Detective*.

Army Personnel Selection Centre
A potential recruit's first two-day exposure to Army life. At this point, he can decide if sleeping on rubberised, piss-proof mattresses is right up his street, thank you very much.

Basic Fitness Test
A 1.5 mile run used to identify the regimental slugs. Failing to complete the run in the time allotted gains instant entry to dregs PT with the other wasters.

Bergan
Large rucksack worn on exercise and speed marches. Its capacious storage capacity encourages training staff to the point where a

single soldier's exercise kit list would have been adequate for the entire British Expeditionary Force of 1939.

Black Masking Tape
Substance that holds the entire British Army together, which can be used to cover any crack smaller than the San Andreas Fault.

British Army (British military version)
Heroic and chisel-jawed band of lovable rogues. Great Britain's safety, reputation and defence is its Number 1 priority. Getting pissed up and tapping off is Number 2, and gives Number 1 a run for its money.

British Army (British civilian version)
Heroic and chisel-jawed band of lovable rogues. Getting pissed up and tapping off is its Number 1 priority. Great Britain's safety, reputation and defence is Number 2, and gives Number 1 a run for its money.

Buckshee
Military unit of currency consisting of any piece of spare equipment that's not nailed down, from a pencil to a Panzer.

Bullnight
Frenzied attempt to clean the single soldiers' accommodation to an unachievable standard and an unrealistic deadline. The combination of cleaning chemicals required to scrub the block will leave all participants resembling Emile from *Robocop* (the balding ginger one who gets run over near the end).

Captain
Officer rank denoted by three pips on the shoulder. Ordinarily perceived by the lads to be good eggs. Mature enough to have experience and junior enough to have some connection with reality. However, all bets are off if the individual is a bit of a bell-end.

Chinook
Fucking big helicopter that looks less capable of flight than a moth with an underslung bowling ball. This belies their ability. A single Chinook could actually transport Catterick Garrison to Baghdad in a oner.

Commanding Officer
The bloke in charge of the whole Regiment. Every instruction he gives is interpreted by his underlings to generate the same outcome: fuck the lads about.

Commcen
Communications Centre. A military typing pool that distributes messages about the CO's birthday around the world. Though it offers undemanding indoor work, most Corps members would rather be struck about the head and body with a pick helve (see *pick helve*) than shine their arse in a commcen seat.

Compo
Army-issued field rations. Designed to bung up a recruit so effectively, that the eventual bowel movement will generate a turd that can be used as a rudimentary polevault in a POW situation.

Cookhouse
Chamber of culinary horror. Routinely avoided by single soldiers in favour of the NAAFI. Keenly frequented by bean-stealing married personnel, whose desire for free scoff has genetically stunted the development of their taste buds.

Corporal
Second promotion for a soldier denoted by two stripes and an acceptable level of top lip topiary. The most important rank in the Army and the promotional 'Beer Glass' ceiling for serial drunkards.

Craphat
Expression used by para-trained soldiers to describe every other living organism on the planet, based on the perceived crapness of

other soldiers' headgear compared to their own maroon berets. This needn't be confined to animate objects, however. It is allowable within paratrooper grammatical rules to describe a malfunctioning vehicle starter motor, for instance, as a 'fucking useless craphat'.

CS Gas
Irritant substance used to disperse large, unruly crowds. On a British Army recruit's initial NBC training, the instructors employ the same amount on one bloke that would be sufficient to quell a poll tax riot.

Daps
White, wafer-thin-soled pumps issued to recruits. Designed by the National Society for the Advancement of Shin Splints and General Lower Leg Injuries.

Death Pack
Packed lunch issued to soldiers away from camp, usually at the ranges. Named for its unappetising combination of an unspecified brand of cola, a ham and tomato sandwich which has melted the bread and a sausage roll like Tutankhamun's cock.

Detachment
Land Rover-mounted comms station consisting of radio equipment only outdated by the vehicle. Manned by a scientifically-mismatched crew who will have their first argument as the key goes into the ignition.

Double Leg
Massively kudos-generating party trick, not usually part of a magician's repertoire. A feat of penile accuracy, which requires nerves of steel and micron perfect central cock-dressing, and sees the performer deliver an equal stream of wazz down the inner seam of both jean legs.

DPM
Disruptive Pattern Material. Issued camouflage clothing, the

opportunity to wear which is the actual reason that everyone joins the Army in the first place. Seeing the world and enjoying an interesting career are mere smokescreen excuses to cover up the fact that you like the look of that funky clobber that the *Big Issue* bloke wears.

Drill
Efficient method of moving a body of soldiers from one point to another by foot. Mainly used by drill instructors as a mechanism for conducting an inter-sergeant competition entitled *'Who can jail a recruit on the flimsiest pretext.'*

Eating Irons
Knife, Fork and Spoon. Though innocuous, inanimate objects to civilians, to British Army recruits they represent an endless source for grippings and beastings.

Endex
End of Exercise. Pivotal moment in manouevres when Royal Signals soldiers can stop sending morse messages about the size of the RSM's wife's arse and return to camp.

Fezz
A dirty bastard. A soldier made unpopular by having horrific standards of personal hygiene. Most of his colleagues would rather suck a tramp's cock than be his roommate.

Fire Trench
Rain storage facility and sleeping hole for soldiers. Ideal medium for introducing new recruits to the pleasures of trench foot. It also offers a unique insight into what's going to happen to you when you die.

Four Tonner
Ubiquitous mode of military transport, also known as a Bedford or 'Robert Redford'. When used as a troop carrier it gives a matchless riding experience, offering fucked backs all round before you get past the camp gates.

Guardroom
Foul-smelling grotto which the RPs call home. By day it smells of overbrewed tea and floorwax and by night of stale farts and ciggy breath. Kept in its pristine state by stripy-suntanned prisoners.

Gurkha
Universally-loved Nepalese soldiers who fight for the crown. Feared for their ferocious history in battle. If a Gurkha pulls his kukri, it must draw blood. Likewise, if you have a crack at one of their curries it will do the same to your ricker.

Jack Wagon
A repository of lost souls in the shape of an overpainted three-quarter tonne Land Rover, used to mop up stragglers on a run or tab. Usually driven by a 20 stone lance corporal with a Master's in being unsympathetic.

Jail
The darkest recess of the guardroom, inhabited by soldiers whose behaviour has gone past 'high spirits' into the realms of fuckwittery.

Kneeling Gun Drill
Physical exercise routinely performed in British Army PT sessions but rejected by the Khmer Rouge as 'barbaric'.

Lance Corporal
First promotion for a soldier denoted by one stripe and an embarrassing attempt at a moustache, worn as a conspicuous maturity badge. Unless of mediterranean stock, the moustache will resemble a football match, having only eleven-a-side.

Lieutenant
Officer rank denoted by two pips and a lessening of the pasty complexion. Technically in charge of the troop but only in the same way that Princess Anne is in charge of the Corps.

Major
Officer rank denoted by a single crown. Normally in command of a squadron. On posting, a photo opportunity will be hastily arranged, so that they can be carried out of the camp gates on the shoulders of men who are pretending to like them.

MFO Box
Inverted Tardis, issued to soldiers deploying on operations or getting posted. It is intended to provide much-needed storage space and help with the move from one place to another. In reality, it induces a short period of introspection on the part of a soldier as he realises that his entire life can be stored in a box the size of a big coffee table.

Ministry of Defence
Governmental department paradoxically responsible for both the well-being and suffering of all soldiers.

Morse code
Series of audible dots and dashes that form a rudimentary signalling language. For apprentices, it is a skill that takes two years to learn and a lifetime to forget. Its only real use is that it enables a user to swear whilst whistling without the knowledge of the object of abuse.

MP
Military Policeman. Known as 'monkeys' to the blokes and 'redcaps' to TV producers. Advanced crimefighting training allows them to follow a piss trail until it ends at a comatose soldier (see *triple crown*).

MRS
Medical Reception Station. First line of military healthcare where a triage is executed to separate the truly sick from those simply wishing to avoid PT and/or work.

NAAFI
Navy, Army, Airforce Institute. Business which runs bars and shops on Army camps and with which soldiers generally have a

love-hate relationship. They love the pies but hate having to go to jail for smashing up a vending machine to get one.

NBC
Nuclear, Biological and Chemical. Sorts of warfare that nobody really likes much. Used by instructors to put the shits up recruits. The only time that the expression 'involuntary urination and defecation' can be used without pointing to a Triple Crown victim (See *triple crown*).

Oath of Allegiance
Attestation given by all soldiers prior to joining the Army. They agree that however ridiculous an order, they will obey it immediately with only a mild 'tut' allowed to register displeasure.

Officer Commanding
The bloke that the RSM salutes whenever physically possible.

Olive Drab
Shade of green employed by the Army for anything that isn't black. Rumoured to be the colour of the RSM's curtains, carpets, wallpaper and wife's knickers.

Pick Helve
A pick handle. Also a Poundstretcher light sabre, issued to soldiers on guard duty who can't be trusted with bullets.

Picking Up the Brass 1
The job given at the end of a range day, to the soldiers who have established that picking up empty cartridges constitutes the limit of their ballistic abilities.

Picking Up the Brass 2
To conduct financial transactions with women who offer sexual favours in return for money.

Picking Up the Brass 3
To find fault with military higher management. This is usually

done whilst stood around a three-quarter tonne Land Rover trailer and will always fail to progress up the chain of command.

Picking Up the Brass 4
Low-quality swear manual, written by two overweight ex-soldiers who are hoping to escape the mundane careers that they've fallen into since leaving the forces.

POL (POL point)
Petrol Oil and Lubricants. Lofty title given to the liquids required to keep 300-year-old Land Rovers functioning, and obtainable from a substandard garage manned by a cross between Charlie Drake and Peter Sutcliffe.

PRI shop
Camp shop selling regimental paraphernalia. Ideal source for Christmas presents if your girlfriend is into cufflinks, paper weights and squadron plaques.

Proffing
The acquisition of spare military kit using the 'five finger discount'. Not be confused with thieving, the consummate proffer is an individual admired for his resourcefulness, creativity and ability to snaffle almost anything. This includes the holy grail of the prof, the fabled third sausage from the breakfast hotplate.

PTI
Physical Training Instructor. Impossibly tanned and impeccably-groomed individuals who exhibit levels of personal vanity rarely seen outside Oscar Wilde books. Spend every waking moment devising new methods of gym-related torture which would be classified as war crimes if practised on enemy forces.

QMSI
Quarter Master Staff Instructor. Person in charge of all the PTIs. A rank only awarded to soldiers imbued with Wintonesque levels of vanity and body worship.

RAF

The Royal Air Force. Junior partner in the British Military triumvarate. Staffed entirely by people sporting moustaches more commonly seen on Victorian circus strongmen.

RATT

Radio Automatic TeleTypewriter. Method of communicating that seriously undermines a radio operator's self image as a combat communicator. Whilst Morse code can be passed off as slightly spy-like, RATT will never make the operator look like anything but Stan Laurel in combats.

Readers' Wives

Collection of photos to be found in the back pages of any low quality British porn mag and featuring the dubious charms of women who can only be described as MOT failures. It is also worthy of note that Army furniture forms the backdrop to a worrying percentage of the photographs displayed.

ROPs

Restriction of Privileges or 'jankers'. Punishment administered to unwitting drunks by the camp authorities whenever there is a backlog of shitty jobs that need doing, or a royal visit is imminent. The horror of the tasks is only ameliorated by their comedic value to the casual observer: it is really funny to watch a bloke weeding a parade square with a spoon.

Royal Corps of Signals (Rest of Army version)

Bunch of jammy, fucking arseholes who get paid too much and never get the fucking phones working on Ops.

Royal Corps of Signals (Signals version)

Wonderfully urbane collection of friendly individuals whose every living second is filled with selfless acts on behalf of their fellow soldiers.

RP
Regimental Policeman. Job within the British Army given to soldiers who have demonstrated a unique ability to be unable to perform any other task without endangering the lives of others. Soldiers moved into this post, will, regardless of their previous physiognomy, be the double of Wilfred Brambell within six months.

RSM
The only man in the regiment who, despite having no speech impediment, pronounces the words 'Left' and 'Right' as 'Doof' and 'Dipe'.

Sandhurst
Home of the Royal Military Academy. An establishment charged with issuing into society men and women who think purple cords are at the zenith of fashion.

SAS
Special Air Service. Mandatory inclusion in all books about the British Military. Mythical regiment of warriors, whose ranks are filled with taxi drivers and fat blokes who drink in your local, who can't tell you about anything they did, whilst tapping the side of their nose knowingly and shaking an empty pint pot in your direction.

Scaleyback
Derogatory term for Royal Signals soldiers used by the rest of the Army. Sometimes preceded by 'fucking' or followed by 'bastards', and usually both.

Screech
Hybrid substance comprised of Agent Orange, baking soda and Hai Karate aftershave, issued in British Army ration packs to sweeten water and remove barnacles from ship hulls.

Second Lieutenant
Figure of fun for everyone in the Army, including RPs and Slop Jockeys (see *RP* and *Slop Jockey*).

Sergeant

Third promotion for a soldier, denoted by three stripes and a thickening of the moustache. Promotion to this rank is normally accompanied by groundless accusations from junior soldiers that the promotee has 'turned on the fuckin' lads, the bastard'.

Sex Liar

Outwardly normal fantasist who claims to have had 'carnival knowledge' of a farcically-inflated number of women. If his claims were true he would be responsible for 79% of the UK annual birth rate. He frequently awards himself the sex-liar's highest honour, the MDC (Mother-Daughter Combo).

Shell Scrape

The little brother of the fire trench (see *fire trench*) which is equally good at storing water. Meant to be dug to enough depth to shelter a fully-grown man. If done just before last light, a dog with worms dragging its arse across the grass would effect a more adequate excavation.

Shuggy

To attempt to continue running whilst undergoing violent dry retching, giving the sufferer the appearance of Oliver Reed at full moon.

Shit Magnet

Soldier so drenched in bad karma that anything and everything can and will go wrong for him. Shit magnets are destined to complete their service at the rank with which they left training. Any promotion is immediately followed by catastrophe, resulting in a swift snakes and ladders-style return to the original status.

Signalman

The rank achieved by Royal Signals soldiers upon completion of training. Generally considered a transitional rank, most soldiers can hope to progress beyond this stage within a year, unless they are a shit magnet (see *shit magnet*).

Slop Jockey

Slang term for an Army chef. So protective are they of mealtime portions that it is generally perceived that they receive commission on leftover food. As lethal with a hotplate spatula as Bruce Lee was with his nunchucks.

SLR

Self Loading Rifle. Precursor to the SA80 and fondly remembered by all soldiers that were good at shooting. For the less able, its main feature was the rearsight's ability to split your eyebrow in two upon discharge of the weapon, generating much hilarity and derision.

SSM

Squadron Sergeant Major. See *'Windsor Davies'*.

Star Jump

Shamelessly homoerotic dance move used in Army PT lessons, guaranteed to make one of your spuds fall out of your shorts.

Storeman

Deeply-embittered guardian of socks and bog roll. Soldiers fall into this role for various reasons, but all can be attributed to bad luck. During the transition from normal soldier to Storeman, a strange phenomenon occurs. Over the course of a couple of years, in the same way that the Gollum covets the ring, storemen begin to believe that every item in the store was issued to them by a higher being and must never cross the counter to be touched by their colleagues. This often leads to an assumption on camp that they are utter fucking wankrods.

SURF

Selector Unit Radio Frequency. Piece of kit that allows 15% frequency separation between dual mounted HF radios and probably costs a bit less on eBay than a TURF (see *TURF*) if you've lost one on exercise.

Sven Hassel
Author who provides a similar service to British Army camps that the Gideons do for hotels. Within every guardroom, a copy of a Sven Hassel book waits patiently to be read by a soldier tired of masturbation. Though Hassel wrote many books, *Blitzfreeze* is the most popular due to the scary picture on the front.

Territorial Army
Mid 1980s drinking club frequented by moustachioed pisstank warriors, which has transformed into an essential component of the modern fighting Army.

Triple Crown
Popular military award which has nothing to do with rugby. A prize consisting entirely of horrified head-shaking goes to any soldier who manages, over the course of an evening, to involuntarily urinate, defecate and vomit into and onto the same set of clothing.

TURF
Tuning Unit Radio Frequency. Piece of equipment associated with HF communicating which serves the purpose of compensating for inefficiencies in an antenna system. That's what it says on eBay, anyway.

Twat Hat
Number Two dress hat or Forage cap. Smart-looking peaked cap with two flaws. Has the ability to induce migraines when placed on the head for longer than 5 minutes and, worn incorrectly, will make the wearer look like Blakey from *On the Buses*.

Twenty Two
Amount of years' service required to achieve the full pension payout from the Army. When followed by a low rank, ie Lance Corporal or Private, it denotes a class of soldier likely to be more bitter and twisted than a lemon corkscrew.

Windsor Davies
Actor commonly associated with the ridiculously-cliched Sergeant Major character in popular 1970s light entertainment comedy *It Ain't Half Hot Mum*. With no hint of irony, all subsequent Sergeant Majors modelled their behaviour and idiosyncrasies entirely on a fictional personality specifically created to be a caricature.

Yeoman of Signals
Peculiarly archaic but official title of the technical operating authority within a Royal Signals unit. Generally perceived to take life very, very seriously, the Yeomen occasionally smile – such as when someone has lost some crypto, or the bloke who said 'twat' over the Div Command net gets caught.

COMING SOON TO A BOOKSHOP NEAR YOU

EDDY NUGENT

and the

MAP OF AFRICA

Scheduled spring 2009

Visit <u>www.mondaybooks.com</u>
for more information

IN FOREIGN FIELDS: TRUE STORIES OF AMAZING BRAVERY FROM IRAQ AND AFGHANISTAN

Dan Collins (Hardback, £17.99)

OUT IN OCTOBER 2008 IN PAPERBACK, PRICED £7.99

In Foreign Fields features 25 medal winners from Iraq and Afghanistan talking, in their own words, about the actions which led to their awards.

Modestly, often reluctantly, they explain what it's like at the very sharp end, in the heat of battle with death staring you in the face.

If you support our armed forces, you will want to read this modern classic of war reportage.

"Awe-inspiring untold stories... enthralling"
- The Daily Mail

"Excellent...simply unputdownable. Buy this book"
- Jon Gaunt, The Sun

"The book everyone is talking about... a gripping account of life on the frontlines of Iraq and Afghanistan... inspiring"
- News of the World

"Riveting and unique... magnificent. A book to savour"
- Dr Richard North, Defence of the Realm

'Modesty and courage go hand-in-hand if these personal accounts of heroism are a measure... an outstanding read.'
- Soldier Magazine

'Astonishing feats of bravery... in laconic, first-person prose'
- Independent on Sunday

'Incredible courage and leadership in the face of almost certain death... amazing stories.'
- The Western Mail

WATCHING MEN BURN
A SOLDIER'S STORY

Tony McNally (Paperback, £7.99)

++ The Falklands ++ 1982 ++ Tony McNally is a Rapier missile operator, shooting down Argentinean planes attacking British troops and ships. And it's a tough job - the enemy pilots are fearless and they arrive at supersonic speed and breathtakingly low altitude.

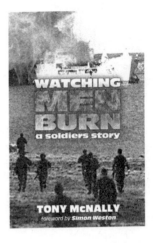

But Tony's war is going well...

Until they bomb the Sir Galahad - a troop ship he is supposed to be protecting. His Rapier fails and he watches, helpless, as bombs rain down on the defenceless soldiers. Fifty men die, and many are left terribly injured.

Tortured by guilt and the horror of the bombing, Tony has relived the events of that day over and over again in his mind.

Watching Men Burn is his true story of the Falklands War - and its awful, lingering aftermath.

**Available from all good bookshops
or from www.mondaybooks.com**

WASTING POLICE TIME...
THE CRAZY WORLD OF THE WAR ON CRIME
PC David Copperfield (£7.99)

PC DAVID COPPERFIELD is an ordinary bobby quietly waging war on crime...when he's not drowning in a sea of paperwork, government initiatives and bogus targets.

Wasting Police Time is his hilarious but shocking picture of life in a modern British town, where teenage yobs terrorise the elderly, drunken couples brawl in front of their children and drug-addicted burglars and muggers roam free.

He reveals how crime is spiralling while millions of pounds in tax is frittered away, and reveals a force which, crushed under mad bureaucracy, is left desperately fiddling the figures.

His book has attracted rave reviews for its dry wit and insight from The Sunday Times, The Guardian, The Observer, The Daily Mail, The Mail on Sunday and The Daily Telegraph;.

'Being a policeman in modern England is not like appearing in an episode of The Sweeney, Inspector Morse or even The Bill, sadly,' says Copperfield. 'No, it's like standing banging your head against a wall, carrying a couple of hundredweight of paperwork on your shoulders, while the house around you burns to the ground.'

"A huge hit... will make you laugh out loud" – **The Daily Mail**
"Very revealing" – **The Daily Telegraph**
"Damning... gallows humour" – **The Sunday Times**
"Graphic, entertaining and sobering" – **The Observer**
"A sensation" – **The Sun**
By PC David Copperfield – as seen on BBC1's *Panorama*
www.coppersblog.blogspot.com

Available from all good bookshops
or from www.mondaybooks.com

DIARY OF AN ON-CALL GIRL
True Stories From The Front Line
WPC EE Bloggs (£7.99)

If crime is the sickness, WPC Ellie Bloggs is the cure... Well, she is when she's not inside the nick, flirting with male officers, buying doughnuts for the sergeant and hacking her way through a jungle of emails, forms and government targets.

Of course, in amongst the tea-making, gossip and boyfriend trouble, real work sometimes intrudes. Luckily, as a woman, she can multi-task... switching effortlessly between gobby drunks, angry chavs and the merely bonkers. WPC Bloggs is a real-life policewoman, who occasionally arrests some very naughty people. *Diary of an On-Call Girl* is her hilarious, despairing dispatch from the front line of modern British lunacy.

WARNING: Contains satire, irony and traces of sarcasm.

"Think Belle de Jour meets The Bill... sarky sarges, missing panda cars and wayward MOPS (members of the public)."
- The Guardian

"Modern policing is part Orwell, part Kafka ... and part Trisha." – **The Mail on Sunday**

£7.99 – and read her at **www.pcbloggs.blogspot.com**

**Available from all good bookshops
or from www.mondaybooks.com**

LIFE AND DEATH IN LONDON:
A PARAMEDIC'S DIARY
Stuart Gray (Paperback £7.99)

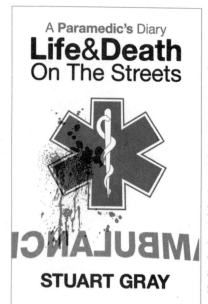

Stuart Gray is a paramedic dealing with the worst life can throw at him. *A Paramedic's Diary* is his gripping, blow-by-blow account of a year in on the streets – 12 rollercoaster months of enormous highs and tragic lows. One day he'll save a young mother's life as she gives birth, the next he might watch a young girl die on the tarmac in front of him after a hit-and-run. A gripping, entertaining and often amusing read by a talented new writer.

**Available from all good bookshops
or from www.mondaybooks.com**

IT'S YOUR TIME YOU'RE WASTING
- A TEACHER'S TALES OF CLASSROOM HELL
Frank Chalk (Paperback £7.99)

The blackly humorous diary of a year in a teacher's working life. Chalk confiscates porn, booze and trainers, fends off angry parents and worries about the few conscientious pupils he comes across, recording his experiences in a dry and very readable manner.

"Does for education what PC David Copperfield did for the police"

"Addictive and ghastly"
– The Times

**Available from all good bookshops
or from <u>www.mondaybooks.com</u>**

COMING SOON FROM MONDAY BOOKS:

PERVERTING THE COURSE OF JUSTICE
Inspector Gadget (Paperback £7.99)
PUBLISHED SEPTEMBER 2008

For the first time ever, a senior policeman – writing as 'Inspector Gadget' for fear of exposure – breaks ranks to tell the truth about the collapse of law and order in the UK.

With access to statistics about frontline police strength (much lower than you think), exclusive inside information on the political targets and interference which are bedevilling officers and detailed analysis of the lies politicians and senior police officers tell, his explosive book will reveal how bad things really are.

Controversial and gripping – and the long-awaited 'follow-up' to PC David Copperfield's *Wasting Police Time* – it will set the news agenda on crime and shock the nation.

SO *THAT'S* WHY THEY CALL IT GREAT BRITAIN
How one tiny country gave so much to the world
Steve Pope (Paperback £7.99)
PUBLISHED APRIL 2009

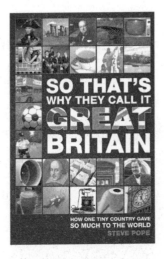

It covers less than half of one per cent of the earth's land mass, but is responsible for more 40% of the world's great inventions. The first car, first train, and first aeroplane *(sorry, Wright Bros)* came from Great Britain, as did the steam engine, the jet engine and the engine of the internet (the www protocols used online).

Britons created the first computer and the first computer game *(noughts and crosses)*, as well as the telegraph, the telephone and the television *(and the mousetrap, the lightbulb and the loo roll)*.

In almost every sphere – from agriculture and medicine to politics, science and the law – we have led the way for centuries.

Most of the world's major sports originated here – along with William Shakespeare and Jane Austen, The Beatles and The Stones, *Fawlty Towers* and *The Office*.

This book shows – without boasting, and with tons of humour, unknown facts and weird stories – just why our country is called GREAT Britain.

Available from all good bookshops
or from www.mondaybooks.com

The Self

SUNY Series, Studying the Self
Richard P. Lipka and Thomas M. Brinthaupt, Editors

The Self

Definitional and Methodological Issues

Edited by
Thomas M. Brinthaupt
and
Richard P. Lipka

STATE UNIVERSITY OF NEW YORK PRESS

Published by
State University of New York Press, Albany

© 1992 State University of New York

For information, address State University of New York
Press, State University Plaza, Albany, N.Y., 12246

Production by E. Moore
Marketing by Fran Keneston

Library of Congress Cataloging-in-Publication Data

The Self: definitional and methodological issues/Thomas M.
    Brinthaupt and Richard P. Lipka, editors.
        p.   cm.—(SUNY series, studying the self)
    Includes bibliographical references and index.
    ISBN 0-7914-0987-2 (hard: alk. paper). —ISBN 0-7914-0988-0
(pbk.: alk. paper)
    1. Self.   2. Self—Research—Methodology.   I. Brinthaupt, Thomas
M., 1958–   . II. Lipka, Richard P.   III. Series.
BF697.S4335 1992
155.2′072—dc20   91-13139
                                                                          CIP

10 9 8 7 6 5 4 3 2 1

Contents

THOMAS M. BRINTHAUPT
RICHARD P. LIPKA

Introduction

For the researcher interested in studying the self, there are a number of important and often controversial issues to consider, many of which were first described by William James a century ago in 1890 (Markus 1990). For example, what are the characteristics and dimensions of the self? How best should the self be measured? What are the effects of the self on a person's motivations, behaviors, and processing of information? Contemporary efforts to study the self vary dramatically in their scope and in how they address these issues.

Since the rediscovery of the self as an object of scientific study over the past two decades (Hales 1985), an explosion of theory and research has occurred among clinical, developmental, educational, and social psychologists as well as other social scientists (Gecas 1982; Greenwald & Pratkanis 1984; Rosenberg 1979; Yardley & Honess 1987). This is an exciting period for anyone interested in studying the self. However, it is also a frustrating and difficult time for those who wish to come up with a meaningful picture of the self. There is wide disagreement about how to define the self, measure it, and study its development. Numerous difficulties also arise when one attempts to integrate the differing theoretical, methodological, and developmental perspectives.

A major reason for this state of affairs is that, too often, self researchers are overly restrictive in their approach to studying the self. One way that problems of studying the self can be addressed is by simultaneously considering theoretical, methodological, and developmental issues. These issues are related to each other in several important ways. Consequently, any discussion of one set of issues necessitates a consideration of the other two. For example, how one defines the self will dictate the methods used to measure it. Differences in how researchers define and measure the self will also increase in importance when the research is couched in terms of developmental issues.

This volume—as well as its companion volume in this series, *Self-Perspectives across the Lifespan*—enlist contributions to studying the self that illustrate and directly address these issues. The contributors describe the theoretical and methodological issues relating to their particular approach to studying the self as well as the lifespan developmental implications of their work.

Our goal is to arrive at a broad understanding of the study of the self. Any approach to studying the self must address a set of important choice points. These primarily concern the questions of *what, how,* and *whom* to study. By way of a general introduction to this volume, we would like to describe briefly the first two of these choice points and how the volume addresses them. The companion volume on the self across the lifespan will devote more attention to the issue of whom to study.

As previous theory and research have shown, the self can be defined in many different ways. Thus, when one studies the self, an important initial question concerns exactly what is to be studied. There is a great deal of variety in how this question is answered in this volume. For example, some chapters focus on the structural properties of the self (Ashmore and Ogilvie, chapter 7; L'Écuyer, chapter 3; and Marsh, Byrne and Shavelson, chapter 2); others emphasize the processing aspects of the self (Freeman, chapter 1); and still others consider both the structural and processing aspects of the self (Hart and Edelstein, chapter 8). Similarly, some contributors devote their attention to self-esteem/evaluation (Juhasz, chapter 6); some focus on self-concept/description (Freeman; and L'Écuyer), and others consider both the descriptive and evaluative aspects of the self (Brinthaupt and Erwin, chapter 4).

Whatever one's preference for defining the self, this definition of *what* to study both influences and is influenced by *how* it can or should be studied. Thus, even if researchers are in general agreement about what they are studying, there are often disagreements about how to best study it. For example, whereas some contributors who emphasize self-structure prefer to employ standardized questionnaires (Byrne, Shavelson and Marsh, chapter 5; and Marsh, Byrne and Shavelson), others rely on open-ended interviews and self-description tasks (Ashmore and Ogilvie; Hart and Edelstein; and L'Écuyer). Among those contributors who are interested in self-esteem, standardized questionnaires, interviews, or a combination of questionnaire and interview are also used (Brinthaupt and Erwin; and Juhasz).

Paralleling the choice points of what and how, this volume is divided into two major parts. "Defining the Self"—or Part I—includes a sampling of contemporary theoretical perspectives. "Measuring the Self"—Part II—examines various measurement and methodological issues and techniques. In the following pages, we describe each of these sections in more detail.

PART I: DEFINING THE SELF

Theoretical Perspectives

What exactly is the "self?" Previous theory and research have identified several theoretical issues pertaining to this question. For example, one issue is the distinction between the descriptive and evaluative components of the self. How are our thoughts, feelings, and perceptions about ourselves related to each other? Several reviewers have addressed this issue in terms of the distinction between self-conception and self-evaluation (Beane & Lipka 1980; Blyth & Traeger 1983; Greenwald 1988; Greenwald, Bellezza & Banaji 1988).

A second issue is the distinction between the self-as-subject (or active agent) and the self-as-object (or observed entity). What is the difference between the *I* and the *me*? In trying to answer this question, theorists have attempted to specify the major dimensions of the self as both subject and object (Damon & Hart 1982, 1986; Harter 1983).

A third theoretical issue concerns the question of change versus stability of self. Is the self purely a reflection of situational and contextual variants (Gergen 1977); or is there a central and stable core self (Markus & Kunda 1986; Markus & Nurius 1986)?

Is the self part of the ego, personality, identity, consciousness, or soul? Or is it separate from these concepts? In their attempts to specify the characteristics and dimensions of the self, theorists have emphasized its structural properties, its processes, or both of these components. For example, self researchers have variously defined the self as (1) a schema (Markus 1983), prototype (Rogers 1981), or cognitive representation (Kihlstrom et al. 1988); (2) a multidimensional hierarchical construct (Marsh & Shavelson 1985); (3) a narrative sequence (Gergen & Gergen 1988); (4) a linguistic description of subjective experience (Young-Eisendrath & Hall 1987); and (5) an elaborate theory (Epstein 1973).

Some theorists are interested in describing and differentiating specific components of the self (Greenwald & Pratkanis 1984); some are cognitively oriented, emphasizing the information-processing characteristics of the self (Kihlstrom et al. 1988); and some are motivationally-oriented, focusing on the self's tendencies for enhancement, consistency, and/or distortion (Sorrentino & Higgins 1986).

Fundamental theoretical issues such as these have stimulated a renewed and active interest in defining the self. As the preceding paragraphs suggest, the field is replete with alternative and sometimes contradictory perspectives. In this section of the volume, we present three very different but representative contributions to defining the self.

In the first selection, Freeman focuses on the claim that the adult self (and, more generally, adult development) is essentially a random phenomenon without any clear trajectory. Drawing on a wide variety of philosophical, psychological, and literary sources, he defines the self as an ongoing story, narrative, or intrepretive creation. According to this perspective, the self is closely tied to past experiences, with its defining characteristics fitting together into a coherent package. As Freeman notes, an important implication of such a definition is that the self researcher must be both a historian and a scientist.

If the self is defined in narrative terms, then how can it be studied? In attempting to answer this question, Freeman reviews several potential criticisms of his definition of the self. For example, a person may embellish, distort, or deceive in his or her self-narrative. Freeman points out that, first, even if present experience affects one's interpretations of the past, this does not necessarily falsify them. Second, and more importantly, it is precisely through these self-narrative processes that a better understanding of the self as a meaning-maker and a significance-generator can be obtained.

Chapter 2 by Marsh and his colleagues is, in some ways, diametrically opposed to the Freeman selection. Rather than focusing on the broader phenomenological and experiential issues related to defining and studying the self, Marsh and colleagues focus on the structure and content of the self. They define the self in terms of its multidimensionality (for example, with physical, social, academic, and nonacademic components) and its hierarchical organization. They assume that there is a set of components that we all share and that is structured in a similar manner across individuals.

Given this structural definition of the self, how can it be studied? Marsh and colleagues describe how their model of the self led to the construction and validation of a set of multidimensional measures of the self. They then review a wide array of research designed to establish the usefulness of their model and the validity of their measures, which they called "Self Description Questionnaires." Much of their review supports the contention that the multidimensionality of the self must be taken into account by researchers of the self. They illustrate how the relationship between theoretical and methodological issues has guided their efforts to define and study the self. Sometimes, their theoretical conceptualization of the self is revised, while at other times, their measures are revised.

In the final contribution to this section, L'Écuyer describes in chapter 3 an approach to defining and studying the self that draws on both the traditions exemplified by Freeman and by Marsh and colleagues. L'Écuyer is unique in that he is one of the few researchers who are actively engaged in studying the self all across the lifespan. In accomplishing this, he has had to deal with several theoretical and methodological issues, and his chapter describes the many choices that he made in addressing these issues.

As do Marsh and colleagues in chapter 2, L'Écuyer defines the self in multidimensional and hierarchical terms. But, as does Freeman in chapter 1, L'Écuyer also allows his subjects to describe themselves in an open-ended fashion. The result is a definition of the self across the lifespan that identifies structure by relying on the self as experienced and described by respondents. It is interesting to note the similarities and differences between his dimensions of the self and those of Marsh and colleagues. In addition, as do Marsh and colleagues, L'Écuyer illustrates one of the major themes of this volume: how one defines the self affects one's preferred methodology and instrumentation, which, in turn, affect how one comes to subsequently define the self.

PART II: MEASURING THE SELF

Methodological Approaches

As the contributions to the "Defining the Self" part of this volume suggest, different theoretical perspectives are associated with quite different approaches to measuring the self. Is there a best way to measure the self?

In answering this question, several methodological issues must be addressed by the researcher of the self (Wells & Marwell 1976; Wylie 1974, 1989). Most of these issues apply equally well to research on other topics. For example, do the instruments being used have sound psychometric properties, such as high reliability and validity, and can the findings be easily replicated?

In addition, researchers of the self must be concerned with social desirability and other response biases. They can choose among methods that differ in the amount of time and effort required of both researcher and participant. Furthermore, it is clear that various methods produce dramatically different quantitative and qualitative data related to the self (Jackson 1984).

Among the approaches available to the researcher of the self are scales and questionnaires, sorting tasks, structured or unstructured interviews, prospective or retrospective tasks, memory and reaction-time experiments, projection measures, experiential sampling, and even psychophysiological and neurological techniques. Throughout this volume, we have selected contributions that reflect this variety of approaches to studying the self. The five contributions in part II focus on a set of general measurement issues, ranging from such theoretical issues as the impact of others on the self to the multidimensional structure of the self.

Most researchers rely on the self-reports of participants as the primary source of data about the self. In chapter 4, Brinthaupt and Erwin extensively review the factors that affect the process of self-report. These factors include the accessibility and organization of self-relevant knowledge; contextual, situational, and cultural factors; and individual and developmental differences. Then, they focus on two popular self-report methodologies for studying the self: the so-called reactive and spontaneous approaches (McGuire 1984). The reactive approach requires subjects to locate themselves on one or more dimensions determined by the experimenter to be important. The spontaneous approach requires subjects to respond to a very general or vague prompt (such as "Who are you?") in a minimally structured format. After evaluating and comparing the spontaneous and reactive approaches to measuring the self, Brinthaupt and Erwin describe a study that compares data obtained from each approach.

A great deal of interest in research on the self concerns the study of differences between groups. For example, does one group of children have higher self-esteem than does another group? For the researcher who defines the self in terms of multiple components, there are certain methodological assumptions that accompany this definition. Two of these assumptions are that the relations among self-components are the same across different groups and that the measuring instrument is perceived in the same way by different groups.

As Byrne and her colleagues note in chapter 5, these assumptions can be violated in several ways. In fact, this may account for some of the inconsistency in research on the self. Using statistical advances such as confirmatory factor analysis and the analysis of co-variance structures, Byrne and colleagues demonstrate, first, that the structure of the self can vary across gender. In particular, they report research in which relations among self-related abilities, such as English and mathematics, are not the same for adolescent males as they are for females.

Second, Byrne and colleagues show that the properties of a measure of self can vary across age groups. For example, a study of gifted children illustrates differences in the perception of item content by fifth- and eighth-graders. These issues have important implications for the study of mean-group differences in research on the self as well as on research into a variety of other topics.

One of the defining characteristics of the self on which nearly all researchers agree is that social interaction and the reactions of other persons play a key role in self-perception (Cooley 1902; Mead 1934; Stryker 1987; Vallacher 1980). Despite this agreement, there has been very little attention devoted to the measurement and conceptualization of these so-called significant others.

In chapter 6, Juhasz reviews how another person can assume a significant role in an individual's self-evaluation. Using student-teacher perceptions as an example, she points out the highly subjective and personal nature of determining the significance of another and the potential for self-perceptual biases in the interpretation of feedback from others. In addition, Juhasz reviews and critiques a wide variety of measures that either assess the perceived significance of others in some way or can be so adapted. Throughout her review, she shows how the multifaceted nature of the self—as well as the situational and temporal influences on the perceptions of others—make measuring significance a formidable task.

In chapter 7, Ashmore and Ogilvie present an important new approach to measuring the self in the context of its relationship with others. They begin with the assumption that the dimensions of evaluation (good/bad) and gender (man/woman) underlie personal identity in terms of how individuals organize their inter-personal self.

Assuming that an adequate understanding of the self must include an individual's internal representations of past and present social relationships, Ashmore and Ogilvie propose a unique unit of measurement, which they call "self-with-other representations." After a thorough description of the methods and procedures designed to operationalize this unit of measurement, Ashmore and Ogilvie demonstrate how these data can be analyzed using hierarchical classes analysis. In so doing, they demonstrate how self-with-other representations can be assessed and visually depicted, even illustrating the feelings of ambivalence that characterize the self in relationship to others. The inferences that can be drawn about self-structure from the resulting hierarchical configurations will be of interest to social, cognitive, developmental, and clinical psychologists.

In the final chapter of this volume, Hart and Edelstein examine the effects of different cultural contexts on the self by reviewing and critiquing theoretical and methodological approaches to cross-cultural research on the self. Then they apply their own approach to defining and measuring the self in different cultural contexts, describing their research with Puerto Rican and Icelandic children and adolescents. Among their conclusions is that, at least in part, cultural ideology and social-class memberships determine adolescents' self-perceptions, such as whether they understand themselves primarily in individual versus social terms. More importantly, they suggest that traditional descriptions of developmental changes in the self must be qualified by the effects of cultural contexts. What are interpreted as developmental changes or advances may, in fact, reflect the effects of cultural socialization and experience. Finally, they make the case that finding—or failing to find—cultural effects on the self is heavily dependent upon the methodology employed.

In summary, each contribution to this volume presents a systematic analysis of specific theoretical and methodological disputes related to the study of the self. The contributors vary in their emphasis on the structural and processing aspects of the self, and a good deal of variety in terms of the methodologies employed and the methodological questions addressed also exists. Theory and research on the self have increasingly come to occupy the attention and interest of several disciplines. As a much-needed sourcebook for those who are interested in studying the self, we intend this book to provide a clear and wide-ranging discussion of many of the issues which researchers of the self will need to confront.

REFERENCES

Beane, J. A., and Lipka, R. P. 1980. Self-concept and self-esteem: A construct differentiation. *Child Study Journal* 10:1–6.

Blyth, D. A., and Traeger, C. M. 1983. The self-concept and self-esteem of early adolescents. *Journal of Early Adolescence* 3:105–120.

Cooley, C. H. 1902. *Human nature and the social order.* New York: Schocken.

Damon, W., and Hart, D. 1982. The development of self-understanding from infancy through adolescence. *Child Development* 53:841–864.

————. 1986. Stability and change in children's self-understanding. *Social Cognition* 4:102–118.

Epstein, S. 1973. The self-concept revisited, or a theory of a theory. *American Psychologist* 28:404–416.

Gecas, V. 1982. The self-concept. *Annual Review of Sociology* 8:1–33.

Gergen, K. J. 1977. The social construction of self-knowledge. In *The self: Psychological and philosophical issues,* edited by T. Mischel. Oxford: Basil Blackwell.

Gergen, K. J., and Gergen, M. M. 1988. Narrative and the self in relationship. In *Advances in experimental social psychology,* edited by L. Berkowitz. Vol. 21. San Diego: Academic Press. 17–56.

Greenwald, A. G. 1988. A social-cognitive account of the self's development. In *Self, ego, and identity: Integrative approaches,* edited by D. K. Lapsley and F. C. Powers. New York: Springer-Verlag. 30–42.

Greenwald, A. G.; Bellezza, F. S.; and Banaji, M. R. 1988. Is self-esteem a central ingredient of the self-concept? *Personality and Social Psychology Bulletin* 14:34–45.

Greenwald, A. G., and Pratkanis, A. R. 1984. The self. In *Handbook of social cognition,* edited by R. S. Wyer and T. K Srull. Vol. 3. Hillsdale, N.J.: Erlbaum. 129–178.

Hales, S. 1985. The inadvertent rediscovery of self in social psychology. *Journal for the Theory of Social Behaviour* 15:237–282.

Harter, S. 1983. Developmental perspectives on the self-system. In *Handbook of child psychology,* edited by P. H. Mussen. Vol. 4. New York: Wiley. 275–385.

Jackson, M. R. 1984. *Self-esteem and meaning: A life-historical investigation.* Albany, N.Y.: State University of New York Press.

James, W. 1890. *The principles of psychology.* Vol. 1. New York: Henry Holt.

Kihlstrom, J. F.; Cantor, N.; Albright, J. S.; Chew, B. R.; Klein, S. B.; and Niedenthal, P. M. 1988. Information processing and the study of the self. In *Advances in experimental social psychology,* edited by L. Berkowitz. Vol. 21. San Diego: Academic Press. 145–181.

Markus, H. 1983. Self-knowledge: An expanded view. *Journal of Personality* 51:543–565.

————. 1990. On splitting the universe. *Psychological Science* 1:181–185.

Markus, H., and Kunda, Z. 1986. Stability and malleability of the self-concept. *Journal of Personality and Social Psychology* 51:858–866.

Markus, H., and Nurius, P. S. 1986. Possible selves. *American Psychologist* 41:954–969.

Marsh, H. W., and Shavelson, R. J. 1985. Self-concept: Its multifaceted, hierarchical structure. *Educational Psychologist* 20:107–125.

McGuire, W. J. 1984. Search for the self: Going beyond self-esteem and the reactive self. In *Personality and the prediction of behavior,* edited by R. A. Zucker, J. Aronoff, and A. I. Rabin. New York: Academic Press. 73–120.

Mead, G. H. 1934. *Mind, self, and society.* Chicago: University of Chicago Press.

Rogers, T. B. 1981. A model of the self as an aspect of the human information processing system. In *Personality, cognition, and social interaction,* edited by N. Cantor and J. F. Kihlstrom. Hillsdale, N.J.: Erlbaum. 193–214.

Rosenberg, M. 1979. *Conceiving the self.* New York: Basic Books.

Sorrentino, R. M., and Higgins, E. T., eds. 1986. *Handbook of motivation and cognition.* New York: Guilford Press.

Stryker, S. 1987. Identity theory: Developments and extensions. In *Self and identity: Psychosocial perspectives,* edited by K. Yardley and T. Honess. Chichester, U.K.: John Wiley & Sons. 89–103.

Vallacher, R. R. 1980. An introduction to self theory. In *The self in social psychology,* edited by D. M. Wegner and R. R. Vallacher. New York: Oxford University Press. 3–30.

Wells, L. E., and Marwell, G. 1976. *Self-esteem: Its conceptualization and measurement.* Beverly Hills, Calif.: Sage.

Wylie, R. C. 1974. *The self-concept: A review of methodological considerations and measuring instruments.* Lincoln: University of Nebraska Press.

—————. 1989. *Measures of self-concept.* Lincoln: University of Nebraska Press.

Yardley, K., and Honess, T., eds. 1987. *Self and identity: Psychosocial perspectives.* Chichester, U.K.: John Wiley & Sons.

Young-Eisendrath, P., and Hall, J. A., eds. 1987. *The book of the self: Person, pretext, and process.* New York: New York University Press.

PART I: DEFINING THE SELF

MARK FREEMAN

1

Self As Narrative:
The Place of Life History in Studying the Life Span

INTRODUCTION: ON THE POSSIBILITY OF SELFHOOD

In an article that was published back in 1980, Kenneth Gergen proclaimed that there was a definite crisis emerging in life-span developmental psychology, and it had to do with the ostensibly obsolete assumption that the process of development was to be characterized in terms of continuity. This cry had indeed been heard earlier, by Bernice Neugarten in 1969, among others, but, whereas Neugarten had been content to urge us to attune ourselves to the possible discontinuities of development, to open ourselves up to the real developmental shifts that might be happening in people's lives, Gergen seemed to be going one step further.

It may well be, he in effect argued, that the process of development—adult development at any rate—is best understood not as a lawful, orderly evolutionary one, but as a type of random walk of accidents and unintended consequences. The implication, of course, is that the idea of development itself may be obsolete, a stale layover, perhaps, from those modes of thinking that insisted that there must be some semblance of unity amidst the flux of experience.

There is a further implication as well. To the extent that the process of development is to be seen as significantly more random,

15

disconnected, and haphazard than has customarily been assumed, so, too, is the self. After all, what else can a fundamentally random process culminate in except a fundamentally formless self?

Given the decidedly disorderly process of living one's life—moment to moment, day to day, and year to year—may it not be the case that the self is little more than an accident waiting to happen? Alongside the attempt to question the orderliness of the process of development, therefore, the very idea of the self—as integrated, consistent, and enduring identity—is rendered suspect. We see evidence of this suspicion not only in psychology—for instance in the person/situation controversy (Mischel 1968; Shweder 1975)—but in sociology, philosophy, literary theory, and a host of other disciplines besides (Barthes 1977; Derrida 1978; Foucault 1973). Both the process of development and the self itself are in the midst of being deconstructed, it would seem, which, for present purposes, can be taken to mean that the operative assumptions by which they have been understood and conceptualized are being undermined.

Should we assume, given what has been said, that our very identities are illusory? That our experience of *I*—this supposedly continuous, integrated, and originating being—is more a wish than a reality? "Not only are selves conditional," John Updike wrote in *Self-consciousness* in 1989, "but they die. Each day, we wake slightly altered, and the person we were yesterday is dead" (211).

Could it be that our conviction in our own unity as selves is a defense against our disunity, or a way of grieving over that part of us that dies each and every day? A similar question could be asked with regard to the issue of development. Could it be that the very idea of development—tied as it is to evolutionary-type concerns with moving forward and upward and with growth and progress—is ultimately a fiction, designed to ensure ourselves that we are indeed headed somewhere?

These types of questions are by no means new. Hume, for instance, in *A Treatise on Human Nature* noted more than 150 years ago that some philosophers "imagine we are at every moment intimately conscious of what we call our SELF; that we feel its existence; and are certain, beyond the evidence of a demonstration, both of its perfect identity and simplicity" ([1739–1740] 1874, 533). Unfortunately for them, however, Hume contended, they are wrong. "For from what impression could this idea be derived?" He further argued, "If any impression gives rise to the idea of self, that impression must continue invariably the same, through the whole course of our lives; since self is supposed to exist after that manner. But there is no impression constant and invariable."

Hume also contended that the only thing we can say with certainty is that, "Pain and pleasure, grief and joy, passions and sensations succeed each other, and never all exist at the same time. It cannot, therefore, be from any of these impressions, or from any other, that the idea of the self is derived; and consequently," Hume proclaimed, "there is no such idea" (533). Needless to say, perhaps, Hume would not be likely to hold the idea of development in terribly high favor either. Only an entity that is (more or less) constant and variable may be said to develop, but surely not the flurry of impressions that Hume is considering.

We may wish otherwise, of course, but we are "nothing but a bundle or collection of different perceptions, which succeed one another with an inconceivable rapidity, and are in a perpetual flux and movement" (534). Thus, the bottom line is "The identity, which we ascribe to the mind of man, is only a fictitious one" (540). It is created, produced, an extrapolation from the flux of experience which deludes us into positing an enduring substantiality when, in fact, there is none.

From other quarters entirely, Nietzsche discussed something quite similar in the late 1880s. Descartes had essentially argued, Nietzsche wrote, " 'There is thinking: therefore there is something that thinks.' " But really, he suggests, all we have here "is simply a formulation of our grammatical custom that adds a doer to every deed" ([1887] 1968, 268). Who exactly is this doer? A soul? A nonmaterial substance? A kind of control tower, calling out directions to be carried out by the body? Not quite, Nietzsche answered.

> The subject: this is the term for our belief in a unity underlying all the different impulses of the highest feeling of reality: we understand this belief as the *effect* of one cause—we believe so firmly in our belief that for its sake we imagine "truth," "reality," "substantiality" in general.—"The subject," [is ultimately just] the fiction that many similar states in us are the effect of one substratum. (268–269)

Why "fiction"? Once again:

> it is we who first created the "similarity" of these states [and as such] our adjusting them and making them similar is the fact, not their similarity (—which ought rather to be denied—)." (269)

As for Nietzsche's own bottom line, "The assumption of one single subject is perhaps unnecessary; perhaps it is just as permissible to assume a multiplicity of subjects, whose interaction and struggle is the basis of our thought and our consciousness in general?" Yes, he decided, that will be the hypothesis. "The subject as multiplicity" (270).

Moving into different quarters still, as we learn from none other than B. F. Skinner (1971, 1974), "Complex contingencies of reinforcement create complex repertoires, and . . . different contingencies create different persons in the same skin, of which so-called multiple personalities are only an extreme manifestation" (1974, 184–185). Again, not unlike Hume and Nietzsche, "A person is not an originating agent; he is a locus, a point at which many genetic and environmental conditions come together in a joint effect." This is not to say that we are not unique for, as Skinner acknowledged, "No one else (unless he has an identical twin) has his genetic endowment, and, without exception, no one else has his personal history." However, the uniqueness, he believes, "is inherent in the sources" (185). Consequently, "There is no place in the scientific position for a self as a true originator or initiator of action" (247–248).

In this and companion volume, we are seeking to study the self across the life-span. But is it even possible? If the self is ultimately a type of fiction, and development ultimately a second-order fiction—a fiction about a fiction—how are we to proceed? To my mind, there is probably no better way for us to find some direction than by drawing upon the work of William James.

SELF AS NARRATIVE

"Let us now be the psychologist," James wrote, "and see if it makes any sense at all to say: *I am the same self that I was yesterday*" ([1890] 1950, 332). One thing is certain, he immediately noted. There is a definite warmth and intimacy to our own thoughts and experiences. We can entertain another person's thoughts, and, on some level perhaps, they may eventually become our own. But there is still no mistaking someone else's thoughts for the ones that belong, indubitably, to ourselves.

Now, when this sense of warmth and intimacy is no longer present, James continued, neither is the sense of personal identity. When we hear anecdotes about our infancy, for instance, the resultant feelings are different from those which derive from memories. Moreover, James added, these memories—some of which may, in fact, be interwoven with fantasy and hearsay—are often questionable in their own right. Finally, as concerns prior experiences for which there is no memory at all—as in amnesia—one's sense of self may virtually disappear.

In light of what James has told us thus far, the idea of self qua identity depends on memory above all else. In this respect, his account is not radically different from Hume's. Perhaps then, James mused, there is indeed a soul of some sort, a nonmaterial spiritual substance behind the scenes of thought. Unfortunately, however, not only can its existence never be proven, but even if it could, James realized, what would it explain? The idea of the soul, therefore, doesn't quite work for James's interpretation—the primary reason being that, even if it exists, it is utterly superfluous for scientific purposes.

What, then, was James's complaint about Hume and his fellow sensationalists? Hadn't they managed to avoid the pitfalls of going the route of the soul? Their problem, James said, is that, instead of focusing on sameness (the enduring soul) at the expense of difference (the flux of consciousness) as the spiritualists do, they emphasize difference at the expense of sameness. They fail to see that our lived experience of continuity is no less real than the somewhat fleshier discrete perceptions which they love to talk about so well. In this failure, they have also managed "to pour the child out with the bath" (James [1890] 1950, 352).

Did Kant do any better than Hume? The problem here, according to James, is that Kant's idea of the self, despite being integral to any and all experiences we might have, is effectively:

> ... denied by him to have any positive attributes [all that remains is] "the simple and utterly empty idea: I; of which we cannot even say we have a notion, but only a consciousness which accompanies all notions." (James [1890] 1950, 362)

In short, Kant does not help much either. The self emerges as little more than the condition of experience, fundamentally devoid of content.

Judging from what has been said, there is the need somehow to strike a balance in our consideration of the identity of the self between sameness and difference. For, is it not the case that we are, in fact, both of these? Even though we perpetually die, as Updike wrote, doesn't part of us seem to live on?

We must pursue this metaphor of death. For our thoughts and experiences to fuse together, James argued, there must be some sort of *medium*. This, he believed, can only be "the real, present onlooking, remembering 'judging thought' or identifying 'section' of the stream of consciousness" ([1890] 1950, 338). What happens, therefore, is that:

> Each pulse of cognitive consciousness, each Thought, dies away and is replaced by another. The other, among the things it knows, knows its own predecessor, and finding it "warm," in the way we have described, greets it, saying: "Thou art *mine*, and art the same self with me." (339).

> [Thus] The identity which the *I* discovers can only be a relative identity, that of a slow shifting in which there is always some ingredient retained. The commonest element of all, the most uniform, is the possession of the same memories. However different the man may be from the youth, both look back on the same childhood, and call it their own. (372)

In these final words, James told us at least three things that would seem to be integral to any inquiry into the possibility of selfhood. The first is that the identity of the self, far from being a stable and enduring object-like thing, is better understood as the terminal point of an ongoing, ceaseless process issuing from the past. We should note that the future is, of course, involved as well, because the "ingredient retained" will likely be a function of whatever project the self is formulating. Along these lines, we can rightfully say that, in some sense, it is the future that determines which ingredients will be retained for inclusion in the self (Markus & Nurius 1986, 1987).

Second—and relatedly—James also told us that the very condition of possibility of selfhood derives, in large measure, from the identity of the past. The memories which we possess are primary foundation for the construction of self. Simply stated, without a past to look back upon and to identify as one's own, there would be no self.

We can extend this perspective to the idea of development as well. Contingent as it is upon a more or less continuous self, which is in turn contingent upon the identity of the past, the idea of development would be unthinkable in the absence of memory. There would be no possibility for transformation, but only replacements, as it were—one self following another.

Third, James proclaimed that the self is irrevocably a product of interpretation. It is a kind of text, we might say, issuing from a process wherein the *I* seeks to determine just who and what its *me* is all about (Freeman 1985; Gergen 1988; Ricoeur 1981). Stated another way, self-reflection requires that the *I* take the role of other—the outside observer—to my own self, seizing upon the available facts and synthesizing them into a workable, coherent narrative.

James's formulation, while insightful, is not entirely satisfactory. The idea of ingredients retained is useful, because it says that identity, rather than being a condition of permanent self-sameness, is, in fact, constituted through the changes we undergo and the presence of residues of what we have been. These, in turn, become linked with what we are now and what we imagine that we will become in the future. We run into problems in this formulation, however, with the allegedly commonest ingredient of them all—what James called the "same memories."

Given the fact that our memories occur in the present—an ever-changing present at that—how can we expect to look back on the same past? Doesn't that same childhood change through the years, even if only in the slightest way?

Indeed, might it not be that the identity of the self derives from the fundamentally different renditions of the personal past created in memory? If so, it must follow that one sensible way of studying the self is to study the changing narratives which people use to tell about who and what they have been and become.

In studying the self across the life span, we must therefore be willing to adopt not only the role of scientist seeking to predict what will be, but the role of historian seeking to understand and explain what was. But we must now ask major questions.

How can this historical perspective be of service in systematically studying the self across the life span? More specifically, given that the sense we derive from life histories is founded upon interpretation—on the part of both the self, whose history it is, as well as that of the researcher who is studying the self—how can we ever hope to derive valid and useful forms of psychological knowledge?

In order to address these questions, I will focus on four distinct problems that frequently emerge in the study of life histories: (1) language, as it is manifested in life-historical recollection; (2) intrusion of the present upon the past; (3) explanation and understanding in historical inquiry; and (4) the problem of self-deception.

Language and Selfhood

Despite the fact that a sense of self, as a psychophysical entity set apart from the outer world, may well be a transhistorical and transcultural phenomenon—at least among those of us who have developed beyond the sensorimotor stage, primary narcissism, symbiosis, and so on—there is ample evidence to suggest that concepts of self are relative to time and place (Baumeister 1987; Geertz 1979; Mauss 1979; Shweder & Bourne 1984; Weintraub 1975. Also see chapter 8 of this volume).

There is an interesting implication to be noted immediately. It may very well be that the entire endeavor in which each of the authors included in this volume were engaged may be most appropriately seen as a type of ethnopsychology. Baldly put, in studying the development of the self across the life span, we are studying a localized entity, one that we, in some sense, have created. This in no way invalidates the endeavor nor does it render it unimportant. It simply means that the particular entity under consideration—what Geertz referred to as a "bounded, unique, more or less integrated motivational and cognitive universe" (1979, 229)—is a cultural product.

So, too, is the idea of a life history. Weintraub, for instance, suggested that it was not until the eighteenth century, with Goethe, that we saw the emergence of the idea of life history as we now know it. It was only then, he argued, that the proper method of accounting for a life came to be to tell its story, historically, from beginning to end. We need not go back to the eighteenth century, however, to see that the idea of life history is by no means a universal one.

Of the Trobriand Islanders, Lee wrote in 1959 that there was no boundary between past and present. Whereas we tend to arrange the events of our lives climactically, with certain of them being deemed more significant than others, for the Trobriander, he said, "there is no developmental arrangement, no building up of emotional tone . . . stories have no plot, no lineal development, no climax" (Lee 1959, 116). In a word, there is no history. It is simply not a meaningful category of self-understanding.

What are we to make of these ideas? First and foremost, there is the need to recognize that a life history, far from being a merely neutral, objective rendition of what was, is enmeshed within a specific and unique form of discourse. It is but one among countless possible modes of understanding the self.

This is not to say that we could just as easily have adopted a radically different mode of understanding the self as we have come to know it. Our own modern, Western conception, in a certain sense, demands as its most appropriate mode of understanding something akin to history—that the modern self and the idea of life history are, thus, mutually constitutive.

However, given that we are dealing here with a unique, local mode of self-understanding that is inextricably bound to the language which we employ, it may be useful to ask a question. In considering life histories, are we learning about selves or about language?

In this context, we might consider the case of Helen Keller, who, at the age of nineteen months, was stricken with an illness that was to take away her hearing and her sight. She apparently did retain some faint memories of the way things sounded and looked before she fell ill, and she continued to explore the world as best she could through those senses that had been spared. By all indications, however, she had to undertake the task of understanding the world virtually anew, primarily through the medium of language.

In addition to the pain and loneliness of having suddenly been thrust into the quiet darkness of this new reality, a strange realization gradually dawned upon her as she grew older. She had become thoroughly confused about who and what she was. Why? Helen Keller wrote in her autobiography, "It is certain that I cannot always distinguish my own thoughts from those I read, because what I read becomes the very substance and texture of my mind" ([1902] 1974, 69).

Therefore, Helen's mind, as well as her very self, rather than being unified and whole—her "own"—appeared, instead, to be a type of "patchwork," as she came to call it, constructed in significant part from the words and thoughts of others.

Even the story she was writing, she implied, was not strictly her own. It derived from others, too, in the form of the meanings they supplied in order that she might come to terms with her experience. While she looked greatly forward to the day when she would be able to put aside the words and thoughts of others, and think and experience in a manner that was genuinely hers alone, it is not completely clear what this could really mean.

If experience and memory take place in and through language, and if language derives essentially from outside the self, how could Helen Keller ever hope to speak her own truth, uncluttered by the influences of others?

In his seminal essay, "On Memory and Childhood Amnesia" published in 1959, Ernest Schachtel essentially argued that life histories must inevitably be considered suspect as sources of true information about the self. Indeed, he went so far as to claim that it is difficult, if not impossible, for the modern individual to remember the earliest years of the past.

Drawing in part on Freud's earlier speculations on infantile amnesia in 1901–1905, there is the idea that we need to hide our threatening beginnings, particularly in the sphere of sexuality (Freud 1962). In fact, if we were to remember all that went on in those difficult years, Freud had argued, we would all be swallowed up in the unavoidable frustrations and disappointments of our adult lives. Nothing would be able to match that earlier intensity. Fortunately for some—unfortunately for others—we forget.

Schachtel took his own speculations on this issue considerably beyond Freud's, however. The repression of sexuality, he argued, does not adequately account for childhood amnesia. Rather, "the biologically, culturally, and socially influenced processes of memory organization results in the formation of categories (schemata) of memory which are not suitable vehicles to receive and reproduce experiences of the quality and intensity of early childhood" (Schachtel 1959, 284). Because we come to inhabit a vastly different world as adults, a world in which language and convention gradually achieve the upper hand in the construction of our experience, there is no returning to the earlier ways.

As for memory after childhood, while amnesia per se is less of a threat, there is a definite incapacity to reproduce anything that resembles a really rich, full, rounded, and alive experience. "Even the most 'exciting' events are remembered as milestones rather than as moments filled with the concrete abundance of life" (Schachtel 1959, 287). The result is that "signposts" are remembered rather than experiences themselves. Sadly enough, these rarely reveal what is truly significant in our lives. They point instead to the events that are supposed to be significant. The result is that our memories are often stereotyped and ridden with cliches. In sum, due to the schematization and conventionalization of life historical memory—both of which are tied to the "obscuring" function of language—much of our past is "condemned to oblivion" (Schachtel 1959, 296). The gap between experience itself and the words we employ to describe it can never be bridged.

There is ample reason to question some of what Schachtel had to say, particularly in regard to the alleged pristineness of childhood and the inevitable fall into the deadened scripts of adult life. To be fair, he does address the articulating function of language along with its obscuring function. Therefore, he knows that the movement of memory is not necessarily downhill, farther and farther away from the real. But the theme of loss and failure, the occlusion of reality wrought by the socially ratified designs which we impose upon our experience, remains paramount. As for the result, it would seem that life-historical data must be rendered suspect.

For present purposes, however, the more important point to be gleaned from Schachtel's discussion is that life-historical data inevitably reflect those culturally specific modes of self-understanding present in a given locale. As Murray (1986) has argued in his comments on "popular life constructors", the particular manner in which a life is told will vary as a function of the specific storylines deemed most appropriate and valuable at a given time and place.

Sheehy's (1976, 1981) books, for instance, can be read in terms of the narrative conventions of romance, with the battle between good and evil culminating, one hopes, in the discovery of inner truth. This does not mean that she necessarily distorted the lives she described. Rather, Murray's claim is only that Sheehy elected to narrate the movement of the lives which she told about in a quite specific manner. She has adopted a certain literary strategy to give these lives artistic form and value.

Two interesting corollaries emerge from this idea. The first is that the specific genres of narrative employed at a given time and place can serve as a sort of barometer of prevailing beliefs, values, and ideals. First, in studying the self via life history, therefore, we have in hand not only psychological information, but also sociological data. The second corollary is that, even if a particular life-historical narrative is a manifestly mythologized and fictive rendition of that life, it may nevertheless provide useful information about how personal experience is organized in a given locale.

It could still be argued, of course, that avowing the literary dimension of life histories renders futile our attempts to utilize them as sources of information about the self. If one cannot help but poeticize the past or to assimilate it into the context of a story with a plot, then how are we ever to genuinely learn about the people we study?

Although it will undoubtedly remain unsatisfactory to some, the answer to this question is a relatively straightforward one. We are able to learn about them precisely through the narratives which they reveal to us. The reason is that, in all of their literariness, these narratives are, in fact, a part of the very fabric of the self.

Simply stated, on some level we *are* the stories we tell about ourselves. This is so whether the tales are accurate (roughly speaking) or inaccurate. Similarly, Rosenberg suggested in his consideration of "implicit developmental theory" in 1988 that life-historical narratives, even if they are outright lies, might still be revealing.

Does this mean, then, that every life history we are told is to be taken strictly at face value? Of course not! As we will see later on in this chapter, the possibility of self-deception and distortion always exists, and it may very well be important to identify those qualities when they occur. But none of what is being said here should be taken to imply that, beneath the veneer of literariness, there exists an "a-literary self," unequivocal and unadorned. This discussion only means that some of the stories we tell are arguably more consonant with the known facts of lives than are others. For the time being, therefore, suffice it to say that, even if the stories we tell appear by all indications to be in the service of truth, they are, nevertheless, literary.

Intrusion of the Present upon the Past

A further difficulty exists in the present context, and it is one that some might regard as the most pernicious of all aspects of life-historical recollection. In recollecting the past through the eyes of the present—replete with its various interests, anticipations, and desires—the possibility exists that, when taken in their usual senses, the past story which one is fashioning is more akin to fiction than to history. Gusdorf wrote in his reflections on autobiography in 1956:

> The difficulty is insurmountable. No trick of presentation even when assisted by genius can prevent the narrator from always knowing the outcome of the story he tells—he commences, in a manner of speaking, with the problem already solved. More-over, the illusion begins from the moment the narrative *confers a meaning* on the event which, when it actually occurred, no doubt had several meanings or perhaps none. [As a result, we must] give up the pretence of objectivity, abandoning a sort of false scientific attitude that would judge a work by the precision of its detail. (Gusdorf [1956] 1980, 42).

For my part, the notions of "difficulty," "illusion," and so forth are problematic in themselves, for it is only with that "false scientific attitude" in mind that this language emerges. Set in opposition to history, to the allegedly real past that cannot be recovered owing to either the fallibility or the deviousness of memory, the past which one recalls can only be deemed illusory, false, and a fiction (Spence 1982).

However different their respective accounts may be, Schachtel and Gusdorf agree on the issue at hand. Memory, it would appear, cannot help but deform the reality of the past. For the time being, however, I will simply suggest that the disjunction observed between life as lived, moment to moment, and life as recollected in no way entails a necessary falsification of the past.

It is imperative to recognize that immediate experience is no less rooted in interpretation than is recollection. In the very act of identifying our experience as possessing such and such a meaning, we are already in the thick of language and convention. To understand recollection in relation to the aim of recovery is, in fact, to misunderstand what it is all about: namely, the positing of an intelligible order to the past from the vantage point of the present. Along these lines, we can justifiably say that the past exists in the present only in memory. It is therefore not to be confused with the "past presents" which we formerly lived.

Again, in the interest of fairness, Gusdorf said as much when he treated recollection as a type of "aerial view" or a second reading of experience that may even be truer, on some level, than the first because it provides a context within which prior experience may be understood. In immediate experience, he suggested, there may be too much agitation and uncertainty to allow one to fully grasp what is transpiring. On the other hand and precisely because of its distance from experience, memory permits one to consider new meanings not only because of the absence of this agitation and uncertainty, but because prior experience can be read in relation to what has subsequently transpired and as an episode in an evolving narrative.

Practically speaking, this means that we ought not to expect perfect congruence between prospective and retrospective data on the self. They provide two fundamentally different vantage points on experience. Indeed, it could be argued in this context that, even if we, as researchers, were to have in hand an exhaustive record of everything that happened in someone's life—a videotape, say, that was as long as the life itself—we would still be missing out on an integral dimension of selfhood: namely, the way in which experience is understood, organized, and appropriated into the fabric of one's life.

With this in mind, it could also be argued that retrospective data are even more instrumental in studying the self across the life span than are prospective data. Consider, for instance, some of the problems attendant to studying children. The analysis of a child, Freud wrote, is most often not very rich in material. "Too many words and thoughts have to be lent to the child, and even so the deepest strata may turn out to be impenetrable to consciousness" (Freud [1918] 1955, 8).

One of the main advantages, therefore, of analyzing the adult rather than the child is that the adult no longer needs to have words and thoughts lent to him or her. To some extent at least, the adult becomes the rightful owner of his or her words and thoughts, the result being that less guesswork is needed. In certain respects, of course, it would seem more convincing, particularly for those who distrust retrospective data, to learn about childhood by analyzing children. But the fact of the matter is, these data are "by far the more instructive" (9).

In line with Gusdorf's "aerial view" idea, Freud also suggested that we may, in fact, be better able to understand a particular period of our lives only after it is over and done with. Again, this is because what becomes available—in addition to the aforementioned words and thoughts—is a narrative context within which the meaning of past experiences may be placed. Therefore, the data of immediate experience, however convincing they may appear to be at a cursory glance, are not as instructive as recollections because they are not yet meaningful episodes in a story.

It should be emphasized that Freud did not claim that immediate experience is meaningless or irrelevant, nor that we should abandon a prospective studying of the self, as is done in most of developmental psychology. Instead, Freud claimed that, because it takes place in the light of known outcomes, recollection provides a vantage point from which the determination of the significance of past experience becomes possible.

Once again, it may be useful to offer a qualification of the point which we have been discussing. Vaillant, for instance, has argued that, "It is all too common for caterpillars to become butterflies and then to maintain in their youth that they had been little butterflies" (1977, 197). He suggested, in other words, that we often fall prey to distorting the past by rendering it to be more in line with present experience. Given what we are now, it may be difficult to imagine that we have ever been anything else. So it is that one's perceived continuity may be an artifact of the act of recollection, or, following what was said earlier, a defense against the recognition of our discontinuity. It may be all too disconcerting to avow our past selves, filled as they often are with ignorance and immaturity.

Returning to Updike for a moment, not only is the self irreducibly multiple, as he has already told us, but we may even dislike our old selves. His high-school self—"skinny, scabby, giggly, gabby, frantic to be noticed, tormented enough to be a tormentor, relentlessly pushing his cartoons and posters and noisy jokes and pseudo-sophisticated poems upon the helpless high school" (1989, 221)—now struck him as considerably obnoxious. He described a subsequent self as "another obnoxious showoff, rapacious and sneaky and, in the service of his own ego, remorseless" (222).

Fortunately for Updike, there was no need to disavow these old selves. In fact, they have culminated in a rather decent fellow.

But should we really expect most people to do the same? Isn't it easier to disavow these old selves, by peopling the past with inchoate versions of the more desirable self which one has hopefully become?

The reverse scenario must also be taken into consideration. In Tolstoy's *The Death of Ivan Ilych* ([1886] 1960), for instance, pleasure turns to pain as Ilych nears death. Initially, as he reflected on his life, he was able to say that everything seemed to have worked out all right. The episodes of his life seemed to work together neatly and cleanly, which resulted in his being able to feel that all he had been through, both good and bad, had been right. However, as the end of his life drew closer and as the prospect of his dying a lonely and painful death became more realistic, this security and comfort gave way to a profound sense of despair.

Ilych was troubled to find that certain moments he had experienced as a child—moments that had been filled with happiness—could no longer be seen for what they had been. "The child who experienced that happiness existed no longer, it was like a reminiscence of somebody else" (Tolstoy [1886] 1960, 147). It was the beginning of the end, he implied—the first stirrings of a grim story. Indeed, juxtaposed against the dismal reality of his present situation, particularly his realization that his life may not have been quite ideal, these moments cannot help but emerge as being much more tragic, for they point to his seemingly inevitable demise.

Tolstoy's story is instructive not only for its methodological insights into life-historical narration, but for its theoretical insights into the different meaning and function of narration across the course of life. As an older man facing the prospect of death and thus of fashioning a suitable ending to the story of his life, Ilych gazes over the terrain of his life and, finding it a wasteland, grows distraught over what has been. As with others who look back upon their lives in old age and find them wanting, the endings they envision may be decidedly bleak. There simply is not enough time remaining to shift the weight of the past.

Needless to say, the narratives told at other periods of the life span would likely have other focal concerns than the ones just described. For instance, in a study of a group of adolescents (Freeman, Csikszentmihalyi & Larson 1986), the aim was to understand how their experiences both alone and with family and friends had changed over a two-year span during high school. Two methods were involved. The first utilized their own descriptions of their experiences at the beginning and end of this period, while the second method assessed their recollections of change.

Without going into any great detail, what my colleagues and I found was that, while their descriptions of immediate experiences were much the same for the two periods in which we had gathered them, they perceived themselves in retrospect to have undergone considerable change, change that they could in fact explain and substantiate. I cite but one example.

While their experiences with their parents may still have been difficult and fraught with conflict, they felt that they had developed the capacity to bring more understanding to the relationships, to situate them within a broader, more comprehensive framework of interpretation. Therefore, in the context of adolescence, life-historical recollection may be tied not so much to determining how meaningful and worthwhile life has been, as in Ilych's case, but to a growing capacity to "see behind" experience, to use one's increased powers of interpretation to better understand and situate the events of one's rapidly changing life.

In any case, in light of the examples which we have been considering, what Gusdorf meant when he referred to the "illusion" inherent in autobiographical reflection may become somewhat clearer. In a distinct sense, the ends to which we have become determine the beginnings which we ascribe to the stories of our lives. However, is it necessary to think of this condition in terms of illusion?

We have seen how present experience can color—or discolor, as the case may be—the meanings of the past. It also seems evident enough that, sometimes, this process of coloration may be nothing short of a patent falsification of the past. But *must* it be so? My own inclination is that it is not.

Yet there remains an important problem for us to consider before proclaiming that life-historical narratives are not merely falsifications of the past. The problem is that, in dealing with life-historical data, the task of making sense of them is not so much *explanatory* as it is *interpretive*. Let us therefore pursue this distinction, and see if we can shed further light on the problems and possibilities of using life-historical data in studying the self.

Explanation and Understanding in Historical Inquiry

Philip Roth began *The Facts* with a letter to one of his fictional creations, Nathan Zuckerman. After so many years of clothing reality with his imagination, he finally chose to write an autobiography and thus revisit the bare facts of his personal past. Much to his surprise, he said, "I now appear to have gone about writing a book absolutely backward, taking what I have already imagined and, as it were, desiccating it, so as to restore my experience to the original, prefictionalized factuality" (Roth 1988, 3). This was a strange and difficult turnabout, therefore, for Roth, the fiction-writer.

Whereas fiction, he suggested, involves the transformation of the real into the imagined, autobiography involves the exact opposite—the attempt to denude one's imagination so as to behold the pristine origins from which it sprang. It is an act of "desiccation," Roth told us—an act of wringing out his own fertile mind toward the end of seeing what lay buried beneath the countless layers of fiction which he had written over the course of his life.

In large measure, the reason he undertook this task was to inform the present. We all go through spaces of darkness, it seems, where the self becomes virtually opaque, and, at times like these, "you need ways of making yourself visible to yourself" (Roth 1988, 4).

A number of months before writing *The Facts*, Roth had found himself terribly confused about his life. He could no longer understand just how he had become the person he now was. Whereas in the past, he had been capable of remaking himself, this time it was impossible. He was in the midst of having a nervous breakdown, as his very self had been lost somewhere along the way.

Roth's objective, as he understood it initially, was to retrace the steps of his past in order to explain how he arrived at his present situation. In this respect, his position was reminiscent of Hempel who argued, in 1942, that history should be conceptualized as an enterprise just as are any other forms of science. It is true enough, Hempel noted, that historical explanations are often incomplete—at least as compared to those offered by the hard sciences. However, the operative principles and goals are the same.

More than twenty years later, Hempel argued that the historian must try to explain the past in a manner as lawful and exhaustive as possible, with each stage being shown to " 'lead to' the next and thus be linked to its successor by virtue of some general principles which make the occurrence of the latter at least reasonably probable given the former" (Hempel 1965, 449). In brief, Hempel's position is founded upon a prospective causal framework rooted in the traditional scientific goals of prediction and control.

In 1986 and 1988, Gergen and Gergen theorized on the concept of development along narrative lines that was largely in agreement with Hempel's ideas. For instance, they noted that the positing of a goal state is intrinsic to the concept, as is the idea of causal dependency. The successful narrative, they wrote, must therefore *"select and arrange events in such a way that the goal state is rendered more or less probable"* [italics in original] (1986, 26).

This perspective is useful, but with one important qualification. The choice of what sort of narrative is to be told can be made only after the data are in—that is, retrospectively. With this in mind, does it still make sense, epistemologically, to speak about causation?

On some levels, yes. We can still speak cautiously about what seems to have led to what. At the same time, however, the mode of causation which we are considering here is not necessarily to be understood in terms of the classic "if/then" model customarily employed. The causation is predicated on a function of interpretation relying completely on a narrator who, from the vantage point of the present, is undertaking the task of establishing meaningful connections between past experiences.

Let us return to Philip Roth for a moment to further flesh out these issues. First, in line with what has just been said, it must be recognized that the "facts" of which he wrote are themselves products of his own imagination because it is only through the act of remembering that facts take on meaning and significance. In selecting for inclusion in his narrative some facts rather than others, he had, in other words, already determined what sort of story he wanted to tell. The task Roth faced, therefore, was not so much to reveal the facts of his life in and of themselves, but to posit possible beginnings—possible causes—in light of the end which he has become.

In short, however much it might have aimed toward a necessary and sufficient explanation of who and what Roth *is*, the project at hand was irrevocably interpretive and narrational. His experiences were brought together through a fundamentally literary act in which the twists and turns of the remembered past became part of a story.

Roth realized this:

I recognize that I'm using the word "facts" here, in this letter, in its idealized form and in a much more simple-minded way than it's meant in the title. Obviously the facts are never just coming at you but are incorporated by an imagination that is formed by your previous experience. (1988, 8)

He also realized that a historical project such as his, far from being a disinterested pursuit, issues from a desire to find answers to the riddle of existence. As is the case with anyone trying to figure out how they have managed to go astray in their lives, the past is examined with specific questions in mind. "Indeed, you search out your past to discover which events have led you to ask those specific questions" (8).

Finally, Roth also realized that, however factually based and explanatory a life-historical narrative may be, it is inevitably permeated by interpretation.

It isn't that you subordinate your ideas to the force of the facts in autobiography, but that you construct a sequence of stories to bind up the facts with a persuasive *hypothesis* that unravels your history's meaning. (1988, 8)

Roth was therefore caught in an epistemological dilemma of sorts. While on the one hand he was interested in letting the facts of his life speak for themselves, it is also clear that those very facts were being selected in the light of present prejudices and preconceptions, including the most appropriate narrative forms for telling his story. For instructive comments on the writing of history, see Gadamer (1979) and Ricoeur (1984).

We ought not to suppose that facts are irrelevant or that they are merely blank screens onto which we project our various prejudices and preconceptions. The point is only that facts acquire whatever sense they have as a function of the whole to which they contribute and of which they are a part. This movement from part to whole and whole to part is sometimes discussed under the rubric of the hermeneutical circle. The main idea is that in interpreting reality—be it a literary text, a body of scientific data, or, as in this case, the facts of one's previous existence—there is a process of going back and forth between the particulars before us and an emerging context within which these particulars can be situated.

With this hermeneutical circle in mind, it is questionable whether Roth's notion of what he called "unravelling" is suitable for our present concerns. Ordinarily, when we speak of unravelling, the connotation is of having arrived at an exhaustive solution as in, for instance, the unravelling of a mystery. At the end of a mystery novel—in most cases, at any rate—all of the disparate pieces of the puzzle and the clues, the significances of which had been unknown, suddenly make sense. We may well wish our lives were like this. As a general rule, however, they are surely not.

There is an important implication here. No matter how successful we may believe ourselves to be in explaining the course of history, the interpretive dimension of the venture remains unsurpassable (Danto 1985; Gallie 1964; Mink 1965; Ricoeur 1981). In turn, this means that, no matter how comprehensive and explanatory a historical account may be, the very fact that it is a product of interpretation precludes the possibility of the account ever being deemed to be complete and exhaustive. The same holds true, I would argue, for accounts of the self and its development.

Therefore, in studying the self via life history, it is imperative to remember that, far from being a neutral and detached recounting of what was, the narrative which one tells is, instead, an interpretive creation founded upon the meaning and significance which one is able to confer upon the experiences of the past.

The question that must now be raised is: How useful are life-historical data in studying the self? Surely they can help us learn about implicit theories of development, selfhood, and more. But given that they are avowedly interpretive products, how can life-historical data reveal anything about the self itself? And finally, how are we ever to know whether the narratives told by those whom we study are to be believed?

Life Historical Narration and the Problem of Self-deception

When gathering life histories, it often seems impossible to tell, with a fair degree of certainty and conviction, whether the person being studied is speaking the truth. It must be emphasized that by *truth*, we do not necessarily mean faithfulness in recounting the discrete events of the past. As has already been suggested, history involves significantly more than this sort of accuracy. In considering the idea of truth in this context, we are, instead, concerned with the truth of the narrative itself as a global, comprehensive, and interpretively based rendition of a life.

There are some who might argue that the idea of truth is entirely inappropriate in this context. The interpretive dimension of life-historical narration, they might hold, is exactly what obviates its possibility. Furthermore, it might be argued that, since the meaning and significance of one's past frequently changes over the course of life, this also renders the idea of truth suspect. If what is palpably true now may change at some point in the future, what justification do we have to speak about it at all?

In response to the first criticism, we can say that, although the primacy of interpretation in life-historical narration does militate against the possibility of speaking about the truth in absolute unequivocal terms, it in no way removes from us the burden of taking the idea seriously. The simple fact that people who are blatantly deceived about who they are do exist should suffice to remind us that we cannot completely sidestep the issue.

In response to the second criticism, I would argue that, far from diluting its importance, the changeability of truth over the course of life says only that, in speaking about the truth of the life-historical past, one must realize that it is not simply *there* for all time. To assume that it is would render the past into a fundamentally static aspect, untouched by an ever-changing present. We know that this is not so.

We also know that what often happens in the course of recollection is that a rendition of the past which we had previously taken to be true and complete is exposed for its falsity or inadequacy. More positively, we often begin to understand more about ourselves. Corollarily, this new realization gives rise to a different and more enlarged conception of who we are.

But the question still remains: How can we begin to distinguish life histories that speak something akin to the truth from those that do not? This is exactly the question that Roth's fictional interlocutor, Zuckerman, raised after having read Roth's autobiography.

Due in part to the need to be discreet about the lives of the people Roth wrote about, Zuckerman felt that there was simply not enough being disclosed in the work. In Roth's fiction, he noted, there isn't the need to worry about being too revealing. Whatever real-life characters his fictional creations may be based upon, they are clothed in enough imaginary garb to prevent people from being offended. More seriously, however, from what he knows of Roth's life—particularly his hopelessly botched marriage—Zuckerman felt that the entire account was just too simple and turmoil-free.

Thus, he asked, not only of Roth but of autobiographers in general, "How close is the narration to the truth? Is the author hiding his or her motives, presenting his or her actions to lay bare the essential nature of conditions or trying to hide something, telling in order *not* to tell?" (Roth 1988, 163–164).

These questions are difficult ones, for as Zuckerman himself realized, perhaps we all *tell* in order *not* to tell—that is, perhaps when we narrate our lives, we are asserting who we *wish* ourselves to be, who we *wish* to present to those who are listening to our story.

All too suspicious of this element of social desirability, Zuckerman laid this suspicion on the line by asking, "Is this really 'you,' or is it what you want to look like to your readers at the age of fifty-five?" (Roth 1988, 164).

Wasn't Roth aware of his own literary tricks? "Even if it's no more than one percent you've edited out, that's the one percent that counts—the one percent that's saved for your imagination and that changes everything. But this isn't unusual really," Zuckerman acknowledged. "With autobiography," he said, "there's always another text, a countertext, if you will, to the one presented." This is why it must be deemed "the most manipulative of all literary forms" (172).

Even this insight, however, cannot allay the most salient source of Zuckerman's discomfort. He refers to Roth's fiction. "The truth you told about all this long ago, you now want to tell in a different way" (173). His complaint, therefore, is that Roth has succumbed to the lure of rewriting his past. He has left behind the raw immediacy of the events that had fueled his earlier work, and has given them new meaning through the distance that has been conferred by time. But is Roth to be faulted for this act of rewriting the past, which, as we have repeatedly seen, appears to be a regular feature of life-historical narration?

In the case presented in *The Facts*, Zuckerman would undoubtedly answer, "Yes." His reason would be that, in light of what he knows about Roth's past as a participant in his fiction over the years, there is simply too huge of a gap between then and now for this story to be believed. His complaints notwithstanding, Zuckerman believes, fortunately, that he is, in fact, able to see both the text and the countertext of what Roth has written.

As I have suggested in another work (Freeman 1984), if life-historical data are to be used in order to derive information not only about self-conception and implicit developmental theories, but about the self itself, it would seem imperative to complement them in some fashion with data that are rooted in ongoing immediate experience. Ideally, this would mean having in hand both prospective data, pertaining to ongoing immediate experience, and retrospective data, which would embody the past in narrative form. Less ideally, perhaps, it would simply mean becoming attuned to the possible disjunctions between the past—or, more appropriately, the "past presents"—as lived and the past as told. When these are not readily-forthcoming, researchers must probe for them. Only then, will we place ourselves in the position of being able to understand, as fully as we might, how previous interpretations of experience have become transformed into present ones.

In suggesting the need for this sort of dual method, I am emphatically not claiming that prospective data are to be privileged over retrospective data as if they constituted some sort of pure, true baseline of experience. As noted earlier, these data are, while useful in their place, only one source of information. Neither can we privilege retrospective data over prospective data in studying the self. While it is clear enough that the narratives which people tell can certainly be in the service of providing that "aerial view" from which the truth can emerge, they can also actually hide the truth, both from others and from oneself.

However, in revealing apparent instances of self-deception among those whom we study, it should be noted that these instances may be every bit as telling about the selves in question as are those instances in which self-deception is manifestly absent. In other words, provided we have the means for identifying self-deception as such, we may still be able to speak cogently about the selves being studied and their needs, desires, and defenses. Of course, this is only so to the extent that we are able to establish a "countertext," as Zuckerman called it, to the one being presented to us.

Generally, this means that, in studying the self via life-history—assuming that we are interested in more than one's present self-conceptions—it is necessary to maintain a type of interpretive vigilance over the data at hand, and to be aware of the dynamic interrelationship of text and countertext. In dealing with life-historical interview data, for instance, it is often possible to detect disjunctions between what one is manifestly saying about his or her life and the meaning of that life.

An adolescent's proclamation of his or her burgeoning independence discloses a latent uncertainty. A middle-aged man's insistence on his contentment, in fact, discloses his discontent. An elderly woman's conviction in the meaningfulness of her life actually discloses a nagging fear that she will die alone and in despair.

Some researchers, of course, may consider it audacious to derive accounts of lives that are other than the ones manifestly provided by the people being studied—and, in some cases, it may very well be so. In other cases, however, it is important to "read between the lines" of what is being said so as to determine, to the best of one's ability, the true meaning and significance.

Furthermore, by studying the self via life histories with the type of interpretive vigilance already described, and by becoming attuned to the developmental processes embodied within those life histories, we might also be able to secure useful information about the factors, both internal and external, that facilitate or impede these processes. As noted earlier, a life history is to be seen, not only as a psychological document, but as a sociological one as well. A life history can reveal the conditions within which the self assumes its specific form. As such, the life history may be considered to be an important tool for studying both selves and their developmental processes along with the social, cultural, and historical factors giving rise to them.

CONCLUSION: THE PLACE OF LIFE HISTORY IN STUDYING THE LIFE SPAN

As I have argued in this essay, despite the numerous methodological and epistemological difficulties encountered in studying the self via life history, this method remains a viable and important mode of inquiry. In life history, I include not only research endeavors such as structured and semistructured interviews designed to explore changes occurring in particular spheres of life experience, but whatever personal documents—diaries, memoirs, autobiographies, and more—as can reveal information about lives. All too often, these types of materials are considered to be too subjective and unwieldy, perhaps suitable for humanists but not acceptable for scientists such as ourselves. However, after Allport's work in 1942, among others, it may be that these materials can provide us with precisely the type of real-life data that can yield insight into those dimensions of selfhood that are closest to who we really are.

By way of offering a qualification, it should be emphasized that, for those inclined to pursue their inquiries into the self in a more systematic experimental framework, the difficulties at hand may appear to be no less insurmountable than they were at the outset. Inasmuch as the difficulties which we have encountered have been largely interpretive in nature, it may be that others, for whom the scope of these difficulties brings us outside the practice of scientific psychology altogether, do remain. In response to this hypothetical criticism, I will say only that it has not been my aim to replace science with something else, but rather to call for a form of science broadly enough conceived to properly accommodate the phenomena being studied.

With regard to the first problem discussed—that of language—I suggest that, although it might be held that life-historical data are hopelessly tainted by the employment of linguistically conventionalized idioms of self-understanding, the problem at hand is, in principle, no different than for any inquiry into the self, the very concept of which receives its form in and through language. Thus, even while acknowledging that it is possible for language to dilute, distort, and falsify experience, it is also clear that we cannot help but disclose experience—whether it is immediate or recollected—through available cultural idioms. Far from necessarily entailing their invalidity as such, the fact that life-historical narratives are linguistic, even literary, artifacts simply means that there is no understanding of narratives and the selves who tell them apart from being culturally specific, linguistically mediated modes of understanding.

The second problem discussed—the effect of present experience on the interpretation of the past—has also been considered by some researchers to present an insuperable obstacle to obtaining valid life-historical data. The very fact that recollection occurs in the present—replete with its various prejudices—renders its truth value to be doubtful. However, as I argued in response to this problem, while there is no denying that present experience does indeed color one's interpretation of the past, it does not necessarily falsify it.

The conferral of new meaning and significance to the events of the past may actually serve the exact opposite function by shedding further—and indeed truer—light on one's history. In this sense, following Freud's viewpoints, the use of retrospective data may, in some instances, be preferable to prospective data in that they can make use of a narrative context which is unavailable in the agitation of immediate experience.

With regard to the third problem discussed—the distinction between explanation and interpretation in historical inquiry—it was suggested that historical understanding, in so far as it is fundamentally retrospective in nature, differs in certain important respects from scientific explanation, as it is customarily conceived. While science—with its traditional goals of prediction and control—looks forward in time, history looks back, aiming to comprehend the interrelationship of past events in narrative fashion.

This does not mean that we should think of history as mere interpretation. Nor should we suppose that the idea of explanation is wholly irrelevant, nor are we spared the burden of deciding which interpretations are valid and which are not. In avowing the interpretive dimension of historical understanding, we are simply acknowledging that narrative knowing is a different form of realization than that which is usually subsumed under the aegis of science. However, to reiterate, the point here is not to claim that narrative knowledge is beyond the purview of science, but only to call for a broad, comprehensive conception of science that includes narrative knowledge within its scope.

Finally, with regard to the fourth problem addressed—that of deception and truth in life history—it was suggested that, although the problem at hand is a serious one, it may still be possible to ensure that we, as researchers, are not misled by the life-historical narratives which we are told. On some level, it will be recalled, the present problem may be considered as irrelevant. If our interest is solely in how people conceive themselves and their developmental processes, the question of truth is beside the point. If, however, we believe that one's self-conception and history can sometimes be at odds with what can consensually be regarded as a more truthful account of who one has been—and if, in fact, we wish to learn not only about self-conceptions but about selves and the factors that shape them—it would seem to be important to devise methods and establish modes of interpretive attention that can aid us in the task.

This task is not an easy one. In addition to the hermeneutic circle within which the self is enmeshed, the researcher is also enmeshed within just such a circle. He or she must seize upon the narrative that has been told, and attempt to make sense of it by working back and forth between part and whole, as described earlier in this chapter. This means that studying the self via life history involves a double hermeneutic or an interpretation of an interpretation. It must be emphasized, however, that this condition is part and parcel of virtually any inquiry into the self that relies upon the self's own version of experience.

To the extent that the self is bound with its history—as I believe it is—it behooves us, as students of the self, to include life-historical data within the scope of our inquiries. By no means am I arguing that life histories should be the *only* source of information about the self, nor even that they are the *most important* source of data. The importance of a given source of information can only be determined in line with the particular questions which are asked.

I am arguing that we ought not to fear life-historical data for either their unwieldiness or their uncertain truth value. These data are no more unwieldy nor uncertain than is the phenomenon which we call "self."

REFERENCES

Allport, G. 1942. *The use of personal documents in psychological science.* New York: Social Science Research Council.

Barthes, R. 1977. *Image, music, text.* New York: Hill and Wang.

Baumeister, R. F. 1987. How the self became a problem: A psychological review of historical research. *Journal of Personality and Social Psychology* 52:163–176.

Danto, A. C. 1985. *Narration and knowledge.* New York: Columbia University Press.

Derrida, J. 1978. *Writing and difference.* Chicago, Ill.: The University of Chicago Press.

Foucault, M. 1973. *The order of things.* New York: Vintage.

Freeman, M. 1984. History, narrative, and life-span developmental knowledge. *Human Development* 27:1–19.

————. 1985. Paul Ricoeur on interpretation: The model of the text and the idea of development. *Human Development* 28:295–312.

Freeman, M.; Csikszentmihalyi, M.; and Larson, R. 1986. Adolescence and its recollection: Toward an interpretive model of development. *Merrill-Palmer Quarterly* 32:167–185.

Freud, S. [1901–1905] 1962. Three essays on the theory of sexuality. *Standard Edition.* Vol. 3. London: Hogarth Press.

————. [1918] 1955. From the history of an infantile neurosis. *Standard Edition.* Vol. 17. London: Hogarth Press.

Gadamer, H. G. 1979. The problem of historical consciousness. In *Interpretive Social Science,* edited by P. Rabinow and W. M. Sullivan. Berkeley, Calif.: University of California Press. 103–160.

Gallie, W. B. 1964. *Philosophy and the historical understanding.* New York: Schocken.

Geertz, C. 1979. From the native's point of view: On the nature of anthropological understanding. In *Interpretive Social Science,* edited by P. Rabinow and W. M. Sullivan. Berkeley, Calif.: University of California Press. 225–241.

Gergen, K. J. 1980. The emerging crisis in life-span developmental psychology. In *Life-span development and behavior* Vol. 3, edited by P. B. Baltes and O. G. Brim. New York: Academic Press. 30–63.

————. 1988. If persons are texts. In *Hermeneutics and psychological theory*, edited by S. B. Messer, L. A. Sass, and R. L. Woolfolk. New Brunswick, N.J.: Rutgers University Press. 28–51.

Gergen, K. J., and Gergen, M. M. 1986. Narrative form and the construction of psychological science. In *Narrative psychology: The storied nature of human lives*, edited by T. R. Sarbin. New York: Praeger. 17–56.

————. 1988. Narrative and the self as relationship. In *Advances in experimental social psychology*, Vol. 21, edited by L. Berkowitz. San Diego, Calif.: Academic Press. 22–44.

Gusdorf, G. [1956] 1980. Conditions and limits of autobiography. In *Autobiography: Essays theoretical and critical*, edited by J. Olney. Princeton, N.J.: Princeton University Press. 28–48.

Hempel, C. G. 1942. The function of general laws in history. *Journal of Philosophy* 39:35–48.

————. 1965. *Aspects of scientific explanation*. New York: New York University Press.

Hume, D. [1739–1740] 1874. *A treatise on human nature*. London: Longmans, Green, and Co.

James, W. [1890] 1950. *The principles of psychology*. New York: Dover.

Keller, H. [1902] 1974. *The story of my life*. New York: New American Library.

Lee, R. 1959. *Freedom and culture*. New York: Spectrum.

Markus, H., and Nurius, P. 1986. Possible selves. *American Psychologist* 41:954–969.

————. 1987. Possible selves: The interface between motivation and the self-concept. In *Self and identity: Psychosocial perspectives*, edited by K. Yardley and T. Honess. Chichester, U.K.: John Wiley & Sons. 157–172.

Mauss, M. [1938] 1979. *Essays in sociology and psychology*. London: Routledge and Kegan Paul.

Mink, L. O. 1965. The autonomy of historical understanding. *History and Theory* 5:24–47.

Mischel, W. 1968. *Personality and assessment*. Stanford, Calif.: Stanford University Press.

Murray, K. 1986. Literary pathfinding: The work of popular life constructors. In *Narrative psychology: The storied nature of human lives*, edited by T. R. Sarbin. New York: Praeger. 276–292.

Neugarten, B. 1969. Continuities and discontinuities of psychological issues into adult life. *Human Development* 12:121–130.

Nietzsche, F. [1887] 1968. *The will to power.* New York: Vintage.

Ricoeur, P. 1981. *Hermeneutics and the human sciences.* Cambridge: Cambridge University Press.

———. 1984. *Time and narrative.* Vol. 1. Chicago: The University of Chicago Press.

Rosenberg, S. 1988. Self and others: Studies in social personality and autobiography. In *Advances in experimental social psychology,* Vol. 21, edited by L. Berkowitz. San Diego, Calif.: Academic Press. 57–95.

Roth, P. 1988. *The facts.* New York: Farrar, Straus, & Giroux.

Schachtel, E. G. 1959. *Metamorphosis.* New York: Basic Books.

Sheehy, G. 1976. *Passages.* Toronto: Bantam.

Sheehy, G. 1981. *Pathfinders.* New York: Morrow.

Shweder, R. A. 1975. How relevant is an individual difference theory of personality? *Journal of Personality* 43:455–484.

Shweder, R. A., and E. J. Bourne. 1984. Does of the concept of the person vary cross-culturally? In *Culture theory: Essays on mind, self, and emotion,* edited by R. A. Shweder and R. A. LeVine. New York: Cambridge University Press. 158–199.

Skinner, B. F. 1971. *Beyond freedom and dignity.* New York: Bantam.

———. 1974. *About behaviorism.* New York: Vintage.

Spence, D. P. 1982. *Narrative truth and historical truth.* New York: W. W. Norton & Co.

Tolstoy, L. [1886] 1960. *The death of Ivan Illych.* New York: New American Library.

Updike, J. 1989. *Self-consciousness.* New York: Alfred A. Knopf.

Vaillant, G. 1977. *Adaptation to life.* Boston, Mass.: Little, Brown.

Weintraub, K. J. 1975. Autobiography and historical consciousness. *Critical Inquiry* 1:821–848.

HERBERT W. MARSH
BARBARA M. BYRNE
RICHARD J. SHAVELSON

2

A Multidimensional, Hierarchical Self-concept*

INTRODUCTION

The self-concept construct is one of the oldest in psychology and is widely used in many disciplines. Despite its popularity, reviews prior to the 1980s typically emphasized the lack of theoretical basis in most studies, the poor quality of measurement instruments, methodological shortcomings, and a general lack of consistent findings except, perhaps, support for the null hypothesis. This situation called into question the usefulness of the self-concept construct.

In dramatic contrast, the last decade has seen considerable progress in theory, measurement, and research. This progress is due, at least in part, to a stronger emphasis on a multidimensional, hierarchical self-concept instead of global measures of self and the development of measurement instruments based on this theoretical approach. The purpose of this chapter is to review different theoretical and empirical approaches that have contributed to this emphasis.

A HISTORICAL PERSPECTIVE

A positive self-concept is valued as a desirable outcome in many disciplines such as educational, developmental, clinical, and social psychology. Self-concept and related processes are frequently posited as a mediating variable that facilitates the attainment of other desired outcomes such as academic achievement. Researchers with a major focus on other constructs are often interested in how constructs in their research are related to self-concept. Methodologists are also concerned with particular measurement and methodological issues inherent in the study of self-concept.

This interest in self-concept has a long and controversial history, and it is one of the oldest areas of research in the social sciences. The longest chapter in William James's textbook (1890), the first introductory textbook in psychology, was devoted to self-concept and introduced many issues of current relevance. An overview of James' theory, although necessarily brief and superficial, serves to introduce critical issues of theoretical importance across the subsequent decades.

William James is generally recognized as the first psychologist to develop a theory of the self-concept. Four notions developed by James were particularly important: (1) The *I* (self-as-knower or active agent) and *Me* (self-as-known or the content of experience) distinction; (2) The multifaceted, hierarchical nature of self-concept; (3) The social self; and (4) The definition of self-esteem as the ratio of success to pretensions and a function of an activity's subjective importance.

According to James, the total person must necessarily contain self-as-knower, the active agent of experience, and self-as-known, the content of the experience. This important distinction poses a difficult problem for self-concept theories in that the self-reflexive act of identifying the content of experience must also involve the self-as-knower so that the two components cannot be separated. For James, self-as-known—the *Me*—"is the sum total of all that he CAN call his" ([1890] 1963, 291).

James divided the self-as-known into the material *Me* (body, clothes, family, home, and property), the social *Me*, and the spiritual *Me*. The spiritual self refers to "a man's inner or subjective being, his psychic faculties or dispositions" (296). The social self "is the recognition which he gets from his mates" (293), so that there are "as many social selves as there are individuals who recognize him ... [or] distinct groups of persons about whose opinion he cares" (294).

The social self can also be a generalized or potential social self that represents the evaluations of a hypothetical higher authority, a future generation, or God. These *Me* components are hierarchically structured "with the bodily Self at the bottom, the spiritual Self at the top, and the extracorporeal material selves and the various social selves between" (313).

For James, a person's overall self-evaluation reflects all the different *Me's* weighted according to their subjective importance to the person. Since a person cannot be all things, he or she must select carefully "the strongest, truest, deepest self . . . on which to stake his salvation" (310).

James noted that: "I, who for the time have staked my all on being a psychologist, am mortified if others know much more psychology than I. But I am contented to wallow in the grossest ignorance of Greek" (310). For James, self-esteem is influenced not by absolute success and failure, but the ratio of success to pretensions.

In this view, objective accomplishments are evaluated in relation to an internal frame of reference. Thus "we have the paradox of a man shamed to death because he is only the second pugilist or the second oarsman in the world . . . Yonder puny fellow, however, whom everyone can beat, suffers no chagrin about it, for has long ago abandoned the attempt to 'carry that line' " (310).

Putting these two ideas together, James concludes that our self-feeling "depends entirely on what we back ourselves to be and do" (310). Also associated with the *Me's* are feelings and the emotions they arouse—called "self-feelings"—and the actions that they prompt. These actions prompted by the *Me's* are self-preservation (or self-defense) and self-seeking (or providing for the future as distinguished from maintaining the present). Hence James' self-system is both an organized structure for interpreting experience and a dynamic process that prompts feelings, emotions, and action.

William James explicitly or implicitly anticipated most subsequent developments in self-concept theories. His social self anticipated the importance of the evaluations by specific and generalized others that was an important focus of symbolic interactionists such as Cooley and Mead. The self-as-knower and self-as-known distinction is acknowledged in nearly all accounts of self-concept and corresponds approximately to the dynamic/process and structural/trait orientations that are currently popular in self-concept research.

The development of the self-system described by James is consistent with recently developed cognitive approaches to the study of self. The definition of self-esteem as a function of both accomplishments and aspirations—and also the subjective importance of the activity—proved to be very heuristic. The simultaneous self-seeking and self-preserving actions proposed by James may reflect the distinction between self-enhancement and self-consistency that has been the focus of much research. Of particular relevance to this chapter, James also anticipated the multifaceted hierarchical model of self-concept.

Despite the rich beginning provided by William James, advances in theory, research, and measurement of self-concept were slow during the heyday of behaviorism. It is only in the last twenty-five years that there has been a resurgence in self-concept research. Even during this more recent period, however, there are interesting peculiarities that appear to have undermined the usefulness of this research for understanding self-concept.

Unlike many areas of research, self-concept research has not occurred primarily within the structure of a particular discipline. Although many thousands of studies have examined self-concept, only a few researchers have published a significant number of studies or have conducted self-concept research over an extended period of time. In many studies the major focus is on some other construct (such as academic achievement or delinquency) and a measure of self-concept is included because of its assumed relevance to the other construct.

It also appears that many self-concept studies lacked sophistication in theory, measurement or methodology. Particularly prior to the 1980s, reviews of self-concept research typically emphasized the theoretical and methodological shortcomings (Burns 1979; Shavelson, Hubner & Stanton 1976; Wells & Marwell, 1976; Wylie 1974, 1979). This disappointing lack of rigor can, perhaps, be explained by the lack of a disciplinary base for self-concept research.

Self-concept, as with many other psychological constructs, suffers in that "everybody knows what it is." Thus, many researchers do not feel compelled to provide any theoretical definition of what they are measuring. Because self-concept is a hypothetical construct, its usefulness must be established by investigations of its construct validity.

These investigations can be classified as within-network or between-network studies. Within-network studies explore the internal structure of self-concept. They test, for example, the dimensionality of self-concept and may seek to show that the construct has consistent, distinct multidimensional components, for example, physical, social, or academic self-concept. These studies typically employ empirical techniques such as factor analysis or multitrait-multimethod (MTMM) analysis.

Between-network studies attempt to establish a logical, theoretically consistent pattern of relations between measures of self-concept and other constructs. The resolution of at least some within-construct issues should be a logical prerequisite to conducting between-construct research. However, between-network research has predominated self-concept research.

Despite the importance and popularity of the self-concept construct, empirical support for its usefulness based on research conducted prior to the 1980s was weak. Research up to that time had made limited progress toward resolving either the within- or between-construct issues. In fact, most research was directed toward the between-construct issues of relating self-concept to other constructs, whereas insufficient attention had been given to the within-construct issues that should have been the basis of constructing appropriate measurement instruments.

In retrospect, this emphasis on between-construct research to the exclusion of within-construct research may have been counterproductive and appears to be one reason why findings were not more consistent across different studies. In contrast, studies in the 1980s have made important advances in theory, measurement, and research.

The purpose of this chapter is to summarize a multifaceted hierarchical model of self-concept and empirical support for the model. Unlike most earlier research, the initial research emphasized the resolution of within-construct issues. This research contributed to support for the multifaceted, hierarchical model of self-concept and led to the construction of multidimensional self-concept instruments. More recent research based on this model has demonstrated the importance of this multidimensional perspective in considering between-construct issues.

For the purposes of this chapter:

1. The focus is on the self-as-known—the structure of experience—rather than the self-as-knower. Said another way, the emphasis is on the structure and content of the self-concept rather than dynamic self-processes.
2. Self-concept is both differentiated and integrated so that it is meaningful to discuss the multiple dimensions of self-concept and a unified self (Epstein 1980).
3. The multiple dimensions of self-concept are hypothesized constructs—traits—that are testable with analytic procedures such as factor analysis, MTMM analysis, and other approaches to construct validation.
4. The dimensions of self-concept are assumed to be enduring, relatively stable trait dispositions. (Some researchers distinguish be-

tween chronic or characteristic levels of esteem and acute esteem that can be manipulated in laboratory settings using false feedback (Wells & Marwell 1976; Wylie 1979)).
5. The dimensions described here are assumed to be nomographic in that they are shared by all individuals. This is not to deny the importance of idiographic dimensions emphasized in phenomenological approaches to self. As noted by Epstein (1980) and others, the two approaches should be viewed as complementary. It is likely that both approaches are correct in that very narrowly defined dimensions may be idiosyncratic to individuals, whereas dimensions are common when the stimulus situations are more broadly defined.
6. Self-concept is assumed to have an evaluative character. This evaluative component may be based on absolute (e.g., an ideal) or relative (e.g., peers) frames of reference. The distinction between self-description and self-evaluation has not been adequately substantiated empirically or theoretically. Hence, the terms self-concept and self-esteem are used interchangeably (Shavelson et al., 1976).

THE MULTIFACETED STRUCTURE OF SELF-CONCEPT

The earliest theoretical accounts of self-concept emphasized its multidimensional nature (James [1890] 1963). Particularly in the period between 1960 and 1980, researchers sought empirical support for this contention, but support for it was weak. Despite this early theoretical emphasis on a multidimensional self-concept, empirical research prior to the 1980s emphasized a general, overall, or total self-concept, and did not adequately address within network constructs reflective of the structure of self-concept. In contrast, the multidimensionality of self-concept is a basic assumption of Shavelson's and colleagues' model (1976) of self-concept which served as the theoretical basis for the development of the Self Description Questionnaire (SDQ) instruments. The primary purpose of this section is to summarize theoretical and empirical support for the assumption.

The Shavelson and Colleagues Model:
A Multifaceted Hierarchical Self-Concept

Reviews of self-concept research in the 1960s and 1970s continued to identify shortcomings no less dramatic than the lack of a theoretical basis for defining and interpreting the construct and the poor quality of instruments used to measure it. In an attempt to remedy this situation, Shavelson and colleagues reviewed existing research and self-concept instruments and developed a multifaceted, hierarchical model of self-concept which they published in 1976.

Self-concept, broadly defined by Shavelson, is a person's perceptions of himself or herself. These perceptions are formed through experience with and interpretations of one's environment. They are especially influenced by evaluations by significant others, reinforcements, and attributions for one's own behavior. In the model, self-concept is further defined by seven major features.

1. It is organized or structured, in that people categorize the vast amount of information they have about themselves and relate these categories to one another.
2. It is multifaceted, and the particular facets reflects a self-referent category system adopted by a particular individual and/or shared by a group.
3. It is hierarchical, with perceptions of personal behavior at the base moving to inferences about self in subareas—for example, English and mathematics components contribute to academic self-concept, whereas physical, social, and emotional components contribute to nonacademic self-concept—then to inferences about self in general.
4. The hierarchical general self-concept—the apex of the model—is stable, but as one descends the hierarchy, self-concept becomes increasingly situation specific and, as a consequence, less stable.
5. Self-concept becomes increasingly multifaceted as the individual moves from infancy to adulthood.
6. Self-concept has both a descriptive and an evaluative aspect such that individuals may describe themselves ("I am happy") and evaluate themselves ("I do well in mathematics").
7. Self-concept can be differentiated from other constructs such as academic achievement.

Shavelson and colleagues also presented one possible representation of this hierarchical model (figure 2.1) where general-self appears at the apex and is divided into academic and nonacademic self-concepts at the next level. Academic self-concept is further divided into self-concepts in particular subject areas, such as mathematics, English, and so forth. Nonacademic self-concept is divided into three areas:

1. Social self-concept which is subdivided into relations with peers and with significant others;
2. Emotional self-concept; and
3. Physical self-concept which is subdivided into physical ability and physical appearance.

Figure 2.1
Structure of Self-Concept. One possible representation of the hierarchical organization of self-concept as posited in the original Shavelson, Hubner, and Stanton model of self-concept.

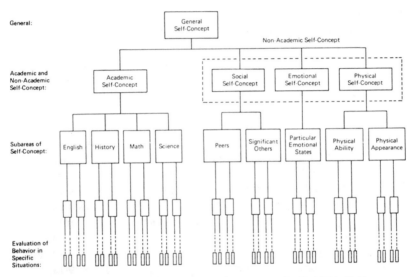

From: Shavelson, R. J.; Hubner, J. J.; and Stanton, G. C. 1976. Self-concept: Validation of construct interpretations. *Review of Educational Research* 46:413. (Copyright 1976 by the American Educational Research Association. Reprinted by permission of the publisher.)

Further levels of division are hypothesized for each of these specific self-concepts so that, at the base of the hierarchy, self-concepts are of limited generality, quite specific, and more closely related to actual behavior. This model posits a structure of self-concept that resembles British psychologists' hierarchical model of intellectual abilities (Vernon 1950) in which general ability (such as Spearman's "g") is at the apex.

The self-concept facets proposed in the Shavelson and colleagues model, as well as their hypothesized structure, were heuristic and plausible, but they were not empirically validated by research summarized in Shavelson et al. (1976). In their evaluation of five frequently used instruments, modest support for the separation of self-concept into social, physical, and academic facets was found. However, these three facets were not clearly identified in any one of the instruments.

At the time, Shavelson et al. were unable to identify any instrument for measuring multiple facets of self-concept as posited in their model, and the multifaceted nature of self-concept was not widely accepted by other researchers. Some researchers argued that the facets of self-concept were so heavily dominated by a general factor that they could not be adequately differentiated (Coopersmith 1967; Marx & Winne 1978).

Coopersmith, on the basis of preliminary research with his Self-Esteem Inventory, argued that "preadolescent children make little distinction about their worthiness in different areas of experience or, if such distinctions are made, they are made within the context of the over-all, general appraisal of worthiness that children have already made" (Coopersmith 1967, 6).

Marx and Winne classified the scales from three commonly used self-concept instruments into the academic, social, and physical facets supported by Shavelson et al., and then used multitrait-multimethod (MTMM) analyses to compare responses from different instruments. They found that responses to each of the three facets demonstrated some agreement across instruments (or convergence). However, responses to the different scales could not be adequately differentiated (for divergence). This led them to conclude that "self-concept seems more of a unitary concept than one divided into distinct subparts or facets" (Marx and Winne 1978, 900).

Prior to the 1980s, self-concept instruments typically consisted of a hodgepodge of self-referent items. Whereas factor analyses of responses to such instruments usually resulted in more than one factor, the factors were typically not replicable, easily interpreted, or consistent with the design of the instrument (Marsh & Smith 1982; Shavelson et al. 1976; Wylie 1979). Byrne noted that "Many consider this inability to attain discriminant validity among the dimensions of SC [self concept] to be one of the major complexities facing SC researchers today" (Byrne 1984, 449–450).

More recently, researchers have developed self-concept instruments to measure specific facets that are, at least, loosely based on an explicit theoretical model, and then used factor analysis to support these *a priori* facets (Boersma & Chapman 1979; Dusek & Flaherty 1981; Fleming & Courtney 1984; Harter 1982; Soares & Soares

1982; and research summarized here). Reviews of this research support the multifaceted structure of self-concept and indicate that self-concept cannot be adequately understood if its multidimensionality is ignored (Byrne 1984; Marsh & Shavelson 1985; Shavelson & Marsh 1986).

Even among those who accept the multifaceted nature of self-concept, there is no agreement on the identity of the specific dimensions that comprise self-concept and how these dimensions are structured. One purpose of the SDQ instruments was to provide reliable, valid measures that are suitable for testing assumptions underlying the conceptual structure of self-concept posited by Shavelson et al. Because the set of SDQ instruments was designed for different age groups, it is also possible to test the model at different developmental levels. In her review of self-concept models, Byrne concluded that "Although no one model to date has been sufficiently supported empirically so as to lay sole claim to the within-network structure of the construct, many recent studies, in particular those of Marsh and his colleagues, are providing increasingly stronger support for the hierarchical model" (1984, 449).

The Development of the SDQ Instruments

In the development of the SDQ instruments, it was reasoned that the determination of whether theoretically consistent and distinguishable facets of self-concept exist, and their content and structure—if they do exist—should be prerequisite to the study of how these facets or overall self-concepts are related to other variables. In adopting such an approach, atheoretical and/or purely empirical approaches to developing and refining measurement instruments were rejected. Instead, an explicit theoretical model was taken to be the starting point for instrument construction, and empirical results were used to support, refute, or revise the instrument as well as the theory upon which it is based.

In applying this approach, the Shavelson et al. model was judged to be the best available theoretical model of self-concept. Implicit in this approach is the presumption that theory building and instrument construction are inexorably intertwined, and that each will suffer if the two are separated. In this sense, the SDQ instruments are based on a strong empirical foundation and a good theoretical model. Consistent with this approach, SDQ research described in this chapter provided support for the Shavelson et al. model, but also led to its subsequent revision.

SDQ instruments have been developed for preadolescents (SDQ I), adolescents (SDQ II), and late-adolescents and young adults (SDQ III) (Marsh 1988, in press-b, in press-c). The three SDQ instruments were originally developed to measure different areas of self-concept that were derived largely from the Shavelson et al. model. (The different scales measured by the three instruments are presented later). Many of the scales—such as physical abilities, parent relations, math, and general—are common to all three SDQ instruments. Consistent with the Shavelson and colleagues hypothesis that self-concept becomes increasingly differentiated with age, the number and diversity of self-concept facets increases across the three instruments.

Testing the hypothesis of a multidimensional self-concept and the facets which the SDQ instruments are designed to measure was an important emphasis in this research. Although it is not the focus of this chapter, more than two dozen factor analyses of diverse samples of different ages have consistently identified the factors which each SDQ instrument is designed to measure (Marsh 1988, in press-b, in press-c). These factor-analytic results provide very strong support for the multidimensionality of self-concept, for the Shavelson and colleagues model used to develop the SDQ instruments, and for the ability of the SDQ instruments to differentiate multiple dimensions of self-concept.

The internal consistency of the scales from the three SDQ instruments is good—typically in the 80- and 90-percentile ranges (Marsh 1989). The stability of SDQ responses is also good, particularly for older children. For example, the stability of SDQ III responses was examined on four occasions during a twenty-month interval (Marsh, Richards & Barnes 1986). Short-term stability over a one-month interval was high (median $r = .87$) and nearly as high as the internal consistency estimates of reliability (median $r = .90$). Across intervals of at least eighteen months, long-term stability was somewhat lower (median of .74), but still substantial. Particularly since these late-adolescents frequently reported significant life changes—such as moving out of their family homes, starting university, taking their first permanent jobs, or getting married—this long-term stability was remarkably high. It is also important to note that general self-concept had the lowest long-term stability (median of .51) of any of the SDQ III scales, despite the fact that its internal consistency was among the highest. Similarly, the general academic scale was less stable than more specific facets of academic self-concept, even though its internal consistency was high.

These findings apparently contradict the Shavelson and colleagues model of 1976 and other theoretical accounts that posit more general components of self to be more stable. The findings suggest that the more general facets are more affected by short-term response biases, short-term mood fluctuations, or some other short-term time-specific influences. Whatever the eventual explanation for the surprisingly poor stability of the general facets, the findings offer support for the use of multidimensional measures of self-concept instead of general measures of self.

The Hierarchical Structure of Self-concept

The Hierarchical Structure of SDQ I Responses. The Shavelson and colleagues model posits that self-concept is hierarchically ordered as well as being multidimensional. The exploratory factor analysis techniques employed in most research (Marsh, Barnes, Cairns & Tidman 1984) are not suitable for testing hierarchical structures. Important advances in the application of confirmatory factor analysis, however, provide solutions to these problems. In 1985, Marsh and Hocevar tested the first-order structure of responses to the SDQ I by students in grades two through five (see also Marsh & Shavelson 1985). The goodness-of-fit of this first-order factor model was examined for each grade level separately, and across all four grade levels. The parameter estimates and goodness-of-fit indices demonstrated that the first-order factor structure was supported at each grade level.

The correlations among the SDQ I factors were estimated in the first-order models, but no special assumptions about the pattern of correlations were made. However, both the Shavelson et al. model and the design of the SDQ I assume that there is a systematic hierarchical ordering of the facets of self-concept which underlie these correlations among first-order factors.

For example, the SDQ I measures four nonacademic and three academic facets of self-concept. Thus, one reasonable hypothesis would be that the seven first-order factors would form two second-order factors, a finding which would be consistent with the Shavelson et al. model. However, the results of previous research suggest complications for this model (Marsh, Barnes et al. 1984). In particular, whereas the math and verbal factors (the reading self-concept factor on the SDQ I is referred to as verbal self-concept to be consistent with labels used on the SDQ II and SDQ III) were each substantially correlated with the general-school factor, they were not substantially correlated with each other. These data suggest that the higher-order structure underlying the SDQ I factors may be more complicated than was previously assumed.

In order to examine the hierarchical structure of self-concept, several competing models were tested. In one model, a single, general self-concept factor was proposed to explain the relationships among the seven first-order factors. This model, however, did not provide an adequate fit at any of the grade levels and was rejected.

In a second model, two second-order factors were proposed—one defined by the four nonacademic factors and one defined by the three academic factors.

This model fitted the data better than did the first model, but it was still inadequate. The final model (figure 2.2) took into account previous research showing verbal and math self-concepts to be nearly uncorrelated. Two second-order academic factors—math/academic and verbal/academic self-concepts—and a second-order nonacademic factor were posited. In this model it was also proposed that the three second-order factors were correlated, which is equivalent to saying that they combine to form a third-order, general self-concept. For each of the four years in school, this model fitted the data significantly better than did any of the other second-order models.

The results of these hierarchical factor analyses were consistent with Shavelson's and colleagues' assumption that self-concept is hierarchically ordered. However, the particular form of this higher-order structure is more complicated than was previously proposed. The Marsh/Shavelson revision of the Shavelson et al. model (figure 2.2) differs from the original Shavelson and colleagues model (figure 2.1) primarily in that there are two higher-order academic factors—math/academic and verbal/academic—instead of just one.

The Hierarchical Structure of Academic Self-concept. Shavelson and colleagues posited self-concept to be a multifaceted, hierarchical construct having academic and nonacademic components. To date, more emphasis—stemming largely from research in educational psychology—has been placed on the academic components, and important revisions have been made in the Shavelson and colleagues model. Shavelson and colleagues originally posited that subject specific self-concept (such as reading and mathematics) could be incorporated into a single higher-order dimension of academic self-concept. However, considerable research, based largely on SDQ responses, suggested that math and verbal self-concepts

Figure 2.2
Structure-of-Self-Concept. An empirically based representation
of the hierarchical organization of self-concept inferred from
responses to the Self Description Questionnaire I that served
as the basis of the Marsh/Shavelson revision of the original
Shavelson and colleagues model shown in Figure 2.1.

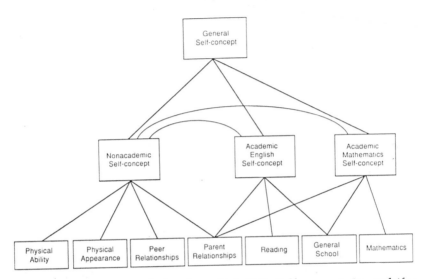

From: Marsh, H. W., and Shavelson, R. J 1985. Self-concept: Its multifaceted, hierarchical structure. *Educational Psychologist* 20:114. (Copyright
1985 by Lawrence Erlbaum Associates, Inc. Adapted by permission of the
publisher.)

were nearly uncorrelated and could not adequately be incorporated
into a single higher-order dimension. Hierarchical factor analyses
indicated the need for two higher-order academic facets—math/
academic and verbal/academic.

In 1988, Marsh, Byrne, and Shavelson more completely tested
the need for this revision by asking a large group of Canadian high-
school subjects to complete the verbal, math, and general school
scales from three different self-concept instruments—the SDQ III
and two other instruments. This research was important because it
provided a strong test of the generality of results based on SDQ research in Australia to responses to other self-concept instruments by
North Americans.

Hierarchical confirmatory factor analysis was again employed
in this study. A first-order factor model provided good support for the

nine *a prior* factors—math, verbal, and general school factors from each of the three self-concept instruments. The critical test was whether correlations among these nine first-order factors could be adequately explained by a single higher-order factor as posited in the original Shavelson et al. model, or whether two higher-order factors as posited in the Marsh/Shavelson revision were required.

The results showed conclusively that the Marsh/Shavelson revised model was superior. In fact, all three verbal self-concept scales were nearly uncorrelated with each of the three math self-concept scales. Similarly, in the hierarchical model based on the Marsh/Shavelson revision, the verbal/academic and math/academic higher-order factors were not significantly correlated. These results provided strong support for the generality of earlier SDQ research and for the revised model.

Marsh, Byrne, and Shavelson went on to critically evaluate the Marsh/Shavelson model. Support for this revised model was based primarily on demonstrating apparent problems with the original Shavelson et al. model. Whereas there was strong evidence that a single higher-order academic component was insufficient, there was no strong support for the premise that just two higher-order academic factors were sufficient.

Part of the problem, they argued, was that the revised model had not been presented in sufficient detail. To remedy this problem, they presented figure 2.3 which offers a more detailed development of the academic structure in the revised model.

The specific academic facets in figure 2.3 were selected to broadly reflect a typical academic curriculum, and the subject areas are roughly ordered from relatively pure measures of the math/academic component to relatively pure measures of the verbal/academic component.

Future research designed to evaluate this model must answer two important questions. First, are students able to differentiate their self-concepts in specific academic subjects so as to produce a well-defined structure of first-order factors? Second, assuming that the first-order factor structure is well-defined, will the two higher-order academic factors adequately explain the relations among the self-concepts in specific subjects?

In Search of a General Self Concept

The emphasis of SDQ research has been on the multifaceted nature of self-concept, on the measurement of distinguishable facets

Figure 2.3
The academic portion of Shavelson's, Hubner's, and Stanton's original
model (1976) and an elaboration of Marsh's and Shavelson's revision in
1985 that includes a wider variety of specific academic facets.

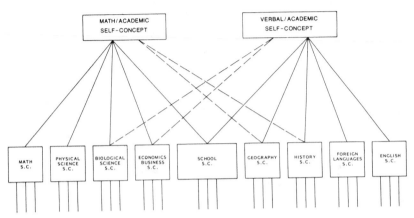

From: Marsh, H. W.; Byrne, B. M.; and Shavelson, R. 1988. A multifaceted
academic self-concept: Its hierarchical structure and its relation to academic achievement. *Journal of Educational Psychology* 80:378. (Copyright
1988 by the American Psychological Association. Reprinted by permission
of the publisher.)

of self-concept, and on the relationships between these specific facets and a wide array of domain-specific external criteria. However,
there is also a need for theoretical and empirical research examining
an overall, total, or general self-concept. Whereas such a construct is
widely inferred, it is typically ill-defined.

In published research, many investigators still represent self-
concept with a single score that is called overall, total, or general
self-concept. Research on self-concept, at least implicitly, has used a
variety of different definitions of general self-concept (Marsh 1986b;
Marsh & Shavelson 1985). Five of them are discussed here.

The first and most common—an agglomerate self-concept—is
a total score for a broad, typically ill-defined collection of self-report
items. The second—a relatively unidimensional self-concept
scale—refers to a separate, distinguishable facet that is comprised of
characteristics such as self-confidence and self-competence that are
superordinate to—but not specific to—a particular content area.
This type of general self-concept is sometimes referred to, albeit am-
biguously, as self-esteem. The third—a higher-order self-concept—

refers to an inferred construct which is not directly measured. The general self-concept that appears at the apex of the Shavelson et al. model and the general factor in the hierarchical factor analyses of the SDQ responses described earlier are examples of this third use. The fourth, a weighted-average general self-concept, follows from William James' assumption that the contribution of a specific component of self-concept to overall self-concept should be based on the saliency, value, or importance of the specific component to a particular individual. Finally, the fifth—a discrepancy general self-concept—refers to a general self-concept that is a function of discrepancies between actual self-concepts and ideal self-concepts in different areas. Alternatively, William James proposed that general self-concept is a function of the ratios of actual self-concept to ideal self-concepts or aspirations, instead of discrepancies.

An Agglomerate General Self-concept. In practice, the agglomerate use of general self is most common. Here, the construct is vaguely defined and there is little rationale for the potpourri of items that are used to measure it. On many commonly used instruments there is an attempt to measure a diverse set of facets, but the different facets have not been empirically verified, nor have their contributions been balanced. Instead, responses are simply summed to form a total score that is taken to be a measure of general self. Such a construct cannot be adequately characterized, and is idiosyncratic to particular instruments.

For example, Marsh and Smith (1982) compared responses to the Coopersmith Self-Esteem Inventory (1967) and the Sears Self-Concept Inventory (1963). A preliminary inspection of the content of each suggested only a modest overlap in the aspects of self tapped by the two, and so it was not surprising that even total scores from the two instruments correlated only .42. This agglomerate use of general self-concept is particularly dubious, and probably has led to many of the contradictory findings which abound in self-concept research.

Unidimensional Esteem Scales. A more justifiable use of general-self is with scales that are specifically designed to measure a relatively unidimensional construct that is superordinate to specific facets of self-concept. Items in such scales do not refer to self-concept in particular facets, but rather infer a general sense of self-worth or self-competence that could be applied to different areas. This is the approach employed by Rosenberg (1965, 1979), Harter (1982, 1983), and the general-self scales on the SDQ instruments.

(Examples of items from the SDQ III are "Overall, I have a lot of self-confidence" and "Overall, nothing I do is very important.")

Factor analytic studies reported elsewhere with the SDQ instruments and with the Perceived Competence Scale for Children (Harter 1982), all demonstrate that such a factor can be clearly identified and that it is distinguishable from other dimensions of self-concept. Particularly in SDQ research, responses to the general-self scale are both internally consistent and have surprisingly low correlations with many of the more specific facets of self.

A Hierarchical General Self-concept. Whereas the use of a hierarchical general self—as with the apex of the Shavelson and colleagues model—has important theoretical implications, the distinction between this and the other uses of general self needs clarification. Unlike the other uses, this general self cannot be tied to a specific set of items but is an unobserved construct that is, in itself, defined by unobserved constructs (that is, it is a higher-order factor). As in the weighted and unweighted total scores, it represents some average of specific facets of self-concept, and its breadth is limited by the scope of specific scales that are included in the analysis.

Thus, in a study that examined only different areas of *academic* self-concept, such a general self would necessarily be limited to a general academic self-concept. Like the general-self scale, the apex in figure 2.1 implies a self that is superordinate to the specific self facets. The hierarchical factor analysis of SDQ III responses by Marsh (1987b) is particularly relevant to this discussion because it included both a separate general-self scale and a hierarchical self. The general-self scale was hypothesized to contribute directly to the hierarchical general self-concept that was at the apex of the hierarchy. This hypothesis was supported, and correlations between the two forms of general self-concept were consistently close to .90, suggesting that the two are very similar when inferred on the basis of responses to the SDQ III.

A Weighted-average General Self-concept. James (1890) argued that failure in areas deemed to be unimportant has little impact on general esteem and this contention is frequently echoed in current research. In the general paradigm used to test this hypothesis, subjects respond to a general esteem questionnaire, such as the Rosenberg scale or the general-self scales on the SDQ instruments; respond to content-specific areas of self-concept, such as those on the SDQ instruments; and rate the importance of each of the content-specific areas of self-concept. The critical issue is whether or not the specific areas of self-concept are better able to predict global esteem when they are weighted by their importance.

Methodological problems in previous research render dubious any clear conclusions, but research reviewed by Marsh (1986b) provided no support for this intuitively appealing hypothesis. In research that prompted the Marsh (1986b) study, Hoge and McCarthy (1984) found—paradoxically—that, when specific facets were weighted by each individual's importance rating, the weighted average was significantly *less* correlated with esteem than was the simple unweighted average of the specific facets.

Marsh identified important methodological problems in the Hoge and McCarthy study and related research, including the use of single-item ratings to infer specific areas of self-concept and ambiguities in how the hypothesis should be tested. In subsequent research with SDQ III responses, Marsh devised solutions to these problems, but still found little support for the weighted-average model.

Using SDQ III responses from a variety of different studies, Marsh found that an unweighted average of the twelve specific SDQ III scales correlated about .7 with the general scale, but weighting each scale by the importance assigned to it by the entire group, diverse subgroups, or by each individual resulted in little or no improvement. Marsh reformulated the hypothesis and proposed a multiple regression model in which specific areas of self-concept, importance ratings, and the specific component by importance interaction were used to predict global esteem.

The critical test was whether the interaction term contributed significantly to the prediction of esteem—that is, whether the relation between a specific component and esteem depended on the importance of the component. For only two of thirteen components—physical ability and religion—did the contribution of a specific area of self-concept interact with the rated importance of the area of self-concept.

The solution to two potential problems in existing research may be useful to pursue. The first problem has to do with the narrowness of the specific facets used to test the model. SDQ scales were specifically chosen to be at least reasonably important to most respondents. In contrast, the two facets originally proposed by William James to illustrate his proposal were his skills as a psychologist, his profession, and his skills as a Greek linguist—the latter being an area in which he had no pretensions. The selection of more narrowly defined scales which most people would find to be unimportant but a few would see as very important—such as those proposed by James—may provide a better test of the weighted-average model. Support for the usefulness of the importance rating for the spiritual values and physical ability scales may offer some support—albeit weak—for this suggestion in that the importance ratings for these two scales had the most variance. The second potential problem is that importance ratings may not provide an adequate index of the salience that a specific component of self-concept has for a particular individual. Whereas we have no better indicators of salience to offer, new methodology emerging from social cognition research may produce better alternatives.

Harter (1985, 1988) devised an alternative formulation for relating self-concept and importance of success in particular areas of self to esteem. Instead of using subjective importance ratings to weight self-concept ratings by computing importance × self-concept cross-products, she computed self-concept/importance differences. In the language of the analysis of variance Harter predicted that the main effect of importance would contribute to esteem instead of positing an importance × self-concept interaction as in most previous formulations. (This is, however, the formulation typically used to study the influence of actual and ideal self-ratings as described later in this chapter).

Harter noted that her formulation "bears a close resemblance to that of Tesser and Campbell (1980, 1983), who have adapted the term *relevance* for a similar construct" (1985, 153). In fact, the Tesser and Campbell formulation implies an interaction—relevant dimensions contribute substantially to esteem whereas irrelevant dimensions do not. Also, Tesser and Campbell focus on relations among self-concept, relevance, and relations to others who serve as a basis of comparison, and not the relation of these variables to esteem. Whatever the theoretical basis for the Harter formulation, its critical test is whether importance ratings—or equivalently, self-concept/importance discrepancies—contribute significantly to the prediction of self-esteem beyond the prediction of merely self-concept ratings.

Whereas Harter reported that self-concept/importance differences were significantly related to esteem, she did not demonstrate that importance ratings made any unique contribution. Marsh (1986b), however, did test this prediction with responses to the SDQ III. While self-concept responses contributed substantially and uniquely to the prediction of esteem, the unique contribution of importance ratings was very small and typically did not reach statistical significance. Although Harter did not adequately test her formulation, appropriate tests conducted by Marsh failed to support it.

A Discrepancy Model of General Self-concept. Historically, self-discrepancy indices of self-esteem have been widely used (Wells & Marwell 1976; Wylie 1974). Theoretically, such scores are frequently based on Rogers's definition in 1951 of esteem as dependent on the discrepancy between how one actually is and how he or she should ideally be, even though a similar notion was expressed by James (1890). This approach was typically operationalized by: (1) subtracting actual self-ratings from ideal self-ratings and summing the differences, or (2) asking subjects to do independent Q-sorts on a set of items in terms of actual and ideal selves, and then correlating the two sets of scores to index the congruency of the two sets of responses. High self-esteem was inferred from low actual/ideal discrepancies and from high actual/ideal congruency.

Psychometric problems with the use of actual/ideal discrepancies are frequently noted (Wells & Marwell 1976; Wylie 1974), but psychometric properties of the congruency measures are not so well understood. The major drawbacks to instruments based on these approaches were the added time and complications in collecting data (particularly the Q-sorts), potential or actual psychometric problems, and the failure to demonstrate the advantages of discrepancy scores over actual self-ratings that are so much easier to collect. In Wylie's review of self-concept instruments which was updated in 1989, instruments using this approach were excluded because previously identified methodological problems had either not been addressed or they had seldom been used in the last fifteen years. Given the intuitive appeal of this approach, it is disappointing that the measurement procedures were not more rigorously developed and tested.

More recently, a resurgence of cognitive approaches to dynamic self processes has led to a renewed interest in actual/ideal discrepancies and related measures (Higgins 1987; Higgins, Klein & Strauman 1985; Markus & Nurius 1986; Markus & Wurf 1987. See also Ogilvie's & Clark's chapter 7 in the companion volume to this book, *Self Perspectives Across the Lifespan*.) Although not focusing on discrepancies per se, Markus and Nurius (1986) introduced the notion of possible selves—what you might become, what you hope to become, or what you are afraid of becoming. They demonstrated that ratings of the probability of possible selves contributed to self-esteem beyond what could be predicted by actual self-ratings. The aspect of possible selves, however, was viewed as a new component to the self-system rather than a standard against which to evaluate the actual self.

Higgins's (1987) self-discrepancy theory provides conceptual advances beyond previous research. Higgins expanded the typology of discrepancy scores by considering actual, ideal, and ought selves from the standpoints of both self and significant others. In this expanded framework, self/actual is contrasted with five potential standards (such as self/ideal and other/ought).

Higgins also introduced new approaches to inferring discrepancies that are idiographic instead of nomographic. Subjects are asked to list up to ten traits representing different selves, such as attributes describing who you actually are—self/actual; and who you mother believes your should or ought to be—other/ought. Discrepancy was inferred from the number of mismatching (antonym) attributes minus the number of matching (same or synonymous) attributes in two different lists—self/actual versus self/ideal—when the lists were compared by external scorers. Higgins demonstrated that different discrepancy scores were differentially related to various affects. For example, self/actual versus self/ideal discrepancies were related to disappointment and dissatisfaction, whereas self/actual versus self/ought discrepancies were related to feelings of guilt.

Higgins (1987) also described preliminary analyses suggesting that self/actual versus self/ideal discrepancies contributed to the prediction of esteem beyond what could be explained by just self/actual responses. Because Higgins did not actually estimate self/actual scores, he used Anderson's norms of adjective likability published in 1968 to determine whether attributes listed under the self/actual conditions were positive or negative. He also defined self/actual as either the number of negative attributes listed, or the percentage of negative attributes listed. The use of this crude normative approach to inferring actual self is ironic in a framework that emphasizes idiographic measures. It is, perhaps, not surprising that these self/actual estimates were only modestly related to self-esteem and much less correlated with esteem than measures derived from well-constructed nomographic scales (Marsh 1986b).

Two alternative approaches would provide more interesting tests of this claim. First, applying an idiographic standard, subjects could simply be asked to rate the favorability of each of the adjectives in their self/actual list. The sum of these favorability ratings would then provide an estimate of actual self. The critical question is whether Higgins's discrepancy scores contributed to self-esteem beyond what could be predicted by the self/actual scores. Second, using a nomographic comparison, multiple regression could be used to test whether Higgins's discrepancy score contributed to the prediction of self-esteem beyond the contribution of a set of well-defined nomographic scales such as the domain-specific scales on the SDQ III.

The focus of Higgins's research has been to expand and explicate processes that are part of a self-system rather than to develop psychometrically sound measurement procedures. His findings do suggest, however, that his measures have discriminant validity with respect to different emotional responses. A serious limitation, however, is a lack of evidence for reliability and validity. Discrepancy scores are based on the number of matches, mismatches, and non-matches in different lists, but this requires considerable subjectivity in scoring. The interrater correlation between scores from two different scorers was $r = .80$ (Higgins, Klein & Strauman 1985). Because this coefficient takes into account only unreliability due to subjectivity in scoring, the reliability of the discrepancy score is likely to be substantially lower than the reported value. Higgins is still refining his measurement procedures (such as the incorporation of relevance and confidence in ratings into the calculation of discrepancy scores) and further attention to psychometric properties will enhance the usefulness of this potentially important new approach.

Summary and Implications of the Multifaceted Structure of Self-concept

Self-concept, as with many other psychological constructs, suffers in that "everyone knows what it is." Thus, some researchers do not feel compelled to provide any theoretical definition of what they are measuring nor even the psychometric properties of self-concept responses. As a result, many reviews of self-concept research emphasize the lack of theoretical basis and the poor quality of measurement.

Apparently, the multifaceted hierarchical conceptualization of self-concept is consistent with the perspectives of many researchers, even though it was not well-represented in instruments developed prior to the 1980s. Such instruments typically had no clearly articulated theoretical basis, and this made the examination of construct validity difficult. One approach to this problem has been to take responses to existing, largely atheoretical instruments and attempt to test hypotheses from theoretical models (Marx & Winne 1978). Because of the poor quality of measurement instruments in relation to this purpose, the approach is of dubious value, and the generally inconsistent results may be attributable to poor theory, poor instrument construction, or both.

In contrast, the SDQ instruments are based on strong theoretical and empirical foundations, and SDQ research has shown self-concept to be a multidimensional hierarchical construct. The hierarchy is, however, much weaker than anticipated by Shavelson and colleagues, and the structure of the academic facets differs from that which was originally posited. This led to a revision of the Shavelson et al. model.

Research summarized here has increasingly led to the conclusion that general self-concept—no matter how it is inferred—is not a particularly useful construct. General self-concept apparently cannot adequately reflect the diversity of specific self facets. If the role of self-concept research is to better understand the complexity of self in different contexts, to predict a wide variety of behaviors, to provide outcome measures for diverse interventions, and to relate self-concept to other constructs, then the specific facets of self-concept are more useful than is a general facet. Interestingly, work leading to the Marsh/Shavelson revision suggested that these criticisms of an overreliance on general self-concept also apply to the usefulness of a general academic self-concept. Because math and verbal self-concepts are only weakly correlated, they cannot be adequately explained by a general academic self-concept. We are not arguing that researchers should abandon measures of general self-concept and general academic self-concept, but rather that more emphasis needs to be placed on content-specific dimensions of self-concept. Researchers should be encouraged to consider multiple dimensions of self-concept, supplemented, perhaps, by general measures. Further support for this recommendation comes from the evaluation of between-network studies that relate general and content-specific dimensions of self-concept to other constructs (Marsh in press-a).

THE RELATION BETWEEN MULTIPLE DIMENSIONS OF SELF-CONCEPT AND ACADEMIC ACHIEVEMENT INDICATORS

Wylie noted that "many persons, especially educators, have unhesitatingly assumed that achievement and/or ability measures will be strongly related to self-conceptions of achievement and ability and to overall self-regard as well" (1979, 355). Not surprisingly and particularly for studies of school-aged children, some measure of academic achievement is one of the most frequently posited criteria used to validate self-concept interpretations, as well as the focus of much SDQ research. The purpose of this section is to briefly review this research.

In the model of Shavelson and colleagues, academic self-concept is one component of overall self-concept, and it is divided into self-concepts in particular content areas such as math and verbal. Support for the construct validity of SDQ interpretations and the Shavelson et al. model requires (1) academic achievement to be more positively correlated with academic self-concept than with nonacademic or overall self-concept, and (2) verbal and math achievement indicators to be more highly correlated with self-concepts in matching content areas than with other facets of self-concept.

In the most extensive meta-analysis of the achievement/self-concept relationship, Hansford and Hattie (1982) found that measures of ability/performance correlated at about .2 with measures of general self-concept, but about .4 with measures of academic self-concept. Similarly, Shavelson and Bolus (1982) found that grades in English, mathematics, and science were more highly correlated with matching areas of self-concept than with general self-concept, and Bachman (1970) reported that IQ correlated at .46 with academic self-concept but only .14 with general self-concept. In her review of studies relating self-concept to academic achievement, Byrne (1984) also found that nearly all studies report that self-concept is positively correlated with achievement, while many others find achievement to be more strongly correlated with academic self-concept than with general self-concept. SDQ research has emphasized the distinctiveness of self-concepts in verbal and mathematical content areas. For example, Marsh, Relich, and Smith (1983) demonstrated that mathematical achievement was substantially correlated with math self-concept (.55); less correlated with self-concepts in other academic areas (verbal, .21; and general school, .43); and nearly uncorrelated with self-concepts in nonacademic areas. These findings support the construct interpretation already described, and indicate the need to distinguish academic from nonacademic and general self-concept, and to distinguish among specific components of academic self-concept.

Research summarized here demonstrates that academic self-concepts are at least moderately correlated with corresponding levels of academic achievement. The correlations, however, almost never approach the reliabilities of the respective measures, suggesting that academic self-concepts reflect more than just academic achievement. Similarly, Shavelson and colleagues (1976) posited that academic achievement and academic self-concept are clearly distinguishable constructs.

Patterns of Achievement/Self-concept Correlations

Most SDQ studies of self-concept/achievement relations are based on SDQ I responses by preadolescents (Marsh 1988). In eleven different studies, achievement in verbal, math, and general academics was assessed by objective tests, teacher ratings, or both. There were 136 correlations between academic achievement indicators and the four nonacademic SDQ facets. Few of these correlations reached statistical significance, most were negative, and only one correlation was significantly positive. Given the range of studies and the diversity of indicators of academic achievement, these results provided convincing evidence for the relative independence of academic achievement and the nonacademic SDQ scales.

Indicators of verbal or mathematics achievement were systematically related to self-concept responses in these studies. There were sixteen correlations between verbal self-concept and verbal achievement indicators; these varied from .18 to .57 (median = .39), and they were all statistically significant. The median correlations between these same verbal achievement measures and math self-concept was .04, and only four of sixteen correlations were statistically significant. The corresponding sixteen correlations between reading achievement indicators and general-school varied from −.04 to .52 (median = .21), and eleven were statistically significant. There were a total of twelve correlations between math achievement and math self-concept. These varied from .17 to .66 (median = .33), and all were statistically significant. The twelve correlations between math achievement and verbal self-concept varied from −.01 to .36 (median = .10), and five were statistically significant. The twelve correlations between math achievement and general-school self-concept varied between −.02 and .59 (median = .26), and ten were statistically significant.

SDQ III responses by eleventh- or twelfth-grade high-school students were related to mathematics and English achievement in two different studies. In the first (Marsh & O'Neill 1984) responses by 296 students in a Catholic girls' school were related to the thirteen SDQ III scales (table 2.1). Math achievement correlated .58, with math self-concept and English achievement correlated .42 with verbal self-concept. The pattern of relations between the different self-concept facets and the two achievement scores provide even stronger support for the content specificity of self-concept/ achievement relations than did the SDQ I studies. It is also interesting to note that general self-concept is not significantly related to either math or English achievement.

In the second study, responses by a large sample of eleventh- and twelfth-grade Canadian students (Marsh, Byrne & Shavelson 1988) to four SDQ III scales (math, verbal, general school, and general self) were related to school grades in mathematics, English, and all school subjects (table 2.1). The average grade in all school subjects correlated .53 with general school self-concept (not shown in table 2.1); math grades correlated .55 with math self-concept; and English grades correlated .24 with verbal self-concept. Grades in mathematics and all school subjects were most highly correlated with math and general-school self-concepts respectively, but English grades were more highly correlated with general-school self-concept than with verbal self-concept. Again, general self-concept was not significantly related to any of the achievement indicators.

In summary, the correlations between SDQ scales and academic achievement indicators support a dramatic distinction between academic and nonacademic facets of self-concept, and also demonstrate the clear separation of math and verbal self-concepts.

Verbal and Math Self-concepts: An Internal/External Frame-of-Reference Model

Even after individuals obtain information from various sources about their levels of academic ability or achievement, these impressions must be compared to some standard or frame of reference. To the extent that individuals have different frames of reference, the same objective indicators will lead to different academic self-concepts. In most such proposals, it is assumed that students evaluate their own performance with that of others through social comparison processes (Marsh 1987a; Marsh & Parker 1984). Such proposals do not explain, however, why academic self-concepts are so content-specific. In order to explain this phenomenon, the internal/external frame of reference model (the I/E model) was developed (Marsh 1986d; Marsh, Byrne & Shavelson 1988).

Verbal and mathematics achievements are typically correlated .5 to .8. Thus, it is reasonable to expect that verbal and math self-

Table 2.1

Correlations between Self-concept Scores and Academic Achievement Measures in English and Math

Self-Concepts	From Marsh and O'Neill 1984. (n = 51)				From Marsh, Byrne, and Shavelson 1988. (n = 991)			
	Correlations		Beta Weights		Correlations		Beta Weights	
	Math	English	Math	English	Math	English	Math	English
Math	.58**	.19**	.72**	-.24**	.55**	.20**	.61**	-.12**
Verbal	.11	.42**	-.25**	.55**	.20**	.24**	-.14**	.31**
Academic	.27**	.24**	.14*	.19**	.34**	.47**	.40**	.13**
Prob. Solve.	.03	.17**	-.11	.24**				
Phys. Ability	.02	-.11	.13	-.19*				
Phys. Appear.	.05	.02	.06	-.02				
Same Sex	-.04	-.01	-.05	.02				
Opposite Sex	-.08	-.03	-.10	.04				
Parents	-.08	-.12	-.01	-.12				
Religion	.00	.00	.01	.00				
Honesty	-.08	-.09	-.04	-.07				
Emotional	.08	.06	.07	.02	-.04	-.04	-.02	
General	.02	.06	-.08	.10	-.04			-.03

Note: Beta weights are standardized beta weights resulting from a multiple regression in which both academic achievement scores were used to predict each of the self-concept scores. In the Marsh, Byrne, and Shavelson (1989) study, only four SDQ III scales were administered.

* p < .05; ** p < .01

concepts would also be substantially correlated. This expectation was incorporated into the original model by Shavelson and colleagues in which academic self-concepts in particular subject areas were posited to form a general academic self-concept. Hence, it is surprising that math and verbal self-concepts are only weakly correlated with each other.

This unexpected lack of correlation between math and verbal self-concepts has been observed in numerous studies with various SDQ instruments, and Marsh (1986d) proposed the I/E model to explain its occurrence. This finding also led to a revision of the original Shavelson et al. model (Marsh & Shavelson 1985; Shavelson & Marsh 1986) described earlier in this chapter (see figure 2.2). According to the I/E model, verbal and math self-concepts are formed in relation to both external and internal comparisons—or frames of reference—that can be characterized as follows:

1. External Comparisons—According to this social comparison process, students compare their self-perceptions of their own abilities in math and in reading with the perceived abilities of other students within their frames of reference, such as other students in their classroom or grade in school. This external relativistic impression is then used as one basis for their self-concept in each of the two areas. It is also assumed that this process is used by external observers to infer the self-concept of someone else.
2. Internal Comparisons—According to this process, students compare their self-perceived abilities in math with their self-perceived abilities in reading, and use this internal relativistic impression as a second basis for arriving at their self-concepts in each of the two areas.

In order to clarify how these two processes operate, consider a student who accurately perceives himself or herself to be below average in both math and reading skills, but he or she may be better at math than at reading and other academic subjects. This student's math skills are below average in relation to other students' skills (an external comparison) but *higher* than average for his or her own skills in other academic areas (an internal comparison). Depending upon how these two components are weighted, this student may have an average or even above-average self-concept in mathematics despite his or her poor math skills.

The operation of social comparison processes, as inferred in the external comparison process, has been supported in numerous studies (Marsh 1987a; Marsh & Parker 1984). Since verbal and math achievements are substantially correlated, the external comparison process should lead to a positive correlation between verbal and math self-concepts. However, the internal process should lead to a negative correlation between verbal and math self-concepts, since math and reading ability and achievements are compared with each other, and it is the difference between math and verbal skills that contributes to a higher self-concept in one area or the other.

The external process predicts a positive correlation between verbal and math self-concepts, while the internal process predicts a negative correlation. Hence, the joint operation of both processes—depending upon the relative strength of each—will lead to the near-zero correlation between verbal and math self-concepts that has been observed in empirical research. The I/E model does not require that the verbal/math correlation be zero, but only that it be substantially less than the typically large correlation between verbal and math achievement levels.

The I/E model also predicts a *negative* direct effect of mathematics achievement on verbal self-concept, and of reading achievement on Math self-concept. For example, a high math self-concept will be more likely when math skills are good (the external comparison) *and* when math skills are better than reading skills (the internal comparison). Thus, once math skills are controlled, it is the *difference* between math and reading skills which is predictive of math self-concept, and high reading skills will actually detract from a high math self-concept.

The I/E model generates a specific and perhaps unexpected pattern of relations among variables representing verbal self-concept, math self-concept, verbal achievement, and math achievement (see figure 2.4). In this model, academic achievement is hypothesized to be one causal determinant of academic self-concept, but the model does not argue against a more dynamic model in which subsequent levels of academic achievement and self-concept are each determined by prior levels of achievement and self-concept.

According to the path model, math and reading skills are highly correlated with each other while math and verbal self-concepts are only weakly correlated. Verbal achievement has a strong and positive direct effect on verbal self-concept, but a small and negative direct effect on math self-concept. Similarly, math achievement has a strong positive effect on math self-concept, but a weaker, negative effect on verbal self-concept. Hence, the I/E model makes many testable predictions besides the lack of correlation between verbal and

Figure 2.4
Path Model of Relationships among Achievements and Reading and
Math Self-concepts: Internal/External Frame of Reference Model.

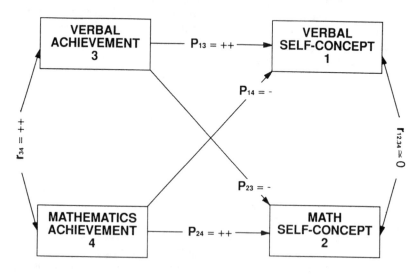

Coefficients indicated to be "++", "-", and "0" are predicted to be high positive, low negative, and
approximately zero respectively.

From: Marsh, H. W. 1986. Verbal and math self-concepts: An internal/exter-
nal frame of reference model. *American Educational Research Journal*
23:134. (Copyright 1986 by the American Educational Research Association. Reprinted by permission of the publisher.)

math self-concepts. An examination of empirical support for these
predictions is presented here.

A Lack of Correlation Between Math and Verbal Self-concepts.
Marsh (1986d) summarized the correlations between math and verbal self-concepts in all previous SDQ studies. Across all SDQ I studies of responses by preadolescents, the correlation between math and
verbal self-concept was close to zero (.06) and only three of twelve
correlations based on individual studies reached statistical significance. However, it is important to note that the correlations based
upon the one sample of second-grade students (.49) and the one sample of third-grade students (.46) were substantial, but that the correlations varied between −.13 and +.17 for the other ten samples

based on responses by fourth-, fifth-, and sixth-grade students. When considered separately, results for the total sample of males and of females indicated that the lack of correlation was consistent across gender. These findings demonstrate that, with the exception of the youngest children, self-concepts in math and verbal are uncorrelated for responses by preadolescents to the SDQ I.

In one large study, the SDQ II was administered to high-school students in grades seven through twelve. The verbal/math correlations did not reach statistical significance at any grade level, and across all respondents the correlation was almost exactly zero (−.0002). The SDQ III has been employed in three studies with university students, with grade eleven high-school students, and with a nonstudent population of young adults who were participants in an Outward Bound program. Again, the five verbal/math correlations were consistently and remarkably close to zero (−.03 to .03), and did not reach statistical significance for any of the studies.

Correlations between math and verbal self-concepts described earlier have been based upon responses by students in an academic setting. The importance of the internal comparison process (in which self-perceived skills in math and reading are compared to each other) and the distinctiveness of the two academic self-concepts may be exaggerated in an academic setting. Hence, the results based on the Outward Bound study are particularly important. This study is based on responses from young adults (aged sixteen through thirty-one; median = 21 years) who were primarily nonstudents and who were participating in a program that emphasized primarily physical outdoor activities, and, perhaps, social relationship skills rather than academic skills. Even for this sample of predominantly nonstudents completing the SDQ III in a nonacademic setting, support for the relative lack of correlation between verbal and math self-concepts was strong.

The results from a wide variety of studies—based on responses from preadolescents, adolescents, and young adults—have consistently demonstrated that there is little correlation between verbal and math self-concepts, and that this lack of math/verbal correlation is consistent across ages (beyond third grade) and gender, and across academic and nonacademic settings. This finding is counterintuitive, and contrary to the original Shavelson and colleagues model that posited that verbal and math self-concepts combine to form a single, higher-order academic self-concept. However, the findings are consistent with the I/E model and the revision of the Shavelson and colleagues model, and offer support for the validity of interpretation based on the I/E model.

An interesting yet unresolved question is why math and verbal self-concepts are substantially correlated for second- and third-grade children, but not for older subjects. These results may reflect the increased differentiation in self-concept with age hypothesized by Shavelson and colleagues and others (Silon & Harter 1985). It may represent difficulties in appropriately responding to rating-scale instruments for very young children. A relevant area for further research is to examine alternative forms of presentation and alternative administration procedures to determine at what age children begin to clearly differentiate between math and verbal self-concepts.

Empirical Support for the I/E Model: The Achievement/ Self-concept Relationship for Verbal and Math Scores. The lack of correlation between verbal and math self-concepts is consistent with the I/E model, but much stronger tests are possible in studies that contain both math and verbal achievement scores as well as math and verbal self-concept measures. Figure 2.4 illustrates an explicit and counterintuitive pattern of relations among the four variables representing academic achievements and academic self-concepts in the form of a path model. Results from thirteen different studies employing the SDQ instruments were used to test the model (Marsh, 1986d).

Different studies were based upon the SDQ I, the SDQ II, and the SDQ III. They also used different indicators of math and reading ability including objective test scores, teacher ratings, and school performance.

As predicted by the I/E model (see figure 2.4), correlations between indicators of verbal and math achievement (r_{34}) were substantial, ranging from .42 to .94, while correlations between residual measures of verbal and math self-concepts $(r_{12.34})$ were much smaller, ranging from $-.10$ to $+.19$. The path coefficients representing the relationship between verbal self-concept and verbal achievement (p_{13}), and between math self-concept and math achievement (p_{24}), were both positive and statistically significant in all thirteen analyses. In dramatic contrast, the path coefficients representing the math achievement/verbal self-concept link (p_{14}), and the verbal achievement/math self-concept link (p_{23}) were both *negative* and statistically significant for twenty-five of the twenty-six parameter estimates.

In summary, these parameter estimates provide remarkably strong support for predictions derived from the I/E model. The support for the predictions is consistent across studies in which age differs substantially, a wide variety of indicators of academic achievement are employed, and different self-concept instruments are used, thus demonstrating the generality of the effects (Marsh, Byrne & Shavelson 1988).

Discussion and Implications of the I/E Model. The I/E frame-of-reference model is able to explain what seemed to be paradoxical relationships between verbal and math self-concepts and the corresponding indicators of academic achievement. The I/E model was originally promoted by the observation that verbal and math self-concepts are minimally correlated with each other, even though verbal and math achievement indicators are substantially correlated with each other. Furthermore, the direct effect of reading achievement on math self-concept and the direct effect of math achievement on verbal self-concept were each significantly *negative*. This pattern of results was consistent, however, with predictions from the I/E model. The results based on the I/E model and related research also present a number of other interesting implications.

1. It is sometimes suggested that math and verbal self-concepts merely represent potentially biased self-reports of school marks and other objective achievement indicators. To the extent that the intent of the self-concepts is to provide a surrogate for more objective indicators, the implied criticism is reasonable, but this is not the intent. The finding that math and verbal self-concepts are minimally correlated whereas the corresponding achievement scores are substantially correlated demonstrates that academic self-concepts are affected by different processes than are achievement measures in the academic areas which they reflect.

2. Understanding the I/E model can facilitate teachers' understanding of their students and how to provide appropriate feedback. Other research indicates that, when teachers are asked to infer the self-concepts of their students, their ratings primarily reflect student ability and do not incorporate the internal comparison process. According to the internal comparison process, however, even the least able students will be relatively better at some than other school subjects. In their best subjects, they may have an average or even above-average academic self-concept even though their skills are below average. Teachers can use this information in providing positive reinforcement that is credible to the student. Similarly, even the best students will be relatively poorer in some school subjects. In their poorest subjects, they may have academic self-concepts that are average or below average even though their skills are above average. This observation may also help teachers to better understand the self-perceptions of the most able students.

3. The independence of math and verbal self-concepts calls into question the role and usefulness of general academic self-concept. General academic self-concept apparently cannot adequately reflect the diversity of specific academic self facets. If the role of academic self-concept research is to better understand the complexity of self in an academic context, to predict academic behaviors and accomplishments, to provide outcome measures for academic interventions, and to relate academic self-concept to other constructs, then the specific facets of academic self-concept are more useful than a general academic facet. Thus, in the same way that our research has led us to question the usefulness of a general (primarily nonacademic) self-concept, this research also leads us to question the usefulness of a general academic self-concept.
4. Further investigation is also needed to examine how the internal comparison process embodied in the I/E model generalizes to other facets of self-concept. Thus, students who see themselves as particularly able academically may see themselves as less able in nonacademic areas. Indeed, if a person is particularly good at any specific endeavor, that person will see himself or herself as relatively less able in other spheres. This process may explain why the average correlation among the different SDQ scales is so low.

A DEVELOPMENTAL PERSPECTIVE

The Shavelson and colleagues model is not primarily a developmental model. One of the postulates of the model, however, is that self-concept becomes increasingly multifaceted as the individual moves from infancy to adulthood. Implicitly, this was used in the design and construction of the various SDQ instruments. As noted earlier, the number and diversity of self-concept dimensions increases for the three SDQ instruments designed for preadolescents, adolescents, and late-adolescent/young adults. In subsequent research designed to test the Shavelson and colleagues model and the SDQ instruments, three related developmental issues were studied.

1. The ability of young children to respond to the SDQ I and particularly to negatively worded items;
2. Changes in self-concept with age and the consistency of these effects across sex; and

3. Formal tests of the Shavelson et al. (1976) hypothesis that self-concept becomes increasingly multifaceted with age.

The Bias of Negative Items in Rating Scales for Preadolescent Children: A Cognitive-Developmental Phenomenon

Test construction specialists argue for the use of some negatively worded items on personality, attitude, and other rating-scale instruments in order to disrupt response sets such as responding to all items with the same response category—particularly for single-scale instruments where all items are designed to measure one construct. The use of negative items assumes that they measure the same construct as positive items. However, this assumption is rarely tested and its validity seems questionable when respondents are preadolescent children. Examination of this issue is of pragmatic importance for researchers studying the self-concepts of young children. To the extent that this potential problem reflects the cognitive development of young children, it is also of theoretical importance to developmentalists. In one test of the ability of young children to respond appropriately to negatively worded items, Benson and Hocevar (1986) concluded that the inclusion of negative items adversely affects the validity of responses by preadolescent respondents.

In the early development of the SDQ I— unlike the SDQ II and the SDQ III—negative items were found to be ineffective in defining the different areas of self-concept which they were designed to measure. Preliminary analyses indicated that negative items contributed less to the internal consistency of the scales, and exploratory factor analyses sometimes revealed a negative item factor, that is, a factor on which only negative items loaded. Younger children in particular often responded *true* to negative items, indicating a very poor self-concept, when their responses to positive items consistently indicated a positive self-concept. This suggested that the problem might be a cognitive-developmental phenomenon. Numerous attempts to revise the negative items failed to solve the problem and led to the recommendation that these items should not be included when scoring the SDQ I (Marsh 1988; Marsh, Barnes et al. 1984).

Marsh (1986a) reported a series of item analyses conducted on responses from students in grades two through five. The exclusion of the negative items consistently improved reliability estimates for each grade level, but the improvement was largest for the youngest children. Total scores representing the sum of positive items and sum of negative items—to the extent that they are measuring the same construct—should correlate at about .80 or higher with each other. For the total sample, the correlation between responses to the two total scores was only .27, indicating that they were measuring different constructs. Furthermore, the results illustrated a dramatic developmental effect.

For the youngest children the two total scores were uncorrelated (−.02), whereas the correlations were much larger for the oldest children (.60). Thus, for the youngest children the negative items were measuring a construct that was unrelated to self-concept, whereas for the oldest children, the negative item responses were substantially related to positive item responses. Marsh also found that the negative item bias was nearly unrelated to other areas of self-concept but was significantly correlated with verbal skills inferred on the basis of two test scores and teacher ratings. These findings clearly justify the decision to exclude the negative items in scoring the SDQ, but they also suggest that the effect is a cognitive-developmental phenomenon.

Age and Sex Effects in Multiple Dimensions of Self-concept

Marsh (1989) examined age and sex effects in the 12,266 responses comprising the normative data for the three SDQ instruments. The often considered question of how self-concept varies with age and gender has diverse theoretical, practical, and methodological implications. It is difficult, however, to derive a clear picture of these relations from the collage of studies that are often based on small, idiosyncratic samples and that use different methodological approaches and different self-concept instruments. This analysis provides much needed continuity by examining responses from large samples of children to similar multidimensional self-concept instruments over all grade levels and into young adulthood. The empirical findings, coupled with a more extensive literature review than had previously been available provide a clearer picture of how multiple dimensions of self-concept vary with sex and age (Marsh 1989).

In her review of age effects, Wylie (1979) summarized research conducted prior to 1977 and concluded that there was no convincing evidence for any age effect, either positive or negative, in overall self-concept in the age range of six to fifty years old. Reports of age effects in specific dimensions of self-concept were too diverse and too infrequent to warrant any generalizations. Despite Wylie's (1979) conclusion to the contrary, subsequent research reviewed by Marsh (1989) found systematic age effects in self-concept responses. The most clearly documented effects are the systematic increases in self-concept during late-adolescent and early-adult years (O'Malley & Bachman 1983).

There is also good evidence for decreases in self-concept during preadolescence. These results imply a curvilinear age effect in which the decline in self-concept must reverse itself sometime during early or middle adolescence. This supposition may also be consistent with the suggestion that adolescence is a time of stress and storm. Empirical research, however, has provided little support for such a curvilinear relation. Nevertheless, because of the emphasis on overall self-concept and the ad hoc nature of specific dimensions that have been considered, the generality of age effects based on overall self-concept to more specific facets is not justified.

In her review of sex differences, Wylie (1979) also concluded that there was no evidence for sex differences in overall self-concept at any age level. She noted, however, that sex differences in specific components of self-concept may be lost when forming a total score. In research reviewed by Marsh (1989), there were small sex effects favoring boys for total self-concept measures and for measures of esteem derived from the Rosenberg (1965) scale. There also appeared to be larger, counterbalancing sex differences in more specific facets of self that are generally consistent with sex stereotypes. For preadolescent responses to the SDQ I, girls had higher self-concepts in verbal and general school, and lower self-concepts in physical abilities, math, and appearance. For responses by high school students to the SDQ II, girls tended to have higher scores for the verbal, honesty/trustworthiness, same-sex relationships, and, perhaps, general-school scales, whereas boys tended to have higher scores in physical ability, appearance, math, and, perhaps, general and emotional scales.

Norms for the SDQ I and SDQ II—at least through grade ten—appear to be broadly representative of school-aged children in metropolitan Sydney, Australia, but the representativeness of the SDQ III norms may be more dubious due to the ad hoc nature of the samples considered. The internal consistency estimates of reliability and factor analyses for this data were summarized by Marsh (1989). Separate sets of analyses of variance were conducted on responses to each SDQ instrument to determine sex and age effects. For the SDQ I and SDQ II responses, age was taken to be grade in school, whereas age for the SDQ III responses was divided into three discrete categories (younger than eighteen years, 18 to 21.5 years, and older than 21.5 years). In each set of analyses the main effect of age was divided into the linear, quadratic, and cubic effects of age for the SDQ I and SDQ II responses, and into the linear and quadratic components for the SDQ III responses.

Age and Sex Effects in SDQ Responses. For SDQ I responses by preadolescents, there is a clear linear decline in self-concept with increase in age (table 2.2). This decline is consistent across SDQ I scales as well as the total score, and is consistent for boys and girls.

For SDQ II responses by adolescents, there is a reasonably consistent U-shaped or quadratic relation. The decline in self-concept observed in preadolescence continues through grades eight and nine. After that, self-concepts increase. This quadratic relation is statistically significant for eight of the eleven SDQ II scales and the total score, and occurs for boys and girls (table 2.2).

The linear age effects on SDQ II responses are much smaller and less consistent across different scales. The variance explained by age in the SDQ II data tends to be smaller than for the SDQ I or the SDQ III responses. For SDQ III responses by late adolescents and young adults, there is a reasonably consistent linear increase in self-concepts with increase in age. The linear age effect is statistically significant for eleven of the thirteen SDQ III scales, and the direction of this effect is positive for nine of these scales and for the total score (table 2.2).

For most of the SDQ I, SDQ II, and SDQ III scales, there are statistically significant sex effects. Some favor girls, but more of them favor boys.

Reflecting this tendency, total self-concept scores favor boys, although this sex difference consistently explains only about 1 percent of the variance in each of the three data sets. The direction of sex differences in specific scales tends to be consistent with traditional sex stereotypes.

For the six scales that are common to the three SDQ instruments, stereotypic sex differences are reasonably consistent. First, boys have higher physical ability, appearance, and math self-concepts for all three data sets. Second, there are no sex differences for the parents scale in any of the three data sets. Third, girls tend to have higher verbal self-concepts (for SDQ I and SDQ II data) and school self-concepts (for SDQ I and SDQ III).

For the scales that are not common to the three instruments, differences also appear to be consistent with sex stereotypes. For the

SDQ II and/or SDQ III data, boys have higher emotional stability, problem solving and esteem scores, whereas girls have higher honesty/trustworthiness, and religion/spiritual-value scores. Sex differences on the social scales, however, are mixed and not fully consistent with traditional sex stereotypes favoring girls.

It was anticipated that sex differences might vary with age. In these three data sets, however, few age-by-sex interactions were statistically significant and typically accounted for less than 1 percent of the variance (table 2.2). Across all three data sets, appearance is the only scale in which sex differences vary substantially with age. At the very youngest ages, girls have more positive self-concepts of appearance, but, particularly during adolescence, they show much lower appearance self-concepts than do boys. With the exception of appearance, these findings suggest that sex stereotypes have already affected self-concepts by preadolescence, and that these effects are relatively stable from preadolescence into early-adulthood

Age and Increased Differentiation

Shavelson and colleagues (1976) posited that self-concept becomes more differentiated with increasing age (Werner 1957), but offered no clear rationale for testing this hypothesis. Markus and Wurf (1987) similarly note that the structure of self depends on both the information available to an individual and the cognitive ability to process this information. Harter (1983, 1985) proposed a model in which self-concept becomes increasingly abstract with age. Her review of previous research suggests that self-conceptions shift from concrete descriptions of behavior in early childhood, to trait-like psychological constructs—such as popular, smart, good looking—in middle childhood, to more abstract constructs during adolescence.

According to Harter (1985), the concept of global self-worth does not evolve before the age of about eight. Consistent with this claim, Harter and Pike (1984) reported that, at younger than age eight, children either do not understand general self-worth items or provide unreliable responses. Subsequent research suggested that mental age may be more important than chronological age (Silon & Harter 1985).

Factor analyses of Harter's self-concept scale for mentally retarded subjects aged nine through twelve (with mental ages of younger than eight) revealed only two self-concept factors instead of the four factors found in subjects with normal IQs. These mentally retarded children did not distinguish between cognitive and physical competence, and the general self-concept items did not cluster to-gether or load on other factors. According to Silon and Harter, the two factors that emerged were less differentiated than the original four factors. The failure to replicate a factor structure is, however, a weak basis of support for this contention. For example, as noted ear-lier, young children have difficulty in responding to negatively worded items, even though the factor structure underlying responses to positively worded items was well defined. Also, Marsh and MacDonald-Holmes (in press) reported that young children have dif-ficulty with the idiosyncratic response scale used on Harter's self-concept instrument, even though the respondents apparently had no difficulty in responding to instruments with more conventional for-mats. This difficulty was related to academic achievement, particu-larly in English.

Table 2.2
Summary of Sex and Age Effects (Percentage of Variance Explained)

	Main Effects				Interaction Effects		
Scale	Sex	Age-linear	Age-quad	Age-cubic	Sex × Age-linear	Sex × Age-quad	Sex × Age-cubic
SDQ							
Phys. Abil.	8.89**	4.66**	0.12	0.01	0.17*	0.17*	0.01
Appear.	2.63**	3.00**	1.14**	0.25*	1.40**	0.03	0.01
Peers	0.83**	1.40**	0.14	0.00	0.05	0.00	0.00
Parents	0.03	2.97**	0.63[c]**	0.02	0.04	0.00	0.01
Reading	1.40[a]**	3.30**	0.04	0.01	0.12	0.03	0.00
Math	0.99**	3.99**	0.00	0.00	0.03	0.00	0.06
School	0.09	6.70**	0.04	0.01	0.13	0.05	0.03
Total	0.92**	8.61**	0.05	0.01	0.40**	0.05	0.01
SDQ II							
Phys. Abil.	2.16**	0.58**	0.89**	0.13	0.06	0.03	0.01
Appear.	7.81**	0.30[b]*	0.19*	0.10	0.17	0.05	0.00
Opp. Sex	1.15**	1.83**	0.00	0.05	0.26[d]*	0.13	0.03
Same Sex	2.76[a]**	0.29**	0.62**	0.73**	0.16	0.33*	0.02
Honesty	3.61[a]**	0.06	1.45**	0.04	0.17	0.01	0.00
Parents	0.20	1.28**	0.67**	0.04	0.18	0.10	0.06
Emotional	2.35**	0.00	0.04	0.00	0.00	0.07	0.38*
General	1.05**	0.12	0.59**	0.26*	0.19	0.05	0.02
Verbal	0.77[a]**	0.00	0.04	0.15	0.06	0.14	0.26*
Math	1.58**	0.13	0.54**	0.05	0.01	0.01	0.05
School	0.09	0.29*	0.42**	0.33*	0.06	0.01	0.02
Total	1.04**	0.00	1.00**	0.31*	0.19	0.00	0.07

(*continued*)

Table 2.2 (Continued)

Scale	Main Effects				Interaction Effects		
	Sex	Age-linear	Age-quad	Age-cubic	Sex × Age-linear	Sex × Age-quad	Sex × Age-cubic
SDQ III							
Phys. Abil.	4.90**	1.55[b]**	0.02	—	0.83[d]**	0.14	—
Appear.	7.64**	12.0[b]**	1.35[c]**	—	2.12[d]**	0.24	—
Opp. Sex	0.20	0.16	0.15	—	1.32[d]**	0.13	—
Same Sex	0.01	0.90**	0.00	—	0.22	0.03	—
Honesty	0.44	2.14[b]**	0.02	—	0.07	0.20	—
Parents	0.12	0.17[b]**	0.05	—	0.00	0.02	—
Spiritual	4.42	1.14**	0.25	—	1.30**	0.16	—
Emotional	2.04**	2.85[b]**	0.01	—	0.50	0.30	—
General	2.35**	2.11[b]**	0.21	—	0.45	0.13	—
Verbal	0.01	1.77[b]**	0.00	—	0.00	0.79*	—
Math	2.21**	1.61[b]**	0.07	—	0.57*	0.00	—
School	0.02	2.98[b]**	0.00	—	0.00	0.28	—
Prob. Solv.	5.12**	3.23[b]**	0.27	—	0.04	0.06	—
Total	1.07**	3.62[b]**	0.10	—	0.13	0.14	—

[a]Girls have significantly higher self-concepts than boys. Other significant sex effects are in favor of boys.

[b]The linear effect of age is positive. Other significant linear age effects are negative.

[c]The quadratic effects of age are negative (that is, the slope becomes more negative or less positive with age as in an inverted U-shaped effect). Other significant quadratic age effects are positive (that is, the slope becomes more positive or less negative with age as in a U-shaped effect).

[d]The significant linear-age × sex interactions indicate that sex differences shift in the favor of girls as they grow older (with larger differences in favor of girls or smaller differences in favor of boys). Other significant linear-age × sex interactions indicate a shift in favor of boys as they grow older.

Note: A series of two-way analyses of variance were conducted in which the separate contrasts were used to test the effects of sex; the linear-, quadratic- and cubic-components of age; and the sex-by-age interaction. For the SDQ and SDQ II data, age was taken to be the year in school, whereas for the SDQ III data, age was divided into three categories. Effect sizes, the percentage of variance explained (that is, eta squared × 100 percent), are all based on single-degree-of-freedom contrasts.

* $p < .01$, ** $p < .001$.

Marsh, Barnes and colleagues (1984) found support for the Shavelson et al. hypothesis in that the average correlation among SDQ I scales decreased dramatically with increasing age during early preadolescent ages (grades two through five). Tests of the generality of these findings across the preadolescent to early adult periods are considered here along with alternative tests of the Shavelson et al. hypothesis.

One possible test of the hypothesis of increased differentiation with age is that correlations among SDQ scales will become smaller with increasing age. This was tested with three sets of correlations for responses to each of the SDQ instruments (see table 2.3) for:

1. All scales measured by each SDQ instrument;
2. The six scales common to the three SDQ instruments; and
3. A set of seven correlations hypothesized a priori to be the smallest.

For each of the SDQ instruments and corresponding age range: (1) The mean correlation among scale scores is higher than the mean correlation among factor scores; (2) the mean correlation among all scales is similar to the mean correlation among just the scales common to the three instruments; and (3) the mean correlation among scales selected a priori to be lowest are substantially lower than the mean correlation among all scales or among scales common to the three SDQ instruments. This consistency—particularly—facilitates the comparison of correlations across the different ages.

There is a substantial decrease in the size of correlations from grade two to grade three, and smaller decreases between grades three and four, and between grades four and five. There is no support, however, for any further declines in the average correlation among scales for the rest of the preadolescent (SDQ I) data, nor for the adolescent (SDQ II) and the late-adolescent (SDQ III) data. In summary, the data provide no support for this test of the hypothesis that self-concept becomes increasingly differentiated with increasing age beyond the early preadolescent years.

An alternative test of the hypothesis of increasing differentiation is that differences among the scale scores for the same person will become larger with age. That is, younger subjects are more likely to have uniformly high or uniformly low self-concepts across all areas, whereas older subjects are more likely to have relatively high self-concepts in some areas and relatively low self-concepts in other areas. In order to test this operationalization, the standard deviation of scale scores for each subject—that is, a within-subject standard deviation—was computed for all scales and for the scales common to the three SDQ instruments. Separate within-subject standard deviations were computed for raw scale scores and for factor scores—that is, those which were standardized to have a mean of

Table 2.3
Summary of Scale Distinctiveness Analyses of Three SDQ Instruments

| Instrument and Age Level | Mean Correlation among: | | | | | | Standard Deviation of: | | | |
| | All Scales | | Common Scales | | Selected Scales | | All Scales | | Common Scales | |
	Raw	Fact	Raw	Fact	Raw	Fact	Raw	Fact	Raw	Fact
SDQ I										
Grade 2	.55	.43	.55	.43	.49	.37	0.52	6.50	0.52	6.36
Grade 3	.37	.27	.39	.29	.30	.20	0.62	6.91	0.61	6.59
Grade 4	.34	.24	.31	.20	.23	.12	0.75	8.07	0.78	8.09
Grade 5	.27	.18	.25	.15	.18	.08	0.75	8.02	0.78	8.07
Grade 6	.28	.18	.25	.16	.17	.07	0.81	8.42	0.84	8.53
Grade 7	.39	.28	.38	.27	.31	.19	0.74	7.70	0.76	7.76
Grade 8	.33	.22	.31	.21	.29	.17	0.80	8.82	0.83	8.93
Grade 9	.28	.19	.27	.18	.23	.13	0.78	8.62	0.81	8.89
Total	.33	.22	.31	.20	.24	.13	0.76	8.11	0.79	8.17
SDQ II										
Grade 7	.30	.18	.29	.17	.21	.09	0.98	8.55	1.04	8.28
Grade 8	.32	.19	.31	.19	.26	.12	0.96	8.49	1.03	8.29
Grade 9	.32	.19	.29	.16	.24	.11	0.92	8.39	0.99	8.38
Grade 10	.31	.18	.28	.16	.21	.09	0.90	8.05	0.96	8.10
Grade 11	.28	.16	.24	.12	.19	.07	0.87	7.99	0.95	8.18
Total	.31	.18	.29	.17	.23	.10	0.94	8.34	1.00	8.25
SDQ III										
LT 18 yrs.	.21	.10	.20	.10	.10	.00	1.16	8.93	1.17	9.12
18–21.5 yrs.	.28	.16	.27	.14	.21	.08	1.07	8.18	1.00	7.96
GT 21.5 yrs.	.27	.16	.26	.13	.22	.10	1.07	8.04	0.96	7.65
Total	.25	.14	.26	.14	.20	.08	1.10	8.37	1.04	8.22

Note: The mean correlation was computed separately for each of three sets of scale scores: correlations among all scales measured by a particular instrument (All); correlations among the set of five scales common to all three instruments (Common); and correlations selected a priori to be the lowest (Selected). The standard deviation of responses by each respondent was also computed for all scales and for the set of common scales (meaning, a respondent who had the same score for all scales would have an SD of 0). Separate analyses were conducted for raw scales scores (Raw) and factor scores (Fact).

fifty and a standard deviation of ten across all respondents to each instrument. For the SDQ I data, within-subject standard deviations increased between grades two and three, and between grades three and four, but did not appear to increase systematically for older subjects. For both the SDQ II and SDQ III data, within-subject standard deviations decreased with greater age, instead of increasing with age as posited. Whereas caution must be exercised in comparing within-subject standard deviations at different ages, the present comparisons offer no support for the increased differentiation of self-concept beyond early preadolescence.

Summary of Age and Sex Effects

Despite claims that self-concept does not vary with increasing age, there appear to be systematic age effects in self-concept responses (Wylie 1979). SDQ responses indicate that self-concept declines during preadolescence, continues to decline in early adolescence, and then increases during middle adolescence through early adulthood. The SDQ results are important because they provide support for the posited age effects on self-concept that were pieced together from a collage of different studies, they show this effect to be reasonably consistent across well-differentiated self-concept scales and across responses by boys and by girls, and they are based on responses to well-standardized multidimensional instruments.

For the total self-concept scores, the results summarized here indicate that boys have modestly higher self-concepts than girls. Marsh and Shavelson (1985) argue, however, that self-concept cannot be adequately understood if only a global component is considered. Consistent with this claim, previous research suggested that the relatively weak sex effects in global self-concept might be a composite of counterbalancing sex differences in more specific areas, some favoring boys and some favoring girls, that are consistent with sex stereotypes. Because self-concept researchers have typically considered only a global self-concept or measured multiple dimensions of self with instruments with psychometrically unconfirmed properties, there has been a weak empirical basis for testing this suggestion. The results of the present investigation provide strong support for this contention and demonstrate that the posited sex effects are reasonably consistent across the preadolescent to early adult period considered here.

Shavelson and colleagues posited that self-concept would become increasingly differentiated with age. An important problem with tests of this hypothesis is how to operationalize the notion of increasing differentiation. Two alternative interpretations considered here each suggested that self-concept might become increasingly differentiated during early preadolescence. The findings, however, failed to substantiate further increases beyond the preadolescent period.

The failure to support this hypothesis, except for early preadolescent years, was disappointing. Indeed, the rationale for including an increasing number and diversity of scales on the SDQ II and SDQ III was based in part on this hypothesis. The clearly defined factor structure for an increasingly complex set of dimensions in the SDQ II and SDQ III may even provide tangential support for the proposal. It may be that alternative measures of increasing differentiation or methodologies emerging from different areas of research may provide better support for this intuitively appealing hypothesis.

It is also relevant to examine the research implications of the decline in self-concepts that occurs in preadolescence and early adolescence. It is tempting to establish value judgments on this finding and look for culprits, such as schools, parents, or society. Because this decline occurs during the school years, it is particularly tempting to blame the educational system (Stipek & Daniels 1988). Such assertions, however, are unwarranted, and this decline should not necessarily be seen as bad or unfortunate.

Indeed, it appears that the very high self-concepts of the youngest children are unrealistically high. As children grow older, they gain more realistic appraisals of their relative strengths and weaknesses, and this information is apparently incorporated into their self-concepts (Marsh, Barnes et al. 1984; Nicholls 1979; Ruble 1983; Stipek 1981, 1984). Perhaps, it would be unfortunate if self-concepts did not become more realistic on the basis of additional life experience.

SUMMARY AND IMPLICATIONS

The central theme of this chapter has been the description of and empirical support for a model positing a hierarchical multidimensional structure of self-concept. Historically, self-concept research has emphasized a global dimension of self. More recent research—such as described here—emphasizes specific dimensions of self and may call into question the usefulness of a general dimension of self.

Marsh, Byrne, and Shavelson (1988) similarly concluded that academic self-concept cannot be adequately understood if specific dimensions of academic self-concept are ignored, suggesting that at least verbal and mathematical components of academic self-concept should be considered. Marsh and Shavelson (1985) concluded that self-concept cannot be adequately understood if its multidimensionality is ignored. The further substantiation of this conclusion has been the major thrust of this presentation and related research (Marsh in press-a).

Interest in self-concept stems from its recognition as a valued outcome, from its assumed role as a moderator variable, from interest in its relation to other constructs, and from interest in methodological and measurement issues. Historically, self-concept research has been noted for a lack of rigor in its theoretical models and measurement instruments. Even though it did not resolve important within-construct issues such as the dimensionality of self-concept, the majority of self-concept research focused on the relation between self-concept and other constructs.

The position taken in SDQ research is that theory and measurement are inexorably intertwined. Each will suffer if the other is ignored. Research described here supports the construct validity of responses to SDQ instruments and the Shavelson et al. model upon which they are based. The research has also clarified many theoretical issues in self-concept research and led to the revised Marsh/Shavelson model. In this sense, SDQ research represents an interplay between theory and empirical research, and supports the construct validity approach that guided SDQ research.

NOTE

*The authors would like to thank Raymond Debus, Rhonda Craven, and Rosalie Robinson for helpful comments on earlier drafts of this review.

REFERENCES

Anderson, N. H. 1968. Likableness ratings of 555 personality-trait words. *Journal of Personality and Social Psychology* 9:272–279.

Bachman, J. G. 1970. *Youth in transition.* Vol. 2: *The impact of family background and intelligence on tenth-grade boys.* Ann Arbor, Mich.: Institute for Social Research.

Benson, J., and Hocevar, D. 1986. The impact of item phrasing on the validity of attitude scales for elementary school children. *Journal of Educational Measurement* 22:231–340.

Boersma, F. J., and Chapman, J. W. 1979. Student's Perception of Ability Scale Manual. Edmonton, Canada: University of Alberta.

Burns, R. B. 1979. *The self-concept: Theory, measurement, development and behavior.* London: Longman.

Byrne, B. M. 1984. The general/academic self-concept nomological network: A review of construct validation research. *Review of Educational Research* 54:427–456.

Coopersmith, S. A. 1967. *The antecedents of self-esteem.* San Francisco: W. H. Freeman.

Dusek, J. B., and Flaherty, J. F. 1981. The development of self-concept during adolescent years. *Monographs of the Society for Research in Child Development* 46. (4, serial no. 191).

Epstein, S. 1980. The self-concept: A review and the proposal of an integrated theory of personality. In *Personality: Basic issues and current research,* edited by E. Staub. Englewood Cliffs, N.J.: Prentice Hall. 81–132.

Fleming, J. S., and Courtney, B. E. 1984. The dimensionality of self-esteem: II: Hierarchical facet model for revised measurement scales. *Journal of Personality and Social Psychology* 46:404–421.

Hansford, B. C., and Hattie, J. A. 1982. The relationship between self and achievement/performance measures. *Review of Educational Research* 52:123–142.

Harter, S. 1982. The Perceived Competence Scale for Children, *Child Development* 53:87–97.

———. 1983. Developmental perspectives on the self-system. In *Handbook of Child Psychology,* edited by P. H. Musser. Vol. 4, 4th ed. New York: Wiley. 275–385.

———. 1985. Processes underlying the construction, maintenance, and enhancement of the self-concept in children. In *The development of self,* edited by J. Suls and A. G. Greenwald. Hillsdale, N.J.: Lawrence Erlbaum. 137–181.

———. 1988. The construction and conservation of self: James and Cooley revisited. In *Self, ego, and identity: Integrative approaches,* edited by D. K. Lapsley and F. C. Power. New York: Springer-Verlag. 43–70.

Harter, S., and Pike, R. 1984. The pictorial scale of perceived competence and social acceptance for young children. *Child Development* 55:1969–1982.

Higgins, E. T. 1987. Self-discrepancy: A theory relating self and affect. *Psychological Review* 84:319–340.

Higgins, E. T.; Klein, R., and Strauman, T. 1985. Self-concept discrepancy theory: A psychological model for distinguishing among different aspects of depression and anxiety. *Social Cognition* 3:51–76.

Hoge, D. R., and McCarthy, J. D. 1984. Influence of individual and group identity salience in the global self-esteem of youth. *Journal of Personality and Social Psychology* 47:403–414.

James, W. [1890] 1963. *The principles of psychology.* New York: Holt, Rinehart & Winston.

Markus, H., and Nurius, P. 1986. Possible selves. *American Psychologist* 41:954–969.

Markus, H., and Wurf, E. 1987. The dynamic self-concept: A social psychological perspective. *Annual Review of Psychology* 38:299–337.

Marsh, H. W. 1986a. The bias of negatively worded items in rating scales for young children: A cognitive-developmental phenomena. *Developmental Psychology* 22:37–49.

———. 1986b. Global self esteem: Its relation to specific facets of self-concept and their importance. *Journal of Personality and Social Psychology* 51:1224–1236.

———. 1986c. Verbal and math self-concepts: An internal/external frame-of-reference model. *American Educational Research Journal* 23:129–149.

———. 1987a. The big-fish-little-pond effect on academic self-concept. *Journal of Educational Psychology* 79:280–295.

———. 1987b. The hierarchical structure of self-concept and the application of hierarchical confirmatory factor analysis. *Journal of Educational Measurement* 24:17–19.

———. 1988. *Self Description Questionnaire: A Theoretical and empirical basis for the measurement of multiple dimensions of preadolescent self-concept: A test manual and a research monograph.* San Antonio, Tex.: The Psychological Corporation.

———. 1989. Age and sex effects in multiple dimensions of self-concept: Preadolescence to Early-adulthood. *Journal of Educational Psychology* 81:417–430.

———. In press-a. A multidimensional, hierarchical model of self-concept: Theoretical and empirical justification. *Educational Psychology Review.*

———. In press-b. *Self-Description Questionnaire (SDQ) II: A Theoretical and empirical basis for the measurement of multiple dimensions of adolescent self-concept: An interim test manual and a research monograph*. San Antonio, Tex.: The Psychological Corporation

————. In press-c. *Self-Description Questionnaire (SDQ) III: A Theoretical and empirical basis for the measurement of multiple dimensions of late adolescent self-concept: An interim test manual and a research monograph*. San Antonio, Tex.: The Psychological Corporation.

————, and Hocevar, D. 1985. The application of confirmatory factor analysis to the study of self-concept: First and higher order factor structures and their invariance across age groups. *Psychological Bulletin* 97:562–582.

————, and MacDonald-Holmes, I. W. In press. Multidimensional self-concepts: Construct validation of responses by children. *American Educational Research Journal*.

————, and O'Neill, R. 1984. Self Description Questionnaire III (SDQ III): The construct validity of multidimensional self-concept ratings by late-adolescents. *Journal of Educational Measurement* 21:153–174.

————, and Parker, J. W. 1984. Determinants of self-concept: Is it better to be a relatively large fish in a small pond even if you don't learn to swim as well? *Journal of Personality and Social Psychology* 47:213–231.

————, and Shavelson, R. J. 1985. Self-concept: Its multifaceted, hierarchical structure. *Educational Psychologist* 20:107–125.

————, and Smith, I. D. 1982. Multitrait-multimethod analyses of two self-concept instruments. *Journal of Educational Psychology* 74:430–440.

————; Byrne, B. M.; and Shavelson, R. 1988. A multifaceted academic self-concept: Its hierarchical structure and its relation to academic achievement. *Journal of Educational Psychology* 80:366–380.

————; Relich, J. D.; and Smith, I. D. 1983. Self-concept: The construct validity of interpretations based upon the SDQ. *Journal of Personality and Social Psychology* 45:173–187.

————; Richards, G.; and Barnes, J. 1986. Multidimensional self-concepts: A longterm followup of the effect of participation in an Outward Bound program. *Personality and Social Psychology Bulletin* 12:475–492.

————; Barnes, J.; Cairns, L.; and Tidman, M. 1984. The Self Description Questionnaire (SDQ): Age effects in the structure and level of self-concept for preadolescent children. *Journal of Educational Psychology* 76:940–956.

Marx, R. W., and Winne, P. H. 1978. Construct interpretations of three self-concept inventories. *American Educational Research Journal* 15:99–108.

Nicholls, J. 1979. Development of perception of attainment and causal attributions for success and failure in reading. *Journal of Educational Psychology* 71:94–99.

O'Malley, P. M., and Bachman, J. G. 1983. Self-esteem: Change and stability between ages 13 and 23. *Developmental Psychology* 19, 257–268.

Rogers, C. R. 1951. *Client-centered therapy.* Boston: Houghton Mifflin Co.

Rosenberg, M. 1965. *Society and the adolescent self-image.* Princeton, N.J.: Princeton University Press.

————. 1979. *Conceiving the self.* New York: Basic Books.

Ruble, D. N. 1983. The development of social comparison processes and their role in achievement-related self-socialization. In *Social Cognition and Social Development,* edited by E. T. Higgins, D. Ruble, and W. W. Hartup. New York: Cambridge University Press. 134–157.

Sears, P. S. 1963. *The effect of classroom conditions on the strength of achievement motive and work output of elementary school children.* U.S. Office of Education Cooperative Research Project, project no. OE–873. Stanford, Calif.: Stanford University.

Shavelson, R. J., and Bolus, R. 1982. Self-concept: The interplay of theory and methods. *Journal of Educational Psychology* 74:3–17.

Shavelson, R. J., and Marsh, H. W. 1986. On the structure of self-concept. In *Anxiety and cognitions,* edited by R. Schwarzer. Hillsdale, N.J.: Lawrence Erlbaum.

Shavelson, R. J.; Hubner, J. J.; and Stanton, G. C. 1976. Validation of construct interpretations. *Review of Educational Research* 46:407–441.

Silon, E. L.; and Harter, S. 1985. Assessment of perceived competence, motivational orientation, and anxiety in segregated and mainstreamed educable mentally retarded children. *Journal of Educational Psychology* 77:217–230.

Soares, L. M., and Soares, A. T. 1982. *Convergence and discrimination in academic self-concepts.* Paper presented at the Twentieth Congress of the International Association of Applied Psychology. Edinburgh, Scotland.

Stipek, D. J. 1981. Children's perceptions of their own and their classmates' ability. *Journal of Educational Psychology* 73:404–410.

————. 1984. The development of achievement motivation. In *Research on motivation in education,* edited by R. E. Ames and C. Ames. Vol. 1. Orlando, Fla.: Academic Press. 145–174.

————, and Daniels, D. H. 1988. Declining perceptions of competence: A consequence of changes in the children in the educational environment. *Journal of Educational Psychology* 80:352–356.

Tesser, A., and Campbell, J. 1980. Self-definition: The impact of the relative performance and similarity of others. *Social Psychology Quarterly* 43:341–346.

————. 1983. Self-definition and self-evaluation maintenance. In *The development of self,* edited by J. Suls and A. G. Greenwald. Hillsdale, N.J.: Lawrence Erlbaum. 1–31.

Vernon, P. E. 1950. *The structure of human abilities.* London: Muethon.

Wells, L. E., and Marwell, G. 1976. *Self-esteem: Its conceptualization and measurement.* Beverly Hills, Calif.: Sage Publications.

Werner, H. 1957. The concept of development from a comparative and organismic point of view. In *The concept of development,* edited by D. B. Harris. Minneapolis: University of Minnesota Press.

Wylie, R. C. 1974. *The self-concept.* Revised edition, vol. 1. Lincoln: University of Nebraska Press.

————. 1979. *The self-concept,* Vol. 2. Lincoln: University of Nebraska Press.

————. 1989. *Measures of self-concept.* Lincoln: University of Nebraska Press.

3

An Experiential-developmental Framework and Methodology to Study the Transformations of the Self-concept from Infancy to Old Age

Trying to define and give answers to the many problems raised in life-span oriented research is not an easy task. During my research career, I have not met all the different and possible difficulties. So I cannot pretend to have identified and solved all the problems raised in such a setting. The reader must then consider the present chapter as offering useful indications, solutions, and proposals derived from a twenty-five year on-going experience in the study of the self-concept across the life span. This material is submitted with the hope that it will help to convince the reader that these difficulties are not insurmountable—and with an even greater hope that it will contribute to the emerging literature on the study of the development of the self-concept across the life span.

These purposes will be achieved through the following steps which constitute the main divisions of this chapter: a brief description of the general goals of my research program on the development of the self-concept across the life span; a review of the theoretical and methodological problems raised in a life-span perspective; a presentation of the tentative answers developed in the realization of my research program; and a conclusion in which the advantages, limits, and implications for future research will be discussed.

GENERAL GOALS OF THE RESEARCH PROGRAM

Since 1967, the main goals pursued in my research program have been to:

- Study the development of the self-concept across the life span in normal people and from the individual's point of view, not the researcher's;
- Use the same methodology to explore the self in order to obtain more comparable results across different ages. (The methodology finally developed was the self-perception genesis method, hereafter referred to as the GPS Method—an adaptation of Bugental and Zelen's (1950) "Who Are You?" technique—which will be explained in the third part of this chapter.);
- Identify the different dimensions of the self-concept from the content analysis of the obtained protocols;
- Organize these dimensions within a similar conceptual framework—to make results more comparable—but flexible enough to integrate new dimensions that could appear at other periods of development. (This conceptual framework will be presented in a later part of this chapter.);
- Construct perceptual profiles characteristic of each age and study their transformations with age;
- Construct developmental profiles for each dimension;
- Study the degrees of importance of these perceptions and their variations from age to age or for different groups of ages;
- Stay in contact with perceptual contents within each dimension to observe the quantitative and the qualitative transformations of the self across the life-span; and to
- Compare men and women on all these aspects in terms of similarities and differences.

Before explaining the method as such, the conceptual framework gradually developed, and the different types of analyses of the results (which will be proposed as examples in a later part of this chapter), it is first necessary to have a look at the general theoretical and methodological problems with a life-span perspective.

THEORETICAL AND METHODOLOGICAL PROBLEMS RAISED WITH A LIFE-SPAN PERSPECTIVE

At least two aspects are to be considered concerning the problems raised in a life-span perspective study of the self-concept: the nature of those problems which pertain to the study of the self-concept as such, and how these problems change with increasing age. Let us take a closer look at these problems.

Problems Pertaining to the Study of the Self-concept

The researcher who wants to study the development of the self across the life span is automatically faced with theoretical and methodological difficulties which he or she has to overcome.

Theoretical Problems. When the aim is a life-span study, operational definitions and other problem-distillation decisions must be clearly made at the start of the project because future modifications of the research program might be impossible to make if inadequate choices have been previously made. These theory-oriented decisions have implications for the possible methods to be used. Thus, it seems necessary to point out some of these theoretical problems.

The notion of the self-concept. The researcher is automatically faced with the problem of considering the self as an individual or social phenomenon, an affective or cognitive structure, a unique or multidimensional organization. As an example, one may legitimately want to study the development of only one dimension of the self all across the life span (such as body image, self-esteem, or self-identity) and obtain very fruitful results to help understand the development of the self. But problems such as the following may occur.

- First, the researcher may discover too late that the development of the selected dimension could be better understood in light of one or several other dimensions; or
- Second, he or she may tend to consider the obtained curve as the standard curve characterizing the development of the entire self. A multidimensional approach clearly shows there are no standard developmental curves but, rather, several very different patterns depending on the dimensions considered (L'Écuyer 1975a, 1981, 1989b, 1990).

The self-concept as a hierarchical organization and the centrality of specific self-perceptions. Such ideas were raised by William James as far back as 1890 in his famous chapter on the self. According to

James, the different types of perceptions which an individual has about himself are not all at the same level of importance. Some are very important and vital, while others are less important or even secondary within this whole *gestalt* which constitutes the self-concept. Since 1890, this idea has regularly been suggested and investigated (Allport 1955; Combs and Snygg 1959; Gordon 1968; Marsh 1986; Marsh & Shavelson 1985. See also chapter 2 of this volume).

James also proposed a possible hierarchy of the different dimensions of the self, while Allport (1961) suggested developmental stages in which specific dimensions are judged to be central. Because the psychological place of every dimension of the self regularly changes in the developmental patterning of the self (L'Écuyer 1975a, 1978, 1981, 1989b, 1990, in press), the importance attributed to certain dimensions of the self (in research, bearing on only one dimension) may be entirely disproportionate when reconsidered in the light of multidimensional and hierarchical approaches to the self-concept in a life-span perspective.

Methodological Aspects. The measurement of the self-concept has always been accompanied by great controversies (see part II, chapters 4 through 8, of this volume). I will raise only a few of these considerations here to help understand the choices made concerning the instrument which I finally used.

The problem of validity: inference versus self-report. This is the classical opposition which has been regularly analyzed (Combs and Snygg 1959; L'Écuyer 1975a, 1975b, 1978, in press; Wylie 1961, 1974). In my review of this controversy, I noted three tendencies.

1. Self-reports are said to have several serious weaknesses;
2. The capacity of the inference techniques to really overcome self-reports' weaknesses seems to be far less evident than some have claimed; and
3. Inference techniques, such as behavior observation and projective methods, cannot replace self-reports because they do not measure the same qualities—that is, the same aspects or levels (L'Écuyer 1978, in press) of the self-concept.

Nevertheless, the debate about validity goes regularly against self-reports because subjects are not *supposed* to be able to describe themselves validly (see chapter 4 of this volume). This certainty is, of course, greater when the subjects are children.

The problem of reliability. It is quite easy to measure reliability in a standard questionnaire. Answers from the retest are the same as that of the test, or they are different. But even with a very simple setting, such as a *yes* or *no* response-format questionnaire, many problems seem to emerge and put the statistical devices into doubt (Wylie 1974. See also chapter 5 of this volume).

The evaluation of the reliability of a self-report in which the individual is entirely free to describe himself as he wants presents much more difficulty. For instance, must the individual repeat the same sentence, with the same words on test and retest? Must the researcher check the reappearance of the same general contents rather than the same words to get a better account of the reliability of such free descriptions? Attention must then be greater to that problem with free self-report methods, and controversies about the accuracy of the decisions taken may also be easily greater.

Despite the validity and reliability problems, I finally chose to work with an entirely open-ended self-report method for the following reasons:

1. The validity of inference techniques is definitely no greater than that of self-reports (Moskowitz 1986, Wylie 1974); and
2. Self-reports cannot be put aside because they bring points of view which are unique in the understanding of the self-concept. These points of view involve the individual's self-perceptions—what he perceives and thinks about himself—no matter what impressions he may give to others.

Qualitative and quantitative analyses. Most researchers study only short developmental periods. In such cases, it seems appropriate to consider the psychological contents of the dimensions of the self to be quite the same from one age to another. Consequently, the analysis of the results takes only their frequencies into account. But can one assume that the psychological contents of a given dimension of the self will remain the same over longer developmental sequences? . . . And all across the life span? Thus, it is necessary for the researcher to take these changes into account. Content or qualitative analysis of the material classified in each dimension of the self seems to be a very good, adequate, and sometimes vital device for this purpose as we will further see.

How Do Research Problems Change in a Life-span Perspective?

This part will discuss the major problems (both theoretical and methodological) which are or can be met while studying the self-concept across the life span.

The Conceptual Framework versus Development. Because life-span developmental research is a relatively new endeavor, it is necessary to be especially cautious about the initial conceptual framework sustaining all future planning of the research. To help overcome possible difficulties, the following topics will be discussed:

1. The construction of the conceptual framework as such;
2. The definitions of the dimensions of the self-concept that are to be evaluated or measured; and
3. The addition of developmental content analysis as a possible solution to solve these two problems.

Conceptual framework versus changes across the life span. The conceptual framework is the theoretical structure which determines all the organization of the research. We are used to defining very precise and specific frameworks and deducing all their counterparts from reviews of the literature, to include the dimensions of the self, their definitions, the contents which will be considered to be part of each dimension, and the methods or tests best suited to measure them. The statistical analyses are also regularly decided at the start of the research.

The situation cannot be as clear in a life-long research program because we do not benefit from the same long research experience heritage. To build a clear-cut conceptual framework at the outset of a life-span-oriented study might, thus, lead to a dead-end because the phenomenon changes too much and no longer fits into previously organized concepts. Frameworks to study the self in very long terms timewise must be flexible enough to integrate new aspects of the self that may appear during the research and which might not be predictable at all.

Definitions of each dimension of the self-concept versus development. The problem of defining each dimension of the self-concept to be suitable for every age from infancy to old age is even more acute. The self-concept does not change only quantitatively. What then happens to the previously identified criteria determining which type of content fits into the definition of each given dimension when, at the same time, these psychological contents regularly change with age? Is it possible to anticipate all these subtle changes and define these criteria accordingly? It is important that researchers remain aware of this factor because it not only greatly impacts on the methods or tests used to measure the self, but also particularly on the types of questions to be included in developing the questionnaire.

As an example, it might appear to not be too difficult to prepare a questionnaire suitable enough to properly evaluate the body image of children, adolescents, adults, and elders. But the construction of a questionnaire to measure identity processes, on the other hand, could raise far more difficulties, at least for adults and elders. This could be because we are not really familiar with adults' and elders' various ways of searching identity. Which type of questions can properly translate this need?

Defining each dimension too rigidly may lead to completely inadequate questions depending on the age groups to which they are applied. As will be discussed in the next section of this chapter, open-ended questions may become necessary to identify totally unpredictable types of answers in translating unknown aspects of the developing self.

Developmental content analysis. Because all the possible dimensions of the self-concept cannot easily and necessarily be entirely predictable, and because the operational definitions and criteria of each dimension of the self can hardly be satisfactorily established at the beginning of a life-span-oriented research program, traditional tests or questionnaires are frequently unsuitable. We met just these difficulties in attempting to build a conceptual framework and formulate operational definitions which were suitable for a life-span perspective (L'Écuyer 1975a).

As an example, a category named *conformity/nonconformity to external demands* had been identified and properly defined to take into account children's reactions to their parents' and teachers' requests. But this category appeared to be unsuitable for adults, particularly elders. Some sentences referred to ways of facing reality and relating to different defense mechanisms. Other sentences such as "I have been obliged to quit my home and move into institutions" or "I would have liked to make long studies, but at that time we had to replace our parents on the farm" refer to conformity/nonconformity to reality, but not in the same meaning of external demands defined for children. Different solutions to these types of issues are possible.

The first choice is to identify specific categories for each peculiarity, define them operationally, and formulate questions specific enough to be able to measure these aspects. For instance, each defense mechanism would have to be identified as specific categories, as well as conformity/nonconformity to external demands and conformity/nonconformity to reality. This would clearly necessitate a great number of questions for only one of the many aspects of the self. It is then easy to imagine the length that such a questionnaire would grow to if it were to be suitable to investigate all the other facets of the self, especially over the life span.

The second choice seems to me to rely on open-ended questionnaires (such as a sentence-completion task) or, preferably, on entirely free questionnaires to which developmental content analysis is applied. To allow individuals to answer as they want to or to describe themselves freely as to how they perceive themselves to be ensures with greater accuracy the possibility of getting material containing the vastly different aspects of the self and the many variations and particular facets which they can assume as the self changes throughout the life span. It also leads to more accurate identification and definitions of all the dimensions of the self because the individuals are not obliged to limit their answers and fit them into the format of questions which they have been asked.

The researcher must then submit these free verbalizations to what I call *developmental content analysis*. This method seems, to me, to be the only device capable of considering the many changing aspects of the self, especially of how they are modified as the self grows and evolves across the life span. The usual methodology of content analysis is applied to the material of the protocols for each age.

Developmental content analysis (L'Écuyer 1987, 1989a, in press) refers to a "deeper review of the coding system," and steps must be taken for a better account of the changes that might have occurred due to such development. What is properly defined for a given response at a given age may not necessarily be appropriate to other ages. The steps independently followed at each age occasionally have to be redesigned over larger developmental scales to ensure that the definitions and criteria of differentiation still fit and still capture the changing aspects of the self itself. Sometimes these criteria must be readapted. At other times, new dimensions must be identified because previous ones no longer match with the particularities of the new material obtained at other ages. The difficulty lies in establishing when it is necessary to modify or adapt the definitions and criteria to the already identified dimensions or categories of the self, and when it is preferable to identify or open a new category. Simply said, when does the material change enough to legitimate a new category in the system? And when are these changes merely nuances of the same basic phenomenon or process? In the latter case, an adjustment of the criteria of differentiation or of the definition of the existing category might be the solution.

Three guidelines to solve this problem are proposed in the section entitled *Conceptual Framework* later in this chapter.

This is not an easy task, but I believe the developmental researchers on the self-concept across the life cycle must deal with it and undertake, at least occasionally, such type of content analysis if they are to construct questionnaires which are suitable for taking developmental changes into account.

Methodological Difficulties of Investigating the Self and Changes in These Difficulties with Age. Other methodological difficulties must be taken into account while studying the development of the self-concept across the life span. These include:

1. The suitability of the instructions to groups of very different ages;
2. The problem of sampling and of other research controls; and
3. Issues relating to the use of the traditional research designs in a life-span developmental study.

The applicability of instructions to different ages. As we have seen previously, the construction of a measure suitable to explore the development of the self across wide age ranges raises difficulties. An additional difficulty is that the measure's instructions are understandable to everybody regardless of age. Here is a simple illustration of this.

The results of our first efforts to help very young children understand the question "Who are you?" were that everyone (including mentally retarded adolescents) drew their faces with or without their bodies as if they were administered the Draw-a-Person Test! Adapted instructions now are: "When I don't know a friend of yours, you tell me a lot of things about him so that I finally have quite a good idea of the way he is. I don't know you at all. Do the same and tell me a lot of things about you so that I will finally have a good idea of who you are."

This example illustrates the types of difficulties which are raised while trying to develop meaningful instructions and adapt them to every age group (from childhood to old age) without changing the basic meaning to everybody of what is asked. Imagine the difficulties for whole questionnaires!

As a matter of fact, problems of comprehension changed with age. During the interviews with very young children three and five years old, the main difficulty was to have them understand the meaning of "Who are you?" and of the following explanation "describe yourself the best way you can." The other challenge concerned how to make them speak of different aspects of themselves, besides only their toys, without any suggestion as to what they might speak about. Reactions such as "Good. Keep on" and "Is there something else you would like to say about you?" proved to be good interventions because they were not "directive," nor did they suggest to the children what to say.

With other groups, from adolescents to 100-year-old individuals, there were no specific problems as to the understanding of the instructions as such. Adolescents and adults were seen in small groups of ten to fifteen, and they each had to write their descriptions on paper.

Adolescents tended to be very extensive in their descriptions of themselves in a free self-report situation with many repetitive sequences which frequently add no new information. The solution finally appeared to be to give them only one or two sheets of paper to write their descriptions of themselves. In such a situation, only those who really needed more space for their answers asked for additional paper. It seems to have helped them to avoid repeating answers within the same categories and to cover more different categories with greater facility.

With adults, a certain proportion tended to answer simply by a short listing of general characteristics about themselves, such as intelligent, honest, sometimes lazy, and the like. For these groups, it was necessary to add instructions explaining that we do not want a listing but a real *description* as to how they perceive themselves.

With elders from ages sixty to one hundred, the difficulty was not really in their understanding of the question "Who are you?" but rather in conveying to them that the question was part of a study of the self-concept, not a two- or three-hour social conversation around the individual's whole-life review. In the latter situations, the answers to the question were finally forgotten or at least became difficult to identify and extract from all the material given. After many trials, the special intervention developed to overcome this handicap was to ask the individual to write his description. But, before he or she even had time to answer, the interviewer gently offered to do the writing if he or she would care not to speak too fast. It seemed that elders appreciated this offer so much that they remembered that the interview was for a scientific purpose. Thus, they remained much more closely on the task of describing the way in which they perceive themselves.

Even with the precautions cited—and of many others not described here—the reader must know that there were still problems.

For different reasons, about 50 percent of the protocols were rejected from very young children and about 30 percent from elders. Among such reasons were:

- Difficulties in establishing a sufficiently good contact (depending sometimes on the interviewer and sometimes on the subject);
- The interviewer's difficulties in explaining the meaning of the instructions without giving clues which would influence the contents of the subject's description; and
- The inability of certain subjects to understand the instructions.

All these adaptations must be made with great care to ensure that the testing situation is as standardized as possible, and that the specific meaning of the request is understood with the greatest possible uniformity across ages. There are no general tricks here. The interviewers must analyze each specific situation and adopt instructions which will not interfere with and compromise the fundamental goals of the research. This last observation leads us to other research design problems, such as sampling and particularly the research controls.

The problem of sampling and research controls in a developmental study of the self across the life span. In their book on normality, published in 1966, Offer and Sabshin wrote about the difficulties of getting samples—such as comparable and paired samples—which could be truly representative of normal subjects.

When studying the development of the self of normal people across the life span, the difficulties in identifying criteria that will ensure the normality of the subjects as well as the comparability of the samples is obvious. Can the criteria to establish physical fitness and mental health in young children be the same with elders? How does the researcher establish that each age group is truly equivalent and comparable to each other? This is easy for dimensions such as age and sex, but more difficult for intelligence and even more hazardous for health or for cultural background. What is the procedure by which to determine a three-year-old child's comparability to a ninety-year-old person?

The impossibility of meeting all these usual standard criteria became rapidly evident. In such a wide perspective as that on the life span, we must accept many compromises or the research itself becomes impossible.

Because one of my goals was to study the development of the self-concept in normal people, I had to ensure a minimum of comparability of the subjects between each age group, as on physical fitness and mental health. As an example, the following flexible criteria were applied to establish subjects' physical fitness in our samples. For children and adolescents, it was necessary not to have contracted severe illnesses in the past to be considered as physically healthy subjects. In old age, physical fitness can hardly be associated with never having been sick during the past. Thus, it is preferable to include some reasonable limits, such as not having been gravely ill during the past five years, not being physically handicapped, and a general feeling of physical well-being. Again, feeling well cannot be judged in the same way for youngsters and elders.

The same assessment remains true for mental health. Instead of engaging in very complicated testing procedures—which would be extremely time-consuming and open to theoretical criticism—it was necessary to be more flexible. Thus, assessing mental health included references to developmental antecedents for very young children; test results and teachers' evaluations whenever possible for adolescents; and judgment, general contact with reality, and capacity for coping with daily tasks for elders. Similar problems apply to other aspects of the usual research controls—standardization of instructional procedures, location of testing sessions, and characteristics of the experimenters (whether men or women, or the same or different ones for a given range of ages). Sometimes, it proved better to mix these variables instead of trying to control them to avoid constant biases because their control over the life span is, for the most part, impossible.

All this does not make these samples entirely comparable nor identical. But they become comparable enough to make life-span research possible and to get results sufficiently reliable to become very good clues to the development of the self-concept and, of course, to stimulate more research in such a direction.

The problem of developing methods and designs applicable to large age ranges. Many developmental researchers have noted that one of the great difficulties in such research over wide age ranges is the so-called impossibility of using the same measuring devices, coupled with the obligation to use different tests for different groups of ages, thus making it impossible to compare results between these periods of life. For most traditional research, our study was focused on a few very specific groups which were as similar as could be possible: ideally, paired samples. Then, the most rigorous experimental procedures and controls were applied to isolate the studied phenomenon.

Eventually, these procedures became the standard way of doing research. Developmental research evolved in that context and, for a long time, focused only on very short periods of life—infancy, young children, adolescents, and groups of adults or elders. Within such limited developmental ranges, researchers have attempted to apply the same traditional procedures with varied success.

The new orientation taken in developmental research—that is, trying to study the entire life cycle within the same research program—necessitates questioning these traditional controls. Because we want to respect the same exigencies required for usual research, life-span developmental research is thus squeezed by procedures which are no longer adequate for such new goals. As developmental research is now enlarging its goals to cover the entire life cycle, research designs and controls must consequently be adapted as well as enlarged to cope with these new and very different particularities of life long realities (including the self-concept).

This viewpoint concludes the more theoretical portion of this chapter. In the remainder of the chapter, I will explain the results of our investigation of the self-concept from ages three to one hundred.

TWENTY-FIVE YEAR RESEARCH PROGRAM OF THE SELF-CONCEPT RESEARCH LABORATORY

In this section, I will present the work done in my laboratory in terms of the conceptual framework and the methodology developed to face the different problems previously described, according to the specific goals pursued in my study of the development of the self-concept across the life span. Then, I will explain the different types of analyses which are now possible. Examples taken from the results obtained from ages three to one hundred will serve as illustrations (L'Écuyer 1975a, 1978, in press).

The Self-concept Research Laboratory

For purposes of organization, clear divisions are made here between the discussions of the conceptual framework and of the method used to study the self. In reality, however, the reader must realize that the research evolved in a spiral process with constant mutual influences between theoretical concepts, methodological problems, and content analysis made from the obtained results.

Conceptual Framework. From the theoretical considerations condensed in the previous sections of this chapter, a first general conceptual framework of the self was constructed in which the self appeared to be composed of four main regions—the structures—each of which were divided into substructures. Our research rapidly showed that this initial model was suitable but had to be greatly enlarged to take a better account of all the particularities of the contents covered in self-reports.

Content analysis of the free self-descriptions indicated the necessity to add a third group of dimensions to this model: the categories. It also indicated that new dimensions or categories appear with increasing age as the self develops. Five new dimensions have to be added at age five, three others at age eight, and four others at age twelve.

It even became necessary to identify a fifth main region of the self—a structure called *self-nonself* to take into account sentences in which the subjects, while describing themselves, did not speak about themselves directly, but indirectly. Samples are: "My friend has a nice bicycle." "All my friends go to school." "All my children have succeeded well in their lives."

Over the course of our research, new substructures were also identified—such as social attitudes, references to sexuality, references to others, and other's opinions of one's self.

These gradual extensions of the conceptual framework of self-development have not always been an easy task. As previously stated, we had to decide when new material should be identified as a new category or as a new substructure or—for one occasion—as a new structure. Three criteria were gradually developed for this type of problem:

1. The uniqueness of this material compared to existing material;
2. The frequency of the material across several age ranges; and
3. Whether it constitutes a more specific aspect of the existing dimensions.

Each time a new dimension was identified, it frequently meant that we had to reclassify or recode previously analyzed material to more accurately account for these new aspects. For example, the adolescent data have had to be recoded four times because of adjustments of dimensions and of their definitions. These adjustments were necessary because material obtained at later ages (with adults and even elders) clarified what was unclear within the complex material of adolescence—an age in which respondents are at the crossroads of childhood and adulthood and the material may have several different meanings.

Even if my first model were incomplete, it nevertheless helped me to understand the material obtained. Conversely, the analysis of this material helped to progressively enlarge this model as different ages brought new aspects to light. As new results were accumulated from other ages, the model and the definitions have been consequently adapted (L'Écuyer 1975a, 1978, 1981, in press).

All of the interviews of subjects from ages three to one-hundred are completed. The final conceptual model is presently composed of forty-three dimensions divided into three levels of organization: the structures, the sub-structures, and the categories. The model has now the great advantage of being accompanied by what I call *experiential developmental definitions* of the dimensions. This refers to definitions which take into account the nature of the changing material (or the underlying perceptual contents) across the life span according to the individual's feelings or experiences. It would consume too much space to give the fifty pages of these definitions here (L'Écuyer in press). For purposes of this chapter, a presentation of the conceptual framework or developmental model of the dimensions of the self derived from our research will be sufficient (see table 3.1).

Other researchers have studied the self with multidimensional and hierarchical approaches (Gordon 1968; Rodriguez-Tomé 1972). Gordon even had the same preoccupations of tracing perceptual profiles and identifying the central dimensions of the self. It is interesting to note that the multileveled conception of the self is more recently becoming popular and that the study of the self in terms of the degree of importance of each perception has also been considered (Marsh 1986; Shavelson 1985. See also chapter 2 of this volume). The development of the self over the life span is also becoming a central preoccupation with researchers, as can be seen from recent symposia on the development of the self-concept across the life span in Cardiff in 1984, and in Finland in 1989.

Based on previous approaches as well as our own analyses of the material from ages three to one hundred, I now define the self-concept as a complex perceptual organization composed of several aspects. The self-concept is:

1. A multidimensional system composed of a wide variety of perceptions which the individual feels about himself or herself (multidimensional aspect);
2. Perceptions from which contents emerge both from the individual's personal experience and from the influence of others over

Table 3.1
Experiential-developmental Model of the Self Concept

Structures	Substructures	Categories
Material Self (SM)	Somatic Self (SSo)	Physical appearance and traits (tra) Physical condition (cph)
	Possessive Self (SPo)	Possession of objects (obj) Possession of persons (per)
Personal Self (SP)	Self Image (ImS)	Aspirations (asp) Activities (listing) (ena) Feelings and emotions (sem) Interests (int) Capacities and aptitudes (apt) Qualities and failings (def)
	Self Identity (IdS)	Simple denominations (nom) Role and status (rol) Consistency (con) Ideology (ide) Abstract identity (ida)
Adaptative Self (SA)	Self Esteem (VaS)	Competency (com) Personal value (vap)
	Self Activities (AcS)	Adaptative strategies (sta) Autonomy (aut) Ambivalence (amb) Dependency (dep) Actualization (act) Lifestyle (sty)
Social Self (SS)	Social Attitudes (PaS)	Receptivity (rec) Domination (dom) Altruism (alt)
	Ref. to Sexuality (RaS)	Simple references (res) Sexual attractions + experiences (sex)

(continued)

Table 3.1 *(continued)*

Structures	Substructures	Categories
Self/Nonself (SN)	References to Others (ReA) Opinions of Others (OpA)	

the individuals' own perceptions (experiential and social aspects, process of emergence);

3. These perceptual contents are gradually organized and hierarchized into a coherent gestalt around a small number of structures delimiting the fundamental areas of the self-concept, each of them covering more limited portions of it—the substructures—fractioned into a variety of much more specific elements called the *categories* (hierarchical aspect);

4. This hierarchical organization and the degree of importance of each of its elements vary and evolve according to changing of ages and basic needs which vary all the life long (developmental aspect and degrees of importance);

5. The transformations of these hierarchical organizations are done by progressive differentiations that occur at different developmental stages (differentiating aspect);

6. As a function of daily experience directly felt, then perceived and finally symbolized or conceptualized by the individual (cognitive aspect); and

7. Where the internal cohesion of this complex perceptual organization is essentially oriented toward maintaining and promoting the adaptation of the whole individual (active and adaptative aspects) (L'Écuyer 1985, in press).

From the preceding text, it becomes clear that the method used was a great help in developing this conceptual framework and making it useful for the study of the self-concept across the life span. It means this method also had to be suitable to every age. It is now time to describe it properly.

The Self-perception Genesis (GPS) Method. The GPS is a self-report method derived from Bugental's and Zelen's (1950) "Who are you?" (WAY) technique. This self-report approach has been chosen instead of an inference technique according to our definition of the self-concept, which refers to the manner in which the individual perceives himself or herself. Originally, the WAY technique consisted of asking subjects to give three responses to the question "Who are you?" (Bugental and Zelen 1950), or giving ten or twenty responses in its most popular version, Kuhn's and McPartland's (1954) Twenty Statements Test (TST).

All of these forms resulted in sentences such as "I am this," "I am like that," and so on. It seemed to me that the number of possible responses allowed does not necessarily give the individual the opportunity to describe himself or herself completely, and that the form of the obtained responses does not allow one to evaluate the many possible facets, distinctions, or nuances within the various ways in which the individual perceives himself.

For the final form of the GPS, I kept the question "Who are you?" but added instructions asking the individual to describe himself or herself freely. "Describe yourself in the most complete way you can, no matter what others may think." I also added a second question to countercheck whether the central perceptions identified from the quantification of question one really corresponded to what the individual considered to be important. This second question was "Within all you said in answering the first question, what is the most important to you?". Subjects were free to mention one or more than one thing in answering this question. In fact, they regularly mentioned several things without any importance rating by simply saying "That's important to me, and that is, and this is" and so forth. A retest for questions one and two has also been made for purposes of reliability.

Finally, what I call a *test of the limits* was also developed to check the degree of completeness of this self-report. A current objection about WAY-like questionnaires is that the question "Who are you?" is so general and vague that it is easy to forget many things about oneself through such a spontaneous description (see chapter 5 of this volume). This test of the limits consists of specific questions covering each region or dimension of the self. If the subject really forgot to speak about these things in his or her first spontaneous self-description, he or she now has the opportunity to do it.

The instructions were: "Some individuals of your age speak about things like . . . their body. Do you have something to say about yourself concerning this topic? If yes, feel free to do so in the way you like." The interviewer presented every item on the list of the test of the limits, each of them accompanied with the same instructions. Aside from the body, these items included references to health, interests, friends, activities, and more. (For a complete list of these items, see L'Écuyer in press).

This test of the limits was previously constructed from the content analysis of several protocols obtained with questions 1 and 2 over a wide age range to ensure that it could cover the different dimensions of the self-concept. During the research phase, this test of the limits was administered *after* questions 1 and 2 were asked so that it would have no suggestive influence on the spontaneous self-descriptions of the first two questions.

The coding of the data was done according to the meaning which the individual gave to what he or she said, not to the psychological interpretation that could be made by the researcher. As has been recommended by several specialists of content analysis methodology (Bardin 1989; Ghiglione & Matalon 1978; Mucchielli 1979; Poirier, Clapier-Valladon & Raybaut 1983), this individual meaning is obtained from the sentence itself and from the general context of the protocol into which it is expressed because a sentence may have an entirely different meaning if it is considered out of or within its context. My approach is a thematic type of content analysis, each theme contributing to the final identification of the dimensions of the self presented in table 3.1.

The usual quantification process is achieved by counting the number of sentences coded in each category appearing in table 3.1. Because, in such a case, the use of frequencies is questionable (Havighurst, Robinson & Dorr 1946; L'Écuyer 1975a, 1978, in press), the quantification of results refers here to the number of subjects with at least one response coded in a given category. The quantification for the substructures, then, refers to the total number of different individuals with at least one response coded into an underlying category of a given substructure. Finally, the quantification for the structures refers to the total number of different individuals with a response in at least one of the underlying substructures. Table 3.2 gives an example of this quantification process.

One must start the quantification at the level of the categories, then of the substructures, and finally of the structures. In this example, for a group of fifteen subjects, the numbers of subjects for the different categories are respectively two, seven, ten, and six. The total for the substructure SSo is eight, not nine (sum of tra + cph), because subject #6 (who has responses in both categories) counts for only one different subject in the total of SSo. The same procedure is followed for SPo (through obj and per) and for SM (through SSo and SPo). Because the samples are not always the same size, these totals

Table 3.2
Quantification of the Number of Subjects with Responses
on Some Dimensions of the Self

Structures	*Substructures*	*Categories*	
	Somatic Self (SSo)	Phys. traits (tra) 6, 12	N = 2
	1, 2, 6, 7		
	9, 12, 14, 15	Phys. cond. (cph) 1, 2, 6	
	N = 8	7, 9, 14, 15	N = 7
Material Self (SM)			
1, 2, 3, 4, 5, 6, 7,			
8, 9, 10, 12, 14, 15		Objects (obj) 1, 2, 3, 4, 5,	
N = 13	Possessive Self (SPo)	6, 7, 8, 9, 10	N = 10
	1, 2, 3, 4, 5, 6, 7,		
	8, 9, 10, 14, 15	Persons (per) 1, 3, 5, 7,	
	N = 12	14, 15	N = 6

can be transformed into percentages for simpler comparisons between groups. In this case, results become: tra: 2/15 = 13 percent; cph: 7/15 = 47 percent; obj: 10/15 = 67 percent; per: 6/15 = 40 percent; SSo: 8/15 = 53 percent; SPo: 12/15 = 80 percent; SM: 13/15 = 87 percent.

Beyond this quantification process, it is important to have an idea concerning the reliability and validity of the results obtained with the GPS. Test-retest reliability data have been obtained from children, adolescents, and elders (aged three to twenty-one and sixty to one hundred). The subjects producing responses on a given dimension during the test session had to be the same at the retest session. This was done for the forty-three dimensions. Only three dimensions may present occasional problems of reliability for some groups, but not for most groups between ages three and one hundred. These dimensions are the structure somatic self, its physical condition category and substructure social attitudes. (Interpretations of the results on these dimensions must therefore be made with caution.) As a whole, this model or conceptual framework thus appears to be highly reliable. More detailed analyses of reliability can be found elsewhere (L'Écuyer in press.)

Despite the great controversy concerning the validity of self-reports (see chapter 4 of this volume), I really believe—as do many others, such as Super (1963)—that such measures undoubtedly possess face or construct validity. But another aspect of validity would also need to be investigated. I call this *experiential validity*.

Because the self-concept is a very deep personal experiential phenomenon, the validation process should not always refer to external criteria. I have tried to go that way with question two administered to every subject from age three to one hundred. The number of possibilities that the subjects' answers to question two could be different from the central perceptions, identified at question one, was 34,091. Such differences appear *only 17 times* in 34,091!

The total number of possibilities (34,091) refers to the total number of subjects interviewed from age three to one hundred multiplied by the number of dimensions of the self. This means that, despite the possible controversy, the choice to count the number of subjects instead of the number of sentences nevertheless corresponds to the individuals' opinion as to what is important to them.

I explained earlier that each sentence was coded by referring to the meaning which the subject seemed to have given in his or her own protocol. But we do not know if he or she would always agree with our coding, except for central perceptions. I suggest that experiential validity could be used for all the material by following these steps:

1. Make an initial coding of the responses;
2. Then meet with the subject and ask what precisely he or she meant by each response in the self-description;
3. Recode each response while taking the subject's explanations into account; and
4. Compare this second codification to the first one.

If there is no real difference between these codifications, we are thus more certain that what we are saying about the individual's self-concept really refers to how he actually perceives himself.

Types of Analyses of the Self-concept across the Life Span

There are several types of analyses which can be made from the data obtained with the GPS method. Among the possible analyses are the study of perceptual profiles, the study of central and secondary perceptions, the development of the self-concept from age to age across the life span, and content analyses of perceptual contents. The following sections of this chapter provide examples of these types of analyses. Since they are only illustrative examples, these analyses are deliberately incomplete.

Table 3.3
Percentage of Sixty-Year-Old Men (M) and Women (W) with Responses in
the Different Dimensions of the Self-concept

Dimensions	M	W	Dimensions	M	W
SM[1]	80	94	SA	87	94
SSo	53	62	VaS	67	69
tra	0	6	com	13	37
cph	53	56	vap	53	69
SPo	80	87	AcS	60	69
obj	47	62	sta	53	44
per	60	87	aut	27	37
			amb	0	6
			dep	7	0
			act	0	0
			sty	27	12
SP	100	100	SS	73	100
ImS	100	100	PaS	67	100
asp	40	44	rec	53	81
ena	87	81	dom	13	19
sem	47	87	alt	20	81
int	53	75			
apt	20	19	RaS	27	12
def	33	94	res	13	12
			sex	13	6
IdS	87	94	SN	67	75
nom	67	69	ReA	67	62
rol	73	94	OpA	0	31
con	0	12			
ide	40	31			
ida	20	44			

[1]Symbols: 2 capital letters = The structures of the self
2 capital letters + 1 small letter = The substructures
3 small letters = The categories
For complete names of the dimensions, refer to table 3.1

The Study of Perceptual Profiles Specific to Age and Sex. The
coding according to table 3.1 and the quantification of the responses
for groups of 60-year-old men (n = 15) and women (n = 16) are presented in table 3.3. For each group studied, three types of perceptual
profiles can be made: profiles of the structures of the self, of its substructures, and finally of its categories. These profiles are also based
on the percentages of subjects (see figure 3.1 extracted from table
3.3). When more groups are to be compared, it is preferable to use

developmental profiles (see The Study of Development of the Self Concept later in this chapter). The percentages in table 3.3 clearly indicate that the profiles of the structures and the sub-structures would be quite similar for men and women. The general perceptual organization of the self is thus nearly the same between sixty-year-old men and women. But a greater number of differences appears when the more specific aspects of the self, the categories, are examined (see figure 3.1).

My hypothesis is that perceptual profiles of the categories will change more rapidly from age to age than will profiles of the sub-structures, because the categories are more specific. The profiles of the structures will take an even longer time to change, probably because these types of profiles correspond to different levels of basic or larger needs in the development of the self or self-realization. Nevertheless, these profiles—of the categories, the substructures and structures extracted from table 3.3—give a very meaningful portrait of the similarities and differences which characterize these two groups.

The Study of the Central and Secondary Perceptions. From these same data, an analysis of the perceptions which are more important or central for these groups is also possible. Interviews with subjects from ages three to one hundred show that central perceptions are those in which 70 percent or more of the subjects give responses on a given dimension of the self. Secondary perceptions correspond to 30 percent or less of subjects using a dimension, and dimensions used by between 31 and 69 percent of subjects are called intermediate perceptions.

Of course, the basis to determine the central perceptions may appear to be doubtful, but these central perceptions are highly confirmed in the comparison of answers between questions one and two (L'Écuyer in press). One can also argue that the individual may speak of things which are not important to him or her and may not speak of things much more important. Ghiglione and Matalon (1978), Unrug (1974), and Mueller (1969) have pointed out this problem.

First, it must be admitted that it is impossible to take into account things the individuals do not mention. Second, it must be recognized that it is very doubtful that the majority of individuals, from ages three to one hundred, regularly chose to name things which were less important to them in their answers to question two instead of things which were really important. Based on these percentages, results from table 3.3 can be reorganized into structures,

Figure 3.1
Profiles of the Categories, In Percentages of Subjects,
for Sixty-Year-Old Men and Women

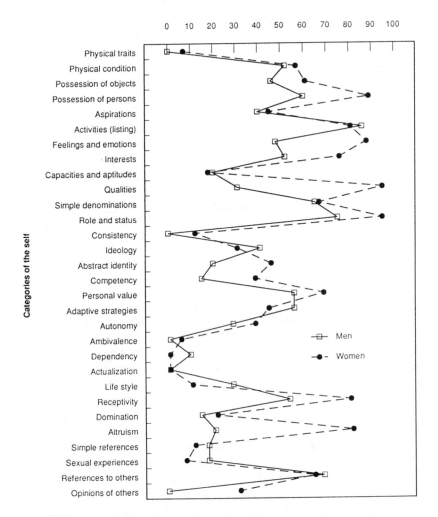

substructures and categories which are central, secondary, and intermediate (see tables 3.4 and 3.5).

When comparing two or more groups, examining the central,
intermediate, and secondary perceptions can be quite informative.
Despite many similarities, groups may differ as to which dimensions
are central to them. In this example, the highest levels of the self

(the structures and substructures, table 3.4) obtain the same levels of importance in sixty-year old men and women. Despite slight differences for the structure "self-nonself" and the substructure "reference to sexuality," the only major difference in importance is for the substructure "social attitudes" which is a central perception for women (100 percent) and an intermediate one for men (67 percent).

Several more differences appear at the levels of the categories (Table 3.5). Only two of twenty-eight categories are central in sixty-year-old men compared to eight in women of the same age. This suggests that men of this age have difficulties in determining what is concretely important in the perception of themselves as compared to women. Is it momentary or also true at different ages? The analysis of additional groups of ages would give the answer. Closer analysis of this table could also point out other similarities and differences between these two groups.

A more organismic analysis of these data can also be made by combining the analysis of the structures, the substructures, and the categories with their simultaneous degrees of importance. A partial example of this type of analysis appears in table 3.6 (derived from table 3.3). In this table, the original percentages are replaced by the degrees of importance of these social-self dimensions.

It is possible to find that a given structure is central in both groups but not according to the same underlying substructures and categories. From the partial example of table 3.6, it can be observed that, at age sixty, the social self is a central region of the self for men and women. Its degree of importance is due to the importance attributed to only one of its substructures, "social attitudes," which are central for both men and women at this age, as compared to the substructure, "reference to sexuality," which is a secondary perception.

At the level of the structure and of its substructures, the perceptual organization is, thus, similar for both sexes. But at the level of its categories, we note that the substructure "social attitudes" is not central for the same reasons. For women, its centrality is due to two categories which are experienced as very important—"receptivity to others" and "altruism." For men, the centrality of the substructure "social attitudes" is due to a much more diffused contribution of its underlying categories, such as "receptivity" which is an intermediate perception, and "domination" and "altruism" which are only secondary perceptions. It can then be said that, if social preoccupations are of central importance for men and women at this age, it is for very specific reasons or attitudes for women and for much more diffuse ones for men.

Table 3.4
Central, Intermediate, and Secondary Structures and Substructures for Sixty-Year Old Men and Women

Structures	Men	Percentages	Women	Percentages
Central	Personal self (SP)	100	Personal self (SP)	100
	Adaptative self (SA)	87	Social self (SS)	100
	Material self (SM)	80	Material self (SM)	94
	Social self (SS)	73	Adaptative self (SA)	94
			Self/Nonself (SN)	75
Intermediate	Self/Nonself (SN)	67		

Substructures	Men	Percentage	Women	Percentage
Central	Self-image (ImS)	100	Social Attitudes (PaS)	100
	Self-identity (IdS)	87	Self-image (ImS)	100
	Possessive Self (SPo)	80	Self-identity (IdS)	94
			Possessive Self (SPo)	87
Intermediate	Self-esteem (VaS)	67	Self-esteem (VaS)	69
	Social Attitudes (PaS)	67	Self-activities (AcS)	69
	References to others (ReA)	60	Somatic Self (SSo)	62
	Self-activities (AcS)	67	References to others (ReA)	62
	Somatic Self (SSo)	53	Opinions of others (OpA)	31
Secondary	References to sexuality (RaS)	27	References to sexuality (RaS)	12
	Opinions of others (OpA)	0		

Table 3.5

Central, Intermediate, and Secondary Categories for Sixty-Year-Old Men and Women

Categories	Men	Percentage	Women	Percentage
Central	Activities (listing) (ena)	87	Qualities + failings (def)	94
	Role + status (rol)	73	Role + status (rol)	94
			Possession of persons (per)	87
			Feelings + Emotions (sem)	87
			Activities (listing) (ena)	81
			Receptivity (rec)	81
			Altruism (alt)	81
			Interests (int)	75
Intermediate	Simple denom. (nom)	67	Simple denominations (nom)	69
	Possession of persons (per)	60	Personal value (vap)	69
	Physical condition (cph)	53	Possession of objects (obj)	62
	Interests (int)	53	Physical condition (cph)	56
	Personal value (vap)	53	Aspirations (asp)	44
	Adaptative strategies (sta)	53	Abstract identity (ida)	44
	Receptivity (rec)	53	Adapt. strategy (sta)	44

Possession of objects (obj)	47	Competency (com) 37
Feelings + emotions (sem)	47	Autonomy (aut) 37
Aspirations (asp)	40	Ideology (ide) 31
Ideology (ide)	40	
Qualities + failings (def)	33	
Autonomy (aut)	27	Capacities + aptitudes (apt) 19
Life style (sty)	27	Domination (dom) 19
Capacities + aptitudes (apt.)	20	Consistency (con) 12
Abstract identity (ida)	20	Life style (sty) 12
Altruism (alt)	20	Simple references to sexuality (res) 12
Competency (com)	13	Physical traits (tra) 6
Domination (dom)	13	Ambivalence (amb) 6
Simple references to sexuality (res)	13	Sexual experiences (sex) 6
Sexual experiences (sex)	13	Dependency (dep) 0
Dependency (dep)	7	Actualization (act) 0
Physical traits (tra)	0	
Consistency (con)	0	
Ambivalence (amb)	0	
Actualization (act)	0	

Secondary

Table 3.6
Organismic Analysis of a Structure According to the Degree
of Importance of Its Underlying Dimensions

Dimensions	Degrees of Importance	
	M	W
Social Self (SS)	C	C
Social Attitudes	C	C
Receptivity (rec)	I	C
Domination (dom)	S	S
Altruism (alt)	S	C
References to Sexuality (RaS)	S	S
Simple references to sexuality (res)	S	S
Sexual experience (sex)	S	S

C = Central Perceptions
I = Intermediate Perceptions
S = Secondary Perceptions

When such organismic analyses are conducted for every other group of perceptions or dimensions of the self, a very elaborate picture of the type of total organization of the self-concept emerges at a given age or developmental period—see L'Écuyer 1975a, 145–195, for a detailed analysis—and it can be very enriching when grounded in a developmental perspective, as will be seen in the next section of this chapter.

The Study of the Development of the Self-concept from Age to Age across the Life-Span. Each of the forty-three dimensions of the self can also be analysed in a developmental perspective across the life span by comparing the responses of subjects from ages three to one hundred. The following examples illustrate developmental profiles and the transformations of the central perceptions across the life-span.

Developmental profiles. To be really meaningful in the study of the development of the self across the life span, developmental profiles must be constructed with figures representing each structure with its two substructures, and figures showing each substructure with its underlying categories. In this way, the development of the total organization of the self-concept across the life span can be illustrated through fifteen or seventeen figures for a specific sex. These developmental profiles are also based on the percentages of subjects giving responses on each dimension. Table 3.7 and figure 3.2 consti-

Figure 3.2
Development of the Substructure *Somatic self* with Its Underlying
Categories of Physical Traits and Physical Condition in Three-
to Ninety-Year-Old Males

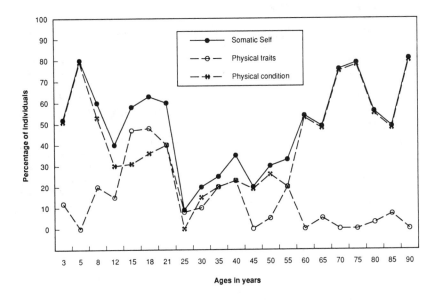

tute an example which illustrates results on the development of the substructure of somatic self accompanied with its two categories—physical traits and physical condition—for men between the ages of three to ninety-five.

A V-shaped curve clearly appears for two dimensions, the substructure somatic self and its physical condition category. The development of the physical traits category does not follow the same pattern at all, and physical condition is more frequently used than physical traits for all ages except during adolescence. Comparison with women would be interesting here. Such analyses of each dimension across the life span or at specific periods of life, are particularly revealing and exciting (see L'Écuyer 1975a, 1980, 1988, 1989b, 1990).

The transformations of the central perceptions across the life span. Percentages in table 3.7 can be replaced by the degrees of importance to which they correspond. The development of the somatic self and of its categories can then be studied in terms of their changing importance across the life span. The same can be done for every

Table 3.7
Percentages of Males for the Substructure Somatic Self
and Underlying Categories

Dimensions of the self	Ages in years	3	5	8	12	15	18	21
Somatic Self		53	80	60	40	57	64	60
Physical traits		13	0	20	15	49	50	40
Physical condition		53	80	53	30	31	36	40
	Ages	25	30	35	40	45	50	55
Somatic Self		8	20	25	35	20	30	33
Physical traits		8	10	20	25	0	5	20
Physical condition		0	15	20	25	20	25	20
	Ages	60	65	70	75	80	85	90
Somatic Self		53	47	75	80	56	47	82
Physical traits		0	5	0	0	4	7	0
Physical condition		53	47	75	80	56	47	82

Table 3.8
Changes in the Degree of Importance of the Substructure
Somatic Self and Underlying Categories in Men

Dimensions of the Self	Ages in Years	3	5	8	12	15	18	21
Somatic Self		I	C	I	I	I	I	I
Physical traits		S	S	S	S	I	I	I
Physical condition		I	C	I	S	I	I	I
	Ages	25	30	35	40	45	50	55
Somatic Self		S	S	S	I	S	S	I
Physical traits		S	S	S	S	S	S	S
Physical condition		S	S	S	S	S	S	S
	Ages	60	65	70	75	80	85	90
Somatic Self		I	I	C	C	I	I	C
Physical traits		S	S	S	S	S	S	S
Physical condition		I	I	C	C	I	I	C

C = central perceptions
I = intermediate perceptions
S = secondary perceptions

other dimension or group of dimensions, comparing each other or comparing different groups.

From the present example in table 3.8, very interesting observations can be made. Perceptions concerning the body become very rarely central perceptions across the life span within the whole gestalt which constitutes the self. The analysis of the forty remaining dimensions shows others which are regularly more important than are those related to the body during the development of the self (L'Écuyer 1975a, 1978, 1989b, 1990). Table 3.8 also shows that the degree of importance varies from age to age or between blocks of ages. The somatic self is an intermediate-central-intermediate perception among ages three, five, and eight, passes from an intermediate level of importance for eight- to twenty-one year old block of ages to the secondary level for the twenty-five to thirty-five-year-old block, and so on.

As in previous analyses for single groups, more organismic analyses can also be made in this developmental perspective. A closer look reveals that the "somatic self" is an intermediate perception at age three and also between ages eight to twenty-one, but not for the same combination of importance of its underlying categories, which are "physical traits" and "physical condition" (table 3.8). The reader can make other observations as to the development of the somatic self and to other combinations of the importance of its categories as ages increase within this same table 3.8.

Such analyses of the development of the self in terms of variations in its most important aspects—the central dimensions or perceptions—provide us with a deeper understanding as to the manner in which the self evolves all across the life span. Some elements of the self never become central. However, it can be observed that other dimensions—and sometimes groups of dimensions—are central during a certain period of time and are later replaced by other dimensions which are entirely different. Differences between men and women can then appear to be more significant. For deeper analyses of this type, see L'Écuyer (1975a, chapter 7; 1978, chapter 10; 1989b, 1990).

Content Analysis. Up to this point, all the analyses have been quantitatively based. But the fact that sentences are put together under the same category does not necessarily mean that all these sentences are identical or that the individuals speak of the same things. There may still exist qualitative variations which escape the quantitative analyses but from which we have much to learn. An example of this is taken from table 3.3 indicating that 40 percent of men and 44 percent of women give responses in the aspiration category. From this quantitative point of view, the conclusion is that there is no difference between sixty-year-old men and women for this category which show the same percentages and same degree of importance. But content analysis of the sentences coded under this category indicates that the similarity between these two groups ends with the computed percentages. Men aspire to change careers, to have less tiresome work, or to retire when possible, while women aspire to stay in good health, experience greater possibilities of social activities, and aspire to financial situations enabling them to still help their children. It is clear here that, beyond the quantitative similarities between these two groups, there still are very important dynamic or psychological differences revealed only by content analysis.

Traditional quantitative analyses take only statistical differences—or their absence—into account, and the interpretation is made in terms of total similarities or total differences. Content analysis, added to quantitative analysis, can take into account four types, instead of two, of similarities and differences between groups.

1. Total similarities between groups: This is the case in which there is no quantitative nor qualitative differences between the groups for the dimension of the self which is analysed;
2. Relative similarities offer: No quantitative differences, but qualitative ones;
3. Relative differences: quantitative differences but no qualitative ones; and
4. Total differences: quantitative and qualitative differences appear on the same dimension between the analysed groups.

This is the second use of content analysis which can—and, I would even say, *ought*—to be made for a deeper understanding of the organization of the self within a group, between groups, and of course concerning the development of the self across the life span. Quantitative analysis informs us only of a difference of intensity. The addition of qualitative analysis brings important new information as to the psychological and more dynamic characteristics on which individuals resemble or differ from others in terms of the ways in which they perceive themselves. For a very detailed analysis of short-term developmental and intertwined quantitative and qualitative analyses of the self-concept, see those made for three-to-eight-year-old children (L'Écuyer, 1975a, chapter 8).

CONCLUSION: LIMITS OF THIS APPROACH, ADVANTAGES, AND IMPLICATIONS FOR FUTURE RESEARCH

In this chapter, we have reviewed the GPS method and the various types of analyses which can be done—in particular, group analyses (profiles of the group, central perceptions, analysis of the psychological contents, and comparisons between groups), and developmental analyses (developmental profiles, transformations of the central perceptions with age, and comparisons between groups). These types of analyses greatly contribute to the improvement of our understanding of the development of the self-concept across the life span. But this method is not a panacea. As a conclusion, I would like to give a brief idea of the GPS method's limits, its advantages, and its implications for future research.

The limits of the GPS method are quite important.

• It is a time consuming method. A great part of the work has to be done on an individual interviewing basis (at least for children and elders), and the obtained material has to be coded by referring to content analysis which takes a good deal of time. One must not be in a hurry to use this approach.

• It is a global and spontaneous approach. The GPS produces a global portrait of the self. The subjects explore their selves their own ways, giving each element their importance as they see or feel it. Thus, some elements are treated extensively, while others are just lightly touched upon. For those who want to deeply investigate specific aspects of the self—such as body image, self-esteem, levels of aspirations, and more—the GPS will be too general of an approach. In such cases, it is preferable to use specific questionnaires with precise questions according to the areas to be investigated.

• Group profiles versus individual profiles. Because quantification is based on the number of subjects giving responses that are coded under a specific dimension (instead of the number of responses under each dimension), the construction of the perceptual profiles is possible only for groups, not for individuals. Thus, it is impossible to compare profiles of two particular individuals, or to make clinical profiles of individuals for different situations. The only possibility would be the quantification of the results on the basis of the number of responses for each individual—which is the current procedure even if it has its problems. For now, this is more of an exploratory than a diagnostic approach.

• Reliability and experiential validity. Due to situational constraints during the research process, reliability has been tested for ages three to twenty-one and sixty to one hundred, but not for ages twenty-five to fifty-five. Because the former periods are generally considered to be the most unstable developmental periods of life, the high reliability obtained for them is quite a good warranty as to the probable reliability of the results obtained during the more stable period of adult maturity between ages twenty-five and fifty-five. It nevertheless needs to be demonstrated in the future. Experiential validity is presently well established for the central perceptions. However, it would also have to be extended to the intermediate and secondary perceptions.

Despite the limits, it is useful to remember the very important advantages of the GPS Method and its possibilities for future research.

• Variety of the types of analyses. The great variety of the types of analyses which are possible from the obtained results provides us with a very detailed picture of the self as such; of its particularities for a given group; and, of course, for more or less long developmental sequences and even all across the life span. The analysis of the degrees of importance of each dimension, the changing of their importance through development, as well as the addition of perceptual content analysis (or qualitative analysis) to usual quantitative analysis—all of these aspects help to improve the understanding of the whole psychological organization of the self and the way it changes as life progresses.

• Adaptability for other problems. The GPS method is not only suitable for developmental studies of the self. It can be used, with the various types of analyses, to study and compare the characteristics of the self-concept of almost every kind of group—ethnic groups, groups with success or failure in academic or professional achievements, mentally deficient people, schizophrenics, and so on.

If it is adapted for individual diagnosis, it will be possible to study self-concept compatibilities for those who want to get married, who want to follow the gradual transformations of the different aspects of the self in the course of psychotherapy, and more.

The question "Who are you?" can also be adapted to various situations and thus make possible other types of analyses. For example, individual perceptions of development can be traced by asking subjects how they perceive themselves in a first session. In a second session, they could be asked how they perceived themselves five or ten years ago. In a third session, the question could be what they think they will be five or ten years in the future.

In addition, the situations can be widely varied. For example, how they perceive themselves as to different roles—student, worker, spouse, or parent.

• Suitability across the life span. This is surely the greatest advantage of the GPS method. It opens the door to the possibility of investigating the development of the self-concept across the entire life span. Only the first two years of life are not reached. The simplicity of the question, its comprehension by everybody no matter the age, and the opportunity to describe oneself freely enable anybody to give a genuine picture of himself or herself. Also, it enables the researcher to obtain a whole picture of the dimensions of the self and to follow their transformations all across the life span in the most comparable manner because all of the results are obtained by the same method.

Longitudinal developmental research could also be done with the GPS. Nevertheless, I do not know the impact of repetitive administrations of the GPS to the same individual over a wide age range. What type of influence could it have concerning the orientation of his or her self-description and the psychological contents of the responses? When would changes in the responses be attributed to developmental changes or to the fact the individual could have decided to speak of other aspects than those during the previous interviews? This is a normal problem for every type of instrument in longitudinal research. One should be careful about what happens with the responses to the GPS in such situations because we are never entirely sure as to what actually causes the changes.

As Botwinick (1977) and Dixon, Kramer and Baltes (1985) noted, longitudinal, cohort, and sequential methods of research tend to underestimate certain types of developmental changes while cross-sectional methods tend to overestimate others.

As for myself, I do not intend to pursue research to enhance the suitability of the GPS. My intention is to write my next book on the development of the self-concept across the life span and I will discuss the results obtained through the various types of analyses explained in this chapter.

I hope the content of this chapter will encourage others to investigate the development of the self-concept all across the life span. I also hope that the description of the GPS method, its applicability to every age, reliability, experiential validity of results, and the various types of possible analyses presented here will make researchers more confident about using such an approach.

But this is surely not the *only* way to proceed. My greatest hope is that this chapter will not only increase interest in the investigation of the self-concept all across the life span, but also inspire the desire to do it and instill the belief that it is possible to accomplish.

I have done it. With enough patience, many others can do what I have accomplished.

Outstanding work has been achieved—in psychology, education, reeducation, and psychotherapy—without really knowing the normal development of the self. As more developmental research is completed, no matter what methodology is used, more will be discovered about the development of the self and our understanding of human beings. I hope my own research will help to further this highly important movement toward the study of the development of the self-concept across the life span.

REFERENCES

Allport, G. W. [1955] 1961. *Becoming: Basic considerations for a psychology of personality.* New Haven: Yale University Press.

————. 1961. *Pattern and growth in personality.* 2d ed. New York: Holt.

Bardin, L. 1989. *L'analyse de contenu.* 5th ed. Collection *"Le Psychologue"* 69. Paris: Presses Universitaires de France.

Botwinick, J. 1977. Intellectual abilities. In *Handbook of the psychology of aging,* edited by J. E. Birren and K. W. Schaie. New York: Van Nostrand Reinhold. 580–605.

Bugental, J. F. T., and Zelen, S. L. 1950. Investigations into the "self-concept" I: The W-A-Y technique. *Journal of Personality* 18:483–498.

Combs, A. W., and Snygg, D. 1959. *Individual behavior: A perceptual approach to behavior.* 2d ed. New York: Harper.

Dixon, R. A.; Kramer, D. A.; and Baltes, P. B. 1985. Intelligence: A life-span developmental perspective. In *Handbook of intelligence,* edited by B. J. Wolman. New York: Wiley and Sons. 301–350.

Ghiglione, R., and Matalon, B. 1978. *Les enquêtes sociologiques: Théories et pratique.* Paris: Armand Colin.

Gordon, C. 1968. Self conceptions: Configurations of content. In *The self in social interaction.* Vol. 1: *Classic and contemporary perspectives,* edited by C. Gordon and K. J. Gergen. New York: Wiley. 115–136.

Havighurst, R. J.; Robinson, M. Z.; and Dorr, M. [1946] 1965. The development of the ideal self in childhood and adolescence. In *The self in growth, teaching, and learning: Selected readings,* edited by D. E. Hamachek. Englewood Cliffs, N.J.: Prentice-Hall. 226–239.

James, W. [1890] 1952. *Principles of psychology.* London: Encyclopaedia Britannica. Vol. 53.

Kuhn, M. H., and McPartland, T. S. 1954. An empirical investigation of self-attitudes. *American Sociological Review* 19:68–76.

L'Écuyer, R. 1975a. *La genèse du concept de soi: Théories et recherches. Les transformations des perceptions de soi chez les enfants âgés de trois, cing et huit ans.* Sherbrooke, Quebec: Naaman.

———. 1975b. Self-concept investigation: Demystification process. *Journal of Phenomenological Psychology* 6:(1)17–30.

———. 1978. *Le concept de soi.* Collection *"Psychologie d'aujourd'hui."* Paris: Presses Universitaires de France.

———. 1980. *Les souvenirs du passé chez les personnes âgées: Reflet de conflits intérieurs ou facteur d'adaptation. Revue québécoise de psychologie* 1:(3)42–57.

———. 1981. The development of the self-concept through the life span. In *Self-concept: Advances in theory and research,* edited by M. D. Lynch, A. Norem-Hebeisen, and K. J. Gergen. Cambridge, Mass.: Ballinger. 203–218.

———. 1985. *Concept de soi et vie scolaire. Revue tirés à part* 6 (September):3–15.

———. 1987. *L'analyse de contenu: Notion et étapes.* In *Les méthodes de la recherche qualitative,* edited by J. P. Deslauriers. Québec: Presses de l'Université du Québec. 49–65.

———. 1988. *L'évolution de l'estime de soi chez les personnes âgées de 60 à 100 ans. Revue québécoise de psychologie* 9:(2)108–126.

———. 1989a. *L'analyse développementale de contenu. Revue de l'association pour la recherche qualitative* 1:51–80.

———. 1989b. Ages and stages in the development of the self-concept across the life span. Unpublished paper presented at the symposium "Transformations of the self across the life span" held in the tenth biennial meetings of the International Society for the Study of Behavioral Development (ISSBD), 9 to 13 July 1989. Jyväskylä, Finland.

———. 1990. *Le développement du concept de soi de 0 à 100 ans: Cent ans après* William James. *Revue québécoise de psychologie.* Special edition on the self-concept, Spring 1990.

————. In press. *Méthodologie de l'analyse développementale de contenu: Méthode GPS et concept de soi.* Québec: Presses de l'Université du Quebec.

Marsh, H. W. 1986. Global self-esteem: Its relation to specific facets of self-concept and their importance. *Journal of Personality and Social Psychology* 51:1224–1236.

Marsh, H. W., and Shavelson, R. J. 1985. Self-concept: Its multifaceted, hierarchical structure. *Educational Psychologist* 20:107–125.

Moskowitz, D. S. 1986. Comparison of self-reports, knowledgeable informants, and behavioral observation data. *Journal of Personality* 54:294–317.

Mucchielli, R. 1979. *L'analyse de contenu des documents et des communications: Connaissance du problème.* 3d ed. Paris: Les Editions ESF.

Mueller, J. E. [1969] 1978. The use of content analysis in international relations. In *The analysis of communication content,* edited by G. Gerbner, O. R. Holsti et al. Huntington, N.Y.: R. E. Krieger Publishing Co.

Offer, D., and Sabshin, M. 1966. *Normality: Theoretical and clinical concepts of mental health.* New York: Basic Books.

Poirier, J.; Clapier-Valladon, S.; and Raybaut, P. 1983. *Les récits de vie: Theorie et pratique.* Paris: Presses Universitaires de France.

Rodriguez-Tomé, H. 1972. *Le moi et l'autre dans la conscience de l'adolescent.* Paris: Delachaux et Niestle.

Super, D. E. 1963. Self-concepts in vocational development. In *Career development: Self-concept theory,* edited by D. E. Super et al. New York: College Entrance Examination Board.

Unrug, M. C. d'. 1974. *Analyse de contenu.* Paris: Éditions Universitaires.

Wylie, R. 1974. *The self-concept.* Vol. 1: *A review of methodological considerations and measuring instruments.* 2d ed. Lincoln: University of Nebraska Press.

————. 1961. *The self-concept.* Lincoln: University of Nebraska Press.

PART II: MEASURING THE SELF

THOMAS M. BRINTHAUPT
L. JEANETTE ERWIN

4

Reporting about the Self:
Issues and Implications

Imagine that you would like to get to know someone who is currently a stranger to you. How might you go about doing this?

One approach might be to observe the person unobtrusively, summarize your observations, and come to some conclusions about him or her. A second approach might be to rely on information about the person obtained from other people who know him or her. A more direct approach would be to engage in interaction with the person, introduce yourself, ask the person to describe himself or herself orally and informally, and then come to your own conclusions. An alternative, although unusual approach, would be to ask the person to fill out a written questionnaire (with items concerning personal demographics, preferences, characteristics, and so on), and then summarize this information into some conclusions about him or her.

Is any one of these approaches to getting to know someone the most accurate or reliable? Which approaches would best tell you what this person is *really* like? Are the different approaches likely to give you the same information? Which approach would you most likely use? Why?

Answering these questions is difficult unless it is clear what you are going to do with the information obtained. For example, the approach or approaches which you favor if you are a police detective investigating the person as a criminal suspect will probably differ from the approach which you might employ in order to determine whether or not you would like to establish a romantic relationship with him or her.

Now imagine that you are a researcher interested in studying the self. How might you go about getting to know your subjects? The approaches already suggested are also relevant to this question. In fact, as they have attempted to study the selves of strangers, researchers of the self have used each of these approaches (such as behavioral observation, use of other individuals who are knowledgeable about the subject, and self-reports in the forms of direct interaction or interview and questionnaire).

Is any one of these approaches the most accurate and reliable way to study the self? Which approaches best tell us what a person's self is actually like? How comparable are the data obtained from the different approaches? Which approaches are researchers of the self most likely to use?

Answers to the first three of these questions are equivocal. The answer to the final question is that most researchers prefer to use the self-report approach. One of the purposes of this chapter is to critically review the self-report approach to studying the self.

Before directing our attention to the process of reporting about the self, it would be useful to briefly note the relative advantages and disadvantages of self-reports, behavioral observations, and ratings by others. Because of the various cognitive and motivational biases associated with the self-report (to be discussed later in this chapter), some researchers have argued that less biased and more supposedly accurate data on the self (at least in terms of predicting subsequent motivation and behavior) can be obtained from behavioral observations and the ratings of others (Kagan 1989; Phares, Compas & Howell 1989). For example, Kagan showed that young boys' self-reports of a negatively evaluated characteristic (such as unpopularity or a reading disability) were often contradicted by peer reports about them as well as by their own nonverbal responses to a filmed model who also possessed the negatively evaluated characteristic. Kagan proposed that disguised procedures (such as monitoring a child's behaviors or facial expressions without his or her knowledge) increase the accuracy of measuring children's self-views, at least with respect to negative characteristics.

In general, direct behavioral observations are preferred over ratings by others, because the latter are presumed to be less reliable and valid measures of self. However, research on the reports of knowledgeable informants (such as teachers, parents, and peers) suggest that others' ratings can be reliable and valid if multiple raters are used and ratings are based on multiple observations of the target's behavior (Moskowitz & Schwarz 1982).

In a comprehensive comparative review of self-reports, behavioral observations, and others' ratings, Moskowitz (1986) described the problems associated with each approach. The reader who is further interested in the differences among these approaches, and the relative merits of one over the others, should consult Moskowitz's review, as well as Shrauger and Osberg (1981) and Shrauger and Schoeneman (1979). For the purposes of this chapter, we are primarily interested in the behavior of reporting about the self and the implications that the process has for studying the self.

The self-report is by far the most frequently used methodology for studying the self. There seems to be good reason for its popularity, given that individuals' self-reports have been shown to be accurate predictors of behavior in many circumstances (Osberg & Shrauger 1986). In fact, the research described in each of the chapters of this volume relies on self-reports in one form or another.

What happens when a person is asked to report about his or her self? What factors are likely to affect the self-report process? We address these questions in the first part of this chapter.

Whereas there are several different self-report approaches, the questionnaire approach is the most popular, although the reasons for its popularity are not immediately apparent. In the next part of this chapter, we examine the reasons for the questionnaire's popularity, and we discuss its advantages and disadvantages by comparing it to another popular approach, the self-report interview. Finally, in an effort to assess the relative merits of these two approaches, we briefly present a study that directly compares data obtained from the questionnaire and interview approaches.

The Process of Self-report

When someone is asked to describe, rate, or report on some aspect of himself or herself, how does the person do it? What exactly is involved in the process of self-report?

There are three major factors that affect reporting about the self. First, self-reports are affected by the accessibility and organization of self-relevant knowledge in memory. Second, self-reports are affected by a number of expectations and cues associated with specific contexts, situations, and cultures. Third, self-reports are affected by a variety of individual and developmental differences. In reviewing each of these three factors, we will note the biases and problems associated with each in terms of using self-reports to study the self.

Accessibility and Organization of Self-relevant Knowledge. Any attempt to understand the self-report process assumes that memory is in some way involved. In order to describe oneself or make decisions about one's own characteristics, a person must access information from memory (Rogers 1974). Ericsson and Simon (1980) argued that, to report information about cognitive processes—such as discrimination learning or problem solving—it must be accessible to short-term memory. Such information is most likely to be accessible if the processes are currently occurring, attended to, and can be verbalized. If one or more of these conditions is absent, then information must be retrieved from long-term memory (or permanent storage). When this information must be retrieved from long-term memory, inferences, filtering, and intrusions are likely to occur.

Whereas Ericsson and Simon were primarily interested in reports about cognitive processing (or "thinking") per se, their arguments are also applicable to reporting about the self. For example, they argued that information about one's emotions, plans, and evaluations is normally held in short-term memory and is therefore available for self-reporting. Research conducted by Schoeneman (1981, Schoeneman, Tabor, & Nash, 1984) suggested that, for both children and college students, the most frequently reported source of knowledge about the self is self-observation—as opposed to feedback from others and social comparison—possibly because of such attentional and memory biases. (See also Gibbons 1990.)

Social-cognitive psychologists have focused on several properties of the self in memory that have important implications for the process of self-report. For example, Wyer and Srull (1986) proposed that a person's self-relevant information search results in the retrieval of information from "self bins" in long-term memory. These bins differ in their levels of generality, are spread throughout the memory system, and can refer to aspects of the self across many different situations, roles, or in relation to many other persons. Wyer and Srull proposed that, when reporting about ourselves, any number of cues or processing objectives can govern our search for self-relevant information. For example, frequently activated information about the self is likely to be more accessible and reportable than infrequently activated information (Rhodewalt & Agustdottir 1986).

Based on the notion that self-relevant information is structured in terms of a mental representation or "schema," studies have shown that the self affects the processing of information about both oneself and others. In fact, researchers find that a self-schema has strong effects on memory (as well as on perception and inference) (Fiske & Taylor 1984; Greenwald & Pratkanis 1984; Kihlstrom & Cantor 1984; Kihlstrom et al. 1988). For example, the self-reference effect (Rogers, Kuiper & Kirker 1977) refers to the finding that making self-relevant decisions about stimulus items enhances subsequent memory for those items compared to items that do not involve self-relevant decisions (such as whether or not an item is printed in capital letters or rhymes with another item).

The self-generation effect (Greenwald & Banaji 1989) refers to the finding that associating arbitrary stimulus items with self-generated knowledge enhances later recall of the items compared to associating them with knowledge that is provided by the experimenter. For example, the stimulus item *refrigerator,* when paired in a sentence with the name of a subject's friend, was more likely to be later recalled than when it was paired with a person's name that was provided by the experimenter.

However, this and related research is concerned with the acquisition and interpretation of information related to the self (and others) rather than the provision of information about the self to others. As such, it is relevant to the process of self-report only to the extent that what is likely to be reported is information with which the self has been involved.

In describing the process of self-report, most cognitive and social-cognitive psychologists have emphasized the biases that can affect this process. If it is the case that what is most likely to be reported is what is currently accessible and/or has been retrieved, then factors that influence accessibility and recall can bias one's self-report. For instance, Ericsson and Simon (1980) noted that the completeness of self-reports can be reduced because not all of the information in short-term memory is actually reported (as, for example, in cases of high memory load).

In addition, there may be data that are not accessible for self-report, such as information that is automatically activated or cannot be verbalized. For example, some self-relevant information may be activated without the control or even awareness of the individual (Bargh 1989). Respondents may also be engaging in self-deception in terms of simultaneously holding contradictory beliefs but being aware of only some of them (cf. Gur & Sackeim 1979). Ross and McFarland (1988) proposed that a person's recall of the past—and, by extension, one's reports about the self—can be reconstructed based on one's current status on a given attribute as well as his or her implicit theories of the stability of specific self-attributes. Given such biases, self-relevant information might be less likely to be included in a self-report or might be distorted.

There is a great deal of research on the effects of unconscious influences on memory (Bargh 1989; Nisbett & Wilson 1977). For example, Nisbett and Wilson (1977) found that individuals were unaware of the reasons for a variety of choices and decisions that they made across a number of tasks. However, this research deals primarily with memory for and explanations of previous behavior and decisions.

It is unclear how unconscious factors affect reporting about the self per se. Typically, when describing or rating the self, the respondent is not asked to provide reasons for his or her descriptions or ratings. Of course, this does not imply that the respondent does not spontaneously generate reasons or explanations when reporting about the self.

In summary, the accessibility and organization of information in memory about the self plays an important role in determining what an individual will say when reporting about his or her self. Information that is easily accessed and attended to and that has involved the self in the past is more likely to be reported. However, for a variety of reasons, some aspects of the self typically cannot or will not be reported.

Contextual, Situational, and Cultural Factors. The process of reporting about the self is also affected by the context, situation, and culture in which the self-report is embedded. Several researchers have advocated that the self (and thus the self-report) is extremely sensitive to contextual effects. In fact, some definitions of the self suggest that it is essentially a collection of selves or identities that are differentially activated by the setting (Stryker 1980; 1987).

According to this argument, contextual and situational factors influence the cuing and filtering of self-relevant information. For example, Markus and Nurius in 1986 and 1987, as well as Cantor and colleagues in 1986 proposed that only a subset of a person's self-knowledge will be salient at any one time. This "working" self-concept can vary dramatically based on the nature of the situation— as well as a person's affective or motivational state—and its contents are a function of the self-conceptions that are currently active or accessible in thought and memory (Hewitt 1976; Gibbons 1990; Wells in press). In addition, some research suggests that motives (such as the desire to appear competent) can influence the accessibility of self-descriptive information as well as how individuals describe themselves at a given point in time (Kunda & Sanitioso 1989; Markus & Kunda 1986).

McGuire and his colleagues (McGuire & McGuire 1988; McGuire, McGuire & Cheever 1986; McGuire & Padawer-Singer 1976) have shown that a person's phenomenal sense of self—that is, the self as experienced by that person—differs depending on the social context. For example, when they are questioned in the family context rather than in school, children are more likely to describe themselves passively—in terms of *state* rather than action verbs. McGuire et al. (1986) argued that this is because the former context is less activity oriented than is the latter context.

Research on self-presentation suggests that situational factors can affect self-reports in many ways. Schlenker (1980, 1986) argued that different situations evoke different self-related motives (such as accurate appraisal versus self-enhancement) as well as different audiences (one's self versus significant others), which, in turn, affect how individuals think about and present themselves (Baumeister 1982). For example, Zanna and Pack (1975) found that female subjects adjusted their self-descriptions to be consistent with the views of an attractive male's traditional or nontraditional views about women.

Finally, some research suggests that affective states can influence the process of self-report. For example, Schwarz and Clore (1983, 1988) have shown that situationally induced bad moods—such as a rainy day or remembering a recent sad event—decrease reported happiness and satisfaction with self (Natale & Hantas 1982).

In addition to more immediate and specific contextual and situational effects on reporting about the self, there are also cultural influences on the process (Andersen 1987; Cousins 1989; Roland 1988; Shweder & LeVine 1984; Triandis 1989; Turner 1976; Zurcher 1977). In an analysis of culture and the self that has important implications for reporting about the self, Triandis (1989) offered several hypotheses. For example, in an individualistic culture (such as the United States), the probability is high that the private self—one's traits, states, or behavior—will be reported. In a collectivist culture (such as Brazil), the probability is high that the collective self—the self in relation to family, co-workers, or society—will be reported.

In chapter 8 of this volume, Hart and Edelstein critically review previous cross-cultural research on the self and describe their own research on New England, Puerto Rican, and Icelandic youths. They find that respondents from cultures that emphasize community and communal values report more social characteristics in their self-reports than do respondents from a more individualistic culture such as the northeast United States. A more extreme view of the situational and cultural nature of the self was put forth by Gergen in 1977 and 1985. (See also Gergen & Gergen 1988).

According to Gergen's social-constructionist position, the self is simply a construction put together at any given moment and based on current social rules or intelligibility systems. In other words, there is no "true self" and, by extension, reporting about the self is a reflection of conventional rules of understanding. Therefore, it is these rules and intelligibility systems which should be the concern of those researching the self and which are revealed in the process of self-report. For a related perspective, see chapter 1 in this volume.

In summary, the immediate context, situational cues, and cultural factors all can affect what an individual will say when reporting about the self. Thus, different perceived requirements or demands in a specific context or situation will call to mind different aspects of the self. In addition, broader cultural norms appear to affect not only how individuals report about themselves but also how they actually think about themselves.

Individual and Developmental Differences.   The third set of factors that influence the process of reporting about the self concerns individual and developmental variations. Many researchers and reviewers have acknowledged the effects of these factors on the process of self-report. Among the individual-difference variables that are most relevant to reporting about the self are self-monitoring (Snyder 1974, 1979); public and private self-consciousness (Fenigstein, Scheier & Buss 1975); self-completion (Wicklund & Gollwitzer 1983); feelings of uniqueness (Snyder & Fromkin 1980); and previous self-report experience (Yardley 1987).

Self-monitoring refers to the extent to which an individual's self-presentation is consistent with his or her internal states and attitudes (low self-monitoring) as opposed to being consistent with situational cues about the appropriateness of specific behaviors (high self-monitoring). Thus, the self-reports of low self-monitors should be less affected by contextual and situational factors than the self reports of high self-monitors (cf. Snyder 1979).

The public and private self-consciousness distinction refers to an individual's general tendency to focus on external or public as pects of the self (one's own self as a social object) or on internal or private aspects of the self (one's own internal states or experiences).

This dispositional factor parallels cross-cultural differences discussed earlier.

Individuals high in private self-consciousness appear to provide more private and internal—as well as more accurate—aspects of themselves in their self-reports than do individuals high in public self-consciousness (Agatstein & Buchanan 1984; Carver & Scheier 1978; Gibbons 1990; Greenwald, Bellezza & Banaji 1988; Shrauger & Osberg 1982).

Self-completion refers to the notion that individuals' favorable self-reports can reflect their nonpossession of relevant characteristics and their efforts to complete themselves by claiming desired properties. Wicklund and Gollwitzer (1983) argued that feelings of incompleteness on particular dimensions can adversely affect the validity of individuals' self-reports. Snyder and Fromkin (1980) proposed that individuals are motivated to feel a sense of uniqueness from others. This need can be manipulated by feedback pertaining to the similarity of oneself to positive and negative others. The sense of difference from others is also likely to affect the process of self-report to the extent that respondents are motivated to report unique aspects of themselves, as well as aspects that they have in common with others.

There is also some evidence that individual differences in previous self-report experience can affect current self-reports. For example, Pryor (1980) suggested that reporting about the self is, in part, a learned or habitual response that gets easier and better with practice. (See also Mabe & West 1982.) Yardley (1987) reported that respondents who had previous psychological counseling or therapy found the task of self-report to be easier—as well as less threatening and unpleasant—than did respondents who had not had such experience. An additional individual-difference variable that might be related to self-report is self-esteem. We will consider this variable in a study reported on later in this chapter.

Research on developmental differences suggests that, especially in childhood and adolescence, the contents of self-reports show dramatic age changes. For example, as they grow older, children's self-reports shift in emphasis from specific and concrete behavioral and physical characteristics to general and abstract psychological and trait-like characteristics (Harter 1983; Montemayor & Eisen 1977; Rosenberg 1979).

Exactly what these differences in the contents of self-report indicate is an open question. For example, older children are likely to have greater reasoning and information-processing abilities than are younger children. Older children are also more likely to have different theories of the self (Broughton 1978) as well as different expectations, assumptions about, or experiences with self-reporting. In addition, and because of cultural factors, younger children may be more likely to ground themselves in social situations than are older children who, when describing themselves, may be more likely to think of themselves as free from a particular context. This difference in perspective might account for the shift with increasing age from specific, concrete characteristics to general, abstract characteristics. Whatever the reason or reasons, both the process and the content of self-reports appear to vary with age.

The role of memory in developmental differences in self-reporting is a particularly interesting issue, especially when given contemporary views that relate self with memory. Research on self-reports of young children suggests, for example, that children's memories for general self-relevant information *precede* their memories for specific self-relevant information (Eder, Gerlach & Perlmutter 1987). This pattern is opposite to that of the content-related changes in self-reporting described above. Eder and colleagues proposed that children as young as 3 1/2 years have "global, context-independent concepts of themselves" (1987, 1049).

In addition, Mueller and his colleagues (In press) reported evidence that memory accessibility and information processing decrease in efficiency among the elderly as compared to young adults, suggesting that what is accessible for self-report may change with age. Ogilvie and Clark (In press) highlighted additional differences in the self-reports of young and elderly adults. Of course, different developmental periods are also likely to experience different contextual, situational, and cultural influences as well.

In summary, several individual and developmental differences affect the process of reporting about the self. Differences in individuals' attention to internal and external self-related cues, as well as their previous self-report experience, will affect the process. In addition, developmental changes are associated with qualitatively different self-reports.

Given the multiplicity of factors that can affect the process of reporting about the self, one might wonder why researchers would rely on self-reports to study the self. In some ways, it is ironic that the many factors described here have been identified and documented primarily with self-reports. Despite concerns about validity, the reliance on self-reports has been quite productive for researchers, both in terms of studying the self and studying the process of self-report.

At the beginning of this chapter, we asked about the extent to which different methodologies yield different data about the respondent's self. In the next section, we address this issue by comparing the effects of two different methodologies on the self-report process.

Reactive and Spontaneous Methodologies

There are many ways to categorize the different approaches to self-report, such as based on response formats, instructions, types of self-related processes under consideration, and more. Following McGuire (1984), we will focus on what we believe to be the most important of these categorizations—the distinction between reactive and spontaneous methodologies.

Historically, the more popular methodology for studying the self through self-report is reactive in nature. This approach requires subjects to react to a few or a great many researcher-provided dimensions, usually through a constrained or closed-end response format in which subjects are asked to locate themselves on a scale representing these dimensions. Popular examples of this approach include the Piers-Harris Children's Self-Concept Scale (Piers 1984), the Coopersmith Self-Esteem Inventory (Coopersmith 1967), and the Self-Description Questionnaire (Marsh 1988. See also chapter 2 of this volume).

A somewhat less popular approach is spontaneous in nature. This approach does not rely on researcher-provided dimensions, and it requires subjects to respond spontaneously to a very general or vague prompt such as "Who are you?" or "Tell me about yourself." Some bounds may be established, such as how long subjects should respond to the prompt or the number of discrete responses that are expected. Or the approach may be virtually unconstrained in terms of time, length, and response format. Examples of this approach include the Who Are You? (WAY) Method (Bugental & Zelen 1950); the Twenty Statements Test (Kuhn & McPartland 1954; Montemayor & Eisen 1977; Spitzer, Couch & Stratton 1970); and the "Tell me about yourself" interview in written or oral format (Brinthaupt & Lipka 1985; McGuire & McGuire 1988).

Reactive and *spontaneous* are not entirely accurate ways of describing these self-report techniques. For example, some approaches—such as projective techniques—use researcher-provided stimuli but also involve a good degree of spontaneity and open-endedness. Even with the most general of spontaneous approaches, the person is still reacting to a question or prompt, such as "Tell me about yourself" or "Tell us about school." Thus, we recognize that there are self-report measures that do fall between the two extremes as we are conceiving them. Nonetheless, we believe that these labels best capture the major difference between the two general approaches—responding to a number of researcher-generated items through a constrained-response format versus providing one's own items to the researcher through an unconstrained format.

In order to structure our discussion of these two general approaches, we will first describe each approach from the perspective of the respondent. In particular, we will conceive the measurement effort as an interaction between researcher and respondent, in which the respondent engages in self-presentation or self-interpretation (Cheek & Hogan 1983; Johnson 1981; Mills & Hogan 1978).

In the traditional reactive approach to studying the self, the respondent is given a paper-and-pencil questionnaire in a group setting, accompanied by a set of oral or written instructions. The questionnaire usually consists of a large number of contextually and temporally ungrounded items, and the respondent's task is to make some type of self-related decision about each one. Presumably, in thinking about oneself on a given dimension, the respondent searches for evidence that is relevant to his or her understanding of that dimension.

In the traditional spontaneous approach, the respondent is given a verbal or written prompt in an individual or group setting, and the respondent's task is to say or write whatever comes to his or her mind. The prompt is purposely designed to be vague and nondirective, and it is also usually contextually and temporally ungrounded. Presumably, in responding to the prompt, the person searches for information that is relevant to his or her understanding of the prompt.

There are several noteworthy aspects to these approaches when they are examined from the perspective of an interaction between researcher and respondent. With the reactive approach, the social interaction between researcher and respondent is kept to a minimum and is, for the most part, indirect. There are usually instructions given by the researcher, but the bulk of the interaction and the attention of the respondent are directed toward the questionnaire itself.

With the spontaneous approach, the interaction between researcher and respondent is more direct as the researcher takes the place of the questionnaire. At least in the case of the individual interview, the researcher is likely to be physically closer, there is the potential for exchange of nonverbal information, and the attention of the respondent is directed both toward the researcher and oneself.

In both the reactive and spontaneous cases, the interaction is almost exclusively one-way. The respondents are being asked questions by the researcher (not vice versa) and they are thus likely to be in a state of self-focused attention (Duval & Wicklund 1972).

In the reactive case, there are discrete interactions in the sense that the person is prompted and responds to each item, for the most part independently of previous items. In the spontaneous case, however, the interaction is continuous in the sense that the respondent continues to respond to the initial prompt throughout the session.

As the previous paragraphs suggest, reactive and spontaneous self-report methodologies can be distinguished along several dimensions. Among the more important differences between the two approaches for studying the self are:

1. The response format and the constraints associated with it;
2. The content and meaning of the measures;
3. Potential response biases; and
4. The handling of the data generated by the approaches.

Response Format. Reactive approaches have made use of a large number of primarily written response formats, including true false, multiple choice, adjective checklist, and semantic differential. There has been a good deal of discussion about the relative advantages and disadvantages of the different reactive formats. For reviews and critiques relating to measures of the self, see Wells and Marwell (1976) and Wylie (1974, 1989).

Regardless of the particular variant selected, there is a limited set of response options available to the respondent. From the perspective of the researcher interested in studying the self, the major constraint associated with the use of specific limited-response options involves the respondent's understanding of those options, as well as the task instructions. Young children, for example, may be unable to read or understand the available response options, necessitating the development of alternative formats (Harter & Pike 1984).

Spontaneous approaches make use of much less constrained response formats, whether written (Montemayor & Eisen 1977) or oral (Brinthaupt & Lipka 1985). In these cases, respondents are free to report about the self as they please. The major constraint associated with the use of this open-ended response format is that respondents must provide intelligible data to the researcher.

Thus, while it is usually not an explicit aspect of the instructions, respondents assume that they should use the rules of grammar to structure their written or oral responses. It is also probably the case that this approach requires more from the intelligence, energy, and/or verbal skills of respondents than does the reactive approach. Arguments can be made that such differences among respondents are both beneficial and harmful to the researcher of the self who uses a spontaneous approach.

Content of Measures. A second dimension on which reactive approaches to studying the self differ from spontaneous approaches concerns the contents of the measures. There are some interesting differences between the two approaches in terms of this dimension.

First, with the reactive approach, the *researcher* selects the contents of the measure. This allows him or her to focus directly on those dimensions considered to be most important or relevant, and it assumes that the researcher is the best judge of how to assess those dimensions. With the spontaneous approach, the *respondent* selects the contents of the measure. This allows the respondent to focus directly on those dimensions considered to be most important or relevant, and it assumes that he or she is the best judge of how to assess those dimensions.

This difference in who selects the contents of the measures also means that the types of information obtained can differ. To take an extreme example, it is probably less difficult to obtain information about specific sexual practices with reactive than with spontaneous measures (Spitzer et al. 1970, 113). There are likely to be a great many aspects of the self that respondents will not volunteer in their spontaneous self-reports, perhaps because these aspects are not normally shared with others, are inaccessible, or are thought to be too unimportant to mention. The researcher who is armed with a reactive approach can assess these content dimensions directly. Whereas the reactive approach prompts or cues a respondent's memory search, the spontaneous approach essentially involves a respondent-directed memory search.

A second difference between the contents of reactive and spontaneous approaches involves the meanings of the terms used. With reactive measures, the concern is that *respondents* understand the *researcher's* terms. There may be differences in understanding of terms or items attributable to a variety of differences among respondents, such as differences on cognitive, developmental, social, or cohort dimensions. Here, the question involves the *researcher's* certainty about the *respondents'* understanding of his or her terms.

On the other hand, with spontaneous measures, the concern is that the *researcher* understands the *respondents'* terms. The respondents' meanings of the terms which they use to describe themselves may also vary for a number of reasons, such as cognitive, developmental, social, or cohort differences. Here, the question involves the *researcher's* certainty about what *respondents* mean by the terms which they use.

Because each approach involves interpretation and understanding of terms from both the researcher's and the respondents' perspectives, it is unclear which is the better one or the more reliable one—at least when studying the self.

Response Biases. The issue of bias associated with approaches to studying the self is a critical one for researchers. As we noted earlier, there are several concerns about self-report data in general, such as whether the respondent is aware of or has access to the reasons for his or her behavior. Assuming, as most researchers do, that these concerns are not fatal to the use of self-report data, what are the biases that are unique to reactive and spontaneous approaches?

To answer this question, refer to the notion of the self-report as an interaction between researcher and respondent. As with any interaction, there are both implicit and explicit rules. Compared to the spontaneous approach, the rules of the reactive approach are more detailed and explicit. These rules are usually given in the instructions, and commonly include statements such as "Be sure to answer all of the items"; "This is not a test. There are no correct answers"; "Try to be as honest and accurate as you can in your responses"; and "Your responses will be kept in the strictest confidence. No one else will see them."

There are also more implicit rules about responding to reactive measures. These rules, which are generalized from normal testing situations and which may or may not appear in the instructions, include not talking to others during the task, answering the items in the order in which they are presented (and usually not returning to previously answered items), and asking for clarification of items if necessary. It is interesting to note that the instructions for the typical reactive measure include a variety of interaction rules, whereas the instructions for the typical spontaneous measure do not mention such rules. This reflects a greater concern about response biases when using the more structured reactive measures.

Among the more frequently noted response biases associated with reactive approaches are acquiescence (or "yea-saying"), extreme responding, and giving the socially desirable response (Moskowitz 1986; Wells & Marwell 1976). These biases are primarily a concern of reactive approaches because of the response formats that are typically used. That is, the respondent has the opportunity to easily respond in a patterned manner that is irrelevant to his or her report about the self. Such effects are likely to be magnified to the extent that respondents believe that their biases will not be detected, or that accurate self-reports are seen as being less important than is socially desirable responding (Johnson 1981; Mabe & West 1982; Shrauger & Osberg 1981).

The effects of prior items on responding to subsequent items with reactive measures have been extensively investigated by Tourangeau and his colleagues (Tourangeau & Rasinski 1988; Tourangeau, Rasinski, Bradburn & D'Andrade 1989). For example, they have shown that earlier material in a questionnaire can produce either carryover (or consistency) effects or backfire (such as inconsistency) effects, depending on such factors as changes in the object or issue under consideration or changes in the dimensions or standards used in making a judgment.

In the case of spontaneous approaches to studying the self, the biases associated with reactive-type response formats are likely to be of less concern. For example, it might be more difficult for the respondent to fake the correct response or respond in a socially desirable fashion on spontaneous measures than on reactive measures.

However, as the constrained-response format of reactive approaches allows for the introduction of specific response sets or biases, the unconstrained-response format of spontaneous approaches allows unique problems of its own. It is not uncommon, for example, to see excessive repetition of items or perseveration on a specific content domain among respondents, especially those who are younger. The spontaneous researcher might even encounter a child who has 25 dogs, cats, and fish, and who knows—and proceeds to describe—each one by name. In addition, there are likely to be responses that are uncodable and/or irrelevant, at least from the perspective of the researcher.

One of the premises of the spontaneous approach to studying the self is that the respondent is not directed or cued to respond in any particular way. To the extent that this is true, what is revealed in the process of self-report is how the respondent tends to think about the self. For example, McGuire and McGuire (1988) argued that the reactive approach tells the researcher only how respondents would think of themselves on a given dimension—if they thought about it at all—and nothing about how frequently they actually think about themselves on that dimension. The spontaneous approach, according to the McGuires, indicates what dimensions respondents do use when thinking about themselves. In other words, the self that is measured by reactive approaches is an "as-if" hypothetical self, whereas the self that is measured by spontaneous approaches is an "as-is" phenomenal self.

The effects of instructions on the contents of one's spontaneous reports about the phenomenal self have been investigated by Yardley (1987). She compared subjects' oral responses to two unconstrained versions of the "Who Are You?" (WAY) spontaneous approach (individual interview variant).

First, subjects responded to the prompt without time or length constraints. Second, subjects were asked to imagine a situation where they felt free to be themselves and, while imagining themselves in this situation, to respond to the WAY prompt. Yardley found that, in the latter condition, subjects described themselves in terms of immediate experiences and subjective states, whereas in the former condition, subjects described themselves with generalizations and objective disclosure of information (Salancik 1974; Spitzer et al. 1970).

The Yardley (1987) study suggests that the responses to the typical spontaneous measure are less "as-is" than they are generalized descriptions of the self as an object. If respondents were reporting about the self as currently experienced, then they should say things pertaining to their current cognitive or emotional state or bodily awareness, such as "I don't know how to answer your question" or "I'm nervous and confused about this interview" (Waterbor 1972). In fact, the implicit message of the spontaneous prompt is for the respondent to describe the self as an object or a referent abstracted from the immediate interview context.

Content analyses of responses to spontaneous measures support this argument (Gordon 1968; McGuire & Padawer-Singer 1976; Montemayor & Eisen 1977). Thus, we suggest that the spontaneous approach does not measure the self as it is currently experienced so much as it measures the self as an object to the respondent.

Data Handling. There are large differences in the characteristics of the data that result from reactive and spontaneous approaches to studying the self. One of the most important reasons for the popularity of reactive measures is the ease of handling the resulting data. Not only are these measures easier to score than are spontaneous measures, but they also allow for greater intersubject comparability. However, reactive measures are limited in terms of the flexibility of the data and their applications.

Although more difficult to quantify and less comparable across subjects, the qualitative nature of the data collected with spontaneous methods gives them much greater flexibility (Damon & Hart 1988, chapter 4; Spitzer et al. 1970). Multiple aspects of respondents' self-reports can be quantified. For example, previous researchers have coded responses to spontaneous approaches in terms of linguistic characteristics (McGuire, McGuire & Cheever 1986), evaluative content (Greenwald, Bellezza & Banaji 1988), descriptive content (Brinthaupt & Lipka 1985; Gordon 1968; Montemayor & Eisen 1977), and the amount of clustering of content dimensions (Jones, Sensenig & Haley 1974).

However, unlike reactive measures, which can provide ratings of specific self-relevant dimensions, spontaneous approaches typically rely on frequency counts. Especially with developmental research, in which the psychological meaning of spontaneous responses may vary with developmental level, relying on frequency counts of spontaneously generated content categories may lead to interpretation difficulties (Harter 1983). Of course, as noted before, the same argument can be applied to reactive measures, since the respondents' understanding of particular items may vary as a function of developmental level.

In summary, reactive and spontaneous approaches to studying the self differ in several ways. There are advantages and disadvantages associated with the response formats of each approach, the interpretation of the contents of the measures, the biases that are likely to occur with respondents, and the handling of the data that each approach provides. However, in addition to these methodological differences between the approaches, it is also possible that they differ in terms of what aspects of the self are being studied. In the next section, we consider this possibility.

Comparing a Reactive and a Spontaneous Self-report Measure

Researchers interested in studying the self have traditionally focused on the implications of a particular self-view. For example, if someone evaluates himself or herself negatively, this should have implications for motivation and behavior. Researchers have also been interested in detailing those aspects of the self that can be manipulated, such as when changes in self-evaluation can be brought about by external factors. On the other hand, there has traditionally been less interest in studying the process of self-description per se.

This research is less concerned with how a person evaluates himself or herself than it is with one's description or understanding of the self that is evaluated. Despite some promising early efforts to study the self-as-described (Bugental & Zelen 1950; Kuhn & McPartland 1954), researchers continue to be primarily interested in the effects and manipulations of the self-as-evaluated (cf. McGuire 1984).

Most of the research that is related to the question of self-description is developmentally-oriented. For example, Damon and Hart in 1982 and 1988 conducted extensive research on developmental differences in self-understanding. (See also chapter 8 in this volume.) They found that young children do not see the various components of the self as related to one another and there is no integrated conception of the self. However, the early and late adolescent integrates the various components of the self into a consistent unity. Other researchers suggest that the self-as-described shifts from an emphasis on objective, concrete attributes in childhood to an emphasis on subjective, abstract characteristics in adolescence (Harter 1983; Montemayor & Eisen 1977; Rosenberg 1979).

Recently, there has been a renewed interest in studying the process of self-description. The extensive program of research conducted by McGuire and his colleagues (McGuire & McGuire 1988) has raised a number of interesting issues concerning the self. One of these issues is the relationship between self-description and self-evaluation. For example, McGuire and McGuire argued that the traditional emphasis on studying self-evaluation is misplaced. In their research, they find that, when subjects are asked to describe themselves with a spontaneous format, explicit references to self-evaluation are relatively rare.

They also argued that the phenomenal self (the self as experienced) is not as evaluatively laden as researchers suggest with their emphasis on studying self-esteem. This raises the question of to what extent self-description and self-evaluation are the same or different.

Several reviewers have discussed the distinction between self-description and self-evaluation (Beane & Lipka 1980; Blyth & Traeger 1983; Breytspraak & George 1982; Calhoun & Morse 1977; Shepard 1979). They suggest that this distinction can be thought of as the difference between self-concept and self-esteem. Accordingly, self-concept refers to the descriptive aspects of the self, whether these are toned evaluatively (such as "I love to read") or nonevaluatively (as in "I am an athlete"). Self-esteem, on the other hand, refers to the evaluation of one's described self (for example, "I don't like myself"), when evaluation refers to the degree of liking for or satisfaction with the self or to the discrepancy between an actual and an ideal or "ought" self (Higgins, Strauman & Klein 1986; Ogilvie & Clark in press; Shepard 1979).

How can the descriptive aspects of the self be separated from its evaluative aspects? To use the cited examples, a person may negatively evaluate his or her descriptions of self (for example, "My love for reading is bad because it keeps me from getting any work done" or "As an athlete, I get injured very often") or positively evaluate them (as in "I learn a lot of good things by reading" or "I am proud to be so good at sports"). Note, however, that these self-evaluative statements can just as well be thought of as self-descriptive. Because it is possible to both describe and evaluate oneself in the same statement, separation of the two processes is a methodological problem. (See Shepard's discussion of the empirical separation of self-description and self-evaluation published in 1979).

To what extent do spontaneous and reactive approaches measure the same or different aspects of the self? Previous researchers, such as McGuire and colleagues (1976), suggested that self-description and self-evaluation are separate aspects of the self, as revealed by the fact that very little explicitly self-evaluative data are generated using spontaneous methodologies. However, the relationship between self-description and self-evaluation is not as clear-cut as it would seem to be.

Some researchers have argued that self-evaluation (or self-esteem) underlies even spontaneously generated self-descriptions. For example, in a study of the evaluative content of the self, Greenwald, Bellezza, and Banaji (1988) asked subjects to produce items in several of the categories found by researchers to commonly occur with the spontaneous "Tell me about yourself" prompt (such as, likes and dislikes, activities, and good and bad qualities). The number of items produced by subjects for each category was correlated with scores on two reactive measures of global self-esteem, the Rosenberg Self-Esteem Scale and the Texas Social Behavior Inventory. Greenwald and colleagues found that global self-esteem was positively and significantly correlated with the number of affectively positive items spontaneously produced by subjects. Thus, they argued that self-evaluation is indeed a common component of spontaneous self-description.

We believe that a comparison of reactive and spontaneous self-report measures is important for two reasons. First, it appears to be an effective way to address the theoretical issue of whether self-evaluation affects self-description. Second, most researchers have assumed that reactive and spontaneous approaches—because they consist of quantitatively and qualitatively different data—measure quite different aspects of the self. The empirical comparison of reactive and spontaneous approaches is necessary before results from each approach can be accepted as compatible or complementary. For example, are age or cultural differences on a reactive measure comparable to age or cultural differences on a spontaneous measure? (See also chapter 8 of this volume.) If the McGuire claim is correct in saying that reactive approaches measure the "as-if" hypothetical self, whereas spontaneous approaches measure the "as-is" phenomenal self, then the two approaches and the results and implications based on them, may not be comparable.

We have chosen to approach these issues in a way that is similar to the study done by Greenwald and colleagues (1988). In particular, we have conducted a study that directly compared a reactive (the Piers-Harris Children's Self-Concept Scale) and a spontaneous ("Tell me about yourself") approach to studying the self. The Greenwald and colleagues study did not compare subjects' reactive self-evaluations with their own evaluations of spontaneous self-descriptions. Our investigation was designed to allow such a comparison. The spontaneous approach was constructed in such a way that both descriptive and evaluative self-esteem-related aspects of the self were captured. Among the questions we attempted to address were: How often do subjects spontaneously give "Piers-Harris-like" statements? What is the relationship between the two measures in terms of evaluative content? And can subjects' Piers-Harris scores be used to predict their spontaneously generated self-reports?

Measures and Procedures. Respondents for the study were 152 students from a school district in the southeastern portion of Kansas. The sample included all students from grades five, six, eight, and nine who were present during the two testing sessions. Students completed the Piers-Harris (PH) Children's Self-Concept Scale in their classes at school. The PH is a widely used self-report questionnaire consisting of eighty self-evaluative statements (such as, "I am a happy person" or "I am dumb about most things") related to several aspects of the self. Students indicated in writing how each statement applied to them by responding "yes" or "no."

The PH has been found to be psychometrically sound, with high reliability and adequate validity (Hughes 1984; Piers 1984; Wylie 1989). In addition to an overall self-esteem summary score, six subscores can be computed on the following clusters: behavior;

intellectual and school status; physical appearance and attributes; anxiety; popularity; and happiness and satisfaction. Some scale items appear on more than one subscale (Piers 1984).

In addition to data from the PH, all students provided data based on a variant and extension of the open-ended "Tell me about yourself" methodology approximately four months after taking the PH. This spontaneous methodology provided us with several types of data. First, the students' responses to the prompt provided us with elements of self-description to which we will refer as "self-concept content." Second, the students made ratings of importance for each specific element of self-concept mentioned. Third, they evaluated each element of self-concept which they provided by stating whether they wanted to change that element or keep it the same. We considered these latter judgments to be self-esteem judgments. Finally, for each element of self-concept that students wanted to change, information about *why* they wanted to change that particular element was collected.

Students were individually interviewed outside of their regular classrooms by a female graduate student. The interviewer first introduced herself, greeted the student, and briefly described the task. If the student understood the task and indicated a readiness to begin, then the interviewer prompted him or her with the statement "Tell me about yourself."

At this point, the interviewer wrote down (as close to verbatim as possible) all statements made by the student. There were no time or length constraints imposed on the student. Once the student appeared to be finished—that is, gave no responses for a thirty-second period and/or said that he or she was finished—the interviewer moved on to the second part of the task.

She showed the student an index card on which was typed the scale to be used for the importance ratings. This was a five-point scale ranging from "not important" (1) to "very important" (5). We used a separate sample of fifth graders (who chose among several possible labels for the five-point importance scale) to determine what categories would be conceptually meaningful and distinguishable for our sample.

To collect the importance ratings, the interviewer then returned to the first statement given by the student and, for this and each subsequent statement, asked him or her "How important is this to you?" Once the student rated each statement, the interviewer moved on to the next part of the task by asking the student to answer "another question about the things you said about yourself."

After reading the first statement of the student's protocol, the interviewer asked "Is this something you'd like to change or keep the same?"

The interviewer proceeded through each of the self-concept statements with the same question. When finished with this portion of the task, the interviewer once again returned to the top of the response protocol and proceeded through it. If a response was one that a student wanted to change, it was read to the student and he or she was asked by the interviewer, "Why would you like to change this about yourself?"

The interviewer recorded all reasons given by the student for wanting to change that particular aspect of the self. Reasons for change judgments were collected for purposes unrelated to the current study. When finished with all of the change statements—or if there were no aspects of the self that the student wanted to change—the interviewer ended the session by thanking the student for his or her help.

It should be emphasized that the students were unaware that one type of question would be followed by another until their responses to the previous type of question were complete. Although, in some ways, the most interesting data would be those self-descriptive statements that were highly important and that the student wanted to change, we did not want to explicitly solicit such data because of the purposes of the research.

Results and Discussion

In comparing the two self-report measures, our interest was in the relationship between self-description and self-evaluation. Thus, our coding of the interview data focused explicitly on the evaluative nature of the students' self-descriptions. The Piers-Harris data (overall $M = 59.3$, $s.d. = 14.1$) closely resembled the normative PH data reported by Piers (1984) for children of these ages. The typical student provided approximately eight responses to the "Tell me about yourself" prompt. This number is similar to the number obtained with other research that has used these ages and the open-ended oral interview methodology (Brinthaupt & Lipka 1985).

Very few of the open-ended responses could be categorized as Piers-Harris-like, either in terms of vocabulary or meaning (such as, "I'm a good person," "I'm smart," or "I have many friends"). In fact, only 4 percent of the total responses could be so classified.

This finding supports the claims of McGuire and McGuire (1988) that most of what respondents provide in a spontaneous measure is not explicitly *self*-evaluative. The students' responses were also coded in terms of whether they were positive (as in, "I like to run"), negative (for example, "I dislike school"), or neutral ("I live in Centreville") in evaluative tone. The majority of the responses were either neutral (53 percent) or positive (43 percent) in tone, with only 4 percent of the students' responses negatively toned. Thus, students appeared to avoid both self-evaluative and negatively-toned responses in their self-descriptions. In addition, the typical response was rated by students as "pretty much important" to them ($M = 3.93$ on the five-point scale).

The "keep" and "change" judgments made by students represented their evaluations of their spontaneously generated self-descriptions. The majority (85 percent) of the students' judgments were for keeping traits indicating that they were satisfied with most of the aspects of themselves that they described. This percentage of keep judgments is very similar to that found in previous research using these ages and this methodology (Brinthaupt & Lipka 1985). Forty percent of the students had no change judgments in their evaluations of their self-descriptions. Students' keep judgments tended to correspond to responses that were rated as more important to them than were those responses that were change judgments. The difference in importance ratings for keep and change responses (based on those students with at least one keep and one change judgment) was significant: $t(90) = 6.84$, $p < .001$. Thus, it appeared that the students' self-descriptions were characterized by statements about themselves with which they were satisfied and which were important to them. Ninety-four percent of the positively-toned responses were keep judgments and 44 percent of the negatively-toned responses were change judgments.

Considering the effects of gender on the students' PH data and open-ended self-descriptions revealed no significant differences. However, there were a few interesting differences in the interview data due to age. In order to analyze age effects, the fifth and sixth graders ($N = 57$) were categorized as younger, while the eighth and ninth graders ($N = 95$) were categorized as older. Analyses revealed that the younger respondents rated their responses as less important to them ($M = 3.77$) than did the older respondents (M 4.03), $t(150) = -2.25$, $p < .05$. In addition, younger respondents made proportionately fewer keep judgments (80 percent) than did the older respondents (88 percent), $t(150) = -2.67$, $p < .01$. Finally, younger respondents showed a greater percentage of negatively-toned responses that were change judgments (16 percent) than did older respondents (4 percent), $t(150) = 2.64$, $p < .01$. There were no age differences on the PH total or subscale scores.

In summary, the picture that emerges from the interview data is that students gave responses that were not explicitly self-evaluative or negatively toned but involved aspects of themselves that were important to them and with which they were satisfied. Compared to the older students in the sample, the younger students described aspects of themselves that were less important to them but with which they were less satisfied. To what extent can these patterns of responding be predicted by the students' reactively measured global self-esteem scores? Our next set of analyses attempted to answer this question.

The correlations between the PH total score and the interview variables revealed that students' global self-esteem was unrelated to length of protocol ($r = .08$), number of Piers-Harris-like responses ($r = .10$), and evaluative tone of the responses (average $r = .04$). This latter finding is in contrast with the findings of Greenwald et al. (1988) who found that self-esteem was positively and significantly associated with the producton of positively toned open-ended responses, using college-aged subjects and a different methodology.

The correlation between global self-esteem and rated importance of responses was positive and significant ($r = .19$, $p < .05$). In terms of the proportion of keep judgments, students with high PH total scores tended to be more satisfied with aspects of themselves than were students with low PH total scores ($r = .27$, $p < .01$). Self-esteem significantly predicted both importance and the proportion of keeps after removing the effects of age. Thus, it appeared that self-esteem was related to the students' open-ended responses.

This effect could have occurred in at least two ways. First, self-esteem may have been associated with students' descriptions of themselves. That is, students with high self-esteem may have produced more important or better self-descriptions than did students with low self-esteem. This was then reflected in their subsequent importance ratings and keep/change judgments. Alternatively, self-esteem may not have been associated with students' descriptions of themselves. That is, when describing themselves, students with high self-esteem may have produced the same types of self-descriptions as students with low self-esteem. Instead, self-esteem may have been associated only with students' importance ratings and keep/change judgments. Students with high self-esteem may have simply evaluated their self-descriptions as more important and more positive than did those with low self-esteem.

Because of the lack of a relationship between self-esteem and the number of PH-like responses and the number of positively-toned responses, we believe that the latter alternative is the more likely one. In other words, in contrast to Greenwald and colleagues (1988), self-esteem does not appear to exert a direct influence on respondents' open-ended self-descriptions. Rather, respondents' *evaluations* of their open-ended self-descriptions do appear to be influenced by self-esteem.

Even though our results are limited, they seem to confirm and extend the arguments of McGuire and his colleagues. Of course, given the differences between our study and that of Greenwald et al. (1988), comparing the results between the two studies must be done cautiously. However, we believe that any methodology that induces an evaluative perspective toward the self will indicate a substantial relationship between global self-esteem and spontaneous self-description. In other words, whereas using a spontaneous self-evaluative prompt such as "Tell us what you like and dislike about yourself" is likely to show a positive relationship between esteem/ and description, using a prompt such as "Tell us about yourself" is unlikely to show such a relationship.

Conclusion: Self-report across the Lifespan

In the first part of this chapter, we reviewed three sets of factors that can affect the self-report process. By way of conclusion, we would like to return to these factors and briefly note some issues related to studying the self across the life span.

In terms of the accessibility and organization of self-relevant knowledge, there are several reasons to think that the self-report process will differ depending upon the age of respondents. For example, it is unlikely that young children have well-defined and well-elaborated self-schemata. This suggests that their self-reports will be much less organized and relevant to the self than the self-reports of adults.

Alternatively, if there are memory decrements associated with old age, the self-reports of the elderly are also likely to differ from those of younger adults (Mueller et al. In press). It is also likely that cognitive biases will affect age groups differently. For example, among adolescents, certain data about the self (such as physical appearance and peer relationships) may be more salient and easily accessible than among children or adults. Similarly, for purely cognitive reasons, adults' self-reports are likely to include dimensions of career and work, whereas children's self-reports are likely to include dimensions of school and academics.

To the extent that different age groups are subjected to differing contextual, situational, and cultural factors (Wells & Stryker 1988), the self-report process is likely to show substantial cross-sectional variation across the life span. In our previous discussion of these factors, the age of respondents was assumed to be constant. However, it is quite likely that these factors operate differently across the life span. For example, do adults show the same self-description patterns in the family versus the school (or work) context that children do? It is possible that, after a stable sense of self has developed in early adolescence or early adulthood, the influence of contextual or situational factors diminishes in magnitude. However, Wells's (In press) research suggests that these factors are important in adulthood. Of course, culture does not remain static as an individual passes through the lifespan, and cultural change can include changes in how the self is defined and understood by a given society. The possibility that cultural factors are more influential on the self-report process at certain ages than others is an intriguing one.

The third set of factors, individual and developmental differences, is clearly related to the process of self-report across the lifespan. For example, most (if not all) individual difference variables are subject to developmental trajectories. Age is likely to be positively associated with previous self-report experience. In addition, with increases in age come greater reasoning and information-processing abilities. The implications of individual and developmental differences for the self-report process seem especially crucial for developmental and personality researchers. For example, how can developmental differences in self-report be separated from differences in self-development or personality?

The final sections of our chapter concerned the advantages and disadvantages of the reactive and spontaneous self-report methodologies. From a lifespan perspective, there are many unresolved issues concerning the use of these methodologies. On the one hand, we believe that spontaneous approaches are superior to reactive approaches in terms of flexibility. On the other hand, the ease of administration and data handling makes reactive approaches more attractive. We would argue that empirical comparison of the two approaches is interesting and important for self researchers, if for no other reason than to establish the optimal circumstances for the use of each approach. Finally, regardless of one's preferences, controlling or in some other way taking into account the factors that can affect the self-report process must be a high priority for those who study the self.

NOTE

We wish to thank Ginny Poole Brinthaupt, Richard Lipka, and Richard Moreland for their comments on an earlier draft of this chapter. Preparation of this chapter was supported by National Institute of Mental Health Grant PH2-T32 MH14588-13.

REFERENCES

Agatstein, R. C., and Buchanan, D. B. 1984. Public and private self-consciousness and the recall of self-relevant information. *Personality and Social Psychology Bulletin* 10:314–325.

Andersen, S. M. 1987. The role of cultural assumptions in self-concept development. In *Self and identity: Psychosocial perspectives* edited by K. Yardley and T. Honess. Chichester: Wiley. 231–246.

Bargh, J. A. 1989. Conditional automaticity: Varieties of automatic influence in social perception and cognition. In *Unintended thought: Causes and consequences for judgment, emotion, and behavior,* edited by J. S. Uleman and J. A. Bargh. New York: Guilford.

Baumeister, R. F. 1982. A self-presentational view of social phenomena. *Psychological Bulletin* 91:3–26.

Beane, J. A., and Lipka, R. P. 1980. Self-concept and self-esteem: A construct differentiation. *Child Study Journal* 10:1–6.

Blyth, D. A., and Traeger, C. M. 1983. The self-concept and self-esteem of early adolescents. *Journal of Early Adolescence* 3:105–120.

Breytspraak, L. M., and George, L. K. 1982. Self-concept and self-esteem. In *Research instruments in social gerontology,* Vol. 1, edited by D. J. Mangen and W. A. Peterson. Minneapolis: University of Minnesota Press. 241–302.

Brinthaupt, T. M., and Lipka, R. P. 1985. Developmental differences in self-concept and self-esteem among kindergarten through twelfth grade students. *Child Study Journal* 15:207–221.

Broughton, J. 1978. Development of the concepts of self, mind, reality, and knowledge. *New Directions for Child Development* 3:75–100.

Bugental, J. F. T., and Zelen, S. L. 1950. Investigations into the self-concept: The W-A-Y technique. *Journal of Personality* 18:483–498.

Calhoun, G., and Morse, W. C. 1977. Self-concept and self-esteem: Another perspective. *Psychology in the Schools* 14:318–322.

Cantor, N.; Markus, H.; Niedenthal, P.; and Nurius, P. 1986. On motivation and the self-concept. In *Handbook of motivation and cognition*, edited by R. M. Sorrentino and E. T. Higgins. New York: Guilford Press. 96–121.

Carver, C. S., and Scheier, M. F. 1978. Self-focusing effects of dispositional self-consciousness, mirror presence, and audience presence. *Journal of Personality and Social Psychology* 36:324–332.

Cheek, J. M., and Hogan, R. 1983. Self-concepts, self-presentations, and moral judgments. In *Psychological perspectives on the self*, Vol. 2, edited by J. Suls and A. G. Greenwald. Hillsdale, N. J.: Erlbaum. 249–273.

Coopersmith, S. 1967. *The antecedents of self-esteem*. San Francisco: W. H. Freeman & Company.

Cousins, S. D. 1989. Culture and self-perception in Japan and the United States. *Journal of Personality and Social Psychology* 56:124–131.

Damon, W., and Hart, D. 1982. The development of self-understanding from infancy through adolescence. *Child Development* 53:841–864.

———. 1988. *Self-understanding in childhood and adolescence*. Cambridge: Cambridge University Press.

Duval, S., and Wicklund, R. 1972. *A theory of objective self-awareness*. New York: Academic Press.

Eder, R. A.; Gerlach, S. G.; and Perlmutter, M. 1987. In search of children's selves: Development of the specific and general components of the self-concept. *Child Development* 58:1044–1050.

Ericsson, K. A., and Simon, H. A. 1980. Verbal reports as data. *Psychological Review* 87:215–251.

Fenigstein, A.; Scheier, M. F.; and Buss, A. H. 1975. Public and private self-consciousness: Assessment and theory. *Journal of Consulting and Clinical Psychology* 43:522–527.

Fiske, S. T., and Taylor, S. E. 1984. *Social cognition*. Reading, Mass.: Addison-Wesley.

Gergen, K. J. 1977. The social construction of self-knowledge. In *The self: Psychological and philosophical issues*, edited by T. Mischel. Oxford: Basil Blackwell.

————. 1985. Theory of the self: Impasse and evolution. In *Advances in experimental social psychology,* Vol. 16, edited by L. Berkowitz. New York: Academic Press.

Gergen, K. J., and Gergen, M. M. 1988. Narrative and the self in relationship. In *Advances in experimental social psychology,* Vol. 21, edited by L. Berkowitz. San Diego: Academic Press. 17–56.

Gibbons, F. X. 1990. Self-attention and behavior: A review and theoretical update. In *Advances in experimental social psychology,* Vol. 23, edited by M. P. Zanna. San Diego: Academic Press. 249–303.

Gordon, C. 1968. Self-conceptions: Configurations of content. In *The self in social interaction,* edited by C. Gordon and K. J. Gergen. New York: Wiley. 115–136.

Greenwald, A. G., and Banaji, M. R. 1989. The self as a memory system: Powerful, but ordinary. *Journal of Personality and Social Psychology* 57:41–54.

Greenwald, A. G. and Pratkanis, A. R. 1984. The self. In *Handbook of social cognition,* Vol. 3, edited by R. S. Wyer and T. K. Srull. Hillsdale, N. J.: Erlbaum. 129–178.

Greenwald, A. G.; Bellezza, F. S.; and Banaji M. R. 1988. Is self-esteem a central ingredient of the self-concept? *Personality and Social Psychology Bulletin* 14:34–45.

Gur, R. C., and Sackheim, H. A. 1979. Self-deception: A concept in search of a phenomenon. *Journal of Personality and Social Psychology* 37:147–169.

Harter, S. 1983. Developmental perspectives on the self-system. In *Handbook of child psychology,* Vol. 4, edited by P. H. Mussen. New York: Wiley. 275–385.

Harter, S., and Pike, R. 1984. The pictorial scale of perceived competence and social acceptance for young children. *Child Development* 55: 1969–1982.

Hewitt, J. 1976. *Self and identity: A symbolic interactionist social psychology.* Boston, Mass.: Allyn & Bacon.

Higgins, E. T.; Strauman, T.; and Klein, R. 1986. Standards and the process of self-evaluation: Multiple affects from multiple stages. In *Handbook of motivation and cognition,* edited by R. M. Sorrentino and E. T. Higgins. New York: Guilford Press. 23–63.

Hughes, H. M. 1984. Measures of self-concept and self-esteem for children ages 3–12 years: A review and recommendations. *Clinical Psychology Review* 4:201–226.

Johnson, J. A. 1981. The "self-disclosure" and "self-presentational" views of item response dynamics and personality scale validity. *Journal of Personality and Social Psychology* 40:761–769.

Jones, R. A.; Sensenig, J.; and Haley, J. 1974. Self-descriptions: Configurations of content and order effects. *Journal of Personality and Social Psychology* 30:36–45.

Kagan, J. 1989. *Unstable ideas: Temperament, cognition, and self.* Cambridge, Mass. Harvard University Press.

Kihlstrom, J. F., and Cantor, N. 1984. Mental representations of the self. In *Advances in experimental social psychology*, Vol. 15, edited by L. Berkowitz. New York: Academic Press. 1–47.

Kihlstrom, J. F.; and Cantor, N.; Albright, J. S.; Chew, B. R.; Klein, S. B.; and Niedenthal, P. M. 1988. Information processing and the study of the self. In *Advances in experimental social psychology*, Vol. 21, edited by L. Berkowitz. San Diego: Academic Press. 145–181.

Kuhn, M. H., and McPartland, T. 1954. An empirical investigation of self-attitudes. *American Sociological Review* 19:68–76.

Kunda, Z., and Sanitioso, R. 1989. Motivated changes in the self-concept. *Journal of Experimental Social Psychology* 25:401–421.

Mabe, P. A., and West, S. G. 1982. Validity of self-evaluation of ability: A review and meta-analysis. *Journal of Applied Psychology* 67:280–296.

Markus, H., and Kunda, Z. 1986. Stability and malleability of the self-concept. *Journal of Personality and Social Psychology* 51:858–866.

Markus, H., and Nurius, P. S. 1986. Possible selves. *American Psychologist* 41:954–969.

———. 1987. Possible selves: The interface between motivation and the self-concept. In *Self and identity: Psychosocial perspectives*, edited by K. Yardley and T. Honess. Chichester, England: John Wiley & Sons. 157–172.

Marsh, H. W. 1988. *Self Description Questionnaire: A theoretical and empirical basis for the measurement of multiple dimensions of pre-adolescent self-concept.* San Antonio, Tex.: The Psychological Corporation.

McGuire, W. J. 1984. Search for the self: Going beyond self-esteem and the reactive self. In *Personality and the prediction of behavior*, edited by R. A. Zucker, J. Aronoff, and A. I. Rabin. New York: Academic Press. 73–120.

McGuire, W. J., and McGuire, C. V. 1988. Content and process in the experience of self. In *Advances in experimental social psychology*, Vol. 21, edited by L. Berkowitz. San Diego: Academic Press. 97–144.

McGuire, W. J.; and Padawer-Singer, A. 1976. Trait salience in the spontaneous self-concept. *Journal of Personality and Social Psychology* 33:743–754.

McGuire, W. J.; McGuire, C. V.; and Cheever, J. 1986. The self in society: Effects of social contexts on the sense of self. *British Journal of Social Psychology* 25:259–270.

Mills, C., and Hogan, R. 1978. A role theoretical interpretation of personality scale item responses. *Journal of Personality* 46:778–785.

Montemayor, R., and Eisen, M. 1977. The development of self-conceptions from childhood to adolescence. *Developmental Psychology* 13: 314–319.

Moskowitz, D. S. 1986. Comparison of self-reports, reports by knowledgeable informants, and behavioral observation data. *Journal of Personality* 54:294–317.

Moskowitz, D. S., and Schwarz, J. C. 1982. Validity comparison of behavior counts and ratings by knowledgeable informants. *Journal of Personality and Social Psychology* 42:518–528.

Mueller, J.; Johnson, C.; Dandoy, A.; and Keller, T. In press. Trait distinctiveness and age specificity in the self concept. In *Self-perspectives across the life span*, edited by R. P. Lipka and T. M. Brinthaupt. Albany, N. Y.: State University of New York Press.

Natale, M., and Hantas, M. 1982. Effects of temporary mood states on selective memory about the self. *Journal of Personality and Social Psychology* 42:927–934.

Nisbett, R. E., and Wilson, T. D. 1977. Telling more than we can know: Verbal reports on mental processes. *Psychological Review* 84:231–259.

Ogilvie, D., and Clark, M. D. In press. The best and worst of it: Age and sex differences in self-discrepancy research. In *Self-perspectives across the life span*, edited by R. P. Lipka and T. M. Brinthaupt. Albany, N. Y.: State University of New York Press.

Osberg, T. M., and Shrauger, J. S. 1986. Self-prediction: Exploring the parameters of accuracy. *Journal of Personality and Social Psychology* 51:1044–1057.

Phares, V.; Compas, B. E.; and Howell, D. C. 1989. Perspectives on child behavior problems: Comparisons of children's self-reports with parent and teacher reports. *Psychological Assessment* 1:68–71.

Piers, E. V. 1984. *Piers-Harris Children's Self-Concept Scale.* Los Angeles: Western Psychological Services.

Pryor, J. B. 1980, Self-reports and behavior. In *The self in social psychology* edited by D. M. Wegner and R. R. Vallacher. New York: Oxford University Press. 206–228.

Rhodewalt, F., and Agustdottir, S. 1986. Effects of self-presentation on the phenomenal self. *Journal of Personality and Social Psychology* 50:47–55.

Rogers, T. B. 1974. An analysis of two central stages underlying responding to personality items: The self-referent decision and response selection. *Journal of Research in Personality* 8:128–138.

Rogers, T. B.; Kuiper, N. A.; and Kirker, W. S. 1977. Self-reference and the encoding of personal information. *Journal of Personality and Social Psychology* 35:677–688.

Roland, A. 1988. *In search of self in India and Japan: Toward a cross-cultural psychology.* Princeton: Princeton University Press.

Rosenberg, M. 1979. *Conceiving the self.* New York: Basic Books.

Ross, M., and McFarland, C. 1988. Constructing the past: Biases in person memories. In *The social psychology of knowledge,* edited by D. Bar-Tal and A. W. Kruglanski. New York: Cambridge University Press. 299–315.

Salancik, J. R. 1974. Inference of one's attitudes from behavior recalled under linguistically manipulated cognitive sets. *Journal of Experimental Social Psychology* 10:415–427.

Schlenker, B. R. 1980. *Impression management: The self-concept, social identity, and interpersonal relations.* Belmont, Calif.: Wadsworth.

———. 1986. Self-identification: Toward an integration of the private and public self. In *Public and private self,* edited by R. F. Baumeister. New York: Springer-Verlag. 21–62.

Schoeneman, T. J. 1981. Reports of the sources of self-knowledge. *Journal of Personality* 49:284–294.

Schoeneman, T. J.; Tabor, L. E.; and Nash, D. L. 1984. Children's reports of the sources of self-knowledge. *Journal of Personality* 52:124–137.

Schwarz, N., and Clore, G. L. 1983. Mood, misattribution, and judgments of well-being: Informative and directive functions of affective states. *Journal of Personality and Social Psychology* 45:513–523.

————. 1988. How do I feel about it? Informative functions of affective states. In *Affect, cognition, and social behavior,* edited by K. Fiedler and J. Forgas. Toronto: C. J. Hogrele. 44–62.

Shepard, L. A. 1979. Self-acceptance: The evaluative component of the self-esteem construct. *American Educational Research Journal* 16:139–160.

Shrauger, J. S., and Osberg, T. M. 1981. The relative accuracy of self-predictions and judgments by others in psychological assessment. *Psychological Bulletin* 90:322–351.

————. 1982. Self-awareness: The ability to predict one's future behavior. In *Aspects of consciousness* Vol. 3, edited by G. Underwood. London: Academic Press. 267–313.

Shrauger, J. S., and Schoeneman, T. J. 1979. Symbolic interationist view of self-concept: Through the looking glass darkly. *Psychological Bulletin* 86:549–573.

Shweder, R. A., and LeVine, R. A. 1984. *Culture theory: Essays on mind, self, and emotion.* New York: Cambridge University Press.

Snyder, C. R., and Fromkin, H. L. 1980. *Uniqueness: The human pursuit of difference.* New York: Plenum.

Snyder, M. 1974. The self-monitoring of expressive behavior. *Journal of Personality and Social Psychology* 30:526–537.

————. 1979. Self-monitoring processes. In *Advances in experimental social psychology,* Vol. 12, edited by L. Berkowitz. New York: Academic Press. 85–128.

Spitzer, S., Couch, C.; and Stratton, J. 1970. *The assessment of the self.* Iowa City, Iowa: Sernell.

Stryker, S. 1980. *Symbolic interactionism: A social structural perspective.* Menlo Park: Benjamin/Cummings.

————. 1987. Identity theory: developments and extensions. In *Self and identity: Psychosocial perspectives,* edited by K. Yardley and T. Honess. Chichester, England: John Wiley & Sons. 89–103.

Tourangeau, R., and Rasinski, K. A. 1988. Cognitive processes underlying context effects in attitude measurement. *Psychological bulletin* 103:299–314.

Tourangeau, R.; Rasinski, K. A.; Bradburn, N.; and D'Andrade, R. 1989. Belief accessibility and context effects in attitude measurement. *Journal of Experimental Social Psychology* 25:401–421.

Triandis, H. C. 1989. The self and social behavior in differing cultural contexts. *Psychological Review* 96:506–520.

Turner, R. 1976. The real self: From institution to impulse. *American Journal of Sociology* 80:989–1016.

Waterbor, R. 1972. Experiential bases of the sense of self. *Journal of Personality* 40:162–179.

Wells, A. J. In press. Variations in self-esteem in daily life: Methodological and developmental issues. In *Self-perspectives across the life span*, edited by R. P. Lipka and T. M. Brinthaupt. Albany, N. Y. State University of New York Press.

Wells, L. E., and Marwell, G. 1976. *Self-esteem: Its conceptualization and measurement*. Beverly Hills, Calif.: Sage.

Wells, L. E., and Stryker, S. 1988. Stability and change in self over the life course. In *Life span development and behavior*, Vol. 8, edited by P. B. Baltes, D. L. Featherman, and R. L. Lerner. Hillsdale, N. J.: Erlbaum.

Wicklund, R. A., and Gollwitzer, P. M. 1983. A motivational factor in self-report validity. In *Psychological perspectives on the self*, Vol. 2, edited by J. Suls and A. G. Greenwald. Hillsdale, N. J.: Erlbaum. 67–92.

Wyer, R. S., and Srull, T. K. 1986. Human cognition in its social context. *Psychological Review* 93:322–359.

Wylie, R. C. 1974. *The self-concept: A review of methodological considerations and measuring instruments*. Lincoln: University of Nebraska Press.

———. 1979. *The self-concept: Theory and research on selected topics*. Lincoln: University of Nebraska Press.

———. 1989. *Measures of self-concept*. Lincoln: University of Nebraska Press.

Yardley, K. 1987. What do *you* mean "Who am I"?: Exploring the implications of a self-concept measurement with subjects. In *Self and identity: Psychosocial perspectives*, edited by K. Yardley and T. Honess. Chichester, England: John Wiley & Sons. 211–230.

Zanna, M. P., and Pack, S. J. 1975. On the self-fulfilling nature of apparent sex differences in behavior. *Journal of Experimental Social Psychology*, 11:583–591.

Zurcher, L. A. 1977. *The mutable self: A self-concept for social change*. Beverly Hills, Calif.: Sage.

BARBARA M. BYRNE
RICHARD J. SHAVELSON
HERBERT W. MARSH

5

Multigroup Comparisons in Self-concept Research: Reexamining the Assumption of Equivalent Structure and Measurement

In their review of self-concept (SC) research, Shavelson, Hubner, and Stanton (1976) reported that most studies were of a substantive nature, with the primary focus being directed toward the investigation of mean group differences. They further noted that findings from this vast literature were, for the most part, inconsistent and indeterminate. Subsequent reviews have led to similar conclusions (Byrne 1984; Hansford & Hattie 1982; West & Fish 1973; West, Fish & Stevens 1980; Wylie 1974, 1979, 1989). Suggesting that SC research had addressed itself to substantive issues before problems of definition, measurement, and interpretation had been resolved, Shavelson and associates called for construct validation studies in order to identify the ills of this area of research. They argued that, unless these methodological issues were addressed, the generalizability of SC findings would continue to be ambiguous and contradictory.

Following this call, a number of construct validity studies have subsequently determined several methodological weaknesses with respect to substantive SC research. The first of these relates to problems of operational definition as documented by reviews of the literature that reveal no clear, concise, and universally accepted definition of SC (Byrne 1984; LaBenne & Greene 1969; Shavelson et al. 1976; Wells & Marwell 1976; West et al. 1980; Wylie 1974, 1979; Zirkel 1971). Indeed, in two separate reviews of the literature, Shavelson and colleagues (1976) and Zirkel (1971) reported more than fifteen definitions of SC that were explicitly cited, not to mention several others that were implicit in the selected instruments and study designs. For example, despite an intent to study a global SC, researchers have referred to the construct by a wide variety of terms, such as *self-perception, self-esteem,* or self-assessment. For a more extensive list, see Wells and Marwell (1976).

A second limitation of SC research has been the failure to interpret findings within a particular theoretical framework (Byrne & Shavelson 1986; Hughes 1984; West & Fish 1973). As such, it has been difficult to evaluate both the goals and methodological aspects of many studies. Furthermore, any valid interpretation of findings from such studies has become virtually impossible. For example, some researchers have investigated differences in global SC when, logically, an examination of a more specific facet of SC would have been more appropriate. Others have examined a particular facet such as academic SC, yet used an instrument designed to measure general SC.

A third problem with SC research relates both to the quality and quantity of the measuring instruments. Many such measures have lacked adequate evidence of sound psychometric properties (Byrne 1984; Hughes 1984; West & Fish 1973; Wylie 1974). Others have been developed for the sole purpose of assessing a specific population and/or to serve the purposes of a particular research problem. In addition to being infrequently tested for reliability and validity, the latter have often been poorly described and difficult to locate, thus rendering replication research extremely difficult, if not impossible.

Finally, many substantive studies of SC have employed inappropriate and/or statistically limited analytical procedures (Byrne & Shavelson 1986; Hansford & Hattie 1982). For example, Shavelson and colleagues reported in 1976 that most research relied on the analysis of zero-order correlations, or simple univariate tests for differences. As such, analyses have been more descriptive than explanatory in nature. Furthermore, despite interpretative statements concluding causal direction between SC and academic achievement, most analyses have been based on simple indices of association (Pearson r), rather than on causal modeling procedures that could more appropriately answer this question (Byrne 1984; Hansford & Hattie 1982; Shavelson & Stuart 1981). Indeed, a recent review of methodological procedures used in SC research has revealed only a modest increase in the application of these statistically more sophisticated procedures (Byrne 1990).

Yet a further explanation of inconsistent findings from SC research may derive from studies whose primary focus is the detection of mean group differences. Indeed, multigroup comparisons are a central concern to research on the development of SC, as well to other areas such as gender or ethnic diversity. In all cases, mean comparisons among groups may mislead if elastic yardsticks are used, or if a yardstick and a ruler provide the comparative measurement. Implicit in the testing for mean group differences is the assumption that (1) the pattern and size of relations among multiple facets of SC are the same across groups (that is, equivalent structure); and (2) the items on the measuring instrument or instruments are perceived in the same way and to the same degree of accuracy by both groups (that is, equivalent measurement).

Only recently, however, have researchers been provided with the methodological means for testing these assumptions statistically. Advances in the application of confirmatory factor analysis (CFA) have now made it possible to test hypotheses related to the equivalence of both the theoretical construct of SC, and its measurement across groups.

The purpose of this chapter is to demonstrate how groups may differ from one another with respect to both the structure and measurement of SC. Specifically, we provide such evidence by examining findings from two independent studies, each of which were designed to test these hypotheses.

Results from the first study exemplify how the structure of SC can vary across gender. In particular, we examine the equivalence of general SC and multidimensional academic SCs across adolescent males and females.

Results from the second study illustrate ways by which a single assessment instrument can differ across age or grade-level groups. Here, we examine the invariance of test items with respect to their scaling units and reliabilities, as well as relations among its subscale scores across grade levels for preadolescent gifted children.

Since the testing for group invariance presupposes that SC measurement will be linked to a specific theoretical framework, we begin by first describing the hierarchical model of SC proposed by Shavelson and colleagues (1976) which provided the theoretical underpinning for the two studies to be examined here. In light of the thorough discussion and review of construct validity research bearing on this model (see chapter 2 of this volume), our treatment of this topic is necessarily brief. However, for optimal understanding of the procedures used—and the results presented here—we strongly suggest that readers examine—or, perhaps, reexamine—chapter 2 before proceeding with this chapter. Next, we explore the issue of group invariance as it bears on the comparison of mean group differences in SC research. Finally, for each of the two selected studies, we present information related to the sample, assessment measures, and methodological procedures. We also discuss in some detail the results of these studies as they bear on the conduct of research designed to investigate the presence of mean group differences.

THE HIERARCHICAL MODEL OF SELF-CONCEPT

Although there exists a number of SC theories (Wells & Marwell 1976; Wylie 1979) and postulated models of SC (Byrne 1984), few have been rigorously tested empirically. Indeed, this seems rather startling, given the plethora of SC measures available to researchers and the fact that sound instrumentation derives from its development within the framework of a well-validated theory.

One theoretical model of SC, however, that has undergone a substantial amount of validation research was proposed by Shavelson and associates in 1976. According to this theoretical perspective, SC is hypothesized as being both multidimensional and hierarchical with perceptions of behavior at the base, moving to perceptions of self in specific areas, such as mathematics; then to perceptions of self in academic and nonacademic areas; and finally, to perceptions of self in general. Furthermore, SC is postulated as becoming increasingly multifaceted with increasing age, and as being differentiable from other psychological constructs such as academic achievement. Recent validation research on this theoretical model, however, has resulted in a structure that is slightly more complex than was originally hypothesized (Marsh, Byrne & Shavelson 1988. See also chapter 2 of this volume).

Although hypotheses related to the hierarchical model of SC have been tested extensively, both within and across populations, most construct validity research has focused on the academic, in contrast to the nonacademic, component. (See chapter 2 of this volume, especially figure 2.1.) While the first of the two studies to be examined in this chapter focuses on the academic component of the model, the second involves both the academic and nonacademic components.

THE CONCEPT OF BETWEEN-GROUP INVARIANCE

In the behavioral sciences, researchers are often interested in comparing SC scores of experimental and control groups across treatments; across nonexperimental groups (such as cross-sectional age comparisons) which are specifically selected for a particular purpose; or over time, (as in longitudinal age comparisons). Implicit in such comparisons is the assumption that the structure, as well as the measures, are equivalent across groups and/or time.

In other words, proposed construct interpretations are group-or time-invariant (Bejar 1980; Cole & Maxwell 1985; Drasgow & Kanfer 1985; Marsh & Hocevar 1985). Bejar (1980), however, has demonstrated that even in experimental studies with the random assignment of subjects to treatment and control groups, the equivalence of structure bearing on the construct under study and its measurement is not guaranteed.

In nonexperimental studies, of course, the assumption is more problematic. Yet, it has been argued that observed group means cannot be considered as comparable without invariant structure of the underlying construct (Bejar 1980; Byrne, Shavelson & Muthén 1989), and invariant measurement (Byrne et al. 1989; Drasgow & Kanfer 1985). To consider otherwise leads to interpretations that are hazardous at best. We turn now to these two aspects of between-group invariance.

The Issue of Invariant Self-concept Structure

Invariance bearing on the structure of SC addresses the equivalence of between-group relations among the multiple facets of SC. It is important whether the pattern and size of the correlations are the same across groups. In other words, in testing for observed mean differences in, say, general SC, academic SC, and social SC, it is important for the researcher to know whether these constructs are related in the same way and to the same extent across all groups under study. If they are not, this bears importantly on the interpretation of SC test scores.

For example, Shavelson and associates postulated in 1976 that SC becomes increasingly differentiated with increasing age. Thus, to compare differences in particular facets of SC between, say, late adolescents and early preadolescents may be risky since it assumes that both share the same SC structure.

The Issue of Invariant Self-concept Measurement

The measurement issue concerns the group equivalence of items on the selected SC assessment instrument in terms of scaling units and reliability—that is, it queries whether test items are being perceived in the same way and to the same degree of accuracy across groups. For example, if the content of particular SC items are interpreted somewhat differently by two groups of subjects, the scaling units will differ, and the measurement operates differently within the groups. That is, the items are differentially valid across groups.

Similarly, if the reliability is significantly greater for one group than for the other, this is evidence of differences in the measurements. As such, the instrument is said to be biased in favor of one of the groups (Green 1975). This leads to substantive conclusions about differences in means that are due, not to the groups, but rather, to the differential functioning of the measurements for each group.

However, age, once again, may bear indirectly on these issues of differential measurement. For example, the interpretative meaning that a respondent attributes to a particular item will necessarily be a function of his or her reading ability, formal academic training and/or informal experiential learning. Such differential perceptions, in turn, contribute to differential scaling units. Likewise, the developmental factor of age can bring about the differential reliability of items. For example, Shavelson et al. (1976) argued for the increasing stability of SC with age. Thus, a finding of higher item reliabilities for a group of older adults compared with a group of preadolescents may, in fact, derive from a difference in the stability of the SC dimensions being measured.

Testing for Invariant Self-concept Structure and Measurement

A number of ad hoc methods have been developed for comparing subscale scores, using exploratory factor analyses, across independent samples (Marsh & Hocevar 1985; Reynolds & Harding 1983). The process, however, has rarely been used in either substantive or construct validation research. Nevertheless, Alwin and Jackson (1981) have argued that such procedures do not adequately address issues of group-invariance.

On the other hand, CFA procedures do provide the means for testing related hypotheses statistically. Since the application of CFA to tests of invariance requires some basic knowledge of its application to single-group analyses, we now digress briefly for the benefit of those readers who may not be familiar with these procedures.

The Concept of CFA.   CFA is based on the analysis of covariance structures with latent variables. This means that, rather than analyzing relations among observed measurements (that is, correlations among scores for each item or subscale), one analyzes relations among the unobserved underlying constructs (as in latent variables or factors measured by more than one observed measure).

Furthermore, CFA demands that the researcher have some knowledge of the underlying latent structure. This knowledge may be based on theory, empirical research, or some combination of both. For example, suppose a measuring instrument is designed to measure four facets of SC (say, general, academic, physical, and social), and this factor structure has been validated in the literature. The researcher can then feel confident in proceeding with a CFA analysis. As such, he or she postulates a priori that certain test items will be highly related to the latent variables which they are designed to measure, and only negligibly related—or better still, not related at all—to the remaining factors.

In factor analysis, these relations are termed *factor loadings.* Thus, we say that the items will load highly on those factors which they were designed to measure (that is, target loadings), and will load negligibly on the other factors (or nontarget loadings). Putting this in context with our example of SC, the researcher would specify a priori that the items designed to measure general self-concept would load highly on that factor but would yield loadings of approximately zero on the academic, physical and social SC factors.

Statistical Modeling in CFA.   Since the analysis of covariance structures involves the specification of statistical models that portray how the observed measurements are related to the underlying latent constructs, researchers typically use schematic diagrams to communicate this information. Thus, to familiarize the reader with basic concepts in CFA, and the symbolic representations generally used, consider a simple example.

Suppose that we have a two-factor model of self-concept:

Let the two factors (latent variables) be general SC (GSC) and academic SC (ASC)

Suppose that each factor has two observed variables:

Let the two measures of GSC be *(a)* the General Self subscale of the Self Description Questionnaire (SDQGSC) (Marsh & O'Neill 1984); and *(b)* the Self-esteem Scale (SESGSC) (Rosenberg 1965).

Let the two measures of ASC be *(a)* the academic self-concept subscale of the Self Description Questionnaire (SDQASC), and *(b)* the Self-concept of Ability Scale (SCAASC) (Brookover 1962).

A schematic presentation of this model is shown in figure 5.1.

Figure 5.1
Hypothesized Two-factor Model of Self-Concept

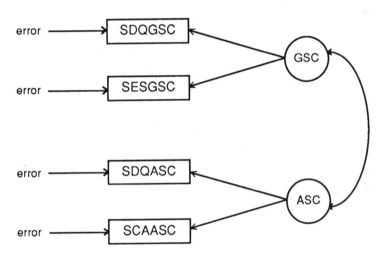

Here, then, we have a two-factor model consisting of general SC and academic SC, each factor being measured by two observed variables. The observed measures for general SC are SDQGSC and SESGSC. For academic SC they are SDQASC and SCAASC. The curved two-headed arrow indicates that general SC and academic SC are correlated. The single-headed arrows represent regression coefficients which denote "causal" influences. That is, GSC—SDQGSC is interpreted to mean that a change in GSC generates a change in SDQGSC. For a more extensive treatment of basic concepts, modeling, and applications, see Byrne (1989).

Model-fitting In CFA. The general idea in the analysis of covariance structures using CFA is that the researcher first postulates a model that specifies (1) how the observed measures are related to the unobserved latent factors; and (2) how the latent factors are related to each other—that is, whether they are correlated. This model—termed a *restricted model* since it constrains certain parameters (such as some factor loadings in our example being zero) in keeping with the researcher's a priori information—is then estimated and its fit to the observed data is evaluated for goodness-of-fit using an appropriate statistical computer package. To date, LISREL (Jöreskog & Sörbom 1985) is the method most widely used.

By this process, then, the restricted model is compared against the observed data. The extent to which the restricted model represents the observed data is reflected in a chi-square (χ^2) value indicative of the goodness-of-fit.

Although CFA analyses based on LISREL modeling have historically relied on the χ^2-likelihood ratio test as a criterion for assessing the extent to which a proposed model fits the observed data, its sensitivity to sample size, as well as to various model assumptions—such as linearity, multinormality, and additivity—are well known (Bentler & Bonett 1980; Marsh & Hocevar 1985; Muthén & Kaplan 1985).

Over the past few years, several alternative goodness-of-fit indices have been—and are still being—proposed. Their adequacy as criteria of fit is a source of continuous debate in the literature (Marsh, Balla & McDonald 1988). One such index that has been widely used is the Bentler and Bonett (1980) normed index (BBI). Its scale ranges from 0.0 to 1.00 with a value close to .90 representing a good fit of the hypothesized model to the data.

We refer to the BBI when we discuss model-fit related to the baseline model specific to each group. Overall, however, researchers have been urged not to judge model-fit solely on the basis of χ^2 values (Bentler & Bonett 1980; Jöreskog & Sörbom 1985; Marsh et al. 1988), or on alternative-fit indices (Kaplan 1988; Sobel & Bohrnstedt 1985). Rather, assessments should be based on multiple criteria, including "substantive, theoretical, and conceptual considerations" (Jöreskog 1971, 421). This caveat bore importantly upon our determination of baseline models which is our next topic to be discussed.

The Baseline Model.   As a prerequisite to testing for factorial invariance it is important to consider a baseline model which is estimated separately for each group. It represents the best possible fit to each group's data in the sense that it is the most substantively meaningful model that most parsimoniously reproduces the means and covariances that summarize the data for each group. Since measuring instruments are often group-specific in the way in which they operate, baseline models are not expected to be identical across groups. For example, whereas the baseline model for one group might include correlated measurement errors and/or secondary factor loadings,[1] this may not be so for a second group. As will be shown later, a priori knowledge of such group differences is critical to the conduct of invariance testing procedures.

In multiple group analyses using LISREL, it is essential that the data from both groups be analyzed simultaneously and that they be based on the covariance matrices in order to obtain efficient estimates (Jöreskog & Sörbom 1985). This is because with multiple-group analyses, which include the testing for invariance, between-group constraints are imposed on particular parameters and, thus, the model is no longer scale-free as it was with the analysis of separate groups. That is, the analyses conducted to determine the baseline model for each group separately could have been based either on the covariance or correlation matrix. Evaluation of the simultaneous group analyses takes advantage of the additive character of the χ^2 statistic and its corresponding degrees of freedom. By adding the χ^2 goodness-of-fit statistics across groups, and their corresponding degrees of freedom, a goodness-of-fit for the combination of baseline models can be obtained.

Testing for invariance involves first, specifying a model in which certain parameters are constrained to be equal across groups, and then comparing that model with a less restrictive model in which these parameters are free to take on any value. The difference or change (Δ) in chi-square values between competing models ($^{\Delta}\chi^2$) is itself χ^2-distributed with degrees of freedom equal to the difference or change (Δ) in degrees of freedom ($^{\Delta}df$). The test provides a basis for determining the tenability of the hypothesized equality constraints. A significant $^{\Delta}\chi^2$ indicates noninvariance. Although space limitations preclude further elaboration of these analyses in this chapter, the reader is encouraged to read Marsh & Hocevar (1985) for a description of the invariance procedure in general and Byrne and colleagues (1988a, 1988b, 1989; Byrne & Schneider 1988; Byrne & Shavelson 1986; Byrne et al. 1989) as it relates to self-concept in particular.

We are now ready to turn our attention to two studies that can illustrate how SC structure and measurements can be noninvariant across groups.

STUDY 1: TESTING FOR THE INVARIANCE OF
SELF-CONCEPT STRUCTURE

The primary purpose of study 1 was to test the assumption of an invariant SC structure for senior-high-school adolescent males and females (Byrne & Shavelson 1987). Specifically, CFA procedures were used to test for the equivalence of *(a)* a four-factor SC structure composed of general SC, academic SC, English SC, and mathematics SC, as measured by multiple assessment instruments; *(b)* the item scaling units for the multiple measures of each SC facet; *(c)* the pattern of factor loadings such that each of the instruments was measuring the same SC facet (congeneric test)[2] for both sexes, and *(d)* relations among the four specified facets of SC.

The Data Base

The sample included 832 (412 males and 420 females) grade-eleven and grade-twelve students from two suburban high schools in Ottawa, Canada. The data approximated a normal distribution (Muthén & Kaplan 1985) with skewness ranging from -1.27 to 0.06 ($\bar{X} = -0.30$) for males, and from -1.12 to 0.05 ($\bar{X} = -.34$) for females; and kurtosis ranged from -0.86 to 2.30 ($\bar{X} = 0.17$) for males, and from -0.82 to 1.13 ($\bar{X} = 0.06$) for females.

A battery of SC instruments (described in the next section of this chapter) was administered to intact classroom groups during one fifty-minute period. To ensure the relevancy of SC responses related to English and mathematics, it was first determined that all students were enrolled in both of these subject areas. The testing was completed approximately two weeks after report cards were issued in April. The students, therefore, had the opportunity of being fully cognizant of their academic performance prior to completing the tests for the study. This factor was considered to be important in the measurement of academic and subject matter SCs.

Measuring Instruments

The SC test battery consisted of twelve scales with three measures for each of general SC, academic SC, English SC, and mathematics SC. All were self-report rating scales and were designed for use with a high-school population.

General SC was measured using the general self subscale of the Self Description Questionnaire III (SDQ III) (Marsh & O'Neill 1984);

the self-concept subscale of the Affective Perception Inventory (API) (Soares & Soares 1979); and the Self-esteem Scale (SES) (Rosenberg 1965).

Measures of academic SC were the SDQ III academic self-concept scale, the API student self subscale, and the self-concept of ability scale form A (SCA) (Brookover 1962).

English SC was measured with the SDQ III verbal self-concept subscale, the API English perceptions subscale, and the SCA form B. Items on form B are identical to those on form A, except that they elicit responses relative to specific content (such as "How do you rate your ability in English compared to that of your close friends?").

Finally, measures of mathematics SC included the SDQ III mathematics subscale, the API mathematics perceptions subscale, and the SCA form C (items specific to mathematics ability). For a more extensive description of these measures, and a summary of their psychometric properties, see Byrne and Shavelson (1986).

Analyses of the Data

Responses to negatively worded items were reversed so that, for all instruments, the highest response code was indicative of a positive rating of SC. Additionally, the first item on the API self-concept subscale was recoded, contingent on the sex of the respondent.[3] The SDQ III, API, and SCA were factor analyzed in an earlier study of these data. Based on these findings, the API student self subscale was deleted as a measure of academic SC.[4]

Using the LISREL VI program (Jöreskog & Sörbom 1985), analyses of the covariance structure of the data were conducted in two stages. First, the best-fitting model was determined separately for males and females. Second, the invariance of SC measurements and structure across gender was tested.

Results

The Baseline Models. We sequentially respecified and reestimated models until the final best-fitting model for each sex was obtained. These results demonstrated a satisfactory fit to the data for both males (χ^2/df = 1.97; BBI = .98) and females (χ^2/df = 2.27; BBI = .98). In fitting the baseline model for both sexes, however, we found a substantial drop in χ^2 when the English SC subscale of the SDQ was free to load on the general SC factor. One additional cross-loading of the mathematics SC subscale of the SDQ (SDQMS) on the English SC factor was found for males only. This finding cannot be explained, and we strongly suspect that this effect will disappear upon replication.

Finally, correlated errors between subscales of the same measuring instrument allowed for a well-fitting model. These parameters represent nonrandom measurement error introduced by a particular method of response format and are commonly found in attitudinal data. These baseline models are schematically presented in figure 5.2.

Test for Invariance. Procedures used for testing hypotheses were identical to those used in model fitting. That is, a model in which certain parameters were constrained equally across gender was compared with a less restrictive model in which these parameters were free to take on any value.

For example, the hypothesis of an invariant pattern of factor loadings was tested by, first, constraining all factors loadings (except SDQMSC) to be equal, and then comparing model 2 with model 1, in which only the number of factors was held invariant across gender. Since the difference in χ^2 ($\Delta\chi^2 = 7.11$) was not significant, the hypothesis of an invariant pattern of factor loadings was considered tenable. Likewise, the hypothesis of invariant factor SC variances and covariances (model 3) was tested but found untenable. Since we were interested in pinpointing differences in the SC structure (more specifically, SC facet relations) between males and females, we proceeded to independently test the invariance of the covariance parameters in the factor variance-covariance matrix. These results are shown in table 5.1

A different pattern of relations was found across gender between mathematics SC and each of the other SC facets, that is, general SC, academic SC, and English SC. To further investigate this differential structure, as well as the hierarchical structure of SC, we examined correlations among the latent SC facets and subject grades. In general, while these findings supported the hierarchical hypotheses, relations involving English and mathematics SCs varied across gender. These results are summarized in figure 5.3.

In reviewing figure 5.3, a number of important gender differences in SC structure are noteworthy. First, while for females, English SC correlated higher with general SC and academic SC than did mathematics SC, the reverse was true for males.

Second, for females, English and mathematics SCs correlated higher with their corresponding grades, than with grades in the other subject. For males, however, this pattern did not hold. While grades in mathematics correlated higher with mathematics SC than

with English SC for males, grades in English correlated to the same
degree with mathematics as with English SC.

Third, although for both sexes the correlation between mathematics SC and mathematics grades was higher than the correlation

Figure 5.2.
Baseline Models of Self-concept Structure for Males and Females

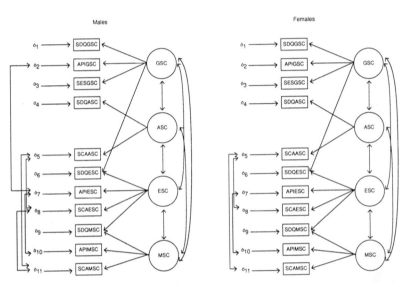

GSC	= General self-concept
ASC	= Academic self-concept
ESC	= English self-concept
MSC	= Mathematics self-concept
SDQGSC	= Self-description Questionnaire (SDQ), general self concept, (SC) subscale
APIGSC	= Affective Perception Inventory (API), general SC subscale
SESGSC	= Self-esteem Scale (SES)
SCAGSC	= Self-concept of ability scale (SCA), general SC subscale
SDQASC	= SDQ academic SC subscale
SCAASC	= SCA academic SC subscale
SDQESC	= SDQ English SC subscale
APIESC	= API English SC subscale
SCAESC	= SCA English SC subscale
SDQMSC	= SDQ mathematics SC subscale
APIMSC	= API mathematics SC subscale
SCAMSC	= SCA mathematics SC subscale

Table 5.1
Simultaneous Tests for the Invariance of Self-concept Structure

	Competing Models	χ^2	df	$^\Delta\chi^2$	$^\Delta df$	p
0	Null Model	6465.41	110	—	—	—
1	Factors invariant	138.26	65	—	—	—
2	Factors and pattern of loadings invariant[a]	145.37	73	7.11	8	NS
3	Model 2 with all latent variances and covariances invariant	195.30	83	49.93	10	<0.01
4	Model 2 with latent construct parameters made independently invariant					
	Covariances					
(a)	Academic/general SC	148.55	74	3.18	1	NS
(b)	English/general SC	145.37	74	0.00	1	NS
(c)	Mathematics/general SC	149.54	74	4.17	1	
(d)	English/academic SC	146.89	74	1.52	1	NS
(e)	Mathematics/academic SC	167.39	74	22.02	1	
(f)	Mathematics/English SC	157.56	74	12.19	1	

[a]All factor loadings invariant with the exception of the additional cross-loading for males.

between academic SC and mathematics grades, the same pattern did not hold for English. English grades correlated higher with academic SC than with English SC. This discrepancy was more dramatic for males than for females.

Fourth, whereas English and mathematics SC were correlated (albeit minimally) for males, they were uncorrelated for females. Finally, for both sexes, grades in English and mathematics were moderately correlated.

Conclusions

Although SC was found to be both multidimensional and hierarchically structured for both sexes, the relations among the facets of SC differed for adolescent males and females. These results, therefore, demonstrate that the assumption of invariant SC structure cannot be taken for granted. Relations among SC facets can differ between groups.

Overall, our results support substantive findings that girls have higher English SCs and lower mathematics SCs than do boys. It

Figure 5.3
Correlations Among Latent Self-concept Facets for Males and Females

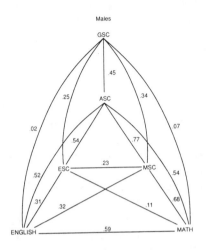
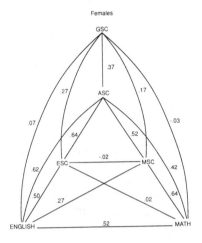

GSC = General self-concept
ASC = Academic self-concept
ESC = English self-concept
MSC = Mathematics self-concept
ENGLISH = Grades in English
MATH = Grades in mathematics

seems apparent that, despite changing societal norms geared to de-emphasize specific sex-role behaviors, sociocultural factors communicated through expectations and reinforcements of significant others may still influence perceptions of academic ability for high-school adolescents. The strength of these sociocultural factors is demonstrated by the finding that, even though girls demonstrate higher mathematics grades, boys still maintain a higher level of self-perceived success in that subject area than do girls.

STUDY 2: TESTING FOR THE INVARIANCE OF SELF-CONCEPT MEASUREMENT

The original purpose of study 2 was to test for the factorial validity and invariance of the Perceived Competence Scale for Children (PCSC) (Harter 1982) across grades five and eight for gifted and average elementary school children (Byrne & Schneider 1988).

Specifically, CFA procedures were used to test for the equivalence of *(a)* a four-factor structure composed of perceived cognitive competence, physical competence, social competence, and general self-worth; *(b)* a pattern of factor loadings such that the items designed to measure a particular facet of perceived competence actually loaded as expected; *(c)* item reliabilities; and *(d)* relations among the subscale factors (latent factor covariances).

Data Base

Byrne and Schneider (1988) found the PCSC to be completely invariant across grades five and eight for a sample of average students. Consequently, data on only the gifted sample provide an interesting illustration of the analysis of invariance related to measurement characteristics. The sample contained 249 gifted children from the two public schools systems in Ottawa, Canada, in grades five ($n = 132$) and eight ($n = 117$). Overall, an examination of item skewness and kurtosis revealed a distribution that was approximately normal (Muthén & Kaplan 1985). For details concerning descriptive statistics, selection criteria and sampling procedures, see Byrne and Schneider (1988).

The Measuring Instrument

The PCSC (Harter 1982) is a twenty-eight-item self-report instrument that measures four facets of perceived competence: cognitive competence (or academic ability), physical competence (or athletic ability), social competence (or social acceptance by peers), and general self-worth (or global self-esteem). Each seven-item subscale has a four-point structured alternative question format, ranging from not very competent (1) to very competent (4). For a summary of psychometric properties, see Byrne and Schneider (1988) and Harter (1982).

Items comprising the cognitive subscale are designed to measure perceived cognitive competence in school only (that is, the ability to do well in school or thinking that one is smart). Items measuring the physical domain focus solely on perceived competence in sports (or the ability to do well at sports and getting chosen for sports teams). Those measuring social competence focus solely on social relations with peers (as in having lots of friends or being easy to like).

In contrast to these subscales, the general self-worth subscale contains items that do not tap perceived competence in particular skill areas. Rather, these items measure the degree to which the child likes himself or herself as a person (that is, thinking of oneself as a good person or wanting to remain as one is).

Analyses of the Data

All responses to negatively worded items were reversed so that the highest response code indicated a positive rating of perceived competence or general self-worth. With the exception of one item in each subscale, analyses were based on an item-pair structure. As such, the seven items in each subscale were paired off, with items 1 and 2 forming the first couplet, items 3 and 4 the second couplet, and items 5 and 6 the third couplet. Item 7 remained a singleton.

The decision to use item-pairs was based on two primary factors: *(a)* the low ratio of number of subjects per test item for each subsample, and *(b)* preliminary EFA results derived from single-item analyses indicating, for the most part, that items were reasonably homogeneous in their domain-specific measurements of perceived competence (Byrne & Schneider 1988).

Furthermore, Marsh and colleagues (1984) have argued that the analysis of item-pairs is preferable to single items for at least four additional reasons. Item-pair variables are likely to *(a)* be more reliable, *(b)* contain less unique variance since they are less affected by the idiosyncratic wording of individual items, *(c)* be more normally distributed, and *(d)* yield results having a higher degree of generalizability.

The CFA model in the present study hypothesized a priori that *(a)* responses to the PCSC would be explained by four factors; *(b)* each item-pair (and item singleton) would have a nonzero loading on the perceived competence factor that it was designed to measure (that is, target loading) and zero loadings on all other factors (that is, nontarget loadings); *(c)* the four factors would be correlated; and *(d)* error/uniqueness terms for the item-pair (and item singleton) variables would be uncorrelated.

Results

The Baseline Models. In fitting the baseline models, two item singletons and one item-pair were found to have substantial loadings on nontarget factors. Specifically for gifted students in both grades, item PPC4 ("Some kids are among the last to be chosen for games") loaded on the social competence factor, and item PGS4 ("Some kids are usually sure that what they are doing is the right thing") loaded on the cognitive-competence factor. Item-pair PGS2 ("Some kids feel good about the way they act" and "Some kids think that maybe they are not a very good person") loaded on the social-competence factor for grade eight only.

The fact that the originally hypothesized model 1 did not fit the observed data equally well across grade led to two additional sets of analyses. First, a specification search was conducted to determine the best-fitting model for each grade. Second, given the known risks of capitalization on chance factors and other artifacts incurred by such procedures (MacCallum 1986), a sensitivity analysis was conducted to investigate, under alternative specifications, changes in the estimates of important parameters (Byrne et al. 1989).

From these analyses, the baseline model for each group was determined. For children in both grades, this model included the cross-loadings of item PPC4 on the social-competence factor, and of item PGS4 on the cognitive-competence factor. Whereas these two cross-loadings represented an optimal fit for children in grade five, this was not so for those in grade eight. An additional cross-loading of item-pair PGS2 on the social-competence factor represented a maximally best-fitting baseline model for these children.[5]

Tests for Invariance.   Once the baseline models were established, analyses proceeded in testing for the equivalence of the PCSC across grade levels. Of interest here was the question of invariant item-scaling units (or factor loadings), item reliabilities, and latent factor covariances. Noninvariant scaling units and reliabilities are an indication that the items are biased in the sense that they are differentially valid across groups (as seen in how the perception of item content varies across groups). Noninvariant factor covariances suggest a differential structure of perceived competence across groups (that is, how relations among the factors underlying the subscale scores vary across groups).

As noted in study 1, any discrepancies in parameter specifications of the baseline models for each group remain so throughout the invariance testing analyses. Thus, the secondary loading of PGS2 on the social-competence factor remained unconstrained for all tests of invariance.

Equality of Item-Scaling Units.   The simultaneous four-factor solution for each group yielded a reasonable fit to the data ($\chi^2_{190} = 232.08$). These results suggest that, for both grades, the data were well described by the four self-perceived competence factors. This finding, however, does not necessarily imply that the actual factor loadings are the same across grade. Thus, the hypothesis of an invariant pattern of loadings was tested by placing equality constraints on all factor loadings (including the two common secondary loadings, but excluding the secondary factor specific to grade eight), and then comparing this model 2 with model 1 in which only the number of factors was held invariant. The difference in χ^2 was highly significant $(\chi^2_{14} = 38.93, p < .001)$. Thus, the hypothesis of an equivalent pattern of scaling units was untenable.

In order to identify which scaling units were noninvariant, it seemed prudent to first determine whether or not the two common secondary loadings were invariant across grade. As such, equality constraints were imposed on these factor loadings, and the model was reestimated. This hypothesis was found tenable $(\chi^2_2 = 5.10, p > .05)$.

Tests of invariance proceeded next to *(a)* test each congeneric set of scaling units (parameters specified as loading on the same factor); and then, given findings of noninvariance, to *(b)* examine the equality of each item-scaling unit individually.

For example, in testing for the equality of all scaling units measuring perceived general self (PGS), all items designed to measure that factor were held invariant across groups. Given that this hypothesis was untenable $(\Delta\chi^2_5 = 24.66, p < .001)$, each factor loading was subsequently and independently tested to determine whether it was invariant across grade. These tests for the invariance of items measuring general self-worth revealed only one item-pair (PGS2) to be noninvariant across grade. Likewise, the scaling units of all remaining item-pairs (or singletons) were tested for between-group invariance. Only one other item-singleton, PSC4, which measures perceived social competence, was found to be noninvariant.

Equality of Factor Covariances. The first step in testing for the invariance of structural relations among subscales was to constrain all factor covariances to be equal across grade. Equality constraints were subsequently imposed independently on each factor covariance parameter. The hypothesis of equivalent factor covariances was found tenable $(\Delta\chi^2_6 = 5.12 \, p > .05)$. These results indicate that relations among the facets of general SC, academic SC, social SC, and physical SC were equivalent across grade levels. They are consistent with those of Marsh and associates (see chapter 2 of this volume) and provide further support for the claim that SC does not become increasingly differentiated with age beyond the early preadolescent years.

Equality of Reliabilities. When the multiple indicators of a CFA model represent items from a single measuring instrument, it may be of interest to test for the invariance of item reliabilities. For example, this procedure was used by Benson (1987) to detect evidence of item bias in a scale designed to measure self-concept and racial attitudes for samples of white and black eighth-grade students, and by Munck (1979) to determine whether the reliability of items comprising two attitudinal measures was equivalent across different nations.

Since it has been shown that the imposition of equality constraints on both the factor loading and error parameters is justified only when the factor variances are group-invariant (Cole & Maxwell 1985; Rock, Werts & Flaugher 1978), this hypothesis was tested first, and was found tenable $(\Delta\chi^2_4 = 5.20, p > .05)$. Tests of invariance then proceeded by testing, first, for the equivalency of item reliabilities related to each separate subscale. Only the perceived cognitive competence subscale (PCC) was found to be equivalent across the grade $(\Delta\chi^2_7 = 8.49, p > .05)$. Subsequently, then, the reliability of each item-pair (or singleton) comprising the three noninvariant subscales was tested for its equivalence across the grade. Findings revealed noninvariance related to three item-pairs measuring perceived general self-worth (PGS1, PGS2, and PGS3); and one item-pair (PSC3) and one item-singleton (PSC4) measuring perceived social competence. A summary of the PCSC items found not to be equivalent across grades (or noninvariant items), with respect to scaling units or reliability, is presented in table 5.2. Readers interested in a more detailed summary should see Byrne and Schneider 1988.

Conclusions

The important finding of study 2 was that, although the four-factor structure of perceived competence was equivalent for gifted children across grades five and eight and as assessed by a single instrument, some measurements were found to be differentially valid. Specifically, one single item and one item-pair demonstrated noninvariant scaling units—an indication that the items were being perceived differently by the two groups of children. Six item-pairs and two item-singletons were found to have reliabilities that were not equivalent across grade levels. Such differential item reliabilities may invalidate traditional analyses in which subscale scores represent the sole observed measurement of a construct. Admittedly, while the issue of noninvariant reliabilities demands a good deal of

Table 5.2
Summary of Noninvariance for Subscales of the Harter (1982)
Perceived Competence Scale for Children[a]

Subscale	Noninvariant Item Scaling Units	Noninvariant Item Reliabilities
Perceived general self-worth	PGS2	PGS1
		PGS2
		PGS3
Perceived cognitive competence	—	—
Perceived social competence	PSC4	PSC3
		PSC4
Perceived physical competence	—	PPC2
		PPC3
		PPC4

PGS1 = Item 4—"Some kids feel there are a lot of things about themselves that they would change if they could."
Item 8—"Some kids are pretty sure about themselves."
PGS2 = Item 12—"Some kids feel good about the way they act."
Item 16—"Some kids think that maybe they are not a very good person."
PGS3 = Item 20—"Some kids are very happy being the way they are."
Item 24—"Some kids aren't very happy with the way they do a lot of things."
PSC3 = Item 18—"Some kids wish that more kids liked them."
Item 22—"Some kids are popular with other kids their age."
PSC4 = Item 26—"Some kids are really easy to like."
PPC2 = Item 11—"Some kids think they could do well at just about any new outdoor activity they haven't tried before."
Item 15—"Some kids feel that they are better than others their age at sports."
PPC3 = Item 19—"In games and sports, some kids usually watch instead of play."
Item 23—"Some kids don't do well at new outdoor games."
PPC4 = Item 27—"Some kids are among the last to be chosen for games."

[a]Each item actually comprises two alternative statements, one the inverse of the other. The respondent identifies himself or herself with one or the other. Only one of the two alternatives is presented here.

any instrument and can be considered to be an excessively stringent criterion, the analyses here are meant to illustrate that item measurements, although derived from the same measuring instrument, can differ across groups.

Nevertheless, the question of why items should be perceived differently across groups remains an intuitively intriguing one. While some might contend that such findings are indicative of poorly phrased items, this may not necessarily be so. Indeed, evidence of noninvariant items have been reported for well-known and psychometrically sound assessment measures. Such is the case for the PCSC examined here in study 2.

As noted earlier in this chapter, one possible explanation of differential item interpretation might be related to age. This seems particularly relevant to the data presented in study 2. Given the eagerness of gifted children to learn, combined with the zeal of most of their parents and teachers in maximizing their exposure to academic and experiential learning, it seems logical that the age difference between children in grade five and those in grade eight should reflect this cumulated knowledge. Such knowledge can't help but influence a child's perception of intended meaning derived from a self-report item.

IMPLICATIONS FOR SUBSTANTIVE RESEARCH

In this chapter, we have demonstrated how SC structure and measurement can vary across groups, including age and grade levels. Consequently, researchers must give serious attention to these assumptions underlying the conduct of multigroup comparisons.

Differences in SC structure across groups suggest that what is measured as SC in one group may not be the same as that measured in another group. As such, mean between-group comparisons lose their importance. Thus, attention must be focused on an interpretation of the between-group structural differences. Simply put, differences in *relationships*, not *means*, become the focus of comparison and interpretation.

When SC *measurements* vary across groups, this reflects on the biasedness of the items. In contrast to the conceptual definition of item bias generally associated with cognitive instruments (as when individuals of equal abilities from different gender or ethnic groups have unequal probabilities of success), item bias associated with affective instruments, such as the PCSC, reflects on their validity and on the question of whether measurements have the same meaning across groups. Evidence of such item bias is a clear indication that the scores are differentially valid (Green 1975).

Both noninvariant scaling units and reliabilities contribute to item bias. Whereas the former reflect on a differential interpretation of item content, the latter reflect on the accuracy of the measurement. Unlike reliabilities computed within the framework of classical test theory, those determined through the use of CFA are based on measurement of latent rather than of observed SC structure.

Within the context of this chapter, noninvariant item reliabilities, then, are not merely a function of differences in sampling variability (Bejar 1980). Rather, they represent error variance after the true score variance associated with the latent SC structure has been taken into account. Nevertheless, since reliability casts the upper bounds for validity, noninvariant findings translate into differential validity, which, in turn, implies item bias in favor of one group over another.

In summation, if the assumption of equivalent SC structure and measurements across groups is ignored, it is possible that a researcher may actually be measuring different things for different people. While we recognize that, from a practical perspective, it is impossible for a researcher to know whether both assumptions have been met prior to the data collection, we argue that the testing of these hypotheses should precede all multigroup analyses. Should evidence of noninvariance be found, the researcher can then address the problem. Indeed, we believe that, by being cognizant of issues related to noninvariance, SC researchers can take several steps to minimize this possibility; these include:

1. Selecting measuring instruments that have been widely tested, preferably across groups, and have demonstrated sound psychometric properties;
2. Paying particular attention to the administration of testing instruments to ensure that members of all groups receive the same explanations, and the same amount of time in which to respond to the allotted items. In the case of young children, or those who may be mentally handicapped, SC items should be read aloud and explained by way of a related example; and
3. Allowing for a post hoc investigation of psychometric artifacts by the conduct of secondary analyses.

Should differential properties in the measuring instrument or differential relations among the multidimensional facets of SC be detected, such artifacts should be reported as an aid to future research. Moreover, in the case of noninvariant measurement, the researcher might consider reanalyzing his or her data with problematic items deleted from the analyses.

IMPLICATIONS FOR SELF-CONCEPT
RESEARCH ACROSS THE LIFESPAN

In the previous section we noted that SC can differ across groups with respect to both its structure and its measurement. We also suggested ways in which to minimize these differences for substantive research in general. We turn now to the more specific implication of these findings for substantive research involving multigroup comparisons at various stages of the life cycle.

Potential Differences in SC Structure

In the initial postulation of their hierarchical model of SC, Shavelson and colleagues (1976) hypothesized that SC structure becomes increasingly differentiated with increased age, and such multidimensionality stabilizes by late adolescence. Indeed, ample empirical evidence now supports their thesis (Damon & Hart 1982; Hughes 1984. See also chapter 2 of this volume.). This fact has very serious implications for SC research involving group comparisons, particularly as it relates to children. To ensure findings that can be meaningfully interpreted, it is imperative that researchers conduct comparisons among groups known to have the same dimensional structure of SC. For example, in the development of SC instruments for school-age children, researchers have distinguished between preschoolers, early and late preadolescents, and early and late adolescents (Hughes, 1984. See also chapter 2 of this volume.).

Unfortunately, empirical research bearing on the validation of SC structure across various stages of adulthood is blatantly absent in the literature. To date, it has been assumed that the structure remains invariant across this age span. Nevertheless, the question of whether SC structure changes as one approaches old age has yet to be tested.

Potential Differences in SC Measurement

While it is generally recognized that multiple and maximally different measures of a construct provide more accurate assessments for both children (Ollendick & Meador 1984) and adults (Haynes 1984), the measurement of SC has been most commonly limited to self-reports and ratings by significant others, such as teachers, parents, spouses, and health care workers. Nevertheless, a wide variety of self-report measures is available (Breytspraak & George 1982; Wylie 1974). These instruments in particular can have an important impact on differential SC measurements across the life span. Since caveats related to the use of these self-report measures vary somewhat for children, young to middle-aged adults, and the elderly, we now address the issues for each of these groups separately.

Children. The most distinguishing characteristic of children is developmental change which reflects itself most saliently in terms of their cognitive abilities, attention span, memory capacity, and test-taking skills (Hughes 1984; Ollendick & Meador 1984). These developmental considerations are important in the measurement of children's SCs for at least two reasons.

First, they bear importantly on a child's ability to understand the question posed by a test item, and the method of response required to answer it. Second, the psychometric properties, as well as the developmental sensitivity of self-report measures, are known to vary with age (Ollendick & Meador 1984).

Thus, in testing for mean group differences in SC using self-report measures, it is critical that the groups represent the same age cohort and that empirical evidence of psychometric soundness based on that age group be known for the assessment measure used.

Adults. Different life experiences can have an important bearing on both the interpretation and response to psychological test items by adults comprising different age cohorts. Two factors that are known to be particularly relevant are educational background and health status (Lawton & Storandt 1984). The extent and quality of one's education can reflect on his or her ability to both understand and respond to a particular test item. For example, many late middle-aged adults have obtained much less formal education than have their younger counterparts. Thus, a comparison of SC scores across these two age cohorts may render the scores differentially valid.

Likewise, health-related factors may bear importantly on perceptions of self by different age cohorts of adults. For example, in a review of thirty years of research on well-being, Larson (1978) reported health as having a major influence on life satisfaction. Indeed, there is evidence to suggest that certain disorders that increasingly accompany late middle-age (such as arthritis, glaucoma, and hypertension) may influence the SC scores (Lawton & Storandt 1984).

In addition to considerations of education and health status, the assessment of SC for adults is further complicated by the lack of appropriate age norms as well as published data on validity and

reliability as related to the measuring instruments. Thus, to minimize the possibility of differentially valid test items across adult age
cohorts, it is recommended that the researcher determine information related to both the educational and health factors prior to drawing his or her comparative samples.

The Elderly.   In addition to the factors of educational background and health status already noted, methodological effects of visual presentation and time limits—as well as the physiological
effects of fatigue, cautiousness, psychomotor speed, and memory—
have been shown to have an important impact on SC scores derived
from the self-reports of elderly respondents (Lawton & Storandt
1984). For these reasons, it has been recommended that certain
compromises related to the length and response demands of self-
report inventories be made for older persons. For example, the use of
fourteen-point rather than nine-point type in printing the items, allowing for more time to complete the items, and reducing the overall
length of the test itself have all been shown to improve test performance (Lawton & Storandt 1984).

While it is important to be cognizant of the test-taking problems of the elderly, the researcher, at the same time, must be careful
not to overcompensate for age handicaps where none exist. Thus, in
multigroup comparative research it is once again important to emphasize the need to screen for such handicaps prior to the selection
of the groups under study.

We have offered a number of caveats bearing on multigroup
comparisons in general, and as they relate to particular stages of the
life span in particular. We hope that, by heightening awareness to
problems associated with mean comparisons across groups, and by
emphasizing the importance of the SC structures being measured,
SC research will benefit richly from the evolution of more consistent findings. Ultimately, this should lead to more fruitful efforts in
advancing our present knowledge of the self.

In summation, multigroup comparisons—whether across age
or across other grouping variables—are tricky because the innocent
comparison of means is based on a vast set of assumptions about the
structure underlying the measurements in particular populations.
More insightful might be the comparison of SC structures.

Indeed, based on our limited research, we know that SC structure does change across at least a portion of the life span, namely
from preschool age through late adolescence. We have consistently
found SC to be increasingly more differentiated with age to the point

where, by late adolescence, some facets of SC are virtually uncorrelated with other facets. We wonder whether this independence among SC facets continues into later adulthood. As we have spelled out in this chapter, such evidence clearly underscores the importance of comparing SC structures in an attempt to understand differences in SC across the life span.

NOTES

1. Secondary factor loadings are synonymous with cross-loadings and represent the nontarget loading of an item onto a factor for which it was not designed to measure.

2. Congeneric tests are defined as those measuring "the same trait except for errors of measurement" (Jöreskog 1971, 109).

3. The item was "I am masculine——— I am feminine."

4. The four-factor solution was not clear for the API. For both sexes, only ten to twenty-five items designed to measure academic SC loaded on that factor. Of the remaining items, ten loaded on general SC, four on mathematics SC, and one on English SC. A subsequent three-factor solution yielded three clearly defined factors for each sex.

5. The PCSC has recently been revised, and many of the modifications address the areas of concern cited in the present study. Two new subscales designed to measure perceived physical appearance and behavioral competence have been added (Harter 1985). Of particular importance here, however, is that the problematic items reported by Byrne and Schneider (1988) have either been deleted (PPC4) or incorporated into the behavioral competence subscale (PGS4; PGS2—item 2). Additionally, items 17 and 21, which measure cognitive competence, have been respectively reworded or deleted. The revised instrument has also undergone a name change; it is now titled *Self-Perception Profile for Children*.

REFERENCES

Alwin, D. F., and Jackson, D. J. 1981. Applications of simultaneous factor analysis to issues of factorial invariance. In *Factor analysis and measurement in sociological research: A multidimensional perspective*, edited by D. D. Jackson and E. P. Borgatta. Beverly Hills, Calif.: Sage. 249–280.

Bejar, I. I. 1980. Biased assessment of program impact due to psychometric artifacts. *Psychological Bulletin*, 87:513–524.

Benson, J. 1987. Detecting item bias in affective scales. *Educational and Psychological Measurement 47:55–67.*

Bentler, P. M., and Bonett, D. G. 1980. Significance tests and goodness-of-fit in the analysis of covariance structures. *Psychological Bulletin* 88:588–606.

Breytspraak, L. M., and George, L. K. 1982. Self-concept and self-esteem. In *Research Instruments in Social Gerontology.* Vol. 1. Clinical and Social Psychology, edited by D. J. Mangen and W. A. Peterson. Minneapolis: University of Minnesota Press.

Brookover, W. B. 1962. *Self-concept of Ability Scale.* East Lansing, Mich.: Educational Publication Services.

Byrne, B. M. 1984. The general/academic self-concept nomological network: A review of construct validation research. *Review of Educational Research 54:427–456.*

———. 1988a. Measuring adolescent self-concept: Factorial validation and equivalency of the SDQ III across gender. *Multivariate Behavioral Research 24:361–375.*

———. 1988b. The Self Description Questionnaire III: Testing for equivalent factorial validity across ability. *Educational and Psychological Measurement 48:397–406.*

———. 1989. *A Primer of LISREL: Basic applications and programming for confirmatory factor analytic models.* New York: Springer-Verlag.

———. 1990. A comparative review of methodological approaches to the validation of academic self-concept: The construct and its measures. *Applied Measurement in Education 3:185–207.*

Byrne, B. M., and Schneider, B. H. 1988. Perceived Competence Scale for Children: Testing for factorial validity and invariance across age and ability. *Applied Measurement in Education 1:171–187.*

Byrne, B. M., and Shavelson, R. J. 1986. On the structure of adolescent self-concept. *Journal of Educational Psychology 78(5):474–481.*

———. 1987. Adolescent self-concept: Testing for assumption of equivalent structure across gender. *American Educational Research Journal* 24:365–385.

Byrne, B. M.; Shavelson, R. J.; and Muthén, B. 1989. Testing for the equivalence of factor covariance and mean structures: The issue of partial measurement invariance. *Psychological Bulletin* 105:456–466.

Cole, D. A., and Maxwell, S. E. 1985. Multitrait multimethod comparisons across populations: A confirmatory factor analytic approach. *Multivariate Behavioral Research* 20:389–417.

Damon, W., and Hart, D. 1982. The development of self-understanding from infancy through adolescence. *Child Development* 53:841–864.

Drasgow, F., and Kanfer, R. 1985. Equivalence of psychological measurement in heterogeneous populations. *Journal of Applied Psychology* 70:662–680.

Green, D. R. 1975. What does it mean to say a test is biased? *Education and Urban Society* 8:33–52.

Hansford, B. C., and Hattie, J. A. 1982. The relationship between self and achievement/performance measures. *Review of Educational Research* 52:123–142.

Harter, S. 1982. The Perceived Competence Scale for Children. *Child Development* 53:87–97.

———. 1985. *Manual for the Self-Perception Profile for Children.* Denver, Colo.: University of Denver.

Haynes, S. N. 1984. Behavioral assessment of adults. In *Handbook of Psychological Assessment,* edited by G. Goldstein and M. Hersen. New York: Pergamon 369–401.

Hughes, H. M. 1984. Measures of self-concept and self-esteem for children ages 3–12 years; A review and recommendations. *Clinical Psychology Review* 4:657–692.

Jöreskog, K. G. 1971. Simultaneous factor analysis in several populations. *Psychometrika* 36:409–426.

Jöreskog, K. G., and Sörbom, D. 1985. *LISREL VI: Analysis of Linear Structure Relationships by the Method of Maximum Likelihood.* Mooresville, Ind.: Scientific Software.

Kaplan, D. 1988. The impact of specification error on the estimation, testing, and improvement of structural equation models. *Multivariate Behavioral Research* 23:69–86.

LaBenne, W. D., and Greene, B. I. 1969. *Educational implications of self-concept theory.* Pacific Palisades, Calif.: Goodyear.

Larson, R. 1978. Thirty years of research on subjective well-being of older Americans. *Journal of Gerontology* 33:109–125.

Lawton, M. P., and Storandt, M. 1984. Clinical and functional approaches to the assessment of older people. In *Advances in Psychological Assessment,* edited by P. McReynolds and G. J. Chelune. San Francisco: Jossey-Bass. 236–276.

MacCallum, R. 1986. Specification searches in covariance structure modeling. *Psychological Bulletin* 100:107–120.

Marsh, H. W.; Barnes, J.; Cairns, L.; and Tidman, M. 1984. Self Description Questionnaire: Age and sex effects in the structure and level of self-concept for preadolescent children. *Journal of Educational Psychology* 76:940–956.

Marsh, H. W.; Byrne, B. M.; and Shavelson, R. J. 1988. A multifaceted academic self-concept: Its hierarchical structure and its relation to academic achievement. *Journal of Educational Psychology* 80:366–380.

Marsh, H. W., and Hocevar, D. 1985. Application of confirmatory factor analysis to the study of self-concept: First-and higher order factor models and their invariance across groups. *Psychological Bulletin* 97(3):562–582.

Marsh, H. W., and O'Neill, R. 1984. Self Description Questionnaire III: The construct validity of multidimensional self-concept ratings by late adolescents. *Journal of Educational Measurement* 21:153–174.

Munck, I. M. E. 1979. *Model building in comparative education: Applications of the LISREL method to cross-national survey data.* Stockholm, Sweden: Almquist & Wiksul International.

Muthén, B., and Kaplan, D. 1985. A comparison of methodologies for the factor analysis of nonnormal Likert variables. *British Journal of Mathematical and Statistical Psychology* 38:171–189.

Marsh, H. W.; Balla, J. R.; and McDonald, R. P. 1988. Goodness-of-fit indexes in confirmatory factor analysis: The effect of sample size. *Psychological Bulletin* 103:391–410.

Ollendick, T. H., and Meador, A. E. 1984. Behavioral assessment of children. In *Handbook of Psychological Assessment,* edited by G. Goldstein and M. Hersen. New York: Pergamon. 351–368.

Reynolds, C. R., and Harding, R. E. 1983. Outcome in two large sample studies of factorial similarity under six methods of comparison. *Educational and Psychological Measurement* 43:723–728.

Rock, D. A.; Werts, C. E.; and Flaugher, R. L. 1978. The use of analysis of covariance structures for comparing the psychometric properties of multiple variables across populations. *Multivariate Behavioral Research* 13:403–418.

Rosenberg, M. 1965. *Society and the adolescent self-image.* Princeton: Princeton University Press.

Shavelson, R. J., and Stuart, K. R. 1981. Application of causal modeling methods to the validation of self-concept interpretations of test scores. In *Self-concept: Advances in theory and research,* edited by M. D.

Lynch, A. A. Norem-Hebeisen, and K. J. Gergen. Cambridge, Mass.: Ballinger. 223–235.

Shavelson, R. J.; Hubner, J. J.; and Stanton, G. C. 1976. Self-concept: Validation of construct interpretations. *Review of Educational Research* 46:407–441.

Soares, A. T., and Soares, L. M. 1979. *The Affective Perception Inventory— Advanced Level.* Trumell, Colo.: ALSO.

Sobel, M. E., and Bohrnstedt, G. W. 1985. Use of null models in evaluating the fit of covariance structure models. In *Sociological methodology,* edited by N. B. Tuma. San Francisco: Jossey-Bass. 152–178.

Wells, L. E., and Marwell, G. 1976. *Self-esteem: Its conceptualization and measurement.* Beverly Hills, Calif.: Sage.

West, C. K., and Fish, J. A. 1973. *Relationships between self-concept and school achievement: A survey of empirical investigations.* Final Report for the National Institute of Education. Urbana, Ill.

West, C. K.; Fish, J. A.; and Stevens, R. J. 1980. General self-concept, self-concept of academic ability and school achievement: Implications for "causes" of self-concept. *The Australian Journal of Education* 24(2):194–213.

Wylie, R. C. 1974. *The self-concept: A review of methodological considerations and measuring instruments.* Lincoln: University of Nebraska Press.

————. 1979. *The self-concept.* Vol. 2: Theory and research on selected topics. Lincoln: University of Nebraska Press.

————. 1989. *Measures of self-concept.* Lincoln: University of Nebraska Press.

Zirkel, P. A. 1971. Self-concept and the "disadvantage" of ethnic group membership and mixture. *Review of Educational Research* 41:211–225.

6

Significant Others in Self-esteem Development: Methods and Problems in Measurement

INTRODUCTION

The importance of significant others in self-esteem development is grounded in symbolic interaction theory (Cooley 1912; Mead 1934; Sullivan 1947). According to this perspective, there are three aspects to how significant others affect people's self-esteem: self-appraisals, the actual appraisals of significant others, and reflected appraisals. Reflected appraisals are one's perceptions of others' perceptions conveyed through responses to the self. These appraisals will be important to a person's self-esteem, provided the focus is a self-dimension considered to be important to that individual's feeling of worth. Also, the "other" must be considered as significant relative to that self-attribute at the specific time and place.

In self-esteem development, significance is important from four perspectives:

1. The esteem value of the specific characteristic or behavior,
2. The "fit" between the latter and the situation,
3. The person's perceptions of the other's appraisal, and
4. The person's perceptions of the other's significance.

In order to have a significant impact on another's self-esteem, one must know what the other considers to be important to his or her feelings of worth. Providing appraisals and feedback about behaviors, attitudes, or knowledge which are of no interest or concern to the other will not impact on his or her esteem. Also, feedback which is situationally incongruous is unlikely to be effective.

Familiarity with role requirements and the other's personal and maturational factors specific to the situation is necessary to identify the focus of another's evaluative appraisal. In other words, the situation must also be significant. The other must consider you to be significant and value your appraisal of him or her.

Determining the relationship between significant others and self-esteem development requires various measures. Two measures provide the baseline data. First, we must know on what the individual stakes his or her feelings of worth—that is, the content of the esteem constellation—in general as well as in specific situations. Second, we need to know on what characteristics and behaviors the individual bases his or her evaluations of another's significance. Because both esteem and significance are highly subjective and personal in nature, designing psychometrically sound measures that are useful with different populations poses many problems.

Although no psychometrically sound instruments are available to prove the point, social interaction theory suggests that the significant others in one's life affect the level of self-esteem and the focus of its development. From a broader perspective, significance can be examined in terms of self-attributes considered as significant enough to provide a base for esteem. Also, we must ask if others are the only or an essential influence on self-esteem.

Questions about the who and why of significance and the relationship of significant persons to another's self-esteem are more difficult than they appear to be, especially when measurement is involved. The uniqueness of the self, the multifaceted situation-specific nature of esteem, and the range of possible significance attributes contribute to a massive pool of interrelated factors. Even more complex are solutions to measurement problems which rest on the accuracy of the appraisal processes which are embedded in self-esteem development. Research and theory offer only partial answers to these difficulties.

SIGNIFICANCE, OTHERS, AND ESTEEM

Do others influence what goes into the self-esteem constellation? Do we need others to bolster our esteem, or can we manage on our own? Do the intersecting paths of the developing individual and the changing society determine significant-other constellations? These intriguing questions concern the design of measures of significant others and self-esteem.

A variety of theorists conceive of the individual as functioning autonomously to fulfill his or her needs and reach his or her potentials. They have conceptualized the self as process, as object, and as knower, distinguishing between the actively perceiving, experiencing, and thinking part of the self and its material, social, and spiritual dimensions (Baldwin 1897; Cooley 1912; James 1890; Mead 1934). The unconscious, the biologically based, and the intuitive, creative, and impulsive aspects of self function not only within society interactively but also autonomously.

Allport's conception in 1961 of "functional autonomy" suggests that a given form of behavior may become a goal in itself, and his idea of propriate striving views the individual pursuing self-defined projects geared to enhancing one's own becoming. Individuals at the self-actualized stage of Maslow (1954) or the highest level of moral development as described by Kohlberg (1973) would be self-motivated. Others would not influence a person's feelings of worth.

From these theoretical bases emerges the view of individuals in charge of their own esteem development. The process of comparison of self with ideal self does not necessarily require another's opinions.

Social comparison theory suggests that reference groups—both those to which an individual belongs and those in which he or she does not have membership—can also influence self-appraisals (Festinger 1954; Hyman 1942; Suls & Miller 1977). In 1985, Niedenthal, Cantor, and Kihlstrom proposed a process of "prototype matching." They reasoned that people match their concepts of themselves with their concepts of people who have selected specific options. In the process, the individual questions whether or not he or she is the kind of person who would select the option which others have selected. The basis for real–ideal self-comparison may also originate in external factors, such as the mass media, impersonal groups, or historical events.

While real–ideal self-comparison probably takes place at both the conscious and unconscious levels, status by association may also impact on esteem. A Chicago Cubs fan, a member of Hitler's youth group, and a Viet Nam veteran engender diverse feelings of worth or value even if no significant other shares their experiences or provides feedback to them. Interest should also be placed on the formation of the esteem base, incorporating behaviors or characteristics modeled after media personalities as a measure of self-worth.

In establishing the importance of the self versus others, we must know if the specific characteristics that are valued, and are therefore significant, are related to global self-esteem—the "I like me. I'm a worthwhile person" feeling. We also need to focus on the importance of group norms and group identity. Hoge and McCarthy, working in 1984 from James's assumption in 1890 that the significance of specific characteristics depends upon what is important to an individual (or on what one has a stake in), found that group identity salience is important to adolescents. Group identity provides an effective but rather narrow, highly valued specific range of self-dimensions.

Ratings of the importance of specific dimensions are matters of strong group consensus. Hoge and McCarthy (1984) conclude that, the wider the range of specific dimensions available to any one person and the greater the freedom to choose among them, the stronger will be the influence of individual (versus group) identity salience on global self-esteem. Thus, one can see that the influence of individual identity salience may vary across age, gender, race, and class.

Do we need others' feedback in order to maintain a positive, realistic level of self-esteem? Probably so, especially if being realistic is a requirement. However, the feedback of others, especially that which is related to achievement, may be no more realistic than our own.

Most of the significant others in one's life are enmeshed in shared social groups and relationships. From these develop a self which has both unity and heterogeneity. Individuals have a variety of specific abilities and habits, physical and personal features, and roles. These may vary across situations. Thus, we can view the person as a multiplicity of selves, corresponding to different situations, tasks, or relationships. These may change, expand, or be reduced in conjunction with developmental, occupational and familial life history.

Throughout the life span, the individual is simultaneously interacting with and reacting to the changing society, actively processing information about the situation and the others in it in relation to the changing self. This leads to the possibility of a varied, changing potential pool of others who may assume temporal or permanent significance to one's esteem.

Theory and research have identified developmental competencies for specific age levels and important others in children's social environments. There also appears to be a common content core on which self-esteem rests. Burns (1979) provided an overview and summary of relevant research. (See also Shirk & Renouf in press; Demo & Savin-Williams in press).

With the publication of Shavelson's hierarchical multitrait model of the self-concept (Shavelson, Hubner & Stanton 1976), student/teacher self-rating scales have focused on teachers, parents, and peers as significant others, with academic achievement, appearance, and physical abilities as content areas. Marsh's Self Description Questionnaire (Marsh, Smith & Barnes 1983) is the most widely used self-report measure at the moment. This measure recognizes that feelings of worth can be specific to certain attributes and situations and allows for comparison of ratings. However, the aspect of significance cannot be measured. We do not know if the factors really matter to the child or impact upon his feeling of esteem, although Marsh argued in 1986 that the importance of specific self-esteem dimensions does not increase prediction of global self-esteem relative to unweighted dimensions (see chapter 2 of this volume).

In 1976, Hewitt distinguished between situations (current interactions) and biographies (the sum total of internalized evaluations of the self) which make up an individual's current self-esteem. This distinction is especially important in a life-span perspective on self-esteem development and the significant others who impact upon it. The older an individual, the more identity stages will have passed, the more complex one's biography and range of interaction partners, and the more persistent a particular style of self-evaluation will be. Individual uniqueness characterizes these developmental processes and outcomes, including a unique set of significant others, some of whom were chosen and some of whom were imposed. The situated self and the biographical self both react to significant others relative to the self's interpretation of the situational identity and the enduring identity. Whitbourne's cognitive conception in 1985 of the life-span construct as a unified sense of past, present, and future events linked by their common occurrence to the individual is similar to this notion.

Relevant to this discussion of situational identity is the part played by roles which are generated by norms, beliefs, and preferences, and which are defined differently in time and place. For example, Fallow-Mitchell and Ryff referred in 1982 to "social clocks" that serve to sanction the appropriate times for events in the female life cycle. However, they noted wide variation according to one's cohort membership.

Juhasz (1989a) proposed a triple-helix role model of adult development in which the drive for positive self-esteem is the power that energizes and directs individuals to concentrate on selected work, family, and self-development roles at various times in their lives. For some of the time, some individuals will be able to balance and coordinate all three major roles, combining esteem elements from each and feeling good about the self relative to each. At other times a single role may assume importance, and individuals with whom one interacts in a specific setting will become most significant for esteem feedback. Viewing role priority as the focus of self-esteem allows identification of others who may be significant.

From the Eriksonian perspective on life-span psychosocial development, one would predict greater situational complexity with a wider range of significant others and a different self-perspective beginning at adolescence. The concept of a complementarity of what Erikson calls history and life history suggests that the development of psychosocial identity is not feasible before adolescence. This raises important questions about the stability of self-esteem, the constancy of choice of significant others, and the most productive and reliable indices of adolescent self-esteem (Demo & Savin-Williams in press). These same questions could be relevant to adults at transitional stages in life, when loss of identity occurs through job displacement, death of a spouse, or disability. In these cases, the adolescent identity cycle must be worked through again, but this time with a different life history (Juhasz 1982a) and a different set of significant others.

Developmental theory leads us to expect that the ability to maintain realistic positive feelings of self-esteem, independent of feedback from significant others, varies across the life span. Erikson's psychosocial stage theory, published in 1950, designates tasks to be resolved and others who play a role in these processes, and also provides one set of competencies on which esteem rests. He designated specific others as being significant, beginning at infancy with the maternal care giver, centering the person in more and increasingly complex social systems through midlife, and ending in old age with self-reflection and decreased involvement with others.

It is helpful to have a generalizable framework as a starting point when examining the impact of others on self-esteem relative to different sources of influence. Age-related developmental shifts will influence children's ways of evaluating self and their dependence on others. Lynch postulated in 1981 that children between the ages of six and nine are developing the concept of an idealized self, and thus the discrepancy between the idealized self and the real self can be measured. In 1985, Saba pointed out that children from nine to thirteen years of age are in a "transitional state from childhood to adolescence" (Saba 1985, 564). Thus, while these children still need security, they are also developing needs for independence from adults. Shirk and Renouf (in press) describe several developmental tasks that children in this age range must resolve.

One could expect less reliance on significant others' feedback as individuals move through the life cycles (Suls & Mullen 1982). However, at certain times when physiological and cognitive developmental changes are impacting on identity formation (such as in adolescence), we can predict greater reliance on others' opinions.

Erikson noted in 1968 that adolescents in search of self "try to find someone more knowledgeable than family members, someone who can somehow peer into the past and predict future events" (Erikson 1968, 257). Similarly, any crisis or unexpected event in the life of the individual or in the social network could shift the balance of esteem from positive to negative or to an entirely different focus. Divorce, job change, illness, or a move to a new location may shake up the esteem components necessitating rebuilding and reassurance from others.

Mature adults should have something for which they stand even if they stand alone. These values become a part of one's identity. Some would call these the basic personality traits, global self-esteem components, or habitual ways of responding. Earlier in the life cycle, such attitudes, values, or behaviors were probably reinforced by significant others, until they gradually become incorporated into the stabilized, consistent conception of the self on which esteem rests. Honesty, dependability, and fairness are attributes of this type. In old age, there may be a shift toward increased autonomy and reliance on one's own self-evaluations. There may be few others left who are significant. With spouses dead, children wed, and friends spread far and wide, many seniors must stake their feelings of worth on their own evaluations of past achievements or just on having outlived many of their cohorts. (Suls & Mullen 1982).

At any point in time, the individual can identify appropriate role models and conduct real/ideal self-appraisals. One can also grant significance to others and incorporate their appraisals into evaluations of self-worth. Moreover, and more importantly, it is obvious that the interactionist view of significance is not comprehensive enough. It only includes the processes of feedback and appraisal relative to the content of one's esteem. Significance begins when one decides to stake oneself upon something specific. Someone or something is instrumental in motivating that decision.

NEW PERSPECTIVES ON OLD PROBLEMS

The problems with measures of significance originate with the nature of significance and the accuracy of perception. Significance is multifaceted and multifunctional, in both product and process. It is a factor in determining the content and basis of esteem as well as in developing and maintaining it.

The importance of significance for self-esteem rests on philosophical and psychological premises which also give rise to difficult questions. These bear directly upon the roles of significant others in the development of self-esteem and upon measurement. The situational self, the biographical self, and the historical self which intersect in the search for identity are incorporated in the esteem base. Our research efforts focus on situational components, especially when seeking to identify significant others.

Biographically, one's life history—those genetic and environmental factors which have had an impact from birth until the present—also become significant esteem components (see chapter 1 of this volume). The historical past assumes special importance at adolescence, and its potential for significance is often overlooked (Erikson 1968; Juhasz 1982a, 1982b). These varied views of self extend the arena of significant others and the value base for self-esteem.

An important question concerns the control and sequencing of the components of self-esteem. We do not know if there is a logical sequence or an optimal number of significant self-esteem components. Nor do we know who or what controls the possibilities for experiencing or incorporating attributes of self which ought to be included in the esteem constellation. Equally important is the developmental progress from being other-directed to becoming significance-director. All of these concerns open avenues for productive research on the role of both self and other in self-esteem development.

The first seeds of significance lie in the values which adults instill in children and youth through teaching and example. Interactions with parents, teachers, relatives, and others, and the reinforcement of desired behaviors and attitudes, earn significance for these adults. Beginning in childhood and continuing throughout the life span, individuals' core role structures evolve from their concepts of who they are in relationship to significant others. The continuing process of self-evaluation, comparing real with ideal behavior and receiving feedback from others, is directed by the need for self-consistency.

Intriguing research questions are contained in Erikson's conception of mutual adaptation of self to others and vice versa published in 1968, and Broughton's allusion in 1983 to persuading the other to view one the way one views oneself. Does the significant other who sends me an esteem-building message perceive this action as self-enhancing, thus impacting on his or her own esteem? Is there reciprocity of significance?

Furthermore, is the initial feedback of the significant other motivated by the desire for self-enhancement? If I am able to convince you to view me as I view myself, do I get a "double dose" of esteem "medicine?" Do I feel good about myself because I have persuaded you (my need for power) as well as because your feedback compliments my behavior or attitude?

Accurate perception of esteem-related messages and their meanings by interactants is the key to addressing these issues and also raises more questions for researchers. For example, do we presently have available the insight, evidence, and theoretical base needed to examine the perceptual processes inherent in self-esteem development? Do we have effective methods and materials for investigating these processes and their influence on feelings of worthwhileness? A communications-system model of information processing which focuses on perception of significance and esteem provides a basic theoretical perspective.

In a simple one-on-one encounter, players in the self-esteem game, through their verbal and nonverbal communication patterns, can assume the role of the perceiver or the perceived. Each can provide for the other feedback that is meant to convey esteem-building or esteem-destroying messages. The receiver of the message will determine the extent to which he or she, as a result, feels worthwhile or significant. This in turn may be translated into a significance rating for the message sender.

In the basic communications-system model (McCreary & Surkan 1965; Shannon & Weaver 1949), processing involves sampling, filtering, coding, matching, and decoding. The individual receiving feedback about self-worth from a significant other uses these same basic processes as he or she decodes varied perceptions into an appraisal of self-worth. The significant other's response or feedback may be both verbal and nonverbal, and it can consist of multiple cues and clues. The individual samples these, filtering out those that are relevant in content and context, coding these into self-descriptor categories, and matching those which relate to specific esteem dimensions. This results in a decoded message about self-worth.

An individual's habitual reaction pattern coalesces into the self-system. This tends to focus attention on those interactions with the significant other person which get approbation or disfavor. Selective filtering and inattention are used by the self-system in order to maintain the self-image which is founded on others' reflected appraisals.

In an investigation of the self-perpetuating development of encoding biases in person perception, Hill, Lewicki, Czyzewska, and Bos in 1989 defined encoding as *interpretive*. Much of the encoding that we do, before being placed in storage, must be further processed, interpreted, and categorized. In a series of experiments, subjects' interpretations of cognitively directed materials were biased in a self-supportive direction. These researchers note that, "Given the ambiguity of many (particularly social) stimuli, the self-perpetuation process may play a ubiquitous role in the development of interpretive categories and other individually differentiated cognitive dispositions" (Hill et al. 1989, 373).

Perceptual biases could develop and perpetuate in a similar fashion when others' appraisals of self are the subject of interpretation. It is important and relevant that supportive evidence for the bias is not necessary in order for self-perpetuating encoding to continue and to strengthen. Hill and colleagues believed that much of this encoding is nonconscious. If this is true for cognitive materials, then we can expect processing appraisals by others who are significant (with a strong affective component) to have similar characteristics such as being nonconscious, independent of supportive evidence, and biased in a self-perpetuating direction.

In 1988, Kenny posed seven basic research questions in interpersonal perception concerning issues of consensus, assimilation, reciprocity, accuracy, congruence, assumed similarity, and self-other agreement. He addressed some of these questions at the dyadic level and all of them at the individual level using a social relations model. A basic issue that he identified—significant others' perceptions—is relevant to our topic. "In person perception, there are multiple perspectives. One can view the other, the self, and the other's view of self. How can these perspectives be integrated?" (Kenny 1988, 248).

Kenny's model incorporates ideas on perspective-taking exemplified by Laing and his colleagues. "Human beings are constantly thinking about others and what others are thinking about them and what they think they are thinking about others, and so on" (Laing, Phillipson & Lee 1966, 30).

Kenny noted that because of methodological problems in research on interpersonal perception, little has been accomplished since the 1950s. His research attempted to confront these problems.

He partitioned perspectives on social relations into three components.

1. *Other appraisal* (how *A* views *B*);
2. *Reflected appraisal* (how *A* thinks *B* views *A*). This includes the actor (*A*'s view of how others view *A*), the partner (how *B* is viewed as viewing others), and the relationship (*A*'s unique view of how *B* views *A*); *and*
3. *Self-appraisal* (how *A* views *A*).

The major problems in accuracy of perception in interpersonal communication revolve around consensus, objectivity, accuracy, and bias.

Kenny pointed to the importance of consensus when determining self-other agreement. He asked, "If others do not agree when rating a person, how can we expect the self to agree with others?" (1988, 256). If there is agreement, is it because, as symbolic interactionists would argue, the other influences the self? Or is it, as Felson suggested in 1981, that both perceivers judge the target using a common set of cues?

Kenny's concept of congruence is also important in influencing perceptions in that, if *A* likes *B*, *A* thinks that *B* likes *A*. However, the congruence effects noted for affective variables are much smaller when looking at other domains. For example, DePaulo, Kenny, Hoover, Webb, and Oliver (1987) found that if a person believes that his or her partner is competent at a task, the person does not necessarily think that the partner sees him or her as competent. Thus, objectivity does not necessarily result in consensus nor vice versa.

The problems of reciprocity and objectivity were also noted by Broughton in 1983. According to Erikson (1968), one's ability to maintain inner sameness and continuity is matched by the sameness and continuity of one's meaning for others. This requires mutual adaptation of self to others. Broughton pointed out that, while this type of match can be negotiated, "neither the augmenting of one's own confidence and self-esteem, nor persuading the other to view one the way one views oneself, can guarantee objectivity" (1983, 247).

Moreover, since consensus is vital, meaning and contextual integration are stressed, demanding adherence to traditional forms of social meaning. In turn, this results in the sacrifice of objectivity in the understanding of self by both the self and the other, which, according to Cassirer (1923), amounts to an equally deleterious sacrifice of true subjectivity. Influenced by social contexts, true objectivity appears to be unachievable.

Affective components of interpersonal interactions also hinder true objectivity. Results of research by Hymel in 1986 indicated that, as with adults, both children and adolescents vary their perceptions and explanations of the behavior of peers as a function of whether they like or dislike the individual. This interpretive bias operates in the service of maintaining affectively congruent perceptions of others. Behavior of disliked peers, relative to that of liked peers, is interpreted in a negative fashion. Children are more likely to minimize or deny responsibility for negative actions of liked peers and to attribute negative actions of disliked peers to stable basic characteristics. Thus, it appears that, once a child is disliked by peers, a no-win situation is established whereby positive actions are interpreted as accidental and negative ones as predispositioned (Demo & Savin-Williams in press). These interpretations are perceptions which influence children's responses to peers. This trend toward bias in interpretion of peer behavior emerges at about seven or eight years of age (Livesley & Bromley 1973) and increases with age (Hymel 1986). In summary, the complex interpretations of behavior by interacting peers are colored by their feelings for one another.

Perceptions are key components in the interactionist approach to self-esteem development. We experience our world through the meaning which we attach to the behavior of others (Kelly 1955) and, through experience and interactions with others, we learn how they see us and what they expect (Allport 1961). However, what is *perceived* may not be what *is*. Both the current state of the organism and the environment, as well as previously established self-perceptions, will influence self-evaluations. Sources of bias and inaccuracy of perception are persistent problems. Other problems will emerge as multicultural life-span research increases.

Accuracy of perception rests, in large part, on the ability to take the other's role. Zurcher distinguished between *making* and *taking* roles, saying that when we *make* roles, we try to create the roles in line with our own inclinations. When we *take* roles we attempt to conform to our perceptions of others' expectations for our behavior (1977, 14).

Cooley pointed to the difficulty of accurately perceiving what another thinks, noting that one can make a judgment only of the other's view. His "looking-glass self" involves "the imagination of our appearance to the other person [and] the imagination of his judgment of that appearance. . . . it is the imputed sentiment, the imagined effect of this reflection upon another mind" (1912, 152).

Developmental level and cultural, social, situational, and motivational factors can color our expectations of role-related behaviors and our perceptions of them. These differences in perception may account for reported variation in self-esteem of children under different circumstances. Brittain (1963, 1966) found that the relative influence of parents and peers on adolescents is determined by the situation. Emmerich (1978) reported sex and age as important variables, and Silvernail (1986) noted lower female self-esteem when teachers were also female. Kawash, Kerr, and Clewes (1986) reported that variations in levels of children's self-esteem can be reliably related to variation in their perceptions of parental control, acceptance, and discipline behavior. These research examples demonstrate only a few of the many variables that influence perceptions of self and others. It is important that researchers systematically isolate the most important factors and determine how they impact on self-perception and how others are perceived.

Biases that we bring to our interactions can interfere with our interpretations of others' behaviors, resulting in inaccurate perceptions. This can have serious repercussions and long-lasting effects, especially in the school setting where teacher-pupil perceptions impact on feelings of competence and ability which are the major bases of esteem for children. The research findings on teachers and students provide clarity and understanding to the complicated perceptual network in teacher-pupil, pupil-teacher, and pupil-self perceptions.

Competence is a key component in esteem, and mastery of academic content is critical for children and adolescents. In this setting, the teacher should be perceived as significant, and unbiased accurate perceptions of students should be one key to significance. Comparison of student attitudes toward school and teachers' perceptions of these (Darom & Rich 1988) yield correlations indicating that, in a typical classroom, the teacher evaluates girls' school-related attitudes as more positive than those of boys. Moreover, these differences are greater than those reported by the children. Also, discrepancies between teachers' perceptions and student reports were more exaggerated for some attitudes than for others. The researchers hypothesized that teachers view childrens' problem behaviors as dispositional in nature rather than as situationally influenced, and that this factor directs their perception of relations and attitudes. They also offer the intriguing possibility that this cycle of misperception is intricately interwoven with the concept of "problem ownership" and teachers' unmet needs, as conceptualized by Brophy and Rohrkemper (1981).

The problem of bias is also present in children's misperceptions of teacher behavior. Teachers' verbal feedback, especially that which is public, provides the main clues that lead students to conclude that they are smart and are doing well. Perceptions of teachers' verbal and nonverbal behavior are the main sources used by students in determining how intelligent they are and how well they are doing in class (Weinstein 1981). Silvernail (1986) also noted that children react differently to various types of feedback and situations. The level of kindly, understanding teacher behavior affects Anglos and blacks differently. A medium level had the most positive influence on black self-esteem. A high level had a negative effect for blacks but was positively related to the self-esteem of Anglos. The research of Pintrich and Blumenfeld in 1985 also suggested that children distinguish among different types of feedback and focus on the differential effects of feedback on achievement related self-perceptions.

Students' abilities to perceive and interpret teachers' nonverbal behaviors are influenced by developmental as well as cultural factors. Younger students focus on the speaker's words and voice tones. They also find it easier to interpret the behaviors of individuals from the same cultural background or language community. Girls, on the average, may be better judges of nonverbal meaning, even as early as the preschool years (Woolfolk & Brooks 1985). Children bring to school with them patterns and ways of perceiving others that are linked to culture and background. In a multicultural setting, researchers must take such differences into account.

In summary, many complex personal and situational factors determine children's self-perceptions. The self-contained classroom provides a laboratory for the discovery and analysis of those which are critical in the study of the teacher's impact on the child's self-esteem. Research with this focus has examined teacher characteristics and feedback about children's behavior. Findings indicate a specificity of perceptual focus in the child's interpretation of teacher response to his or her performance. Some children focus on ability, some on effort.

Also, children's self-perceptions of ability and effort are closely related to teachers' feedback about work. The types of feedback, the interactions between classroom context variables, teachers' differential treatment of students, individual classroom experiences, and children's interpretations of these factors will all influence choices of significant other and perception of reflected appraisals about self-worth. Problems of accuracy and bias are linked closely to those of consensus and objectivity. These constructs overlap and intermesh as do the problems inherent in striving to be free of bias, to reach consensus, to be objective, and to be accurate. In interpersonal interactions, perception is clouded, and many factors inhibit realization of the latter goals.

THE CONNECTION: APPRAISAL, SIGNIFICANCE, AND SELF-ESTEEM

The problems of bias and accuracy of perception and their impact on self-esteem hamper the study of significance and its measurement. Questions of the "chicken-egg" order emerge. For example, does self-esteem level influence perception and/or vice versa?

There are also nagging "how" questions such as that posed by Harter and Pike. They asked, "How do the perceived characteristics of others influence one's judgments of social acceptance?" (1984, 1981).

Our focus has been on the impact of perceptions of others' appraisals on level of self-esteem. However, early work by Ludwig and Maehr in 1967 revealed a reverse relationship. The level of self-esteem can influence the interpretation of information about self. Ludwig and Maehr found that, when a person has a high self-evaluation, inconsistent or negative information lowers self-esteem only a little. The reverse holds for low self-evaluation and positive appraisal by others. The self-esteem rating is higher.

Cognitive dissonance theory could explain the tendency to try to maintain or achieve a favorable self-image. Individuals are motivated to form self-enhancing perceptions of others' feedback. Further research may provide insight into two related questions. Is the relationship between feedback from significant others reciprocal?

That is, does the child's level of self-esteem affect the amount of positive feedback which he or she perceives from adults? Or is it a one-way relationship, in which the positive feedback, as measured by children's reports, affects the child's self-esteem?

Significant others are generally viewed in terms of the positive effect which their opinions have on the self-esteem of an individual. Rarely are children questioned about those who impact negatively on feelings of competency or value. Even if this negative component is investigated, the significance aspect is not considered. In order to obtain feedback, one must present oneself to the other, either physically, verbally, or behaviorally. Self-presentations may make little or no difference on the way in which individuals view others. Preconceived stereotypes and biases may make any or all self-presentations irrelevant.

However, Young and Bagley pointed out in 1982 that there are limits to how many other individuals whom one can define as significant as well as how often one can define another person as significant. There are some people whose opinions cannot be ignored forever, no matter how painful they may be.

These researchers also raised an interesting point about the long-range impact on self-esteem by persons who are not viewed as important. Young and Bagley made specific references to teachers who might be considered as insignificant but whose appraisals raise doubts about competence. These doubts might even affect self-esteem long after the child has left school. It appears that we must extend our range of possible significant others and include both positive and negative dimensions in our concept of significance.

Researchers have generally found that the relationship between self-appraisals and reflected appraisals tends to be strong, whereas their relationship to the actual appraisals of significant others are slight (Schrauger & Schoeneman 1979). In 1989, Felson and Zielinski noted low correlations between reports of children and reports of parents on actual parental support, suggesting that these perceptions are not very accurate. Felson and Zielinski postulated a type of reciprocity which could influence both appraisals and perceptions. They stated that "Support increases self-esteem, which increases support (or perceived support), which in turn increases self-esteem" (1989, 733). Based on their analysis of children's and parents' reports, Felson and Zielinski concluded that the accuracy of perceptions does not affect how influential parents are.

This work is promising in that the frustrating role of perception in the solution of the self-esteem puzzle may be a minor concern. This viewpoint makes a great deal of sense. Self-esteem is affective in nature, just as fear, anger, and frustration are.

Is accuracy of perception really that important in self-esteem development, or is faulty misperception an equally powerful determinant of how one feels about oneself? If the message giver is considered to be significant, and if his or her opinion carries weight in one's evaluation of self, then, regardless of the causes of the misperception, it is the only perception available at the moment.

It follows that the significance attributed to the other will color one's interpretation of verbal and nonverbal feedback. When influenced by situational and personal variables, response set, and performance effects, perceptions which might or might not be accurate will be formed and will influence self-esteem.

MEASURES: A REVIEW AND CRITIQUE

Behaviors and characteristics of teachers, parents, and peers have been related to children's levels of self-esteem. However, certain assumptions that these individuals are significant and that the content of the esteem measures is important to the subject's feeling of worthwhileness cast doubt upon the validity of these measures. The accuracy of perceptions and freedom from bias can also be questioned. However, selecting on the basis of developmental and personality theory *(a)* persons who are likely to be significant, *(b)* attributes and behaviors reportedly associated with significance, and *(c)* variables on which esteem should rest, allows the researcher to try different techniques and measures.

Researchers have proposed an impressive list of attributes which are believed to be contributory to significance. They include autonomy, control, participation, and support (Gecas & Schwalbe 1986); appreciation, communication, companionship, and respect (Juhasz 1988); closeness, dominance, independence, love, and responsibility (Pipp et al. 1985); companionship plus emotional, informational, and instrumental support (Reid et al. 1989); and power (Smith 1983; Spady 1973). Parents, peers, and teachers are considered to be the primary forces in development of these esteem-related factors, at least for children.

Many measures compare self-perceptions and the perceptions of others. Inventories, questionnaires, interviews, and projective tests have employed forced-choice, retrospective, drawing, and manipulative methods. Interactions with, feelings about, and perceptions of relationships between individuals and others have been the focus of these measures. Understanding the processes in perception and ensuring accuracy is a pervasive problem. Also, most measures do not directly address the significance factor. However, methods and procedures could be adapted for this purpose from existing measures.

Self-perception inventories (Soares & Soares 1965) ask students, using bipolar scales, to rate themselves, how they think teachers see them, and their ideal selves. Similar forms are available for peers, teachers, counselors, and other individuals to rate the student. Short sentences are the format for young children. Adjectives are added for older subjects. These measures are purported to "allow comparison of self-ratings with 'self as others see it,' testing the accuracy of both an individual's perceptions and also his/her self-ratings" (Robinson & Shaver 1975, 104). However, neither accurate self-appraisal nor true perception of others' appraisals can be guaranteed.

This criticism applies also to self-other discrepancy scales such as the one developed by Miskimins and Braucht in 1971 to measure self-concept from a clinical perspective. Ratings of self and how family and friends see the person focus on general, social, and emotional selves. This scale was used for clinical self-confrontation using videotape playbacks of subjects.

Robinson and Shaver also noted that, "since subjects rate how others see them, and most of the rating dimensions are accessible to observers, objective comparisons can be made between subjects' and judges' ratings. This and other aspects of the self-confrontation can be useful both for the subjects and for measurement validation" (1975, 95).

This type of scale could be useful for measuring observable behavior. However, the meaning attached to the behavior—which is an important aspect in the perception of significance—cannot be objectively measured.

The influence of others on adolescents has been measured using hypothetical situations in which an adolescent is faced with a choice of two possible alternatives, one favored by parents and the other favored by peers. Subjects are asked to choose the most likely alternative for themselves in each situation (Emmerich 1978).

This procedure is based on the assumption that adolescents' choice of alternative action in conflict situations (favored by peers or by parents) signifies which of the two is more influential. However, this assumption is erroneous because other factors may motivate selection of alternatives. Also, the forced-choice form of response limits the inclusion of other individuals who may be significant. This problem could be eliminated by using a series of pairs of people, adding to parent and peers any others whom subjects might volunteer. By a process of elimination, the adolescent would indicate the most favored person and the selected alternative. This would allow each subject to include all those who are important.

Using a retrospective method, Pipp and colleagues in 1985 assessed late adolescents' developmental theories about their affective relationship with their parents. College students used circle drawings to represent their theories at five points in time, beginning with infancy. To determine whether the subjects differentiated their own perspectives from the perspectives of their parents, twenty-one five-point Likert scales were also constructed.

Subjects first rated how they felt about each parent and, second, how they perceived their parents' feelings about them. This scale consists of theoretically derived attributes of those who are significant in the lives of others, including dominance, independence, responsibility, closeness, and love. Using the two methods described, these late adolescents constructed theories of the affective components of their relationships with their parents over time. Such a retrospective approach might be useful in tracking developmental changes in the basis of esteem and significant others over the life span.

Reid and colleagues developed in 1989 a psychometrically sound instrument called *My Family and Friends* for evaluating children's subjective impressions about social support from family and friends.

Consisting of twelve dialogues based on Vygotskian principles, *My Family and Friends* yields information about *(a)* children's perceptions of the availability of individuals in their networks to provide different types of social support, and *(b)* their satisfaction with the help they receive. Needing things or help was the key construct underlying the development of this measure. Children's responses to an interviewer's questions about whom they went to and how often, their spontaneous comments, and their own questions provided the content for the instrument.

Dialogues were constructed about related social situations, and the satisfaction questions incorporated terms and phrases used frequently by the children. Dialogue scripts were then used to guide child-interviewer collaborative interaction.

Special props were also designed for this study and included (1) social network cards with the names (or drawings or photographs) of all individuals in the child's social network; (2) a wooden ranking board in which the cards could be inserted; and (3) a large satisfaction barometer with a movable red level indicator with key labels indicating gradations at ten-point intervals from zero to fifty.

Based on the work by Reid and colleagues in 1989, it appears that social support could be one factor that impacts on self-esteem development in children. Were social support to be used as a focal point, the concept should be extended to include reciprocity and mutuality. At the lowest developmental level. others assume significance because of what they can provide or do for the receiver. This generates feelings of worthwhileness. Social, emotional, and cognitive developmental growth, with changing views of self and what is valued, shift the balance to include "What I can do for myself?" and "What I can do or be to others?" However, the opportunity to indicate the negative impact of a significant other on self-esteem would appear to be minimized when support is the construct being measured.

Comparison of self-evaluations with perceptions of those conveyed by significant others is thought to determine the accuracy of one's self-concept. In his ground-breaking research of 1979, Rosenberg queried children about others (such as parents, teachers, and classmates) who might be significant.

He tried to determine children's different perceived selves by asking "Would you say your (for example, mother) thinks you are a wonderful person, a pretty nice person, a little bit of a nice person, or not such a nice person?" He also asked how much the child cared about what others thought, as well as about source credibility and the relationship of children's feelings to their perceptions of feedback. One limitation of Rosenberg's research was that the significant others were preselected and might not have included all possibilities.

In terms of exploratory approaches, considerable evidence suggests that, in assessing self-esteem, direct information from the person is the best source of data (Wylie 1961). This should be true also for measuring significance. Questions such as "Who is important to you?" or "Who would most influence your decision about (whatever situation)?" certainly produce more accurate and personalized responses than do objective-type test measures. However, they fail to reveal the *what* and the *why* of significance. Nor do these questions provide information on the impact of the individual's feelings of worth, whether positive or negative.

The challenge for the researcher is to formulate questions that will elicit the individual's unique reactions to the significant other's feedback (his or her reflected appraisal of self-worth), and identify those aspects of personality and behavior which earn significance for another, as well as identify feelings related to an individual's self-worth.

With questions derived from Kinch (1963)—such as "How do others respond to you? What does the other do or say? How does this make you feel about yourself?"—and with significance as the focal point, I have designed procedures and questions in an attempt to further extend understanding of the significant other's impact on self-esteem.

The pencil-and-paper procedures used key questions designed to elicit individual input. These provided structure without restricting the response. The questionnaire called *Important People for Me* (Juhasz 1989b) was pretested on nine- to thirteen-year-olds, and wording and design were revised to eliminate problems in clarity and content. This questionnaire elicited the subjects' list of important people, then had them rank-order persons on the list, selecting for each (1) the degree of importance (from "very" to "somewhat"), and (2) their own feelings of self-worth in reaction to this significant individual (ranging from "great" to "awful"). Subjects also answered an open-ended question about what the person did or said to make the individual feel good or bad. A system for coding these responses as positive or negative was based on needs theory.

A revised questionnaire designed for college students required descriptions of others' behaviors, self-feelings, and reactions:

1. Who is it that makes you feel like a really great person, and what do they do that makes you feel this way?;
2. Who is it that makes you feel like a good-for-nothing person, and what do they do that makes you feel this way?;
3. Do any of the adults whom you are with in school make you feel good about yourself—that you are a worthwhile, valuable person? What does each of these adults do and/or say that makes you feel this way? Describe your feelings and how you act then.;
4. Do any of the adults whom you are with in school make you feel bad about yourself—that you are worthless and good for nothing? What does each of these adults do and/or say that makes you feel this way? Describe your feelings and how you act then.

The method and formats were successful in eliciting qualitatively rich responses. More sophisticated and complex relationships and reasoning were evident in the answers of older students. Herbig

(1990) used the dialogue, follow-up, query, interview method, and the college level questions with two groups of adolescent males, including some who were in therapy. The next step will be to design a composite high-school/college-level questionnaire based on the responses and input from the pilot groups.

Ten- to fourteen-year-olds in Australia, New Zealand, and the Philippines, and caucasians, blacks, and Chinese in the United States, have used versions of the "Important People for Me" measure (renamed "Significant-Other Scale") (Juhasz 1989a, 1990; Watkins & Barrett 1988). Analysis of data from these studies revealed gender, age and cultural differences in those who were considered to be significant or important. In addition both negative and positive self-perceptions were recorded.

Wells and Marwell contended in 1976 that we can define self-esteem, not in direct terms of attitudinal or perceptual processes, but rather in terms of what such processes feel like or how persons react to them. This affective-feeling dimension assumes great importance both in measurement design and in interpretation of behavioral outcomes. With young children and special populations, affective status affects cognitive status (Harter & Connell 1982). Adult feedback about children's behavior is perceived in "bad me," "good me" terms, giving rise to feelings such as happiness, sadness, anxiety, or depression. According to Selman (1980), children as early as five years of age are capable of inferring another person's feelings, intentions, and thoughts with some degree of accuracy. Fifth- and sixth-graders can respond when asked "What happens to make you worry, feel bad, or nervous?" They can also rank each item on a subsequent list according to intensity of feeling and frequency of occurrence (Lewis, Siegel & Lewis 1984).

The usefulness of drawing techniques has been demonstrated with special populations who may experience difficulty with traditional pencil-and-paper measures because of language, culture, age or ability. They also provide a neutral approach to cross-cultural studies where social values and cultural norms are likely to influence the significance attributed to family members (Juhasz 1990; Nuttall, Chieh & Nuttall 1988; Watkins 1988). In 1990, Juhasz and Munshi published results of work in which they had classes of five- and six-year-olds draw their own pictures of persons whom they agreed were important to them, such as mother, father, teacher, friend, family, and others. They also drew pictures for class-generated common situations—home, school, vacation, math, reading, and free time. The children discussed and decided upon the drawing of eyes, nose, and mouth for three faces (circles) to represent happy, sad, and OK feelings.

In the "Faces and Feelings Test," children first decided how each person and situation made them feel about themselves (in particular, sad, happy, or OK) and then matched faces with their pictures of situations and people. Different matching methods were used, such as placing a face beside a picture, drawing the mouth (the distinguishing factor) on a face for each picture, and pasting the appropriate face beside each picture. A happy face is associated with "good me," a sad face with "bad me." It represents both the reflected appraisal of the significant other person and the child's self-evaluation. Because this test was designed by and for children, it therefore does not suffer from shortcomings like inappropriate stimulus materials, being useful only with a limited age group, or based on a specific theory (McArthur & Roberts 1982).

From this review of measures, useful techniques and approaches for the study of significant others and self-esteem development can be extrapolated. The adaptation and/or combination of these could result in unique and effective new designs for life-span research focused on the identification of esteem components, significant-other determinants, and relationships among these variables.

Social support measures appear to tap some attributes of significance which may be related to self-esteem (Demo & Savin-Williams in press; Felson & Zielinski 1989). Attributes of significance which may be related to self-esteem appear in the dialogue stems of the instrument developed by Reid and colleagues in 1989. They obtained interval data from subjects' manipulations of the personalized props and reported acceptable test-retest reliability and alpha coefficients in evaluating children's ability to differentiate types of social support as well as who provides them. If we could establish the bases of esteem, similar methodology could be used to develop a psychometrically strong instrument. Social-support dimensions alone reflect only utilitarian, needs-meeting aspects of self which are much too narrow to accommodate the possible range of esteem factors.

The most frequently used preestablished lists of significant others appear to be inclusive enough for the subjects surveyed. Content analysis of support network data by Reid and colleagues in 1989 indicated that parents, siblings, friends, relatives, and teachers are important. In studies of self-esteem development, these persons also emerge as significant (Blyth, Hill & Thiel 1982; Juhasz 1989a). However, a major problem is the lack of cross-cultural validation of the universality and stability across the life span of both the attributes of significance and those who are granted it.

Directed questions, individualized materials, and props have been used successfully to have subjects generate their own pool of others whom they consider to be significant (Juhasz 1989b, 1990; Reid et al. 1989). However, the assumption that noninclusion connotes nonsignificance can be questioned. This is particularly relevant when negative influence on self-esteem is considered. For example, a child might not list a father who is serving time in prison even though this may have an impact on his or her esteem level. Follow-up interviews could address this problem.

The "Faces and Feelings" and "My Family and Friends" materials and methods eliminate some of the cross-cultural, age, and ability problems mentioned earlier. The props designed for the social support study could be adapted for use in the study of self-esteem and significant others, having the advantages specified by the authors of "reducing distractability and making abstract concepts more concrete" (Reid et al. 1989, 898). The network cards are subject-designated and, thus, can accommodate any range of significant others. The barometer markings could extend below zero to include negative feelings of esteem. Watkins (1988) used the "How I See Myself" approach developed by Juhasz in 1985 in New Zealand, Hong Kong, Nepal, and the Philippines. Age, race, and gender differences emerged with an American sample (Juhasz 1990).

There must be a much wider range of significant others, if we are to consider school drop-outs, run-away or throw-away children, institutionalized persons, and the many age and social groups who are not included in studies of self-esteem. Conversely, we could probably find a sizeable percentage of the population who either have no significant others or depend upon self-evaluation relative to impersonal, group, or mass media role models. Also, values such as pride in ethnicity could be highly significant without involvement with others.

One cannot establish measurable relationships without valid instruments. At the heart of the matter is a problem not directly addressed in this chapter. Self-concept is not the same as self-esteem, and we have not been successful in developing measures to uncover the differences in the two constructs (see chapter 4 of this volume). Since the other's significance is in terms of the individual's self-esteem base, precision in significance measurement also seems to be impossible.

My research has attempted to reveal the individual's unique list of others and bases of esteem. However, relationships among these variables were explored using established self-measures, such as Rosenberg's self-concept scale of 1963, the Piers Harris (Piers 1969) self-concept scale, and Marsh's and colleagues' Parent and Peer subscales of 1983. These have established reliability and most researchers consider these scales to measure self-esteem.

The underlying assumption is that self-esteem is the same as the less specific construct of self-concept. Thus, student-generated significant others, and knowledge of why these people were considered to be significant, could only be related to researcher-generated self-descriptors which might or might not have been important to esteem development. When we broaden our research base, the methods discussed here will be useful—and so will the guidelines for instrument development and clinical interviewing proposed by Damon & Hart (1988) and Reid et al. (1989).

CONCLUSION

The theory and research presented in this chapter provide insight into some of the so-called noise factors (developmental, environmental, and social) which bias and influence esteem-related self-other processes. If the goal of measurement is prediction, does this mean that the desired changed attitudes toward self must be objectively measurable? And is this possible?

For example, change in children's behavior could be perceived by a teacher as an indication of her significance when, in fact, the children might view neither the teacher nor the behavior as particularly important to their self-esteem. It is difficult to predict behavior when motivating factors are varied and complex and when situations are real rather than laboratory settings. Many intervening variables can influence the individual's response to feedback in terms of its impact on self-esteem. Personality factors and momentary personal agendas might determine which of the available responses is acted out.

Given that instruments to measure the relationship between children's significant others and their self-esteem are in the embryo stage, it is not surprising that measures of the relationship between adults' significant others and their self-esteem are nonexistant. At this time only the baseline components and relationships (such as significance ranking of others and rating of self-worth feelings) can be psychometically measured and only at a simplistic level. The multifaceted nature of self-esteem, the specificity of others' significance, and the situational and temporal impact on individuals' perceptions and evaluations makes this a highly complex phenomenon.

Research on constructs such as significant others and self-esteem has social relevance with implications beyond the research setting. Thus, Wells and Marwell have advised a sense of caution but also urged continuation, charging that, "We cannot throw up our hands at the difficulties posed by the nature of the topic because debates and decisions will continue with or without research on these topics" (1976, 252).

In this instance, our task is to find some systematic means of discovering the relationship between significance attributed to others and self-esteem. Attempts at measurement are hampered by disagreements and by lack of clarity in delimiting the critical variables, in defining them concisely, and in deciding upon the key relationships. Scholars from different disciplines, using varied approaches, are developing creative measurements and systems of analysis in attempts to solve these problems. Current research efforts are at the divergent stage. With a comprehensive conceptual framework as a guide, an interdisciplinary team could approach measurement problems from different perspectives with a concerted, coordinated effort to systematically unravel the significant-other/self-esteem relationship.

REFERENCES

Allport, G. 1961. *Pattern and growth in personality.* New York: Holt, Rinehart, & Winston.

Baldwin, J. 1897. *Social and ethical interpretations in mental development.* New York: MacMillan.

Blyth, D.; Hill, J.; and Thiel, K. 1982. Early adolescents' significant others: Grade and gender differences in perceived relationships with familiar and nonfamiliar adults and young people. *Journal of Youth and Adolescence* 11:425–450.

Brittain, C. 1963. Adolescent choices and parent-peer cross-pressures. *American Sociological Review* 28:385–391.

———. 1966. Age and sex of siblings and conformity toward parents versus peers in adolescence. *Child Development* 37:709–714.

Brophy, J., and Rohrkemper, W. 1981. The influence of problem ownership on teachers' perception of and strategies for coping with problem students. *Journal of Educational Psychology* 73:295–311.

Broughton, J. 1983. The cognitive-developmental theory of adolescent self and identity. In *Developmental approaches to the self*, edited by B. Lee and G. Noam. New York: Plenum.

Burns, R. 1979. *The self-concept.* Suffolk: Richard Clay, Ltd.

Cassirer, E. 1923. *Substance and function.* New York: Dover Press.

Cooley, C. 1912. *Human nature and the social order.* New York: Scribner's.

Damon, W., and Hart, D. 1988. *Self-understanding in childhood and adolescence.* New York: Cambridge University Press.

Darom, E., and Rich, Y. 1988. Sex differences in attitudes toward school: Student self-reports and teacher perceptions. *British Journal of Educational Psychology* 58:350–355.

Demo, D. H., and Savin-Williams, R. In press. Self-concept stability and change during adolescence. In *Self-perspectives across the life span*, edited by R. P. Lipka and T. M. Brinthaupt. Albany, N.Y.: State University of New York Press.

DePaulo, B.; Kenny, D.; Hoover, C.; Webb, W.; and Oliver, P. 1987. Accuracy in person perception: Do people know what kind of impressions they convey? *Journal of Personality and Social Psychology* 52:303–315.

Emmerich, H. 1978. The influence of parents and peers on choices made by adolescents. *Journal of Youth and Adolescence* 7:175–180.

Erikson, E. 1950. *Childhood and society.* New York: Norton.

————. 1968. *Identity: Youth and crisis.* New York: W. W. Norton.

Fallow-Mitchell, L., and Ryff, C. 1982. Preferred timing of female life events. *Research on Aging* 4:249–267.

Felson, R. 1981. Self and reflected appraisal among football players: A test of the Meadian hypothesis. *Social Psychology Quarterly* 44:116–126.

Felson, R., and Zielinski, M. 1989. Children's self-esteem and parental support. *Journal of Marriage and the Family* 51:727–735.

Festinger, L. 1954. A theory of social comparison processes. *Human Relations* 7:117–140.

Gecas, V., and Schwalbe, M. 1986. Parental behavior and adolescent self-esteem. *Journal of Marriage and the Family* 48:37–46.

Harter, S., and Connell, J. 1982. *A model of the relationship among children's academic achievement and their self-perceptions of competence, control and motivational orientation.* Unpublished manuscript. University of Denver, Denver, Colo.

Harter, S., and Pike, R. 1984. The pictorial scale of perceived competence and social acceptance for young children. *Child Development* 55:1969–1982.

Herbig, R. 1990. A study of young male adolescents' perceptions of significant others. Doctoral dissertation. Chicago: Loyola University.

Hewitt, J. 1976. *Self and society.* London: Allyn & Bacon.

Hill, T.; Lewicki, P.; Czyzewska, M., and Bos, A. 1989. Self-perpetuating development of encoding biases in person perception. *Journal of Personality and Social Psychology* 57:373–387.

Hoge, D., and McCarthy, J. 1984. Influence of individual and group identity salience in the global self-esteem of youth. *Journal of Personality and Social Psychology* 47:403–414.

Hyman, H. 1942. The psychology of status. *Archives of Psychology, 38* (Whole No. 269).

Hymel, S. 1986. Interpretations of peer behavior: Affective bias in childhood and adolescence. *Child Development* 57:431–445.

James, W. 1890. *Principles of psychology.* Vol. 1. New York: Holt.

Juhasz, A. 1982a. Male identity at mid-life: An Eriksonian interpretation. *Mensa Research Journal* Summer:10–20.

——— . (1982b) Youth identity, and values: Erikson's historical perspective. *Adolescence* 17:443–450.

——— . 1985. Measuring self-esteem in early adolescents. *Adolescence* 20:877–887.

——— . 1988. *Parents as significant others in children's self-esteem: An exploratory study.* Unpublished manuscript. Chicago, Ill.: Loyola University.

——— . 1989a. Black adolescents' significant others. *Social Behavior and Personality* 17:211–214.

——— . 1989b. Significant others and self-esteem: Methods for determining who and why. *Adolescence* 95:581–594.

——— . 1990. *Significant others and self-esteem of American and Australian early adolescents.* Under review.

Juhasz, A., and Munshi, N. 1990. *Measuring self-esteem in young children: A cross-cultural methodological study.* Under review.

Kawash, G.; Kerr, E.; and Clewes, J. 1986. Self-esteem in children as a function of perceived parental behavior. *The Journal of Psychology* 119:235–242.

Kenny, D. 1988. Interpersonal perception: A social relations analysis. *Journal of Social and Personal Relationships* 5:247–261.

Kinch, J. 1963. A formalized theory of the self-concept. *American Journal of Sociology* 68:481–486.

Kohlberg, L. 1973. Continuities in childhood and adult moral development revisited. In *Life-span developmental psychology*, edited by P. Baltes and K. Schaie. New York: Academic Press.

Laing, R.; Phillipson, H.; and Lee, A. 1966. *Interpersonal perception.* New York: Harper & Row.

Lewis, C.; Siegel, J.; and Lewis, M. 1984. Feeling bad: Exploring sources of distress among pre-adolescent children. *American Journal of Public Health* 74:117–122.

Livesley, W., and Bromley, D. 1973. *Person perception in childhood and adolescence.* London: Wiley.

Ludwig, D., and Maehr, M. 1967. Changes in self-concept and stated behavioral preferences. *Child Development* 38:353–357.

Lynch, M. 1981. Improving self-esteem and reading. *Educational Research* 27:194–200.

Marsh, H. 1986. Global self-esteem: Its relation to specific facets of self-concept and their importance. *Journal of Personality and Social Psychology* 51:1224–1236.

Marsh, H.; Smith, I.; and Barnes, J. 1983. Multitrait-multimethod analysis of the Self-Description Questionnaire: Student-teacher agreement on multidimensional ratings of student self-concept. *American Educational Research Journal* 20:333–357.

Maslow, A. 1954. *Motivation and personality.* New York: Harper.

McArthur, D., and Roberts, G. 1982. *Roberts apperception test for children—manual.* Los Angeles: Western Psychological Services.

McCreary, A., and Surkan, A. 1965. The human reading process and information channels of communication systems. *Journal of Reading* 8:363–372.

Mead, G. 1934. *Mind, self and society.* Chicago: University of Chicago Press.

Miskimins, R., and Braucht, G. 1971. *Description of the self.* Fort Collins, Colo.: Rocky Mountain Behavioral Science Institute.

Niedenthal, P.; Cantor, N.; and Kihlstrom, J. 1985. Prototype matching: A strategy for social decision making. *Journal of Personality and Social Psychology* 48:575–584.

Nuttall, E.; Chieh, L.; and Nuttall, R. 1988. Views of the family by Chinese and U.S. Children: A comparative study of kinetic family drawings. *Journal of School Psychology* 26:191–194.

Piers, E. 1969. *Manual for the Piers Harris Children's Self-Concept Scale.* Nashville, Tenn.: Counselor Recordings and Tests.

Pintrich, P., and Blumenfeld, P. 1985. Classroom experience and children's self-perceptions of ability, effort, and conduct. *Journal of Educational Psychology* 77:646–657.

Pipp, S.; Shaver, P.; Jennings, S.; Lamborn, S.; and Fischer, K. 1985. Adolescents' theories about the development of their relationships with parents. *Journal of Personality and Social Psychology* 48:991–1001.

Reid, M.; Landesman, S.; Treder, R.; and Jaccard, J. 1989. "My family and friends": Six- to twelve-year old children's perceptions of social support. *Child Development* 60:896–910.

Robinson, J., and Shaver, P. 1975. *Measures of social psychological attitudes.* Ann Arbor, Mich.: Institute for Social Research.

Rosenberg, M. 1963. Parental interest and children's self-conceptions. *Sociometry* 26:35–49.

———. 1979. *Conceiving the self.* New York: Basic Books.

Saba, B. 1985. The guided training techninque for use with nine- to thirteen-year-olds. *Individual Psychology* 41:564–569.

Selman, R. 1980. *The growth of interpersonal understanding: Developmental and clinical analysis.* New York: Academic Press.

Shannon, C., and Weaver, W. 1949. *The mathematical theory of communication.* Champaign, Ill.: University of Illinois Press.

Shavelson, R.; Hubner, J.; and Stanton, J. 1976. Self-concept: Validation of construct interpretations. *Review of Educational Research* 46:407–441.

Shirk, S., and Renouf, A. G. In press. The tasks of self development in middle childhood and early adolescence. In *Self-perspectives across the life span,* edited by R. P. Lipka and T. M. Brinthaupt. Albany, N.Y.: State University of New York Press.

Shrauger, J., and Schoeneman, T. 1979. Symbolic interaction view of self: Through the looking glass darkly. *Psychological Bulletin* 86:549–573.

Silvernail, D. 1986. *Developing positive student self-concept.* Washington, D.C.: National Education Association.

Smith, T. 1983. Parental influence: A review of the evidence of influence and a theoretical model of the parental influence process. *Sociology of Education and Socialization* 4:13–45.

Soares, A., and Soares, L. 1965. Self-perceptions of culturally disadvantaged children. *American Educational Research Journal* 6:31–45.

Spady, W. 1973. Authority, conflict and teacher effectiveness. *Educational Researcher* 2:4–10.

Sullivan, H. 1947. *Conceptions of modern psychiatry.* Washington, D.C.: W. H. White Psychiatric Foundation.

Suls, J. M., and Miller, R. L, 1977. *Social comparison processes: Theoretical and empirical perspectives.* Washington, D.C.: Hemisphere.

Suls, J. M., and Mullen, B. 1982. From the cradle to the grave: Comparison and self-evaluation across the life span. In *Psychological perspectives on the self,* Vol. 1, edited by J. Suls. Hillsdale, N.J.: Erlbaum. 97–125.

Watkins, D. 1988. Components of self-esteem of children from a deprived cross-cultural background. *Social Behavior and Personality* 16:1–3.

Watkins, D., and Barrett, R. 1988. Significant others of New Zealand and Filipino adolescents. *Psychological Reports* 62:588–590.

Weinstein, R. 1981. *Student perspectives on "achievement" in varied classroom environments.* Paper presented at the annual meeting in April of the American Educational Research Association in Los Angeles.

Wells, L., and Marwell, G. 1976. *Self-esteem: Its conceptualization and measurement.* Beverly Hills, Calif: Sage Publications, Inc.

Whitbourne, S. 1985. The psychological construction of the life span. In *Handbook of the psychology of aging,* edited by J. Birren and K. Schaie. 2d ed. New York: Van Nostrand Reinhold.

Woolfolk, A., and Brooks, D. 1985. The influence of teachers' nonverbal behaviors on students' perceptions and performance. *The Elementary School Journal* 85:513–528.

Wylie, R. 1961. *The self-concept.* Lincoln: University of Nebraska Press.

Young, L., and Bagley, C. 1982. Self-esteem, self-concept, and the development of black identity. In *Self concept, achievement, and multi-*

cultural education, edited by G. Verma and C. Bagley. London: The Macmillan Press.

Zurcher, L. 1977. *The mutable self: A self-concept for social change*. Beverly Hills, Calif.: Sage Publications, Inc.

RICHARD D. ASHMORE
DANIEL M. OGILVIE

7

He's Such a Nice Boy . . . When He's with Grandma: Gender and Evaluation in Self-with-Other Representations*

It is the Wednesday before Thanksgiving, and a young man is driving home from college with three of his fraternity brothers. Barry feels good and strong, even a bit cocky.

As the radio blares country and western music, he and his friends engage in nonstop banter, and their language is frequently profane. At times, their conversation has a distinctly competitive edge, almost like the intense competition they exhibited in a pick up basketball game earlier that day. But the mutual affection is also clear throughout.

Once at home, Barry seems, to his friends, to be very quiet and restrained when he is around his parents, especially his dad. Playing pool with his brothers and sisters, however, he acts just like he does at the fraternity.

That evening, after spending a long time in the bathroom getting cleaned up, he brings a former girlfriend to the house. His college friends are surprised not only at his dress (not the jeans-T-shirt-sneakers uniform, but slacks and a dress shirt) but also at how conservative and traditional he acts with her.

After everyone else has gone to bed, Barry and his mom continue an earlier discussion of politics, and they get into an argument. She sees him as aggressive and angry—and he is. But he's also a bit frightened, although he can't quite label the feeling. She can't understand what has gotten into him, and neither can he. Barry doesn't like himself when he acts like this.

Although all the others sleep late on Thursday, Barry gets up at 6 A.M. with his mom. While she prepares the dressing for the turkey, he works on a term paper. He always gets up early and works.

At dinner later that day, Barry not only dresses up again but doesn't utter a single four-letter word (neither of which is like him back at college), but he is also soft spoken and interpersonally gentle. He is especially solicitous of his grandmother who is clearly very proud of him ("He's such a nice boy . . . ").

As he sits at the end of the long table opposite his father, Barry looks around at all those present. He is struck by the thought that these are almost all the people who really matter to him, and he feels happy.

Although the time frame is short—about twenty-four hours—this hypothetical scenario illustrates how variable an individual's self-experience and behavior can be as a function of who he or she is with. This variability could be unique to the individual depicted here, or it could be that the variation is easily understood in terms of situational norms (such as, one should not swear at the dinner table on Thanksgiving) and general roles (such as, all young men in America are supposed to be competitive). Certainly individual differences and cultural prescriptions are important, and we will return to these themes later in this chapter. At the same time, however, we believe that the scenario about Barry illustrates another important phenomenon concerning self-concept. As in the case of the hypothetical college student Barry, each of us is, in part, a confederacy of self-with-others. That is, we experience and enact our self in somewhat different ways with the specific other people with whom we have important relationships. Over time, these patterns of thought, feeling, and action are represented internally (although not necessarily consciously) as part of one's overall sense of personal identity. We use the label *self-with-other representation* to refer to this structured set of thoughts and feelings about self when with others.

In an earlier work (Ogilvie & Ashmore 1991), we described this construct, its relation to other similar self-concept theories and variables, and presented a detailed account of how we measure this complex and complicated facet of the social self. In this chapter, however, we present a second progress report on our efforts to explore self-with-other representations. Our plan is as follows: First, we briefly describe the self-with-other representation construct, and we then situate this notion within a more inclusive multiplicity model of gender identity (Ashmore 1990).

A central assumption of this framework is that one's gendered self-concept[1] can fruitfully be partitioned into five separate general components: biological/physical/material, personal-social attributes, interests and abilities, symbolic and stylistic behavior, and social relationships. In this report we highlight the final such component by offering the self-with-other concept and attendant empirical procedures as a new approach to measuring the self in social relationships.

Next, we explain why, in this report, the focus is on two general contents within self-with-other representations—evaluation (positive/negative) and gender (male/female). Then we describe our integrated idiographic/nomothetic strategy for assessing these. The introductory portion of the chapter concludes with an overview of the overall research project within which the present data were collected, the phrasing of the major issues to be addressed, and a detailed example of how we assess self-with-other structures.

In the next major section, the method employed is described in more detail. We then present some illustrative findings. Here, the emphasis is on describing what the self-with-other representational structures of a sample of individuals look like. Of particular interest are nomothetic indices pertaining to evaluation and gender that can be derived from the idiographic analysis of self-with-other representations. The chapter concludes with a brief recapitulation and suggestions for next steps.

THE SELF-WITH-OTHER REPRESENTATION CONCEPT

The last decade has witnessed a large increase in the amount and variety of research and theory concerning self and identity. Two of the most exciting recent developments in the subarea concerned with self as known—content and structure of self as distinguished from self-motives (Berkowitz 1988)—is the grappling conceptually and empirically with self as multifaceted and the social nature of personal identity. Important contributions have been made by many others (Gergen 1977; Gergen & Gergen 1988; Markus & Nurius 1986; Markus & Cross 1990; Rosenberg 1988; Rosenberg & Gara 1985; Stryker 1987; Tunnis, Fridhandler & Horowitz 1990). (See also chapter 2 of this volume.) Our conceptualization fits in this tradition, and we acknowledge our debt to others who have been tilling adjacent intellectual fields (Ogilvie & Ashmore 1991).

As did the others noted, we begin with the assumption that identity, although a property of the individual, is thoroughly social. Also, while recognizing that most people have a solid belief that they are one person and experience feelings of personal unity over time, we believe, as do the others, that it is fruitful to assess multiple facets of this overall self. Our primary twist, however, concerns the precise content of these multiple social-self units.

Since at least the time of James and Cooley, it has been recognized that others provide important inputs to self knowledge. The most famous statement of this general position is the "looking-glass self"—we learn who we are (that is, we develop our self-concept), in part, by looking at how others regard us. Although we acknowledge that this reflected appraisal is a major input to self as known, we believe that this position, at least as most often interpreted, paints a much too mechanical and impersonal view of the *how* and *what* of the social self. Our view is that, when we interact with others, we do more than use them as a looking-glass and simply notice what they think we are like.

In addition, we encode (sometimes consciously, but more often unconsciously) how we are when in the company of a particular person. Such internal representations involve multiple codes, including propositional/verbal ("I am competent"), affective/emotional (feelings of comfort and interest), and behavioral/motor (speaking in a forceful voice) (Ashmore & Del Boca 1986, 8–9). These multiple-channel internal representations of what one is like in interaction with another person are the building blocks of what we term *self-with-other representation*.

For most isolated and routine contacts with others who are unfamiliar to us, these internal representations of self-with-other do not greatly impact the self as known. However, for interactions with important others—especially when contacts occur over considerable time and in multiple settings—the individual comes to create an internal cognitive/affective category of "self-with-whomever)." Some of these self-with-other units may be consciously held, but, for most people most of the time, individuals are unaware of their major self-with-other units.

The next step, according to our framework, is combining individual self-with-other units into groupings (which we term *self-with-other constellations*), and these, in turn, are organized as an overall structure. That is, it is assumed that, not only does a person create discrete self-with-specific-other units in her or his head and heart, but, over time, she or he builds up a more articulated or differentiated and integrated structure of self-with-others by grouping specific self-withs together and then organizing these into a more complex representation with cognitive/affective links among all the self-with units.

Although the precise structure of this overall self-with-other representation is unknown, we have found it useful to think of it as categorical in nature and as hierarchically arranged. This view fits nicely with most existing models of memory as consisting of propositional networks (see Fiske & Taylor 1984, especially 214–216). Unlike many hierarchical categorical models, however, we do not believe that the internal categories are organized into groups that obey strict set inclusion rules. Quite simply, "How I am with so-and-so" can fall into two different mental clusters. As a consequence, we utilize a hierarchical-classes method to analyze and visually represent the overall self-with-other structures of individuals (DeBoeck & Rosenberg 1988; Ogilvie & Ashmore 1991; Rosenberg 1988).

A return to the introductory scenario can illustrate portions of the proffered framework. First, the hypothetical student, Barry, behaves quite differently and he experiences a wide range of emotions with the different important people in his life. We suggest that, in part, these actions and emotions are driven by the student's sense of self-with each person. He may be aware of some of these internal representations. In fact, it kind of tickles him "to put on a show for grandma." However, most of his internal representations lie below consciousness. He is, in fact, very surprised when one of his friends teases him about being an old-fashioned suitor with his former girlfriend.

Second, the scenario gives clues about the student's overall self-with structure. For example, when he is with his mom, he is hardworking, he can feel happy, he can be quiet and reserved, and he can also act angry. This suggests that self-with-Mom is, for this person, part of a high-order internal cluster that ties into low-order self-withs having quite different affective tones. That the focal character always gets up early and works hard and also feels happy when with all the important people in his life suggests that hard-working and positive affect may be relatively pervasive aspects of his self-with-other structure.

SELF-WITH-OTHER REPRESENTATION AS
PART OF GENDER IDENTITY

Although the self-with-other notion can stand alone (Ogilvie & Ashmore, 1991), we have found it useful to consider it as but one facet of an individual's overall personal identity. Our efforts to date have focused more specifically on self-with-other representations as part of gender identity. Here we differ from those who employ a narrow definition of this concept as one's phenomenological sense of being a biological male or female (Money & Ehrhardt 1972; Spence 1985). We define gender identity as "the structured set of gendered personal identities that result when the individual takes the social construction of gender and the biological 'facts' of sex and incorporates these into an overall self-concept" (Ashmore 1990, 512). We believe that an individual's gender identity not only summarizes past learning about self and gender, but also that gendered personal identities can drive current behavior, including that such as described at the outset of this chapter. Other general explanations of sex, gender, and the individual have been offered and these are briefly described and critiqued before returning to a more detailed presentation of our model of gender identity, which is offered as an alternative to these accounts.

Alternative Conceptions of Sex, Gender, and the Individual

One of the possible explanations for the student's behavior in the beginning scenario is the male role, in that our society does specify that men should be competitive, hard-working, cocky, and willing and able to express anger. The notion that the conduct of individual men and women can be accounted for by two broad and general gender roles (the male and female roles) is especially popular among sociologists (Giele 1988).

More prominent in psychology have been two other perspectives on how individual conduct reflects sex and gender—sex differences and gender as a global personality variable (Ashmore 1990; Deaux 1984). According to the first approach—which has been around for a century and still commands attention (Eagly 1987)—an important task for researchers is to test for average sex group differences on a wide variety of psychological variables. The gender as a personality variable framework begins with Terman's and Miles's introduction in 1936 of the concept of psychological masculinity/

femininity, and can be traced through the masculine/femininity (M/F) scales so popular in the 1950s and 1960s, to the androgyny construct that commanded attention in the 1970s and 1980s, and ultimately to Bem's notion of "gender schema" published in 1981 and 1985. Although these various theories and associated measuring devices differ in many ways (Beere 1990; Cook 1985), they share an underlying assumption that sex and gender are somehow represented in the individual in terms of one or a small number of stable personality traits (Ashmore 1990).

Although the perspectives of gender role, sex differences, and gender as a personality variable each provide valuable insight, they share important limitations with regard to illuminating individual thought, feeling, and behavior as impacted by sex and gender. From our point of view, the most important shortcoming is that they unnecessarily oversimplify and homogenize the individual as a gendered creature. Although there are clear exceptions (Ashmore 1990, note 4), this is evident with regard to the presumed causes, contents, and consequences of the individual's thoughts and feelings about, and as a result of, sex and gender.

In terms of causes, the dominant sociological perspective assumes that (1) American culture presents a clear definition of two gender roles, (2) the sex difference approach tacitly presumes that biological sex is a simple cause of average female-male differences, and (3) gender-as-a-personality-variable theories are based on the view that sex and gender present to individuals clear and unambiguous messages about masculinity and femininity and that these are directly assimilated or rejected.

Our view, however, is that neither biological sex nor cultural prescriptions concerning gender speak with a single voice. Quite simply, individuals—especially Americans in this last decade of the twentieth century—are exposed to a wide variety of exemplars of maleness and femaleness, such as cultural inputs concerning gender that are not homogeneous (Sherif 1982; Spence 1985), and the lessons we get from our bodies are not unitary and simple (Jacklin 1989).

Given this heterogeneity of inputs, it is not surprising that the contents of sex and gender are not as tightly interconnected within individuals as would be expected on the basis of the gender role, sex differences, and gender-as-a-personality-variable perspectives. That is, a large and growing literature shows that a wide variety of individual-level gender constructs—such as masculinity/ femininity, sex stereotypes, and gender attitudes—do not covary strongly (Cook 1985; Downs & Langlois 1988; Frable 1989; Huston 1983; Spence 1985).

Another factor contributes to the lack of tight within-person connections among sex and gender concepts—the creative individual. Not only are individuals exposed to many different models and messages, but they are active in processing this information. Thus, they can ignore some inputs and modify others, as well as simply swallowing others whole or spitting them out.

The final or consequences step at the individual level is also complex—how individuals act can not be reduced to points along a single modern-versus-traditional dimension, and social action is not easily and directly shaped by a homogeneous internal representation of sex and gender. Rather, extending Ajzen's and Fishbein's (1977) notion of attitude-behavior correspondence, it is asserted that, in seeking to understand how specific gender contents predict particular social behaviors, one must consider how the content variable and the behavior match (Ashmore 1990). For example, voting for a female candidate for governor corresponds in terms of target with the gender attitude of acceptance of women as politicians. Thus, this internal gender construct should be more predictive of such voting than most, if not all, gender identity indices, because the target for these is self, not women politicians.

Our view, then, is that, while sex and gender are potent inputs into the individual, they do not provide simple and unitary messages. This, together with the active and creative organizational work accomplished by the individual, means that sex and gender within the person are bound by a sort of loose glue. Thus, we would, as a first step, expect sex stereotypes (as beliefs about the social categories of men and women), gender attitudes (evaluations of these social categories as well as of gender-related issues such as chivalry and the Equal Rights Amendment), and gender identity (self-concept as informed by sex and gender) to be not highly intercorrelated. Indeed, the available evidence suggests that, at an aggregate level, they are not. We take this "loose-glue view" of gender a step further by proposing that, even within one's personal identity, sex and gender do not have simple and widely shared effects, and, thus, gender identity is best construed as multicomponented.

Multiplicity Model of Gender Identity

Rather than beginning with the sociological role metaphor, a sex-differences view derived from differential psychology, or a trait personality perspective on masculinity and femininity, our alternative model of sex, gender, and the individual begins by construing gender as an instance of intergroup relations (Ashmore & Del Boca 1986; Deaux 1984; Sherif 1982). This view suggests three crucial individual-level constructs—stereotypes, attitudes, and identity. Here, we focus on the third one, or how self-concept is informed by sex group membership as well as societal prescriptions and proscriptions concerning the social categories of male and female.

Our assumption that many diverse messages about sex and gender are available and that people can be active and creative processors of these inputs leads to the guiding hypothesis that, for most people most of the time, gender identity is nonhomogeneous in content. Since the proposed model specifies that gender identity is complex and complicated, it is necessary to make some simplifying assumptions at the outset in order to be able to study this so-called mysterious monster. To this end we have partitioned the self into five general content categories. We do not believe that these contents are completely independent of one another nor that they are somehow stored inside the person in discrete locations. Instead, we argue that, for the sake of analysis, it is possible and fruitful to consider the self as known to be composed of distinguishable contents. More specifically, we follow and slightly amend the five content areas of sex typing which Huston presented in 1983 as a conceptual scheme that also fits well with the self-concept contents identified by personality and social psychologists (James 1890) and those studied by developmentalists concerned with self and other understanding (Hart & Damon 1985).

The first hypothesized content area is personal-social attributes, or "What I am like on the inside that gives my life stability across time and situations." These are relatively enduring internal qualities of the individual that are reflected in behavior across relatively diverse situations and with a wide variety of people. One very important personal-social attribute for adults is personality traits. This facet of this content area has received considerable attention from gender researchers. Indeed, almost all major M/F measures use trait adjectives (Cook 1985). Our view is that this emphasis has obscured the potential importance of other personal/social attributes, especially identities and roles (such as "jock" or "Mother") and characteristic ways of feeling and expressing emotion. This emphasis has also led researchers to overlook the other components of gender identity.

The four relatively ignored general areas of self as impacted by sex and gender are (1) biological/phsyical/material attributes (or

"What my body is like," "What I do to and with my body," and "What are the important 'things' in my life?"); (2) symbolic and stylistic behavior (or "How I use my body, voice, and the like"); (3) interests and abilities (or "What I like to do" and "What I am good at"); and (4) social relationships (or "What I am like with other people"). Ashmore (1990) describes these broad areas of self content. In this chapter, the focus is on the fourth aspect.

The social-relationship component refers to how the individual enters into, maintains and experiences multiple types of relationships, including close personal relationships (Kelley et al. 1983) and role relationships (Giele 1988). Major current theories of gender focus on male and female styles of relating to others (Gilligan 1982), and there is considerable data that boys and girls as well as adult men and women engage in relationships in quite different ways (Huston & Ashmore 1986; Maccoby 1987). Although the social relationship component (which we also refer to as the *social self* and *interpersonal self*) comprises many facets, we highlight the self-with-other representation concept and measurement procedures which we offer as a step toward the scientific study of this crucial aspect of personal identity.

GENDER AND EVALUATION IN SELF-WITH-OTHER REPRESENTATIONS

With regard to the *what* of individuals' overall self-with-other representational structures, we expect that some patterns will be unique or idiosyncratic, others will be shared by a small set of people, and still others will be present in the self-with structures of many individuals (Kluckhohn and Murrary 1953, 53). In this relatively early progress report on the self-with construct, we focus less on the personal and unique but more on consensual themes in how individuals organize their interpersonal self. More specifically, we suggest that in American society—and perhaps in all or most cultures—two general issues must be confronted in building and maintaining a personal identity: (1) evaluation, as in "Am I a good or bad person?," and (2) gender, as in "Am I a man or woman?"

All known cultures distinguish male and female as significant social categories, and all societies have shared belief systems that specify what members of these categories are like and how they should behave (Sherif, 1982). These cultural belief systems not only provide a basis for individuals to know what other people are like and how they should behave, but they also supply information per tinent to self definition. Thus, gender, along with the biological factors subsumed by the rubric of sex, should be significant to personal identity in general and self-with in particular.

What is the content of cultural messages about the sexes? As personally noted, we do not feel that there is one such message. At the same time, there is considerable evidence that, in terms of how the sexes are perceived, the social category distinction of female versus male is mentally associated with the personality differentiation of soft versus hard (Ashmore, Del Boca & Wohlers 1986).

If one focuses on just the positive side of the male end of this cognitive/affective continuum, the attributes not only connote hardness and strength but also intellectual and task capability. This positive male cluster has most often been named *instrumentality* or *agency*. The female positive grouping has been labelled *expressiveness* or *communion*. The dark side of cultural sex stereotypes reflect, for the most part, the extreme or unrestrained versions of these attribute clusters. For example, for males, arrogance is an extreme manifestation of self-assertion which is a central part of agency.

That sex stereotypes coincide with the distinction hard-soft is important because hard-soft is also a marker for the potency (P) dimension of connotative meaning, and there is considerable evidence that potency is the second major dimension of connotation. The first such continuum is evaluation (E). Since Osgood, Suci, and Tannenbaum introduced the semantic differential technique in 1957, a large number of studies have demonstrated that evaluation (Is it good or bad? Pleasant or unpleasant?) is the major dimension of affective meaning. This is true in response to a wide variety of targets, including perception of other people and of self (Ashmore 1981; Rosenberg 1977; White 1980).

Thus, it is asserted that evaluation (E) and potency (P)—with the latter including the more general topic of gender—are two issues that all Americans must confront in forming and maintaining a personal identity structure. If so, it should be possible to measure evaluative and gender-related aspects of self-with-other representations. This paper represents an initial attempt to do just this.

OVERVIEW OF THE SELF-PERCEPTION PROJECT

Having covered the *what* of present concern (evaluation and gender in self-with-other representations as part personal identity), we turn now to the *how*—how we investigated this general topic.

There were two overarching methodological principles. First, since our model specifies that gender identity is multicomponented, it was necessary to assess as many facets of the hypothesized five content areas as possible. Second, because gender identity is a property of the individual and because we conceive of the individual as active and creative, we felt it necessary to adopt an idiographic approach to data collection and data analysis (Allport 1962). That is, we sought to explore self through each participant's own eyes and in the person's own words. Further, and where possible, data were analyzed within-person. At the same time, we were able to derive nomothetic indices from each person's self-structure. These measured important psychological variables by using a yardstick that had the same meaning across persons. Thus, these nomothetic properties allowed us to test across-person generalizations (Rosenberg 1988). Our strategy, then, was an integrated idiographic-nomothetic one (Ashmore 1990; Ogilvie & Ashmore 1991).

These guiding principles were implemented in the Self-Perception Project (Ashmore & Ogilvie 1988). We assembled a panel of college students who agreed to participate in a multisession investigation of self-concept. The first four sessions were concerned with the social-relationship component and provided assessment of each participant's overall self-with-other representation. Consistent with our idiographic approach, the crucial units in this regard were supplied by the participant and included the specific individuals important to the person as well as the words and phrases the respondent used to describe these people and self-with each. In order to explore how evaluation and gender were encoded in each participant's self-with structure, we supplied two evaluative selves (*Me as I would like to be* and *Me at my worst*) and a set of descriptors that varied systematically with regard to evaluation and sex stereotypy. These supplied targets and descriptors are analogous to radioactive tracers used in some medical diagnostic procedures. Basically, the supplied selves and features are injected into each participant's self-with-other representational structure, and the person's pattern of responses allows us to determine where they end up in the structure.

In later sessions, we measured multiple facets of the biological/phsyical/material, personal/social attributes, and interests and abilities components of the proffered multiplicity model. (It was impossible to assess symbolic and stylistic behavior.) Eventually, these data will allow us to tie our findings to previous work, and also provide evaluative and gender indices for each component that roughly parallel those explored in the self-with-other representations.

ISSUES TO BE ADDRESSED

The primary aim of the research to be reported is to explore the self-with-other facet of the social self. Thus, this is hypothesis generation rather than hypothesis testing work. At the same time, it is possible to offer some general predictions. It is expected that it will be possible to measure individuals' self-with-other structures and to represent the complexity and organization of these in a relatively simple and easily comprehended fashion. With regard to this very general hypothesis, an important follow up question is "What do self-with-other representations look like?" A major goal of this chapter is to address this query. Considerable attention is paid to how an individual's overall self-with-others structure is obtained, and then we describe the contours of these structures for the participants in the Self-Perception Project. This examination focuses on the overall differentiation of self-with-other representations, and the various ways in which evaluation and gender are integrated into these structures.

BARRY AT THIRTY-SIX: AN EXAMPLE OF ASSESSING SELF-WITH-OTHER STRUCTURES

The assertion that an individual's self-with-other representational structure can be assessed and visually depicted in a relatively simple manner is our central hypothesis in this chapter. Thus, the following extended discussion is designed to explain how this is done.

We revisit Barry, the hypothetical young man featured at the outset of this chapter. Barry is now a thirty-six-year-old faculty member in a history department and was recently granted tenure. Barry is interested in the possible application of psychological research methods for studying biographies of four United States presidents. In order to familiarize him with some of our methods, he agrees with the suggestion that he use himself as a subject in order to understand our approach. His first task is to make a list of eight important people in his life. As he constructs this list, he is encouraged to consider for inclusion people who are having negative as well as positive influences on his life.

After Barry completes his list, his interviewer asks him to select the name of a person who is easy for him to describe. He selects his department chairperson with whom he has recently been having some difficulty. Barry describes her as intense, hardworking, and not as fair as he would like her to be. His interviewer writes down the words (henceforth called *features*) that Barry uses to describe her. The list includes *intense, hardworking,* and *unfair.*

Barry is then asked how he perceives himself in his interactions with his chairperson. He replies, "Recently, I have found myself being tougher than I would like to be and far more withheld in my interactions than I was a couple of years ago. I have to be that way for self-preservation. She wants me to teach two courses I have never taught before, and, at this stage of my career, I have to be careful with my time. You see, I am very time-conscious." From these comments, the interviewer extracts the features *tough, withheld,* and *time-conscious.*

By now, the interviewer has six features on her list: *intense, hardworking, unfair, tough, withheld,* and *time-conscious.* The aim is to collect twelve to fourteen descriptors from Barry. We term this his *personal vocabulary.* Given that there are seven more people on his list, that is an easily realizable goal.

The next person Barry selects for description is a neighbor with whom he engages in friendly competition each summer over gardening. He does not know this individual particularly well, but he gets a kick out of their game of "one up." While his neighbor is not one of the most important people in his life, gardening *is* important to him, and his neighbor is a person highly associated with that activity. He describes his neighbor as *supportive* and himself as *committed* to the summertime battle.

The other people Barry describes are his daughter (a three-year-old that he plays with for an hour after dinner every evening), an advisee (a graduate student who is chronically late in completing his assignments and has to be pushed each step of the way), his father (a seventy-two-year-old man whose disabilities have forced him to live in a nursing home), a former mentor (a well-known historian with whom Barry has collaborated on several occasions, and now Barry experiences a desire to establish a name of his own, independent from his mentor), a tennis partner (a person whose tennis skills are equal to Barry's and with whom there is intense rivalry twice a week), and, in his words, "the students in my favorite lecture course." In regard to the students in his course, Barry is permitted to violate the rules and create a category of people instead of one person. He states that he is able to go "all out" in this large course, and what he sees in front of him is a "sea of interested faces." As Barry discusses these individuals and his relationships with them, several additional features are added. Most notable among them are *extra-verted, sociable, nurturant,* and *impatient.*

By the end of the data collection session, Barry has named twelve features. His interviewer has four features (*warm, boastful, feminine,* and *masculine*) that she wants to include in this type of exercise. These items are taken from a consensual vocabulary (or descriptors widely used and having shared gender and evaluative meaning in American society) and are examples of the radioactive tracers referred to previously in this chapter. The two features dropped from Barry's list are *unfair* and *extraverted. Unfair* is deleted because he used the word only one time, and *extraverted* is sufficiently synonymous with *sociable* for it to be excluded. The interviewer also adds three items to Barry's list of eight people. They are *Me as I usually am, Me as I would like to be,* and *Me at my worst.*

The twelve features, the eight names, and the three self-categories are now entered in a computer. Henceforth, the names and self-categories will be called *targets.* Seated in front of the computer, Barry's task now is to rate eleven targets on all fourteen features. In this exercise, however, Barry does not rate the eight people as he perceives them to be. Instead, he forms an image of himself when he is with each target and rates whether or not each feature describes *him* in his interactions with them.

The first target to appear on the screen is *daughter.* Feature *committed* is shown under *daughter,* and Barry enters 1 indicating that *committed* applies to him when he is with his daughter. Had *committed* not been a quality that Barry feels is descriptive of him in that relationship, he would have entered 0. After *committed* is rated, that feature disappears and is replaced with *sociable* and all remaining features. After he rates *impatient,* the last feature on the list, a beep is sounded, and a new target, *Chairperson,* replaces *Daughter* on the screen. In this manner, Barry works his way through all the targets. When a category of self (such as *Me as I would like to be*) is shown, instead of rating himself with his ideal self, Barry simply determines whether or not a given feature characterizes how he would like to be. Barry's computer-assisted ratings are complete after he makes 154 separate ratings. Table 7.1 reconstructs his ratings in matrix form.

Analyzing Self-With-Other Ratings

The next step is to analyze the matrix using an algorithm dubbed HICLAS, for Hierarchical Classes Analysis (DeBoeck &

Table 7.1
A Hypothetical Self-with Targets and Features Matrix

Feature

Targets	Committed	Sociable	Nurturant	Withheld	Hardworking	Tough	Intense	Warm	Masculine	Time-conscious	Supportive	Feminine	boastful	Impatient
Daughter	1	1	1	0	0	0	0	1	1	1	1	1	0	0
Chairperson	1	0	0	1	0	1	0	0	1	1	0	0	0	1
Advisee	1	0	0	0	1	0	1	0	1	0	1	0	0	1
Me as I usually am	1	1	1	0	1	0	1	1	1	1	1	1	0	1
Neighbor	0	0	0	0	0	0	0	0	1	0	0	0	1	0
Mentor	1	1	1	1	0	1	0	1	1	1	1	1	0	1
Me at my worst	1	0	0	1	0	1	0	0	1	1	0	0	0	1
Tennis partner	1	0	0	1	1	1	1	0	1	0	1	0	0	1
Me as I would like to be	1	1	1	0	0	0	0	1	1	1	1	1	0	0
Students in lecture course	1	1	1	1	1	1	1	1	1	1	1	1	0	1
Father	1	1	1	0	0	0	0	1	1	1	1	1	0	0

Rosenberg 1988). Unlike many multidimensional scaling and clustering algorithms that require as input distance or similarity measures among items, the input for HICLAS is the two-way binary matrix itself. An advantage that HICLAS has over alternative methods is its unique ability to recover the contents of a two-way matrix by simultaneously computing subset/superset relationships contained in both the rows and columns of the matrix. It does so by alternating between rows and columns of a matrix as it locates the best-fitting row and column classes and their hierarchical relations. Described as a set theoretical model, HICLAS first determines the optimal number of bottom classes (called *ranks*) and proceeds from there to compute the relationships between these bottom, subset classes and bundles of targets and features that are connected with two or more of them. In this way, a hierarchy of bundles is formed as higher order or superset clusters are layered upon the basic units of bottom classes.

Moving from an abstract discussion of HICLAS back to the concrete world of Barry's ratings, figure 7.1 shows the results of a HICLAS analysis of his matrix. A rank-three solution was used in this analysis, and that was sufficient to represent nearly all of Barry's ratings. Only two items (target *Neighbor* and feature *boastful*) could not be fit into the representation. These items are listed as *residuals* on the top and bottom right side of the figure. Had a four-rank solution been used, these items would have been included in the body of the representation, but, in this case (as with all of our work with HICLAS), a rank-three solution is judged to be sufficiently accurate and rich to stop at that point.

A careful scrutiny of table 7.1 shows that a HICLAS solution could be done by hand. Note, for example, that Barry's ratings of himself with *Daughter*, with *Father*, and *Me as I would like to be* are exactly the same. Likewise, there is a complete overlap between his ratings of himself with *Chairperson* and *Me at my worst*. These clusters appear as the first and second rank bundles at level 1 in the top half or target portion of figure 7.1. Below both of these clusters are level-1 feature clusters that contain the descriptors that essentially define both rank-one and rank-two clusters.

Now note that Barry judges himself to be *time-conscious* with all targets in the first two level-1 target clusters. At the feature level, *time-consious* belongs to rank-one and rank-two feature clusters and, therefore, is a superset of both. Its inclusion in the developing hierarchical configuration brings *Mentor* in as a superordinate or elevated target connecting clusters A and B. At this point—assuring

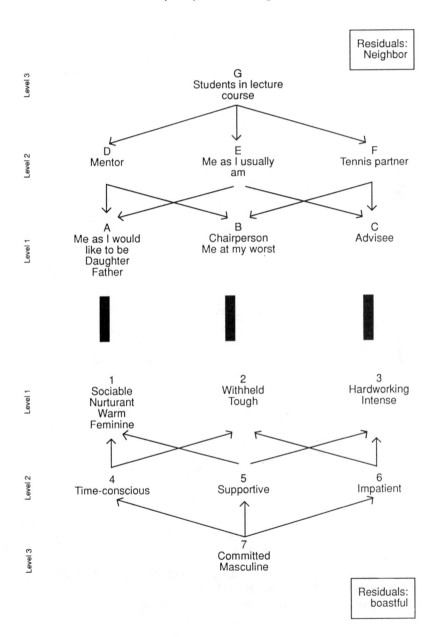

Figure 7.1
Barry's Self-with-Other Representational Structure as
Portrayed by HICLAS Algorithm

you that it can be done—we leave it up to readers who enjoy working with such puzzles to re-create figure 7.1.

Nomothetic Possibilities of HICLAS Self-with-Other Representations

Barry's world of interpersonal relationships is deceptively simple. We have kept it that way so that the reader can understand our procedures and follow the logic behind HICLAS operatons. Later, it will be seen that the matrices created by real-life participants in our research are more complex. Not only do they rate more targets using more features, but the resulting matrices are then doubled for reasons to be described. Further, in our research, we have many Barrys. Since we began with seventy-two project participants, seventy-two different self-with-other representations have been computed. Ogilvie and Ashmore (1991) discuss the self-with-other structures of two individuals in some detail and, in so doing, demonstrate the usefulness of the approach for understanding individual lives. But the goals of the Self-Perception Project go beyond idiographic analyses. We certainly want to preserve the unique ways in which individuals organize their interpersonal relationships and take meanings from them, but we also want to create knowledge at a more general level. This requires that a nomothetic approach to these data be developed. This task involves identifying strategies for making cross-person and group comparisons based on certain characteristics or properties of each individual's self-with-other configuration. Later in the chapter we will address three questions:

1. On average, what is the size, shape, and organization of self-with-other configurations?
2. How is self-perceived gender organized into the social selves of the individuals in our study?
3. How can people be meaningfully compared in terms of self-evaluation?

In the next section, we introduce the reader to some of the approaches which we have taken to answer these questions, and we do so by continuing to use Barry as an example.

Some Common Structural Components of Self-with Other Representations. How does Barry's self-with-other representational structure compare with the average self-with-other configuration? Is it typical, or does it vary from normative depictions?

In order to answer this type of question, several critical and scorable components of self-with-other representations must be identified. Although no rules or standard procedures have been adopted by workers in the area, it is possible to build on ideas put forth by others (Rosenberg 1988) to state three general working principles for identifying nomothetic qualities of individuals' HICLAS displays.

1. Number or How Many Included. This can be approached in many ways. How many targets or features are included in the structure (versus in residual)? How many target/feature clusters are there? How many items are in a particular cluster? For example, how many superordinate features does each person have?
2. Level or How High Up. An overall structure can have, given the rank-three solutions used here, anywhere from one to three levels. An individual target or feature can be located in any one of these three levels, or it can be outside the person's self-with-other system, that is, in the residual category.
3. Evaluative Tone or How Positive versus Negative. Either for the structure as a whole or any part, is the content positive, negative, uncertain, or ambivalent?

These principles can be used to derive nomothetic indices for overall structures and for specific targets or features, and we return to these issues below. These principles also point to ways of identifying the crucial components of self-with-other displays. Here, we will follow the lead of Gara (1987) as cited in Rosenberg (1988) who has identified five nomothetic types of clusters in HICLAS structures. The labels Gara gives these are *positive, negative, unelaborated, prominent,* and *prominent-ambivalent.* In the following discussion we apply these labels, with some slight variations and refinements, to various clusters within Barry's HICLAS configuration in order to show how cross-person comparisons can be made and how average representations can be configured. We start by looking at level-1 target clusters in figure 7.1.

Positive. There are three level-1 target clusters in Barry's self-with-other representational structure. They are labelled *A, B,* and *C* in figure 7.1. In the terminology of HICLAS, these clusters, respectively, are called *rank one, rank two,* and *rank three.* Let us look first at the rank-one target cluster (labelled *A* in figure 7.1) and determine if it fits any of Gara's categories. The feature cluster (feature cluster 1) most directly linked with target cluster A contains *sociable, nur-turant, warm,* and *feminine.* If Barry were a real person, we could ask him if these are positive or negative features for him. But since we created him, we must answer the question ourselves, and the answer is that Barry considers all of these features to be positive. Affirming this answer is the fact that his rank one target cluster contains *Me as I would like to be*—his image of his Ideal self. On the basis of this evidence, then, rank-one target cluster is labelled *positive.*

Unelaborated. We can also determine if cluster A is elaborated or not. Although Gara's labelling system assumes that a cluster is elaborated if it is not coded as unelaborated, we explicitly label clusters with a large number of items as elaborated. The primary index of elaboration is the number of items in a cluster. In this instance, cluster A is elaborated in that it contains several items. If it contained only one item, it would be coded *positive-unelaborated.* If Barry is to be judged as typical with regards to rank-one target cluster being positive and elaborated, a majority of other displays would have to show the same pattern.

Negative. The rank-two target cluster in figure 7.1 fits Gara's negative category. *Withheld* and *tough* are discomfitting features for Barry, and they are directly linked with *Me at my worst,* as well as descriptive of him with his disliked *chairperson.* With so few targets to begin with, it is difficult to determine if this cluster is elaborated or not. It has but one fewer items than does its counterpart (cluster A), but let us judge this reduction of items to be sufficient to give Barry's rank-two target cluster the label of *negative-unelaborated.*

Prominent. Prominent clusters are any clusters that are located above level 1. Thus, in Barry's display, clusters D through G are all prominent clusters. In addition, all clusters above level 1 in Barry's representation are also unelaborated in that all of them contain only one item. Therefore, each cluster would be coded *prominent-unelaborated.*

Features can also be looked at from the perspective of prominence. In this regard, we draw special attention to feature cluster 7 in figure 7.1. The two features in that cluster are *committed* and *masculine.* These two features are Barry's invariants in that, no matter who he is with, he perceives himself as always masculine and, with one exception, always committed. The term we will use for level-3 feature clusters is *superset.* The descriptors contained in superset feature clusters are highly informative insofar as they reflect raters' perceptions of their most durable and unchanging qualities. We stress again, however, that the person is not necessarily aware of the special status of superset features.

Prominent-ambivalent. The rule for categorizing a cluster as *prominent-ambivalent* requires that (*a*) it is located above level 1, and (*b*) that it links directly to both a negative and positive target cluster. Cluster D in Barry's diagram meets this requirement. This one-item cluster contains *mentor*, and Barry rated himself when with his former mentor as *sociable, nurturant, warm,* and *feminine* (cluster 1), as well as *withheld* and *tough* (cluster 2). The summary label given to Barry's cluster D, then, is *prominent-ambivalent-unelaborated.*

Gender in Self-with-Other Representations. In questions 2 and 3 listed previously, we ask "How can gender and how can self-evaluation be measured in order to provide some bases for group comparisons?" We have developed two complementary strategies for answering these questions. One involves the use of ordinal scales and the other employs a categorical approach. While both approaches are used to investigate gender and evaluation, for the purpose of this illustration, we separate them and briefly discuss an ordinal method for studying integration of gender descriptors in the social self. Then, we describe a categorical approach to investigating evaluation.

Recall that two gender terms, *masculine* and *feminine* were injected into Barry's rating vocabulary. Barry rated himself as masculine in *all* of his relationships and as feminine in fewer relationships. Therefore, masculine appears in a prominent feature cluster and feminine in a nonprominent one. Indeed, masculine is a superset feature for Barry, making it one of his fundamental beliefs about himself. The question now is how can this gender-related information be transformed for the purpose of making cross-person or group comparisons? Our ordinal solution is as follows.

In terms of degree of prominence or elevation, there are four possible locations for any feature. It can be listed as residual or it may appear in a cluster located in any one of the three levels. Residual descriptors are the least prominent of features in that they are used so infrequently that they cannot be located into the body of the structural configuration. Thus, if a gender term appears as a residual, we give it a score of *1*. It is scored *2* when it appears at level 1, *3* when at level 2, and *4* when at level 3. In other words, the higher the level, the more pervasive is the gender term as part of the self-with structure. Thus, in Barry's case, *masculine* is given the score of 4 and *feminine* is scored 2. These scores represent a nomothetic interval property that can be created as are any other scaled items. For example, they can (and will) be used to show sex similarities and differences with regard to the degree of integration of the features *masculine* and *feminine* into the social self.

Evaluation in Self-with-Other Representations. In addition to rating himself with important people in his life, recall that Barry was also given three self-related categories to rate. They were *Me at my worst, Me as I would like to be,* and *Me as I usually am.* The first two categories assume that most individuals possess some qualities that they do not like and other qualities that they do not only like but desire to maximize. *Me at my worst* comprises the undesired self (Ogilvie 1987), and *Me as I would like to be* is equivalent to the ideal self. *Me as I usually am* assumes that most individuals are able to envision and rate themselves as they are in general—that is, within and across various situations and relationships.

One approach to investigating evaluation in self-with-other representations involves the creation of categorical templates that describe different structural relationships among these three variables. Barry's data fit one of the most common of these templates. Return to figure 7.1 and note that *Me as I usually am* is prominent and links directly with rank-one target cluster (labelled *A*), a cluster that contains *Me as I would like to be.* By virtue of this arrangement, Barry is telling us that his usual self exhibits several features including most or all of the features that are manifest when he is at his best. Also note, however, that neither of these selves are linked with *Me at my worst.*

The template that describes the juxtaposition of Barry's three selves is one that depicts a usual-self linkage with the ideal self and with the undesired self isolated from them. In other words, while *Me at my worst* is integrated into Barry's structural space (that is, it is not a residual), it remains separate from his usual and best selves. As we will explain later, we refer to this type as *content/defended.*

Of course, the pattern just described is but one of several possible arrangements. For example, another categorical template which we will discuss later is one in which all three self-related judgments are linked. This integrated pattern depicts *Me as I usually am* in a prominent cluster that is linked to lower order (usually level 1) clusters, one containing *Me as I would like to be* and the other containing *Me at my worst.* Our working label for this type is *integrated.*

We have used our fictitious Barry to introduce our procedures for collecting self-with-other ratings, to exemplify the HICLAS method of analyzing these ratings, and to show how nomothetic infomation can be derived from the resulting structures. In this extended prelude to our program of research on aspects of the social self, we have introduced the reader to some new terms and concepts that will be used again when some of our findings are presented. However, before we come to that section, we must leave Barry's neatly organized world of interpersonal relationships and describe the much larger puzzle we have created.

Upping the Ante: The Self-with-Other Structures of Real People

Real-life relationships are a great deal more complex than we have made them in Barry's example. Most people have many more than eight important people in their lives, and personal vocabularies are never limited to ten words. We attempt to tap the richness of relationships and vocabularies by having participants in our research identify twenty-five important people and rate each on sixty features. In Barry's scenario, he performed 154 separate ratings. Our research participants make 1,680 separate ratings. Imagine attempting to determine the underlying hierarchical structure of these resulting matrices by hand! Indeed, we have made the matter of analysis even more complex as the result of the following decision.

Input for HICLAS is restricted to two-way binary matrices such as used with Barry's scenario. But, unlike Barry, participants in our research use a *0, 1,* and *2* rating system. In this scheme, *0* means *not at all or never descriptive,* *1* stands for *somewhat or sometimes descriptive,* and *2* indicates *very or always descriptive.* Thus, for our participants, when a name appears on the screen, the rater must decide if a given feature does not describe her or him in the relationship *(0),* sometimes describes how she or he is or feels in the relationship *(1),* or is highly descriptive of her or him in interactions with the target *(2).* We are not alone in the usage of a *0–1–2* rating system. Most researchers who use HICLAS employ it. The primary reason for this is that most respondents feel more comfortable making ratings on a three-point continuum rather using a two-point scale which they experience as being too "yes-no." The resulting matrices, however, are not binary. HICLAS simply does not know what to do with *2* responses. Procedures that have been followed up to now have been to automatically covert *2s* to *1s,* making judgments of *always* equivalent to assessments of *sometimes.*

We have been uncomfortable with these conversions, but, like others, have not dealt directly with the potential problems in published reports (Ogilvie & Ashmore 1991). Our discomfort stems largely from the fact that the distinction between a *1* (sometimes) and a *2* (always) is phenomenologically an important distinction. For most people, the difference is quite meaningful, and this distinction is completely lost when *2s* are converted to *1s*.

There are no perfect solutions to the problem. But we have now settled on a partial solution that we consider to be an improvement over automatic *2 = 1* conversions. Briefly, our strategy involves creating two matrices from the original which, unlike Barry's, contains *2s* as well as *0s* and *1s*. In effect, the original matrix is doubled. this is done as follows: *0=0,0;1=1,0,* and *2=1,1.* The first of each pair of digits are placed in the first matrix, and the second of each pair is placed in a second. A *0* remains *0* in both matrices. A *1* remains *1* in the first matrix and changes to *0* on the second. A *2* becomes *1* on both. The expanded matrices are then merged into a now-doubled two-way binary matrix. This enables us to roughly preserve judgments of degree of feature applicability to a given self-with-other relationship.[3]

All of the HICLAS-derived results to be discussed have been converted in the manner already described. The only additional piece of information necessary to report is that the structural representations we now work with contain two types of features. Features that are scored predominantly as *1s* are listed in their original form. Features that arrive in clusters primarily on the basis of *2* ratings are preceded by a *v* which stands for *very*.

METHODS AND PROCEDURES

Participants

When the Self-Perception Project began in January 1989, it included seventy-two Rutgers University students. Forty-seven of these had taken part in all nine sessions of the Person Perception Project, which ran from September 1987 through December 1988 and explored the role of the sex of targets in person-perception (Ashmore & Del Boca 1986). An additional ten were recruited from an adult development class taught by the second author; five responded to letters sent to a sample of university juniors; and ten were referred by friends in the project. When the project began, nine of the participants were seniors, fifty were juniors, and thirteen were sophomores. In terms of sex, fifty were female, and twenty-two were male. The ethnic distribution was as follows: thirty-nine white, twenty-one black (African-American), eight Hispanic, three Asian-Indian, and one Asian. Sixty-eight individuals completed all eleven sessions of the project. Of these forty-seven were female and twenty-one were male; thirty-seven were white, nineteen were black (African-American), eight were Hispanic, three were Asian-Indian, and one was Asian. Forty-six have graduated from college, and twenty-two are still enrolled as undergraduates.

Assessing Self-with-Other Representations

The first four of eleven sessions of the Self-Perception Project involved collecting and analyzing data pertaining to participants' perceptions of other people and themselves with these people. A detailed description of the methods and procedures used in these sessions as well as a discussion of the purposes behind each appears in the Ogilvie and Ashmore work of 1991. In this chapter, however, the description of the four sessions can be brief because the reader has already been introduced to several of the procedures through the discussion of Barry's interview and his subsequent ratings.

Session One. Prior to the first session, a letter was sent to all participants asking them to bring with them a list of the most important people in their lives, both present and past. The letter gave some examples of the sorts of people to include, such as parents, relatives, friends, or even enemies.

When a participant arrived for the first session, she or he was interviewed by a staff member for a maximum of eighty-minutes. The goals of the interview were to (1) winnow the participant's list of people down to (or increase it up to) twenty-five names; (2) take notes on who these people are and the nature of the participant's relationships with them; and (3) obtain a sample of the participant's own vocabulary for describing other people and herself or himself when with each person. These goals were accomplished by having the participant discuss each person on the list, one by one, while the interviewer recorded information about the relationship and, on a separate form, created a list of words the interviewee used to describe the "other" and "self-with-other." Near the end of the interview, work was done to delete some less important people in instances when a list exceeded twenty-five.

After session one was concluded, several steps were taken to prepare for the next session that took place about three weeks later. One of the most important tasks was to reduce each of the participant's personal vocabularies to forty-two words or phrases. This was accomplished by crossing out duplicates and by reducing synonyms into exemplar words. A back-up list of several words was retained in case some personal vocabulary words matched our list of eighteen words, which included those drawn from the results of William's and Best's research in 1982 using Gough's Adjective Checklist to assess sex stereotypes. Eight words were high-consensus male stereotypic attributes, and eight others were high-consensus female stereotypic characteristics. These were further subdivided into positive and negative evaluations. Male-positive words were *active, confident, independent,* and *strong.* Female-positive words were *affectionate, gentle, sympathetic,* and *warm.* Male-negative words included *boastful, coarse, egotistical,* and *hardhearted.* Female-negatives were *fussy, nagging, weak,* and *whiney.* Two more words—*feminine* and *masculine*—brought the total number of words in this consensual vocabulary to eighteen.

Finally, the sixty descriptors (both personal and consensual), now called *features,* and the twenty-five targets were entered into a computer.

Session Two. In this session, the participant was trained as to how to perform computer-assisted ratings. As already explained, a name appeared on the screen followed by a feature. The rater was instructed how to rate a target in terms of that feature (and the remaining fifty-nine features) by entering a *0* (not at all descriptive), *1* (somewhat or sometimes descriptive), or *2* (very or always descriptive). After the first target had been rated using all sixty features, another name appeared on the screen and that individual became the target for feature ratings. However, unlike our hypothetical testing of the fictitious Barry, session two was devoted to obtaining ratings of the participant's perception of their important people. The task of rating others on a list of attributes is a standard procedure in person-perception research. Eventually, the results of this data gathering session will be intergrated into a final report of the Self-Perception Project. For present purposes, however, no further reference will be made to this session as we turn our attention to the self-with-other ratings performed in session three.

Session Three. A few weeks after session two was completed, the participant returned to make more computer-assisted ratings. The procedures were nearly identical to those described above in the scenario with Barry. That is, a target appeared on the screen and the rater's task was to form an image of themselves in a modal scene with that person and, using the sixty features, to rate *themselves* when with each individual target. As with Barry, three more targets were added—*Me as I usually am, Me as I would like to be,* and *Me at my worst.* For most participants, this resulted in a matrix of twenty-eight targets times sixty features.

Session Four. Session Four was primarily a feedback session. The participant first performed four paper-and-pencil ratings of self with each of the twenty-five others—*not masculine/masculine,not feminine/feminine*—and two other rating scales tailored for the individual and based on the analyses of his or her data from previous sessions.

Next the interviewer introduced two diagrams, one showing the results of HICLAS analyses of session two, and the other a HICLAS display of session-three ratings. A predesigned format was used to walk the participant through the diagrams drawing attention to certain structural properties contained in them.

The reader has already been given a taste of what occured in session four in the section in which we described some structural properties of Barry's self-with-other representational display. In our discussion of Barry, we made up a story about his self-with-other configuration. We determined what the display meant. We did not do that with our participants. Instead, *they* became the meaning-makers. The interviewer served merely as a "walk-through guide." The participant was the interpreter.

One further comment is warranted about session four. It is an example of one of the ways in which we formed investigative partnerships with the participants in the study. While we did not forego our responsibilities as researchers, we realized that our participants are the specialists on their own lives. Of course, there are some aspects that they will not tell us about and other nonconscious factors that they cannot tell us. Still, there is an enormous amount of information readily accessible to subjects that, once obtained, operate as correctives to researchers' speculations. In summation, we have learned that the benefits of creating a dialogue with participants in which we rely on them to tell us what certain results mean far outweighs any possible advantages of forming and maintaining a sacred line between experimenter and subject.

WHAT'S TO BE FOUND: ILLUSTRATIVE NOMOTHETIC FINDINGS

The goal in this section is not to present all the results but rather to illustrate the nomothetic possibilities of the self-with-other concept as we have operationalized them. This description of "what's to be found" is divided into two primary subsections. The first, which takes a macroscopic perspective, is devoted to the contents and contours of self-with-other representations as assessed by means of the HICLAS algorithm. This description of what self-with-other structures look like is further partitioned into three subsections.

1. What is the average self-with-other representation?;
2. What is the overall size and shape of the HICLAS representations of the interpersonal self? and
3. Of what do the primary nomothetic subparts of these overall structures (as identified in the discussion of the fictitious Barry) consist and how are they organized?

The second major part of this presentation of illustrative nomothetic findings takes a more microscopic view as we describe how evaluation and gender are encoded within individuals' self-with-other structures. For both the good-bad and male-female issues, this is done in two ways.

1. Using individual tracer elements (such as the feature *masculine*), descriptive statistics for nomothetic properties indexing single continuous variables are presented; and
2. Using multiple tracer elements (such as *masculine, feminine,* and the *very* versions of each), we identify major patterns of incorporating these into the social self structures revealed by the HICLAS algorithm and use these as categorical nomothetic indices.

Macroscopic View of Self-with-Other Representations: Overall Contents and Contours

The HICLAS analysis of the session three self-with ratings yielded seventy-two depictions like that presented in figure 7.1, one for each of the participants in the Self-Perception Project. Each diagram is unique in terms of both content and organization.

With respect to content, in addition to each person having different important people in his or her life, forty-two of the sixty words and phrases the respondents used to describe these people and their relationships with them were drawn from their own vocabularies. Participants also organized their perceptions of themselves in their relationships differently, resulting in nonduplicating constellations and overall structures. At the same time, however, it is possible to identify patterns of self-with organization, and these patterns can be used both to better understand individuals and to make cross-person comparisons.

We begin this analysis of what the self-with-other structures produced by the HICLAS algorithm look like by describing the "big picture." More specifically, we present a visual depiction of the self-with-other structure for a modal Self-Perception Project participant and discuss this as well as a second average pattern that is a slight variant on this overall scheme. Finally, we describe in depth the nomothetic properties that were used to derive the modal pattern and its variants.

It will be seen that the modal self-with-other structures are less complex than were Barry's as depicted in figure 7.1. Some readers may prefer to simply know that and have a firm feel for the "big picture" as presented in figure 7.2. However, given our present nomothetic focus, we think it is essential to spell out the various steps that have been taken to compute average structures. (Hence, the second and third following subsections of this chapter which some readers may choose to skip).

Average Self-with-Other Structures. The previously described nomothetic principles (*how high up, how many, how positive versus negative*) and the nomothetic cluster types were used to identify an average overall self-with-other structure for the Self-Perception Project participants. This is presented in figure 7.2 which is a HICLAS diagram that describes a modal participant in our project. That is, figure 7.2 fits the average results for a large subset of the sample as a whole, including those for the primary nomothetic types of clusters in self-with-other structures. It is essential to note that the figure is highly schematized, and, while it does fit a substantial portion of the people in our research, it certainly does not in its entirety fit all or even most of the respondents. In short, figure 7.2 is a prototype of which there is considerable variation. In fact, as will be explained shortly, it is just one of two closely related average configurations.

Figure 7.2 was derived as follows. First, for each participant, we noted which target clusters (*A* through *G*) and feature bundles (*1* through *7*) contained items or were filled (versus empty). Next, again for each individual, we categorized each target cluster as per the previously described typology of *positive, negative, ambiguous in evaluative tone, elaborated* (containing five or more targets), or

Figure 7.2
Schematized Average Participant's Self-with-Other Representational Structure as Portrayed by HICLAS Algorithm

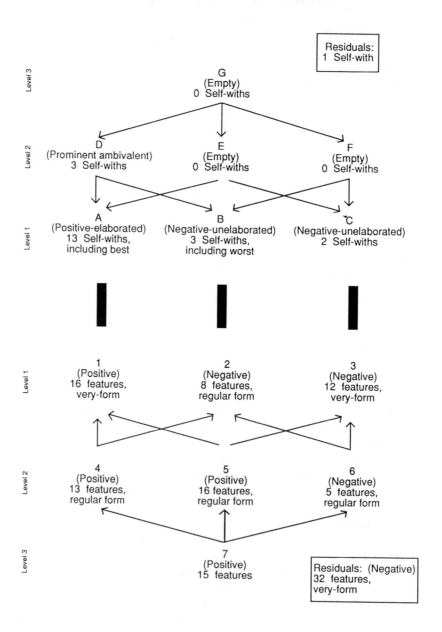

unelaborated. We also classified each feature cluster in terms of evaluative tone and form of descriptors. Finally, we counted the number of items in the target and feature bundles.

Beginning with the issue of filled versus empty clusters, for the clear majority of participants, the feature and target residuals contained items, as did all seven of the feature groupings and the three level 1 target clusters (namely, *A, B,* and *C*). For most respondents, target cluster *G* (superset) was empty. Level 2 target clusters were as follows: All three empty: three females and no males; one filled and two empty: nineteen females and twelve males; two filled and one empty: twenty-three females and nine males; all three filled: five females and one male.

These results suggest two average patterns. In both, all feature clusters and the residuals are filled and target cluster *G* is empty. In the first modal pattern, which characterizes ninteen or 38 percent of the females and twelve or 54 percent of the males, only one level 2 target cluster contains self-withs. This pattern is depicted in figure 7.2. We have chosen *D* to be filled because this is the most common situation, especially for females.

In the second modal pattern, there are two nonempty level 2 clusters. This pattern fits twenty-three or 46 percent of the females and nine or 41 percent of the males. Again, it is to be emphasized that there is much variation around these average overall configurations.

The modal patterns—especially the simpler one presented in figure 7.2—suggest the following general conclusions about the social self as operationalized by the present procedures. With regard to targets or self-withs (the top part of the figure), the internal representation of self-with-important others is relatively simple and particularized. Beginning with the level 1 building block clusters, there is a single positive *social me* (cluster A) which is brought out by a large number of others. This self-with constellation is defined by a large number of positive features (clusters 1, 4, and 5). Although it is not apparent in the figure, the targets in cluster A are also relatively heterogeneous, containing various mixtures of friends, parents, other relatives, teachers, and the like. In addition, there are two much smaller negative interpersonal selves. In sum, the pattern for level 1 targets is one big amorphous positive and two small but differentiated negative self-with groupings. Moving to level two, the modal participant has just one or two higher order groupings (cluster D in the figure, or *D* plus either *E* or *F* in the other major pattern). These contain a small number of people who bring out both positive and negative facets of self. Thus, our average participant had just one or two self-with constellations that represented a mixing or blending of affect and experience in interpersonal relationships.

Moving finally to level three, the fact that cluster *G* was empty for the overwhelming majority of respondents suggests that almost no one in the Self-Perception Project had important people in their lives who brought out their full ranges of social-self possibilities.

Turning to the bottom of figure 7.2, the features were somewhat more differentiated in the sense that all level 2 and 3 clusters contained descriptors. With regard to evaluative tone, there is a clear bias toward positivity. Negative features tend to be rejected (hence, the large number of predominantly negative descriptors in the residual category for the modal individual in the project). The cardinal traits of most participants (those in cluster 7) also tend to be positive.

With regard to form of feature, the *Very*-form predominates at lower levels in the hierarchy and in the residual category. This pattern of *very*-descriptors as more common in more specific self-with constellations makes sense because features preceded by *very*- can be thought of as more extreme characteristics (the respondent always gave them a 2). This logical finding provides indirect and partial validation for our overall assessment procedure and particularly for the decision to double the matrix.

Size and Shape of HICLAS Representations of the Interpersonal Self. The foregoing modal (figure 7.2) and slight variant other average structures were based on findings for a large number of nomothetic indices calculated from the HICLAS display of each participant. We now present the findings for these measures in detail. (As already noted, some readers may prefer to skip over this detail and move ahead to the microscopic view in which we describe how individuals integrated gender and evaluation into the described modal self-with-other overall structures.) We begin by presenting in table 7.2 the descriptive statistics for several individual continuous variables derived from these structures for each participant.

In terms of number of targets described, the means were 26.54 and 25.82 for female and male respondents respectively, with an overall sample mean of 26.32. Since our procedure (especially time constraints) placed a ceiling of twenty-eight on the number of possible targets (which was violated in a small number of cases), it is not clear whether college age students such as the present respondents would have substantially more important-others and whether

Table 7.2

Descriptive Statistics for Nomothetic Properties Pertaining to Overall Self-with-Other-Representation Structure

Property	Females (n = 50)				Males (n = 22)			
	Mean	SD	Minimum	Maximum	Mean	SD	Minimum	Maximum
Targets (Self-withs)								
Number described	26.54	2.41	19.00	30.00	25.82	3.94	16.00	30.00
Number of clusters	4.70	0.95	3.00	7.00	4.64	1.05	3.00	7.00
Number of targets in level 2 and 3 clusters	5.50	4.01	0.00	21.00	7.41	5.41	1.00	20.00
Ratio of targets in level 2 and 3 clusters	0.21	0.15	0.00	0.75	0.28	0.18	0.04	0.71
Number of targets in residual	1.40	1.82	0.00	8.00	0.41	0.67	0.00	2.00
Ratio of targets in residual	0.05	0.07	0.00	0.30	0.02	0.03	0.00	0.13
Features								
Number described	120.00	0.00	120.00	120.00	120.00	0.00	120.00	120.00
Number of clusters	6.46	0.71	5.00	7.00	6.14	0.89	4.00	7.00
Number of features in level 2 and 3 clusters	42.64	12.70	18.00	65.00	44.73	13.05	19.00	79.00
Ratio of features in level 2 and 3 clusters	0.36	0.11	0.15	0.54	0.37	0.11	0.16	0.66
Number of features in residual	32.54	10.37	4.00	40.00	32.05	9.85	11.00	40.00
Ratio of features in residual	0.27	0.09	0.03	0.33	0.27	0.08	0.09	0.33

sex differences might emerge if the upper bound that we imposed were lifted. Our hunch is that neither alternative would have surfaced.

In the open-ended listing of important-others in session one, the average number of people listed was 30.1, and this did not vary by participant sex. (Excluded from the calculation of this average was the list of 120 people compiled by one participant who misread our instructions and named all of her present and past acquaintances. During her interview, she was able to identify twenty-five of these as most important.) Thus, the number of important-others included in our procedures may somewhat underestimate the size of the universe of such others for participants such as those that we utilized, but this does not appear to be appreciable.

The table also indicates how these multiple self-withs are psychologically organized. These targets were clustered into an average of 4.70 and 4.64 bundles by female and male respondents, with an overall sample mean of 4.68. In comparison with the hypothetical Barry, then, our participants were considerably less differentiated in terms of the number of target clusters, although some individuals did distinguish the maximum possible seven self-with groupings. There was great variation in terms of elevated or prominent targets, which was simply indexed as number and ratio of targets appearing in level 2 or 3 categories. The respective means were 5.50 and 0.21 for females, and 7.41 and 0.28 for males (6.08 and 0.23 for all participants). These averages, however, must be considered in the light of the large individual variations around them. The standard deviations and ranges for both sexes were quite large. Thus, the people in the Self-Perception Project varied considerably in the degree to which they differentiated themselves in their relationships with important others.

For those with a small number of higher order targets (as in figure 7.2), self-with-important-others is experienced in very discrete, local, and distinct ways, what we have labelled as *particularized*. On the other hand, for those having a relatively large proportion of level 2 and 3 targets (as in the second average pattern and for respondents with even more prominent targets and groupings), their interpersonal self is not only more differentiated but the higher order self-withs are more complex and involve greater nuances of feeling and behavior since they build on more than one level 1 cluster.

Turning to the features, the mean number of clusters was just over six for both sexes. For all participants, the mean was 6.36, with a range of four to seven. In terms of elevation or prominence of features, somewhat more than forty (full sample average = 43.28) or about 36% fell into level 2 or 3 clusters. Again, the range was wide—eighteen (15%) to seventy-nine (66%). Thus, as was true for elevation of targets, participants differed greatly one from another in the extent to which many or just a few of their features were placed in higher order and, hence, more complex categories. In contrast with the pattern for targets, a relatively large number and proportion of descriptors were not integrated into the structure revealed by HICLAS. For both sexes, 27% of the features appeared in the residual category.

Primary Nomothetic Subparts of Self-with-Other Structures: Targets. Following the reasoning already laid out in using the example of Barry to identify nomothetic cluster types within HICLAS displays, we coded each of the target clusters in each participant's self-with-other structure. More specifically, each participant's clusters A through G (as in figures 7.1 and 7.2) were coded in terms of both evaluative tone—predominantly positive; predominantly negative; or ambiguous/uncertain—and degree of elaboration, with clusters having five or more targets designated as *elaborated* and those with four or less self-withs as *unelaborated.* The frequency of each nomothetic cluster type for each such cluster is presented in table 7.3.

Target Cluster A (rank one). As can be seen in table 7.3, cluster A is positive and elaborated for the clear majority of participants. It is so coded for forty of fifty females and sixteen of twenty-two males. *Me as I would like to be* falls into this cluster for twenty-four females and ten males. For those cluster As coded as positive-elaborated, the mean number of included targets was 13.43 and 12.63 for female and male participants, respectively. Thus, as was the case for the hypothetical Barry, rank 1 for most respondents was a relatively large grouping comprising individuals who bring out the positive qualities of the participants.

Target Clusters B and C (ranks two and three). There is more variability regarding clusters B and C. The modal type in both cases is negative-unelaborated for both sexes. For cluster B, the next most common coding is negative-elaborated for females, whereas for males the next most frequent type is ambiguous/uncertain. For females, then, cluster B is negative (thirty-two of fifty), and *Me at my worst* appears in this group for nineteen females. Turning to cluster C, for females, the second- and third-most frequent codings are positive-unelaborated and ambiguous/uncertain. But for males, the two positive types and ambiguous/uncertain show about the same small frequency.

Table 7.3
Nomothetic Cluster Types for Targets; Frequency by Sex of Participant

| | Females | | | | | | Males | | | | | |
| | Cluster Type | | | | | | Cluster Type | | | | | |
Level One	PosEl	PosUEl	A/U	NegEl	NegUEl	Empty	PosEl	PosUEl	A/U	NegEl	NegUEl	Empty
Cluster A Rank 1	40	0	7	1	0	2	16	0	2	1	0	3
Cluster B Rank 2	5	4	8	14	18	1	3	1	6	2	9	1
Cluster C Rank 3	0	13	12	0	22	3	3	4	5	0	10	0
Level Two	PosEl	PosUEl	A/U	NegEl	NegUEl	Empty	PosEl	PosUEl	A/U	NegEl	NegUEl	Empty
Cluster D	3	3	34	0	0	10	3	1	7	0	0	11
Cluster E	5	9	10	0	0	26	2	6	7	0	0	7
Cluster F	0	0	10	0	6	34	0	0	6	0	2	14
Level Three	4 SWs	3 SWs	2 SWs	1 Sw	Empty		4 SWs	3 SWs	2 SWs	1 Sw	Empty	
Cluster G	1	0	2	6	41		0	0	3	3	16	

Note: PosEl = Positive in evaluative tone and elaborated.
PosUEl = Positive in evaluative tone and unelaborated.
A/U = Ambiguous (or clear positive and negative) or uncertain in evaluative tone (elaborated versus unelaborated not distinguished).
NegEl = Negative in evaluative tone and elaborated.
NegUEl = Negative in evaluative tone and unelaborated.
Empty = No targets fell in this cluster.
SWs = Number of self-withs in this cluster.

Target Cluster D, E, and F (prominent). The modal pattern, especially for females, is clear. Cluster D is ambivalent/uncertain with cluster E and F empty. It is this average configuration that is depicted in figure 7.2. There are, in addition, important minority patterns for the latter two clusters. With regard to cluster E, ten females and seven males have this coded as ambiguous/uncertain and fourteen females and eight males have this categorized as positive. Concerning cluster F, the second most common coding is ambiguous/uncertain.

Target Cluster G. Again the modal pattern is clear. This cluster contained no self-withs for forty-one of fifty females and sixteen of twenty-two males. Thus, unlike the hypothetical Barry, most of the people who participated in our project did not have any important-others who brought out the full range of self-experience and emotion. This strong pattern makes the exceptions, those with one or more targets in this superset cluster, candidates for further idiographic exploration.

Primary Nomothetic Subparts of Self-with Other Structures: Features. We also coded each of the feature clusters in each participant's self-with-other structure. Each respondent's clusters 1 through 7 (as at the bottom of figures 7.1 and 7.2) were coded in terms of both evaluative tone (predominately positive, predominantly negative, or ambiguous/uncertain) and form of descriptor (predominantly regular or the *very-* form introduced by the doubling procedure already described). The frequency of each form and evaluative tone categorized for each such cluster is presented in table 7.4.

Level 1 Clusters. With regard to evaluative tone, the modal pattern follows logically from the present information, although the direction of causality is just the reverse since the evaluative coding of each target grouping is based largely on the feature bundle defining that cluster. Cluster 1 is positive, and clusters 2 and 3 are negative for the average participant. The form coding indicates that the *very-*form is quite common in level 1 clusters, especially for females. Given that the *very-*form can be thought of as the more extreme descriptor (since it represents the respondent's assigning the feature in question a 2), it is reasonable that they should be common in clusters that are quite specific to particular others and that are relatively undifferentiated. That the more extreme descriptors predominate in the more specific level one groupings rather than in the more general

Table 7.4
Nomothetic Cluster Types for Features; Frequency by Sex of Participant

	Females								Males							
	Form (a)				Evaluation (b)				Form (a)				Evaluation (b)			
	Regular	Very-	Both	Empty	Posi-tive	Nega-tive	A/U	Empty	Regular	Very-	Both	Empty	Posi-tive	Nega-tive	A/U	Empty
Level One																
Cluster 1	10	29	7	4	40	2	4	4	5	11	4	2	18	2	0	2
Cluster 2	25	11	11	3	8	33	6	3	8	8	3	3	4	12	3	3
Cluster 3	13	28	7	2	13	27	8	2	6	7	6	3	6	9	4	3
Level Two																
Cluster 4	40	3	6	1	34	5	10	1	17	2	2	1	12	7	2	1
Cluster 5	34	9	4	3	35	5	7	3	14	4	2	2	15	4	1	2
Cluster 6	33	4	2	11	4	26	9	11	12	2	0	8	2	9	3	8
Level Three																
Cluster 7	46	0	1	3	39	3	7	1	21	0	0	1	16	1	4	1
Residual	0	46	4	0	4	35	11	0	0	19	3	0	3	11	8	0

(a) Form refers to whether the features in the cluster were regular (the unmodified form) or very- (the form produced by doubling the matrix). Participants were coded into one of the above groupings based on the predominance of one form versus the other, using a 60% decision rule.

(b) Evaluation refers to whether the features in the cluster were predominantly positive or negative in evaluative tone, again using a 60% criterion. An ambiguous/unclear (A/U) code was given when either (a) there was no clear predominance of one tone over the other, or (b) the features did not allow clear determination of evaluative tone.

level 2 and 3 clusters also serves to validate both the HICLAS algorithm and the already described doubling procedure.

The form coding also reveals potentially informative differences between the sexes. Cluster 1 is predominantly the *very-* form for both sexes. For females, this is also true of cluster 3, but cluster 2 consists of regular descriptors for the modal participant. For male respondents, on the other hand, clusters 2 and 3 show no clear pattern concerning form of feature. For females, the average respondent appears to have two types of level 1 negative feature groupings: one consisting primarily of regular form descriptors, the other of the more extreme *very-* features.

Level 2 clusters. In contrast to level one groupings, the level 2 clusters contain predominantly regular form features. With regard to evaluation, clusters 4 and 5 are positive and cluster 6 is negative for the average respondent.

Cluster 7 (superset). The modal pattern is clear. For both males and females, the superset is positive in evaluation and contains regular form descriptors primarily. Thus, as noted, the attributes that our respondents see as true of them no matter whom they are with are positive in connotation.

Residual. This *not me* grouping stands in direct contrast with the contents of cluster 7. It contains, for the most part, negative descriptors and these are generally of the *very-* form. Taken with the findings for the superset cluster, this suggests that most of our participants have a positivity bias with negative attributes rejected and positive features accepted and made prominent in their self-with-other representational structures.

Microscopic View of Self-with-Other Representations: Good/ Bad and Female/Male. In this section we describe how individuals incorporate the good/bad and female/male themes into their interpersonal selves. This is done both in terms of individual continuous variables and on the basis of gestalt patterns involving multiple tracer elements.

Evaluation in Self-with-Other Structures: Individual Continuous Variables. Recall that the majority of rating targets were provided by project participants. These targets consisted of important people in their lives. The only items added to the target list by the investigators were *Me at my worst, Me as I would like to be,* and *me as I usually am.* These items were included in order to provide information regarding participants' present-day perceptions of their undesired selves, ideal selves, and usual selves. Focusing on the former two, we injected ideal self (*I*) and self at worst (*W*) into each person's self-with system.

Where did these evaluative tracers end up? We went about answering this query with individual continuous property scores in two ways: (1) How high up or how elevated were the positive and negative selves and (2) How many other targets were connected to the positive and negative selves?

The top part of table 7.5 reports the descriptive statistics for these nomothetic indices.

In terms of ideal-self elevation (with *1* scored for residual and *4* for level 3 superordinate), the overall mean was 2.36, and the range was quite narrow, from just 2 to 3. Thus, ideal self for every participant was in the structure (no one made it residual). At the same time, it was never a self that pervaded all other self-withs (no one made it a level 3 superordinate). Self-at-worst was a bit less elevated or prominent on average, with a mean score of 1.92, and some participants did not experience this negative self as part of their interpersonal identity. For example, thirteen participants made self-at-worst a residual.

A second approach was to count the number of self-with targets connected with ideal self and self-at-worst (that is, the number of self-withs in the same cluster or a direct subset bundle). As can be seen in table 7.2, many more self-withs were connected with the positive self (14.04) than with the negative self (2.94).

Evaluation in Self-with-Other Structures: A Gestalt and Categorical Approach. A second general way to study evaluation in self-with-other representations is to focus attention on the relative locations of all three of the supplied self-target items within each representational space and note the various patterns of linkage or gestalts. We have identified and have temporarily labelled four patterns that account for all seventy-two participants. These are described next.

Integrated. An evaluatively integrated structure is one that contains *Me as I usually am (U* for usual) in a prominent cluster that is linked to a lower-level cluster containing *Me as I would like to be (I* for ideal) and another lower level cluster containing *Me at my worst (W* for worst). This configuration suggests that the rater perceives *U* as expressing some elements of both *I* and *W*. Thus, the positive and negative selves are differentiated, but both are seen as part of or integrated into the overall or usual self.

Table 7.5

Descriptive Statistics for Individual Continuous Nomothetic Properties Pertaining to Evaluation and Gender in Self-with-Other Structure

	Females (n = 50)				Males (n = 22)				Sex Difference
	Mean	SD	Mini-mum	Maxi-mum	Mean	SD	Mini-mum	Maxi-mum	t
Evaluation in Self-with-Other Structure									
Ideal self (IS) elevation	2.34	.48	2	3	2.41	.50	2	3	Not computed
Self at worst (SAW) elevation	1.90	.58	1	3	1.95	.38	1	3	Not computed
Number of targets connected to ideal self	13.80	6.11	0	25	14.59	6.22	0	26	Not computed
Number of targets connected to self at worst	3.34	4.81	0	22	2.05	2.72	0	11	Not computed
Gender in Self-with-Other Structures									
Feminine elevation	3.40	.86	1	4	1.36	.58	1	3	−10.14*
Very feminine elevation	2.24	1.08	1	4	1.09	.29	1	2	−6.96*
Masculine elevation	1.40	.83	1	4	3.59	.67	2	4	10.89*
Very masculine elevation	1.06	.24	1	2	2.23	1.02	1	4	5.30*
Expressive-positive elevation	12.24	2.19	7	16	11.14	1.96	7	15	−2.03*
Instrumental-positive elevation	13.00	1.98	9	16	13.95	1.50	12	16	−2.02*
Expressive-negative elevation	7.72	2.48	4	15	7.18	3.11	4	14	−0.78
Instrumental-negative elevation	7.56	2.50	4	13	8.95	2.87	4	14	2.08*

*p < .05
Note: t values in italics are based on samples with unequal variances.

Unintegrated. An unintegrated structure is one in which none of the three items are linked. That is, *U*, *I*, and *W* are isolated from each other. Participants whose diagrams match this pattern indicate that their usual selves are different from both their ideal selves and their worst selves, and the latter two are also different from each other. In this somewhat curious pattern, the good and bad *me's* are distinguished but neither is integrated into the participant's everyday personal identity.

Content/defended. The pattern labelled content/defended is one wherein *U* is linked with *I*, and *W* is isolated from both. There are three major variations of these arrangements. One is with *U* and *I* in the same cluster, and *W* is isolated. The second, and equally common, configuration is one in which *U* is in a prominent cluster that links with *I* but does not connect with *W*. The least common variation is in which *W* remains isolated, and *I* is linked with *U* from a superordinate position. These patterns are labelled *content,* because of the close relationship between *I* and *U*. *Defended* is added to the label to reflect the fact that *W* is in a cluster that is compartmentalized from clusters containing *U* and *I*. In other words, the participant's negative self is cut off from the usual self, and this may indicate a defensive avoidance of unattractive facets of self as an interpersonal creature. Representations fitting a content/defended pattern indicate that the usual self shares features that characterize the ideal self, and the worst self plays no part in that constellation. Whether this represents genuine contentment or a defensive posture, we cannot say at this time.

Unhappy. Discontent, unhappiness, and—in some instances, perhaps—depression is indicated when there is a linkage between *U* and *W*, and *I* appears in a disconnected cluster. The two variations of this pattern are (1) *U* and *W* are in the same cluster, and *I* is isolated; and (2) *U* is linked with *W* from a prominent cluster, and is not linked with either item.

The results of having coded each participant's diagram into one of these categories are presented in table 7.6. What stands out most in these results is the fact that the category *Content/defended* accounts for 86 percent of the males in our sample compared with 46 percent of the females. That is, nineteen of the twenty-two males link their usual selves with their ideal selves and place their worst selves in an isolated or unlinked position. The same pattern is true of twenty-three of fifty, or less than half of the females. The remaining females are distributed fairly evenly across the other three cate-

Table 7.6

Distribution of Participants across Four Categories of Self-evaluation

			Frequency (Percent)	
Category Label	Description	Example	Females	Males
Integrated	U links with I and W	U—I, U—W (cluster)	11 (22%)	1 (5%)
Unintegrated	U, I and W in separate and unlinked clusters	U I W	8 (16%)	2 (9%)
Content/Defended	U links with I, W is isolated	U—I W	23 (46%)	19 (86%)
Unhappy	U links with W; I is isolated	U—W I	8 (16%)	0 (0%)

U = Usual self
I = Ideal self
W = Worst self

gories. Eleven (or 22 percent) of the females are categorized as integrated with only one male in that category. Eight females (16 percent) and two males (9 percent) are labelled as unintegrated. And finally, eight females (16 percent) and no males are coded as unhappy by our system.

Overall, these results show that nineteen females and only one male (38 percent versus 5 percent) integrate their worst selves with their usual selves. These figures represent the total number of females and males coded as either integrated or unhappy. This pattern supports the results discussed by Ogilvie and Clark (in press) wherein it is reported that females are more likely than males to use the undesired self or worst self as pegs for self-evaluation. In effect, females are generally more in touch with and/or less defended against negative feelings and discomfitting features of the self than are males, making these components of the self more accessible to females for the purpose of self-evaluation.

Gender in Self-with-Other Structures: Individual Continuous Variables. Just as three self targets were introduced into each participant's interpersonal self structure, the present procedures involved eighteen consensual features that served as tracers for gender—masculine and feminine, as well as four traits each for expressive-positive, instrumental-positive, expressive-negative, and instrumental-negative. For each of these six concepts, continuous variable indices were computed for degree of elevation or prominence in the structure. The results for these measures are reported in the bottom portion of table 7.5.

The elevation indices were exactly as predicted. *Masculine* was higher up (or more prominent) in the self-with structures of males. *Feminine* was more elevated for female than male participants. For males, *masculine* most often appeared in a level 2 or 3 cluster (hence, the mean of 3.59), and *feminine* was either a residual or in a level 1 category (hence, the mean of 1.36), and the mirror image was true for female respondents. Parallel results were obtained for the expressive and instrumental traits, although a statistically significant sex difference was not obtained for expressive-negative qualities.

Did participants bring the Gender by Evaluation types of items into the self-with structures as bundles or as four individual items? This query was addressed as follows. Gender-related tracer terms were located on the HICLAS structures of all self-with-other displays. Recall that the consensual vocabulary included four words in each of four categories: expressive/positive (*E/P*); instrumental/

positive (*I/P*); expressive/negative (*E/N*); and instrumental/negative (*I/N*). Participants were categorized as schematic in regards to *E/P* or to *I/P* if three or four *E/P* or *I/P* words appeared in the same cluster. Since *E/N* and *I/N* words were used less frequently (that is, they more often appeared in the residual category), the rule for schematicity was reduced to two or more *E/N* or *I/N* words in the same cluster. This method of scoring enables us to assess the extent to which females and males in our sample employ female and male stereotypic words *as packages* to describe themselves in their interpersonal relationships.

Briefly summarized, the major findings are these.

1. Expressive/Positive (*E/P*). Seventy-three percent of the males and 68 percent of females are schematic in regard to female stereotypic/positive words. Females are more likely than males to locate E/P words in higher order cluster (or, 33 percent of the females are schematic at level 3 as compared to 6 percent of the males). In addition, 50 percent of the females have the feature *feminine* in the same cluster as the packaged expressive/positive attributes, and 25 percent of the males associate E/P words with *masculine*.

2. Instrumental/Positive (*I/P*). Eighty-two percent of the males and 62 percent of the females are I/P schematic. Interestingly, 72 percent of the I/P schematic males have *masculine* in the same cluster, whereas *feminine* appears in 71 percent of the I/P clusters for females. Thus, male stereotypic-positive traits are used schematically by both sexes (but more so among males than females), and they are gendered on the basis of the sex of the respondent. That is, males, as would be expected, see masculine and instrumental/positive attributes as going together. For females, however, the culturally stereotypic male qualities are bundled, not with masculine in-self but with feminine.

Gender in Self-with-Other Structures: Gestalt Categorical Patterns. Just as we identified patterns of incorporating evaluative targets into self, we sought to uncover the gestalts for how the cultural concepts of masculinity and femininity were made part of self-with-other structures. This was done by finding the various ways in which feminine, masculine, and the *very*-forms of each were organized in each participant's HICLAS display. Seven types of configurations were found, and these are presented in table 7.7. As can be seen at the right of the figure, the first three types represent traditional sex-typing in that males make *masculine* part of self and reject feminine by making it a residual, and females do just the reverse.

At the left, three variations on this pattern are indicated. In the first, masculine and very masculine (feminine and very feminine) are grouped together. In the second, the regular form is above the *very*-form. In the third, the *very*-form appropriate for one's sex is, along with the two other-sex summary descriptors, pushed into the residual.

The next three types (social-self as masculine *and* feminine) involve the participant making both masculine and feminine a part of the social-self. These types are conceptually similar to some meanings of androgyny as a mix, blend, or combination of masculinity and femininity (Cook 1985; Sedney 1989). The final type, which only occurs for three females, involves the apparent rejection of all four of the summary gender attributes. This gestalt pattern may be something like the Undifferentiated grouping often identified in gender-as-a-personality-variable research of the last 15 or so years or it may be the equivalent of what has been dubbed "sex-role transcendence" (Cook 1985; Sedney 1989).

In terms of the summary categories, the clear majority of both sexes are coded as traditionally sex-typed. In addition, a solid and similar minority for both sexes seem to have made both masculinity and femininity a part of the interpersonal self. In the present sample, it is only a tiny minority of females who appear to reject or transcend the cultural notions of masculinity and femininity. In addition to this last sex difference, there are some hints at male-female differences within the traditional sex-typed classification. Males seem more often to reject extreme masculinity (the *very*-form), and females are more prone to rate themselves as very feminine in a number of their interpersonal relationships.

REVIEW AND PREVIEW

The chapter began with a hypothetical scenario in which a college student exhibited marked variation in self experience and social behavior as a function of an interaction partner. Three general explanations were offered for this.

1. Individual differences. Some people are stable in behavior across others. Some are not;

Table 7.7

Distribution of Participants across Seven Primary and Three Summary Categories of Masculine (Masc.)/Feminine (Fem.) in Self-with Structure

Primary Categories for Male Participants	Males n	Males %	Females n	Females %	Primary Categories for Female Participants	Summary Categories	Males n	Males %	Females n	Females %
Masc. and v. masc. in same cluster; fem. and v. fem. in residual	3	14	12	24	Fem. and v. fem. in same cluster; masc. and v. masc. in residual	Traditional sex typed social self	15	68	35	70
Masc. above v. masc.; fem. and v. fem. in residual	6	27	17	34	Fem. above v. fem.; masc. and v. masc. in residual					
Masc. in structures; v. masc., fem., v. fem. in residual	6	27	6	12	Fem. in structure; v. fem., masc., v. masc. in residual					
Masc. and fem. in structure	6	27	9	18	Fem. and Masc. in structure	Social-self as masc. and fem.	7	32	12	24
Masc. and fem. in same cluster	1	5	2	4	Fem. and Masc. in same cluster					
Fem. above masc.	0	0	1	2	Masc. above fem.					
Masc., v. masc., fem., v. fem., in residual	0	0	3	6	Fem., v. fem., masc., v. masc. in residual	Social-self as not gendered	0	0	3	6
	22	100	50	100			22	100	50	100

2. General social roles. Although his behavior varied, the major actions made sense in terms of the male role; and
3. Internal self-with representation. This not only summarizes past relationships, but also impacts current behavior and experience.

The bulk of the chapter was devoted to describing the hypothetical construct of *self-with-other*, explaining how this can be assessed empirically. Then, it showed how nomothetic properties of individuals' self-with-other structures can be measured.

With regard to the preceding presentation of illustrative findings, we have attempted to address three general questions—What do self-with-other structures look like? How is evaluation made part of self? and How is gender incorporated into the social self?

Although the present data constitute first steps and not final answers, we can phrase some tentative conclusions. Concerning the overall content and contours of self-with structures, the modal pattern was to have a relatively simple and particularized organizational scheme for targets (see figure 7.2).

There were, however, substantial numbers of participants who showed a more differentiated and integrated pattern concerning self-withs. In making good/bad a part of the interpersonal self, individual continuous nomothetic variables indicated that the positive self was higher up in and more connected with self-withs than the *self at worst* for most respondents. This is consistent with other work using HICLAS to assess personal identity (Rosenberg & Gara 1985).

In terms of self-with evaluative gestalts, four different configurations of three selves—usual, ideal, and worst—were identified. Females were well represented in all four categories, while males were located predominantly in the configuration that connects usual and ideal selves and isolates worst self from that pair.

In answer to the final question, males tend to make masculinity more prominent in their self-with structure, and females tend to elevate the feminine. At the same time, the gestalt categorical approach showed important variations in the pattern of making masculinity and femininity part of one's social self.

Since our research strategy involves a balanced concern with accurate description of individuals and making generalizations across the natures of people, the next steps for us involve both idiographic and nomothetic directions. With regard to the latter, the present chapter was concerned with measuring one facet of the social relationships component of our multiplicity model of gender identity. We must develop means of assessing the remaining components and then empirically test how these various indices are intercorrelated. This task is well underway. In the Self-Perception Project, we have used existing measures where available and developed new devices and procedures where they were unavailable to assess multiple parts of each of the major components identified in our model.

Although an integrated idiographic-nomothetic research approach guides our work, the emphasis in this chapter has been on the nomothetic posssibilities of our endeavor. This approach is useful in its own right. For example, it provides continuous and categorical variables to use in testing of the multiplicity model. It can also be used as a springboard for idiographic work.

Every participant in our project is an exception from any general rule. Now that the modal types of self-with structures have been determined, we are better able to identify strong exceptions and explore in depth the life-events and other factors that pertain to unique configurations of social selves.

For example, we can begin to discern how it came to be and what it means when a person perceives herself to be both masculine and feminine in her interpersonal relationships—or himself to be, at the same time, both feminine and masculine in his relationships. That person can be compared with an individual who rejects both masculinity and femininity as meaningful descriptors of the self in interaction with others.

Or how did it come about that a few people rate their usual self as similar to their worst self? Is this a transitory phenomenon? Did they accomplish their ratings on a particularly bad day? Or is this a style that reflects a chronic condition of low self-esteem?

Like the fictitious Barry, the ways in which we express ourselves vary according to whom we are with. Somewhere with these variations is a core *meaning-making* self attempting to organize the social world from the context of *me* being in that world. We are endeavoring to measure and represent portions of the results of that activity.

It is an ambitious undertaking. Our outlook on the future holds the present enterprise as a promising building block for more encompassing models of the self in social interaction that are likely to be developed in the wake of this preliminary work.

NOTES

*The preparation of this chapter as well as the collection and analysis of the data reported herein were supported by National Institute of Mental Health Grant MH40871–03/04. We thank the institute for its support. We also thank the many people who have made the Self-Perception Project successful. First and foremost, this includes the participants who have been willing to share parts of themselves and their lives with us. In addition, we express our gratitude to the many people who have assisted with data gathering and analysis. In particular, we thank Janet Weingrad, Laura Longo, Scott Bilder, and Greta Pennell who were instrumental in preparing the materials necessary for completing this chapter.

1. The modifier *gendered* is used to describe those aspects of an individual's self-concept that have been shaped, in part, by cultural expectations about what males and females are like and how they should behave.

2. Although Rosenberg and his coworkers have used the term *elaborated* to refer to several different aspects of HICLAS structures, we use it here strictly to refer to *how many*, or, more specifically, the number of items (self-withs or features) in a grouping.

3. The reason why we state that this conversion roughly approximates the original matrix is because the *2 = 1, 1* rule means that a *very* also becomes a *sometimes*. An alternative strategy is to make a *2 = 0, 1* conversion. What this does is isolate 2s from 0s and 1s. But it carries with it the disadvantage of indicating that *never* is equivalent to *sometimes* on the first matrix. We have tested this alternative and found that the *1* on the second matrix essentially drives the structure. That is, the structural representation consists primarily of those targets that activate the strongest feelings or views of self and the remaining targets are listed as residuals. The HICLAS solution of the same matrix using the *2 = 1, 1* rule vastly reduces the number of residual targets and results in a more psychologically meaningful structure.

REFERENCES

Ajzen, I., and Fishbein, M. 1977. Attitude-behavior relations: A theoretical analysis and review of empirical research. *Psychological Bulletin 84:* 888–918.

Allport, G. W. 1962. The general and the unique in psychological science. *Journal of Personality 30:*405–422.

Ashmore, R. D. 1981. Sex stereotypes and implicit personality theory. In *Cognitive processes in stereotyping and intergroup behavior,* edited by D. L. Hamilton. Hillsdale, N.J.; Erlbaum. 37–81.

———. 1990. Sex, gender, and the individual. In *Handbook of Personality: Theory and Research,* edited by L. A. Pervin. New York: Guilford Press. 488–526.

Ashmore, R. D., and Del Boca, F. K., eds. 1986. *The social psychology of female-male relations: A critical analysis of central concepts.* New York: Academic Press.

Ashmore, R. D., and Ogilvie, D. M. 1988. *Gender identity, sex stereotypes, and social action.* Research proposal funded by the National Institute of Mental Health.

Ashmore, R. D.; Del Boca, F. K.; and Wohlers, A. J. 1986. Gender stereotypes. In *The social psychology of female-male relations: A critical analysis of central concepts,* edited by R. D. Ashmore and F. K. Del Boca. New York: Academic Press. 69–119.

Beere, C. A. 1990. *Gender roles: A handbook of tests and measures.* New York: Greenwood Press.

Bem, S. L. 1981. Gender schema theory: A cognitive account of sex typing. *Psychological Review* 88:354–364.

——— . 1985. Androgyny and gender schema theory: A conceptual and empirical integration. In *Nebraska Symposium on Motivation,* Vol. 32, edited by T. B. Sonderegger. Lincoln: University of Nebraska Press. 179–226.

Berkowitz, L. 1988. Introduction. In *Advances in experimental social psychology,* edited by L. Berkowitz. Vol 21, San Diego: Academic Press. 1–14.

Cook, E. P. 1985. *Psychological androgyny.* New York: Pergamon Press.

Deaux, K. 1984. From individual differences to social categories. Analysis of a decade's research on gender. *American Psychologist* 39:105–116.

DeBoeck, P., and Rosenberg, S. 1988. Hierarchical classes: Model and data analysis. *Psychometrika* 53:361–381.

Downs, A. C., and Langlois, J. H. 1988. Sex typing: Construct and measurement issues. *Sex Roles* 18:87–100.

Eagly, A. H. 1987. *Sex differences in social behavior: A social-role interpretation.* Hillsdale, N.J.: Erlbaum.

Fiske, S. T., and Taylor, S. E. 1984. *Social cognition.* Reading, Mass.: Addison-Wesley Publishing Company.

Frable, D. E. S. 1989. Sex typing and gender ideology: Two facets of the individual's gender psychology that go together. *Journal of Personality and Social Psychology* 56: 95–108.

Gara, M. 1987. A set theoretical model of person perception. Unpublished manuscript under editorial review.

Gergen, K. J. 1977. The social construction of self-knowledge. In *The self: Psychological and philosophical issues,* edited by T. Mischel. Totowa, N.J.: Rowman & Littlefield. 139–169.

Gergen, K. J., and Gergen, M. M. 1988. Narrative and the self in relationship. In *Advances in experimental social psychology,* Vol. 21, edited by L. Berkowitz. San Diego: Academic Press. 17–56.

Giele, J. Z. 1988. Gender and sex roles. In *Handbook of Sociology,* edited by N. J. Smelser. Newbury Park, Calif.: Sage. 291–323.

Gilligan, C. 1982. *In a different voice: Psychological theory and women's development.* Cambridge, Mass.: Harvard University Press.

Hart, D., and Damon, W. 1985. Contrasts between understanding self and understanding others. In *The development of self,* edited by R. L. Leahy. Orlando, Fla.: Academic Press. 151–178.

Huston, A. C. 1983. Sex-typing. In *Handbook of child psychology.* 4th ed., Vol 4, *Socialization, personality, and social development,* edited by E. M. Hetherington. New York: Wiley. 387–467.

Huston, T. L., and Ashmore, R. D. 1986. Women and men in personal relationships. In *The social psychology of female-male relations: A critical analysis of central concepts,* edited by R. D. Ashmore and F. K. Del Boca. Orlando, Fla.: Academic Press. 167–210.

Jacklin, C. N. 1989. Female and male: Issues of gender. *American Psychologist* 44:127–133.

James, W. 1890. *Principles of psychology.* New York: Holt.

Kelley, H. H.; Berscheid, E.; Christensen, A.; Harvey, J. H.; Huston, T. L.; Levenger, G.; McClintock, E.; Peplau, L. A.; and Peterson, D. R. 1983. *Close relationships.* New York: Freeman.

Kluckhohn, C., and Murray, H. A. 1953. Personality formation: The determinants. In *Personality in nature, society, and culture,* edited by C. Kluckhohn, H. A. Murray, and D. M. Schneider. New York: Alfred A. Knopf. 53–67.

Maccoby, E. E. 1987. The varied meanings of "masculine" and "feminine." In *Masculinity/femininity: Basic perspectives,* edited by J. M. Reinisch; L. A. Rosenblum; and S. A. Sanders. New York: Oxford University Press. 227–239.

Markus, H., and Cross, S. 1990. The interpersonal self. In *Handbook of Personality: Theory and Research*, edited by L. A. Pervin. New York: Guilford Press. 576–608.

Markus, H., and Nurius, P. 1986. Possible selves. *American Psychologist* 41: 954–969.

Money, J., and Ehrhardt, A. A. 1972. *Man and woman, boy and girl*. Baltimore, Md.: Johns Hopkins Press.

Ogilvie, D. M. 1987. Life satisfaction and identity structure in late middle-aged men and women. *Psychology and Aging* 2:217–224.

Ogilvie, D. M., and Ashmore, R. D. 1991. The self-with-other representation as a unit of analysis in self-concept research. In *The relational self: Theoretical convergences in psychoanalysis and social psychology*, edited by R. C. Curtis. New York: Guilford Publications.

Ogilvie, D. M., and Clark, M. D. In press. The best and worst of it: Age and sex differences in self-discrepancy research. In *Self-perspectives across the life span*, edited by R. P. Lipka and T. M. Brinthaupt. Albany, N.Y.: State University of New York Press.

Osgood, C. E., Suci, G. J., and Tannenbaum, P. H. 1957. *The measurement of meaning*. Urbana: University of Illinois Press.

Rosenberg, S. 1977. New approaches to the analysis of personal constructs in person perception. *Nebraska Symposium on Motivation*, Vol. 24. Lincoln: University of Nebraska Press.

———. 1988. Self and others: Studies in social personality and autobiography. In *Advances in experimental social psychology*, Vol. 21, edited by L. Berkowitz. New York: Academic Press. 57–92.

Rosenberg, S, and Gara, M. A. 1985. The multiplicity of personal identity. In *Review of personality and social psychology*, Vol. 6, edited by P. Shaver. New York: Academic Press. 87–113.

Sedney, M. A. 1989. Conceptual and methodological sources of controversies about androgyny. In *Representations: Social constructions of gender*, edited by R. K. Unger. Amityville, N.Y.: Baywood Publishing Co.

Sherif, C. W. 1982. Needed concepts in the study of gender identity. *Psychology of Women Quarterly*, 6:375–398.

Spence, J. T. 1985. Gender identity and its implications for the concepts of masculinity and femininity. In *Psychology and gender: Nebraska Symposium on Motivation, 1984*. Vol. 32, Edited by T. B. Sonderegger. Lincoln: University of Nebraska Press. 59–96.

Stryker, S. 1987. Identity theory: Development and extensions. In *Self and identity: Psychosocial perspectives,* edited by K. Yardley and T. Honess. New York: Wiley. 89–103.

Terman, L. M., and Miles, C. C. 1936. *Sex and personality.* New York: McGraw-Hill.

Tunis, S. L.; Fridhandler, B. M.; and Horowitz, M. J. 1990. Identifying schematized views of self with significant others: Convergence of quantitative and clinical methods. *Journal of Personality and Social Psychology* 59:1279–1286.

White, G. M. 1980. Conceptual universals in interpersonal language. *American Anthropologist* 82:759–781.

Williams, J. E., and Best, D. L. 1982. *Measuring sex stereotypes: A thirty-nation study,* Beverly Hills, Calif.: Sage.

DANIEL HART
WOLFGANG EDELSTEIN

8

Self-understanding Development in Cross-cultural Perspective*

A concern for the cultural context of psychological development is often extolled by reviewers and theorists but rarely realized in empirical investigations. For the domain of self-understanding, this state is particularly striking.[1] Self-understanding offers unique opportunities for exploring the developmental relationship between the individual and the enveloping social environment, of which the historically transmitted behaviors and symbols which form the culture are a part.

On the one hand, self-understanding is intensely personal and individual. The individual is the final arbiter of what will, and what will not be included in self-understanding. The immediacy of personal experience accords a certain authority to the individual's own perspective on the nature of the self.

On the other hand, while it is a conceptual system that is unique in its subjectiveness, self-understanding emerges and matures only within a social world. Self-reflection develops through social interaction (Mead 1934), and attributions about the nature of self can have meaning only in a social and cultural medium (Hart 1988). The study of self-understanding, more so than that of other concepts, can provide a valuable perspective on the nature of development in cultural context.

Not only can the study of the sense of self in its cultural context contribute to a conceptual model of the intersection of the individual and society, but to a richer description of self-understanding development as well. Almost all studies of self-conceptions of children and adolescents have drawn their subjects from middle-class America. The consequence is that most extant accounts of self-understanding are descriptive only for a fraction of the world's children and adolescents. One is left, then, with a description of self-understanding that is impoverished by its limited applicability.

In the first part of this chapter, several different theoretical and methodological approaches to cross-cultural research are considered critically. Our goal here is to explore the possibilities inherent in cross-cultural research, as well as the contributions and flaws of several important studies. In the second half, we shall describe some of our recent research on self-understanding among Puerto Rican and Icelandic children which challenges some common conceptions.

CROSS-CULTURAL AND ANTHROPOLOGICAL INVESTIGATIONS

Just what can be learned about the development of self-understanding from cross-cultural and anthropological investigations? Cross-cultural psychological research offers a number of benefits, as reviewers have noted (Brislin 1983), three of which are particularly evident for self-understanding development. The first concerns the universality of self-understanding development.

As with other domains such as moral judgment, researchers are deeply divided as to the extent to which self-understanding follows a single developmental trajectory as well as the significance of apparent deviations from it. The debate, as we shall see, echoes the confusion noted by Kohlberg (1981) between the prescriptive judgment (how much similarity in self-understanding *ought* to exist between cultures) and the descriptive account (what similarities and dissimilarities can be *discovered* through empirical research).

Those who believe there ought to be great homogeneity in the sense of self among individuals from widely different societies as a consequence of maturational and cognitive universals argue that an account of self-understanding development need not incorporate culture as an influence. Unsurprisingly, those who would prescribe fundamental differences in the sense of self as an inevitable result of dramatic differences in cultural backgrounds emphasize the importance of symbol systems and traditional patterns of interacting as determining forces on the emergent forms of self-understanding. The universality and the related sources of self-understanding development are issues that are best framed in a cross-cultural perspective.

Investigations in other cultures also offer the opportunity to assess the individual contributions of variables that are usually confounded in Western industrialized nations. For instance, at about ages seven to nine, children in the United States begin to describe themselves in terms of their capabilities relative to those of others (Hart & Damon 1986). For example, they might say, "I am a good kickball player."

In this culture, it is impossible to determine whether this tendency is the result of a newly emergent ability to make use of self-comparison information or merely the consequence of entry into elementary school, where such comparisons are incessantly made by teachers and older students. Disentangling the effects on self-understanding of age and education, social class and ethnic background, and similar sets of confounded variables can be addressed best through investigations in other cultures.

Finally, the cross-cultural study of self-understanding can lead to the discovery of new phenomena. So little is known about what people think about themselves—and the domain is so rich—that it is difficult to imagine that previously undiscovered facets will not be revealed through cross-cultural research.

However, there is surprisingly little cumulation of results concerning the sense of self in any of these areas. It seems as if many researchers interested in the sense of self and its variations across cultures have chosen rather extreme paradigmatic positions on the nature of mind and society which prevent easy synthesis of findings.

In Shweder's terms the two positions are divided by their views of mind, with "one advancing the image of man as intendedly rational, the other advancing an image of man as inevitably nonrational" Shweder, 1984, 58). Those who view humans and minds as essentially rational (the "enlightenment" view, in Shweder's terms) have contributed to a paradigm in which the focus is on the identification of universal features of the human mind. From within this framework, the course of development is one along which the individual gains ever more knowledge within increasingly better forms of thinking, interacting, and understanding. Much of developmental psychology—and certainly its theory as offered by Piaget, Chomsky, and Kohlberg—derives from this broad view of the nature of mind.

Investigators in the other (Shweder's "romantic") paradigm are more likely to identify themselves with symbolic anthropology. In arguing that the human mind is nonrational (or at least that many of its interesting characteristics are), these theorists choose to explore the metaphors and symbols that organize conscious life. Concepts of self, society, mind, and obligation, symbolic anthropologists argue, are infused with metaphorical elements that derive from cultural symbol systems. The paradigmatic orientation is culturally relativistic, with the aim of identifying the unique perspectives on self and mind characteristic of each culture.

Although it would be false to characterize all research on the nature of self in different cultures as belonging to one or the other paradigm, it is clear that many investigations can be so categorized. It is worth considering representative studies of each type in some detail, as a means of understanding the implicit methodological and theoretical models that produce widely divergent perspectives on the nature of self in cultural context.

The Discovery of the Universal Self-concept

Some of the most intriguing research-based claims about the influence of culture on the developing self-concept have been made by Daniel Offer and his colleagues (Offer, Ostrov, Howard & Atkinson 1988). The format of their research was simple.

Adolescents in ten cultures were asked to respond to a structured self-concept questionnaire. The structured questionnaire of choice in the study was the international version of the Offer Self-Image Questionnaire (OSIQ), consisting of ninety-nine short, written descriptions to which the subject responds by circling a number from 1 ("Describes me very well") to 6 ("Does not describe me at all").

Scale scores, ranging from positive to negative, are derived from the responses and correspond to eleven facets of self: impulse control, emotional tone, body image, social relationships, morals, vocational and educational goals, sexual attitudes, family relationships, mastery of the external world, psychopathology, and superior adjustment. For instance, a person with a positive scale score for body image would rate as self-descriptive the statement that "I am proud of my body" (Offer et al. 1988, 38), and deny the self-appropriateness of the item "I frequently feel ugly and unattractive" (1988, 39).

To complement their data from American teenagers, Offer and colleagues recruited colleagues from nine countries—Australia, Bangladesh, Hungary, Israel, Italy, Japan, Taiwan, Turkey, and West Germany—asking each to administer the questionnaire in his or her own culture. The OSIQ was translated into the appropriate language with great care in order to ensure that the meaning of the items remained the same in all countries. For the most part, this effort seems to have been successful. Almost six-thousand middle-class adolescents in high school between the ages of thirteen and nineteen from the ten countries completed the questionnaire.

The design of the study and the nature of the questionnaire permit a variety of analytic approaches. For instance, because the scale scores range from positive to negative, it would be possible to compare nations in terms of the global "psychological health" of their adolescents. This type of focus on contrasts among cultures would emphasize the finding that significant differences among countries were found for more than half of the items on the questionnaire, indicating that nationality was a more powerful influence on self-image than either sex or age. Statistically significant sex differences were found for about 25% of the items and significant developmental trends appeared in less than 10% of them.

Generally, however, the authors chose not to elaborate on differences between adolescents from the ten cultures, but on the commonalities among them. Offer and his colleagues point out that, despite the pervasiveness of significant cross-national differences, the magnitude of these differences was quite small. Furthermore, in their judgment, the results do not clearly suggest that the nations can be easily ranked in terms of the global self-images of their adolescents.

Instead, the researchers prefer to argue that the results of their study indicate that there is a "universal adolescent," who thinks of himself or herself as "happy most of the time," "able to exercise self-control," "caring and oriented toward others," "valuing work and school," "expressing confidence about their sexual selves," "having positive feelings toward their families," and "able to make decisions" (Offer et al. 1988, 110–111).

Ultimately, then, Offer and his colleagues argue that there is relatively little variation in the adolescent's sense of self that can be attributed to cultural influences. Instead, biological forces and universals in cognitive development together result in the same "core self" (1988, 112), emerging in divergent cultures. Anthropological arguments to the contrary, the authors argue, are either historically dated or methodologically questionable.

The "Universal Self" Reconsidered. Although the work of Offer and colleagues provides many interesting findings about adolescence in different cultures, their claims about the universality of the sense of self should be regarded skeptically. As Triandis pointed out in 1988, the samples included in the study are all middle-class and

literate. Certainly claims about a "universal self" should be qualified in light of the nature of adolescents who responded to the
questionnaire.

A more troubling problem concerns the data elicited through
the OSIQ. It is not at all clear that the various items composing the
questionnaire tap the adolescent's understanding of self. For instance, when adolescents are asked to rate the extent of their agreement with the OSIQ statement that "very often parents do not
understand a person because they had an unhappy childhood" (Offer
1988, 196), are they revealing something about their understanding
of self? To argue that such a statement elicits an important component of the self-concept appears to result in denotative difficulties. If
beliefs about parental characteristics are self-referential, then *any*
rating apparently made by an individual deserves the same status.
The self-concept becomes all inclusive.

Also problematic is the formation of scale scores from aggre-
gating responses. These scale scores are, in Geertz's terms, "experience distant" (Geertz 1984). This means that the scale scores are not
phenomenally real aspects of adolescent experience. For instance, an
adolescent may be rated in terms of a "psychopathology scale," but
it seems unlikely that he or she thinks of the self in those terms in
the course of day-to-day life.

The structured format of the questionnaires and the formation
of scale scores means that the resulting description of the adolescent
self-concept is saturated with investigator inferences. There is little
opportunity for the subject's own interpretations of self to be revealed. (See chapter 4 of this volume for a further discussion of this
issue.) The consequence is that one adolescent's portrait of the self
must match another's because both are restricted to the paint-
by-numbers canvases provided by the researcher. Although a number of Offer's and colleagues' findings are quite interesting, we
believe that their measure results in an underestimation of cultural
variability in the sense of self.

Symbolic Anthropology and Cultural Incommensurability

In her challenging essay about the nature of self and emotion in
cultural context, Rosaldo argued in 1984 that a lack of cross-cultural
research has resulted in a tradition of psychological theorizing in
which features of mind and emotion found in Western culture are
treated as universals.

This is not to say that Rosaldo and other symbolic anthropologists believe that there are no concepts that all persons hold. Ros-

aldo, as did Levine and White in 1986 and Geertz in 1984, agreed that some concept of self can be found in all cultures. But she and other symbolic anthropologists argued that the concept of self has only two similarities across cultures—a perception of the self's continuity over time and its separateness from others.

Beyond this spare framework, the sense of self is constituted in culturally specific ways.

> Conceptions of the self assume a shape that corresponds—at least in part—with the societies and politics within which actors live their lives, the kinds of claims that they defend, the conflicts they are apt to know, and their experiences of social relations. (Rosaldo 1984, 149)

Why is it that Western investigators have found it so hard to accept the reality of variation of a fundamental type in the sense of self? Rosaldo suggested that this is because of the culturally derived distinction between a "real" self, inside and available only through self-reflection, and a "false" self which is apparent in day-to-day behavior. Therefore, because "we think of a subjective self whose operations are distinct from those of persons-in-the world, we tend to think of human selves and their emotions as everywhere the same" (Rosaldo 1984, 149).

To defend her claims, Rosaldo reported some of her field work with the head-hunting Ilongots from the Philippines. As have many anthropologists, Rosaldo made use of detailed naturalistic observations of day-to-day life in the culture under investigation. These observations become the basis for inferring the basic categories of experience and organization that structure a particular culture.

As Levine noted in 1984, the emphasis of this ethnographic approach is to identify the symbols for which there is a consensus within a community. Because these symbols permeate and saturate most facets of life among members of a culture, Levine argued that their effects are robust and can be identified without recourse to the sorts of tests and measures needed to uncover the relatively weak effects of traditional psychological variables.

Rosaldo argued that there are consensually shared symbols among the Ilongots that do shape communal life. Beyond the fascination it holds due to head-hunting, Ilongot culture challenges common assumptions about the nature of the sense of self and others. For instance, in sharp contrast to persons in Western cultures, among Ilongots, "personality descriptions are extremely rare, as are strategic reckonings of motivation" (1984, 146); nor do they refer to "personal histories or distinctive psychic drives to account for the peculiarities of deeds" (1984, 147).

Instead, the Ilongots understand behavior to be a consequence of environmental, social, political, and spiritual forces. These are seen as direct influences, whose effects on behavior need not be mediated by consciousness or through self-reflection. In this culture, then, the self is not seen as a source of personal volition.

Ilongot culture also differs from Western societies in its lack of emphasis on the individuating functions of the sense of self. As noted previously, persons in all cultures appear to possess a concept of self according to which a person is judged continuously over time and distinctly from others. Rosaldo argued that this latter quality— distinctness from others or individuality—is particularly evident in the Western understanding of self. Many studies with children, adolescents, and adults in the United States report that American children are concerned with being autonomous and individuated, as reflected in self-descriptions such as "individual," "unique," "my own boss," and "independent" (Damon & Hart 1988). It is as if a mature sense of self is one in which that person achieves complete independence from the surrounding social context.

Ilongots, according to Rosaldo, have a different view. While recognizing distinctions between individuals, Ilongots emphasize in their self-definitions connections between self and other. In Ilongot culture, one aspires to be like other adults, to be able to see one's self as similar to the selves of everyone else. To see oneself as unique, distinct, and separate from others (an indicator of successful identity formation in Western culture) is to fail in the task of constructing an adequate sense of self among the Ilongots.

These observations concerning the differences in sense of self from Westerners to Ilongots confirm, Rosaldo claimed, the transforming power of culture and cultural symbol systems in affecting psychological functioning. Her argument suggested that the consequence of different cultural symbol systems is that there will be few similarities in the sense of self across societies. She challenges the validity of applying the same interpretative framework to the self-conceptions of persons from different cultures, claiming that such efforts inescapably produce distorted accounts.

A Second Look at the Cultural Self. Rosaldo's radical critique has not been accepted by all cultural anthropologists. Spiro, for one, argued in 1984 that his careful reading of Rosaldo's description of the

Ilongots revealed that many of the psychological categories that derive from Western psychology can, in fact, be applied in Ilongot culture. Spiro claimed that the substantial differences between Ilongot and Western cultures are, instead, attributable to the content and expression of these categories. The point he advanced was that it may be a mistake to assume that cultural symbol systems determine every facet of self and mind because they may obscure to the investigator's vision important cross-cultural commonalities.

Although the ethnographic approach may be essential for identifying symbols common to members of a community, the data it generates do not easily permit a determination of the extent to which individuals within and across cultures are similar or different. One cannot know, based on Rosaldo's narrative descriptions, the extent to which there is individual variability in the concept of self among the Ilongots. It is possible that some Ilongots have a distinctly different understanding of themselves than the one sketched by Rosaldo. Furthermore, because the ethnographic approach is aimed toward identifying within-culture commonalities, it is not well-suited for assessing differences between cultures. For instance, Rosaldo's judgment that Western and Ilongot cultures are very different rests upon her impressions and readings about the first and a detailed ethnography of the second. These different sources of information may result in an overemphasis on cultural diversity.

Summary. Our review of the studies by Offer and colleagues and by Rosaldo was intended to highlight the theoretical and methodological biases characteristic of the two paradigmatic approaches. The "enlightenment" researchers—Offer and colleagues—claimed that the adolescent's sense of self varied little across culture. This is because the core of the self, they claimed, is constituted by biological and cognitive universals. This view guided their choice of a highly structured questionnaire for use in their research, a decision which, we argued, prevented the adolescent's own understanding of self from fully emerging.

The "romantic" investigation of Rosaldo led to the conclusion that the sense of self varies radically according to the type of symbol system used by a particular culture. Toward demonstrating this variability, Rosaldo reported some of her field observations of Ilongot culture and contrasted these findings with her conclusions regarding Western industrialized societies emerging from her informal observations and readings. This type of comparison, we have suggested, might be misleading.

Our view is that neither paradigmatic "romantic" nor "enlightenment" investigations are likely to advance future accounts of self-understanding development. The "romantic" tradition, in assuming that the sense of self is simply a derivative of cultural symbol systems, fails to acknowledge or to address the role of self-understanding in regulating social interaction (Baldwin 1902; Mead 1934; Triandis 1989).

The concept of self is not merely a cultural epiphenomenon. Persons appear predisposed by the development and structure of the nervous system to acquire knowledge about the self (Gardner 1983; Kagan 1981). Because the sense of self is neurologically based and has adaptational value for social interaction, it is unlikely to assume arbitrary forms dictated solely by culture.[2]

Strictly "enlightenment" approaches to the sense of self seem doomed to failure as well. While constants in biological development and social interaction are likely to provide a framework within which the sense of self emerges, the nature of social life and social behavior varies in significant and important ways across cultures. It is impossible to believe that a person who grows up in a nonliterate society, in which all adults are involved in farming or related activities, with members of the community concerned more with interdependence and interpersonal harmony than with individual achievement, will think of the self in the same way as does a person growing up in an upper-middle-class family in the United States.

Cross-cultural research is most likely to yield significant findings when its goals are more modest than demonstrating that persons are the same or radically different across cultural contexts. An account of self-understanding will benefit most from studies which examine the types of similarities and differences that exist across cultures, the factors that give rise to the observed differences, the relationship of differences to patterns of interaction and behavior, and the implications of culturally specific patterns for the nature of the phenomenon under investigation. Two of our studies of this more modest type, based on a new model of self-understanding development, are described in the following section.

THE DAMON-AND-HART MODEL

One model of self-understanding development that has received extensive exploration was proposed by Damon and Hart (Damon & Hart 1982, 1986, 1988; Hart & Damon 1985, 1986, 1988). The model blends the distinctions proposed by William James in the sense of self with a cognitive-developmental approach. Figure 8.1 presents a graphic representation of the model.

According to the model (and following after William James) the sense of self is composed of two basic types of experiences: the *self-as-object*, represented by the front face of the model, and the *self-as-subject*, depicted on the side face. The self-as-object includes within it those features and characteristics which an individual might ascribe to the self when regarding the self as one might regard any other person. So, for instance, one might think of the self in terms of characteristics such as friendliness or intelligence, just as one thinks of others in the same terms.

As did James, we have proposed that the characteristics composing the self-as-object can be further divided into different self-schemes. In our model, there are four self-schemes: the physical self, which includes physical and material characteristics (such as, "I have brown hair" or "I have a nice car"); the active self composed of the self's activities and abilities (as in, "I am a good swimmer" or "I play basketball often"); the social self comprising the individual's relationships and characteristics affecting social interaction (such as, "I have a lot of friends" or "I am shy"); and finally, the psychological self which includes emotional and cognitive features (as in, "I am moody" or "I am smart.").

Some theorists have argued that the development of self-understanding might be best characterized by a sequential shifting from the physical self to the active self to the social self to the psychological self. Our own position is that the evidence for this sequential shifting is extremely weak (Damon & Hart 1982; Hart & Damon 1986).

The extent to which any one of the four self-schemes is prominent in self-understanding is more a reflection of contextual and cultural factors than of developmental change. For instance, within the United States, we would predict that the psychological self would be prominent for children of parents with high academic standards, just as the active self might be prominent for children deeply involved in athletic pursuits. We do not believe that the former pattern would be suggestive of advanced development just as the latter would not indicate retardation.

To better describe self-understanding development, we have posited four, hierarchical levels, with each level representing a new form of meaning. Movement from one level to the next entails the transformation of meaning and organization of characteristics,

Figure 8.1
Damon and Hart's Developmental Model of Self-understanding

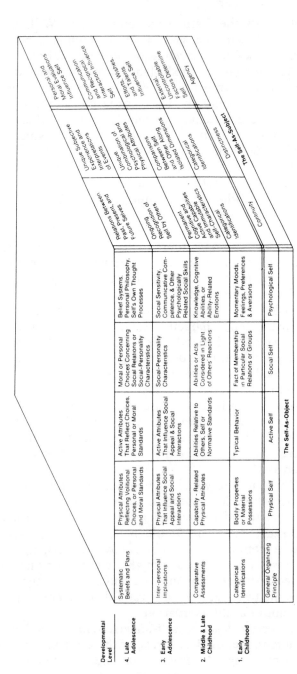

rather than the deletion or addition of new classes of features. We believe that it is this transformation of meaning and organization of characteristics that is fundamentally developmental and most likely to be similar across cultures.

Level 1: Categorical Identifications. This is represented by the bottom row in figure 8.1. At this level, children understand the self as the sum of separate categorical identifications. A child might respond to a self-description question with "I am big, have a lot of friends, and I am happy," with the meaning of each feature being independent of the others. There is little integration among these disparate facets of the sense of self.

Level 2: Comparative Assessments. Self-understanding focuses on comparisons between the activities and abilities of the self versus those of real or imagined others. A child at level 2 might well continue to describe the self as "big," but the characteristic of "bigness" derives its meaning within the context of relative abilities "I am big which helps me be a good basketball player."

Level 3: Interpersonal Implications. This is characterized by the focus of self-understanding on how features of one's self influence his or her interactions with others. There is a concern at level 3 for the facets of self that may define one's place and manner of operating in the social network. A young adolescent might think of the self as "shy," with the meaning of shyness perceived in its contribution to relative isolation—"and I don't want to be shy because I don't have as many friends as I would like."

Level 4: Systematic Beliefs and Plans. Characteristics of self draw their meanings for one's identity through their relationships to systematic beliefs and life plans. Shyness, for example, may be retained as a feature of self, but its importance now stems from the relevance of shyness to goals and values—" . . . and I don't want to be shy because I want to be a minister; to be a good minister, to help people understand God, you have to be somewhat outgoing."

The side face of the model corresponds to the self-as-subject—that facet of self-experience that, as early as 1892, James claimed eludes easy description. Nonetheless, it is very real. James argued that, in addition to judging the self much as one might judge others—a process constituting the self-as-object—each person is aware of being conscious. Of course, James himself acknowledged that it is impossible to study consciousness itself by using traditional psychological methods.

In our own work, we have chosen to study children's and adolescents' understanding of features of self that, James argued, derive from this experience of the self's consciousness. These components include self-continuity, distinctness from others, and agency. The development of understanding of these facets of self-understanding generally parallels development in the self-as-object, and, therefore, four levels are posited here as well. Because this facet of the model does not figure prominently in the discussion that follows, the unique features of its developmental path will not be described. (For more details, see Damon & Hart 1988.)

The testing and revision of the model have relied heavily on the clinical-interviewing of children and adolescents, using open-ended questions such as "How would you describe yourself as a person?"; "What makes you proud about yourself?"; and "How did you get to be the person you are now?" One advantage of this method is that subjects generate their own self-descriptions, using their own vocabularies and guided by their unique perspectives on themselves. This is in contrast to self-concept measures like such as Offer's and colleagues' OSIQ described earlier in which subjects are asked to rate themselves on dimensions that are provided by the investigator, that are phrased in the investigator's vocabulary, and that are derived from the investigator's notions of the nature of the self-concept. (See also chapter 4 of this volume.)

Furthermore, the choice of the clinical-interview format reflects on orientation toward the meaning which children and adolescents ascribe to the various facets of self. From the perspective of the model, what is different about the older child and the young adolescent is not that one describes the self using physical characteristics and the other thinks of the self in terms of its psychological qualities. Indeed, both types of characteristics may be present in their self-descriptions. Instead, what is different is the meaning that the quality has for the individual. For instance, "being big" may be important to the child because "it makes me a good kickball player" (level 2), but important to the young adolescent because "my friends would tease me if I were small" (level 3). In this sense, our interest in the meaning of self is similar to that of the symbolic anthropologists.

A variety of studies have provided support for the Damon-and-Hart model of self-understanding and its associated methodology. Cross-sectional and longitudinal studies have confirmed the developmental nature of the levels and the stability of individual differences (Damon & Hart 1986; Hart & Damon 1986), while studies of conduct disorder and anorectic adolescents have demonstrated that the model is sensitive to clinically useful differences between these samples and normal adolescents (Melcher 1986; Schorin & Hart 1988).

Cross-cultural Extensions of the Model

To what extent can the model be useful in describing the development of self-understanding in different cultures?

The first issue concerns the applicability to other cultures of the divisions in the experience of self proposed by William James and incorporated in the model. We believe that the various facets do represent phenomenologically real components of the sense of self that are likely to be present in every culture.

There is clearly a consensus among investigators that all cultures have a concept according to which the self is continuous over time and distinct from others, which represent two aspects of the *I* component of the model presented in figure 8.1. For the other aspects of the model, however, there is less evidence.

The third aspect of the *I* component—agency—may be present in the self-understanding of persons in non-Western cultures, but in very different forms. Rosaldo's description of Ilongot culture, for instance, suggests that the sense of agency there is construed even among adults in external terms, with social and environmental forces determining the self's actions.[3]

It seems probable that persons in every culture have some knowledge of the self's characteristics that would be included within the *me* component of the model—traits such as physical attributes, abilities, social qualities, and affective and cognitive traits. What is likely to vary is the extent to which these various sets of *me* characteristics are prominent in self-understanding, for two possible reasons.

First, self-understanding is most likely to be elaborated in those areas of the self's expertise (Cantor & Kihlstrom 1987). If a culture places particular emphasis on interpersonal negotiation, then its members are likely to develop expertise in this area, which in turn, will be reflected in an extensive sense of the self's social qualities.

Second, the norms and orientations of a culture may determine which facets of self-understanding are prominent in self-awareness (Triandis 1989). Those facets that stand out in self-reflection then become central to self-definition.

Self-understanding in Puerto Rico. The first study seeking to examine the interpretative value of the self-understanding model for understanding development in another culture utilized forty-eight children and adolescents from a small fishing village in Puerto Rico (Hart, Lucca-Irizarry & Damon 1986). Children and adolescents in this community experience a very different life than those growing up in, for example, urban New England. The village lacks paved roads, health services, and social class stratification. The cultural orientation of the community emphasizes cooperativeness and harmony within family and nonfamily relationships, with children and adolescents expected to contribute to these goals through obedience to parental expectations. Few children attend school for more than three or four years, and most expect to occupy the roles of their parents when they reach adulthood. Boys become fishermen, and girls are their wives.

A sample of forty-eight children and adolescents, matched for age and sex, was drawn from a lower middle to middle-class urban area in New England. There is substantial social class stratification in this industrialized city. The majority of students complete twelve years of schooling, with many eventually attending college. Community values in this area are less centered on cooperation and interpersonal harmony, and reflect instead an orientation toward individualism. This results in a concern with individual achievement and careful self-assessment (Triandis 1989).

The orienting hypothesis of the study, which focused only on the *me* component of the model, was that children and adolescents in Puerto Rico would be more likely than those in New England to think of themselves in terms of their social characteristics, with the children and adolescents in New England expected to evidence greater concern for the psychological features of self-understanding than the youth from Puerto Rico.

The greater emphasis on the social qualities of self within the Puerto Rican sample was predicted because the values of the community, social cooperation and communal harmony, are likely to (1) result in expertise in social relationships which would be accompanied by an elaboration of the sense of self in this area (Cantor & Kihlstrom 1987); and (2) increase the salience of these components of the understanding of self so that they would be reported more frequently in self-descriptions (Triandis 1989). The individualistic bias of the New England community should result in a more elaborated sense of the psychological traits of self as well as an increase in their salience.

Children and adolescents in both cultures were individually interviewed, using the set of clinical interview questions presented elsewhere (Damon & Hart 1988; Hart & Damon 1986). As described earlier, the purpose of these questions is to elicit as fully as possible the individual's own understanding of self. In order to accomplish this, the interviewer followed up each initial response to a question with additional "probe" questions.

For instance, each subject was asked "How would you describe yourself as a person?" If a child responded "friendly and big," the interviewer would ask additional questions such as "What does being friendly mean to you? Why is being big an important part of you?" Generally, the interviewer continued asking additional questions until the child was unable to elaborate further on the meaning or importance of a particular characteristic of self. Each interview session was recorded on audiotape and later transcribed. The interviews from Puerto Rico were then translated from Spanish into English.

The first task in coding the interviews was to subdivide each of them into "chunks."[4] Basically, a chunk consists of a single unit of meaning. Usually, this unit of meaning is an initial characteristic of self (such as, *big*) and all the responses to questions that probed the meaning and importance of the characteristic to the individual. After each chunk is identified, the coder assigns it to a developmental level and to a self-scheme corresponding to the front face of the model. This is done by matching the chunk to prototypical chunks in the coding manual that correspond to the four developmental levels and four self-schemes. Once the chunks have been coded, various summary indices for the interview can be computed.

For the purposes of this chapter, only two need be mentioned: the percentage of chunks in each scheme, and the modal developmental level, defined as the most common developmental level for all the chunks on the interview.

The results of the analyses suggested that there are important similarities in the self-understanding of children from the two different cultures. Children and adolescents in Puerto Rico, as did their counterparts in New England, thought about themselves in ways characteristic of the different developmental levels and the different self-schemes. Among the Puerto Rican youth there were examples of level 1 (*What are you like?* I am swarthy, I am short, I am slender); level 2 (*What are you like?* I am so dumb. *Why?* Because I don't understand what they teach me); as well as level 3 (I respect older persons and teachers. *Why is respect the most important?* People will love me.)

A statistical comparison of the distribution of modal developmental levels between the two cultures revealed no significant differences, indicating that the two samples were, apparently, indistinguishable from a developmental perspective.

Yet, viewed more closely, it is clear that there are important differences in self-understanding between the youth of the two cultures. Although statements characteristic of each of the self-schemes were found in both cultures, and the percentages of chunks in the physical and active self-schemes were the same for both samples, the distributions of chunks across the social and psychological schemes were quite different. As hypothesized, the Puerto Rican children and adolescents offered relatively more social descriptors of self than did the New England sample. Thirty-six percent of the responses of the Puerto Rican children, in comparison to only 21 percent of those for the New England sample, fell within the social self-scheme.

In reading the Puerto Rican interviews, one is struck by the centrality of the self's connections to others, as in the following two examples.

> *Can you tell me what you are like?*
> Good, bad, pretty, and nice with my friends.
> *From all those things, which ones are the most important for you?*
> Give them presents.
> *Why?*
> Because I like to play with my friends. I'm nice with my girlfriends, and they are good to me too.

> *Can you tell me what you are like?*
> I am like any other kid. I like to share and help other kids smaller than me to resolve their problems at the school. I always look for their well-being. I separate them when they are fighting because they should share with each other, and they should be friendly so when they grow up they'll be good friends.

These examples of self-understanding, in which the social features of self are particularly evident, are quite common in the Puerto Rican interviews and relatively uncommon among the interviews with New England youth. Instead, the New England youth were more likely to think of themselves in terms of their psychological qualities (31 percent of the chunks in this self-scheme, as opposed to 17 percent of the chunks for the Puerto Rican sample). For instance:

> *What was different about you?*
> I had no self-confidence, I remember that.
> *What does it mean to have self-confidence?*
> To believe in yourself. Just to keep telling yourself you know you can do it . . .
> *How does that make a difference?*
> It helps you get through things.
> *Like what? What does it help you get through?*
> Schoolwork.
> *Why is it important to be able to get through schoolwork?*
> So you can have an education.
> *Why does that make a difference?*
> Well, if you don't have an education it's not gonna get you very far in life.

In this example of self-understanding, the New England adolescent clearly thinks of herself in terms of a psychological characteristic, specifically self-confidence, which derives much of its meaning within the context of academic success and personal achievement. This sort of response, although not totally absent in the interviews, was far less common among the Puerto Rican youth.

To summarize, this initial foray into cross-cultural research yielded several intriguing findings. First, the results suggested that the developmental model of self-understanding portrayed in figure 8.1 and its associated methodology can be useful for cross-cultural investigation. The first three developmental levels, as well as the four self-schemes, were present in the self-understanding of children and adolescents from the small fishing village in Puerto Rico. Furthermore, the distinctions proposed in the model allowed the identification of interpretable commonalities and differences in self-understanding between youth of the two cultures.

In addition to confirming the value of the model, the findings offered new information about self-understanding development in cultural context. The results suggest that children growing up in small, traditional communities which emphasize communal values are more likely than youth growing up in an individualistic culture such as in urban New England to think of themselves in terms of their social characteristics.

The findings also call into question the validity of inferring that the presence of psychological characteristics in self-understanding is indicative of higher levels of development, as suggested by many investigators (Montemayor & Eisen 1977). The results of the Puerto Rican study suggest, instead, that the tendency to focus on psychological characteristics rather than on others may not reflect a developmental advance, but instead a process of cultural socialization.

Left unanswered by this preliminary investigation are several important questions. What variables or combination of variables give rise to the observed differences in self-understanding—educational differences, social class stratification, community size, or cultural values? Do differences in self-understanding, when they arise, reflect variations in an underlying competence or differential saliencies? We have attempted to answer these two questions in a second study, using children from Iceland.

Self-understanding in Iceland. Icelandic culture is unique in the opportunities it offers for the exploration of the effects of social class and community type on social cognitive development. Most cross-cultural studies, such as the one already described, compare cultures that are radically different from each other on virtually every dimension. The New England and Puerto Rican samples, for instance, differed in terms of social class, cultural values, educational backgrounds, and community size. As a result, it is impossible to determine which factors, or combination of factors, underlie observed differences.

Within Iceland, however, it is possible to compare cultures that differ on only a few dimensions. This is possible because Iceland is a small country, with an unusually homogeneous population. Icelanders share the same language and ethnic background. Furthermore, there is a rich cultural and historical tradition which is common to all. The educational system is standardized, with a single curriculum offered across the country. All children from ages six to twelve attend lower elementary school. Then between the ages of thirteen and fifteen they complete their years of compulsory education in upper elementary school. Many students also continue their education in grammar schools and at the university level.

What makes Iceland particularly unique is that, within this context, there are important social class and community-type distinctions. The extreme egalitarianism of Icelanders has prevented them from explicitly acknowledging the presence of distinct social classes (Broddason & Webb 1975), but sociological analyses has demonstrated their existence. In the most thorough investigation of educational and occupational stratification in Iceland conducted to date, Bjornsson and Edelstein (1977) identified six social classes: (1) unskilled manual workers, (2) skilled manual workers, (3) unskilled clerical workers, (4) technical workers and teachers, (5) business managers, and (6) professionals. Their research has demonstrated that these classes form an ordinal scale, and that the typical relationships between social class and outcome variables found in other countries obtain in Iceland as well.

For instance, children from the upper social classes (whose parents are technical workers, teachers, business managers, and professionals) score higher on IQ tests, have higher grade-point averages in school, are more likely to attend college, have fewer psychiatric symptoms, and are more likely to have parents with high expectations for them. There is abundant evidence, then, that distinct social classes do exist and influence development.

The course of life among Icelandic children is not only affected by their parents' occupations, but also by where they live. For the most part, children live in one of two types of communities: urban, contemporary Reykjavik or traditional, farming, or fishing villages that dot the coastline of the country. These latter communities differ from Reykjavik along a number of dimensions (Edelstein 1983).

In these traditional cultures, children are integral, contributing members to the family's welfare. This is because children can and must perform many of the tasks involved in farming and fishing, the activities upon which the families depend. Value changes between generations are also less consequential, because the nature and demands of family and occupational life are so stable. In many ways, of course, this sort of community greatly resembles the fishing community studies in the Puerto Rican investigation reported on earlier in this chapter.

Because the social class and community-type distinctions exist within an otherwise homogenous Icelandic culture, it is possible to study their unique effects on self-understanding development. Our expectations were that both social class and community-type would influence children's understanding of self. A host of studies have demonstrated that middle- and upper-class parents, in comparison to lower-class parents, use more personal-subjective statements (Hess & Shipman 1965) in conversations with their children, emphasize more frequently social role-taking (Maccoby 1980), and place higher value on independence and autonomy (Kohn 1977). Together, these findings suggest that middle- and upper-class parents make salient to their children the psychological qualities and features of persons. Consequently, we hypothesized that children in the higher social classes would be more likely than those in the lower ones to think of themselves in terms of their emotions, moods, and cognitive abilities (Hart & Edelstein 1989). Based on our research in Puerto Rico, our hypothesis was that children growing up in the small, traditional communities should focus more on the social qualities of self than would those from Reykjavik.

The sample for this study was drawn from the longitudinal investigation of Edelstein and his colleagues in 1983. Ninety-six twelve-year-olds from Reykjavik, divided approximately evenly by sex and social class, and thirty-six twelve-year-olds in the three lower classes from two small villages were recruited for this study.

Each child was interviewed by a well-trained native of Iceland. The interviews were tape-recorded, transcribed, and translated into English by a professional translator. Although here we are interested in children's self-conceptions, the interviews included questions tapping a variety of domains, such as moral and social judgment.

Approximately half-way through the session, the interviewer asked the child "How would you describe yourself?" This question is from the standard clinical interview protocol described by Hart and Damon (1986). This question taps only the front face of the model, corresponding to the *Me* aspect of self-understanding. Unfortunately, in this study no data relevant to the *I* components were collected. If the child had difficulty with the question, the interviewer rephrased the question, and encouraged the child to respond. The child's initial responses were followed by interviewer questions designed to draw out fully the child's meaning. As in the previous study, the responses were divided into chunks, and then assigned (with high interrater reliability) to one of the four self-schemes: physical, active, social, and psychological.

Each child's teacher was asked to provide ratings of the child's general development, self-confidence, general capability, social development, popularity, and behavior in class. Because these various ratings are homogenous (alpha = .86), we have combined them to form a general competence index.

The first of our hypotheses, concerning the relationship between social class and the number of chunks in the psychological self-scheme, was confirmed (r = .26, p < .01). Although the magnitude of this relationship is relatively modest, it does suggest that social class does affect the ways in which children think about themselves.

It might be argued that the relative lack of psychological statements among the children from the lower social classes reflects delayed development or a lack of intellectual expertise. However, none of the correlations between the general competence score (the summed teacher ratings) and the number of self-descriptive psychological chunks was significant. The general competence score was, however, related to the number of self-descriptive chunks in the social self-scheme. This means, at least in Iceland, that the extent to which children think of themselves in psychological terms is not reflective of their intelligence or cognitive skills. Instead, it appears to be the case that the psychological focus is at least in part a consequence of class membership, which makes salient these facets of self-understanding.

The predicted relationship between community-type and the number of self-descriptive chunks in the social self-scheme was not confirmed. This is best interpreted as indicating that community-type alone does not differentially affect the saliency of different characteristics of self. The social focus of the Puerto Rican children and adolescents, then, probably derives more from the cultural values of cooperation and interpersonal harmony than from the size and traditional nature of the community.

An unanticipated difference was found, however. Despite the high quality of the interviewing and the careful phrasing and rephrasing of the question, many children, particularly those from the traditional communities, had great difficulty responding with self-descriptions. This difficulty was completely unexpected, at least for the first author. In hundreds of interviews with New England and Puerto Rican children, few subjects had found questions requesting self-description impossible to answer. Yet, among Icelandic youth, this was relatively common. For instance:

> I earlier asked you to describe your friend. I would now like to ask you to do something which may be a little more difficult, and that is to describe yourself. What are you like?
> I don't know what I'm like.
> Have you no idea about that? If you get into such a situation that there was some stranger—that for some reason you wanted him to know what you were like—then you'd have to say what you are like. How would you do that? How can you describe yourself?
> I could only say what . . . I don't know.
> What kind of person are you?
> I couldn't do that if someone else was to say this.

Couldn't you do it yourself?

No.

But you're the one best acquainted with yourself, isn't that so?

No, hardly.

Still, couldn't you describe yourself?

No.

What is striking about this example is the great difficulty this youth has with the question. Compare this with the facile responding of an American of the same age.

What kind of person are you?

I'm kind of like an easy-going person. I don't like to get into fights or arguments and things like that. I'm pretty easy to get along with.

Why is that important to know about you?

Well, certain people, like, you know, their personality, like if they're more like a person who'll push you around, that can affect, you know, the kind of friends they'll have.

The American youth responds easily to questions demanding self-description. Her ready answers to the question suggest that she sees herself as an authority on her own nature. In contrast, it seems that the Icelandic child doubts whether he is an authority on the nature of his own self, denying that he is the one "best acquainted" with it. This surprising view that the self is not an authority on itself is evident in the following two excerpts with children from Iceland.

How would you describe yourself?

Well, I don't know. I very rarely take a look at myself. I see very little. I just can't imagine how I'd do that [describe myself].

How would you describe yourself?

It's just like in football. If the other team were to judge the game—like—I feel others should be the judge of what one is like.

This belief that others can know better than the self what one is like, in combination with the difficulties inherent in self-description, can lead to behavior that is strikingly unusual. Consider the following example from an interview with a twelve-year-old from Iceland who relates his own and his brother's difficulties with self-description.

> It's really difficult to describe oneself. My brother is going abroad as an exchange student [which requires a written self-description as part of the application]. He asked me to describe him and I did so and he wrote it down.
> Why do you think he did that?
> Well, he just couldn't describe himself.

In a final example, an Icelandic twelve-year-old provides an interesting glimpse into the cultural influence on self-knowledge. When asked to describe himself, he excitedly indicated that he could provide an answer because "I got to know myself a little when I went abroad."

More than 40 percent of the children from the traditional communities were unable to respond to the self-descriptive question and evidenced the difficulties and discomforts seen above with less than 25 percent of the children from Reykjavik experiencing the same problem (a difference that is statistically significant).

Although the phenomenon is quite apparent, its meaning is more elusive. In part, the failure of Icelandic children to describe themselves reflects a general desire to avoid the appearance of self-aggrandizement. The interview questions might have been perceived as soliciting information about what is special about the self, and therefore avoided.

Our interpretation is that there is more to this phenomenon than a reluctance to speak about the self to the interviewer. We believe that the failure of many of the Icelandic youth to respond to the self-descriptive questions suggests that their self-understanding is largely implicit and tacit. Cognitive psychologists frequently distinguish between two types of knowledge, *declarative* and *procedural*, a distinction that respects the different neurological systems involved in each (Squire 1987).

Declarative knowledge consists of facts and memories of events that are accessible to consciousness, and are often arrayed along a continuum from semantic to episodic. Semantic knowledge consists of facts and events that are tied to multiple contexts, and therefore have become independent of any single one. Knowing that there are fifty states, or that George Washington was the first U.S.

president, are examples of semantic knowledge, because these facts can be accessed without any knowledge of the context in which they were originally learned.

The clinical interview questions described here elicit semantic knowledge. Children and adolescents are asked for a general description of themselves, not reports of specific events.

In contrast, episodic declarative knowledge is constituted of facts or events that are linked to a single context. For instance, one's memory of the high school prom is likely to be episodic, because most adolescents attend only one. Procedural knowledge are sequences of behavior that are acquired gradually over a series of trials, are retrieved automatically in appropriate situations, and are not easily accessed through consciousness. Riding a bicycle is an example of this form of knowledge. Although a few measures used during infancy appear to tap procedural knowledge of self (Kagan 1981), to our knowledge, no measures have been used to tap this facet among children.

In these terms, Icelandic youth, particularly those from the traditional communities, may be lacking semantic knowledge of self. If true, the consequence would be that the individual would not have ready access to an understanding of self rich with concepts such as intelligence, friendliness, and so on. In turn, this would explain why the Icelandic children found it so difficult to answer the question "What kind of person are you?" which elicits semantic knowledge.

A lack of semantic knowledge of self would not imply that the Icelandic youth have failed in the task of developing an important conceptual system. Even those twelve-year-olds who could not answer the self-descriptive question were able to succeed in school and interact effectively with friends and family members, and probably utilized self-knowledge to do so, as in "I know the answer to this math question, so I'll raise my hand now before the teacher calls on me for another question" or "I am a better soccer player when I'm on the same team as my friend."

Yet this self-knowledge may be largely episodic and procedural and, therefore, not easily drawn upon in responding to context-free questions such as "What kind of person are you?" In order to elicit these forms of self-understanding, one would have to develop new techniques. For instance, one might ask subjects to recall specific incidents that are revealing of the self's nature—that is, to tap episodic self-understanding—or pose highly structured dilemmas to elicit procedural self-understanding.

This line of analysis must also address the reasons that semantic self-knowledge is less common among Icelandic youth. Our in tuition is that the great homogeneity of the entire culture—but which is particularly true of the traditional communities— decreases the opportunities for the acquisition of this form of knowledge. In such settings, everyone shares the same ethnic background, cultural heritage, and social network.

There may be a few instances in which one's membership in one social group conflicts with one's membership in another; comparisons between oneself and others may yield few dramatic differences; the values of parents and their rearing practices may vary little from one family to the next; one's vision of the self in the future (as a farmer or as a fisherman) may differ little from those of one's peers; and so on. Without these sorts of experiences, semantic self-knowledge may be less rapidly accrued because these sorts of conflicts and concepts may be the sources of the reconstruction process inherent in the acquisition of semantic information (Tulving 1985). We hope to test these speculations in future investigations.

To summarize, then, the research with Icelandic children yielded several significant findings. First, we found that children from higher social classes described themselves more frequently in psychological terms than did children from the lower social classes. Because the number of psychological chunks offered by a child was not correlated with estimates of his or her general competence, we argued that the more frequent psychological focus of the children in the higher social classes reflected the salience of these characteristics for them, rather than greater expertise.

The study also yielded the unexpected finding that Icelandic children in general and those from traditional communities in particular found it difficult to describe themselves. Our tentative interpretation of this finding is that this means that Icelandic children's self-understanding is formed mostly of episodic and procedural knowledge that is not easily accessible for responding to questions such as "What kind of person are you?"

CONCLUSIONS

What have cross-cultural investigations contributed to our understanding of self-understanding development? One of the important contributions of this body of work is its explicit concern with the embeddedness of the sense of self within a social context. Virtually all researchers and theorists acknowledge that the construction of the sense of self occurs only within a matrix of relationships and social institutions, yet the developmental literature is virtually bereft of research informed by such an assumption (Hart

& Damon 1988). Cross-cultural research is one means of redressing this glaring weakness in the literature.

The results of cross-cultural investigations can also dispell misconceptions about the nature of age-related change. For instance, a common assumption is that, as children become adolescents and acquire sophisticated cognitive abilities, they become capable of inferring nonobservable psychological qualities which then become part of self-understanding. This perspective suggests, then, that self-understanding oriented toward the psychological features is developmentally superior to self-understanding with another focus. Yet the findings from the studies in Puerto Rico and Iceland indicate that the psychological focus of the self-understanding of children is, in part, a consequence of cultural ideology and social-class membership. This is an important qualification on the traditional surface-to-depth description of developmental change in self-understanding.

Similarly, Rosaldo's findings concerning the lack of concern among the Ilongots for individuation and their belief that their own actions are controlled by external forces challenge many developmental accounts. The model presented in figure 8.1, for example, depicts age trends for volition that apparently would not emerge in the culture studied by Rosaldo.

Not only can cross-cultural research aid in the revision of developmental descriptions, it can provide new information about underlying processes. Our research in Iceland, for example, suggested that social class membership directly influences children's understanding of themselves—with those in the higher social classes more likely to think of themselves in psychological terms—apart from any indirect influence resulting from social-class effects on cognitive development. The lack of differences between children from the traditional community and those from Reykjavik indicates that community size and lifestyle are not sufficient by themselves to make unusually salient the social characteristics of self. Instead, it seems likely that the social focus of self-understanding among those living in traditional communities is a consequence of the high value of cooperation and interpersonal harmony for them, in contrast to the individualism exalted in our urban New England sample.

Perhaps the most important contributions of cross-cultural research, however, are the challenging new phenomena that emerge which require theoretical and methodological accommodation. How is it possible that Offer and his colleagues found little variation in the sense of self across cultures? What does this finding suggest about their perspective on the sense of self? Exactly what does their instrument measure? Similarly, why is it that Icelandic children have such great difficulty describing themselves? What type of knowledge do self-descriptive questions tap? These problems and questions thrown onto the path of developmental researchers will, in the long run, result in more thoughtful descriptions of self-understanding development.

As we noted in the introduction, cross-cultural approaches to the development of the sense of self are all too rare. We hope that our discussion here will encourage investigators to consider the development of the sense of self—in infancy and adulthood as well as in the age ranges we discussed—in its social context. It is an approach rich with promise.

NOTES

*Preparation of this chapter was made possible by a grant to the first author from the President's Coordinating Council for International Research, Rutgers University.

1. We use the term *self-understanding* rather than *self-concept* when referring to a person's constellation of beliefs, thoughts, and attitudes about the self for several reasons. First, *self-concept* has, unfortunately, been used interchangeably with *self-esteem*. As a consequence, *self-concept* in the literature might refer to one's representation of self, one's positive or negative evaluation of self, or both. This makes the term too broad for our purposes here. Second, we prefer *understanding* to *concept* when referring to the various representations which one has of the self. In our minds, the former emphasizes the active construction and revision that accompanies the development of a composite representation of self.

2. Based on the work of Baltes, Reese, and Lipsitt (1980), it is possible to speculate that the path of self-understanding development might be most predictable in infancy and early childhood, when biological factors are crucial in development. However, these factors wane in influence during adolescence, when the relationship of the individual to society is negotiated. At this time, cultural factors may become the more important influences on the development of self-understanding. Unfortunately, there are too few studies available in the literature to examine this hypothesis.

3. Such a finding, if replicated, would suggest that the basic category is present in the self-understanding of persons from different cultures, but that its developmental trajectory would be very different from the one followed in the United States. An alternative interpretation would be that the same developmental path might be uncovered with extensive interviewing of a broader spectrum of the population, a finding that would be consonant with

that of Kohlberg (1969). Kohlberg found that, among the Atayal, an aborigi-
nal tribe in Formosa, adults believe that, during dreams the soul leaves the
body and experiences real events, a view abandoned by late childhood in the
United States. Yet, by interviewing Atayal children and adolescents, Kohlberg was able to demonstrate that they follow the same developmental trajectory as American youth until early adolescence, at which time cultural
pressures lead them to adopt the belief that dreams are real.

4. The coding procedure is described fully in Damon and Hart 1988. A
copy of the coding manual may be obtained by writing the first author.

REFERENCES

Baldwin, J. 1902. *Social and ethical interpretations of mental life.* New
York: MacMillan.

Baltes, P.; Reese, H.; and Lipsitt, L. 1980. Life-span developmental psychology. In *Annual Review of Psychology,* Vol. 31, edited by M. Rosenzweig and L. Porter. Palo Alto: Annual Reviews. 65–110.

Bjornsson, S., and Edelstein, W. 1977. *Explorations in social inequality:
Stratification dynamics in social and individual development in Ice-
land.* Studien und Berichte, Nmr. 38. Berlin: Max-Planck-Institut fur
Bildungsforschung.

Brislin, R. 1983. Cross-cultural research in psychology. In *Annual Review of
Psychology,* Vol. 34, edited by M. Rosenzweig and L. Porter. Palo Alto:
Annual Reviews. 363–400.

Broddason, T., and Webb, K. 1975. On the myth of social equality in Iceland.
Acta Sociologica 18:49–75.

Cantor, N., and Kihlstrom, J. 1987. *Personality and Social Intelligence.* Englewood Cliffs, N.J.: Prentice-Hall.

Damon, W., and Hart, D. 1982. The development of self-understanding from
infancy through adolescence. *Child Development* 53:841–864.

––––––. 1986. Stability and change in children's self-understanding. *Social
Cognition* 4:102–118.

––––––. 1988. *The development of self-understanding in childhood and adolescence.* New York: Cambridge University Press.

Edelstein, W. 1983. Cultural constraints on development and the vicissi-
tudes of progress. In *The child and other cultural inventions,* edited by
F. Kessel and A. Siegel. New York: Praeger. 48–81.

Gardner, H. 1983. *Frames of mind.* New York: Basic Books.

Geertz, C. 1984. "From the native's point of view": On the nature of anthropological understanding. In *Essays on Mind, Self, and Emotion,* edited by R. Shweder and R. Levine. New York: Cambridge University Press. 123–136.

Hart, D. 1988. The adolescent self-concept in social context. In *Self, ego, and identity: integrative approaches,* edited by D. Lapsley and F. Power. New York: Springer-Verlag. 71–90.

Hart, D., and Damon, W. 1985. Models of social cognitive development. *Genetic Epistemologist* 14:1–8.

———. 1986. Developmental trends in self-understanding. *Social Cognition* 4:388–407.

———. 1988. Self-understanding and social cognitive development. *Early Child Development and Care* 40:5–23.

Hart, D., and Edelstein, W. 1989. *The relationship of self-understanding to community type, social class, and teacher-rated intellectual and social competence.* Under review.

Hart, D.; Lucca-Irizarry, N. and Damon, W. 1986. The development of self-understanding in Puerto Rico and the United States. *Journal of Early Adolescence* 6:293–304.

Hess, R., and Shipman, V. 1965. Early experience and the socialization of cognitive modes in children. *Child Development* 34:869–886.

James, W. [1892] 1961. *Psychology: the briefer course.* New York: Harper & Bros.

Kagan, J. 1981. *The second year of life.* Cambridge: Harvard University Press.

Kohlberg, L. 1969. Stage and sequence: the cognitive-developmental approach to socialization. In *Handbook of socialization theory and research* edited by D. Goslin. Chicago: Rand McNally. 348–480.

———. 1981. *The philosophy of moral development* Vol. 1. San Francisco: Harper & Row.

Kohn, M. 1977. *Class and conformity.* 2d ed. Chicago: University of Chicago Press.

Levine, R. 1984. Properties of culture: an ethnographic view. In *Essays on Mind, Self, and Emotion,* edited by R. Shweder and R. Levine. New York: Cambridge University Press. 67–87.

Levine, R., and White, M. 1986. *Human conditions: the cultural basis for educational development.* New York: Routledge & Kegan Paul.

Maccoby, E. 1980. *Social development: psychological growth and the parent-child relationship.* New York: Harcourt, Brace, Jovanovich.

Mead, G. H. 1934. *Mind, self, and society.* Chicago: University of Chicago Press.

Melcher, B. 1986. *Moral reasoning, self-identity, and moral action: A study of conduct disorder in adolescence.* Unpublished Doctoral Dissertation, Pittsburgh, Pa.: University of Pittsburgh.

Montemayor, R., and Eisen, M. 1977. The development of self-conceptions from childhood to adolescence. *Developmental Psychology* 13:314–319.

Offer, D.; Ostrov, E.; Howard, K.; and Atkinson, R. 1988. *The teenage world: Adolescents' self-image in ten countries.* New York: Plenum.

Rosaldo, M. 1984. Toward an anthropology of self and feeling. In *Essays on Mind, Self, and Emotion,* edited by R. Shweder and R. Levine. New York: Cambridge University Press. 137–157.

Schorin, M., and Hart, D. 1988. Psychotherapeutic implications of the development of self-understanding. In *Cognitive development and child psychotherapy,* edited by S. Shirk. New York: Plenum. 161–186.

Shweder, R. 1984. Anthropology's romantic rebellion against the enlightenment, or there's more to thinking than reason and evidence. In *Essays on Mind, Self, and Emotion,* edited by R. Shweder and R. Levine. New York: Cambridge University Press. 27–66.

Spiro, M. 1984. Some reflections on cultural determinism and relativism with special reference to emotion and reason. In *Essays on Mind, Self, and Emotion,* edited by R. Shweder and R. Levine. New York: Cambridge University Press. 323–346.

Squire L. R. 1987. *Memory and brain.* New York: Oxford University Press.

Triandis, H. 1988. Commentary. In *The teenage world: Adolescents' self-image in ten countries,* edited by D. Offer, E. Ostrov, K. Howard, and R. Atkinson. New York: Plenum. 127–128.

———. 1989. The self and social behavior in differing cultural contexts. *Psychological Review* 96:506–520.

Tulving, E. 1985. How many memory systems are there? *American Psychologist* 40:385–398.

THOMAS M. BRINTHAUPT
RICHARD P. LIPKA

Summary and Implications

The purpose of this volume was to address issues of defining and measuring the self. Its focus has been on the questions of *what* to study and *how* to study it.

To what extent can we answer the questions raised in the introduction now that we have sampled a variety of perspectives and considered a number of issues? In this final chapter, we return to these initial questions and examine critically each of the chapters. We consider several of the similarities and differences in how the contributors have addressed these issues as well as discuss additional issues that they have raised.

DEFINING THE SELF—WHAT HAVE WE LEARNED?

It was our intention to select quite different contributions to defining the self. Our contributors differed most in terms of whether they emphasized the structural or processing aspects of the self. Freeman's discussion of the experiential nature of the self details the self as subject or active agent. He sees it as a fluid construct, perpetually changing and being revised. Several questions arise from this definition of the self. For example, who or what is doing the changing or revising? Freeman is not explicit about exactly how the process of self-narrative is brought about. Instead, his emphasis is on the narrative process and its potential problems.

Is the *I* the storyteller and the *me* the story that is told? Or is the *I* part of the story or interpretive creation as well? The answers to these questions are important in determining the relationship between the structural and processing aspects of the self.

For example, do self-distortion and self-deception primarily affect the structure of the self (as in the resulting story) or do they mainly affect the process of self-narrative (as in the storytelling)? If the answer is the latter, then this suggests that what is important about the "self" is its interpretive function. This is the case that Freeman is making. However, the structure of the self may also be altered by the tendencies to embellish, distort, or deceive.

In addition, there is the question of whether the researcher should emphasize the more internal meaning-making and significance-generating aspects of the self (as Freeman does) or the more public aspects of the self in interaction with others. Who is the narrator's intended or actual audience? It might be oneself, and it might be others. These audiences are probably also not the same when it comes to the processes involved.

One of the important implications of Freeman's definition of the self is that we essentially employ a case study approach to studying it. Because of the unique trajectory of every person's self-narrative, an extensive and detailed analysis is required if we are to identify any common principles of self-narrative.

Freeman suggests that life history can be an important tool for the self researcher. How might this approach be useful? Perhaps researchers should rely more on works of literature, biography, autobiography, and diaries for their data, as Freeman argues. For this to occur, however, more attention needs to be devoted to methodological issues, such as instructions and prompts, time, length, and referent constraints, and the handling of data. For example, what qualitative differences emerge when a person engages in an "online" description of the self as it is currently experienced as opposed to making a retrospective account of oneself? Must the data of immediate experience first become meaningful episodes in a person's story, as Freeman suggests?

A final issue with regard to Freeman's definition of the self concerns differences in life-historical recollection depending on where a person is in the life span. In his chapter, L'Écuyer reported some of the difficulties he had in getting elderly participants to describe themselves. It seemed that they were more likely than his younger participants to fall into a life-encompassing personal narrative, rather than describing specific aspects or dimensions of themselves. Is there a greater preference for the narrative as a mode of self-understanding among the elderly than among young adults? Perhaps seeing the self as an ongoing narrative is easier, more natural, or more meaningful for the elderly. Surely, to be able to look back over "everything" is a different experience for the elderly than it is for the college student.

To approach this issue from another direction, is there any usefulness in studying the narratives of children? Do they engage in self-narratives and, if so, how do these differ from those of adults? As these questions illustrate, there are many issues related to studying the self as narrative that have yet to be addressed by researchers.

In their chapter, Marsh and his colleagues focus on the self as object or structure. They define the self as a multidimensional, hierarchical construct, and they have devoted a great deal of attention to identifying its dimensions and their interrelations. By using a theoretical model of the structure of the self as their starting point, they have been able to construct sound measures and test several interesting hypotheses.

Given the importance of their theoretical model, several issues regarding its completeness and adequacy should be addressed. One interesting issue concerns the extent of similarity and dissimilarity of Marsh's and his colleagues' dimensions to those of L'Écuyer. The latter researcher arrived at his dimensions and hierarchical structure in a manner quite different from that used by Marsh and his colleagues. However, not only did L'Écuyer employ a very different methodology, but he also came to describe the structure of the self in a more data-driven than theory-driven fashion. How do the results of these two perspectives compare to one another?

For Marsh and colleagues, a major distinction in the hierarchical structure of the self is the nonacademic and the academic (math and verbal) facets. Within the nonacademic self are aspects of parent and peer relationships, physical appearance, and physical abilities. In addition, both the math and verbal facets can be broken down into more specific facets, such as math and science or history and geography.

For L'Écuyer, the academic/nonacademic distinction is absent. In fact, he makes no reference to the academic facets of the self-structure. L'Écuyer's conception of the self is primarily a nonacademic one, and it includes those nonacademic facets of the work of Marsh and colleagues, in addition to several others.

What might account for these dissimilarities? Because of their emphasis, Marsh's and colleagues' samples of interest are children and adolescents. L'Écuyer, on the other hand, is interested in the nonacademic experiential aspects of the self, and he is interested in all age groups. These different emphases point to some important questions about and limitations of the Marsh and colleagues approach.

One interesting question about the academic self described by Marsh and colleagues concerns the genesis of these facets. Are the independent facets of the math and verbal self attributable to the organization of schools and curricula? Can the more specific academic facets be mapped directly onto the different classroom subjects of the typical (Western) student? How are these facets related to the children's school experiences?

With regard to the nonacademic self, the implications of Marsh's and his colleagues' approach deserve to be explored. A similar approach to testing and validating the multidimensionality and hierarchical organization of the academic self can also be applied to the nonacademic self. Marsh and colleagues argue that the specific facets of the academic self are more useful for researchers than is the general academic facet. Can a parallel argument also be made for the specific and general facets of the nonacademic self? For example, is achievement in a nonacademic area (such as work) more strongly associated with nonacademic factors than general self-concept? Marsh and colleagues suggest that this is the case.

What implications does the Marsh and colleagues model have for the selves of adults? Despite the support for their model, the emphasis on the academic self raises several questions about its generalizability to adult samples. Are the distinct aspects of the academic self in childhood and adolescence also present in older adults? If not, this might support the argument that the academic structure of the self is the result of on-going school experiences and is therefore unstable in the longer term. Does the nonacademic self increase in differentiation into adulthood? What are the effects of role transitions, career developments, and the like on the self-structure? Does the nonacademic self increase in importance relative to the academic self in adulthood?

Marsh and his colleagues acknowledge that their model is not a developmental one. Nevertheless, the issues raised by their theoretical and methodological approach to defining the self offer several avenues for researchers who are interested in studying the self in adulthood.

L'Écuyer's approach to defining the self relies on aspects of both Freeman's and Marsh's and colleagues' approaches. One of the most interesting parts of L'Écuyer's approach is his attempt to apply the same methodology to individuals across the life span. Whereas he describes many of the problems he encountered with this effort, there are additional issues and implications that deserve discussion.

For example, it may be that the varying problems L'Écuyer encountered with different age groups (such as with the understanding of instructions or the task itself) may tell us something about how these age groups actually think about the self. Could controlling for these problems lead to losing information about the self? In fact,

Hart and Edelstein found that some Icelandic adolescents had a great deal of difficulty describing themselves, suggesting the influence of cultural or sub-cultural factors on the self. Perhaps more in-depth interviewing of the kind used by Hart and Edelstein (who used extensive "why" and follow-up questions) might reveal important life-span differences.

In addition, even by using the same method across the life span, there are still questions as to why there are transformations in the self. As pointed out in the chapter by Brinthaupt and Erwin, the differential use of categories by children and adults may be due to developmental factors, differences in understanding of questions, cohort effects, and so on. Those researchers who are interested in why there are differences in structure across the life span may need to supplement the methods of L'Écuyer.

Another issue concerns the data obtained by L'Écuyer. How distinct and independent from each other are the categories, substructures, and structures? Also, given that this research is cross-sectional, is there any merit in applying this approach longitudinally? For example, what would it mean if a single participant provided a self-description two years later that was virtually identical to his or her first self-description? Does this indicate high reliability on the part of the measure? Would we conclude that the person has the same self-structure now as two years ago? And what if a researcher asked participants to describe themselves retrospectively, as Freeman advocates? Would there be differential usage of categories or substructures if participants from many different ages described themselves as they were when they were, say, thirteen-years old?

The acquisition and coding of the type of data described by L'Écuyer is time-consuming and difficult, as he acknowledges. Yet the quality of data is rich, and many interesting issues can be addressed when the self is defined in both structural and experiential terms. Through the use of qualitative or content analysis, important differences can be identified that might be missed by the quantitative approaches of researchers such as Marsh and his colleagues.

MEASURING THE SELF—WHAT HAVE WE LEARNED?

Several measurement and methodological issues were raised by the contributors to this section of the volume. How can the self researcher make intelligent choices concerning the use of the many available measures and methods? Each contributor offered guidance for the researcher who is confronted with this question.

In their chapter on the self-report process, Brinthaupt and Erwin detail an imposing array of factors that can affect the data of the self researcher. Several aspects of their review have important implications for studying the self. For example, what are the implications of biased or inaccurate self-reports for researchers? It would seem that avoiding self-report bias or inaccuracy would enhance our ability to predict the behaviors of individuals. But not all researchers have this as the goal of their studies of the self. As Freeman argues, the factors that affect the veracity of self-reports tell us a great deal about the process of self-conceptualization and self-understanding, the study of which is also a worthy pursuit.

For those researchers who are concerned about biased or inaccurate self-reports, one alternative is to employ behavioral observations or the reports of knowledgeable others. But this strategy raises a number of questions. For instance, what are we to make of disparities between self-reports and the reports of others? Is one more accurate than the other?

Differences between how we look at ourselves and how others look at us are interesting data in their own right, perhaps telling us something about self-presentation or the social nature of the self. If we take an approach similar to that of Brinthaupt and Erwin with the reactive and spontaneous variants of self-report, there are several types of comparisons that might be made between self-reports and those given by others. Are knowledgeable others aware of discrepancies between their perceptions of a person and his or her self-perceptions? It might be interesting to compare others' perceptions of how a target person really is with their perceptions of how the target looks at his or her self—that is, the differences between how we perceive a target and how we perceive the target's self-perceptions. Of course, comparing these data with the target's actual self-reports would also be useful.

Another implication of the self-report process as described by Brinthaupt and Erwin concerns those aspects of the self that cannot be or are not reported, for whatever reasons. For example, when persons omit bad, embarrassing, or socially proscribed aspects from their self-reports, are we to assume that these are unimportant to their self-perception and self-understanding (to say nothing of their motives and behaviors)? Few would argue that these denied or hidden aspects of the self are unimportant. Does this mean then, that a spontaneous self-report reflects how frequently we think about ourselves only in terms of positive self-aspects as well as safe negative aspects?

Finally, in terms of reactive and spontaneous self-reports, which approach should a researcher use? What factors should affect the choice of methodology? Brinthaupt and Erwin do not describe the optimal circumstances for the use of each approach. However, their review should give the researcher into the self much to consider when deciding to make use of self-reports.

In their chapter on multigroup comparisons in research into the self, Byrne and her colleagues suggested that violations of the assumptions of equivalent structure and measurement might account for some of the inconsistent findings in the self literature. They demonstrated both gender differences in self structure and age differences in the perception of measurement items. In the first case, they suggested that the self of an adolescent male may not have the same structure as that of an adolescent female. What might account for gender differences in the structure of the self? It may be that gender-role stereotypes are responsible (for example, English being more important to females, and mathematics being more important to males). Whatever the reasons, the major implication is that comparisons of mean scores on the academic facets of the self are affected by differing relations among the various self-facets of males and females. This caveat applies as well to other types of comparisons, such as those based on race and age.

In the case of measurement noninvariance, Byrne and colleagues argued that some mean differences between groups are not due to the groups but to the differential functioning of the measures for each group. There is a different interpretation of noninvariant measurement that should be considered. In particular, is the differential functioning of the measures related to differences between the groups?

For example, if the responses of a young age group are less reliable than those of an older group, this might suggest that the younger sample has a less reliable or structured self. The issue is whether nonequivalent measurement is something to control or to consider as theoretically important or useful. If certain items are perceived differently by two groups of children, does this suggest that the items are bad and should be deleted from the measure, or that there are developmental differences that can explain the variance? While Byrne and colleagues do not discuss the possibility, perhaps the contents of nonequivalent items hold useful theoretical and developmental implications for the individual doing research into the self.

What implications do the issues raised by Byrne and her colleagues have for alternative approaches to measuring the self? They rely on what Brinthaupt and Erwin referred to as reactive measures. How do researchers who rely on spontaneous or other methodologies address issues of structural and measurement invariance? The analytic strategy advocated by Byrne and colleagues is certainly more easily used with reactive measures.

However, the issues are also relevant to other measures. For example, L'Écuyer's efforts to handle differences in the interpretation of his questions and his task reflected a concern with measurement invariance. Byrne and her colleagues illustrate how those who prefer using reactive measures can systematically address these issues, but it is unclear how researchers such as L'Écuyer can benefit from this approach, short of giving up his preferred methodology.

Juhasz was interested in measuring the existence of significant others and their effects on one's evaluation of self. She raised many interesting questions, not only about how to conceptualize significance, but how to measure it as well. Much of her discussion is based on the position that significance is *given* to another person. But, as she asks, is there reciprocity of significance? Do others know that they are significant, and do they seek to become so with us? If so, we may need to extend our research efforts beyond interpersonal perception into interpersonal relations.

Another interesting implication concerns the possible negative effects of others on self-esteem. There is a great deal of experimental research on situational manipulations of self-esteem, but very little research has examined the impact of negatively significant others.

In addition to the many issues described by Juhasz surrounding significance, other questions can be raised. For example, when are others significant and when are they not? To answer this question, we might need to specify whether we are concerned with significance today, next month or year, or in the past. Does it matter when we make our judgments of the significance of others? In addition, can others who are not alive (such as, a deceased friend or family member) or not known personally (as in a film or musical star, politician, or religious figure) also be significant? Are these being missed by current measures of significance?

Finally, what is the difference between choosing a significant other and having one imposed on oneself by specific others, events, or circumstances? What effects do choice or control have on the impact of others on self-esteem? The area of significant others and the self is full of such interesting questions. By following Juhasz's measurement suggestions—especially the use of interviewing and drawing techniques—researchers can begin to zero in on the *what* and *why* of significance.

Ashmore and Ogilvie also focused on the social aspects of the self. However, unlike Juhasz, they were less interested in the effects of significant others on self-evaluation than they were in identifying the structure of a person's self in relationship to significant others. Their approach is an interesting combination of structural issues, participant-generated data, and theoretical and clinical concerns related to the social self. Several implications emerge from their self-with-other unit of analysis for research on the self.

For example, to what extent do respondents to a self-related measure (such as the Self-Description Questionnaire or the Twenty Statements Test) rely on self-with-other representations when rating or describing themselves? Are self-with-other representations involved whenever one thinks about the self? Is the self made up of some self-with-other representations and some self-*without*-other representations? Most basically, the issue is how the detailed clusters of targets and features identified by Ashmore and Ogilvie map onto our everyday experiences of the self-with-others. Is there a clear and strong correspondence here or are such structures outside of our awareness?

Establishing the range and boundaries of the self-with-others would provide important information about the social and nonsocial aspects of the self. In their structural models of the self, both Marsh and colleagues and L'Écuyer include the self in relation to others. However, in both cases, this aspect of the self represents only a small part of the overall self-structure. This does not necessarily mean that the self-with-others is relatively unimportant. In addition to the importance of self-with-others in understanding interpersonal relations and gender-related issues, such representations may also underlie or permeate the evaluations or descriptions of participants in Marsh's and colleagues' as well as L'Écuyer's research on the hierarchical, multidimensional self. That is, individuals may base their self-evaluations and self-descriptions across many domains on others and/or their relationships with others.

If we question the definitions of *relationship* or *interaction*, then there are other implications of the Ashmore and Ogilvie approach. For example, Juhasz suggested that significant or important others could be individuals (such as media or religious figures) with whom a person has interacted indirectly at most. Such individuals are apparently not solicited in the Ashmore and Ogilvie procedures. Is it possible to have a relationship or to interact with these types of targets? If so, where would these particular others fall in participants' target clusters?

In addition, it may be that different targets (or clusters of targets) are encountered in different contexts. That is, some targets may be encountered in a particular setting (such as home or school) or at a particular time (the distant past or currently). Perhaps such factors are important in interpreting the resulting target and feature clusters and hierarchies. This might, for example, explain some of the variations in how participants in the Self-Perception Project differentiated themselves in their relationships with important others.

In the final chapter, Hart and Edelstein demonstrated the fruitfulness of cross-cultural research on the self. They illustrated the influence of theoretical and methodological assumptions on the findings and interpretations of self researchers. For example, they argue convincingly that the identification of universal features of the self as opposed to its unique characteristics across cultures is a function of the definitions and measures employed. Their own approach to studying the self emphasizes self-understanding or how we think of the self in the course of day-to-day life.

To what extent can their arguments be expanded to include discussion of other between-group differences besides cultural ones, such as those based on age, race, or gender? For example, if we consider age or developmental differences, we might argue that the measures employed by Marsh and colleagues underestimate developmental variability. That is, one reason why they fail to find increased differentiation in the self beyond early adolescence is because the variation cannot be detected with the SDQ.

Of course, Marsh and colleagues are interested in the structure of the self rather than aspects of self-understanding. Thus, once again, we come up against differences in how researchers define the self and how this affects their methods and conclusions. By emphasizing the meaning-making characteristics of the self, Hart and Edelstein are on ground similar to Freeman and, as such, are more likely to capture differences in the experiential aspects of the self across cultures or ages.

An interesting implication of the Hart and Edelstein approach concerns the relationships between cultural and developmental differences. Can the effects of culture and development be thought of in the same way? As suggested above, the identification of developmental, racial, or gender differences in the self may be a function of the definitions and measures used. How do we know that a seven-year-old's tendency to focus on physical characteristics versus a thirteen-year-old's focus on psychological characteristics reflects a developmental advance rather than a process of cultural socialization? Hart and Edelstein suggest that we do not know for sure which process is operating. Nor can the two be easily separated.

It is also interesting to consider the relationship between cultural and developmental factors at different times in the life span. For example, does the social and cultural context exert a greater influence on the self-understanding of adolescents and adults than of infants and children, as Hart and Edelstein suggest? How do the two factors interact in affecting self-understanding? In addition to the many theoretical and methodological issues raised by Hart and Edelstein, there are clearly a great many other issues that emerge when we consider the effects of culture and socialization on the self.

In conclusion, it appears that, based on the contributions to this volume, researchers do not agree on how to define and measure the self. This may suggest to some that the field of research on the self is in bad shape. In fact, some researchers argue that we need to agree upon a small subset of psychometrically sound and well-validated measures and use only these in our research efforts.

But what is so interesting about the self as an object of study is that researchers disagree on what is the most important aspect of it to consider. Is the self-as-object more important than the self-as-active-agent? Are processing issues more interesting than structural issues? These are difficult questions to assess, as the contributions to this volume indicate.

All of the contributors have made good cases for what they think is interesting about the self and how they think those interesting aspects should be studied. We believe that they have succeeded in illustrating that the many quite different approaches to studying the self continue to raise important theoretical and methodological issues.

Contributors

Richard D. Ashmore
Department of Psychology
Rutgers University
New Brunswick, New Jersey

Thomas M. Brinthaupt
Department of Psychology
Middle Tennessee State University
Murfreesboro, Tennessee

Barbara M. Byrne
School of Psychology
University of Ottawa
Ottawa, Ontario
Canada

Wolfgang Edelstein
Max Planck Institute for Human Development
   and Education
Berlin, Germany

L. Jeanette Erwin
Department of Psychology
University of Houston
Houston, Texas

Mark Freeman
Department of Psychology
College of the Holy Cross
Worcester, Massachusetts

Daniel Hart
Department of Psychology
Rutgers University
Camden, New Jersey

Anne McCreary Juhasz
Department of Educational Psychology
Loyola University
Chicago, Illinois

René L'Écuyer
Laboratory of Research on the
   Self-Concept
Department of Psychology
University of Sherbrooke
Sherbrooke, Quebec
Canada

Richard P. Lipka
Center for Educational Services, Evaluation and
   Research
Pittsburg State University
Pittsburg, Kansas

Herbert W. Marsh
School of Education
University of Western Sydney, Macarthur
Campbelltown, New South Wales
Australia

Daniel M. Ogilvie
Department of Psychology
Rutgers University
New Brunswick, New Jersey

Richard J. Shavelson
Graduate School of Education
University of California
Santa Barbara, California

Subject Index

A

Academic self-concept:
  academic achievement and, 67–78, 184–186;
  cultural effects on, 309–310;
  facets of, 55–58, 67–78, 182–187;
  internal/external frame of reference model of, 70–78;
  versus nonacademic, 55–58, 175, 178–179, 325–326
Age differences: (see also Development of self-concept, Developmental differences)
  in self-concept profiles, 116–128;
  self-perception and, 216
Agency, sense of (see Self-as-subject)
Autobiography:
  and ongoing, immediate experiences, 36–37;
  as self-understanding, 26–34, 297–298;
  interpretation of autobiographical data, 15–40

B

Bodily self (see Physical self)

C

Chomsky, N., 293

Closed-ended (reactive) measures of self: (see also Interviews, Measurement of self, Open-ended measures)
  advantages and disadvantages of, 128–131, 147–154;
  and open-ended (spontaneous) measures, 147–148, 152–162, 330;
  biases associated with, 151–152, 296, 299–300;
  instructions for, 148–149, 151–152, 193, 197–198
Cognitive dissonance, 218
Confirmatory factor analysis:
  and analysis of covariance structures (LISREL), 178–181, 183;
  testing measurement assumptions with, 174, 179–181
Consciousness:
  perspective on, 15–18;
  study of, 304
Construct validity:
  in self-concept research, 47–48, 53–54, 172–199;
  interpretation of, 329–330
Content analysis:
  quantification of data with, 114–116, 127–128;
  with developmental data, 102–104, 109–110
Contextual and situational effects:
  on self-report process, 142–144;

Author Index

A

Agatstein, R. C., 145, 147
Agustdottir, S., 140
Ajzen, I, 243
Allport, G., 38, 99, 206, 215, 247
Alwin, D. F., 177
Anderson, N. H., 65
Anderson, S. M., 143
Ashmore, R. D., 237–245, 247, 254, 260, 261, 331, 332
Atkinson, R., 294

B

Bachman, J. G., 68, 81
Bagley, C., 219
Baldwin, J., 206, 300
Balla, J. R., 180
Baltes, A. B., 131
Baltes, P., 319
Banaji, M. R., 3, 141, 145, 147, 154, 156
Bardin, L., 114
Bargh, J. A., 141, 142
Barnes, J., 54, 55, 79, 85, 89, 208
Barrett, R., 225
Barthes, R., 16
Baumeister, R. F., 22, 143
Beane, J. A. 3, 155
Beere, C. A., 242
Bejar, I. I., 176, 195

Bellezza, F. S., 3, 145, 147, 154, 156
Bem, S. L., 242
Benson, J., 79, 192
Bentler, P. M., 180
Berkowitz, L., 238
Best, D. L., 262
Bjornsson, S., 311
Blumenfeld, P., 217
Blyth, D. A., 3, 155, 226
Boersma, F. J., 52
Bohrnstedt, G. W., 180
Bolus, R., 68
Bonett, D. G., 180
Bos, A., 213
Botwinick, J., 131
Bourne, E. J., 22
Bradburn, K. A., 152
Braucht, G., 221
Breytspraak, L. M., 155, 196
Brinthaupt, T. M., 147, 149, 154, 159, 160, 327–330
Brislin, R., 292
Brittain, C., 216
Broddason, T., 311
Bromley, D., 215
Brookover, W. B., 179, 183
Brooks, D., 217
Brophy, J., 217
Broughton, J., 146, 212, 214
Buchanan, D. B., 145, 147
Bugental, J. F. T., 97, 112, 113, 147, 155
Burns, R. B., 47, 207